THE GOLDEN HAWK
and
A WOMAN CALLED FANCY
[Two Complete Novels]

FRANK YERBY

The Golden Hawk

and

A Woman Called Fancy

[TWO COMPLETE NOVELS]

THE DIAL PRESS · NEW YORK

MANUFACTURED IN THE UNITED STATES OF AMERICA

THE

GOLDEN

HAWK

To Flora

1

THERE WAS NO WIND in all that sweep of sky. Now and again one of the black-gray mountains of cloud, too heavily laden, sank almost to the surface of the Caribbean; but that was where the wind was, and the towering domes and pinnacles of mist were rent into shreds and sent scudding to leeward to be lost in the white boil of spray where the waves crashed in thunderous fury over the rocks of the Isle des Vaches—Cow Island.

Kit Gerado sat very still on the coil of tarred hempen line. In actuality, his lean body was in constant motion as he swayed in counter to the *Seaflower*'s frenzied pitching; but so deftly did he manage the matter of balance against the trim brigantine's devil dance with wind and storm that he seemed not to move at all.

He was so still that Bernardo Díaz, moving aft with great difficulty against the hissing, wind-driven spray, stopped to gaze at him. But for the great mane of tawny gold that whipped in the gale like a cavalry standard in full charge, Kit might have been a wonderfully lifelike figure from a Velásquez canvas; his slim body, lithe even in repose, was etched all the more vividly against the white wall of hammering water by the somber blackness of his doublet and full Spanish pantaloons. He seemed quite the young hidalgo of the Hapsburg courts, except that upon coming closer Bernardo could see that the doublet was open from throat almost to navel, and the broad expanse of Kit's chest, glistening with storm spray, was bronzed from long exposure to a tropic sun.

About his lean belly, board-flat and ribbed and corded with muscle, Kit wore a broad sash of cloth of gold, contrasting vividly with the soberness of his other garments; and even as Bernardo watched, Kit's lean fingers toyed briefly with the knot that held it in place. The knot gave after a moment, and Kit drew the sash off, holding it across his wide-spread knees with both his hands.

Bernardo, who had seen this gesture many times, sighed deeply, for he knew what it meant. From where he stood, he could not see the device of the Black Heron on a field of gold that ornamented the banner Cristóbal Gerado now wore as a sash; but he knew it was there, for he had been with Kit when they had first seen it. No, he could not see the sign of the Black Heron, but he could see Kit's face, see his mouth drawing into a hard line, his blue eyes becoming glacier ice, and the knuckles of his hands tightening until they showed white from the strain.

On that earlier day, Bernardo recalled sadly, the Heron Banner, which as much as anything else on this dreary earth was responsible for their being aboard this hell ship, had fluttered gaily in the afternoon sunlight from the pikestaff of a helmeted and cuirassed horseman. The man had sat boldly on his dancing Andalusian steed, leading a procession of riders through a narrow street in Cádiz.

Cádiz—ah, Cádiz!—rising white-walled and dreamlike, a city of pearl above a sea of indigo, a cluster of low, flat-roofed houses and a tangle of streets. Was there indeed such a place, or was it too false, a trick of the disordered imagination, as empty of reality as the name Kit bore, as difficult to comprehend as the swift flow of liquid Castilian from the lips of a lad whose eyes were as blue as a Norwegian fjord, and whose hair, falling in great curling masses about his broad shoulders, was like Iberian sunlight, heavy with gold?

Shaking his head, Bernardo bent forward against the wind and plodded toward where the young first officer sat. An odd sight indeed was Bernardo Díaz, converted Jew. His shoulders were twice as broad as those of the average man, and his arms were great coils of muscle. His chest was huge, but his legs were pipestems and less, thin and crooked beyond belief. Twelve years in the galleys of His Most Christian Majesty, Philip IV of Spain, and four in those of the Caliph of Barbary, do that to a man. Now, at thirty-nine, Bernardo looked fifty. "Arab or Christian," he would say dryly, "their whips bite deep."

He looked at the bare masts of the *Seaflower*, held to the wind by one flying jib and the small spritsail, then back at the young first officer.

"I have news, Kit," he said. "Bad news. The men are growing ugly."

Kit shrugged. "I know. When are they not half a point from mutiny?"

"Today they are less than that. We're in for a blow, and they know it. At sea that would be bad enough, but to lie here two miles outside the best harbor in two hundred leagues and be beaten to pieces is—well, they don't understand it."

"They know why." Kit's voice dropped even lower, but there was a fine, bright edge to his tone. "Would they take on a fleet of two dozen well-armed vessels?"

"Have the French so many craft in there?" Bernardo asked incredulously.

"Yes. And to them the *Seaflower* is an English vessel. I grant you there are not ten Englishmen aboard, but so long as Lazarus commands her, she is English. And if they granted us consideration of the fact that we do not fly the flag, do you think they'd let this leper bark into their harbor?"

"Lazarus!" Bernardo spat, his voice cold with loathing. "There's the root of the whole matter! True, there are no longer any lazarettos in Europe where he could hide his rotting hideousness, but here in the colonies there are many places where . . ."

Kit's lean, tanned hand reached up and caught at the white-gold spike of a beard that bisected his firm chin. He gave it a gentle tug, and his eyes rested speculatively on Bernardo's lean, Semitic face. Bernardo, who was not wanting in perceptiveness, caught the unspoken reproach at once; but he considered the matter too grave for nicety of sentiments.

"Look, Kit," he went on doggedly, "I am not without sympathy for the dreadful scourge that devours him. But what right has he to expose you to contagion? You and I and every man aboard this pest ship? Who are we that we should implement his vengeance against a world that cast him off in most understandable horror?" Bernardo bent closer, persuasion moving urgently through his tones. "He is an old man. Now, if you were captain of the *Seaflower* . . ."

Kit turned away and stared toward the shadowy harbor. "Were I captain," he said slowly, so that his words came out measured and spaced, ice-hard, and as free of warmth, "I would sail this sea witch into the harbor of Cartagena to the citadel above which the Heron Banner flies, and blast my way house by house to Don Luis's door. Under Lazarus at least they live. Under my command, they'd die like the dogs they are!"

Bernardo looked down at the wings of the Black Heron, spread wide on the cloth of gold.

"You cannot forget him," he murmured, "can you?"

"Forget him!" Kit breathed. "Forget Luis del Toro? Not until my hands have torn his heart from his breast!" He leaned forward, his eyes intent and hard, a little flame of madness leaping in their depths.

Nor am I likely to forget him either, Bernardo thought bitterly. Don Luis is a monster of wickedness—a true son of evil, in whom Satan, his father, will never find cause for shame. He lifts a finger and I am bereft of lands and goods just because I am born a Jew; he gestures and a woman dies of torture, a coward takes his own life, and we, Kit and I, are hurled across half a world into a leper bark from which all men flee in shrieking horror. . . . He bent forward again, shrugging his great shoulders. Del Toro was of no importance at the moment. The matter of the leper captain crowded all else out of his mind.

"Listen to reason, Kit," he said. "You know how it is with us. What happens when we go ashore? Every woman up to the age of sixty flees shrieking at the top of her lungs. We are cheated of our treasure. There is no man who will bargain with us fairly; we are not even permitted the freedom of their rum shops. We are not lepers, but we might as well be for all the chance we have of taking our ease or indulging our manly appetites. Good God, Kit! The men will mutiny before long, and you and I will die along with Lazarus's stinking hideousness. Now, if you were in command . . ."

Kit's eyes rested coolly on the face of his friend.

"If you were in command," Bernardo persisted, "we could sail into Basse-Terre or even Port de Paix and be welcomed. Since De Cussy was killed at Cap Français last year, Saint-Domingue has a new governor. The Sieur Ducasse understands the ways of freebooters, having been one himself. Why, Laurens de Graff, and even Daviot, the worst butcher since L'Ollonais, sail in and out of the harbor of Port de Paix with impunity."

"So?" Kit said.

"Why shouldn't Christophe Giradeaux, Frenchman, do the same thing?"

Kit smiled. "I am but half French, as you well know. What of Cristóbal Gerado, bastard of a Spanish grandee? Or Kit Gerado, the English sea dog the whole Caribbean believes me to be?"

Bernardo grinned at him. "I think that Kit of the golden mane comes of all nations. The choice is up to him."

Kit's smooth forehead furrowed with thinking. He remembered the day when Lazarus had first removed in his presence the mask that hid the face of living death from all mankind. The fingers that fumbled at the strings were terribly swollen and dead-white; moreover, they stopped short at the second joint without a trace of nails. Kit had leaned against the door frame, waiting curiously. Then the mask had fallen away from Lazarus's face, and Kit had peered into what seemed to be the countenance of an ancient lion: the nose was huge, rimmed about by heavy nodules, the brow ridged and furrowed with wrinkles, the cheeks flabby, with spots of ghastly whiteness on them, and the ears huge, thickened and elongated beyond belief.

The blue eyes looking out from under the great shelf of the brows had been for a moment infinitely sad, then rage had flared in them.

"I am to be obeyed, lad," Lazarus had roared, "not stared at!"

That had been the beginning. Now Kit realized Lazarus's loneliness, and the terror that haunted him. He had learned, too, that but for his horrible disease, Lazarus might have been a kindly and greathearted man. He looked up at Bernardo.

"No," he said gently. "I will not sanction the murder of an old and broken man who in his own way has been good to me."

"Who said anything about murder?" Bernardo demanded. "There are thousands of islands in this sea where a man could live out his days in the sun, with fruit and shellfish for food, and fowls too, dropped by a fowling piece. Why, we might even buy him a Negress or a Caribbee maid, young and hot of blood, to warm his old bones. It would be a blessing for him."

Kit frowned. "It's odd how bright a glow a man's oily tongue can rub on villainy," he growled. "No, Bernardo—no more of this." He turned away.

The wind was coming from the east, blowing straight across Hispaniola, so that all the palms bowed together before it. Now and again a long fringe of palm would tear loose from its trunk and be hurled out to sea. The great waves swelled, rising with deceptive, heavy slowness, as though the sea were made of a thick sirup; then they would crash down to batter the *Seaflower's* stern with tons of white water. The brigantine ran baremasted, except for the jib and spritsail that held her due west, so that only her narrow stern took the smashing impact of the waves. She slid down a long, oily gray trough of sea, only her two masts visible, then rose sickeningly, her bowsprit angling skyward, hanging there for long minutes before a caprice of wind and water dropped her downward again.

It was then that the little knot of men pushed their way out of the forecastle and headed unsteadily toward Lazarus's cabin. As if by instinct, Kit glanced up and, in one motion, was on his feet and striding toward the leper captain's door, aware that the long-threatened mutiny was about to flare up. Inside the fetid gloom of Lazarus's cabin, the captain looked at him sadly.

"What is the urgency, Kit?" he asked.

"The men . . ." Kit began, anxiety in his voice.

"Mutiny?" Lazarus growled. "I've been expecting that. Well, Kit, shall we put it down?"

Kit looked at him in astonishment. " 'Shall we put it down?' " he echoed. "Is there any question of that?"

"Yes, Kit," Lazarus said slowly. "There is a question. If I die, you will become captain. Should I deny you that for the dubious pleasure of a few more years of this—this existence? What is my life, Kit, that I should cling to it?"

Kit looked at the leper captain, his blue eyes very clear.

"I would not have it at that price, sir," he said quietly.

"You're a good lad, Kit. I would have liked a son like you. But no matter. You've made my last years good ones." He stood up slowly. "I'll dicker with the swine, though the outcome matters little to me."

"Then let me face them!" Kit barked. "It's time they learned to come to heel for good and all!"

"Time enough for that when you're captain, Kit," Lazarus said, his hideously deformed fingers fumbling at his mask.

"Do you think that will ever be? In any mutiny I'll go over the side one splash behind you. I've led these dogs over the rails of twelve galleons, but what use has it been? They still resent my advancement. They're overdue for a lesson from me now."

"Then they shall have it," Lazarus said mildly. "You are armed?"

"Yes," Kit growled, touching the silver butts of his great pistols.

"We will not kill any unless we must," Lazarus said. "It will be better to cow them. These, I think, will serve." He took down a duck-foot pistol for himself. Kit stared at the curious weapon. It had four barrels spread out fanwise, so that it could cover the entire deck of a vessel with its fire. It had only one flintlock hammer, all four barrels firing at once from a single pull of the trigger. Kit watched Lazarus load it, cramming an unusually large charge of powder into each barrel, as well as half a dozen small shot on top of each charge. One blast from this multiple hand cannon and the whole deck might be swept clean.

"George of England made it," Lazarus said, "for the express purpose of putting down mobs. Now if you'll take down that blunderbuss dag up there, you'll be as well armed as I. Don't be afraid to touch it, Kit. It has been cleaned many times since I put it there."

Kit took down the tremendously heavy little gun, which, though it was as short as a pistol, had a rifle stock. The great bell-shaped barrel had been polished until it shone.

"Load it with scrap iron," Lazarus said, "above a triple weight of powder. It will kick like a Spanish mule, but if we have to fire, there will be none left to oppose us."

Kit loaded the weapon, all the time glancing toward the door.

Lazarus shook his head. "They won't rush us here. They would have to come one at a time through that door, and we could pick them off at leisure. Never fear—they'll await our pleasure."

Kit stood up, the short, ugly weapon draped over the crook of his arm.

"One thing more, Kit," Lazarus said. "When this thing is over, we sail for Port Royal."

Kit's brows rose. "Jamaica? Why?"

"To put me ashore on English soil. I'll give myself up to the authorities while you slip away. Wait, lad, hear me out! Though England and Spain are united in this damned mésalliance against France, the worst that can happen to me is to be exiled to some deserted island. This truce with the dons can't last. I have sunk more Spanish galleons than any Englishman since Drake. Alliance or not, my countrymen feel as I do. Besides," and he grinned wryly, "where will they find a hangman who would dare touch my skin to loop the rope about my neck?"

Kit frowned. "Is that your wish?" he growled.

"It is, Kit. I'm weary of the sea and fighting. And youth must be served. Come now."

They weaved their way, bracing themselves against the pitching of the vessel, to the deck. The men were drawn up in a semicircle facing the cabin, their faces black with scowls. Only Bernardo stood apart from them, his great pistol belt crisscrossing his shoulders. As Kit and Lazarus strode on deck, Bernardo came over quietly and stood beside them. Kit smiled mockingly.

"Have I ever deserted you yet?" Bernardo asked huskily.

"Never," Kit answered. "I should have known you would be on our side."

"You are likely to die with him now, Jew," Lazarus said. Then, to the men, "Speak your piece, lads, and have done with it!"

A man stepped forward. It was Tim Waters, a wizened little Englishman with the scar of a cutlass swipe ridging his face from brow to lip, one eye gone, and the top lip drawn upward by the wound so that his ugly yellow fangs showed forever in a macabre grin.

"Well, Cap'n," he began, "we've been thinkin', me an' the lads . . ."

"Deviltry, no doubt," Lazarus growled. "Go on."

"Lookee, Cap'n, we're in for one hell of a blow, as ye kin see. And here be the best harbor in the Windward Isles, not four leagues off our starboard."

"Correct. And in it are some twenty French vessels ranging from frigates to sloops of war. What do you think of that, Timothy!"

Waters scraped one bare, horny foot against the deck. "Them Frenchies," he said slyly, "is awful easy wit' freebooters. 'Specially wit' them as kin parlay frog. Now, if the *Seaflower* was to beat in wit' a fleur-de-lis streamin' from the masthead . . ."

"And with Captain Lazarus, who has sunk over thirty Frenchmen, in command? You have an answer to that one too, Timothy?"

Waters hesitated, twisting his hideously scarred face to glance at his comrades.

"Me an' the lads," he got out at last, "was thinkin' that ye'd agree to step down. Now, with Dupré here in command"—he nodded to a squat, thickset Gascon—"them frogeaters would welcome us like brothers. We could hide ye in the hold, an' put ye ashore later. Then ye could beat it for the hills. Live like a king up there, wit' twenty black wenches to wait on ye hand an' foot."

"I see," Lazarus said quietly. "And if the French came aboard and searched the vessel, you'd deliver me to them—in irons—wouldn't you?"

Waters glanced uneasily at the others. A mutter rose and ran from man to man. Emboldened, Waters turned back, a wicked grin on his face.

"Well, if ye want to put it that way, Cap'n," he said, "looks like we better git it over right now!"

Kit could see the men gathering for a rush. He stepped forward, the blunderbuss leveled. "I think," he said evenly and clearly, "that it would please me greatly to blow half of you to hell."

"And I the other half," Lazarus snarled, leveling the fan-shaped, four-barreled pistol.

"And if you leave even one," Bernardo added, laughing, "I'll shoot him through his gutless belly!"

The men stopped as though they had run against a wall. Kit could see their eyes, opened in fear, jerking from the enormous bell-shaped muzzle of the blunderbuss to the four black owl's eyes of the duck-foot pistol, and again to the slim dueling pistol that Bernardo held in his hand.

"Now, lookee, Cap'n . . ." Waters quavered.

"You witless, yellow-bellied curs," Lazarus said slowly, "do you think you're a match for Lazarus?"

"No, Cap'n," Waters whined. "We didn't mean to do ye harm. Why, me an' the boys was merely going to tie ye up a bit, so's ye wouldn't git hurt."

Lazarus's pale-blue eyes rested on Waters's face. They were glacial in their coldness. Then a little pinpoint of fire shone in them suddenly.

"Yes, Tim, you're very considerate. I must admit that. Kind as a brother—a blood brother." He thrust one deformed hand sidewise toward Kit. "Your dagger, lad," he whispered. Kit passed it over.

"The Caribbees have a ceremony," Lazarus said quietly, "by which they confer blood kinship upon those they love and trust. . . . Keep them covered, Kit." He took the dagger and drew the edge of it across his own wrist. It went across cleanly, and after a moment the bright blood oozed through. "Now, Tim," he said gently, "put out your hand. I would honor a brave and faithful comrade."

Waters stood there, his face graying, his voice gurgling like liquid in his throat, unable to shape a single recognizable sound, his one good eye bulging from its socket as he looked at that sickening, corpse-white hand, those abbreviated nubs of nailless, diseased fingers, over which the thick blood oozed. He sank to his knees.

"Cap'n," he got out, "Cap'n, for the love of God!"

But Lazarus advanced upon him slowly. When he was close, Waters collapsed in a quivering heap, slobbering like an animal in terror. The leper captain bent down and lifted Waters's left hand. Waters struggled feebly, trying to jerk it away, but those shortened fingers had a grip of iron. The captain slashed Waters's scrawny wrist until the blood came, and then, slowly, impassively, he pressed his own self-inflicted wound against it, so that their blood mingled. Then he stepped back, smiling peacefully.

"Throw down your arms, men," he said. "There'll be no mutiny here."

The pistols and cutlasses clattered to the deck. Kit stared at the men, his own stomach a little sick.

"Back to your quarters!" Lazarus barked. The men slunk back, whipped.

Then, after a moment, Waters raised himself from the deck and staggered after them. They whirled on him, daggers glittering in every hand. "Keep away!" they roared. "Leper!"

Waters faced them, the tears from his one eye penciling his scarred face. "Lads," he quavered, "lads, for the love o' God, I fought wit' ye . . . I broke bread wit' ye . . ."

A bearded man growled: "You did, but never again! Go to your brother. Go to Cap'n Lazarus!"

"Yes, Tim," Lazarus said gently, "come to me. Come and see how it feels to be rotting while you're still alive. Come watch your hands shrink, joint by joint, until they're animal's paws. It's not too bad. You feel no pain. You can put your hands into a candle flame and watch the flesh burn, and laugh. But it grows lonely, Tim. It's hard to have the whole world against you, praying for your death. Will it not please you to go ashore to find that the foulest strolling wench in Basse-Terre, half-blind of the French sickness, will run away from you shrieking? Yes, Tim, come. Come, brother leper!"

Waters's cavernous mouth came open, and a long, high animal howl of pure madness shrilled from his throat. He raised his hands, curved like talons, against the lowering sky, and started for his comrades.

"Whoresons!" he bleated. "You dirty bastards! Bas . . ."

He never finished the word. Kit saw the bearded man's leather jerkin tear open, saw the horny fingers close around the butt of a hidden, unsurrendered pistol. Waters was so close to the man that his tunic caught fire from the blast; then he crumpled all over at once, becoming suddenly boneless, sprawling grotesquely in death.

Lazarus shook his great head mournfully. "Now, who," he asked quietly, "is going to heave him over the side?"

The men stared at the corpse in breath-gone fascination. Not one of them, Kit knew, would dare lay a finger on it.

"Let him lay," the blackbeard growled at last.

"Yes," Lazarus said, "let him. Let him lie there until he rots, and the winds sweep the stink from his bloated belly into your nostrils. I think, lads, I shall not be lonely any longer." He turned then, and went down into his cabin. Kit followed him.

"Take the helm, Kit," Lazarus said, "and head for Port Royal. They've had their lesson."

"But Tim . . ." Kit protested.

"Tonight I'll heave him over myself. But leave him there all day. It will throw a scare into them they'll never forget."

Kit went aft and took his place at the whipstaff, holding the *Seaflower*'s prow due west. On the foredeck, the men stood as though frozen and stared at the body of Tim Waters. All day they rode before the wind, the trim vessel breasting the mountainous waves like a playful dolphin, but when night came they reefed even the flying jib, using only the spritsail to maintain steerageway. Yet such was the force of the gale that when morning broke, the fair coast of Jamaica lay before them.

The crew, finding that Tim's body had disappeared during the night, fell to work willingly. The *Seaflower* scudded toward the harbor of Port Royal. But as they nosed into the bay, Bernardo, who had climbed up the foremast, roared down: "Hard aport! Hard aport, for the love of God!"

Without a second thought, Kit swung the whipstaff all the way over. The *Seaflower* responded at once, swinging about on the first arc of the circle. It was her handiness that saved their lives. A slower, less responsive vessel would have been only halfway around when the tidal wave hit. As it was, the mountain of water struck her three-quarters aft and hurled her ahead like a chip. The whole world for Kit was a white wall of water, blotting out the sky, pounding his eardrums senseless with a torrential deluge of sound. Standing on the little platform between decks, protected only by the low, arched cover, he was hit by a tag end of the wave that had all the weight and apparent solidity of so much stone. If the impact of the water had not been broken by the high sweep of the poop and the arch over his head, so that its force was largely spent, it would have smashed every bone in his body. As it was, it struck him with sufficient force to knock him unconscious.

Minutes later his eyes flickered open. The unmanned whipstaff stood up before him, straight and level, as though the *Seaflower* were drifting in a dead calm. Kit staggered to his feet, shaking his head. He remembered the wave, but now . . . He looked aft. Half the crew was gathered on the poop, staring toward Port Royal. Kit called to one of the men and gave over the whipstaff. He made his way aft.

Behind the *Seaflower* the water was calm, with only a little swell, and the wind that blew in from the sea was gentle. But on the shore a great plume of smoke stood up above what had been the town of Port Royal—an immense plume, a column of white so broad at its base that it covered the entire city. It rose straight up so high that its domed head seemed to touch the very floor of heaven. From where he stood, Kit could see that it was fed by the red tongues of many flames. Then near the shore another wave started, much smaller and weaker than the first. As it raced toward them, Kit saw the few remaining houses on the shore swing back and forth crazily and come crashing down. Off to the left of the city, a hill lifted its head. Now, as they watched, the hill split in half, and the great rocks rumbled downward, directly upon the city. Kit could see the inch-high figures of the people of Port Royal running wildly about while the earth writhed under their feet, and now and again yawning chasms opened up and swallowed them. From the firm decks of the *Seaflower,* it was all curiously remote and unreal—an extraordinarily vivid nightmare; but before his eyes a city was dying.

Bernardo came and stood beside him. Together they watched the mad scramble as the people put out to sea in anything that floated; but near the shore the earthquake tremors raised mountains of surf, and red lava from the yawning chasms turned the shoal water into live steam. Not one of the small boats got through.

Kit turned and saw Captain Lazarus coming out of his cabin.

"What is it, Kit?" he asked.

"I think, sir," Kit said quietly, "that very likely there are no authorities for you to surrender yourself to. Look!"

Lazarus's gaze followed Kit's pointing finger. "Merciful God!" he whispered. "What is it?"

"Earthquake, sir," Bernardo told him. "I saw one once in Italy. But nothing like this!"

Kit stiffened suddenly. From one of the coves near the city a tall Spanish galleon was beating out to sea. That a Spanish vessel should be in the harbor of compatriots of Drake, Hawkins, and Henry Morgan was only another irony of seventeenth-century power politics, which sometimes made allies of hereditary enemies. The growing power of Louis XIV had forced all Europe into an alliance against France, while the rotting hulk that was Spain, for all the vastness of her possessions, was no longer to be feared under such a king as Charles the Bewitched. Straightening, Kit turned to the renegade Spaniard he himself had made third officer.

"Shorten sail, Pat," he said softly.

Patricio Velasco relayed the command to the men. The *Seaflower* lost headway rapidly.

"Gunners at stations," Kit said. The filthy, half-naked buccaneers leaped to their guns, the tarred matches flaring in their hands.

Kit watched the tall Spaniard beating through the boiling surf. She came on, overtaking the *Seaflower* with majestic deliberation. Kit's hands whitened, gripping the rail. Beside him, Patricio and Bernardo stood, scarcely daring to breathe. The Spaniard would have to come much closer before the *Seaflower*'s guns would have much effect on her massive timbers. On she came, moving with maddening slowness, a mighty ocean monarch overtaking a dwarf. Kit wondered why she had not opened fire. There was something contemptuous in the way she ignored the *Seaflower*'s existence. Kit's mouth hardened beneath the white-gold mustache.

Suddenly he felt Bernardo's great hand tightening on his arm with a bone-crushing grip. Startled, Kit half-turned. But Bernardo was staring past him, pointing wordlessly at the pennant that fluttered from the masthead, just beneath the flag of Spain. It was a simple device: a Black Heron on a field of gold! Kit leaned forward, unbelieving, a tumult of fierce joy hammering through his veins—at the sight of the banner of Don Luis del Toro.

"His ship!" he whispered, his voice hoarse with exultation. "*His* ship! By the saints, Bernardo, I will crust his filthy bones with salt before nightfall!"

Bernardo's dark eyes narrowed, watching the galleon with the Heron Banner as it drew abreast. "Better put her over, Kit," he growled. "She's not truly a galleon, despite her lines. I'd say a ship of the line, mounting a hundred guns."

"Damn her guns!" Kit snorted. "Damn her and her guns! I'm going in! Hard aport!" he roared at the helmsman.

The *Seaflower* veered, angling in the direction of the great ship. The lines of their tracks converged.

"Three points to sta'board!" Kit called. The *Seaflower* veered again, coming about on a track parallel to that of the great Spanish vessel.

"Stand by for a broadside!" Kit commanded. The gunners bent over their pieces, their faces ashen with fear.

Bernardo said nothing. He knew that one blast from those huge cannon aboard the Spaniard would lift them from the water. But he knew also that there was no stopping Kit.

Kit lifted his hand in the signal for firing. But he held it there, suddenly arrested by a commotion on the Spaniard's upper deck. She lay a pistol shot off the *Seaflower*'s port side, and the men on the deck were plainly visible. Down the wind the hoarse hallooing of their laughter beat faintly on Kit's ears. Then his hand came down, inch by slow inch, without giving the signal to fire.

For on the deck of the Spaniard there swayed the willow-slender figure of a woman. Kit hung over the rail, his eyes filled with the dazzling whiteness of her flesh amid the tattered rags that were all the Spaniards had left of her clothing. Even as he watched, rough hands seized her again, the brown fingers digging into the golden blaze of her hair, forcing her head backward until the white blob of her face was blotted out by the hooked beak and black mustache of a Spanish seaman.

"Dogs and sons of dogs!" Kit howled. "Bring me a musket!"

A seaman leaped aft and returned with the heavy, clumsy weapon. Kit settled it across the lee rail, taking careful aim. But before he could fire, the woman tore loose from the Spaniard's grasp. Her hand shot skyward, and bright in it glittered the sheen of the Spanish seaman's dagger. It crashed downward, disappearing to the hilt through the snowy globe of one bare breast. Kit saw her crumpling slowly to the deck, and the rage in his throat was as bitter as wormwood. His finger tightened on the trigger; the musket numbed his shoulder with its recoil as the Spaniard went over sideways, one half of his face entirely gone.

Instantly the Spaniards began to scramble toward their guns. Kit lifted his hand and let it drop all in one motion. All the *Seaflower*'s guns opened the sky and the sea with one stupendous bellow, kicking back on their wheeled carriages to the limits of the hempen breeching rope that anchored them to the sides, the brigantine rolling with the recoil, and the clouds of smoke washing out the horizon. But when the smoke had cleared, though there was a pile of dead seamen on her decks, the giant Spaniard seemed scarcely to have been touched. Instantly, from her high deck came a storm of fire from her murthering pieces: swivels, rabinets, falconets, falcons, and minions.

The small shot shrieked through the *Seaflower*'s rigging, inflicting small damage. In another minute though, Kit knew, she would be able to bring to bear her immense full cannon, hurling sixty-four-pound shot. That two or three hits from those great guns would be enough to sink the *Seaflower* he knew even better. He raced toward the helmsman, shouting commands. Those crew members detailed to the task shivered the fighting sails, throwing the *Seaflower* rapidly back so that she dropped astern of the Spaniard almost at once. Then the sleek brigantine veered sharply to port, bringing her prow dead astern of the Spaniard, so that that great vessel could bring only her light chase guns to bear.

It was at this point that Lazarus mounted the deck.

"You handled it well, Kit," he said, "but as you can neither board nor sink her, it is only sense to run away."

"Never!" Kit spat.

Lazarus smiled. "Be reasonable, Kit," he said. "What chance has a brigantine against a ship of the line?"

"That ship," Kit got out, "sails under the colors of a man I am sworn to kill."

"You'll have to wait," Lazarus said calmly. "It's quite impossible now."

Kit opened his mouth to protest further, but a shout from the men on the forecastle stopped him. He ran forward, followed by Bernardo and Lazarus. A group of seamen were clustered near the bowsprit, pointing up at the Spaniard's towering stern. Kit gazed upward, his jaw dropping open.

"Mother of God!" he whispered. "Have they all the women of Port Royal aboard?"

High on the poop deck of the Spaniard, another slender figure struggled in the arms of a broad-shouldered hidalgo. From the short distance separating the two vessels, Kit could see that she was very much like the first, except that her wildly disheveled hair was not golden, but as red as a sunset. So intently did Kit watch her that it was long seconds before something in the hidalgo's appearance struck him as being familiar; then his breath left his lungs in a huge gasp, for the Spaniard who held the slender girl to him was Don Luis del Toro. Kit whirled, his hands searching for a musket, but when one had been put into them he stood there transfixed, unable to fire. There was not one chance in a thousand of hitting Don Luis without also wounding the girl. Then something very like a smile played about the corners of his mouth.

Slowly, carefully, he lifted the musket. It roared, and splinters from the lateen yard showered down on Don Luis's bare head. The grandee whirled, releasing the girl. As Kit reached for another musket, he saw her poised above the carved and gilded gingerbread work just under the stern lantern, then she arched downward, cutting the sea as cleanly as any knife. Kit lifted the second musket, but Don Luis flattened himself behind the lateen mast and called to his own musketeers.

The girl's bright head, the color of a scarlet hibiscus against the blue water, broke surface. Instantly five Spanish musketeers leaped to the poop, their weapons pointed downward. For them to miss at such a distance was an impossibility. But before they could take aim, the *Seaflower*'s chase gun fired. When its lionlike roar had ceased echoing, ten yards of the Spaniard's stern castle had been carried away, and with it the musketeers. In two swift glances, Kit saw Don Luis scrambling downward toward safety and the girl stretching up her arms for help. There was time for only one of the two actions called for. Kit let the musket clatter to the deck and threw a line to the girl.

A dozen hands leaped to grasp the other end, and the slight figure of the girl was hauled swiftly over the side. Kit released the rope and caught her at the armpits, dragging her aboard. He stood her on her feet and stepped back, gazing at her. The long red-gold hair streamed wetly over her shoulders, haloing a slim face with high cheekbones that gave her eyes the illusory appearance of having an odd, Mongolian slant. Now, resting on Kit's face, her eyes widened until they were enormous, making her small face even smaller by comparison. They were a deep green, curiously light-filled; they matched exactly the emerald that Kit wore in his left ear.

Kit's blue eyes sought the crimson curve of her mouth, held tightly against pain and terror, then his gaze fixed on the white column of her neck and her slim figure, only partially concealed by a single shift rent in half a dozen places and clinging with drenched fidelity to every singing line of her young body. Behind him now, a low snarling mutter ran through the ranks of the crew. Kit whirled to face them. Woman-starved, pent-up far past the bursting point with years of unsatisfied desire, how long could he or anyone restrain them? Them—or himself?

But at that moment Lazarus stepped forward and touched the girl's arm with the slender stick he carried.

"Come," he said gently. Silently the girl turned and accompanied him into his cabin. Then the door was closed behind them.

Kit stood there with the rest of the crew, staring at that door, hearing the echo of their muted rage rumbling in his own throat. What can he do with her? he wondered bitterly. Old as he is and rotten with disease? The thought checked him, bringing him up short against an icy wall of terror. That fair skin, white as the snows of the Spanish mountains with the dawn light on them, would it know the touch of those fingers of living death? Would that matchless, marvelous brush-fire hair whiten and fall out, and the skin, stretched taut above those fine-cut cheekbones, deaden into gray-white ringed with purple?

There was need now for cessation of thinking. Turning, Kit barked commands at the crew. They scrambled among the rigging, cracking on all sail until the *Seaflower*'s two masts groaned under the burden of canvas. The helmsman put her over hard to port, and she veered away from the great castled Spaniard with which she had fought so indecisive a battle. Kit headed her toward Hispaniola and stood on the forecastle, his mind black with unbidden thoughts.

After nightfall, he turned and moved aft, step by step, toward Lazarus's cabin. A few of the crew members still ringed it, staring hungrily at the closed door.

"Away!" Kit roared at them. "Get your arses to work, or I'll see how a touch of the cat can speed you! Step along now, right hearty!"

The buccaneers slunk away like sullen hounds, their greedy glances fixed backward on the door. Kit stood there silently for a long moment, then the door crashed open and the huge silhouette of Lazarus was framed in the lantern glow, reeling there and bellowing Kit's name.

"Aye, aye, sir?" Kit answered.

"Come," Lazarus whispered. "Come and take the girl away. I was a fool, but I have been lonely so long . . . and her skin was so fair . . . Before I died, just this once, it seemed that fate owed me some recompense for all my suffering. But no. Come, Kit, and take her to your quarters."

"What happened?" Kit growled.

"She asked me—to remove—my mask."

"Oh!" Kit whispered.

"She did not faint. I could have stood that. No, Kit, she looked into my face—and vomited from sheer disgust. Come and take her, Kit."

Kit entered the dim, foul-smelling interior of Lazarus's cabin. On a chair, the girl was bent over, half-swooning, her shoulders shaking. Kit put out his hand and touched her gently. She whirled, her eyes green blobs of naked terror; then the fear in them subsided a little.

"I have come to take you away," Kit said in the stiff, accented English he had learned from Lazarus. "Have no fear. I will not harm you."

Silently the girl rose and came to him. Kit led her up the ladder and across the deck, one hand resting on the butt of his pistol. Behind him he could hear Lazarus muttering: "She looked into my face—my old, dying beast's face—and she . . ."

Kit opened the door to his quarters and pointed to his hammock. "Lie down and rest," he said. "You are hungry, perhaps? I will get you food."

"Food?" the girl echoed, the word shuddering up from her throat in tones of near-nausea. "I shall never eat again!"

Kit stared at her blankly.

"Where will you sleep?" she asked.

"Outside," Kit said. "Just outside, so that no one may enter."

"And you—you'll not come in?"

Kit shook his head. "No," he said simply. "I shall not trouble you."

The girl turned on him angrily, her emerald eyes firelit in their depths.

"Do you think that I believe that? You're a man, for all your handsomeness, and all men are beasts!"

Kit studied her, his blue eyes somber. "I'm sorry you believe that," he began.

"Believe? I know. Didn't Don Luis put into Port Royal to save us from the earthquake? And you saw how he helped us! Beth, my sweet sister, dead by her own hand on the deck, after those swine had finished with her. While I—I was more highly honored. Don Luis reserved me for himself. And here on this vessel—this English vessel—that horrible, disgusting old man . . ."

Kit's hand stole inside his sash and came out with the great pistol. "Here," he said, "take this. If any man enters—even I—use it!"

The girl looked up at him, her green eyes widening. "Thank you," she whispered.

Something in her eyes sent a glacial chill stealing through Kit's veins. "Not on yourself!" he growled.

"Why not? What have I left to live for? Would a decent man—if there is any such thing—have me now? Could I go back to Jamaica to Reginald and say, 'Here, take me, used, befouled thing that I am'? I could scrub my skin until it reddens and peels and never remove the stain. It's inside upon my soul."

"Give me back the pistol, then," Kit said.

"No," the girl said softly. "I shall not harm myself. If I had the courage, I would have done it before now. No, I will live—and many a man shall suffer for this day!"

Kit looked at her, and his blue eyes were very clear. He left the cabin, closing the door softly behind him. But even as he lifted his hand from the knob he heard the crash of a pistol shot. It came from aft. He started toward the sound, but before he had covered half the length of the deck Bernardo met him.

"Kit," he said, "Kit . . ."

"Lazarus?" Kit growled.

"Yes. Through the mouth."

Kit pushed past him and entered the cabin. The great bulk of Captain Lazarus was sprawled on the floor, a pistol gripped in his hand. Kit covered that huge, shattered head with a blanket and knelt beside him, muttering swift Castilian prayers. Then he took down the captain's hammock and rolled Lazarus's inert bulk onto it.

He called four members of the crew. They lifted the hammock by the guy ropes and walked slowly to the side. They paused there while Kit lifted his head and said in English: "Forgive him, O God of the heretics, for though his sins were many, he was greatly put upon. Amen." Then the body of Captain Lazarus slid over the side to make a muffled splash in the darkened sea.

Kit could see the men scurrying off to wash themselves. He followed them more slowly. When he was clean and had eaten, he went back to the door of his cabin. Wearily he sank down. As he sat there, the creak of his hammock swinging gently against the swell sounded in his ears. It went on all night, a slow, maddening sound. His mind formed the image of the girl, lithe, soft-curving, nestling there amid the bright blaze of her long hair.

Finally, as the first flush of morning was graying in and the ragged outlines of Cow Island were visible on the horizon, Kit got up stiffly. He pushed open the door and entered the cabin. Inside, it was yet dark, but he could hear the girl's regular breathing.

He lit the lantern and stared down. She lay in the hammock, relaxed in sleep, her mouth soft and a little parted, dew-petaled, inviting. Kit stood there staring at her until some of the desire in him slipped away to be replaced by a great and aching tenderness. Then, kneeling beside the hammock, he kissed her mouth. She came awake at once, her green eyes terror-filled and flaring.

"You!" she whispered, her voice hoarse, chest-deep, filled with loathing. "You too!" Then, before Kit could move, she swung the long pistol over and fired at point-blank range. Kit saw the wall of fire exploding before his eyes, felt the white-hot stab of pain, then clouds of darkness closed in upon him from all sides at once. But as he lay there on the floor, slipping out on the tide of roaring blackness, he imagined he felt the soft, fragrant weight of her body pressing upon his in the gloom, and his hand moved briefly, caressing her bright hair. Then night crashed down, complete and utter, with no ray of light and no sound at all.

2

Early in the morning, the Black Heron extricated itself from the folds of the golden banner that had held it so long imprisoned and flew across the tiny space of Kit's cabin. It furled its ominous wings and sat on the foot of Kit's bunk. Kit watched it a long time, staring into the bird's strange eyes, which were lidless, golden, unalive. Then, with a low croak, the heron moved forward and stood on his chest. And try as he would, Kit could not move it.

There seemed to be something the matter with his arms. He could not raise them. He made the effort, the beads of perspiration standing out on his forehead, but his arms lay at his sides like so much mutton, lifeless and inert. The heron sitting on his chest was much heavier now, pressing down with such weight that all his breath seemed to be leaving his lungs. And suddenly, inexplicably, there was a shifting in time and space and the heron was no longer there. The weight was still there, however, somewhat lighter than the heron; but instead of being confined to his chest, it lay on his entire body, warm, fragrant, soft-fleshed, moving. It seemed to be weeping, and the great tears dropped like warm rain into his face. There was a sweeping motion, and a lock of hair, damp and smelling of salt water, brushed across his face. He knew, without being able to see it, that it was like hibiscus petals, like poinsettia, like flame.

He put up his fingers to stroke it, and this time they moved, seemingly without effort. And the pale face above him blurred momentarily into focus, the mouth flame-scarlet and trembling uncontrollably, bending down to find his in the darkness. The warm lips moved closer, parting as they caught his, pressing until all his breath stopped, the body pressing too, making of itself one long caress, breast and trunk and thigh moving upon his, the little snow cones, shell-rose-tipped, soft-stabbing his bare chest like widely separated fire points. And all his life was caught up in one wild surge of flame that roared out into the dark. . . .

The next time he came back, it was to vivid brightness, and the Black Heron fluttered once more on its golden banner from a pikestaff being borne through a street in Cádiz. . . . Kit saw himself, the boy Kit, standing on the roof of his foster father's house with his mother, a lovely creature all pink and white and golden whose tongue still spoke with the accents of Normandy, and with Bernardo Díaz.

Below them, lolling in their saddles in contemptuous arrogance, a party of grandees were riding. Kit could see them now, like figures from a bright tapestry strangely come to life, their faces vague and indistinct above the rich black-velvet tunics, blurred into curious anonymity except for one face.

Remembering that face, a sound tore at Kit's throat—a muted syllable, voluptuous with rage, that started as an animal growl, low and bestial, and rose to a groan that was half a sob, brimming with raw and quivering pain. He half-rose on his bunk, and someone who watched beside him pressed him back. For a moment, the actuality of Bernardo's troubled face came clear before Kit's sight. He opened his mouth to comfort his friend, to say . . .

But the words remained forever unspoken, for before he could utter them, Kit was back again on a rooftop in Cádiz. Below him, once more the Heron Banner danced in the sunlight, and the grandees rode through the crowds that scurried fearfully away at their approach. Kit watched the spectacle idly until a low, explosive gasp from his mother's lips reached him. He could hear her breath strangling in her throat. Then, to his vast amazement, she turned and ran, as fleet as a girl, down the stairs. Bernardo was two steps behind her and Kit followed hard on his heels. But neither of them was swift enough to catch her. She plunged out into the street, and while Kit stood in the doorway as if turned to stone, she threw up her hands and caught at the bridle of one of the horsemen.

"Luis!" she shrieked. "Luis!"

Kit saw the man's whip go up, arching against the sky. Then it sang downward and the lash hissed across his mother's face like a serpent, cutting it to the bone.

Kit saw her sitting in the roadway, holding her face in her hands, the bright blood oozing out between her fingers. Then he was off, the rage roaring in his throat, stretching out his hands for the grandee's neck. He got a vivid impression of the man's face, swart as a Moor's, with a bold, jutting nose and a chin marred by a tuft of inky beard. Then one of the lancers who accompanied the grandee let down his lance so that the shaft came heavily across the boy's bright head. As Kit lay there in the street, with the rooftops reeling in circles above him, he heard the hoarse laughter of the hidalgos. . . .

That sound now was curiously mingled with the soft wash of the seas outside his cabin, and with the noises inside his head. He lay listening to it until he could no longer distinguish which was laughter and which was sea wash, and sank at last gratefully into slumber.

When he awoke again it was morning once more, and for almost an hour he knew where he was. He could discern the oak beams of the bulkheads, see his own garments hanging from a peg, and the weary form of Bernardo slumped over in a chair in a sleep of pure exhaustion.

"Poor Bernardo," he mused, "to what a pass have I brought him!" He raised himself halfway up on the bunk, but the action set the hammers to swinging inside his skull so that he fell back, and darkness crashed down once more. It was a confused darkness, filled with dreams that hurled themselves with lightninglike profusion before his eyes, without regard to time or space. . . .

He saw himself a child in the house of Jeanne Giradeaux and Pierre Labat, wigmaker to the grandees of Spain, come like many another Frenchman of his time to Spain for reasons he guarded jealously. Kit heard once more the whispers: "Don Luis . . . Luis del Toro . . . Del Toro . . ." whispers that ceased abruptly whenever he entered a room, only to linger on like an undefined menace always hovering above his bright head. . . .

He stood, at one and the same time with no sense of transition in time or space, and pumped the heavy pistol balls point-blank at Del Toro, seeing them flatten against the gleaming breastplate the grandee wore, the mighty figure reeling under the impact and clattering ignominiously to the cobblestones, entirely unhurt save in spirit. Afterward, he and Bernardo were fleeing, endlessly fleeing, breath-gone and lost, with thunderous hoofbeats pounding after them through the streets of Cádiz.

Kit saw himself stop and fire, saw Bernardo do likewise, and when finally they had reached the shelter of the ancient tombs the Phoenicians had dug centuries ago above Cádiz, Kit found that he had the Heron Banner in his hands. . . .

This time he sat fully upright in his bunk, and his voice rang out: "Stop it, you beasts! Oh, most foul, murderous, torturing dogs!"

Bernardo sprang at once from his chair and tried to push him down; but in his delirium Kit had the strength of ten. His eyes flamed with pure madness; the anguish on his face under the great swath of bandages was almost greater than Bernardo could bear. Then the vision that passed before Kit's sightless eyes was one that he had never seen in reality, but in the curious, disordered dream world of delirium it was far more clear than any of the others. Kit groaned terribly, pushing his knuckles into his blue eyes and grinding them cruelly in the attempt to shut out the pictures that persisted in coming with such hideous clarity:

He could see, as though he stood there, the subterranean chamber beneath a stone castle and the brawny figure of the executioner, glistening all over with sweat, in the ruddy glow from the brazier in which the irons were heating. He could see the man's face hidden in its cap of leather that fitted over the shaven bullet head and came down to the mouth line, to form a mask through whose slits the small beady eyes shifted; and before him the lovely white figure of Kit's mother stretched hand and foot around the outer circumference of the wheel that creaked as the man tightened the cords. By such an implement, the arms were dislocated at the shoulders, at the elbows, at the wrists, the legs at hip, knee, and ankle, until at last the bones themselves gave. Then the small, willowy rods of iron stroked lightly, just hard enough to break the soft ribs of a woman's chest, until her body was a thing of rubber, utterly wanting in skeletal support. And beside the great glistening brute, the robed and saintly figure of the Inquisitor asking delicately:

"Where is your son Cristóbal? Where is he? Where? Where? Where?"

Kit could see his mother's fine head thrashing about on the slim column of her throat as she moaned:

"I do not know! Truly I do not! By the Virgin! By Saint Anthony! By the Blessed Infant Jesus, I do not know!"

He saw her faint. They loosened the rack and revived her. Then they began again, questioning, insisting, probing through the long hours while the irons that had been heated for application to her white skin, and the other ugly implements, waited. The knout. The boot. The thumbscrews.

The Iron Maiden, that form-fitting coffin studded with five-inch iron spikes. In the field of inhuman bestiality, at least, there was no end to Spanish inventiveness.

Kit sat there on his bunk, half-supported by Bernardo, his bandaged head swaying with the slow weaving roll and pitch of the brigantine, and his words came out hoarse-voiced and agony-laden: "How long did it take, Bernardo? How long for a small and lovely woman to die?" Then, bending down his bright head, he gave way to the convulsive racking of great sobs. Gently Bernardo pressed him back upon the bunk, and this time Kit made no resistance.

Throughout that day and the next, Bernardo was able to follow quite clearly what was happening in Kit's fevered mind. He saw Kit relive their escape from Cádiz Harbor, diving from the Torre del Vigía into the sea and swimming to an outward-bound Netherlander. He saw Kit's face light up with fierce joy as they were told that the *Zeeroover*'s destination was the Indies, for they had already learned that Don Luis del Toro had left Spain for Cartagena the night before the civil authorities tortured Jeanne Giradeaux to death. He saw the battle in which their vessel was overtaken and pulled down by the pirate brigantine *Seaflower,* and the calm air with which Kit accepted service aboard a vessel commanded by a man whose very touch was death.

And finally, joyously, Bernardo saw the young man whom he loved like the son he had never had slip into normal, dreamless sleep, cool of skin, breathing calmly.

So it was that on the fifth day after receiving the wound, Kit looked up from his hammock into the face of Bernardo Díaz. It was a very solid, perceptible face, without any intervening haze of darkness shifting between it and his eyes.

"Thank God!" Bernardo whispered, his voice rich and vibrant with emotion.

A weak ghost of a smile wavered about the corners of Kit's colorless mouth. "I have yet sins to commit," he whispered, "before I gain admission into hell."

"It's a narrow squeak you've had, Kit," Bernardo said. "The ball creased your skull, cracking the bone a little, I think. Anyhow, you're mending now."

Kit's hand stole upward and touched the great wad of bandages swathing his head. "The ball?" he echoed. "Yes! She shot me. Where is she, Bernardo? She is not harmed? You did not permit the crew . . ."

"Youth," Bernardo sighed, shaking his head. "Oh, to be twenty-one again!

. . . The wench comes within a hair of sending him into the next world and he inquires about her health!"

Kit struggled to sit up. "Answer me, Bernardo! She is not hurt?"

"That I do not know. The lady is—no longer with us."

"What!"

"She went over the side as we passed Cow Island. I saw her gain the shore. The red-haired one is a wonderfully expert swimmer."

Kit was sitting fully upright now, swaying in the hammock, supporting his head between his hands.

"But Cow Island, Bernardo!" he got out. "Every French freebooter in the Antilles holes up there!"

"Yes," Bernardo said grimly. "No doubt she received a warm welcome. Do not waste your sympathy on her, Kit. After all, it is not her fault that you are still alive."

Kit sat very still, staring at the bulkhead. "Nor hers that she used that pistol," he whispered. "She was so young, Bernardo—so young and so fair. And she had been foully abused."

"That I know. But there are other fish in the sea, Kit. Now that Lazarus is gone, there will be wenches aplenty to stroke those fair cheeks of yours. What a blessing that she aimed high! Your hair will cover the scar."

"I shall never get her out of my mind," Kit said.

"Never is a long time. In twenty years you will find how easily the faces of a dozen maids run together indistinguishably in the mind's flux. . . . But there are other matters more pressing than this of the lass."

"So?" Kit growled.

"The crew. This tongue of mine, whose oiliness you've seen fit to complain about in the past, alone has maintained your captaincy."

"My captaincy!" Kit said. "Mother of God! I'd forgotten that!"

"Time you remembered it," Bernardo said dryly. "I think you'd better put in your appearence on deck. Can you stand?"

He put out his arm and Kit grasped it. But when Kit's feet had reached the floor, the cabin oscillated dizzily before his eyes and Bernardo had to catch him to keep him from falling.

"Tomorrow, then," Bernardo said. "I'll bring you some hot broth. In the meantime, I'll keep these dogs off."

On the morrow, Kit woke with a head that ached only a little and eyes that were entirely clear. Long before Bernardo entered his cabin he was up, swaying lightly on his feet. Another bowl of the steaming broth, and yet another, sent the strength curling steadily through his limbs. Bernardo helped him dress, and together they went up to the quarter-deck.

Bernardo cupped his big hands and roared to the crew: "Attention! Line up, and hear Captain Gerado!"

The men shuffled into position, their faces blank and hostile.

"Look you, lads," Kit began steadily, "life aboard the *Seaflower* has not been a pleasant one. That I know well." The buccaneers growled assent. "We've piled up treasure only to have it stolen from us because the people of Basse-Terre believe us befouled with leprosy. That must be changed."

"Aye," the black-bearded ruffian growled, "but how?"

"We will heave to near the coast of Cuba," Kit told them, "and clean the ship. All of Lazarus's possessions must be sent over the side, and sulphur burned in his cabin. Then the vessel will be swabbed from hold to crosstrees. After that you men will scrub your filthy hides, trim your hair and beards, and dress yourselves as honorable seamen. When this is done, we will put into Basse-Terre."

"Sacrebleu!" Dupré grunted. "What difference will it make? Still we ride the *Seaflower*—pest ship of the Antilles!"

"I will change that," Kit said evenly. "If I should fail in this, I will step down and allow you to choose another man as captain. But," he added, his voice dropping even lower, his words coming out slow and spare and deadly clear, "I will stand for no grumbling until the matter is put to the test. If I fail to fill your coffers with gold and make it possible for you to take what pleasure you will ashore, I will step aside. Till then, look alive and step nimbly! To your stations now!"

Watching the men keenly, Bernardo could see that the look of sullen hostility on their faces had lessened considerably. They went about their tasks with energy. All day the *Seaflower* tacked through the Windward Passage until she came to a sheltered cove and nosed into the quiet haven. Minutes after she had dropped anchor she was alive with activity, which ceased only after night had fallen. Her decks were swabbed until the oak planking gleamed dully. Fresh gilt was applied to her ornamentation, the black pitch paint was applied to her hull until it took on the look of newness. Kit ran her in so close to shore that by low tide she was almost entirely out of water, and the hammers rang against the chisels as the barnacles were pried loose from her hull. The stifling fumes of sulphur poured out of her ports, and all shot-torn and gale-rent sails were discarded for new canvas, and fresh, newly tarred hemp replaced the worn guy ropes, clew lines, and stays of her rigging. Three days later, the *Seaflower* was as trim a vessel as ever cleaved the sea of the Caribbees.

She put out to sea, heading across the passage between Cuba and Hispaniola. As the low hump of Tortuga came in sight, the crew lined up for Kit's inspection. They were dressed, every man of them, in nondescript finery taken from the holds of vessels they had scuttled. That the colors they had selected were ill-matched, so that they looked like a garish lot of tropical birds, made little difference; the men of the *Seaflower* were a brave sight. Kit passed along the line of the crew until he came to the black-bearded ruffian, Smithers, a fugitive from the gibbets of half the North American colonies and a veritable prince of scoundrels. Smithers was a young man towering by an inch over Kit's own six feet of height, but his face was so buried in the great dark swirls of his beard that it was almost impossible to determine how he looked.

Kit gazed at him, a mocking light dancing in his clear blue eyes.

"Scissors!" he barked. At once one of the ship's boys ran to fetch them. Kit took the gleaming shears in his hand and advanced upon Smithers. Something very like terror leaped in the buccaneer's eyes as Kit growled: "Time we saw what lies behind that vermin's nest. Hold him, men!"

The men flung themselves on Smithers with howls of delight. Kit's hand flashed, and black clouds of whiskers drifted to the deck. Kit did not cut them all off; instead he left the howling, swearing scoundrel a neatly pointed Vandyke, and an upswept flourish of mustachios. Then he stood back, surveying his handiwork. Shorn of his beard, Smithers was an extraordinarily handsome devil. Kit's hand went inside his coat and came out with a small silver mirror. He thrust it out before Smithers' face.

"Here," he said grinning, "see for yourself."

Abruptly Smithers stopped struggling. His mouth dropped open. He stared at himself in unconcealed awe.

"Mother of God," he whispered, "I'm right pretty!" The crew roared.

The rest of the voyage went on with uncommon smoothness. Smithers, who had been root and branch of much of the trouble aboard, stood more than half the time by the mizzen staring at his own image in a flat piece of brass he had polished into a mirror. Now and again he would pat a stray hair back into place in his black spike of beard; his mustachios were smartly waxed and both his hair and his Vandyke were oiled and drenched with perfume.

"Vanity," Kit remarked to Bernardo as they passed him on their rounds, "has its uses!"

When they came into the harbor of Basse-Terre, Kit did not, as Lazarus had done, anchor the *Seaflower* far out and apart from the other vessels. Instead, he slid her in among the other pirate craft, manned by men of a score of nations, that lay tied up in the bay of the city that lived on stolen goods.

Bernardo looked at Kit, who was dressed after a fashion that would have delighted a lord of the court of Versailles, then back to the city.

"To think," he said with a chuckle, "that as a boy I used to dream of digging up pirates' treasure!"

Kit's cool blue eyes lighted with amusement. "Before you knew Basse-Terre, eh? If there is any buried gold in the Antilles, it was by the hands of whores and rum-sellers that it was hidden. God knows they get it all!"

"Though not in the past from the *Seaflower,"* Bernardo mused. "Yet if the daughters of joy do not this night receive their share of our spoils, another foot will tread the quarter-deck tomorrow."

Kit frowned, his eyes catching the pinpoints of fire from the dancing waves. "I do not care for the honor," he said quietly, "if there be any honor in captaining this crew of cutthroats. But there are two matters I must attend to."

"Two?" Bernardo growled. "Del Toro, and . . . ?"

"And she of the flaming hair and the ready trigger finger," Kit answered simply.

"I'll wager that your methods in these pressing matters will vary widely," said Bernardo.

"I'll not deny that," Kit said. "But come, we'd best be putting ashore. It seems that the citizenry of Basse-Terre are preparing their usual hearty welcome."

At Kit's command, a plank was run out from the *Seaflower* to the wharf. He and Bernardo marched down it, followed by the heavily laden crew. As they filed down the wharf, Kit saw a manservant of one of the merchants busily engaged in drawing a line across the sand of the beach.

Kit moved toward him slowly, his eyes light-filled and dancing. As he came closer, the women in the crowd, who had set up their usual screeching at the sight of the *Seaflower*'s crew, fell silent suddenly. Those of them who had started to run away, looking back over their shoulders all the time, slowed to a walk, then to a full halt. Kit walked on with grave deliberation toward the man who was busily drawing his line in the sand. The sunlight broke through the crests of the wine palms and fell full on his great curly mane. Beneath the broad brim of his maroon felt hat and the proud silver of the ostrich plume it gleamed like gold in the morning light. Kit's slim hands, ablaze with great diamonds, rested carelessly on the silver hilt of his Spanish sword, and his mustache and spike beard were white-gold.

He reached the manservant amid a silence that could almost be felt, broken only by the faint echo of the surf offshore. He paused a moment, looking at the man's broad back, before he dealt him a kick that sent him face forward into the soft sand with such force that his chin plowed up a furrow.

The silence exploded into laughter, and high above the hoarse masculine guffaws rang the clear soprano peals of the women. The manservant got up, bellowing. Kit put the tip of his beribboned cane against the man's chest and held him off despite his enraged struggles.

"I do not fight with lackeys," he said. "Tell your master there will be no more lines—ever."

The manservant lunged forward, still bellowing. Kit jerked the point of the cane away so suddenly that the man almost fell. Then the stick whistled through the air, biting into the servant's back and shoulders. For a long moment the heavy-muscled fellow took the savage beating, then he turned and fled howling up the beach.

Kit pirouetted on one high red-leather heel and faced the merchants. Their countenances were beet-red, their fat jowls quivering.

"From this day forth," Kit told them blandly, "you will deal with the *Seaflower* as with any other vessel that puts into Basse-Terre. No lines, fair exchange for our goods. Do I make myself clear?"

A low, rumbling mutter started among the merchants and ran from man to man. Kit caught the words "Lazarus" and "leprosy." He threw back his head so that the heavy mass of golden curls shifted about his shoulders.

"Lazarus is dead," he said flatly, "and buried at sea these many months. His gear has been heaved over the side, and the vessel fumigated. There is no leprosy among us."

The merchants broke into small groups. Kit could hear their voices rise in debate.

"One moment, gentlemen," he said, his voice bland and patient. "I fear that you mistake me still. We do not come as supplicants, bending a knee for your favor. It is our intention to be dealt with fairly and honestly, as all other seamen are. No lines, fair trading—and the freedom of the town. This bickering is bootless. Here are our goods. Come, make your offers!"

One of the merchants stepped forward, his cheeks purple. "And if we refuse?" he growled.

Kit shrugged his shoulders, an eloquently Gallic gesture, and turned back to his crew. "The gentleman speaks of refusing!" he said, his voice light and filled with mockery.

In two strides Smithers and Dupré were flanking the merchant, long knives gleaming in their hands.

"Shall we open his fat belly, sir?" Smithers inquired gravely. "Or just cut his throat?"

"Nay, lads, I think an ear will do for a starter," Kit said, shaking his fair head.

Instantly Smithers' knife rested on top of the merchant's ear. The man squealed like a stuck pig.

"Captain!" he wept. "Good Captain, have mercy!"

"Mercy?" Kit drawled. "A strange word, isn't it?"

Smithers' knife pressed down gently, and a tiny trickle of red stole down the merchant's fat face.

"I agree!" the merchant shrieked. "We agree. Gentlemen, tell him! Speak, for the love of God!"

The others broke out in a confused babble of assent, their faces pale as death.

"That's better," Kit growled. "Leave him his ear, Smithers. He will need it."

Timidly the merchants stepped forward and appraised the goods the *Seaflower* had brought. Then, with trembling voices, they offered higher prices than the *Seaflower*'s crew had ever heard from them. The men bent forward eagerly, ready to pass over the silks, leathers, perfumes, laces, and mounds of plate and bullion. But Kit stopped them with a curt gesture.

"No," he said. "It is too little. Make me another bid."

The merchants fell back, shrieking louder than they had for fear of their brother's ear.

"That's the way, Kit," Bernardo whispered exultingly. "Stick 'em where it hurts—in their miserly purses!"

Kit drove the price upward three times more before he consented to the sale. And he took his own share in golden crowns and louis d'ors. Bernardo did likewise. But the crew, with no thought beyond the present, were content with rum, a handful of écus, sols, piasters, and pieces of eight—and assignations with the the women of the town.

By nightfall, Basse-Terre was loud with revelry. After years of semi-imprisonment aboard the *Seaflower,* her crew found their new freedom sweet. But Kit walked alone on the moon-silvered beach and watched the indigo water break white over the rocks. It was there that Bernardo found him.

"Kit," he said, "it is bad to absent yourself like this. The crew are asking for you. They cheer your name to the echo."

"So?" Kit growled.

"Join them in a glass, Kit. They will think all the better of you for it. And you will have need of the goodwill of your crew."

"Yes," and he sighed, "that I will. Very well, Bernardo." He glanced down at the canvas sack Bernardo carried. "What have you there?" he asked.

"Medicines," Bernardo answered, grinning. "I have here lignum sanctum, called by some guaiacum. It's said to be a specific against the French sickness. Also China root, the tuber of smilax, like our sarsaparilla, which is supposed to cleanse the blood of the great pox. When the lads have finished their pursuit of Venus, we shall have need of both."

"Are all the women diseased?" Kit demanded.

"No, not all. But how is a man to tell?"

"I do not care," Kit said morosely, "since there are none among them with hair like fire and eyes like an emerald sea."

"So!" Bernardo laughed. "The wind still blows to that quarter, eh? Come with me and we shall see how long this moonsickness of yours can withstand the hot caress of reality."

"Always!" Kit growled.

"Always is a long time," Bernardo said. "Come!"

They marched along the streets of Basse-Terre until they came to the largest of the taverns. Through the doorway there sounded the bellow of sea chanteys, the boom of deep male laughter, and the high breathless titter of female voices. Bernardo stood back while Kit put his head inside. Instantly there went up a great bull-like roar of welcome.

Still Kit hesitated. But not for long. While he stood there, a group of young girls, ranging in years from sixteen to not above twenty, hurled themselves on him. They tangled their slim fingers in his golden hair, they caught at his arms, dragging him into the tavern. Grinning, Bernardo entered the tavern in his turn and closed the door behind him.

Early in the morning, when the sun broke through the row of prickle palms that fringed the eastern border of Basse-Terre, Kit sought out Bernardo. This in itself proved to be more difficult than he had anticipated. Kit found it necessary to search through more than a dozen houses and all the rooms above the taverns before he found his second in command.

When at last a wizened, toothless harpy had cackled a "Yes, of a certainty, he is here, M'sieur le Capitaine!" and indicated a rickety stairway leading to the loft of her palm-thatched house, Kit hesitated a moment before mounting the stairs. Then he started up them.

He poked his head up through a trapdoor and looked around. Almost at once he saw Bernardo. There, on a pile of hay, his friend slumbered, his peaceful snores rising from his half-opened mouth. Kit stood very still, his blue eyes widening, for in the crooks of Bernardo's great arms nestled two of the youngest and fairest daughters of Basse-Terre.

Kit's firm mouth spread into a slow grin under his golden mustache. Noiselessly he tiptoed across the rush-strewn floor until he stood over the sleeping trio. Then he brought the open palm of his hand down across the ivory curve of two fair bottoms so smartly that it made a sound like two small pistol shots. The girls leaped to their feet, shrieking. Then, seeing

Kit, they contorted their supple young bodies into ludicrous positions, in a futile effort to cover the most salient points of their nakedness.

Bernardo cocked open one weary eye. He looked at Kit and closed it again, groaning.

"Up with you, shameless one!" Kit roared in mock wrath.

Again Bernardo opened an eye. Then a slow, wicked grin stole across his dark face. Wearily he lifted a hand and pointed to the place where the reddening imprint of Kit's palm and five wide-spread fingers showed on a girl's fair skin.

"It was bad enough to wake me that way," he said, "but did you also have to brand them?"

"Get up, Bernardo!" Kit was grinning. "Time we were off. Otherwise that hooked beak of yours will be imprinted on the countenances of half the next generation of Tortuga."

Bernardo considered this remark gravely. "They could do worse," he said, chuckling. "What of that jutting Hapsburg chin of yours? I suppose you spent the night in prayerful meditation?"

Kit's face reddened under its tan. " 'The sheep's business is none of the goat's concern,' " he quoted. Bernardo sat up, pillowing his head in his hands.

"Off with you, lasses," he growled. "The Captain and I have matters to discuss."

The two girls ran squealing down the ladder. Bernardo turned his head cautiously on the column of his neck.

"It's not unhinged," he muttered. "I would have sworn . . ."

"Enough of that nonsense," Kit growled. "Come, get dressed. I need you."

Bernardo's great hand groped for his pantaloons. He found them, and stood up. Then, poised on one leg like a gigantic crane, he eyed Kit speculatively.

"The last I saw of you," he began, "you were the subject of a tug of war between the tall brunette and that plump, rosy Bretonne. Tell me, which of them won?"

"Enough!" Kit roared. "We have work to do. We must round up the crew. I want to make Cow Island tomorrow. If we wait too long . . ."

"Damn that red-haired witch!" Bernardo said. "She's not half so fair as some of the maids here in Basse-Terre. I tell you, Kit . . ."

"Get up!" Kit blazed.

"Look you, lad," he said quietly as he drew on his doublet, "the crew will be ill-disposed to leave Tortuga so soon. It has been years since any of them has tasted of the fleshpots. The course of wisdom is to let them enjoy the fruits of victory under your command for some time before setting a course that might cause mutiny."

Kit's fair brows crowded together over the bridge of his nose. "You're right about that," he mused. "Still, there are coasting hoys that ply between the ports of Saint-Domingue daily. Come, Bernardo."

"Mother of God!" Bernardo groaned. "Such impatience! I will not stir a step until I have coffee to clear my head of last night's fumes. If the red-haired one made either Cow Island or Aux Cayes, she is beyond the need of haste. Still less if she didn't make them."

"You said she gained the shore," Kit growled.

"Did I? Perhaps I did. It's not important. By now she is dead of either abuse or drowning. What does it matter now?"

Kit's hand moved out and caught the front of Bernardo's leather jerkin. "If you don't hurry," he said, "nothing in this life will matter to you."

Quietly Bernardo freed himself of Kit's grasp and sat down to draw on his jackboots, cursing all the while in a sibilant mixture of French, Spanish, and English. A moment later he stood up.

"I'm ready," he said. "Let's get this over. For till they lay the wench's bones before you in proof, there will be no living with you. Come."

They made the wharves in a few minutes, and woke a fat Frenchman who slumbered beneath the single mast of a round-bellied boat hollowed out of a cypress log. A moment's conversation and the musical clink of gold pieces were enough to rouse him into astonishing activity. He kicked the Negro slave who slept under the long arm of the tiller, and started clumsily to unfurl the single sail. Kit aided him, and five minutes later the fat-hulled hoy was butting its way out of the harbor of Basse-Terre toward the southern part of Haiti, and Aux Cayes.

Kit stood in the bow, gazing at the shore line of Aux Cayes that grew more distinct with a slowness that was pure torture. Before the hoy had pushed its prow into the sand, he was over the side, wading through the surf. Bernardo followed him from a distance, seeing him racing up the beach toward a group of French freebooters who lay in languid conversation under the shadow of the palms.

They looked up at Kit in some astonishment. It was some moments before the tangled jumble of his words became clear. Then broad grins split their leather countenances.

"The little red one?" one of them said. "But certainly! She came ashore over there—on the Isle des Vaches. We've heard she stabbed five men before she was subdued."

"Subdued? Pah!" one of his companions spat. "That red-haired sea witch was never subdued! She came wading through the surf naked as a newborn, with a knife in her teeth, and . . ."

"Damn your eyes to deep-blue hell!" a third put in. "These creatures of a most incredible imbecility have not yet the right of it, Monsieur le Capitaine! The little Rouge came ashore, and those stupid beasts on Cow Island . . ."

Kit looked from one to another of them. "Do any of you really know what happened?" he demanded. "Were you there?"

"That, no," the filibusters said reluctantly, "but we have the intelligence straight from . . ."

"Damn their intelligence," Bernardo growled. He had come up during the Gallic uproar and had heard most of the dispute. "Let's cross over to Cow Island and get the truth."

"Aye," Kit growled. They retraced their steps to the hoy and silenced the protest of the weary captain with another louis d'or. An hour later they hove to in a sheltered cove off Cow Island. Then they inched their way quietly ashore between the throngs of French vessels that always tied up there.

Kit's queries made him at once the center of a voluble crowd. Of the many who attempted to tell the tale, there were three who spoke with authority.

"But yes," an old Gascon said, "we were there. This child with the red hair swam ashore on the seaward side where a corvette lay at anchor. She hadn't a stitch on her back and her skin was like the milk of eyes, like pearl, like . . ."

"That I know," Kit growled. "Go on."

"She was exhausted, the poor little one. But for the blind stupidity of those insane ones, she would have had no time to rest. Instead of lining up and taking their turn like men of discretion, they began to fight over her. Seven men were killed in the fight. I do believe that this little Rouge enjoyed it. When at last most of them were wounded, she got hold of two pistols that had fallen to the sand and pointed them at the men. She forced a little Parisian to remove his doublet and trousers and dressed herself in them. This done, she made them bring her water and food."

"They did not rush her?" Bernardo demanded. "All of them together could have . . ."

"They were too bemused by her beauty—and her courage. No, the knaves swore on the nonexistent honor of the strolling street wenches who bore them that they would not molest her further, and asked her to choose a husband from among them."

"And did she?" Kit growled.

"No. She laughed at them. The next night, since the captain of the corvette had fallen in the battle over her, the crew of that vessel set about electing a new leader. In the midst of the dispute, the little Rouge strode among them and declared that since she had more wit and courage than any twenty of them, she would be their captain, and that the election was at an end."

"Mother of God!" Kit breathed.

"All seamen," Bernardo declared, "fear the presence of a woman aboard ship worse than the plague."

"But yes," the old Gascon agreed. "Still, they looked at the milky curves of her legs under those tattered trousers, and her young breasts pushing their way half out of her shirt, and decided perhaps that once at sea . . ."

"Where is she now?" Kit demanded.

The old Gascon swept his arm out over the great blue curve of the ocean. "Out there," he said. "And I will wager my life, what there is left of it, Monsieur le Capitaine, that wherever she is, she commands that vessel still."

"Why do you believe that?" Kit said quietly.

"Because in her there is a hatred that is absolutely bottomless, a cruelty that burns bright as the flame of her hair. She has declared war on the whole race of men. That war she cannot win. But many a brave matelot will die in his blood before they swing her from a yardarm."

"That," Kit said slowly, "they will never do. Not while I have life. Come, Bernardo."

"What now?" Bernardo said as they tramped through the sand toward the waiting hoy.

"Back to Basse-Terre. Back to the *Seaflower*. Then, Bernardo, we will comb the sea of the Caribbees. Till I find her again, this little Rouge, there will be no rest for me, nor any joy in my heart."

"*Diablo!*" Bernardo muttered under his breath. "Would God they had cut her throat!"

Kit glanced at him over his shoulder. "What did you say, Bernardo?" he asked quietly.

"Nothing," Bernardo growled. "I need my feeble breath. Let us be off."

But Kit was already gone, running hard toward the place where the hoy danced in the freshening surf.

3

DURING ALL THE TIME that Lazarus had commanded her, the *Seaflower* had been forced to sail shorthanded, but now at last Kit found it possible to take his pick of seamen to man her. Of these, the greater part were Frenchmen from the provinces of Brittany, Normandy, and Gascony; but the remainder included Welsh, Irish, Scots, and Englishmen who had fled to the French Antilles to escape punishment for crimes committed in their homelands. There were boys, too, who shipped as powder monkeys and cabin boys, and one or two runaway Negro slaves. Kit had appointed Bernardo his master's mate, and the two of them stood by while Smithers and Dupré read the sailing articles, the former in English, and the latter in French.

"Each man to bring his own powder and shot," Smithers bellowed, and Dupré repeated the announcement in French. "No prey, no pay!"

The circle of men nodded grimly. They were quite accustomed to such arrangements.

"Our good captain, Christopher Gerado, receives one thousand écus in pay. Our master's mate, seven hundred. Our second mate—myself, lads—five hundred. The carpenter and shipwright, three hundred. The surgeon, two hundred and fifty, including medicines. All others one hundred, except the boys, who get fifty. Recompense to the wounded is as follows: Six hundred écus or six slaves for the loss of a limb; three hundred écus or three slaves for loss of a thumb, an index finger of the right hand, or an eye."

"But matey," a Welshman protested, "I be left-handed!"

"Them as favors the use of the left gets the same as others do for the right," Smithers ruled at once. "One hundred écus for the loss of any other finger. Each man to select a partner or matelot to fight at his side, to nurse him when hurt or sick, and to inherit all his goods if he be killed and has no woman." Smithers paused for breath.

"Now for divvying up the loot," he continued. "After the pay and the recompense to the wounded is taken out, we share in this fashion: Six portions to the cap'n. Two to the master's mate. One and three-quarters to the second mate; one and one-half to the shipwright; one and one-quarter to the surgeon. All others one share, except the boys, who get one half-share. Fair enough?"

"Fair enough," the throng of grimy men agreed.

"Then aboard with you!" Smithers bellowed. "Look alive and pull right hearty!"

Kit watched them as they came aboard, then turned to Smithers. "You may up-anchor now, Mr. Smithers," he said quietly. The courtesy was deliberate. Lazarus had taken care to instill into Kit all the niceties of seamenship, even to the courtesies usual among officers of Their Majesties' Royal Navy. That this formal turn of speech was somewhat out of place aboard a freebooter apparently never had entered the old leper captain's head. As for Kit, he followed what he had been taught without question.

The winch clanked and the thick coils of tarred hemp tightened. Slowly the ring of heavy, hand-hammered wrought iron broke water. At Kit's side, Bernardo Díaz cleared his throat.

"What is it, Bernardo?" Kit asked.

"This—quest of yours for Rouge," Bernardo said in a tone inaudible to Smithers, who stood not two yards away. "You do not intend to tell the men?"

Kit's firm mouth widened into a slow smile beneath the white-gold mustache. "No, I do not," he said. "Always long of head aren't you, Bernardo?"

"I've reached nigh on to forty winters by taking thought," Bernardo said dryly. "See that you do as well. You have a responsibility to the men, Kit. You cannot sacrifice them to your desire to take vengeance on Del Toro or your quest for Rouge. Unless they find enough loot to make the voyage worth while. . . ."

"They'll mutiny," Kit finished for him. "That I know right well. But consider this, Bernardo: If Rouge is herself seeking treasure, will she not ply the same sea lanes frequented by the Spanish plate ships? Can't we kill two birds with one stone?"

"Yes—if you don't consider it a waste of time to board a Spanish vessel instead of continuing your search!"

Kit gazed upward where the men were swarming amid the rigging, bending the *Seaflower*'s broad sails to the wind. When he turned back to Bernardo, his eyes were smiling.

"When I die," he said, "it will be in the great bed of a manor, soft with linen sheets. I have no desire to be hanged, Bernardo. Besides, such limbs as hers should be caressed by silks. What vessels cross our paths, we take. Rest quietly on that score."

"Good!" Bernardo grunted, and cocked his weather eye aloft. "We'll make good speed," he added. "The wind is almost dead astern."

The *Seaflower* slid quietly out of the harbor of Basse-Terre and headed westward, along the long arm of the upper peninsula. Bernardo looked down at her knife-sharp prow. Already it was breasted with foam.

"The wind will hold," he observed. It was the season for the trade winds. They could cross the entire Caribbean with a wind that varied no more than three points off dead astern. On the other hand, the Spanish vessels coming from Mexico and Peru would have to tack into the wind. The advantage in speed would be all in their own favor.

As he retired to his scrubbed and polished cabin, Kit had the feeling that luck was with them. The *Seaflower* seemed a thing alive, rolling gently with the rising swells, and running before the winds like a great white-winged bird. True, most of the Spanish vessels would lie at anchor in the roadbeds of the Mexican and Peruvian harbors, waiting for the winds to shift. But some of them would start to inch homeward toward Spain. The insatiable maws of the homeland would brook no waiting. Spain was too near disaster to wait long for the treasure that she was tearing from her colonies.

The *Seaflower*'s luck held, and in four months she had captured and sunk seven Spanish vessels. The booty was excessive, the Spanish ships having been loaded with the treasure that was now so urgently needed in Spain. Kit was firmly entrenched with the crew, for in addition to their rich spoils, the losses aboard the *Seaflower* had been light. But during all this time there had been no sign of Rouge or of a ship sailing under the banner of the Black Heron.

Late one day they espied a dainty caravel, convoyed by a fleet of four Spanish ships of the line. The *Seaflower*, with her tremendous advantage of speed, bided her time during the late afternoon and early evening, then under cover of night swooped in among the cumbersome ships of the line and cut the caravel out of a miniature armada. When Kit and his men boarded her it was early morning, and she was already listing dangerously. By the time the *Seaflower*'s crew had combed her for booty and taken the captives aboard, she was heeling for her last plunge into the deep, night-black waters of the Caribbean.

Among the captives were two women, whom Bernardo half led, half dragged before Kit, who was standing at the rail.

Kit turned to the women. The elder, a lean and formidable matron of some fifty winters, spread her arms as though to shield her charge from his impious glance. Kit put out an arm and set the duenna gently aside. He stood there a long moment, staring at the younger, a mere slip of a girl no more than eighteen or nineteen.

Bernardo Díaz watched his face keenly. Now, the Jew exulted, now the red-haired witch will be forgotten. If blood flows in his veins, he will forget her for this one! . . .

Kit's blue eyes, cool and grave, studied the girl before him. She was as slender as a willow sapling and as graceful. Her hair hung loose about her shoulders, as black as a vulture's wing against the spring snow of her face. Under her slim brows her eyes smoldered blacker even than her hair, and firelit in their depths. Kit watched the corners of her mouth, blood-rose red, tender-soft. Her lips were moving, shaping words, but it was long before their sense came over to him.

"I have no English, Señor Captain," she whispered. "But if you do not know Spanish, I will try French, although poorly."

Kit's mouth spread into a smile under the white-gold mustache. "Your Spanish will serve, señorita," he said in flawless Castilian. "Go on."

The girl drew herself up proudly. "I would like to know the meaning of this!" she said. "What manner of man are you, to wage war upon women? Why did you sink our ship?"

Kit took a step toward her, looking down on her small face from his great height. "I ask the questions here," he said quietly. "What is your name?"

"And if I do not choose to answer?"

"The señorita will not be so unwise. I should regret having to employ harsh measures."

The girl's black eyes flashed somber fire. "You would not dare!" she spat.

"Would I not?" Kit asked softly. Then, turning to Bernardo, he said, "Bring me the whip!"

Bernardo hesitated, searching Kit's face. But the blue eyes were impassive. Shrugging, Bernardo went forward, and returned after a moment with the weighted lash. Kit slipped the loop over his wrist and played the nine-foot lash out along the deck. The girl hung there, her face ghost-white, staring at it in breathless fascination.

"Your name, señorita?" he said quietly.

Mutely the girl shook her head. Kit drew his hand far back, and held it there; but it was the duenna who broke.

"It is Valdiva!" she screeched. "Do not strike her, you murderer! You'll pay for this, just you wait! The house of Del Valdiva is mighty."

"And so is your tongue," Kit said wearily, and brought down the whip so that its loaded tip cut through three of the duenna's many petticoats. The duenna leaped skyward, shrieking.

"Tie her up," Kit commanded. "And gag her. I'm tired of her noise." He turned back to the girl. Putting out his hand, he lifted her chin and gazed into her small oval face.

"No," he said, shaking his head, "I'll not whip you. Your skin is much too lovely to be striped." The girl jerked her head away angrily. "What is your name?" Kit asked again. "The rest of it, I mean?"

The girl stared up into his face, seeing it pale bronze, the mustache and Vandyke white-gold, the hair gold too, like a great mane about his shoulders, and the plume white above the maroon of his broad-brimmed hat.

"It is Bianca," she whispered.

"Bianca," he muttered, "the fair one—it fits."

Bianca del Valdiva stood looking up at him, her black eyes endlessly dark, searching his lean face.

"Señor Captain," she said, "I am innocent. If you plan to be dishonorable toward me, I ask that you take my life instead."

Kit looked at her and slowly, deliberately, began to laugh. "Dishonor you?" he chuckled. "Señorita, you flatter yourself."

The girl stiffened as though she had been struck, her warm mouth tightening into a thin line.

"Then set me ashore," she snapped. "I am betrothed to a good and generous man, who will reward you for your kindness. By your speech you are from Spain, though your hair and eyes belie it. Surely you must have heard the name of Don Luis del Toro."

Kit stared at her. Then, slowly, his head came back and laughter crashed from his throat. It was a hard, bitter sound, entirely without mirth. Hearing it, the girl drew back in terror. Her eyes widened.

"You—you know him?" she stammered.

"Know him?" Kit echoed. "His stars and mine have been entangled since my youth—so much so that I cannot pluck a mermaid from the bosom of the sea upon whose hand he has not set his seal. But I have sampled that grandee's vaunted kindness many times in the past. God save you from such a marriage!"

Bianca's hands flew up like two white birds and covered her ears. Kit stood there a long time, studying her face before he turned away.

"Very well, señorita," he said, "have it your own way." Then to Bernardo, "Take her to my quarters until I decide what to do with her."

The duenna struggled furiously at her bonds, her lean face livid above the gag that stopped her mouth. The girl looked at him imploringly, her own small face white with terror.

"She may have her woman with her," Kit added. Then he turned on his heel and strode aft.

Bianca del Valdiva stood there staring after him, her black brows knit and puzzled. Then as the old shrew joined her Bernardo heard her whisper: "Why does he hate Don Luis so?"

Bernardo took the women to their quarters and left them there. Then he sought Kit. He found him on the poop staring aft, his face grave and serene. Bernardo came up to him, his own dark face twisted with forebodings.

"Why, Kit," he demanded, "have you taken prisoners of no conceivable use to us—or of any value. More, they are an actual hindrance and a danger. Is it your intention to revenge yourself on Don Luis by molesting her?"

Kit turned to his friend, a slow smile lighting his eyes.

"Truly, my own duenna matches and exceeds hers. Still your long and worried tongue a bit and listen. Can't you understand what a stroke of luck this is? That girl in her own small and dainty person represents half the wealth of Cartagena."

"How so?" Bernardo growled. "You're devious, Kit. Explain."

"The girl is dear to Don Luis. Dear enough to bring a ransom of say a hundred thousand crowns. Did you note the emerald on her finger—those green stones for which the district about Cartagena is so justly famed? Were we to dispatch it to him with a note, might it not occasion some concern within his heart? Followed later by one of her small fingers to speed him?"

"That you would never do!" Bernardo spat.

"Of course not, you know me too well," Kit sighed. "I would not harm her. In some strange way she reminds me of the other, though God knows there is no similarity between them."

"Except that they are both beautiful," Bernardo said.

Kit looked up, his blue eyes questioning. "Is she?" he said. "I had not noticed it."

"Your masculinity!" Bernardo swore. "This one is as beautiful as the angel of dawn moving under the wing of night! Have you eyes? Or has that red-haired witch enchanted even them?"

"Yes," Kit said, "she has. And while she lives, I can see no other woman."

Bernardo frowned thoughtfully, peering out to sea. "This ransom plan sounds good," he said. "But how would you manage it?"

"I would leave her under guard at Basse-Terre," Kit began.

"That would be noticed," Bernardo growled. "And no don would be foolhardy enough to put into Basse-Terre for any reason whatsoever. And neither could we enter the Boca Chica in order to deliver her ashore at Cartagena if Don Luis should pay us the ransom. Between the twin fortresses of San Luis and San José we'd be caught like rats in a trap. And the Boca Grande is too shallow to even think of putting in there."

"Therefore," Kit said, "we must select another cove into which Don Luis might come. What do you think of Cul-de-Sac?"

"Excellent! He could land in Cuba, then beat straight across the Windward Passage with little danger of being intercepted. Cul-de-Sac is of no importance. The French keep no garrison there."

"All of which Don Luis knows well. What troubles me is that if I give Don Luis a safe-conduct to retrieve his bride, upon what pretext can I then cut his evil throat?"

"He will give you excuse enough, once he arrives. But there are other considerations. Under whose guard would you leave the maid?"

"Yours, of course, Bernardo."

"No, Kit, I know my own desires. The maid is too fair—I have a weakness for such. And that ancient she goat, could I restrain myself even from her?"

"You refuse me, then?"

"I must."

"But there is nobody else. Look, Bernardo, these satyrs of mine would ravish the girl, and perhaps even the duenna, by the time we were out of sight of land."

"Then you must stay yourself."

"I?"

"Yes. I can put the *Seaflower* across the Caribbean and heave to off the Boca Grande channel while the message is dispatched by dinghy. Meanwhile, you can learn something of the ways of women—a lesson that you sorely need."

Kit looked at Bernardo, frowning. "But what about Rouge?" he growled.

Bernardo grinned. "I strongly suspect that by the time we return Rouge will be of scant concern to you. If I am wrong, there will be time and to spare to search for her. Meanwhile, we gain a fortune, and maybe your vengeance too."

"Yes," Kit sighed, "it is a pleasant thought."

At this moment Bianca put her head through the cabin door. A shaft of sunlight fell across her face, lighting her eyes. Above her snowy skin her hair was blue-midnight jet, startling in its contrast to her fairness. Bernardo leaned close to Kit's ear.

"It will not be too hard to stay, will it, Kit?" he whispered.

"No," Kit growled, "it will not."

So it was that the helmsman put the whipstaff of the *Seaflower* all the way over so that she came about in a wide circle, heading back toward Hispaniola. After that, the great boom of the fore-and-aft sail on the rear mast swung back and forth constantly as the trim vessel tacked into the teeth of the wind. Her progress was necessarily much slower than it had been before, but she still made good speed.

They slid by the towns of Léogane and Petit Goave in the night, seeing the lights dim-flaring and yellow beneath the palms. When they had rounded the point of the lower peninsula, the sea was quiet and the dreadful pitching that had kept both the girl and her duenna confined to the quarters that Kit—much to the astonishment of his crew—had vacated for them ceased. The waters that lay in that blue crescent between the upper and lower peninsulas were well sheltered from the trade winds. The *Seaflower* beat eastward through a sapphire sea broken only by the long iridescent swirls of sargasso weed, and now and again by the rainbow flash of a flying fish.

The women appeared again on the deck, followed by the eyes of the entire crew. Only Kit ignored them with an almost studied unconcern. Bianca's dark eyes strayed frequently toward his tall figure.

Standing there against the deep blue of the southern sky, with the great masses of tawny gold hair spilling down over his broad shoulders in leonine curls and the trim spike beard and pointed mustache gleaming white-gold in the sunlight, Kit was totally unaware of the confusion he was causing. Bianca's glances were no longer furtive; she was gazing at him openly now, a tiny frown marring the smooth expanse of her forehead.

Doña Elena, the duenna, leaned close. "Have a care, my girl!" she said. "You're making a spectacle of yourself!"

"Oh bother!" Bianca said. "I don't care a fig what these ruffians think."

"Nor what *he* thinks?" Doña Elena said, jerking her head in Kit's direction.

"Of course not!" Bianca snapped. "Why should I?"

"That I cannot tell. But it is strange that you made me spend two hours piling up your hair today. Don Luis is a great grandee, a man of parts and property, while this curled and beribboned jackanapes . . ."

"Hold your tongue!" Bianca ordered. "I dress as I please—and for my own amusement!"

"That may be," Doña Elena said gloomily. "All I know is that I left Spain with a pure and innocent maid in my charge, and I wonder what I shall deliver to Don Luis."

Bianca whirled, the tears sparkling in her black eyes. "You wicked old woman!" she cried. She might have said more, but Kit's step sounded lightly above the soft wash of the seas, and a moment later he stood before them.

He swept off his hat and made them a bow compounded equally of mockery and courtesy. "I trust that the ladies are enjoying their voyage," he said smoothly.

Bianca's black eyes widened in her pale face. "Enjoying?" she got out. "We are expected to enjoy a voyage to God knows where, with only heaven above knowing what fate awaits us?"

Kit's face was grave and unsmiling. "This is the second time you have mentioned the hideousness of your fate—perhaps not in quite the same words," he said slowly. "On that point I cannot reassure you, not knowing precisely what fate you consider hideous. But if you will permit me, señorita, I might state that you are completely safe from any fate that requires my active personal participation, as I am relatively fastidious in such matters."

Thereupon he bowed again and was gone, leaving the girl standing white-faced and close to tears.

The *Seaflower* moved quietly into the harbor of Cul-de-Sac. On the shore the palms had taken on a brownish hue, for it was long since it had rained. The waves ran slowly up the white beach between the long seaward-pointing fingers of the mountains, and all the brush was burned and reddish from the heat. The *Seaflower*'s sails flapped listlessly in a ghost of a breeze, and the midday sun stood just above the mast, fixed in a yellowish-white sky from which every trace of blue was gone, blasted out by the heat.

Bianca waited at the rail, gazing at the rows of tumble-down palm-thatched cabins that looked fitter for occupancy by swine than by human beings. She heard the groan of the winch and the splash as the anchor went over the bow into the water. Turning, she faced Kit, one hand nestling at the base of her throat.

"We—we go ashore—here?" she faltered.

"Yes, señorita," Kit said calmly, "here."

Kit assisted Bianca and Doña Elena into the dinghy, then took his own place. They were rowed in by the old left-handed Welshman who would serve them as servant. Kit had selected him because whatever the man's intentions, his advanced state of senility made their accomplishment impossible. Bianca sat in the bow of the small boat while the old scoundrel grunted and strained, winking his one good eye at her whenever she glanced his way.

The instant the prow of the dinghy had pushed its way into the slushy sand, the entire population of Cul-de-Sac turned out to greet them. This consisted for the most part of blacks, with a thin scattering of mulattoes and here and there a white man. The whites were usually old men, buccaneers who had quit the sea or criminals wanted in the larger towns of Hispaniola, come to this God-forsaken hole to die. They were, Kit surmised, no doubt responsible for the mulattoes; but there were more pressing matters to occupy his attention at the moment.

Addressing the populace in French, he made his wants known. In a few moments every able-bodied man was busy in the erection of two new huts, on a site some distance down the beach from the rest of the town. When they were finished, Bianca noted that they smelled fresh and clean, which was more than could be said for the other huts of Cul-de-Sac. She noticed, too, that Kit and the Welshman had taken up quarters together in one hut. She and Doña Elena, then, were to be granted privacy, at least. She opened her lips to sigh with relief, but the sigh did not come. A little puzzled frown hovered above her eyes. She was safe. Apparently, this outlandish pirate captain meant merely to hold her for ransom—this outlandish young captain whose hair was spun gold, and whose eyes were sea water. Her person and her honor were both safe, but she was not relieved. More, she was rather piqued at his indifference; through her small, intensely feminine mind ran the ghost of a scheme to bring him to heel.

Then later on I shall spurn him, she thought. I shall turn aside from him and leave him in the dust like the fool he is. . . . She stopped short, her black eyes widening into a night beyond her ken. At the moment she saw Kit coming up the beach toward her, and as she ran into the hut, she was not sure whether it was from Kit she fled or from herself.

4

BIANCA STOOD on the beach a little distance away from Kit and watched the *Seaflower* putting out to sea. God grant her a safe voyage, she prayed silently, and a speedy return—so that I may go home to the good man who is to be my husband before . . . But she stopped her mind before it reached the final thought, and went back into the little hut she was to share with Doña Elena.

Sleep, she soon found, was an utter impossibility. Not only was there little abatement of the heat, but the very air sang with swarms of mosquitoes. Her eyelids were soon swollen shut, her lips, her nostrils—every exposed portion of her body was a stinging torment of itching, burning welts. Across from her in the darkness, she could hear Doña Elena groaning in her sleep, but the older woman's age-toughened skin fared better than her own.

She sat up on the edge of her hammock, great tears running down her red and swollen cheeks, her ears ringing with the sound and the impact of her own slaps. He hands were bloody with the crushed corpses of half a hundred mosquitoes, but among the multitude of their fellows their demises went unnoticed. So busy was she that the man was entirely inside the hut before she noticed him.

She stood up with the long swirls of the gown which Kit had presented to her, along with a complete wardrobe—snatched, no doubt, from some poor unfortunate's back—sweeping behind her. There was time for the long rasping intake of breath before the rough hands seized her, then she threw back her head and screamed.

As the man bore her out on the beach, she heard the swift thud of running feet behind her. Then the heavy bark of a pistol sounded and the ball whined overhead. At once the man dropped her unceremoniously to the sand and sped away in the darkness. Kit strode past her, and took aim again.

She got to her feet and stumbled after him. When she reached his side, she said, "You—you would kill him!" Her voice was rich, and freighted with horror.

"Of course," Kit said calmly. "What would you have had me do—kiss him?"

"I know, but to try to shoot him like a dog . . ."

"When men behave like dogs, they should expect a dog's fate," Kit said. "But a thousand pardons, señorita. When another such—suitor comes, I shall not interfere with your—pleasures. Adiós."

He bowed then, and started back up the beach toward his hut. Bianca gazed after him, rage and fear contending for mastery within her. Finally fear won.

"Kit!" she cried. "Kit!"

He halted at once. She came running up to him, her young face pale silver in the moonlight under the blue-jet cascade of her hair.

"I—I'm afraid!" she confessed. "He—he tried to . . . Oh, Kit, it was awful, and there might be others."

Kit took her arm. "I shall not sleep," he said gently. . . . "But, Mother of God, what happened to your face?"

"The mosquitoes," Bianca said. "They're eating me alive."

"I might be able to help you. Wait a bit."

He disappeared into the doorway of his hut, and reappeared almost at once with a round earthen pot called an olla. In his hand was a thick pile of dried leaves.

He crossed to her hut and entered, paying no attention to the hysterical sobs of Doña Elena, who thought he was the would-be ravisher come back again. Kneeling on the floor, he packed the pot with the leaves and ignited them with flint and steel. At once a rich, fragrant smoke curled skyward.

"Tobacco leaves," Kit explained. "And here are more to replenish the olla when these are burned through. That should keep the little beasts at bay." Then he bowed and went out. Bianca found the smell of the smoke pleasant; moreover, it was completely successful in driving the swarms of mosquitoes from the hut. So it was that, worn-out by terror and discomfort, she fell at last into a deep, dreamless sleep.

When she woke, the sun was driving a shaft of white heat directly into the window. She got up and dressed hurriedly. Then, followed by the groaning Doña Elena, she sought Kit. She found him surrounded by a council of the town fathers. She heard his voice ring out:

"Any other man who dares touch her will not get off so easily."

The men, Bianca saw to her vast astonishment, were nodding their heads in assent. She came up to Kit and took his arm, then dropped it abruptly, her face covered with blushes and confusion. Such a gesture, she realized, had been well enough last night under the cover of darkness and the stress of circumstances, but today, in the sunlight, before the eyes of half a hundred men . . . True, they did not know she was betrothed, and to another man. Strange how remote Don Luis had become; she was having difficulty in recalling his face.

Kit looked down at her, smiling. "I trust you slept well?" he inquired.

"Very—thanks to you." Her tone was much warmer than she had meant it to be, so she hastened to correct it. "Of course, if it were not for you I should have been neither in discomfort nor in danger."

"Alas," Kit sighed, "that's all too true. But it will be ended soon. Are you hungry? By now Jim should have our breakfast ready."

On an open fire before the huts, Jim was boiling palm cabbage in an olla. In another, plantains steamed, while on a flat rock thin cakes made of the sawdustlike flour of the cassava or manioc root were baking. Jim saw them coming, and a wide grin split his toothless countenance.

"Come and eat," he called. "'Tain't much, but 'twill serve!"

Bianca sank down before the fire on the sand, and after a moment Doña Elena joined them. The older woman was much the worse for the heat, but Bianca noticed that it did not affect her appetite. Bianca tasted the strange fare gingerly at first, then, finding it surprisingly good, ate well. After they had finished, Jim brought them gourds of a pale liquor that tasted like beer. Bianca raised her eyes questioningly.

"*Veycou,*" Kit explained. "They make it from fermented cassava meal. It aids digestion in this heat."

That might well be, Bianca thought, but after having downed half a gourd, she realized that it also aided the mind to giddiness and the heart to levity. For the life of her, she was unable to keep her lips from smiling as she gazed at Kit. This was a very sorry state of affairs. She forced the corners of her mouth down, but they persisted in crawling up again. Kit's frown deepened. Why in the name of heaven, Bianca thought desperately, can't I stop smiling?

It was at that moment that she felt something very like a white-hot needle entering her arm. She shrieked softly, and Kit bent over, his face filled with concern. With his thumb and forefinger he pulled out the little red insect that was burrowing into her skin.

"What–what is it?" Bianca quavered.

"*Bête rouge,*" Kit growled. "It's a very serious matter. They lay their eggs under the skin and make ulcers. Jim, bring some fat."

Jim disappeared into the hut and returned with a gourd full of thick, vile-smelling hog fat.

"Smear it on your face and arms," Kit commanded. "It will keep them away during daylight and the mosquitoes at night."

Bianca sat there staring blankly at the evil-smelling mess.

"Do as I say," Kit growled. "I don't want you to get sick on my hands."

Timidly Bianca stretched forth a hand and took a handful of the grease. It was cool and soothing to the skin, despite its smell. Doña Elena did likewise, and afterward Jim and Kit.

So began the long days of waiting. This, the chief island of the Antilles, Bianca found, was far from the jeweled isle of romance that the tellers of tales have made of the green chain that dots the Caribbean Sea. In addition to the five thousand varieties of insects, all of which stung or bit, there were the wild hogs that came rooting through the streets and which charged at the swish of her broad skirts; there were the wild dogs that howled all night, the hideous-voiced parrots and crows; there were the pigeons that made it unsafe to sit under the trees, and whose flesh was so tough and bitter that it was impossible to eat it. There were the horses and cows of the townsmen that poked their heads through the windows and frightened her half out of her wits; and there were the little chickens, the *pintadas,* which were always underfoot.

In the swamps the frogs boomed and the alligators bellowed. The great blue herons split the night open with their ugly asslike braying. Moreover, the white skin that all her life she had protected from the hot sun of her native Spain had here no protection from this much hotter sun. She burned bronze, blistered and peeled and burned all over again. Doña Elena kept to her hammock most of the time and this was an additional burden, for in her loneliness Bianca was forced more and more to seek Kit's company. His cool courtesy, his almost maddening indifference, were fast becoming a goad she could not resist.

If she could have bathed in the sea, it might have been better, but even this method of cooling body and nerves was denied her, because the great dorsal fins of the tiger sharks cut the water in plain sight of land. As she sat now in the partial shade of a wine palm, she could see Kit's blue eyes gazing at her, and her breath caught deep in her throat. I wonder what he's thinking, she mused. I'd give half a lifetime to know. . . .

Kit's thoughts at that moment were black and troubled. The *Seaflower* should be back by now, he thought. It must come back! She is so fair, this little one, so soft and so tender. And she is his—*his!* What concern is that of mine? There is still Rouge. Hold on to that. Never forget her, never. With her sea-green eyes that slant upward in the corners, her hair like hibiscus petals, and her skin like ewe's milk. No, never forget her who lay close to me when she thought me dying of her shot and wept out her despair; do not forget her for Bianca, who belongs to my enemy, who cannot be mine—for all her unstarred midnight wave of hair and her mouth, soft, tender, secret-smiling. . . . He got up abruptly and started down the beach.

Bianca stood up and took a step or two behind him, then her small shoulders sagged and she turned away. Behind her the jungle lay thick-tangled, cool and inviting. She started walking, slowly at first, then with gathering speed and deliberation, toward the matted brush. Inside, it was cool and dark, and a few yards from the now invisible beach a little stream ran placidly inland. I'll follow it, she decided. I can always find my way back. . . .

So thinking, she moved along the stream until she came to a place where it widened and deepened into a shaded pool beneath a bamboo thicket. The water was slow-moving, clear, and inviting, and the heat lay like a blanket about her head. Without thinking she kicked off her shoes—her stockings having long since fallen prey to the sand and rocks on the beach—and holding her skirts high, waded into the water.

Bianca could not swim. Such an accomplishment would have been unthinkable in a Spanish noblewoman. So she contented herself with wading back and forth in the cool green water, moving so smoothly and quietly that she did not disturb the giant bull alligator that lay like a gnarled log on the dark bottom. She might have kept up her wading indefinitely had she not moved farther out and inadvertently stepped into a hole. She splashed downward, the water coming up to her waist, drenching her garments.

"Holy Mother!" she cried. Then, as the coolness reached her skin, her temper vanished, and she laughed aloud. I'll take them off, she decided, and really bathe. She started shoreward, held back by the weight of her water-logged clothing.

But the splashing and the laughter had disturbed the ancient cayman.

Slowly he moved upward, his rusty snout sliding easily along the surface. Bianca neither saw nor heard him; she had reached the far end of the pool and put one slim white foot ashore when he reared, bellowing. The girl whirled and hung there a moment frozen as the great jaws, lined with hideous teeth, came open. Then she started to scramble up the bank, and as she gained it, her lips tore open and she screamed.

At the moment that the sound of her cry came to him, Kit was standing on the beach a few yards away, peering out to sea with profound relief in his heart, for there on the horizon was the white blob of the *Seaflower*'s sails. At the cry, he whirled and plunged into the brush. He saw Bianca floundering toward him amid the snarl of the underbrush, held back by the drenched weight of her clothing. She hurled herself upon him, and through all the layers of her clothes he could feel the pounding of her heart. He heard the crashing noise in the brush, and freed himself of her grasp. Then, as the great, clumsy beast came through, he fired one of his pistols, the shot going straight into the gaping mouth.

The alligator thrashed about in a frenzy, flattening the brush for yards around; then at last it lay still and hideous in death. Kit turned back to Bianca and saw that she was swaying, even her lips drained of color. Putting out his arms, he drew her to him.

She nestled against his chest, her shoulders shaking with sobbing. At long last, she quieted and raised her small oval face. Suddenly, without premeditation or conscious thought, he put down his head and kissed her. It was a gentle kiss, light and tender, entirely lacking in desire. She stood very still with her dark eyes closed, her mouth warm against his. Then very slowly she moved away from him, her eyes coming open, studying his face.

"Why did you do that?" she whispered.

"Why? Truly, I do not know, Bianca."

"Can't you say it, Kit?" she murmured. "Can't you say what I want most in all the world to hear?"

Slowly he shook his head. "Forgive me," he said at last. "That was much against my will. . . . Come, the *Seaflower* is in sight." He put out his hand and she took it, her face still averted, the tears rising like jewels over her lashes and spilling down her cheeks.

"Do not weep," Kit said. "It is all over now."

She whirled suddenly and faced him, turning her back toward where the white sails of the brigantine were growing on the horizon. She put up both her hands and let them rest lightly on his broad shoulders.

"I am betrothed," she said slowly, "to a good and honorable man. You should not have done that, Kit. You should not have kissed me. For now you force me to acknowledge what my heart has known all along: I love you and none other—now and forever and always, till the day I die!"

Kit looked down at her, bleak pain in his blue eyes. "You must not say that," he said. "You must not even think it."

"Why not?" Her eyes sought and held his gaze. "There is another," she breathed. There was no questioning in her tone. Her words were a statement, flat and controlled and dreadfully calm.

"There is Don Luis," Kit growled.

Bianca shook her small head slowly. "No, not Don Luis," she said. "What is she like, Kit, this woman? What manner of creature is she?"

Kit looked out past her to where the *Seaflower* danced on the horizon. "Like an angel," he said, "like a witch—I cannot decide. Her eyes are sea emeralds, her hair Greek fire. She kissed me once as I lay dying and brought me back to life. Her beauty is a wound in my heart that will bleed until I find her again."

Bianca gazed up at him, her eyes diamond-bright. "God speed you in your quest," she whispered. "I would not have you unhappy for all the world!" Then, rising on tiptoe, she kissed him, her mouth moving upon his, lingering, soft-parted, until his hands, gone beyond his will, tightened on her waist. Her face was twisted with pain, but she did not resist. At last, slowly, she swung back against his arm, so that he could see the streaks of her tears. He released her almost at once, and stood looking after her as she walked away, her head bent, her slim shoulders shaking. Then he turned back toward the *Seaflower,* feeling with a curious sense of finality that never again in life would he know either happiness or certainty or peace.

5

KIT STOOD on the beach of Cul-de-Sac with Bianca and Bernardo Díaz and watched the great ship *Garza* of Don Luis del Toro inching her way over the horizon.

"He's on schedule," Bernardo growled.

Kit said nothing. Instead he turned his head in a half-circle and gazed wonderingly at this sun-stricken, heat-killed land. It was the same, nothing had changed. And yet, magically, everything had changed. The long blue fingers of the mountains that ran down into the sea on both sides of the bay were an even paler, more pastel shade, until they seemed suspended in time and space like the sea haze that marked their base. Behind the tiny hamlet, the tangled fringe of marsh and jungle, which ran back for a few score yards until it too was halted by the omnipresent mountains of Haiti, seemed greener than he had remembered any jungle to be: a dreamscape out of neverland.

The *Garza* beat in across the Windward Passage with majestic deliberation. Of all the multicolored confusions about him, she was the only certainty. Kit glanced down at Bianca, seeing the girl's face pale and set, her mouth held in a hard line, her black eyes unwavering. Bianca looked up at him and put out her small hand.

"Good-by, Señor Cristóbal," she said brightly. "And many thanks for saving me from the ennui of a most tedious voyage. But for you I would have known nothing of piracy, mosquitoes, alligators, and other interesting matters."

Kit took her hand and held it. His lips broke into a slow smile. "Is this all you have to say to me?" he asked.

"Yes—what I would like to say, I dare not. It would only pain you to listen to it, and shame me to say it. This way is better, isn't it? That we pretend that there was no yesterday. For when you find your Rouge I would not have you troubled by any fleeting memory, by one disloyal word."

"And Don Luis? What of him?"

"I do my duty," Bianca answered simply.

"I see," Kit said.

Bianca looked up at him, her night-dark eyes soft with tenderness.

"I think the world will someday learn great things of you," she whispered. "I think that you will become a prince—how else could you have been born so princely? And I shall make my final voyage to Cartagena of the Indies—out of your life, my Kit. And there I shall be a good and dutiful wife to a great grandee. I shall spend all my days forgetting you. And there will come an hour when I shall succeed in the attempt. Do you know when that will be, Kit?"

"No," Kit said. "When will it be, Bianca?"

"The day I die," she whispered.

Kit put out a sinewy arm and drew her to him. "You have bemused yourself with loneliness," he said. "I am not the man you think me. Remember what I am—a sea rover, brutal, poorly lettered, my soul besmirched into hell with the blood of the innocent, a murderer and a thief, unfit to touch your finger tips. Remember only those things, and forget the wretch who caused you so much pain."

Bianca straightened. "That, never!" she said fiercely.

Bernardo touched Kit's arm. "He's coming in now," he said. "Better get the girl and her woman up into the hills until this business is finished."

"Yes," Kit said. "Jim will take them there. I'll meet this murderous hidalgo face to face."

Bianca turned and joined Doña Elena, and the two of them followed the wizened little Welshman across the beach to where the thick brush nestled at the foot of the mountains. Kit looked after them for a moment, then turned back to where the *Garza*'s boat beat through the white wall of the surf toward the pale-gold sand.

He and his company, which consisted of Bernardo, Patricio, Smithers, and Dupré, walked down to the water's edge. Without hesitation Don Luis del Toro stepped out into the water, not troubling himself to remove either his black kidskin shoes or his fine silk stockings. He was clad altogether in black, after the fashion of the Spanish nobility, and Kit knew at once that here was an opponent to respect.

Don Luis del Toro, though not so tall as Kit, was well above middle height, a compactly built man whose body, even in repose, suggested enormous strength. Beneath the sleeves of his black-velvet doublet, his arms were as big as Bernardo's, and his shoulders were broader than Kit's own. His nose jutted boldly from his brown-granite face and his chin, whose deep cleft was hidden by an inky short beard, was heavy after the Hapsburg fashion. His eyes, brown, and deep-set under his heavy brows, rested quietly on Kit's face.

"Where is she?" he demanded in English.

"First let me see the color of your gold," Kit said in limpid Castilian.

Don Luis leaned forward, peering intently into Kit's face. "I have seen you before," he growled. "But where?"

"Many times," Kit told him, "over the barrel of a gun. In Cádiz, when you whipped my mother with your lash. In the harbor of Cádiz, after your people had taken her life. Off Port Royal, when you made pretended rescue an excuse for ravishment. And you shall see me again, when I am not bound by a safe-conduct to spare you. But enough of this. Where is the money?"

Don Luis nodded to one of the helmeted and cuirassed soldiers who attended him. The man stepped forward, grunting under the weight of an oak chest. When it had been opened, the dull gleam of the roughhewn pieces of eight gleamed dully in the sunlight. Kit picked up a few of the heavy coins, minted at Lima in Peru from a single heavy bar of gold, and all of them so roughly cut that there was not one of them that was truly octagonal, or bore all the letters of the inscription. He felt the sharp edge where the chisel of the mint worker had hacked the single coins away from their fellows, and hefted them for their weight. They were up to standard or even heavier, weighing as much as a hundred and eighteen grams rather than the hundred and thirteen specified by law.

"Fetch the girl," he said to Bernardo.

All this time Don Luis's gaze had never left his face. On the grandee's countenance was an expression less of anger than of regret—a look of baffled pride oddly commingled with admiration.

"You are as I should have expected you," he said, "knowing whence you sprang. But, Cristóbal, I did not order your mother's execution. Indeed, I pleaded for clemency. But the authorities of the town were overzealous. In this I crave your indulgence, and ask that I be not blamed."

"You lie in your teeth!" Kit spat.

Don Luis shrugged resignedly. "That the cub roars and has fangs I should have known," and he sighed, half to himself. Then his brown eyes lighted, for Bianca was coming down the beach, her face pale and colorless, her lips unsmiling.

Kit watched Don Luis sweep her into his great arms. This is nothing to me, he told himself; but a slow, deep feeling of sickness curled at the pit of his stomach. He noted with some satisfaction that Bianca turned her head slightly aside so that the grandee's kiss just missed her mouth.

"He has not harmed you?" Don Luis growled.

"And if I had?" Kit spat.

"You would die," Don Luis said simply. His tone was quite empty of emphasis or of any quality of threat. It was as though he were discussing the weather—a statement of fact so calmly, so confidently self-evident that Bianca's heart turned over within her.

"No, Luis," she said quickly, "he has not harmed me. Save for the abduction, he has been the soul of courtesy."

Don Luis studied Kit's face, as though to inscribe it on his memory. "You have your gold. Have we your leave to depart?"

"Yes," Kit said. "Depart and be damned!"

A slow smile played across Don Luis's dark face. "We shall see upon whose head the damnation will fall," he said quietly. "Come, Bianca." He turned, still holding the girl loosely in the circle of his embrace. But at the last moment she whirled, freeing herself with one swift motion, and ran back to where Kit stood.

She swayed before him on tiptoe, the light in her dark eyes shifting behind the bright film of her tears.

"Good-by, Kit," she whispered. "God speed you, and guide you, and bring you every happiness." Then she was gone, running back toward where Don Luis waited, his face as black as a thundercloud.

Kit said no word. Instead he turned back to his company and said very softly: "To the *Seaflower*. There is work to be done."

The *Garza* was still big on the horizon when the winches of the *Seaflower* drew her anchor free of the blue water. The white sails unfurled beneath the yardarms, dropping downward until the light breeze bellied them out and the great fore-and-aft sail on the mainmast filled, the boom swung far over. Effortlessly, the sleek brigantine began to move out of the harbor of Cul-de-Sac, leaving it drifted in pale light-filled, rainbow-hued mists.

"You've done well," Bernardo said. "By this one coup you've gained us more than on all our last voyage."

Kit did not answer; he was peering at the *Garza*, drifting almost motionlessly on the sun-filled sea. Then he knitted his brows.

"Yes," he said softly, "but we have not yet brought home our treasure. Look, Bernardo."

Bernardo squinted against the light, following Kit's pointing finger with his gaze. "Fiends and whoresons!" he got out. "I knew that dog of a grandee was not to be trusted."

Kit looked out frowning toward the end of the harbor, where the twin lines of war vessels were converging, each of them coming from opposite directions, from behind the long blue fingers of the mountains. From one side four ships of the line came, from the other, three. Quietly he called Smithers to his side.

"Crack on all sail," he ordered. "Gunners to their stations. Stand by to repel boarders."

"If we could gain the open sea," Bernardo groaned, "we might have a chance. But bottled up here, we are doomed! Of what avail is the *Seaflower*'s speed in this deathtrap of a harbor?"

"If we can force them to break that line . . ." Kit mused.

"They are not fools," Bernardo snapped. "The trap was well baited and better sprung!"

Smithers came up on the forecastle and faced Kit. "Begging the Captain's pardon," he began, "I have an idee."

"Then speak, man!" Kit roared.

"Them dons draw twice and three times the water as us. Now if we was to put back into the harbor, they'd have to come in after us. Inside, they'd run aground as sure as all hell—leastwise enough of 'em to let us out."

Kit shook his head. "Ships of the line, Smithers," he said. "They mount basilisks and long culverins aplenty—with chaces of sixteen and twenty feet. They could stand out so far that only our one basilisk could hit them—and what good would an occasional hit with a fifteen-pound roundshot do us?"

"From that distance they couldn't throw heavier!" Smithers argued.

"Yes, but how many could they hurl to our one? Even fifteen-pound shot will smash the *Seaflower* to pieces if she's hit with one every ten seconds."

"Yet if we go out," Bernardo mused gloomily, "they'll lay on a broadside with sixty-four-pounders—full cannon, Kit. Four such shots as they throw can sink us. Suppose we were to lie low and wait for night. In the darkness, perhaps . . ."

"It's our only chance," Kit growled. "But pray God there is no moon!"

At Smithers' shouted order the helmsman came about on the whipstaff, and the *Seaflower* paralleled the line of Spanish vessels. Then she put all the way about and headed back into the harbor. As she neared the shallow water, every man aboard her held his breath. The helmsman put her about again, and she started a slow glide across the harbor, again parallel to the Spaniards, but in water so shallow that they could not follow her.

Now was the time for action, Kit knew. If the Spaniards were seamen, they would kill the *Seaflower* in a matter of hours. All they needed to do was to close in until their immensely long and slim basilisks and long culverins were in range and they could pound her to pieces, entirely without risk to themselves. These long guns threw a very small shot, but they hurled it by such an immense weight of powder through such long barrels that they could outrange guns throwing shot of almost six times greater weight. The *Seaflower* had only one such gun aboard, mounted in her bow as a chase gun; but the seven Spaniards could muster among them more than fifty. If the Spaniards came in before night, the brigantine was doomed.

But to Kit's immense relief, they did not break their line. They continued to patrol the entrance to the harbor with majestic deliberation, crossing and recrossing the open mouth of the cuplike declivity between the Haitian hills.

Smithers ordered a ration of rum to give the men courage, but neither Kit nor Bernardo touched it. The day dragged on. The sun burned red as blood on the western horizon. Imperceptibly, it dropped to the water's edge, laying a track of orange and scarlet across which the Spanish ships crawled like black water spiders. The pastel-blue of the mountains became pale violet, then royal purple, then they lay night-black against the bloody blaze in the western sky. Kit could see the black-crowned silhouettes of the palms leaning over against the deepening blue of the night, then the sky darkened until they were drowned in night, blackness upon blackness, and the great stars rode the bosom of the sea.

He had turned to Smithers to relay an order when he heard Bernardo's groan. Above the reappearing edge of the mighty hills, the great pale-yellow disk of the moon was rising. It grew brighter. The palms stood up again, crowned in silver, the sky silvered into grayness, the water was like the vats of the Peruvian mints, a hard white blaze so bright that on the *Seaflower*'s decks one could have read the finest print without difficulty.

Kit looked around him, seeing the twin fingers of the mountains running darkly down into the sea, the black-trunked, black-silver-crowned palms bending seaward before the trade winds, the night soft and slumberous with spring, the breeze perfume-laden with all the flowers of Hispaniola, singing down across the bay toward where the dark outlines of the vessels of death passed and repassed in the moon-silvered night.

What a night on which to die, he thought. Turning to Smithers, he said quietly: "You may crack on all sail, Mr. Smithers."

Bernardo came up to Kit and put out his hand. "You're a fighter," he growled proudly. "I have seen many who bowed to odds—and died in the torture chambers and under the lash. There is no shame in death on the high seas when a man goes down with all guns blazing. I am proud to go that way, and with you."

Without a word, Kit took the great hand. Then he went into his cabin. A moment later he returned, bearing the *Seaflower*'s pennant—a great golden hawk on a field of blue. He gave it to Bernardo.

"Bernardo," he said, "nail our colors to the mast, so that no man among us may strike them!"

The *Seaflower* stood out from the harbor with the wind quartering off her stern. And out there in the silver blaze of the moon track the Spanish vessels waited.

"Hold your fire," Kit commanded, "until we are too close to miss. We will take one at least of them with us this night."

Cannily, the helmsman held the brigantine in the lee shadow of the mountains, sailing her dangerously inshore, so that before the Spaniards saw her, she was among them. She slid into line so close to one of the great vessels that a stone could have been hurled by hand to the Spaniard's decks without great effort. Kit's hand came down, and all of the *Seaflower*'s port guns spoke at once, making bass thunder, every shot going home.

Kit saw the Spaniard's masts crashing down, bringing with them a wild tangle of sailcloth and cording, and something like hope awoke in his heart. On the impact of the recoil the guns leaped back to the limits of the breeching rope.

"Point-blank range!" Kit roared, and the gunners lifted their hammers, knocking the elevating quoins from beneath the trucks of the guns. As the wedge-shaped pieces of hardwood fell free, the muzzles of the guns dropped until they were pointing at the water line of the reeling Spaniard. The other vessels stood by, unable to fire their guns for fear of hitting the great ship, for the *Seaflower* lay so close to the ship of the line that such nicety of aim by the Spaniards was practically impossible.

Again Kit gave the signal to fire, and the broadside boomed out, shaking the ocean. Plainly, through the echoes after the fire, Kit could hear the crash of the Spaniard's timbers and the screams of her dying crew. Then, to his amazement, a glow of fire showed amidships of the Spanish vessel. Hungrily, it ran upward into the broken rigging; in three minutes the whole vessel was ablaze. This, Kit saw at once, was a stroke of ill luck, for what illumination the moon had so far failed to give was now provided by the blazing Spaniard. The *Seaflower* lay in the middle of the Spanish fleet, etched starkly against the dancing flames.

At once the Spaniards opened up with their great cannon, splitting the night asunder. Kit could see the yellow tongues of fire probing the dark for the range, then afterward sea and sky opened with the slow, rolling bellow, the echoes reverberating endlessly among the encircling hills. White geysers stood up like momentary columns all about the *Seaflower* while she fought back, giving them shell for shell. Such was the accuracy of her fire that in a few minutes not one of the Spanish vessels remained unhurt. But the Spaniards were getting the range now. A blinding explosion of fire, water, and oak splinters filled the air not ten yards from where Kit stood. He saw four of his gunners crumple like broken dolls beside their pieces, the pale scrubbed surface of the planking running thick and red with their blood. Beside them one of the demicannon had overturned on its carriage, lying grotesquely on its side with the wooden wheels still spinning.

Another ship veered into a parallel track, and swept the *Seaflower*'s deck with a hail of small shot. When she had passed, less than half of the brigantine's crew were on their feet. Kit saw Dupré sitting on the deck, his linstock flaring beside him, trying desperately to push the pink sausage rolls of his guts back into the gaping wound in his belly. He sat there a long time, pushing desperately with both hands, not uttering a sound, until at last his hands were too slippery with his own blood to be any longer effective. Then he let his intestines spill out, and sat staring at them glumly, with an expression of acute disgust on his round, swarthy face that did not change even after he died. It was only when a forty-eight-pounder hit the *Seaflower* squarely, causing her to roll and sending him over limply on the deck, that Kit knew he was dead.

"Mother of God," Kit muttered, "why don't they sink us and get it over with?"

But the Spaniards continued to slash at the brigantine with small shot, killing her crew one by one until less than two dozen men remained on their feet, and of these not one was unwounded. Kit and Bernardo were but slightly hurt, only cut in five or six places by flying splinters. The helmsman was dead, hanging over the whipstaff, so that the trim vessel veered aimlessly, losing steerage, wallowing helplessly in a trough of the sea while the Spanish men-of-war went by her one by one in a beautiful line and raked her decks.

Kit heard at last that most hideous of all sounds to a seaman, the splintering crash of a broken mast; then almost at once another, so that the *Seaflower* lay naked on the bosom of the sea, denuded of her white wings, unable to gain headway. He looked around at Bernardo, blackened like himself from head to foot with gun soot. Only the flesh about their eyes showed white, streaked here and there with the rivulets of their own blood. Kit put out his hand and Bernardo took it. He stood there with the young captain whom he had followed and counseled and guided across half a world, waiting for the death that both of them knew was imminent. And looking into Bernardo's eyes, Kit saw no fear.

It was a long moment before either of them realized that the Spaniards had ceased firing. They turned as one man, peering through the deafening silence to where the gigantic bulk of the *Garza* bore down upon them. The huge ship of the line rose in close and the grappling hooks dropped into place. Kit saw Don Luis, splendid in a coat of mail, climb down to the *Seaflower*'s decks, followed by a score of soldiers. Of Kit's men, there was not one left with either the strength or the will to oppose them.

Stiffly Kit and Bernardo advanced to meet the grandee. The moonlight glinted blue-silver on the armor, and white on the great plumes above the helmets. The Spaniards were a brave sight. Kit glanced from them to the broken bodies of his dead and tired, sooty, wounded living; the rage and humiliation in his breast was like white fire and poison.

Don Luis's even white teeth showed brilliant in his dark face. His big hand came up and gave his short beard a contemplative tug.

"You fought well, Cristóbal," Don Luis said. "Few captains I know could have stood us off so long."

"Words!" Kit spat. "Do with us what you will, and have done with it!"

"Be not overhasty," Don Luis said calmly. "I require of you only the ransom money. Where is it?"

Kit's blue eyes widened in his soot-blackened face. He nodded to

Bernardo. The Jew started off and returned after a few moments with the chest.

"Open it," Don Luis commanded.

Kit's tired, stiffened fingers worked clumsily with the lock. When at last it was opened, the gold pieces glinted dully in the light of the moon.

"Take it up," Don Luis said to one of the soldiers. The man bent and grunted under the weight of the chest. Don Luis raised his sword to the visor of his helmet and saluted Kit.

"Adiós," he said softly. "And when you remember your mother, remember also that I spared her son." Then he turned on his heel and went back up the ratlines to the *Garza*, leaving Kit and Bernardo standing there caught in a vast stupor of astonishment.

"Mother of God!" Kit whispered. "Why in the name of everything holy did he spare us?"

"We shall know someday," Bernardo muttered. "But come now, we must bind up the wounded and bury the dead."

Nevertheless, Kit remained motionless, watching the long line of men-of-war beating out to sea, moving slowly, silently past the place where their fellow blazed, bloodying the sea and the sky with the ruddy glow of the flames. Then at last he went down the splintered, slippery deck, moving stiffly, automatically, his eyes blank and unseeing.

6

Kit sat on the beach before Cul-de-Sac with his elbows resting on his knees and his two hands toying with the soiled and bloodstained folds of the Heron Banner. He was almost completely motionless, his blue eyes staring blankly out to sea, while behind him people of the village were digging a huge pit into which the *Seaflower*'s dead would be tossed. Bernardo Díaz looked at him, seeing his whole body freighted with abject dejection. He crossed quietly to where Kit sat and laid a kindly hand on his shoulder. Kit looked up quickly into Bernardo's dark face.

"Bernardo," he said, "I've been a fool!"

"That's the beginning of wisdom," Bernardo remarked. "But then, what man is not?"

"But none so complete, so colossal a fool as I. I am the crown prince of asses."

"And I," Bernardo grinned, "am your prime minister!"

Some of the moroseness left Kit's face at Bernardo's remark.

"He has bested us again," he said slowly. "Whenever we meet, he is always the victor. Why is it so, Bernardo?"

"Because he is older and wiser. You must fight him with his own weapons, Kit. When your tongue has become as forked as his, when you are as full of guile, then . . ."

Kit stared at Bernardo, his blue eyes narrowing in his tanned face. "In my hands," he said, "I had the instrument of his destruction. I could have made a cuckold of him before his vows were said, delivered to him a used baggage, deflowered, dishonored, damned! Whenever he looked at her, whenever his hands touched her flesh, he would have been faced with the thought that here were my leavings. Only, Bernardo, she was so fair—so gentle and so fair."

"All the better," Bernardo growled. "A forced maid freezes up her loins to pleasure, but one as willing as she so plainly was redoubles your joy with the fury of her passion. If it had been I, I would have set my mark upon her flesh so that he could never forget it!"

Kit studied Bernardo gravely. "He has wronged you too," he mused, "as grievously, almost, as myself."

"It behoved him to forget," Bernardo remarked dryly, "that the records of my conversion, my baptismal papers, are recorded in the cathedral. Only by forgetting could he appropriate for his own purposes my houses and lands and my ships. And on what pretext? That I am a Jew, a fact I can help as little as he can help being the Spanish grandee he is. But enough of this. What now, Cristóbal?"

Kit stood up suddenly. "First," he said, "we must cut a mast and erect a jury rig to take us back to Tortuga. Then we will commence anew." He looked at Bernardo, his forehead creased with frowning. "I shall put to sea again," he said slowly, "and skirt the coast until I devise some method of luring Del Toro from behind those walls of Cartagena which now so effectively protect him. During this time of waiting, I must take ships, many ships, and pile up a mountain of gold. For when I find Rouge again, I will build her a manor befitting her beauty."

"So you would still find your Rouge? I had thought that perhaps this other had . . ."

"Shaken me in my purpose?" Kit frowned. "No, Bernardo, in this I remain unshaken, though someday I shall perhaps discover why the thought of Bianca as the wife of that swart beast makes a taste like rotten mangoes in my mouth. But come, time enough later for thinking."

The task of making the *Seaflower* seaworthy was not an easy one. Before a day was gone, Kit was forced to give up the idea of duplicating her original rig. His crew was sullen and bad-tempered, held back by their wounds, but held back even more by their renewed conviction that the *Seaflower* was indeed a hell ship, cursed with misfortune at her launching. Fortunately for Kit, they had neither the strength nor the will for open mutiny, so that finally the *Seaflower* limped back into the harbor at Basse-Terre, her green unseasoned mast bending before every stiff breeze, her ragged sloop rig pushing her along at a rate of speed so unbelievably slow that often Kit was in doubt as to whether or not she moved at all. Were it not for the singing perfection of the lines that her French builders had so lovingly shaped, the *Seaflower* would have been unmanageable. As it was, she barely maintained steerageway.

Night and noon and morning Kit and Bernardo had scanned the horizon, fearing the appearance of a line squall, or even mildly heavy seas, or most of all the chance passing of an English or Spanish vessel. But the gods of mischance had had their fill. The low, humpbacked form of Tortuga rose over the rim of the ocean, and grew with a slowness that crawled along Kit's taut nerves.

But when the entrance to the harbor of Basse-Terre was in sight, Bernardo sought Kit out, a most impious grin stretching his swarthy countenance.

"Kit," he said, "do you know what will happen when these rascals of ours go ashore?"

"Yes." Kit nodded. "They will spread abroad the tale of our misfortunes and we will not be able to obtain a crew of blind men, boys, and women, let alone seamen."

"That must be prevented," Bernardo said cheerfully.

Kit let his gaze rest on Bernardo's face, wrath gathering in his blue eyes. "And how would you do that, my good Bernardo? Put them in irons, so that they can't go ashore? Or perhaps we should heave them overboard at this point?"

"That," Bernardo grinned, "is a pleasing thought, considering their actual worth. But I have a milder suggestion. Think a moment, Kit. Why do these he goats go to sea?"

"To obtain gold," Kit said.

"Yes—but do they love gold for itself, or for what it can buy?"

Kit's frown relaxed, recognition lighting his eyes. "I follow your drift," he said. "If they go ashore hurt, beaten, penniless, with nothing to buy the dreams of drunkenness or the favors of women, that is one thing, but . . ."

"Shall I summon them?" Bernardo inquired quietly.

"Yes! Call them up. You are always long of head, Bernardo!"

In a few minutes the survivors of the battle stood sullenly before Kit. Most of them were clad in rags, and all of them displayed filthy, blood-caked bandages. They stood in a wavering line, their eyes filled with cold hostility.

"Men," Kit began, the ghost of a smile hovering about his mouth, "our luck has been bad, fiendishly bad. But that you know right well."

The crew stood there silently, the hostility in their eyes unwavering.

"Our misfortune, however, was not due to any fault of yours. You fought well and bravely. We were outnumbered and beaten. That is no disgrace. Because it was no fault of yours, because you did your part and more, I cannot permit you to go ashore empty-handed. Out of my own coffers you will receive your pay. Moreover, tonight at the Hôtel des Boucaniers we will celebrate our late defeat, and our coming victories—at my expense. Of course, if any of you are not disposed to accept . . ."

The crew turned incredulous faces toward one another, their lean, bearded jaws dropping open. Then the look of amazement was replaced by slow-dawning joy. Smithers stepped out of line.

"Cheers for our Cap'n!" he bellowed. "The best what ever sailed the seas!"

The men responded, roaring out their cheers in half a dozen tongues. Kit smiled quietly.

"When we go ashore," he added, "say nothing to the people. Within the hour you shall have your pay. Back to your places now!"

The men leaped to their stations. The *Seaflower* crawled into the harbor.

"In this expense," Bernardo declared, "I shall share, since it was I who suggested it."

Kit shook his head.

"No, Bernardo," he began, "I must take the responsibilities, since I am captain."

Bernardo grinned at him. "We will need new masts, new sails, new cording. There is ten days of work here for a shipwright and ten sea carpenters. You haven't enough for the twin necessities of these repairs and conciliating the crew. Whether you like it or not, you must accept my help."

Kit looked toward the quays of Basse-Terre, growing slowly before the *Seaflower*'s slim prow. "You are a good friend, Bernardo," he said quietly.

The rest of the day passed quickly. Kit went out to the small monastery where the good Fathers kept his gold. For this service, they received a handsome yearly offering that served the wants of many of Basse-Terre's sick, poor, and aged. To those who censured them for receiving money gained in so barbaric a fashion, the friars said frankly that the good they so selflessly did with the gold at least balanced the evil incurred in its gaining.

Before nightfall, the carpenters and the shipwright were swarming over the hull of the *Seaflower,* healing her hurts with sound, seasoned timber. On the morrow they would begin to erect her tall new masts.

As for the crew, they were already half-drunk, noising abroad in the streets and the alleys the news of Kit's generosity. And many a stout fellow was already turning over in his mind the advantages of shipping aboard her once she was ready to sail.

That night at the Hôtel des Boucaniers the noise of revelry beat deafeningly on Kit's ears. He sat a little apart, cool amusement lighting his eyes. A slim, dark creature who had spent her childhood cutting purses in the streets of Marseille lay beside him, her head pillowed in his lap. On his right, the blonde Bretonne sat quietly, one arm encircling his broad shoulders. That neither of them had so far gained the advantage was the only thing that kept them relatively at peace. A tall beaker of cane rum rested almost untasted in his hand. That this revel was costing him his last écu he knew well, but there was something fitting in the knowledge. Gold gained from the bosom of the sea had a quality like quicksilver, running in bright drops through the open hand.

As for Bernardo Díaz, he joined gleefully in the riot. The gold he had gained at the risk of his life was now gone to the last sou, yet that seemed exquisitely comic to his richly ironic mind. He laughed as loud as any of them, and pinched bottoms and took kisses, his broad, clean-shaven chin red with the rum of the Antilles. He had already chosen a woman to ensure that he would not spend the balance of the night in thinking or in vain regrets.

The revel lasted late. When it was over at last, Kit walked on the moon-silvered beach under the slim-trunked palms—alone. Now, as always, he took out the tattered, bloodstained pennant about whose somber symbol so much of his life had revolved. The moonlight fell on the wings of the Black Heron, so that the bird of evil seemed almost alive and poised for flight. And all that had been clear before was unclear now, murky and confused.

He could imagine Don Luis sitting now in his house in Cartagena, bastion of the Indies, a city whose walled strength could not be matched anywhere on earth either in the Old World or in the New. At one time that had meant little to Kit; he would have climbed over the walls and laid down his life gladly for the privilege of first flinging the hated grandee into hell. His hatred of Del Toro had in no degree diminished, but he was checkmated by his own new-found desire to live. And for that, Rouge was responsible.

"Rouge." Saying the name alone was enough to start kettledrums in his blood. Like white fire in his mind was the image of her swaying before him on the *Seaflower*'s deck, the few tattered rags the Spaniards had left her clinging to her figure: sea-foam whiteness of hip and thigh, and breasts so proud that they flaunted their conical perfection like a challenge. Her mouth, wine-scented, poppy-petaled, a trifle full and petulant, self-willed, spirited; the shell-pink lobes of her nostrils flaring, and above them the oddly Mongolian slant of her emerald eyes beneath the flame of her soft-curling hair.

Before Rouge he had fed his soul on hatred, and battened on dreams of vengeance. Now, because of her, whole new vistas were opened up to him: he heard the ring of hammers and the rasp of saws and in his mind saw the vast edifice that would be her domain erected in fair and pleasant fields; his eye piled up vague, half-imagined furnishings of unbelievable richness—silks soft enough to caress her skin, velvets, satins, jewels whose glitter paled the noonday sun. These he would tear from the holds of the Spanish plate ships, and lay in mounds at her feet. This would he do—after Luis del Toro was dead by his hand, his house in ashes about him, his Bianca widowed.

Kit stopped short, his face heavy with frowning. His imagination conjured up Bianca as he had seen her last, standing there on tiptoe before him, her dark eyes tear-bright, filled with haunting sweetness, with poignant, almost insufferable longing; he could see the clean, innocent outlines of her ethereal young face framed in the soft night cushion of her hair.

Bianca was an angel out of heaven, too beautiful to touch or believe; Rouge was born to sear a man's mind into fevered disorder—and he, Kit, was after all mere flesh and blood.

Of this he must not think too much. That way lay madness. "Rouge," he whispered to the night wind, "come back to me—for I am no fit consort for a saint. But you and I could make such joy on earth that angels looking down would desert their starry thrones. We could spin sunlight into garments, and wear the blue water like sapphires."

His mood changed suddenly and he groaned. This *was* madness. Rouge was far beyond his reach, or indeed she might even be dead. He was stunned by the thought as he listened to the muffled booming of the sea. It was a far, sad sound, not unlike the music of a dirge. Above his head the palm trees caught the sea wind and talked in dark voices. Somewhere inland, a parrot screeched hideously, making a sound like demented laughter.

Slowly, Kit walked up the beach, his high red heels kicking up little spurts of sand that caught the moonlight like silver as he moved. His head bent and troubled, he returned to the town, which lay buried deep in quiet and in slumber.

7

THE *Seaflower* swung southward down the chain of the Antilles, speeding like a great white-winged bird past islands strung like emeralds on a string looping in a great curve toward South America. To Kit's ears, even their names were like jewels: Hispaniola, Puerto Rico, Guadeloupe, Martinique, Granada, Santa Lucia, Trinidad. . . . And the sea that they encircled—cupped by them between the green poignard that is Florida and the long, rugged arm of the Isthmus, the blue crescent of the Gulf of Mexico and the towering peaks and mighty rivers of the mainland—was like sapphire, topaz, lapis lazuli.

Wherever she went, into whatever waters she pushed her prow, the *Seaflower* left a trail of broken ships bloodying the blue waters with the ruddy glow of fires as they flamed downward to destruction. From as far north as the mouth of the Mississippi to as far south as Rancherías, where the Rio de la Plata sweeps downward through the pampas of the Argentine into the sea, the black-hulled brigantine pulled down her prey.

True, she confined her attention to the galleons of Spain, but this discrimination was but little dictated by gallantry. Kit hoped one day to settle in France or in one of the French colonies, and hence wanted no black mark on his record. He spared the English, in part because they were fellow countrymen of Lazarus and Rouge, but more because they were almost without exception privateers embarked on the same errand as his own. The Dutch with their cargoes of hides, tallow, rum, and slaves interested him not at all; but the Spaniards bore bullion of gold and tons of silver plate, and he hated them with all his heart.

By mid-March of 1694, his name was known and feared throughout the Caribbean wherever the Spanish tongue was spoken. He flew the banner of the Golden Hawk, like his golden, lionlike mane. Men spoke of the fury of his attack, of his cold and smiling ferocity. But the ones who could speak with any authority were few indeed, for they owed their lives to occasional lapses on the part of Kit's crew, who, being men and thus liable to error, sometimes failed to make sure that the Spaniards they left on the decks of the plate ships were all dead. It was not a thing that happened often.

Kit stood on the deck, his fingers moving softly over the cloth-of-gold sash that encircled his waist. The wings of the Black Heron on it spread fanwise over the bulge made by the barrels of his pistols. His blue eyes were cloudy with dreaming, for his thoughts were far away.

He was thinking, at the moment, of his mother. After the usual surge of pain at the memory of the cruelty of her death, older questions rose to plague him. How had she come to Cádiz, this gentle, lovely woman, as blonde and fair as her Norse ancestors who had settled centuries ago on the northern shores of France? Why, in the name of God and the Virgin, had she ever come to be married to that posturing peasant, Pierre Labat? That Pierre did not deserve his distaste Kit knew well, for with all his unmanly fussiness, he had treated Kit most kindly. He had adored the lovely aristocratic woman who had become his wife, and had provided for both Jeanne and Kit well, having made money as hairdresser and wigmaker to the grandees of southern Spain. They had come to him from as far away as Valencia and Barcelona to have their great blue-black manes fashionably curled; and those afflicted with baldness paid him princely sums for the magnificent wigs with which he so cunningly concealed their defects. In his small way, Pierre Labat had been an artist, but he had never wholly recovered from his awe at finding himself married to a gentlewoman of Normandy. If he had remained in his native France, that would have been beyond his wildest dreams.

Kit suspected that he himself was the cause of that particular mystery, for it was more than certain that Pierre Labat had never sired him. His own lean and towering height had never sprung from that fat little dwarf Labat; nor did the fine, chiseled purity of line of his features bear any resemblance to the pudgy countenance of his foster father. There had been about Cristóbal Gerado from his earliest youth an arrogance and a swagger that bespoke proud Spanish blood.

Bernardo, Kit was certain, knew in part or entirely the answers to these riddles, for he had been a fast friend of Jeanne Giradeaux from that long-past day when she had first set foot on the shores of Spain. It was characteristic of Jeanne that she had never wavered in her regard for the greathearted Bernardo, though to maintain a friendship with a "new Christian," as the converted Jews were called, could be done only at considerable risk to herself. In the Spain of 1689, there were no others. Masses were being said in the former synagogues, and thousands of these brave and faithful people lay in indistinguishable heaps in common graves outside half the cities of Castile and Aragon. Pierre Labat had almost fainted in pure terror each time Bernardo had approached his door, but both Kit and Jeanne had stoutly championed his right to enter as a friend.

The father-and-son relationship had existed between Kit and Bernardo for as long as he could remember. Kit had lavished on that stout, battle-scarred old campaigner the devotion he instinctively withheld from the effeminate Labat. Yet even this was not enough to make Bernardo divulge any secrets. "Some things," he growled, when asked, "are better left unknown." And neither threats nor persuasion could move him from his stand.

Kit had half-turned toward Bernardo, but now he turned away, sighing heavily. His thoughts fled, unaccountably, to Bianca. Why was it that the idea of Bianca as the wife of Del Toro was so distasteful to him? What precisely was the emotion that he still felt toward that soft and lovely creature? Was it love? How was it possible for a man to love two quite dissimilar women at one and the same time? He could see them both as vivid as life before his eyes, both with their sea-foam whiteness of skin and matchless loveliness. But where Rouge's snowy body was complemented by the hibiscus fire of her head, the vulture-feathered blackness of Bianca's hair made her fairness doubly startling by contrast. Bianca was a song in the darkness, solace to a man's wounded spirit; Rouge was brush fire and volcanoes beneath spring snow. And he, God help him, loved them both!

In that moment a confusion that had long been troubling him was suddenly made clear. Why had he not, after so long a time, made good his vengeance on Del Toro? He realized that to try to take Don Luis in Cartagena was worse than foolhardy, rimmed as that grim gray city was with mountainous walls of stone; but subconsciously he had been troubled by Bianca, and the declaration of devotion she had made to him. If he killed his enemy, would he not of necessity be forced to assume the responsibility of Bianca? And however delightful that prospect might seem, what, then, of Rouge? Rouge was in his blood. The mention of her name was a kind of autointoxication. If only I had been born a Mussulman, he thought bitterly, I could have them both! . . .

He was, he was beginning to realize, driven by fierce surges of emotion that often ran quite counter one to the other, for besides the fact that he loved two women, and hated Don Luis with a hatred as bottomless as the pit, yet another current surged within him, no less strong than the others: a powerful, mounting tide of ambition. His boyhood had been spent under a cloud of mystery, in humble circumstances, but always he had had a hunger for greatness. Wealth? He had that. No, it was more than wealth that he desired. It was a name that men would reckon with, holdings spreading out from horizon to horizon, and tall sons of his loins to carry on his name.

Those sons—would they wear manes of scarlet on their heads, or would their scalps be crowned with night-black curls? That thought again! Angrily, he put it from his mind, and turned to planning the details of his manor, picturing it lovingly in his mind, furnishing it room by room with all the luxuries he had ever seen or heard of. The furniture would be hand-carved and brightly gilded, and on the back of each chair would be carved his crest. That thought brought him up short; a low, mocking laugh escaped his lips. His crest! What heraldic device could he employ? The bar sinister across an empty shield? Nameless, fatherless bastard that he was, what escutcheon had he upon which to charge his nonexistent armorial bearings—the Golden Hawk, emblem of the plunderer bird?

He threw back his head to laugh aloud, but at that moment the unmistakable slow-rolling boom of gunfire came to him. He turned to Bernardo, but there was no need to ask. Bernardo was bending forward, his nostrils quivering, his whole body at attention.

"Crack on all sail," Kit ordered.

It was still daylight when they came on the scene. A low, black-hulled corvette stood in the midst of three huge plate ships and hammered at the gigantic vessels as though her crew were possessed of the fiends. Kit had no need to give the order, his men were already at their stations. One plate ship was a windfall that a man dreamed about for years, but three! Into these great ships the Spaniards crowded the plate and bullion that had once made up the cargo of a fleet of galleons, on the theory that one ship was more likely to escape detection than a fleet. This theory was quite correct—it was hellishly difficult to sight any one vessel on the great blue curve of the ocean. These ships, no doubt, were loaded to the gunwales with silver from Peru, which was explanation enough of the fury with which the corvette fought.

But without aid the little vessel did not have a chance. True, the plate ships were not handy fighters—the small buccaneer was escaping their fire with mocking ease—but neither could the light guns of the corvette dent their heavy timbers. After a while she would be forced to give up. The *Seaflower* swept down on the battle like a white-winged bird. When she was within range, Kit concentrated her fire on the plate ships' rigging. In four broadsides, the *Seaflower* demasted two of the great Spaniards. Seeing this, the third struck her colors.

At once the *Seaflower*'s crew swarmed over the sides and began the labor of bringing the heavy pigs and plates of silver topside. While they were thus gleefully engaged, the corvette slid to the opposite side of the Spaniard, and her crew too swarmed up the ratlines. In a moment, cutlasses and pistols were drawn as the *Seaflower*'s crew prepared to defend their spoils. Seeing the approaching trouble, Kit swung down to the Spaniard's deck.

"Hold!" he cried. "There is enough for us all. We will share it with you."

"Who said anything about sharing?" a voice answered him. "These prizes are ours!"

Something in the tone arrested Kit. The voice was a clear soprano, like that of a cathedral choirboy. He whirled, his eyes widening in his bronzed face, seeing as though through a faint haze the mouth as red as a blood rose, the emerald-green of the eyes, and the long sweep of the hibiscus-red hair.

"You." His mouth shaped the word, but no sound came out, no sound at all. Rouge walked toward him, her bare legs white under the boy's trousers that reached but halfway between hip and knee. He could see the black lash of the Spanish whip that was coiled over one shoulder, diagonally across so that it lay between the young, upthrusting breasts which pushed their way half out of her tattered shirt. A sash of scarlet, exactly matching her hair, encircled the almost unbelievable slimness of her waist, and into it a brace of pistols was thrust. She approached him slowly, swaying lightly on her feet like a young willow in a spring breeze, and as she neared her green eyes widened in recognition.

"Kit," she whispered. "Kit of the golden mane! And I thought that I had killed you!"

"No," Kit exulted, "your aim was bad. I have searched the seas these many years in order to find you!"

He put out his arms and swept her toward him. At once her hands came up, dagger-taloned, reaching for his eyes. He caught them in midair and held them there, slow amusement curving the corners of his mouth.

"Have you forgotten?" she spat. "No man embraces me—not even you!"

"For five whole days," Kit said quietly, "I lay between life and death because of your shot. For that I shall exact payment—and now!"

But Rouge swung backward, wrenching herself from his grasp. She put up her slim white hand, which all the sun in the Caribbean had been able only to freckle a bit, and grasped the butt of the Spanish whip. Then she slipped down and out of its evil coil, playing it along the deck.

"Come no closer, Kit," she warned.

Kit looked at her, seeing her young figure, lithe, soft-curving, revealed in all provocative purity of line by the abbreviated costume she wore, seeing her hair flaming about her shoulders, her eyes making green fire, her mouth scarlet, all the more inviting because of its fury. And, laughing aloud, he stepped toward her.

Her crew lolled against the rail, grinning. This indeed was going to be a show. Kit took another step. The lash whistled through the air and curled about his bare arm; when she drew it away, the slow, thick ooze of blood followed it. Kit did not even glance down. He took another step and another, until Rouge was forced to retreat, the whistling crack of the whip sounding all the time, and the stripes on his arms and shoulders growing until they crisscrossed; his fine linen shirt was a thing of bloody rags, and still he advanced upon her. Finally, in desperation, she swung the whip so that the lash curled across his face, leaving a bloody stripe from cheek to mouth. Kit raised a hand to his face. It came away wet with his own blood. Then, his blue eyes cold with fury, he sprang forward and caught her to him.

His hand came up and caught her chin, forcing her face upward until he found her mouth. She struggled furiously in his embrace for a long moment, then her struggles lessened, ceased, her hands hung limply at her sides so that the loop of the Spanish whip slid down her slim hand and the evil weapon thudded on the deck. Kit kissed her slowly, lingeringly, moving his mouth upon hers, pressing her backward until her lips broke against her teeth. When at last he released her she swung back against his arm, her eyes star emeralds behind the shifting haze of her tears.

"You should not have done that!" she cried. "You should not have shamed me so!" Then, whirling, she ran to the rail and swung down the lines to the deck of her own vessel. Kit watched her go, a crooked grin on his bronzed, bleeding face. Bernardo came up to him and touched his arm.

"Those stripes," he growled. "They want attention. Come, Kit."

Quietly Kit followed him. But before he quitted the Spanish vessel, he called one of Rouge's crew to him.

"Tell your captain," he said, "that I will discuss the terms of the division of the spoils with her—later." Then he turned and walked toward where Bernardo waited, his dark face heavy with disapproval.

"I suppose," Bernardo growled, "that this ends our voyage."

"No, Bernardo," Kit answered, laughing. "It means only that we do not go alone."

Bernardo paused in his sponging of Kit's stripes and looked at his captain gravely. "I know well," he began, "that you will listen to nothing against her. But, Kit, she is not for you. When a man marries he should seek out a young maid, innocent and sweet of mind and body, pure in thought and deed, whom he can lead and instruct in the duties of wife and mother."

"And Rouge, of course," Kit said dryly, "does not fit this description."

"Judge for yourself. Aside from the fact that she goes half-naked, and has probably consorted with whatever member of her crew or . . ."

"Enough!" Kit snarled. "I will not hear this even from you!"

"She has the temper of a fiend, the will of a shrew, and the morals of a she goat."

"Enough, I said!" Kit roared. "Did you not hear me?"

Bernardo shrugged his enormous shoulders and fell silent, his deft fingers moving gently over Kit's bruised and broken flesh.

Through the heavy silence, broken only by the creaking of cording and tackle and the soft wash of the seas, came the noise of a new uproar. Kit could hear the high, clear tones of Rouge's voice, but her words were muffled by the distance. No distance, however, could hide the pistol-shot sounds of her whipcracks. Kit bounded to his feet and raced toward the deck, with Bernardo at his heels.

The two of them swung up to the lofty deck of the captured Spaniard, and running across it, peered down the other side, where the corvette lay. Rouge was walking on the foredeck, moving forward one step at a time, swinging the heavy Spanish whip while her crew slunk backward in a semicircle like a pack of cowed jackals.

"Dogs and sons of dogs!" she shrieked. "Knaves and whoresons, born of filth and abominations! Have I not told you that I am not to be touched? Must you be whipped to rags before you learn who is master here?"

Kit turned toward Bernardo, a slow smile lighting his blue eyes.

"You spoke of her morals," he said quietly.

"In that perhaps I was mistaken," Bernardo conceded. "But not in her temper. I would sooner mate with a fiend out of hell!"

"The matter of mating does not concern you at all," Kit said with a grin. "Come, let us go to her assistance."

Groaning, Bernardo passed Kit a heavy pistol, and the two of them slid down a line to the low deck of the corvette.

"Perhaps," Kit said mockingly, "perhaps we can be of assistance?"

Rouge whirled, her eyes a hard, emerald blaze. "Go back!" she spat. "Haven't you done me enough harm?"

"I?" Kit said. "I harmed you? In what way?"

"I have taught these dogs," Rouge said, "with good and sufficient example, that no man lays a finger on me. Then you come and spoil it all with your pawing and mouthing! Now they would like to follow your example, and I must whip them all, every man jack of them!"

"I see," Kit said gravely, but with cool amusement crinkling the corners of his eyes. "Perhaps I should allow you to shoot me again to convince them you do not lie?"

Rouge glared at him, her small face hot with rage. "Don't tempt me!" she said.

"Nor shall I," Kit said lightly. "I do not like being shot—or whipped. But enough of these incivilities. I came merely to extend an invitation to my fellow captain to dine with me on my vessel this evening."

A little of the anger left Rouge's green eyes. "No," she said shortly.

"Why not? Surely you are not afraid. I shall not harm you."

"You cannot harm me," Rouge said contemptuously. "But I can think of no good reason for dining with you—or with any other man."

"The division of spoils," Kit said softly, "will give you excuse enough to offer your crew. As for yourself, I do not think you need any further excuse. Shall we say at eight, then?"

"At eight," Rouge said. "Yes—at eight hours after you arrive in hell! Off with you, Señor Cristóbal."

Kit made her a mocking bow and turned away; but as he placed his hands on the line, he turned once more toward the girl.

"Before you come," he said cheerfully, "do me the honor of bathing. I do not like my women to smell of gun soot, tobacco smoke, or sweat—it ruins their charm. Adiós, Rouge."

He saw her hand reach down for her dagger, and despite his agility, the broad blade of the knife hissed past him so close that it sheared off a lock of his tawny mane. He bent down and picked up the lock. Then he crossed to where the dagger still quivered in an oak beam. Before her astonished eyes, he quietly wrapped the bright gold of the hair around the hilt of the dagger. Then he hurled the dagger back so that it stood in the mast above her head.

"Keep it," he said, "as a tender remembrance of me—to be pressed to your bosom of nights!" Then he went up the line hand over hand, leaving her trembling with fury.

"She'll not come," Bernardo said.

"No? On that score I'll wager you a hundred écus."

"Done!" Bernardo growled.

Kit went to his cabin and bathed and dressed. When he had finished, he was as fine as any prince, ablaze with jewels, bedecked with yards of snowy lace and fine embroidery. Bernardo held up the mirror of polished silver before him, remarking as he did so: "Of three things there is no end: the cawing of the raven, the braying of the ass, and the vanity of a man in love."

By the end of the seventeenth century, masculine foppery had reached an extent that was never again to be equaled in Western history. Five years later the reaction against its extremes had set in, but in April 1694 it still took Kit two and a half hours to dress himself adequately. So it was that when he again mounted the *Seaflower*'s deck he had a scant half-hour's wait before the time he had set for the dinner. Actually, his wait was shorter.

Fifteen minutes later he felt Bernardo tapping his arm and, looking up, saw the leather bag of coins dangling from that worthy's hand.

"You have a way with women," Bernardo groaned. "Here, take your loot!"

Grinning, Kit pocketed the wager and walked eagerly toward the rail, over which Rouge's crew was laying a plank. He saw them help her up, then the significance of all this ceremony came to him. Rouge was clad in a gown of exquisite Córdoba lace like a mist of midnight, cut in extreme décolleté, its somber hue chosen deliberately to accentuate her natural fairness, so that above its black filigree work made in the pattern of strange, unearthly flowers the whiteness of her neck and shoulders and bosom was like a cry in the darkness of a man's heart.

The dress was caught about her waist and clung like the clasp of a lover; at one and the same time it shielded and flaunted the proud upflare of her full, young breasts; from her waist it arched down like the inverted bell of a black orchid plucked in a dream garden in a season of fevers and delirium.

On her head the great masses of her hair were piled so high that Kit had the impulse to stretch out his fingers and warm them at that living flame.

He put up his hand and helped her down. Then he stood a moment, looking into her face. He took a stride toward her, swift and purposeful, but he halted abruptly without taking another. It was her eyes that had stopped him. They were as clear as sea water, but a light of pure mockery danced in their depths with a glee that was almost diabolical. Do what you will, they challenged him, I can match and top every move you make.

"I changed my attire," Rouge said tartly, "not to please you, but so that we would waste no time in banter. I can masquerade as a woman still, though the woman I was died long ago."

Kit took her arm and guided her toward his cabin. "I doubt that," he said, "for if you are not alive, nothing on earth is."

"I live for one thing only," Rouge said, her voice flat, calm, curiously controlled, "and that is to see Luis del Toro, grandee of Spain, dead in his blood at my feet."

Kit poured out two goblets of wine from a stone flagon that had been cooling since morning. "I share that feeling," he growled, "perhaps with better excuse than you." He lifted the knife and carved slices off the breast of a smoked fowl.

"Perhaps it was only a small deed," Rouge said slowly, "as men count deeds. Only a bit of sport. . . . And what difference does it make if it cost my sister her life? Or that I was to be married in another month? I—who now must remain forever unwed."

"I don't agree," Kit growled. "Was your suitor so poor a man as to reject you for a fault in no way your own?"

"No, but I too have my pride. I could not come to him dishonored." She looked at Kit and her green eyes were very clear. "To him," she added, "or to any other man."

"I see," Kit said quietly.

Rouge lifted the goblet of ruby-colored wine. The dying sunlight came through it and touched her long, graceful fingers with deep rose.

"You said," she mused, "that you share my feeling about Del Toro. Why so, Kit?"

"My mother," he said, his voice husky, "died of torture—at his command."

Rouge drew in her breath sharply, her eyes widening until they dominated her entire face with their emerald blaze. When she spoke, her voice had dropped to a whisper.

"I'm glad I did not kill you," she said.

"And I too," Kit said, smiling. "Dead, I could do nothing for you. Alive, perhaps I can lead you back to happiness."

"I shall never be happy again," Rouge said flatly.

"That may be doubted," Kit said. "On the sea, surrounded on every side by rude men who know how to sink a vessel, cut a throat, and force a maid, but nothing else—perhaps not. But in a home of your own with a man who loves you as your husband . . ."

"You?" Rouge snapped.

"Yes," Kit said softly, "I."

Rouge stared at him a moment, her green eyes filled with soft lights that moved in unbroken progression as her gaze followed the clean, sculptured outlines of his face.

"You love me, I suppose?" she mocked. "How can you? You're a man, and men know nothing of love. Lust, yes—the satisfying of their grosser desires, but love . . ." She threw back her head and her laughter came out hard and mirthless. "Marry you? And when I have grown old and fat have you looking in the village for some younger maid?" She leaned forward. "Tell me, Kit," she said, "would you be so anxious to take me as a wife if I insisted on separate rooms and no intimacies between us? Would you marry me for the pleasure of my company merely, for the music of my sweet voice? Would you?"

Kit's gaze dropped and his whole face was a picture of woe.

Rouge's laughter rang merrily through the tiny cabin. Then abruptly she halted. She leaned forward across the table, and her finger tips traced lightly the lash stripe on Kit's face.

"I have hurt you," she said, "in more ways than one. And I am sorry, for in some ways you seem different from the rest."

She stood up, as if to go. Kit got swiftly to his feet and came around the table. He stood looking at her for a long moment, then, very gently, he drew her into his arms. As light as his touch was, he could feel her body stiffening, and with a swift motion she turned her head aside from his kiss. He released her at once and, bringing both his hands up, cradled the soft oval of her face between them, looking quietly into her eyes.

"You cannot go on forever evading life," he said, "or including me among those who have no other thought beyond their own gratification. You were made for me, Rouge—not for a day only, but as the partner of my soul. I must break through the wall you have built around your heart, so that you live again—warmly, as a woman should."

He bent down then and found her mouth. It was warm and sweet, but with nothing of response there—nothing at all. There was something maddening in her coolness. His hands swept downward and encircled her waist, drawing her to him in a grip that was likely to crush her wholly, and his lips flamed upon hers, moving, searching, until slowly, softly, he felt the trembling start. Start and increase and move upward in wild, surf-pounding surges, her face slanting itself now across his at a sharper angle, so that her mouth fitted more and more closely into the contours of his own, her hands creeping up, moving slowly, caressing the surface of his sleeves until at last they met and locked behind his head, her fingers working through the heavy masses of his hair.

He could feel her lips slackening and parting. Then they were suddenly scalding, fiercely demanding, upon his own. Without freeing himself from her embrace, he dropped one arm to the level of her knees and, lifting her off her feet, laid her gently on the bunk.

"No," she whispered, her voice low and intense. "You must not!"

But he sank down beside her and stopped her protests with his mouth until she lay trembling in his embrace, her lips, soft-sighing, brushing against the hollow of his throat. He straightened after a time, and she lay there staring up at him, her eyes as green as emeralds, as deep as tropic seas. When she spoke, her voice was so low that he had to bend down to hear the words.

"Loose me," she whispered, and turned over face downward, so that all the buttons and laces of her back lay under his trembling hands. . . .

Afterward, when time came blurring once more into focus, she lay very still beside him in the darkness, and a single ray of moonlight stole in through the porthole and fell across her face. He looked down at her, seeing the big teardrops filtering through her dark lashes, more jeweled than any diamonds in the world. And suddenly he felt curiously ashamed and unclean, as though his act differed not even in degree from the brutality of Del Toro.

"Forgive me," he whispered. "I never intended that you should be hurt because of this. Between us two there can be no thought of sins and sinning, for always it was meant to be thus." There was only silence from beside him except for a half-stifled sob. "Say that you forgive me," he pleaded. "Say that you will sail with me to Saint-Domingue, and there we will be married."

Rouge sat up slowly, the tears streaking her face, then she swung the long singing curves of her legs outward and down, and gathering up her clothing, began to dress, still without uttering a word.

Kit got up too and drew on his own clothing. When he had made some semblance of order among all his ribbons and laces, he turned once more to Rouge and drew her into his arms. She made no move to resist, but came quite woodenly, like one half-alive. He bent down and kissed her once more, his lips as light as a breath upon hers, as reverent as a prayer. She lay back against the circle of his embrace, her green eyes deep and somber, a little puzzled light moving in their depths.

"I must have time," she whispered. "Much time—in which to think."

Kit frowned. He had no way of knowing that the fear which moved in her eyes and shook her voice was of herself, of her tremendous capacity for response to him, who, of all men on earth, had broken completely through her defenses. All her ideas were in need of revision. Passion, in spite of the Spaniards' brutality toward her and her dead sister, existed in her after all. Her own blood, then, was as hot and eager as that of any panting animal of a man. . . . Yes, she must think; she must have much time for thinking.

"One year from today," Kit said gravely, "I shall put into the harbor of Petit Goave. If you have changed your mind by then, join me there. Is that time enough?"

"Yes," she whispered, "quite."

"Will you come?" he whispered.

She looked at him, a long, slow, searching look.

"Who knows?" she said. "Wait—and see."

8

THE SEÑORA BIANCA DEL TORO sat alone in her room. She was as still as a statue of marble, and almost as pale. But for the green fire of the emeralds from Muzo and Chiquinquirá, she seemed a masterwork by some priestly artist designed ultimately for the nave of a great cathedral. Only the occasional flutter of her snowy hands and the faint flare of her nostrils showed that she lived.

But her young mind, alert to the point of rebelliousness, was far from inactive. Behind the dark screen of her eyes moved thoughts so daring that they frightened her. Just four years before, the Sister Juana Inés de la Cruz, sitting amid the shadows of the cloister into which masculine disapproval of her brilliance had forced her, had penned her immortal answer to the Bishop of Puebla, Fernández de Santa Cruz, quietly defending a woman's right to have thoughts, and to express them, to cultivate the intellect that God had given her. And here and there throughout tropical New Spain an occasional woman had spoken out against the brazen, multitudinous infidelities that the swaggering grandees took as their inalienable right. But Bianca, lacking the knowledge that she was not alone in her secret revolt, prayed to the Virgin to be delivered from the dark tumult of her thinking.

If, she mused, I were not alone so much. If Luis would lessen his desire to devour the entire earth and take from it all its treasure, I might in time become accustomed to him. I might someday learn to care for him a little, for he is a man of great parts and even a little kindness. What more power can he want? He is president of the Audencia, commander of His Majesty's fleet in the western Caribbean. He owns three haciendas—why, in Spain his holdings would constitute an actual latifundium; there are princes on the continent of Europe who possess less land. He owns mines at Cali, Muzo, and Zipaquirá, and his petition before the King for the title of Count will surely be honored. He has indigo, bananas, and cane, three thousand Negro slaves whose lives are at the mercy of his lightest whim; an *encomendero* over the services of another thousand Indians. What else is there in this world to gain? . . .

Her face darkened perceptibly as the answer to her question came unbidden to her mind. There *is* one thing more, which only you can give him —a son and heir.

But he has sons, Bianca recalled. I've heard him say . . . Mulattoes and mestizos, her reluctant mind taunted. Any Negress can give him a son, but only you can give him the noble Spanish son of his loins, the heir for whom he has built his empire. You alone can mother the straight-limbed, fair-skinned lad he dreams of, you alone can bring him the assurance that the proud name of Del Toro will not vanish . . .

She remembered well the day she had first entered Cartagena with Don Luis. As they had driven down the cobblestoned streets of the city toward the Del Toro mansion, a painted woman, clad in a saya cut so low that her breasts were in danger of complete exposure, came to a halt. Bianca had stared at her. Never before had she seen a woman so shamelessly dressed in public. The woman had moved toward the carriage, calling to Don Luis with obvious familiarity.

"Luis darling, what have you got now? *Diablo,* but she's a beauty! Oh, but you'll tire of her—the pale, pretty thing. Then you'll come back to me. I'll be waiting."

Bianca had turned a frozen face toward her betrothed. Don Luis nodded grimly to a hidalgo who rode alongside. The man spurred his mount forward, uncoiling a loaded whip as he rode.

"Luis!" the woman had squealed. "Stop him! Stop him, for the love of God!"

Bianca had seen the whip rising against the sky. Then it sang downward, wrapping itself halfway around the woman's body. When the rider drew it away, the cloth of the saya had been cut through as cleanly as with a knife, and through the break showed the bright stripe of the woman's blood. Her scream had been a dreadful thing, high and thin and edged with terror. Again Don Luis had nodded. The hidalgo brought down the whip again, the loaded lash whistling through the air. Quietly, Don Luis put his head out of the window and addressed the coachman.

"Drive on," he had said.

Now, recalling the incident, Bianca shuddered again. How can I give myself unconditionally to him? she whispered to herself. His lightest touch freezes my blood, and his caresses bring only fear and trembling. I think that if a woman's heart and mind are not opened to a man, her body will reject his seed. No, he must seek elsewhere for this son of his bosom. . . .

And you? Will you also seek elsewhere for fulfillment—even across the Caribbees, to where he with the star-sapphire eyes and a mane of tawny gold roams? Are you not really glad of your husband's absence?

"Yes!" Bianca said aloud, with a fierce kind of joy. "Yes, I am glad, and

I will think no more of this!" She stood up suddenly and looked about her as though she were seeing the details of her room for the first time. Her eyes wandered over the great beams of quebracho wood—wood so heavy and strong that it sinks when tossed into the sea, so hard that it blunts the edge and shatters the handle of any ax used against it—down over the carved furniture with its gilt and brightly colored leatherwork to the cool red tiles of the floor. Great vases of Indian pottery stood in the corners, silk tapestry ornamented the walls, and everywhere there shone the moonlight gleam of silver mirrors. Through the open arch, Bianca could see the silver dishes glowing softly on the immense table of red lapacho wood, which was as hard as quebracho and as lasting. The dishes caught the flickering light of the candles that gutted and flared in silver sconces.

Beside her now the girl Quita entered the room as silently as a shadow and began brewing the yerba-de-maté tea over a silver brazier, the ruddy fire of the charcoal lending a slow, smoldering glow to the somewhat barbaric beauty of her face. Bianca looked past the mestiza toward the fine swirling lines of the iron grillwork that barred her windows.

And these, of all the handsomely wrought details of her surroundings, registered upon her consciousness. In spite of all the delicate artistry of swirling vine tendril and leaf shape into which the iron had been tortured, they were still—bars. Such bars, she told herself, were necessary for protection against thieves and other intruders. But, her mind mocked, it is against the "other intruders" that they are chiefly designed. Since our fathers insist upon giving us in marriage to men about whom we know nothing, and since our husbands insist upon their right to sire bastards upon every Negress or Chibcha maid who crosses their path, they must pay for these privileges with the endless fear that we may retaliate in their absence, and we must pay in our turn for that fear by being kept prisoner in these splendid cages that they call homes. . . .

She stopped short, once more appalled at her own thoughts. There was something unfeminine in such thinking. It is only, she told herself again, that I am alone so much. . . . And there is nothing, the dark whisper in her mind mocked, of which you are more glad. And this of the bars—if Kit were to appear tonight at an unbarred window, would you not help him up and clasp him to you?

Bianca halted her thoughts at last, her convent-trained mind aghast at the dark, unruly tumult in her blood. Don Luis never woke such wild confusion within her. With him, she was the gentle, submissive wife who knew her duty and did it, repugnant though it might be. Perhaps her repugnance was the reason why, after all this time, there was no child. She would have been glad to present him with the son he so ardently desired; perhaps then there would have been peace between them. She sighed and turned to Quita. The mestiza stood there silently, the fragrant tea steaming in the silver bowl she held in her hands.

"No, not here, Quita," Bianca said. "Outside in the patio."

She got up and walked through the dining room to the enclosed square garden floored with tile, where a multitude of tropical flowers perfumed the night. She took the tea from Quita's hand and sat sipping it slowly, her eyes dark and brooding.

"Señora," Quita whispered.

"Yes?" Bianca said without turning her head.

"Why are you unhappy?" Quita said slowly, shaping the unaccustomed Spanish words clumsily. "You are so lovely—with a beauty like the moon and the stars and the night. Why do you sigh? Why do I sometimes hear you weeping in your chamber?"

Bianca looked at the half-breed girl. "It—it grieves you, Quita?"

"Much."

"Why, Quita? Why are you concerned for me?"

"Because you give me things, and never speak harshly to me, and are kind and gentle and never have me beaten. So my heart is a stone within me at the sight of your grief. But why is it, señora? You, who have so much . . ."

"I, who have everything," Bianca whispered, half to herself, "save that without which all else is nothing."

Quita leaned close, her black eyes warm with sympathy. "There is perhaps a man?" she murmured. "A cacique greater than the Señor Capitán Don Luis?"

Bianca jerked upright, the red wings of anger beating in her fair cheeks. "You are impertinent!" she flared, but the anger died as quickly as it had come. The smooth, kindly face of the mestiza was soft with pity; and, too, realism was replacing the early mysticism of her religious training in Bianca's mind. It posed a baffling question: In what way am I different from this slave girl? I have wealth, which cannot buy the happiness she has. She is enslaved, but am I free? When she finds love, she will go to her man and love him with all her body's passion, and it will be a clean thing, a fine thing, a thing far better than this—this bondage in which fate and custom hold me bound. . . .

Gently she put out her hand and laid it on Quita's arm. "I was hasty," she said. "I have no lover, Quita. But there is a cacique, greater than all the caciques of earth, whom I love. And but for the fact that he did not want me, I would not be here now."

"Then he is a fool!" Quita said fiercely.

"Or a man of honor," Bianca said wryly, "which is, perhaps, only another way of saying the same thing."

"Yet he will come back to you," Quita said firmly. "I will see to it!"

Bianca looked at the mestiza curiously, a pitying smile hovering about the corners of her mouth. "And how," she demanded, "do you propose to work this miracle?"

Quita's slim hands disappeared within the folds of her saya, to reappear after a moment with a necklace of gold. "Here," she whispered, "take it!"

Bianca stared at the necklace, which was made of gold wire drawn to the fineness almost of a human hair, and soldered together in a pattern so intricate as to defy the skill of the makers of the finest European lace. At its apex swung the figure of a woman, cast in heavy gold. The figure was nude, and all the attributes of femininity were vastly overemphasized, but for all its primitive heaviness of form, it was beautiful. Bianca's black brows rose questioningly.

"It is a *tunja,*" Quita explained. "I do not know her name, I am vastly ignorant of the lore of my people. But this I do know—she will aid you in finding your love."

Bianca looked at the tiny Chibcha Astarte, grossly sexual almost to the point of obscenity, then looked up at the statue of the Virgin, standing serenely in her niche. With quick revulsion she started to put the little figurine away from her, but midway in the action she wavered, halted. There was a curious fascination about the little pagan goddess; there was something fresh and free about her—a hint of open fields and blue skies and mountains veiled in rainbow mists like those encircling the Cauca Valley near Cali. And suddenly Bianca understood that whatever evil there was in the little goddess she herself had read into it with her European-trained mind, with its habitual deification of the asceticism it finds so hard to practice. The little Indian figurine would henceforth represent to her the fertility of the earth, the fruitfulness of fields, and a clean and joyous love, free of shame and dark doubts and questionings, wholly good.

"Thank you, Quita," she said. "I shall treasure it always. But is it not of great value? It is gold, isn't it?"

Quita laughed. "I am no Spaniard," she said. "Gold is nothing to me. We get it from the Panches, who grub it up from the earth and sell it to us for blankets, pottery, and salt. And who knows but what they get the better bargain, since they obtain useful things for this yellow dirt?"

Bianca looked at the girl, dawning respect in her gaze. "You are wise, Quita," she said, "very wise."

Quita opened her mouth to say something, but outside in the street they both heard the clatter of hoofs. Quita bent and picked up the silver bowl and fled silently to her own quarters.

Bianca heard her husband's heavy tread in the hallway. Swiftly she dropped the figurine down the front of her dress and, picking up a goose quill, dipped it into a bottle of ink that stood on a table at her side. She put out her hand and drew paper toward her. So it was that when Don Luis entered the enclosed patio he found her busily engaged in writing. He stopped short, his dark face twisted into a scowl.

"You can write?" he asked. "I do not like that. And can you also read?"

"Yes," Bianca said firmly. "Though this is but a poor greeting from a husband away so long."

Don Luis strode to her and took her gently into his arms.

"Forgive me, Bianca," he said. "Seeing you writing shocked me. A woman's mind is too delicate to be troubled with such things, and there are many things set down in print not fit for feminine eyes to see."

"I read only my catechism and my prayer book," Bianca said tartly. "Besides, I am no longer a girl—marriage, naturally, has robbed me of my innocence."

Don Luis threw back his head and laughed aloud. "A ready tongue," he said with a chuckle. "Well, I have the most accomplished wife in Cartagena. There is not another woman in all this region who can read print or scrawl her name. But, knowing your goodness, I will not let it trouble me. Besides, I have news for you. Letters granting me a patent of nobility, carrying with it the title of Count of the Realm, arrived from Spain today."

Bianca freed herself from his grasp and made him a deep curtsy. But Don Luis, who was not lacking in subtlety, detected in its very graveness a hint of mockery.

"My lord," she murmured.

"You do not seem overjoyed," he remarked dryly.

"No, but I am pleased," Bianca said, "for you. As for myself, what can a title add to my life?"

"Nothing," Don Luis growled, "since you have perversely persisted in gloom since the day we were married. But don't mistake me. I care little for the empty honor or for the lying flattery of all the obsequious lackeys who will presently fawn upon me. It is only that it carries with it a grant of *mayorazgo* that warms my heart."

"That means that the land . . ." Bianca began. "I cannot recall—explain this thing, Luis."

"You know what it means. My holdings can never be sold or divided, but must pass down in unbroken succession from eldest son to eldest son—forever."

"From eldest son . . ." Bianca whispered.

"Yes," Don Luis said quietly. "And in that you have failed me—but no more. Tomorrow we set sail for Lima. There are physicians there who will put an end to your barrenness."

"You took me to Cali," Bianca mused, "because there the air was good. And so it was. I loved the Cauca Valley with all my heart. It was a paradise of light and color, and the air was like wine. I hated to leave Popayán, it was so much cooler there, but what good did it do? Or the valley of the Rio Atrato in Chocó when we stopped there for some weeks on our way back?"

"I didn't want to take you to Atrato," Don Luis growled. "You insisted upon going there."

"Yes," Bianca sighed, "and I wish now I had not. Those Indians standing waist-high in the waters all day panning out your gold, with the hot sun beating down on them and the whips of your overseers continually biting into their flesh . . . How many of them died while we were there, Luis?"

"Enough!" Don Luis spat.

"They were beaten," Bianca went on as though she had not heard his command, "for panning out the green gold. Your men made them throw it back, and whipped them for bringing it out of the water. Why must it be thrown back, Luis? Isn't it lovely metal—much like silver?"[1]

"It is worthless. It is much too hard to be worked. Besides, if left long enough it ripens into true gold. But enough of these silly questions. You have work to do. We sail at full tide tomorrow for Porto Bello."

Bianca bent her head in a gesture that was just a shade too submissive. "As you will, my lord," she murmured, but in the doorway she turned and her black eyes lifted to her husband's face. "What reason does my lord give to the *oidores* and the caballeros for this voyage? It is best that I know, so that I may be in accord with you if I am asked."

Don Luis looked at her keenly, a sardonic smile playing about his bearded mouth. "What would you tell them if I did not instruct you?" he asked.

"That I am barren and my lord would have me cured of it," Bianca answered.

Don Luis frowned. "Say rather that my godson Ricardo Goldames, nephew of the Archbishop of Cartagena, has completed his studies for the doctorate at the University of San Marcos in Lima. Of course I must attend the ceremonies—bear the expense, as is befitting a godfather. And that,

[1] The metal was platinum. The Spanish, who did not know its value, threw it back to "ripen into gold." The San Juan and Atrato rivers in Colombia still produce the world's chief supply.

my pretty little wife, happens to be true." He sighed. "The expenses will not be light. . . . But off with you, there is much yet to be done."

Again Bianca made her husband a low curtsy, and swept through the doorway to her bedchamber.

The next day when the tide was at the full, the great ship *Garza,* which is by interpretation the *Heron,* moved silently down the Bay of Cartagena, heading southward toward the Boca Chica channel, which led out into the open sea. Bianca sat on the high deck under an immense silk canopy that shielded her fair face from the sun, and watched the Getsémani section drop behind. The ship inched over to starboard, rounding the long tongue of land on which stood the fortress of Santa Cruz. Beyond it the land sank suddenly almost to the level of the sea, and lay flat and regular until the rounded hump of the Terra Bomba rose out of the ocean.

It was nearly nightfall when they hailed the fortress of Boca Chica, almost a full day having been spent in passing through the treacherous lower reaches of the Bay of Cartagena. But once in the open sea, the *Garza* spread her wings and moved majestically over the face of the waters. Three days later she dropped anchor in the harbor of Nombre de Dios and rested there for the night. The next day she sailed the short distance to Porto Bello.

Bianca was most anxious to go ashore, for if there is any one thing true of the Caribbean, it is that its waters are never calm. Even upon bright, blue days the *Garza* had rolled and pitched with ponderous deliberation, the very slowness of the motion lending misery to the seasickness that it caused. As the great vessel nosed into the lovely harbor that had inspired Columbus to give the port its name, Don Luis stood on the forecastle and swore softly. Bianca lifted a white face with greenish circles about her eyes toward her husband.

"What ails you, Luis?" she demanded.

"It's fairtime," he growled. "We could not have chosen a worse season in which to arrive."

"Why?" Bianca asked.

"Look," Don Luis said, and pointed.

Even from that distance Bianca could see the throngs on the wharves. In front of the vast customhouse, the streets were black with humanity.

"Did a fleet arrive at Cartagena during my absence?" Don Luis asked. Bianca nodded. *"Diablo!"* he swore. "Every thieving merchant from Lima to Mexico City is in Porto Bello tonight. Once they have news of the convoy's arrival they descend on this place like a flock of vultures."

"Why don't they come to Cartagena?" Bianca said. "That is where the fleet first drops anchor."

"Too far," Don Luis grunted. "Besides, the Isthmus has its narrowest neck here, so the merchants from Lima and other cities on the Pacific coast find Porto Bello easiest to reach. If we can find a place to lay our heads tonight, we may thank the Holy Virgin for her kindness."

A few minutes later Don Luis had handed Bianca over the side to the young officer in command of the ship's boat. Then he climbed down beside her. As they came in to the quays, the helmsman had to weave his way through the tightly packed mass of pirogues, hoys, and even rafts that blackened the water, lying so close to one another that it was impossible to glimpse the sea on which they rode.

Ashore it was worse. Though she was flanked fore and aft by her husband and his retinue, Bianca was buffeted and shoved by the howling crowd of merchants. Tents had been set up in the main thoroughfare; open-air stalls were everywhere, piled up with all kinds of cloths, laces, shoes, hardware, wine, machinery, clothing, notions, tools, oils, perfumes. And there were slaves. Before these last, Bianca halted, staring open-mouthed at the slim Dahomey maidens whose glistening naked bodies looked as though they had been carved out of ebony. Nor was she the only one; a crowd of men were clustered about the slave mart, and from their winks, gestures, and bawdy talk, Bianca soon gathered that it was the singing perfection of the black girls' willow-slim bodies, the curve of hip and ebon thigh, the high, conical upthrust of breast, that was evoking the feverish bidding, rather than any work that the Negresses might be able to do. She turned a stricken face toward her husband.

"I should have warned you," Don Luis said grimly. "Come."

At the intersection they had to wait a full hour before there was any break in the parade of mule trains, come from over the Isthmus, laden to the limits of the beasts' endurance with sugar, cacao, cotton, tobacco, hides, indigo, vanilla, pearls, gold, silver, copper, tin, salt, cochineal, and emeralds. Finally they made their way to a smoky hostel, where for a single night's stay Don Luis was forced to pay a thousand pesos.

Their meals, Bianca soon discovered, were to cost them twenty times the price of a much better meal in Cartagena, and when the food was brought she found it inedible. After supper Don Luis left her in the care of Quita, guarded by two stout men-at-arms.

Bianca lay talking to Quita, and then began a short prayer for her husband's safe return. He had, she knew, gone to engage mules to transport them and their goods over the Isthmus to the Pacific side, where they would board another ship and sail southward to Lima. But midway through the prayer the face of Kit interposed itself, and all unbidden, her thoughts set sail upon dark voyages. . . . If, she mused, Luis were not to return—Holy gentle Mother, forgive me!—I might return to Cartagena and send him word. . . . But no, this is wickedness. It is evil to think thus. I must not, I must not. . . .

It was at this moment that Don Luis returned. Overcome with contrition for her secret wickedness, Bianca sprang up and flung herself into his arms. A moment later she discovered her mistake. The smoldering fire in his dark eyes blazed fiercely in an instant. His great arms tightened about her until her breath was almost gone.

"Leave us," he growled over his shoulder to Quita. Bianca heard, with a kind of icy terror, the swift rustle of the girl's departure. Then, slowly, with oddly mingled strength and gentleness, Don Luis laid her down on the great bed.

Afterward, as he lay sleeping beside her in the darkness, Bianca sat upright and stared into the lightless void of night. This time it had been different; this time her traitorous body had leaped with unbidden fire; this time her short whimpering cries of passion had been real. It was hot in the close little room, and her naked body was wet with perspiration, but upward from her heart the glacial chill of terror stole slowly until she was shivering in all that dense tropical heat like one half-frozen.

"Good-by, my Kit," she whispered. "Now and forever, good-by." Then: "Holy Mother of God, blessed among women, grant me that it be a son."

9

Kit sat stiffly on the back of the great white stallion. In his early youth in Cádiz he had ridden frequently on the pack mules that formed the backbone of Spanish overland transportation. And not infrequently he had obtained from one hidalgo or another employment that meant his riding the blooded Andalusian horses of the peninsula. But years at sea do not help a man's horsemanship, and Kit found that managing the spirited animal he had bought from a neighboring planter required more attention than it had formerly.

He was aware, too, that Bernardo Díaz was watching him with a curious expression. Bernardo managed his own animal with ease, a fact that Kit found somewhat annoying. Kit tightened his already firm grip on the bridle and touched the white stallion's sides with the big Spanish spurs he wore. They were of silver, as were the great stirrups hammered from the soft metal into the shape of the toe of a jackboot. To the horse, however, the rowels of the silver spurs felt the same as those of any baser metal; his rearing almost unseated Kit. Kit brought him down again, loosing about the beautiful animal's head a volley of trilingual oaths.

Bernardo grinned wickedly. "You should never leave the quarter-deck, Kit," he said, chuckling. "With horses you display a most unpracticed hand."

"Enough," Kit growled. "What brings you here? I can see by the look of smug contentment on your homely face that you have news."

"Alas," Bernardo said cheerfully, "I have always had an open countenance. It is my greatest misfortune, Kit. In this world a man has great need of dissembling and guile."

"Never mind the philosophy," Kit said. "Get to the news. It must be important to part you from your gaming and wenching."

"A wench or two might cool the fever of your impatience," Bernardo observed. "You were not cut out for monkhood, Kit."

"The news!" Kit roared.

"I have none, but I do have an invitation from His Excellency the Governor for you to dine with him on Monday next at his house at Léogane."

"The Sieur Ducasse invites me to dine with him? How did that come about, Bernardo?"

"I have often ridden through his cane fields. Three times a week, to be exact. Near Léogane there's a small pigeon who puts up enough resistance to the plucking to make it interesting—and the shortest route to her home lies through the Sieur Ducasse's lands."

"Are you sure you did not waylay him with some tortuous scheme?"

"I am grieved," said Bernardo, grinning, "at your suspicious nature. What scheme could I have?"

"Who knows, my old one?" Kit smiled at him. "You of course chanced to meet Ducasse?"

"Yes. And the Governor, who is of Huguenot parentage, can take a mass or leave it, though I think he likes the leaving better than the taking. Therefore neither the question of my birth nor the fact of my conversion concerned him in the least. We talked of ships and sailing. It was a good talk, Kit—the man knows the sea."

"So? How came this invitation to dine?"

"I dropped, in passing, word that I had served aboard the *Seaflower*. The good Sieur was at once all ears, and asked if I knew you. Your fame has spread abroad, Kit. The Governor very probably would like to employ you in some service."

"I don't like that," Kit growled. "I'm done with such a life."

"Patience, Kit. For miles on end one rides through a sea of cane, tilled by blacks brought from Africa. His Excellency hinted that such a plantation was not beyond your attaining. Here in the New World great wealth is much easier earned than in the Old. If I were you, I would lend a most attentive ear to what Ducasse has to say."

"This has a pleasant sound," Kit agreed, "still . . ."

"What harm can come of eating the man's food and drinking his wine, since both are reputed to be excellent?"

"I stand persuaded," Kit said. "You will of course also be present?"

"Of course. Now ride with me a bit while I inform you about His Excellency. Nothing is more pleasing to a man's ear than knowledge of his previous doings—especially when they have been noteworthy. And Jean-Baptiste Ducasse is a great man, I assure you. He began his career as a slave trader for the Compagnie de Sénégal, and at once distinguished himself by helping to drive the Dutch out of the island of Gorée. Then he took all the rest of the islands in the Cape Verde group. He made his first voyage to Saint-Domingue in 1680. . . . Are you listening, Kit?"

"Attentively," Kit said. "Go on."

"There he displayed his intelligence by taking heed of what everybody in the Antilles knew, but what no dealer in black ivory had ever bothered to consider: the fact that to continue to bring in Coromantes, Fantis, Ashantis, and Dahomeans was not only foolhardy but suicidal. Those tribes of blacks fear neither a white skin, God, nor the devil, and wait only for the first dark night to begin cutting their masters' throats. He came back loaded with Whydahs, Nagoes, Pawpaws, Congoes, and Angolans—all diligent, tractable slaves. And to prove that the man can think, he brought not one Ebo, the easiest of all blacks to obtain, and the stupidest. From that one voyage, Ducasse made his fortune—never before or since has a shipload of Negroes commanded a higher price."

"You are oddly expert in these matters," Kit mused. "Have you studied the blacks, Bernardo?"

"Yes," Bernardo replied with a smile. "When you get to be a planter, you will need a manager."

"You were speaking," Kit said slowly, "of Jean-Baptiste Ducasse. The selection of my plantation manager can wait."

"So I was. My wits grow addled with age. With the money that he made, Ducasse outfitted himself as a privateer. Soon he had made such a name for himself that Louis XIV commissioned him a lieutenant in the Royal Navy. By this time Pouançay was dead and Paul Tarin de Cussy had become Governor of Saint-Domingue. We were in these waters with Lazarus when the news of De Cussy's elevation reached us, remember?"

Kit nodded patiently.

"Ducasse was exceedingly busy. He attacked the Dutch in Guiana and chased the English completely out of St. Kitts; then he sailed back to France. When he returned he found that he was now governor, for De Cussy had fallen in the sack of Cap Français in 1691. Ducasse chased the British away from Guadeloupe. Then he settled down to rule, with such effectiveness that Saint-Domingue has become a model colony—even the buccaneers obey him. There the matter rests until this day, except for the forays by Daviot and Laurens de Graff against Jamaica—also at His Excellency's orders. All in all, a most excellent leader, in my opinion."

"Yes," Kit mused, "he seems a real man. Have you any idea what he wants of me?"

"Something touching Jamaica. It would do no harm to find out. Out here the world is young, and there are not the old quarrels, old schemes, and old jealousies to contend with. If filibustering were the only way a man could gain sustenance in the Antilles, I would say depart; but the white crystals of the sugar mills and the great hogsheads of rum will make all the gold of El Dorado paltry by comparison. It will not be amiss to gain the Sieur Ducasse's favor."

Kit did not answer. He bent his bronzed face and stared fixedly at the white arch of the great stallion's neck, feeling the rhythm of the horse's motion.

They rode on in deep silence. The sun burned blood-red into the Caribbean and the night crashed down without twilight or dusk between it and the dazzling day gold. The palms and the mountains and the thickets disappeared in the abrupt darkness, and the profligate heavens flung out their treasure of stars. The horses moved on slow-clopping through a night like man's destiny—filled with sound and motion, traveling unceasingly onward toward a goal whose outlines cannot be discerned.

Exter, Jean-Baptiste Ducasse's residence at Léogane, was a pleasant mansion built of great cypress clapboards, and the Governor himself was a tall, heavy man whose immense brown wig, curling over his back and shoulders, gave him the look of a benevolent lion.

He greeted Kit and Bernardo with bluff cordiality, and led them to the great dining salon. Glancing at the silver service, Kit saw at once that the table was laid for only three. This was strange. For what reason had the Governor thought it necessary to maintain such privacy?

His Excellency was not slow in getting to the point. Over the golden mound of the roast fowl, he eyed Kit quizzically, the light of humor dancing in his small blue eyes.

"The captain of the *Seaflower,*" he chuckled. "You are young for such a command, Monsieur Gerado."

"What do years matter?" Kit answered. "It is the straightness of the aim and the strength of the arm on the tiller that make the difference."

Ducasse reached out a powerful hand and took up a glass. He raised it to his lips and held it there without tasting the amber wine while his eyes studied Kit above the rim.

"There is," he mused, "in my office at Port de Paix a record of French ships lost to enemy action in these waters. I seem to recall a *Cygne,* a *Gallant,* and a *Gloire* sunk by one brigantine called the *Seaflower*. There were more, but those come most easily to mind at the moment."

Kit put his own glass down with deliberate slowness and his eyes were cool and grave. "Not while I commanded her," he said flatly. "I have never fired on the fleur-de-lis."

"So?" Ducasse said calmly. "If not, it is most strange for one who was born in Cádiz, in the realms of His Most Impotent, Bewitched Majesty, that royal idiot Charles II of Spain!"

Kit looked at Ducasse, and smile wrinkles played about the corners of his eyes. "Would you bait me, your Excellency?" he asked. "If so, you take the wrong track. My mother, it happens, was born in Normandy, and my true name is Giradeaux."

Ducasse bounded to his feet. His arm swept across the table, reaching for Kit's hand.

"There!" he roared. "I knew you were no dog of a Spaniard! I should have known it before—your French is better than mine."

"And if your Excellency's records are complete," Bernardo put in dryly, "they should show that the *Seaflower* has sent twenty-two Spanish ships to the bottom within the past three years."

"They do show that," Ducasse said, and laughed. "That was what puzzled me. But no more of this. Now to business. You know that the town of Port Royal was ruined two years ago by an earthquake."

"Yes," Kit growled, "we were in the harbor when it happened."

"So? You were supremely lucky to have escaped, then."

"We were," Bernardo said, "but pray continue. You were speaking of Port Royal."

"Since that explicit manifestation of Divine displeasure, I, in my small way, have implemented the arm of the Almighty. I have sent Daviot and De Graff to slow the English work of reconstruction, but for all that they rebuild much too fast and too well." He leaned forward confidentially. "Not that I fear their fortifications and batteries, but there is a slower thing that over the years can ruin us here." He glanced past Kit and Bernardo and his eyes took on a dreaming look. "All the world will one day make a track over the waters to Saint-Domingue. The Cul-de-Sac and Cap Français and the harbor at Port de Paix will be black with shipping come from Europe to buy our sugar and our rum. There is where our wealth lies! Let the Spaniards grub gold out of the earth—still it will flow back to us. I do not fear the Englishman's guns, but I do fear their sugar mills and their slaves. They must not compete with us here; in this Saint-Domingue must reign supreme!"

"Therefore," Kit said quietly, "you want me to take the *Seaflower* out and raid them once again?"

"No! I would have you join me in a full-scale expedition against Jamaica. I shall have more than twenty ships, and from this blow the English will never recover. But I can use your youth, courage, and skill. What do you say, Captain Giradeaux?"

"I don't know," Kit mused. "I have no quarrel with the English. The only Englishman I have known well was a kindly man. Still, this inaction begins to pall on me."

Ducasse crossed to where Kit sat and took his arm. "Come," he said, helping Kit up. They walked to the window, and Kit followed his finger pointing over the immense expanse of cane fields to the very foot of the mountains. "There is," he said softly, "over against Petit Goave, arpent upon arpent of such rich land, as yet untilled. As governor of this colony, it lies within my power to grant that land to whomever I will—in reward, of course, for services justly performed."

"And if I refuse," Kit said, "you might recall to a court the *Seaflower*'s former misdeeds, and leave it up to me to present proof that I had no hand in them."

Ducasse looked at the lad, seeing him young, fair, and very spirited. "No, Christophe," he said quietly. "Your choice is free. Accept or refuse as you will."

Kit frowned. He tugged thoughtfully at the golden spike of his beard. "When do you sail?" he asked.

"Next month."

The next month was June of the year 1694. There were yet nine more months of waiting before Kit's promise to Rouge was to be fulfilled. And there was little hope that she would appear before the time appointed. He had much to gain and nothing to lose.

"The *Seaflower* will take her place in the line," he said.

10

On the morning of June 22, 1694, Kit and Bernardo lay in a little copse of woods on the island of Jamaica, looking out on a great cane field. Behind them hid the crew of the *Seaflower*.

"Look, Kit," Bernardo was exulting, "you have no country. By birth you are a Spaniard, but Spain's star is setting and you have killed too many dons to face the reckoning. Likewise, you are not French, for men reckon descent after the father, and no man, not even I, knows with any certainty who your father was. But now you have gained a country! Ducasse loves you like a son. He could not be more joyful over the feat of saving Major Beauregard's troops from that ambush if he had performed it himself. He will not forget how many times you have turned the tide of battle in his favor. As a planter of Saint-Domingue, who knows what greatness you might attain?"

"Who knows indeed?" Kit said dryly. "Still, this attack sits unhappily in my gullet. I have known but two people of English blood in all my life. One of them was a great sea captain and the other the woman I want for my wife."

"She will know nothing of this, and she would care less if she knew. What can it matter, since by this you gain the means to make her the greatest lady of Saint-Domingue?"

"Yes," Kit growled, "as to that you have much logic, though small right. But right and logic were always at variance, is it not so, my old one?"

"Always," Bernardo agreed.

To their left the tall chimney of a sugar mill sent volumes of black smoke into the air. Kit paid scant attention to the mill. He was watching the young Englishman who was directing the Negroes as they fed the stalks of cane into the great stone crushers. A team of mules drew the millstones around. Kit could see that their left eyes had been covered with a length of cloth to keep their endless circling from making them dizzy.

A humane people, the English, he reflected, and turned his attention back to the young man. He was, Kit had to admit, an uncommonly handsome youth. A shade too handsome in fact, Kit thought. The young man was shouting at his blacks and his clear tenor voice came over to Kit. It took Kit a moment to understand the meaning of the English words. Had it not been for Smithers' insistence upon speaking English to him, Kit might have forgotten the tongue that Lazarus had taught him with such painstaking care.

" 'Od's bodikins!" the young man swore. "You black beasts! Get it in there—push it closer or I'll have your bloody hides!"

"Yas, Marsa Reginald," the black who was feeding the crushers groaned. "Doin' best I kin."

Kit saw the young man rise in the saddle and bring his riding crop down, full across the Negro's back. The black man cringed, and gave the stalks of cane a convulsive shove. The next moment Kit heard him scream. It was a terrible sound, like a loon night-maddened or like a parakeet loosing his insane, fiendish laughter. Looking closer, Kit could see that the Negro had caught his hand in the crusher.

"Mother of God!" he whispered. "Why doesn't he stop the mules?"

But the young Englishman—wasn't it "Reginald" the Negro had called him?—sat there like one stupefied. The great millstones dragged the black's wrist and forearm and upper arm between them, so that the slave was pulled round and round the outer rim of the crushers and the cane juice came out red with his blood.

"Idiot!" the Englishman shrieked, suddenly completely beside himself with rage. "You've ruined the entire batch! Brutus! Bring the ax!"

Kit and Bernardo watched in cold stupefaction while another Negro hurried off, to return after a moment with a broad-bladed ax.

"Set him free!" the young man ordered. Brutus, his black face the color of old ashes, swung the ax skyward. Kit saw it arching against the sky. Then it whistled downward to strike the imprisoned slave's shoulder with a sound like no other sound on earth—except, perhaps, the sound of the poleax in the slaughter pens.

The black man lay on the earth, his arm sheared off at the shoulder, and the great flood of his life pumped out until all the earth beneath him was muddied. No one made the slightest effort to aid him or to stop the bleeding.

Grimly Kit turned to his buccaneers. "All right, men," he said quietly, "burn the field!"

In a trice the flints snapped against the steel, and the buccaneers blew lustily on the smoldering tinder. One of them got a tiny yellow flame and stuck the tarred end of the huge torch into it. Instantly it flared, and all the buccaneers crowded around the man, lighting their torches from his.

It was the misfortune of the English on the southern shore of Jamaica that their land was exceedingly arid. They were able to grow cane only by irrigation, and even so many of the stalks that stood in the fields were brown and dry. To the north, beyond the mountains, torrents of rain fell; but the Blue Mountains—as the Jamaicans so accurately called the range that separated the north from the south of the islands—effectively stopped all rainfall from reaching the southern shore. It was in the south that the flatlands lay, and the industrious English had made them grow.

The cane about the margins of this field was so much tinder. The system of irrigation was crude and misapplied. So it was that when the Englishman looked up from his blood-ruined cane juice and his dead slave, he saw a wall of flame advancing upon him, and through it a horde of buccaneers, shrieking like fiends and firing their great muskets.

He stood there open-mouthed until Bernardo was upon him. The Jew's great arm swept up, and his open palm made a sound like a pistol shot against the young man's face. The next moment the Englishman was rolling in the dust.

The fierce buccaneers pulled him to his feet and began to bind his arms. He jerked his face around and his eyes fell on Kit, beplumed, beribboned, lace at throat and wrist, a slim Spanish sword dangling at his side.

"Your name," Kit demanded.

"Reginald Parish," the young Englishman spat. "And if I were not bound . . ."

Kit's blue eyes searched his face; they were as cold as ice. "Release him," Kit said quietly. The buccaneers hesitated. "I said release him!" Kit growled. The men hurried to obey.

"I have no sword," Parish said.

"Give him your sword, Bernardo," Kit said. "I would not deny even such a dog as this the chance of an honorable death."

"You're a fool, Kit," Bernardo said. "How do you know this fop is not a maître d'armes?"

"I'll chance it," replied Kit, smiling. "On guard!"

Reginald Parish brought his sword up in a practiced flourish. The blades made blue lightning in meeting, the air was loud with the clang of steel even above the crackle of the flames. Parish pressed the attack so that Kit was forced to give ground, parrying the Englishman's thrusts with negligent, deceptive ease.

"Reginald . . ." he mused aloud as he fought. "That name has a familiar ring." He stretched forward suddenly, his right knee bending, his left leg straightening out until the lace at his knee swept the earth, and the Englishman's sword swept upward from his hand. Kit straightened and put the point of his sword against the earth.

"Recover your weapon," he said coldly.

"You're twice a fool," Bernardo muttered. "Run the bastard through!"

Reginald Parish picked up the sword and saluted Kit with it. Then he lunged forward, beginning a furious attack. Kit gave not an inch; he parried in tierce and his blade continued along his opponent's sword, opening a cut above the man's eye.

"Have you had enough?" Kit asked, lowering his weapon.

Instead of answering, Parish lunged forward with all his might, so that Kit was forced to leap aside, parrying in seconde so late that the rounded bell guards of their weapons' hilts clanged together. Kit came up body to body, forcing his opponent's arm upward while the ribbons of sweat and blood bedewed young Parish's face.

"Without honor, ah, Reginald!" he mocked. "Now to make an end to this."

He started forward, his blade a moving blur, so that Reginald was forced to give ground, meeting Kit's blade in quinte, in sixte, now in prime, his hand held up before his face, the blade angling downward across his breast while Kit laughed and beat him back. Then, in sudden riposte, Kit laid the point of his rapier against Parish's heart. Suddenly, abruptly, he halted.

"Reginald!" he whispered. "Now I know! It's the name of the man Rouge was to wed!"

"Rouge?" Parish panted. "I do not know that name."

"A maid," Kit said, "with hair the color of flame and eyes of emerald."

"Jane!" Parish croaked. "Lady Jane Golphin!"

Kit sheathed his sword. "Take back your life. I will not harm anyone once dear to her."

"Then it was you," Parish cried, "who barbadoed her away!" He sprang forward, the point of his rapier aimed straight for Kit's heart, but the crash of Bernardo's pistol echoed above the raging flames. Reginald loosened all over at once, becoming suddenly boneless, Bernardo's rapier spinning from his hand.

Kit stood there watching him fall slowly toward the earth, then he raised his blue eyes to Bernardo's face. "Thank you, my old one," he said quietly.

Reginald Parish lay on the ground coughing blood. "Rosalind," he gurgled. "You will not harm her? . . . Swear it."

"Rosalind?" Kit said. "Who is she?"

"My wife," Reginald gasped, but the word brought a rush of blood to his throat, so that he strangled from it, his face purpling.

"I swear," Kit said.

Something like peace came into Parish's eyes. He opened his mouth to say something, but whatever it was it was never voiced, for at that moment he died.

"An ugly business," Kit said. He looked out at his men, who were busily overturning the vats and prying loose the millstones with great staves. "The price of becoming a gentleman of Saint-Domingue runs high," he mused.

"He had scant claim upon Rouge," Bernardo observed. Then: "I wonder where the manor house is?"

As if in answer to his question, the high cry of a woman rang through the woods. A moment later the woman came in sight. She was as naked as the day she was born, except for a few rags of clothing that clung to her arms and shoulders. Behind her as she ran pounded two buccaneers. Hope flared suddenly in the woman's eyes. She sped straight toward Kit, forgetful of her nakedness. When she was close she hurled herself into his arms and lay against his iron-hard body, shivering and whimpering like a whipped child. Kit disengaged her grasp gently, and taking off his greatcoat, wrapped it about her.

The buccaneers gathered about Kit and the woman, mutters running from man to man. Kit faced them, one hand about the woman, the other holding a freshly primed pistol that Bernardo had that moment given him.

"I told you last night," he said flatly, "that I would have no rape! Whoever disobeys me dies! Understand?"

The freebooters fell back, their faces black with scowls. Kit heard the woman gasp.

"Reginald!" she whispered. She was looking at the dead Englishman.

"I am sorry, my lady," Kit said in his slow, accented English. "I would have spared his life, but he forced the issue."

Lady Rosalind Parish turned her heart-shaped face toward Kit, seeing the clean chiseled lines of his jaw, the thin falcon's beak of a nose, the mouth firm beneath the white-gold mustache, and the great mane of his hair spilling down over his shoulders like a golden fleece.

Kit looked at her, seeing her face small, lovely, fierce. There were no tears in her blue eyes, the trembling was gone from the corners of her rose-pink mouth, which was curving upward at the corners in a terrible kind of joy.

"I'm glad! Now I'm free!" she said, her voice calm with a dreadful calmness. "How I hated him!"

Kit was puzzled, but said, "Lead me to the manor—if these dogs of mine have not yet burned it."

"No," Lady Rosalind whispered, "they have not—they were far too busy —with me."

Kit turned back toward Bernardo and commanded, "Bury the dead." Then very gently he led Lady Rosalind away from the smoke and cinders of the burning cane field.

She marched ahead of him. Only three buttons of his coat were fastened, so that her white legs gleamed softly in all their slender length each time she took a stride. Once inside the manor house she asked him to sit down while she went to the wine cupboard. She returned with a decanter and two large goblets.

"To my freedom!" she cried, and drained her glass.

Kit sat there with his glass untouched, looking at her in amazement. The three fastened buttons of his greatcoat concealed nothing of her, but she moved before him like a graceful doe, entirely without shame. She downed another glass, then a third, her blue eyes brightening, her gaze moving intently over his face.

"Hadn't you better go and dress?" Kit said slowly.

Rosalind Parish threw back her head and laughed. "No, good Captain," she said, laughing. "I have no shame! Your sea dogs removed all need for it. Besides, it's nice to be naked—so very cool."

"Your husband," Kit said. "Why did you hate him?"

She put down her goblet with a crash. "Because he didn't love me! Because he was always mooning over another woman, Jane Golphin, who was barbadoed during the earthquake! Because he was a weakling and I needed a man!" She leaned forward, her lips dew-petaled, warm and inviting. "Such a man as you—perhaps . . ." She stood up suddenly, her slim fingers toying with the topmost button. "If you had come yourself, instead of sending those evil-smelling rogues, I fear I would not have struggled."

She came slowly up to Kit and put her head against his chest.

"There is no need for haste," she whispered. "You can continue your raid —tomorrow."

Kit put his hands roughly on her shoulders and pushed her away from him.

"This day your husband has been killed. I fear that the dog in the human race is not confined to the male alone."

She looked up at him, her smile sensual and excited. "Yes, I am evil!" She laughed as she said it. "I am glad of it! I have held it pent up too long." She studied Kit's frowning face. "Do not go!" she whispered.

"In my lifetime," Kit growled, "I have sent many a soul to hell. But I have not sunk so low as to kill the husband and take my pleasure with the wife. Good day, madame!" He bowed, and turning, marched through the doorway. And as he strode through the woods, he heard the high, hysterical titter of her laughter.

Four days later, at the head of his ship's company, Kit marched back toward the sea. His men drove a hundred Negroes—all Eboes, selected by Bernardo—before them. The raid, as a raid, had been a success. Two hundred and fifty mills and plantations had been destroyed and more than thirteen hundred Negroes captured. But the attack designed to reduce Jamaica to the status of a French colony was an abysmal failure. The English had been wounded. They had not been defeated.

The long line of buccaneers, their faces lost amid the great dark forests of their beards, filed downward toward the shore in ragged lines, driving the slaves. Behind them, above the royal crests of the palms, Kit could see the huge plumes of black smoke billowing in the still air.

"Fifteen," he counted silently, "sixteen, seventeen, eighteen, nineteen . . ." And every one of them the house a man had loved or the mill he had built or the cane field he had made to grow on the arid soil. How many of the owners lay charred and blackened in the smoking embers of their manors? How many of their women had run shrieking into the thorn thickets and marshes, only to be pulled down by these goats and satyrs he had helped loose among them?

His fingers strayed down to the frayed sash of gold he had made from Don Luis's Heron Banner. Now while he was loosing his fury on the innocent, Luis del Toro was taking his ease in his house at Cartagena. Beside him, no doubt, Bianca was sitting, fair Bianca whose beauty still moved with troublesome brightness through Kit's memory.

If, he mused, it were not for the chance that Rouge might yet join me at Petit Goave, I would scale those walls and strike him down! No, more than that, there is the possibility of a still richer vengeance! What worse could I do, before I send him into hell, than to bind him hand and foot to a pillar, with this banner stuffed in his mouth for a gag, and then take my pleasure with Bianca there before his eyes? Death ends all suffering, but with the sight of her writhing in my arms, even in the grave his sleep would be troubled. . . .

They topped a rise and looked down at the surrounding country. Kit frowned, for there before them lay still another plantation, which somehow had escaped burning. Bernardo looked up at Kit with questioning eyes. Kit's frown deepened, his hand came up and tugged at the golden spike of his beard. Then he looked about at his men.

"Well, lads?" he said.

"God's blood!" Smithers said. "A few more blacks won't hurt none. The more the merrier!"

The others nodded assent. Kit sighed. From the first he had known what they would say.

"Spare the manor," he ordered. "I will drink the owner's wine. And no ravishment—there will be bawds aplenty when we reach Saint-Domingue."

"If we don't bust first," said Smithers, grinning. The men laughed. They were in rare good humor, which increased with the imminence of their homeward voyage.

At Kit's signal they swept down on the cane fields. Kit and Bernardo made straight for the house. Long before they reached it the dry cane fields were a sea of flame, and the crash of the overturning vats and crushers resounded from the mill. They turned down a neat roadway flanked by rows of white-trunked palms, leading to the great white mansion in the center. They had brought with them five or six buccaneers, considering this number sufficient to overcome the scant resistance they expected.

When they were a hundred yards from the manor, a dozen armed Negroes came out. Bernardo peered at them intently, gauging the shape of their heads, their bone structure, and the flare of their nostrils.

"Whydahs," he pronounced. "Have no fear, these blacks are not fighters."

"Fire a volley over their heads," Kit commanded.

The long buccaneering muskets leaped to the freebooters' shoulders. The crash of their fire echoed from the road. As the smoke drifted up through the palms, Kit saw the timid blacks scrambling for safety.

"Life is strange," Bernardo philosophized. "Either a man buys fierce Dahomeans or Coromantes and gets no work, or he buys Eboes, or Whydahs and has no defense from aggression."[1]

Kit did not answer. He was leaning forward, pinpoints of fire in his blue eyes. A woman had come out of the manor and was beating the blacks back to the fray with the flat of her sword. She used the weapon as though she had handled a blade all her life. Kit hung there a moment, staring. Wildly, wordlessly, he began to run toward her. Bernardo looked after him in astonishment. He lifted his eyes toward the woman, then he too broke into a gallop. Even from that distance he could see that her hair was as red as the flames that devoured the cane fields.

Kit came running straight toward the trembling blacks. The muzzles of their muskets came up, pointing at his chest. The woman spoke to them sharply.

"Hold!" she commanded.

Kit came up to her, his blue eyes searching her face. "Rouge," he whispered, "my little Rouge."

"Lady Jane Golphin, you murderous dog!" she said, her green eyes fixed upon his face. "Get away or . . ."

Kit slowed, a smile playing about the corners of his mouth. "Or what, Rouge?" he mocked. "What, my red-haired sea witch turned gentlewoman?"

[1] The troops of Toussaint, Dessalines, and Christophe, a century later, were nearly all of Dahomean descent, as were their leaders.

"You are mistaken," she said evenly, her red mouth moving, shaping the words, her skin white as the petals of water lilies beneath the amazing brush fire of her hair. "I know no Rouge."

"Then I will instruct you, Lady Jane. You are oddly expert with that sword of yours, and your eyes are as green as sea water, your mouth still hungers to be kissed."

He moved toward her, but the point of the rapier came up and rested on his bare chest.

"Come no farther," she spat, "or I'll kill you!"

Kit glanced down at the rapier making a small dent in his bronzed skin. Then slowly, deliberately, he moved forward. A drop of blood showed around the point. Then, as he lifted his foot to move forward again, she drew the sword back, and the next instant Kit held her in his arms. Tears spilled over her dark-gold lashes and penciled her fair cheeks.

"I am weak," she wept, "weak! You should die!"

"Why, my little Rouge?" Kit whispered.

Her pale face lifted, and her eyes blazed with emerald fire.

"For taking away all I had left of belief in the goodness of men! For proving that you too are a murderer, when I was learning in my heart to care for you deeply!" She stared at him, the tears in her eyes like diamonds. "You came here to a land that had never harmed you. You burned and ravished and destroyed. And when you found Reginald Parish, you killed him because I had once loved him! You fool, he was married, and I had long ago become merely his friend and neighbor!"

Kit tried to interpose, but he could not stem the rush of Rouge's words.

"You killed poor, spineless Reginald," Rouge continued, her voice rising, "and then you lay with his wife! Forced her, she says, though I doubt that, for Rosalind has scant need of forcing!"

Kit stared at her, light dawning in his eyes. "She lied," he said gravely. "On all counts, she lied. I did not slay Parish. I left Rosalind untouched."

"I will not listen to you!" Rouge cried. "All men are dogs, and worse! Go away, Christopher—get out of my sight, for my forbearance wears thin."

Kit did not move back. Instead, his arms swept up and drew her to him, and his lips found her mouth. He could feel her body trembling through the rich fabric of her clothing, sense the terrible warfare within her: the fierce demanding surge of desire, the great swift, sweet lassitude of assent struggling with her rage, her hurt, her hate. His mouth moved on hers, feeling her lips slackening into surrender, the beat of her heart beneath the soft-cushioning globes of her breasts becoming a drum roll, swift-pounding against his own. He bent down and swept her into his arms, oblivious of the stares of the buccaneers. With one booted foot he kicked open the door and entered the cool gloom of the great mansion.

"Which way?" he said, his voice hoarse. Mutely, she motioned with her head. He shouldered open the second door, and paused for a moment before the large bed, canopied with netting against the mosquitoes. Then, very gently, he laid her down upon it.

"No," she whispered, "not yet, Kit. Talk to me—say that you love me, that I am not another Rosalind whom you take because you can."

Kit murmured: "No, never that! You are my love, my heart, my bride."

Her white hands came up and lay along the bronzed curve of his cheek. "I am through with fighting against you," she whispered. "I came here to Jamaica to learn again to be a woman, that I might not be ill of grace when I came to you. The lesson went hard. Teach me, my Kit—teach me to be whole again. Kiss me—hold me—never let me go!"

Kit bent down and kissed her mouth. Her pale fingers stole upward and caressed the bright blaze of his hair.

"Now," she sighed, "I am ready. Do what you will. Perhaps this time I shall find true joy in it."

Kit's lean, iron-hard fingers trembled on the fastenings of the gown. Then suddenly her hands caught at his wrists and she sat up, staring out of the window.

"My fields!" she said. Then she turned the great blaze of her slanted eyes on him. "You," she whispered, her voice edged and harsh, "you did this too! You ordered the burning!"

Kit swung about, seeing the great wall of flame riding before the wind, roaring down upon the manor. The house, he saw in an instant, was doomed. He half-turned back toward her, but the motion came too late. He saw the flash of the silver candelabrum as she swung it with all her force. He jerked aside, but not fast enough or far enough. The blow that might have stoved in his skull merely glanced along the side of his head, leaving him swaying dizzily on his feet and shaking his head to clear his reeling sight.

He heard the swift rustle of her garments as she fled from the room, and staggered after her. She fled down a long hallway toward the rear of the house. Kit ran unsteadily after her, and came out into the courtyard in time to see her mount and ride away. He was still there, supporting himself by an arm about a pillar, when the others joined him. Bernardo looked at him with anxiety, but Smithers and the men, seeing the thick ooze of scarlet spreading down his face, roared with unconcealed joy.

"No ravishment, eh, Captain! A good rule, sir! You should practice it sometime!"

Kit looked at them, and a wry grin spread under the blond mustache. "I am bested," he admitted. "But for this, that red-haired sea witch shall pay!"

Then he turned and took Bernardo's proffered arm. An hour later they started their final march to the sea.

11

KIT STOOD MOROSELY on the foredeck, watching the *Seaflower* thread her way delicately between the whitecaps, pushing her prow into the deep-curving troughs of the sea. For three days they had been running due west, almost at right angles to their true course, but now the gale whose fury had driven them some three hundred leagues out of their way was blowing itself out. In another hour, perhaps they would be able to set a new course for Saint-Domingue.

His fingers stole up and touched the swath of bandages that encircled his aching head. I almost had you won that time, my little Rouge, but for a wind and flame and obedience to the orders governing an expedition I joined against my better judgment—which, in fact, I joined only to gain for you the station befitting you. Now I have gained these things only to lose you. . . .

Lose her? Lose Rouge? Never while she lived! Twice now she had lain trembling and lost within his arms, soft with the lassitude of surrender. And the second time would have been the first repeated, made more glorious, but for the hellish mischance of that burning field. That first time on shipboard when she had come to him unwillingly only to surrender at the last, to brand him hip and thigh with her beauty that was both snow and flame—with how bright a glow did the memory flare in his mind still! To the end of his days that thought would warm him, no matter how cool his blood would grow with age.

But what had been could be again—and this time for as long as they both should live. He had burned her house. Very well, he would build her another, and such a house as she could not now imagine in her wildest dreams. He had burned her fields. Now he would fling down at her feet fields bathed in sea mists, fragrant with rains, in which in the space of days the cane would spring up taller than a mounted horseman—fitting recompense for those dry, brown Jamaican fields that had to be watered at the cost of so much labor.

He stopped short. He would do these things, but what then? How was he to find one small corvette on the trackless bosom of the sea? Two years had passed between the time he first saw Rouge standing drenched and trembling on the *Seaflower*'s deck and the time when by purest chance he had stumbled upon her attacking the great plate ships. How many weary years would pass again before he found her? She would not go back to Jamaica, that he knew; she would hurl her renewed fury down upon the heads of men—and he, God help him, must find a tiny craft that might be anywhere within three thousand wind-whipped leagues.

He was interrupted in his reverie by the lookout's shout, floating down through the diminishing shriek of the wind.

"Vessel astern!" he called. "Three points to sta'board!"

Kit and his officers crowded aft, staring at the apparition, their minds refusing to credit the evidence of their eyes. For there, on the crest of the still wildly racing waves, a ship rode with every sail bent to the wind, heeling over at so great an angle that her lee rails were actually awash, boiling after them at a speed no sailing vessel was ever intended to make.

The vessel alternately appeared and disappeared as she drove through the walls of spray, and each time they saw her she was nearer. Now she was upon them, and Kit could see that she was a corvette with lines as clean and trim as the *Seaflower*'s own. Then as she drew abeam a great roar burst from her single line of guns, and she disappeared momentarily behind the cloud of gun smoke. Instinctively, Kit hit the deck, and the balls sang over him by inches, smashing the gunwales into matchwood, and overturning four of the *Seaflower*'s guns.

"Gunners to station!" Kit howled, and the *Seaflower* became an anthill of frenzied activity. The passers and the powder monkeys skidded over the wet decks, their deadly burdens cradled in their desperate arms. The gunners had trouble with their matches, but after several agony-laden minutes they got them burning despite the storm. The touchholes had to be cleared and filled with dry powder, and by the time they were ready, the *Seaflower* had taken another broadside that killed three of the men.

Bernardo swung at Kit's sleeve, pointing. Kit looked down at the glowing object that hissed on the wet deck.

"Mother of God!" he breathed. "They're serving red-hot shot!" Then he turned back to his gunners. "Hold your fire!" he called. "Helmsman, run her in until we can't miss!"

Again the corvette loosed her murderous hail, but the men were better sheltered now. The *Seaflower* veered in toward the attacking vessel, riding in so close that Kit could see the name on her prow.

"*Seawitch,*" he spelled out, his brow knitted with frowning. He lifted his sword high, holding it there while the gunners crouched beside their silent pieces, waiting for his signal. The *Seaflower* fell off a bit, running exactly parallel to the corvette, her guns at point-blank range aimed at the slim and deadly vessel scant yards away. Then, slowly, Kit's sword arm started downward. Halfway down he halted the movement abruptly, his breath a tangled burning within his lungs, for there on the high deck of the corvette the woman stood, her long red hair streaming to leeward like a banner of blood.

"Hold!" he got out, but the word was a mere croak. The wind snatched it from his lips, and before he could reshape it the titanic thunder of the *Seaflower*'s guns rocked sea and sky with their belly-deep roar. The walls of smoke rose before his eyes, and he heard his own voice shrieking like a man gone mad: "Hold! Hold your fire for the love of God!"

Then the smoke cleared, and he saw the light corvette, never designed to match guns with so stout a vessel as the *Seaflower,* heeling over as though mortally wounded. Even as he watched, he saw the fire break out amidships, and as he swayed there, his face gray as death, Bernardo chortled.

"We hit the furnace for the hot shot!" Bernardo yelled. "Knocked it over, hand bellows and all, and the bastard's burning! Give him another, Kit! Finish him off! God's blood, didn't he know enough not to attack the *Seaflower?*"

"Ride her in," Kit called. "Cease fire. Grappling irons ready! Stand by to board her!"

Bernardo turned an incredulous face toward his captain. "You're mad, Kit! You can't board her in such a sea!"

Kit turned his face, gray-pale and haggard, to Bernardo. "It's *her* ship," he whispered. "And board her we must, though we drown in the attempt."

The *Seaflower* drew closer, her own crew watching the mountainous seas with fear-stricken eyes. From where they stood, Kit and Bernardo saw Rouge walking up and down the deck, swinging the long Spanish whip, the crack of the lash sounding even above the storm. Somehow she got five gunners back to their stations, and the guns roared out one after another. At such a distance, it was impossible to miss. Kit kept his gaze fastened on the dying *Seawitch,* but as he watched, the *Seaflower* veered suddenly, the distance between the two vessels widening.

Kit turned to growl at the helmsman, then his jaw dropped blankly. Where the *Seaflower's dos d'âne* had been there was only a smoking mass of timbers, the whipstaff itself was a thousand ragged splinters, and the brigantine was entirely out of control. He stood watching the blackening seas growing broader between the two vessels. The tarred stays, shrouds, halyards, and clews of the corvette were burning rapidly, the sails catching, too, despite their wetness. A great weakness stole up through his limbs. He sat down abruptly on the deck, watching the boiling masses of mist and cloud blotting out the *Seawitch*'s outline. For a long time he could mark her by the bloody glow that she cast upward on the enveloping cloud, then all was mist and grayness and silence and death.

He sat very still on the *Seaflower*'s deck, without moving, until Bernardo touched his arm and led him away. Bernardo knew it was not well for the *Seaflower*'s crew to see her captain weep.

In the morning the sun broke through the high, fleecy mare's-tails and all the sea to the east was a rosy pink, breaking in gentle swells so mild that the brigantine scarcely rolled at all. On the deck the ship's carpenter and a crew of hands sweated and swore as they fitted a new whipstaff into place.

Kit trod the deck forward and aft, his blue eyes blank and unseeing, his thin mouth held in a tight line, his fingers clenching and unclenching. He stopped before the laboring group.

"How long now?" he demanded.

The ship's carpenter looked up and wiped the sweat away from his brow with a grimy hand. "God knows, Cap'n," he said. "Another four-five hours."

"Mother of God!" Kit whispered. Bernardo, who kept constantly at his side, put out a restraining hand.

"It's no use, Kit," he said kindly. "By now that corvette has gone down with all hands. It was vile luck, but you must not blame yourself."

"Not blame myself!" Kit exploded. "Whose fault was it, then? Had I not seen that vessel before? Had I not set foot on her deck? And the name—how often have we both applied it to Rouge herself? That little sea witch—that little red-haired sea witch! If I were not a prince of asses, she might be here now—alive and with me. Holy Mother of God! What have I done to deserve this?"

"Gently, Kit, gently. In this life there is much that a man can never understand. You are young, and all of life is before you. Time heals all wounds, and . . ."

"Enough of your ancient saws! There is nothing left in life for me. Rouge is dead, and her blood is on my hands."

"She tried to kill you often enough," Bernardo remarked.

"Would to God she had succeeded! Better that than this!"

Bernardo shrugged and turned away. Then, after three long strides, he stopped short, perched on one leg like a grotesque waterfowl.

"Kit," he whispered.

"Be quiet!"

"No, Kit, this you must see!" He pointed, and Kit, raising his head, saw what it was that had stopped Bernardo. There on the horizon lay four bright sails. Kit stared at them fixedly, watching them grow larger.

"Ducasse's squadron?" Bernardo ventured.

Kit shook his head. "No," he said. "I fear they are English, from their cut. Order more men to help the carpenter."

For two hours more a beehive of men sweated and fumbled and swore, trying to complete the repairs, while the sails of the four vessels grew ever larger. Finally, they were upon the *Seaflower*, four fast English frigates, bristling with guns. While the stubborn timber resisted all efforts to fit it into the badly bent socket of the former whipstaff, the first of the English vessels drew close enough to open fire with her chase guns.

"Gunners to their stations," Kit ordered quietly. His voice was a husky whisper, flat and calm, drained of all feeling. The men scurried to their places, but at the moment only the guns beneath the stern castle could be brought to bear. Kit watched the Englishmen's roundshot tearing through his rigging with an expressionless face. If, his whole bearing seemed to say, this be doom, then I am ready. . . .

But Bernardo turned a face dark with fury upon him. "You have no right to do this," he said coldly. "We cannot maneuver, while they can. They outgun us four to one. They can beat in and pound us to pieces!" Kit shrugged eloquently. "If you are tired of life," Bernardo pleaded, "at least consider the men!"

Kit studied the face of his friend, his own eyes cool and grave. "I think they would prefer to die as seamen should," he said, "rather than to hang on the end of a yardarm."

"Stop, Kit," Bernardo said, "the English are not wanting in honor. Do we not bear letters of marque from both His Excellency and the King? As the crew of a commissioned privateer, all they can do is hold us prisoners of war until this conflict ends."

"But will they honor these letters?" Kit asked mildly. "The *Seaflower* is well known in all these waters."

"We have never taken an English prize," Bernardo reminded him. "We have preyed chiefly upon the Spanish, with some minor forays among the Dutch. I think they will treat us well."

Kit gazed toward the fat mushroom of smoke that ballooned out of the mouth of one of the English chase guns, and heard the whine of the ball as it passed overhead.

"Very well, Bernardo," he said quietly, "you may order Smithers to strike our colors." Then, turning on his heel, he marched below.

The English vessels moved alongside and slung over their grappling hooks. Then their boarding parties came over the side, to find the *Seaflower*'s crew drawn up ready to receive them. Kit had returned to the deck.

"So," the young English captain said, smiling, "this is the celebrated *Seaflower!* I had expected a hotter reception, Captain Gerado."

Kit made a slight bow. "We were disabled," he said shortly, "in a chance encounter with one of your vessels yesterday. I wished to spare my crew needless bloodshed."

"So," a cold, sneering voice spoke up from the English captain's elbow, "you deliver them up to be hanged!"

Kit turned and looked at the Spanish officer who stood there in breastplate and helmet, his black beard curling fiercely.

"Who said anything of hanging, Don Enrique?" the English captain demanded.

"Is it not the fate commonly dealt out to pirates?" the Spaniard countered.

"The court at Port Royal will have that to decide," the Englishman said coldly.

Kit smiled. "I trust that the good Captain . . ."

"Neilson."

"That Captain Neilson will be so good as to remind the court that the *Seaflower* has never taken an English prize."

"But what of Spanish vessels?" Don Enrique demanded. "What of England's ally and true friend?"

"I have had the pleasure," Kit mocked, "to send to hell above a hundred of the vessels of that monarchy which lacks both wit and honor. I think that Their Majesties of England will one day thank me for a signal service, once their eyes have been opened to the tragedy of this mésalliance."

Don Enrique sprang forward and struck Kit full across the mouth with his open palm.

Kit smiled softly. "With Captain Neilson's permission, I will rid England of one more false friend," he said quietly.

"No," Neilson growled. "Enough of this farce. Captain Gerado, you will be good enough to accompany me to my vessel, the *Glorious*. You may bring with you such of your officers as you designate."

Kit nodded to Bernardo and Smithers. An hour later, they sat with Captain Neilson in his own cabin drinking his good wine.

"I will do what I can," Neilson said. "I like this alliance as little as you do. The letters will be presented in evidence. I think they will do some good."

Four days later the crew of the *Seaflower* stood before the King's magistrate at Port Royal, listening to a fierce denunciation by the royal prosecutor.

"These men have shed English blood!" he roared. "They have burned plantations and ravished Englishwomen! If your lordship is so disposed, I would call in evidence Lady Parish who suffered dishonor at the hands of this man and his crew."

The barrister assigned to their defense made a perfunctory gesture of protest. It was quickly overruled. There was a rustle of skirts and the whole court rose as Rosalind Parish was led to the witness box. She raised her hand and took the oath in a quavering, tear-laden voice. The court was hushed and silent.

"And now, my fair lady," the Crown prosecutor began, his voice sinking to a low rumble that he evidently intended to sound benign, "the court wishes to spare you as much embarrassment as possible. If you will answer my questions as simply as you can, I think we can word the matter so as not to offend your—ahem—delicate sensibilities."

"Object!" the defense squeaked.

"Overruled," the magistrate boomed.

"Do you, my dear lady," the prosecutor began, "recognize this man?"

Rosalind's blue eyes lifted and met Kit's cool stare. "I—I do," she whispered.

"Is he not the man you saw shoot down your husband!" the prosecutor thundered.

Again that quick nod. Kit smiled grimly.

"And—ahem—afterward did he not force his way into your bedchamber—and hah—ahem—force you to submit to—ah—certain indignities—at—ahem pistol point?"

Kit looked at Rosalind and threw back his head and laughed aloud. A furious buzz ran through the courtroom. The magistrate thundered with his gavel. Rosalind's face was scarlet, her blue eyes alight with anger.

"He did!" she said in a high, clear voice. "And afterward he turned me over to his crew!"

The whole court became bedlam. The magistrate pounded his gavel in vain. It was long minutes before order was restored.

"Captain Gerado," the magistrate boomed, "what have you to say to these charges?"

Kit stood up with almost insolent deliberation. "I am not so ungallant," he smiled, "as to contradict a—lady." The pause was deliberately, insultingly prolonged. "But I might say that my crew and I were here in open warfare, at the orders of the King of France. The letters of marque submitted bear that out. I say that this court has not established our guilt upon the charge for which we were brought to trial, that of piracy against the Crown. Since we have not been charged with violation of the articles of warfare, it seems strange that we should be tried for it. As for our having violated the honor of Madame Parish, I dare say that half the young blades of Port Royal have personal knowledge that such a feat is beyond possibility—since one cannot destroy what does not exist."

Again the thunderous uproar. The head of the gavel broke away from the shaft under the magistrate's furious pounding. As the room quieted, Kit could see Don Enrique standing with his right leg forward, his head bent in a half-bow in the magistrate's direction. At once the magistrate recognized him.

"Don Enrique!"

"I beg to suggest that His Spanish Majesty's Government could but regard it as an unfriendly act if these men receive less than the extreme penalty," the Spaniard said smoothly.

The magistrate waved a hand airily, as though to dismiss all thought of that remote possibility. Kit watched Rosalind's face as the magistrate rose. It was chalk-white and her eyes were seeking his. He gazed at her coolly, ignoring the agonized pleading in their depths.

"The prisoners will rise and face the bar," the bailiff intoned. The *Seaflower*'s crew rose in a ragged semicircle.

"In view of your high crimes and misdemeanors against Their Majesties' Government and against that of our royal ally, Charles II of Spain, I hereby sentence you to be taken from the gaol at dawn tomorrow, paraded through the streets for the edification of the populace, and finally hanged by your necks until you are dead. And may God have mercy on your souls!"

The silence had thickness and texture. It could be felt. Every man in that court drew in his breath and held it, none daring to be the first to let it out. So it was that Rosalind's explosive gurgle had all the carrying power of a musket shot. Every eye in the court swung in her direction. She stood up, swaying a moment, before she crumpled in a dead faint at the foot of the bar.

Silence then—heavy as death. Then the uproar, complete and terrible.

12

AFTERWARD BIANCA preferred not to think of that journey across the Isthmus by mule train. Here was country the like of which she had never seen before—steaming jungle through which a path had to be hacked with brush hook and machete; fetid swamplands alive with mosquitoes, filling her delicate nostrils with their ugly marsh stench; monkeys and harsh-voiced parrots howling overhead; fer-de-lance and venomous bushwhacker slithering their deadly, twisting bodies through the undergrowth.

To make matters worse, her miserable morning sickness brought her daily proof that she was indeed with child, and the jolting of the mule did nothing to add to her comfort. She said nothing of her condition to Don Luis, and bore his chafing with silent dignity. Finally, however, her condition had become so bad that Don Luis was forced to use a litter for her, which was suspended between two mules. After that the journey was easier.

They came down to the Pacific side, passing the blackened ruins of the old city of Panamá, which stood in silent rebuke to Henry Morgan's infamy. Bianca turned away, and the weary mules clopped the last league of their journey into the small but bustling hamlet that was growing into the new Panamá. When Bianca sat up in her litter and saw the great ship that was awaiting them on the blue waters of the Gulf of Panamá, she wept from sheer joy.

Once aboard ship, she recovered her health with the boundless elasticity of youth. By now, her morning sickness had passed, and she felt so well that she was a little ashamed of her high spirits, having been taught that delicacy, especially during pregnancy, was the hallmark of the patrician.

The galleon crawled southward over sunlit seas balmy with eternal spring. Here, off the northwestern coast of the vast Viceroyalty of Peru lying along the rugged Pacific shores, the sea was of a blueness that stunned the imagination, rolling majestically inland in waves like long folds of lapis lazuli until it reached the shoal waters. There, as clearly and as sharply as though the line of demarcation had been drawn by the hand of a giant, it blazed pale-green, as bright as emerald.

On the shore, in the declivities between the mountains, thick forests of palms and thickets of bamboo tossed their bluish-jade crowns against the azure sky. Birds like feathered jewels, crimson and maize-yellow and topaz, exploded their rainbow brilliance against the somber trees. They sang and screeched and arched their bright trajectories between sun wash and tree shadow until, watching them, Bianca wept.

Don Luis laid his arm gently across her shoulders and drew her to him. He looked down at the small face from which all color had drained, leaving it like Andean snow except for the almost savage scarlet of her trembling mouth. His big hand came up and stroked the hair—black almost to the extent of suggesting blueness, so that in its sheen no hint of brown or red showed—that fell like starless night shadow about her shoulders. He felt again the momentary start of surprise that this foaming cascade of blue midnight was so warm to the touch; his eyes registered for the thousandth time the startling juxtaposition of ebony and spring snow, so that when he spoke the boom of his great bass had an underlying hint of pain in it.

"Are you thinking of another bird of fine plumage, Bianca?" he said.

The quick black eyes lifted to his suddenly and their gaze rested cool and grave upon his face.

"All that—is past," Bianca said, her voice utterly wanting in expression.

Don Luis frowned. The little nagging whisper that had lain buried since the day he had retrieved his captive bride from the cove of Cul-de-Sac probed its ugly way to the surface of his consciousness.

"Is it?" he growled. "Are you sure of that, Bianca?"

The dark eyes darkened even more, becoming night-black. Bianca searched her husband's face, and the corners of her mouth stole upward in the merest ghost of a smile, but she did not answer. She stared at him coolly, gravely, quietly, until the great veins of his temples stood out and beat with his blood.

"Answer me!" he thundered. "Have you forgotten him, Bianca; forgotten this nameless bastard of a worthless Frenchwoman?"

"At any event," Bianca said quietly, "you have not, my lord."

Don Luis glared down at her, his face dark with anger above the jutting night cloud of his beard.

"I am not sure," he said evenly, slowly, spacing his words with the menacing deliberation of a man accustomed to control all things, even his rages, "that I have heard a convincing account of what happened in Hispaniola while you were—detained."

"Didn't you?" Bianca answered tartly, and turned her gaze toward the tangled jungleland of the shore.

Don Luis stared at her, lovely and defiant, the green bile of tortured jealousy boiling inches below the level of his throat. His hands shot out and spun her around, none too gently.

"Speak!" he roared. "What happened there?"

"Your voice is overloud," Bianca said with exasperating sweetness. "Would you share our tête-à-tête with the crew?"

"Enough of your raillery!" Don Luis said, but his voice was lower. "I think an answer on that score is due me."

"Why?" Bianca asked innocently.

"Because . . ." Don Luis began. Then he realized the trap into which he had fallen. It was impossible to maintain dignity and at the same time admit his jealousy. "It is enough that I await an answer and command that you give it," he said.

"And if I refuse?"

"To refuse," Don Luis said heavily, "is to lend weight to the supposition that I—perhaps—took a dishonored woman for my wife."

Bianca paled, her eyes black fire coals in the whiteness of her face. "Has it ever occurred to you," she whispered, "that such a supposition is a most vile insult?"

"That I do not know," Don Luis blustered. "I know only that he is young and fair to look upon, and that you are young and susceptible." He paused, searching her pale face, and the rage died within him, leaving only the sickness and the hurt. "Say again that nothing happened there," he whispered, "and I will believe you."

Bianca studied this great, strange man who had become her husband, who would sire whatever children she would have, and the intimacy of both these reflections did not detract from his strangeness. He might have been a graven image for all the warmth that kindled in her eyes. She could answer him, she knew. She could say in all honor and all truth that nothing had happened between her and Kit—nothing, save only a kiss. So her thoughts ran. But Bianca was not lacking in that strange quirk of utterly feminine cruelty which is so much a part of every woman.

"Think what you will, my lord," she said at last. "I will not deny you the solace of your thoughts."

Then, very deliberately, she turned away from him. Don Luis took a half-step toward her, but his dark eyes fell on a little group of harquebusiers who had stood staring curiously at him and Bianca. He stopped short and turned his furious countenance toward the slowly backward-slipping land.

The ship butted her way southward across the equator, and suddenly all the warmth was drained from the air. Bianca stood on the deck with a shawl about her shoulders and watched the steaming tropical forest disappear to the northward while directly abeam of the vessel lay scrub trees, dwarfed by the chill. She was conscious of her husband's dark, tormented gaze as she stood there, but she would not turn.

Under the prow of the ship the water was icy-green, and the bleak, forbidding, bone-dry land stretched southward in austere beauty as far as Bianca's eye could see. She gazed at the gray skies lowering above land that might have been the Sahara for all the moisture it contained. Then she turned puzzled eyes upon her husband.

"So many clouds," she mused, "and yet there is nothing here but sand and rock. Why is that, Luis?"

Don Luis spoke up quickly, almost jovially, delighted that Bianca had at last broken the strained silence between them.

"It has not rained in Peru," he said, "for seven years. Often, it is said, babies have grown to manhood in these parts without seeing rain. Yet in this season the clouds are always there. God and Virgin alone know why no rain falls from them."

"Then," Bianca queried, "how do the people live?"

Don Luis put out his hand and pointed.

"See those mountains beyond the lower foothills of the coast? In the season of clouds, a mist but little heavier than a fog descends upon them. It is called in this country the *garua*. Where it sits on the mountains, the soil is drenched with moisture, and overnight, almost, plants and grasses spring up. Men call these grasses the *loma*. They make excellent feed for the cattle, the sheep, and the llamas."

"Llamas?" Bianca echoed.

"A beast not unlike a camel, but without a humped back. Truly there are many wonders in Peru."

Within the first hours of the next morning, Bianca was given proof of the truth of her husband's words. She was awakened by the cries of sea birds, and the beat of uncounted wings. She dressed hastily and mounted the deck. Looking up, she could no longer see the sky, except as momentarily revealed patches of light between the wings of the birds. The whole heaven was blackened by them. From horizon to horizon they brushed each other with their wing tips and made the air hideous with their screeching. Over the port bow a line of pelicans passed, their ugly sacked beaks thrust out and their small heads resting on their curved necks in the recess between their wings. Bianca watched them pass with a growing sense of amazement. Idly, she began to count them, but she wearied when she reached five hundred, and she missed count frequently because of the sameness of the birds. So she stood quietly and watched the pouch-beaked sea birds fly past until her knees ached with the standing. She shifted position and hung on, unable to tear her gaze away from the spectacle. At last she gave way to her weariness and sat down on a coil of rope. She was still sitting there watching the pelicans when she heard the clang of the watch bell, and realized with a sudden disbelief in the evidence of her senses that she had been watching a line of pelicans fly across the ship for two full hours and that the last bird was not yet in sight.

She turned her astonished eyes toward the other side of the ship and saw that the water ahead was boiling ceaselessly. She watched this for another half-hour until the ship nosed into this white-whipped whirlpool. Then she saw that the wild white foam was the continuous splash being made as one gannet after another dived into the sea after fish. She stared at them until she realized that this too was not going to end, and turned her eyes to a stop just abaft of the starboard beam where a black cloud hovered over the water. She heard a step at her side, and Don Luis was pressing a telescope into her hand.

"Cormorants," he said. "Look!"

Through the glass the black cloud became broken up into a mass of individual birds, whirling across the lens so fast that they made Bianca dizzy. And above them all soared albatrosses, frigate birds, man-of-war birds, terns, plovers, and the omnipresent gulls. There was nowhere she could look without seeing the flash of wings. Even the surface of the ocean, for a full twenty miles, bore the floating shapes of the sea birds, resting quietly on the dancing wavelets with folded wings. Bianca turned an awed face toward Don Luis.

"How many are there?" she said.

"God alone knows,"[1] Don Luis replied. "A man standing in one spot might wear out ten lifetimes counting them—and yet would not have begun. . . . Come, it is time you went below. We should reach Callao before nightfall."

But the galleon made even better speed than he had hoped. It was still bright afternoon when the cold, greenish Peruvian current flattened out into still, almost waveless waters. On their starboard the great island of San Lorenzo lay, with its low foothills breaking the force of the waters. Off to the port side Bianca could see the promontory aimed like a dagger straight at the heart of San Lorenzo, and beyond it the low, thatched huts of Callao. The galleon beat in against the wind, which on this stretch of coast blows forever from the southwest, and came gracefully up alongside the wharf without having to drop anchor at all.

On the wharf there was a great bustling, but a bustling in slow, dance tempo. The Indian roustabouts took the hawsers of the galleon and belayed

[1] A twentieth-century naturalist has counted 5,600,000 birds on one small island near Lima. This flock alone consumes a thousand tons of fish a day.

them about the piles in a manner that stated plainly that tomorrow or the day after would have served as well.

Standing beside her husband, Bianca let her dark eyes stray over the nondescript crowd. Then, abruptly, her gaze halted. For there on the wharf a young man had swept off his great plumed hat and made her a sweeping bow. As he straightened, she could see that he was uncommonly handsome, with brown hair so light that it was almost the color of honey and eyes as blue as Kit's own. I shall always, Bianca thought miserably, have a most uncomfortable weakness for eyes of that particular shade. . . . Then she turned toward her husband in time to see that he was smiling and returning the young man's salute with rare good humor.

"My godson," Don Luis said.

Bianca took Don Luis's hand and came down the gangplank. At its foot, Ricardo Goldames waited, his blue eyes widening with every step she took toward him.

"My esteemed godfather," he whispered. "I am overwhelmed!"

"With your joy at my coming, no doubt," said Don Luis, chuckling, his deep voice filled with irony.

"Of course!" Ricardo was smiling. "But also at the sight of my new godmother. I trust that the closeness of our relationship will permit me to kiss her hand." Thereupon he did so though with a great deal more ardor than any religious dutifulness could have inspired.

"Señora," he said cheerfully, "I am desolate!"

Bianca looked at his young, handsome face on which not the slightest trace of sadness showed. "Why, señor?" she said gently.

"Because this old he goat of a godfather of mine has snatched the fairest flower of all earth's beauties, and hereafter I must mourn my loss in vain."

This quite outrageous statement was made so calmly and with such a pleasant expression that Bianca took a half-step backward, glancing fearfully at Don Luis. But her husband merely threw back his head and roared with laughter.

"You are not changed, Ricardo!" Again he chuckled. "You are still a scoundrel. I warrant that the proctors at San Marcos grew so weary of your deviltry that they closed one eye at your lack of knowledge. But come, you have transportation to Lima for us, haven't you?"

"The best," Ricardo said. "I have prevailed upon the Viceroy himself to lend me his own coach. And His Excellency hopes that you will honor him with your presence in his house during the festivities."

Bianca glanced up at her husband. This was high honor indeed. In his own right, the Viceroy of Peru was an actual monarch—many times more powerful, in fact, than many a princeling of the worn-out houses of Europe. Don Luis took the invitation calmly, as no more than his due.

"We accept, of course," he said. "Lead on."

The Viceroy's coach was a splendid conveyance, carved of quebracho wood and much ornamented with giltwork and metal fittings of pure silver. It was drawn by four of the finest horses Bianca had ever seen. The coachman and the footman were Negroes of a blackness defying description, but the sable hue of their skins set off their splendid livery all the more vividly.

The whip cracked over the backs of the horses, and the coach moved off toward Lima. Despite the dust and the jolting of the heavy vehicle—which was entirely wanting in springs or any reasonable substitute—Bianca found the eight-mile journey from the seaport of Callao to the mighty capital of Lima most interesting. Ricardo talked incessantly, but Bianca heard scarcely a word. She was far too busy gazing out the window at the strange new world into which she had come. So far she had not seen another white face. All about her were Indians talking quietly in their liquid Quechuan tongue, moving slowly over the dusty highroad driving their herds of llamas or alpacas before them.

She noticed that one of the strange camellike beasts was lying down and, despite a shower of blows from his driver, was refusing to get up.

"This," Ricardo said, grinning, "is worth seeing." Putting his head out the window, he called to the driver to halt. As the coach ground to a stop, the incensed Indian made a grievous mistake. He moved around to the beast's head and began to tug furiously at the bridle. At once the llama lifted its slim head and spat a mouthful of foul green liquid into the Indian's face. The Indian sprang back, wiping his blinded eyes. Then he whipped out a knife and sprang at the animal's throat.

"Stop!" Ricardo cried. "You know better than that! Ease him and he will stand."

The Indian turned a sullen face toward the young Spaniard. Slowly he sheathed his knife, and walked around to the side of the squatting beast. He opened the great bag it carried and handful by handful began to throw out the dried maize it contained. He had thrown out no more than ten small handfuls when the llama gave a low, contented grunt and got awkwardly to its feet.

"You see," Ricardo said triumphantly. "A llama has far more brains than an Indian. He knows how much he can carry. There are times," he added ruefully, "when I myself have been less wise." Then he put his head out the window again and ordered the coachman to go on.

They followed the curves of the Rimac River past the thatched adobe huts of the Indians. The stench of the cooking fires smote them in the nostrils. Bianca lifted a perfume-drenched handkerchief to her nose and glanced inquiringly at Ricardo.

"*Taquia,*" he said. "Dried llama dung. This land is starved for wood. Were it not for the beasts, they would have no fuel. Everything here depends upon nature. You have seen the birds? Well, we send ships out to their nesting places, which return loaded with their offal. We call it *guano* —and with it we enrich the land."

"I think," Don Luis growled, "that this is hardly a subject to talk about to your godmother, Ricardo."

"A thousand pardons, señora," Ricardo said. "Here in our barbaric land it is easy to forget our manners."

"Not that you ever had any," Don Luis observed. "Isn't that Lima ahead?"

Bianca put her head out the window and took her first look at the capital of the great Viceroyalty. Lima, she saw at once, was a great city—a great Spanish city. The spires of the cathedral, the cabildo, the Casa Real, rose in the faintly misty air.

As they moved into the city, the first impression—that of the Spanish nature of Lima—was altered but not dispelled. Through the streets shuffled hundreds of Indians, the descendants of the proud Incas, now broken and dispirited. They moved with bent heads, their colorful serapes and rebozos picking up the light, gleaming dully brown and blue and white and green over their bent shoulders. Before them moved the herds of mules, sheep, cattle, llamas, and alpacas. These latter, unlike the hardier llamas, were bearing no burdens, being driven in merely for the shearing.

Here in this quarter the filthy huts of plastered mud, shared alike by Indians, goats, pigs, and chickens, assailed Bianca's gaze. The naked children stared back at her with great wondering eyes. Then the earthen streets of the Indian quarter gave way to the paved avenues of the Spaniards, and the barred-and-shuttered houses of the mighty stared forbiddingly down upon them. Through the middle of the street the stinking gutters ran, and now and again a window of an upper story opened, to reveal some Indian or Negro serving-woman with a bucket of garbage. Then, with a mumbled cry of "*Agua va!*" she would unceremoniously dump the foul-smelling contents into the street, and woe betide the passer-by who failed to dodge!

Bianca shuddered, seeing all this. However, Lima was alive with pageantry, too: the caballeros on their fine steeds, dressed in velvets stiffened with embroidery and sitting tall in their splendid gold-inlaid saddles; the dark eyes of the *limeñas* peering coquettishly through the curtains of their coaches at the magnificent *charros* in their broad-brimmed hats edged with silver and gold lace, fur-trimmed and embroidered jackets, silver-buttoned pantaloons, leather leggings and immense silver stirrups and spurs, raising their ivory-inlaid whips in gallant salute to the señoritas. Lines of goldsmith shops vied with the even more numerous ones of workers in silver. Portuguese Jews, whose wealth and business acumen had won them a measure of security from the grasping fingers of Inquisition, hurried through the streets intent upon their drafts and papers. Nuns and bearded friars lent a note of sobriety to the otherwise brilliant throng.

And everywhere were the beggars, sticking their filthy and diseased paws even into the windows of the coach, so that Don Luis was forced to strike them with his cane. Here too were the Negroes, permitted by law to wear the cast-off garments of their masters, so that it was easy to tell a mulatto from a mestizo, though in coloring and features they might be identical. Here were the women of the town, gay, abandoned, noisy, of every race and hue and combination thereof.

Jewels sparkled on hatbands; mere merchants adorned themselves with almost priceless pearls. Even the half-breed women, and lovely mestizas, wore sandals and belts of silk and gold, with pearls and rubies—presents, no doubt, from doting hidalgos, as were their ornamented skirts and jackets of fine cloth. On the walls of the public buildings the rude scrawls prohibiting public nuisance testified to the want of even the rudiments of delicacy or restraint among the people, but half a glance sufficed to show that these warnings had no effect. Bianca turned her scarlet face aside and gazed out no more until an uproar smote her ears.

Looking out, she saw a crowd of Negro retainers engaged in a furious brawl. One group, dressed in bright liveries of green and gold, was having much the better of it. They were armed with short swords, pikes, and daggers, while the others, whose much more splendid livery was of gold and royal purple, had only staves. Don Luis turned questioning eyes on his godson.

"The blacks in green," Ricardo explained, his tone full of good-humored enjoyment of the bloody riot, "are the retainers of the rector of the university. Of all the slaves in Lima, they alone are permitted to wear sidearms. The others are the servants of the Viceroy, who hold it ill that they are not so honored. They fight every time they meet. All the blacks—those of the Archbishop, the *oidores,* and the regents of the Audencia—hate the Negroes of the rector worse than poison. They always attack them, which is most stupid, since the rector's Negroes always win. Ah, here come the officers of the guard!"

The officers of the guard, heavily armed and wearing coats of mail, swept down on the brawling Negroes. For a moment the uproar increased, then abruptly it ended. The guards had brought the shafts of their heavy pikes down over the heads of half a dozen blacks, leaving them sprawling in the street. The rest stared down the gaping muzzles of the muskets of the guards and discretion took precedence over valor. The driver of the coach cracked his whip, and the heavy vehicle moved on toward its destination.

That night Bianca sat at the fiesta table and tried to follow the light chitchat of the conversation. At the head of the table the Viceroy himself was suffering from mild social confusion. The recent elevation of Don Luis to the rank of count had upset protocol. The Count of Monclovia knew how to talk to his inferiors. If Don Luis had been a mere grandee, he could have dealt with him with graceful condescension, but with the Count del Toro, his newly made equal, he was at a loss. Don Luis's dry, half-ironic remarks did nothing to help the situation. Little by little he was letting Monclovia know that in wealth, in extent of holdings, in everything except the office of viceroy, he exceeded his superior officer. The silences between the two men lengthened.

Bianca too found the evening difficult, but for a different reason. Across the table from her, Ricardo Goldames's glances dwelt more and more on her face. And his eyes were naked with adoration. She wanted to warn him, to tell him to turn aside his gaze, but the women prattled on. Bianca was sure that they had noticed, that every señora in the great salon was aware of this wild and secret indiscretion. The evening dragged on, every moment crawling with leaden feet over her tortured nerves. When at last it was over Bianca found that she was to be alone except for Quita, for Don Luis had been summoned to discuss urgent matters of state.

Sitting in her nightdress, with Quita brushing out her long night-black hair, Bianca was not even surprised when small stones thudded against her window. Quita smiled slowly and prepared to depart.

"No!" Bianca said, her voice high, breathless, filled with terror. "Stay—I need you."

Then step by slow step she crossed to the barred window and stared down at Ricardo Goldames.

13

Sometime during the night of July 1, 1694, the great clock of time stopped for Cristóbal Gerado. He was made aware of it by the stars. On many a night before, while the *Seaflower* swung at her creaking hawsers, anchored in some quiet cove, he had seen them wheel in great white circles above the masthead. Sometimes under full press of canvas, the sails tugging at the sheets, he had watched them reel and dip with the cadenced rise and fall of the leeward rail. There had been a slow and awesome majesty about their dance, as though if a man listened hard enough, he might be able to attune his hearing to the mighty music of the spheres.

Tonight, however, they were still. It was, Kit knew, simply because he saw them from the land—more exactly, through the stout iron bars of the Port Royal gaol. Strange, he mused, that never since my youth have I watched the stars from land. . . . The stars were the seaman's friends, guideposts in the great inverted bowl of heaven, but now they were still, for time had stopped . . . and his life, too, would presently stop with it.

Sighing, he looked at the humped silhouettes of his crew, black and motionless in the fetid darkness. The gaol was scarce a year old, but already it had taken on the noisome stench common to dungeons everywhere, reeking with human smells and more—the indefinable gaol odor, the sweet-sick putrefaction scent of liberty dead and hope lying rotting.

He shook his head to clear it of such thoughts. Oddest of all, it seemed to him, was the fact that he did not want to die. Why this strange, instinctive clinging to life? Rouge was dead, and by his own hand. Bianca was perhaps worse than dead—living in the loveless thralldom of his ancient enemy. In either case, he was powerless to remedy the situation. On the morrow it would be remedied for him. The choking embrace of hemp would assuage his griefs forever.

He heard the swift-scurrying passage of rats in the darkness, then the low intonation of Patricio Velasco's prayers: "Hail Mary, full of Grace, the Lord is with thee. Blessed art thou among women. Blessed is the fruit of thy womb, Jesus. Holy Mary, Mother of God, pray for us now, and at the hour of our death. . . . Amen."

He found his own lips repeating the solemn words, murmuring, "*Sancta Maria, Mater Dei, ora pro nobis peccatoribus, nunc et in hora mortis nostrae!*" He crossed himself reverently at the end, and saw from the movement of Bernardo's great shoulders that the Jew was doing likewise. In this hour the differences of faiths had melted: Bernardo could pray in two religions with no sense of conflict. The heretic Smithers knelt alongside the Catholic Velasco, and the sins of them all were heavy burdens of scarlet on the nakedness of their souls.

Kit heard the rustle of motion as Bernardo rose and approached him. The great hands groped through the darkness and found his shoulders.

"Kit, my son," Bernardo whispered, "forgive me. I brought you to this."

"We could not have fought," Kit reminded him. "They would have sunk us with ease."

"Yes, but better that death than this. Better a clean death at sea than this filthy, dishonored dying."

"Fret no more about it, my old one," Kit said gently. "It is good that we end the voyage as we began it—together."

"Kit," Bernardo began, but the sound of footsteps halted him. Every man in the dank common cell was on his feet as the fat bulk of the turnkey loomed before them.

"Avast, ye rogues!" he bellowed. "Stand back! I have a visitor to see Christopher Gerado—and mark ye that ye show her every courtesy! It would please me to add a taste o' the cat to what awaits ye tomorrow."

The key turned in the massive lock, and the door creaked open a little, just wide enough to admit the slender figure of Rosalind Parish. She held a lantern in her hand, and by its light Kit could see that her blue eyes were filled with tears. The moment she saw him she passed the lantern to Bernardo and sank on her knees before Kit, her whole body shaken with sobs. Kit stretched out his hand to her.

"Get up," he growled. "This is not fitting."

Instead of rising, she caught at his hand and covered it, back and palm, with kisses. Kit bent and raised her gently to her feet. Then he glanced around at the others.

"Leave them!" Bernardo said, hope glowing in his eyes. "The wench might save us yet!" The men drew apart hastily.

Rosalind's white arms stole up and encircled Kit's neck. "I am sorry," she said, weeping. "God and His Angels witness that I love you!"

"So much," Kit remarked dryly, "that you send me to the gibbet with your lies."

"I—I know," she said at last, her voice scarcely a breath. "I have been to see the magistrate to tell him the truth. He refuses to believe it. Oh, Kit, can you forgive me? Say that you can. . . . Please—for the love of God."

Kit looked down at her, his blue eyes luminous in the semidarkness. "My life is nothing to me," he said gravely. "And for it, I forgive you freely. But why did you do it when a word from you would have freed us?"

"Because you didn't want me," she said. "Consider, Kit, I was never really in love before. I married Reginald thinking I could learn to love him, but I could not. I have taken lovers—out of bitterness, out of hatred for the fop that he was—but I am a decent woman at heart, that you must believe. . . . Say that you believe me, Kit."

Kit smiled above the bright crown of her head. This he could grant her; this small comfort he could give her before he died.

"I believe you," he said gently. "Go on."

Rosalind raised her head and searched his face. It was grave and calm. With a glad cry she went up on tiptoe and kissed him.

"When you came, when you saved me, everything stood still for me."

"And then?"

"And then you scorned me. I know it was my fault. I was lacking in subtlety. I should not have flung myself so hungrily at you, but I had felt your arms and I was on fire. Kiss me, Kit—kiss me."

She was oblivious to the mockery in his deft embrace. At last she sighed, slowly and with deep content. She drew back a little, and her hand disappeared in the bodice of her gown. It came out holding a razor.

"Here," she whispered, "take it and shave off your beard! Your hair and mine are much alike in color. I will strip off these garments and you shall change with me. Before morning you should be far away."

Kit threw back his head and laughed. "You have read far too many romances, Rosalind!" he said. "Look—I am over six feet in height. Your gown would swirl about my knees. That bodice of yours would rip into pieces if I forced it over my shoulders. No, Rosalind, I fear that I must accept my fate."

"Try it!" she wept. "If you wrapped yourself in my cloak and bent your head . . . The skirt contains much cloth. I could let it down so that . . ."

"No," Kit said gently. "Even if I could, I would not leave my men. I hope that you will enjoy the spectacle tomorrow."

Again she hurled herself upon him, convulsed with such a titanic upheaval of grief that her wild sobbing brought the turnkey hurrying to the gate. He put his head through the bars to see the better and opened his mouth to bellow at them, but no sound came out—no sound at all. For Bernardo's enormous hands were encircling his neck. Kit saw the man's eyes bulge from their sockets, saw the sweat rise and glisten on his forehead in the dim light of the lantern, then the man's ugly face turned blue and his tongue came out of his gaping mouth. Bernardo hung on long after he was dead. Then, holding the turnkey effortlessly with one hand, he sought and found the bunch of keys.

"You and your taste of the cat-o'-nine-tails," Bernardo said contemptuously. "Sleep well, you obscenity, until Satan wakes you up in hell!"

"The streets are alive with soldiers," Kit observed. "Let us decide on a plan."

"No," Rosalind said, "there will be no soldiers. Captain Neilson assured me of that. They are all at the tavern, being entertained at his expense."

"And the guards at the doors? . . ." Smithers growled.

"They have drunk by now at least a gallon of sack I brought them with the good Captain's compliments."

"Uncommonly thoughtful of him," Kit mused. "Why should he be so kind to me, Rosalind?"

"Because I asked him to. Also because the verdict angered him. He said that he would be pleased to meet you at the cannon's mouth on the open seas, but that he'd be damned before he'd serve at the hanging of a brave and honorable foe."

"He's a real man!" Bernardo grunted.

Kit stared at Rosalind a moment, then turned to his crew. "Away, lads!" he said softly. "Make no sound. We will seize the *Seaflower*. We can rig two gun tackles at each side of the whipstaff socket and station a man at each. A tug at the ropes and she will heel right handily. And God knows there's no vessel afloat can catch her. Come!"

With the ease born of long practice they went down on their bellies and worked their way through the corridor. The gates opened one by one to the keys on the iron ring that Bernardo had taken from the turnkey. At the gates, the guards fell an easy prey, one to the butt of the turnkey's pistol, the other to Bernardo's encircling fingers.

"Scatter!" Kit commanded. "And make for the harbor. We will reassemble there."

By the time they had all reached the place where the *Seaflower* lay, five more of the men were armed with muskets, pistols, and cutlasses they had taken from the drunken soldiers they had met reeling through the streets.

At the end of the wharf they slipped into the water and swam out to the *Seaflower*. Coming up on her decks, they swarmed over the sleepy Britishers who guarded her. They used belaying pins, musket butts, pistol barrels, and the flat of their cutlass blades, for out of respect to Captain Neilson, Kit had ordered that there was to be no killing. Then they loaded their unconscious victims into a longboat and set it adrift.

Bernardo and a picked group worked feverishly at the jury tackle. In twenty minutes they had it rigged. Soon the square sails bellied out on the foremast, the spritsail ballooned, the white triangles of the flying jibs caught the fresh night wind, the great spanker on the main heeled hard over, its boom almost at right angles, and the *Seaflower* moved out of the harbor, running free before the wind like a spirited thoroughbred that had taken the bit in its teeth.

They made Saint-Domingue in less than two days, steering southward toward the lower peninsula, for at the command of Ducasse their old haunt at Tortuga had been deserted, the entire town of Basse-Terre having been moved to Port de Paix.

When they finally reached the harbor of Petit Goave, the men turned gleeful eyes toward the white town sliding in toward them over the port bow. True, the English had taken back the Negroes with which the crew had hoped to gain a fortune. However, they had not bothered to search for the loot the men had taken from the manor houses, thinking, no doubt, that they would have time and to spare to search the *Seaflower*'s hold after the hangings. There was enough left, the men knew, for one brave rout.

Watching Kit's face, Bernardo was aware that he did not share the mood of his crew. One would think, Bernardo mused, that he was going toward the gibbet rather than away from it.

When the *Seaflower* lay at last at anchor, Kit paid off the men, adding liberally to their loot from his own share. Then, after having told them to hold themselves in readiness if he should require their services again, he and Bernardo went down the ladder into the last of the boats.

That night every bawd in Petit Goave and above half of those from the near-by town of Léogane descended on the tavern in which the *Seaflower*'s crew celebrated their return. These were reinforced by many of the young matrons and maids of the town who so far had escaped the professional status. Kit, however, was not present. Bernardo sighed as he contemplated the plump little maid who was turning a most attentive ear to his flattery. Time enough tomorrow to console his captain, tonight there were more attractive prospects in view.

He was not to go uninterrupted. An hour later he looked up from the lips of his companion into the smiling face of a richly attired courtier. The man was obviously a gentleman. Even to Bernardo's rum-bemused eyes he had a look of authority about him. Bernardo scrambled hastily to his feet.

"A thousand pardons, Monsieur Díaz," the man murmured. "It pains me deeply to interrupt your most pleasant occupation, but I am here in behalf of His Excellency"—Bernardo stiffened in anticipation—"who urgently wants to see Captain Giradeaux. The Sieur Ducasse asked me to congratulate the entire company on their miraculous escape, and to present every man with a purse as a token of his gratitude and esteem. I trust you will see to the distribution of the money?"

Bernardo grinned. "That I will! But as for Captain Giradeaux, I do not know his present whereabouts."

"A pity. Still, there is no great haste. His Excellency is much taken with the young captain. He desires to reward him suitably for the great part he played in the late expedition."

"I will have him at Exter," Bernardo promised solemnly, "the day after tomorrow at the very latest."

"My thanks, Monsieur Díaz. And now, if you will be so good . . ." He held out a huge leather sack, crammed to the bursting with gold pieces. Bernardo saw at once that here were at least a hundred gold louis for every man. Catching the courtier's arm to prevent his escaping, he sprang to a table and bellowed in a forecastle voice:

"Look, my lads! Gold! From the land of His Excellency the Sieur Ducasse! Give a cheer to his messenger!"

The men shook the rafters with their lusty hurrahs. The bewildered gentleman found himself hoisted to the shoulders of two sweating, evil-smelling seamen and paraded about the hall, half the trulls in the place smearing his hands with winy kisses. The courtier took these attentions with good grace, and made them all a flowery speech in beautiful Parisian, which the bearded buccaneers and their blowsy women only vaguely understood. But if he thought he was going to be permitted to escape, he soon discovered his mistake. He found himself seated at a table with a lithe quadroon wench on his lap and a tankard of rum in his manicured hands. After three pulls at the tankard, he began to relax; after five he found, to his amazement, that he was actually enjoying himself. Besides, the quadroon was lovely. When the dawn light poured into the windows, the fine Parisian gentleman, his rich attire in disarray, was roaring a lusty sea chantey with as much fervor as any sea wolf in the tavern.

When Bernardo recovered himself enough to recollect his promise, it was afternoon. He was, he realized, no longer in the tavern, but in a room belonging, in all probability, to the plump maid. By a mighty effort he raised his head, now of ten tons' burden, and surveyed his surroundings. His surmise had been correct. The girl slept, in all her voluptuous innocence, by his side. Bernardo lowered his great head and groaned. Of what worth were pleasures taken in the dark that a man could not remember in the morning?

But such thoughts must be put away. He had a task to do. Groaning again, he heaved himself erect and began to dress. When he had finished and started for the door, he glanced down. The plump maid, her skin dewed all over with a faint film of perspiration, had not even stirred. Bernardo made the doorway in one great lurch, and stood outside blinking blindly at the brilliant light.

He knew where to find Kit. Half an hour later he came to the door of a small hostel that was vastly unpopular in Petit Goave because the angular Huguenot widow who kept it insisted upon at least the appearance of respectability. He had no excuse to enter, because Kit was standing there beside his white stallion, holding the lead rope of a pack mule in his hand. Bernardo's brows made pothooks of questioning.

"It is no concern of yours," Kit said almost cheerfully, "but if you must know, I am bound to Notre Dame de Léogane to pay a call on Father Dumaine."

Bernardo surveyed the heavily laden pack mule. "With all your spoils from the expedition?"

"All," Kit said quietly.

"Why?" Bernardo demanded, his own quest momentarily forgotten.

"It is not too much to ensure perpetual masses for her soul. And certainly not enough to lift the burden of sin from my own."

Bernardo ran the tip of a dry tongue over drier lips. "How long will you stay?" he demanded.

Kit's blue eyes were cloudy with pain. "Until tomorrow. Why?"

"Good!" Bernardo said, relief audible in his voice. "His Excellency sent a special emissary to ask you to call on him. I think he plans to reward you for saving Beauregard's troops from destruction."

Kit shrugged. "What need have I now for rewards?" he said quietly. "The lands that the Sieur Ducasse promised me, what good are they now that she is dead?" He looked out over the blue waters, seeing the white sails of the hoys and sloops creeping over it under the blinding sun. "Here I had planned to build her a great house of gray stone . . ." He looked at his friend and the anguish in his eyes was like smoldering flame.

Bernardo put an arm about Kit's shoulders and gave him an affectionate squeeze. "Easy, Kit," he said. "There are limits to all things, even grief. This was an accident—God in His mercy knows you never would have harmed her willingly. Still"—Bernardo paused a moment and a look of shrewdness crept into his dark eyes—"I would like to see you build that house."

Kit looked at him. "Why, Bernardo?" he asked.

"Life has not been kind to me," Bernardo answered with a sigh, "yet I have not been entirely cheated of a son since chance threw us together. Would you deprive me then of grandsons—for they'll be mine, Kit, because of the great love that I'll bear them. Grieve for a space, that is only natural, but afterward build this house of yours, and spare a room for me."

Kit smiled at him slowly. "So I must provide you with grandsons, you old villain? Why does it fall on me to remedy your neglect in not siring a son?"

Bernardo grinned and waved a deprecating hand. "A son of mine would not have been so fair as you, Kit," he said. "Listen to me, Kit. There are other maids as fair as she."

"Name one!" Kit snapped.

Bernardo rubbed his long clean-shaven chin. When he pronounced the name, he flung it out like a challenge.

"The Señora Bianca del Toro," he said. Kit stiffened, but said nothing. "I think that she will someday become a widow," Bernardo continued, "for Don Luis has many enemies."

Kit's hand strayed down to the sash of gold that he always wore, and his blue eyes hardened.

"Yes," he said, "she will be widowed—and soon!" He turned again to Bernardo, the fury leaving his eyes. "Bianca," he mused. "It has been so long that my memory nearly fails me and I mistrust it. Could there have been such a maid as my mind recalls? Or do I create the image out of my loneliness and my pain?"

"And what sort of maid do you recall, Kit?" Bernardo asked.

"A small maid," Kit said slowly, "scarcely reaching to my shoulders, with a face like an angel's, yet with a spice of mischief in her eyes. And what of those eyes, Bernardo, for here my memory fails me? Black, I think, and so deep and sure. Thus does my mind recall her. Tell me, Bernardo, is this an illusion?"

"No," Bernardo growled. "So indeed she was. I had hoped that when I left the two of you together at Cul-de-Sac she would turn your mind from Rouge, but you were always stubborn, Kit. So, now . . ." He shrugged eloquently.

"So now I shall complete my errand," Kit said calmly.

"His Excellency expects you on Wednesday," Bernardo said quickly.

"Very well," and Kit sighed, "I will be there."

Early Wednesday morning, before the coolness had yet left the land, Kit and Bernardo rode with Governor Ducasse up the steep mountain trail. They rode very slowly, each of them occupied with his own thoughts. Ducasse was thinking that the menace of commercial competition from Jamaica still existed and that all his letters to the court of France asking for aid with which to drive the Spaniards from the southern half of

Hispaniola had gone for nothing. If he controlled the whole island, what greatness might he not attain? Shaking his head, he urged his mount upward through the cool morning air.

Bernardo, for his part, was savoring the thought of settling down at last in a land where men did not consider the question of religion, where no one paid any attention at all to the Semitic cast of his countenance. Here he might even take a wife, for he was still in his early forties, though he looked older. Kit's taunt that he had failed to provide himself with a son had struck home. But what chance has a man to take a wife, or beget sons, Bernardo reflected bitterly, when he is being hunted like an animal from land to land? . . . Now all that might at last be changed! For the prospect of such peace he was willing even to forget Del Toro, who had set the Inquisitorial machinery in action against him.

Kit's thoughts were on a different plane. There is, he mused, a devilish irony in the workings of fate. Here at my finger tips I have the chance to gain all that I wanted, but now that the chance has come it is meaningless to me. How lovingly had I planned this house for Rouge, so that once it had been built, I could go from room to room with no feeling of strangeness or newness. In Spain I was a nameless bastard kept hidden in the house, but here I might have been a lord over men and acres. . . . Might have been? I might be still—life goes on and I must live out my destiny, though God knows I shall find scant joy in it. Without her it will be an empty triumph, entirely without meaning. Yet in this world nothing stands still, so I must achieve what I can before the path of Luis del Toro again crosses mine. . . .

On their right hand now the bayonet-shaped leaves of the agave plant stood in neat, orderly rows. Between the plants the Negroes moved, gathering the leaves for their fiber. Beyond the field, on long lines stretched from pole to pole, the golden fiber dried, for this was a sisal plantation. The horses moved upward, sure-footed as goats, through the thatched villages occupied by the blacks, who had entirely replaced the Arawak Indians. On every hand were the slow, sweet-moving signs of husbandry—the pounding of a black man's stick as he hulled the rice in a mortar hollowed from a cypress log, beside him his wife winnowing the chaff from the grains by throwing them up from a flat pannier woven of reeds. Kit saw the golden chaff blowing away downwind, and the deft black fingers picking the brownish rice grains from the pannier and placing them in a box of carved teak.

At a distance another black ground the yamlike manioc root against a rough barked pole, and caught the wet, dustlike cassava flour in an earthen urn. His small son was squeezing out the poisonous juice from the flour through a coarse cloth, and on the flat, hot rocks placed in the embers of the fire a young woman baked the thin cakes for their evening meal.

Slowly, like poison being drawn from a deep wound, Kit could feel something of his bitterness leaving him, something of his grief. They paused now and drank ice-cold water from a calabash gourd offered them by a slim Dahomey maid.

The village dropped below them. Above them the hills were amethyst, while from brush and tree the tropical flowers flaunted their vivid hues. The whole world seemed like a sea of nodding flowers: hibiscus, poinsettia, bougainvillea, frangipani, and others whose names Kit did not know but whose beauty was a healing song in the hurt darkness of his heart.

They came out at last upon a plateau as flat and level as a table, as though someone had cut off the mountaintops with an incredibly sharp knife, leaving what had been jagged peaks as even and green as a lowland valley. Here was a sweep of pleasant fields, bathed in the rainbowed mists of the mountains through which a little silver stream ran, making a noise like joyous laughter.

"This," Ducasse said gently, "is yours, Christophe—if you still want it."

"Want it?" Kit breathed. He plunged down from his white stallion and walked through the uncut grasses that came up to his waist, toward the stream. On the journey up through the foothills, he had been of half a mind to refuse the Governor's bounty, but how can a man refuse a slice of paradise that he has earned? He came back to the Governor.

"My thanks, your Excellency," he said. "It far exceeds my greatest desire."

"Then it's yours," Ducasse said gruffly—"at a price."

"A price?" Kit echoed, wonderingly.

"That your door will always be open to a tired old man who might want to escape now and then from the duties and cares of officialdom. Is it too much?"

"No." Kit laughed. "Come and welcome to you, but it will be long before my house is built. My coffers run low of gold for the building."

"The Spaniards," Ducasse remarked, "still have as much as they ever did."

That, Kit reflected, was true. He could take to sea again and exact his tribute from his foes. In two years at the most he should be able to recoup the fortune that his generosity to his crews and his long series of misfortunes had so badly depleted.

"Here is where we should erect the house," Bernardo said, gleefully surveying the land with his eye.

"You're mad—as usual," Kit growled. "It should be here." They quarreled good-naturedly over the location of the manor. After a time the shadows lengthened deep-blue on the trail, and they turned to go.

Kit sat on his mount, looking back at the fair fields. When Del Toro lies dead, he mused, I will bring Bianca here. These halls as yet unbuilt shall someday know the noise and scamper of my sons at play. His blue eyes darkened suddenly, somber with pain.

"Yet she shall be," he whispered, "only a tenant in a house I built for you, my Rouge."

Turning, he rode down the trail after the others.

14

BIANCA GAZED thoughtfully at the dark profile of her husband outlined against the light that came through the window of the great coach. It was the day Ricardo Goldames was to receive his doctorate. A tiny frown appeared between her brows and drew them together. Why is it, she mused, that though I do not love him, though time stopped for me that day in Cul-de-Sac, there is something about his face that moves me deeply? . . . She turned away and her glance fell on the pale face of Ricardo, who sat opposite them in the coach.

His blue eyes were like those of a wounded dog, wretched and imploring. Since that night almost a week ago that he had scaled the walls and stood "eating the iron" (as the Spanish called the fruitless braying of a young lover) outside her window, Bianca had not spoken to him. She had dismissed him coldly that night, reading the naked, animal desire in his eyes, the absence of tenderness despite all the stilted poetry he had mouthed. To Bianca, this had been inexpressibly shocking. Convent-bred, she instinctively believed that the demands of a husband were one of the crosses a woman had to bear. A lover, on the other hand, was a kind of cavalier servente who supplied poetry and romance—and demanded nothing in return.

Ricardo had demanded something. Were all men, then, alike? She shook her head, trying in vain to clear it of the confusing burden of thinking. Nothing in this life seemed to fit the patterns of her preconceived notions. For instance, she did not love Don Luis. Therefore his love-making should have been utterly repugnant to her. But was it really? Truthfully, Bianca had to admit that she felt no real distaste toward her husband's passionate embraces—that indeed on more than one occasion she had responded to him with ardor. Was she then depraved? she asked herself. The answer, when it came, was in itself a kind of mystery. There was in him, her subconscious mind told her, something that moved her, something not of himself—something of another.

What other? To that there was no answer. Bianca's mind drifted off, as it always did, to Kit. She had vowed that she would never forget him, but at the moment certain features of his appearance escaped her. She loved him still, that she knew. But what kind of love was it that after two years could not recall the exact shade of his eyes? Blue? Ricardo's eyes were blue, for he was a Galician. Half the inhabitants of that province, the descendants of the Teutonic Visigoths who had ravaged the north of Spain centuries before, had blue eyes, and not a few of them were blond. But to say "blue" meant nothing—what exactly was the shade of Kit's? It is of no importance, she told herself, but her forgetfulness rankled. What was important, her conscience told her, was the fact that if it had been Kit who stood beneath her window she would have sent down Quita to open it for him.

Bianca lay back against the cushions of the coach and closed her eyes. Like the tumultuous throbbing of her own blood, the sound of the kettledrums that headed the parade in which they rode came back to her, and through them the moaning of flutes and oboes. Without opening her eyes, she knew that behind the richly arrayed band that led the procession came the faculty of the University of San Marcos, dressed grandly in their caps and gowns to honor Ricardo. Behind them strode the *bedeles,* the monitors, also decked out in their finery, carrying the maces of the university.

Her eyes came open and she stared at Don Luis. Then, suddenly, they widened and a kind of terror flamed within their depths. For now, beyond all remote possibility of doubt, she knew—she *knew!* She sat there, studying her husband's face and wondering how all this time the recognition had escaped her. Then that too explained itself—it was all a trick of coloring. A person sitting between someone and a strong light is robbed of color, his profile becoming, in effect, a silhouette. So it was that at last the superficial differences were canceled out for Bianca—Kit's blond fairness and Don Luis's almost Moorish swarthiness were as nothing, and the two faces were one face—the same. True, Don Luis's profile was older and a trifle heavier, but the likeness, now that the coloring no longer stood in the way, was almost agonizingly exact.

At once her mind was off, racing down forbidden avenues. On the day that he had abducted her Kit had acknowledged that he knew Don Luis. He had known Don Luis's Black Heron coat of arms. He had secretly nurtured a terrible hatred for Don Luis that she had sensed. The evidence mounted to the skies, exact and damning.

What was it her husband had said? "This bastard son of a worthless Frenchwoman." How did you know that, Luis? How else but that you yourself sired this fair and princely bastard? How had Kit come by his manners, his grace, his courtliness? And why did you spare him when you had him at your mercy? Why else but that you knew he was your son!

She bent her head and the great tears stung and tugged at her eyelids. It all fitted, and it explained so many things. And I am with child now, the bitterness in her heart mocked, because this unrecognized resemblance with Kit melted me into submission—even more, into passionate response to you, Luis. . . . She felt the bitter pain of frustration, but she had to look up now, for Ricardo had reached out and touched her hand.

"We are here," he said.

The footman opened the door and Don Luis climbed down and put up his hand to help her. He could feel her trembling, and a little questioning frown wrinkled his brows, but Bianca turned her face away.

Then the three of them followed the procession into the cathedral. When the ceremony was over, Ricardo, now a Doctor of Letters, was surrounded by an admiring throng who pressed their congratulations upon him in a shower of costly gifts. Finally Don Luis announced that after the banquet to which they were all invited there would be a bullfight. The crowd broke into cheers.

At the bullfight Bianca sat with Ricardo because Don Luis, as a sign of his courage, had entered the lists against the bull. There had been talk at the banquet of the cowardly patron who a few years ago had hired a beggarly fellow to fight his bull for him. The men had cried shame at such lack of manliness.

Ricardo, who was an extremely rational young man, had excused himself from the bullring on the score of fatigue due to the arduous preparation he had made for the ceremony. He had better ideas of how to spend an evening than by risking his fine figure as an offering to the sharp horns of an angry bull. Half the young hidalgos of Lima were in the ring, mounted on their fine chargers, their lances ready in their hands. The bull, Bianca saw, didn't have a chance.

"Afraid, Señor Doctor?" she asked Ricardo.

"I am giving a demonstration of a higher form of courage," Ricardo said sadly, "for I run the risk of being transfixed by the displeasure in your eyes. Believe me, señora, that is a crueler stab than any bull could deal."

Bianca looked at him quietly. "Give me your promise that you will never again behave so disgracefully," she said, "and I will forgive you."

"Alas, how can I promise? Ask me not to breathe. Say to me, 'Die, Ricardo!' and I will kill myself at your feet. But do not ask me not to love you, because such a thing is beyond my power."

Bianca could not help laughing at his extravagant speech. "You are a wicked lad, Ricardo," she said. "Love me if you will, only do not expect me to love you in return. That I cannot do."

"No, you can't, can you?" Ricardo said softly. "Nor my revered godfather and patron either—not while this blond devil of a pirate still lives!"

All the color drained from Bianca's face, leaving it ghost-white. Her lips moved once or twice before they succeeded in shaping the words.

"Who—who told you of that?" she whispered.

Ricardo looked at her. He saw her face white, her lips pale, her eyes widening into great pools of darkness into which all his happiness was sinking.

"Who told you, Ricardo?" The tone was edged like a blue-steel blade glinting in the sunlight.

"I have an informant who served on the *Garza,*" he said finally. "But say it isn't true," he whispered, his voice unrecognizably hoarse. "Say that he lied—that you do not love this buccaneer."

The blue-midnight cloud of matchless hair moved slowly sidewise.

"No, Ricardo," she said gently, sensing his grief and shame, "your miserable informant did not lie."

Ricardo fell back against the seat, hearing the thunderous roar of the cheering far off and faint, like the surf-pounding of a distant sea. Below them Don Luis was standing in his stirrups goading the maddened bull with his lance. Bianca looked down, and the black, rebellious thoughts crowded resistlessly into her mind. If that horse should stumble, or that magnificent animal should raise his mighty head . . .

"Holy Mother of God," she whispered to herself, "forgive me! Do not permit me to will his death."

Ricardo sat up, and his voice was filled with savage mockery.

"So," he said, "you too pray for the bull!" Bianca lowered her head and the great tears ran like strings of diamonds down her pale cheeks. "Forgive me," Ricardo said. "I have been beastly to you. My whole life is not worth one of your tears."

Gently Bianca patted his hand. "No," she said. "I wept for my own wickedness."

"Tell me about him," Ricardo said, "this English sea dog who has stolen your heart."

"Do you really wish to hear, Ricardo?" she said sadly.

"Yes. Perhaps then I can understand."

"Well," Bianca began, "he is not truly English, though he commanded a vessel sailing under that flag. His mother was French. His father—he does not know. He was born in Cádiz, and speaks Castilian that is like music. He is fair like you, though much burnt by the sun. His eyes are like sea water, his hair like the sun's own gold."

"But a sea robber—a pirate! A man of rude manners and coarse speech!"

Bianca shook her head.

"No, you wrong him. He was well reared. He has the manners and the grace of a prince."

"Then why does he follow so vile a trade?"

"Because his father, who is a very great nobleman, cast him off. If this grandee were to acknowledge him, he would rank among the great names of . . ." She stopped short, realizing that she had said too much.

"Of Spain," Ricardo finished for her. "Already you have said his father was a grandee. And yet you say he does not know who his father is."

"He doesn't," Bianca whispered.

"But you do?" Bianca nodded mutely. "Who is it, Bianca? This interests me strangely. Tell me!"

"I cannot do that," Bianca said firmly. "It is my secret, and it will die with me."

"But . . ." Ricardo began.

He was interrupted by a tremendous roar from the crowd. Don Luis had killed his bull. He stood in the center of the ring, holding his horse by the bridle, and bowed right and left to the crowd. He came forward now and bowed low to Bianca. The cheers redoubled as she loosened the blossom behind her ear and threw it down to him.

It was then that the stranger, clad in the rough garb of a seaman, approached Ricardo. With a word of apology to Bianca, Ricardo drew the man apart. They stood there for a moment in whispered conversation. The crowd began to drift away. Then Ricardo led her down to the gates, where Don Luis awaited them.

"A brave fight, my lord," Bianca told him. "You were magnificent."

Don Luis glowed visibly at her words of praise. He bent over her hand. He straightened, and was opening his mouth to thank her when a hand plucked diffidently at his sleeve. Raising her eyes, Bianca saw the same man who had engaged Ricardo in conversation.

"What is it?" Don Luis growled.

"It is of great importance, my lord," the stranger said calmly. "And it is for your ears only. If my lord would step a bit apart . . ."

Something in the man's bearing caused Don Luis to heed him. His assurance, perhaps, the calm surety in his eyes. Bianca saw her husband walk away a little distance. The seaman began to talk swiftly, earnestly. Don Luis's face was a study. It was frozen with intentness. His great dark eyes leaped suddenly with tremendous fire. Bianca saw his hand go into his pockets and come out with a purse, which he tossed to the man. Then he rejoined them. But it was to Ricardo that he spoke.

"You will see Bianca home," he commanded. "This man has brought news that must be looked into—and at once!" Bianca gazed at him, her eyes filled with questioning. "I go to Callao, my love," Don Luis said gently.

"And when will you return?"

"I don't know, but I will send you word." Then he swung himself into the saddle and thundered away. He had reached the first corner and was half around it before it occurred to Bianca to question the nature of the news that could cause Don Luis to ride away without even pausing to kiss her good-by.

"It will be a dreary time," she said, half to herself. "A woman without a husband might as well be imprisoned in a dungeon."

A crafty gleam appeared in the corners of Ricardo's eyes. He looked at Bianca and the gleam kindled, became fire. But when she turned toward him he hid his gaze with a quick toss of his head.

"A woman," he observed softly, "need not have a dreary time."

Bianca's voice was tart. "Not if she is without shame and would abuse her husband's faith in her!"

"You misunderstand," Ricardo said slowly. "A woman should have some pleasure in life. All pleasures are not sinful. What harm would there be if you veiled yourself and allowed me to show you the town?"

"None—except that would encourage you to make other requests. And those gained, you would proceed to still others, Ricardo, until . . ."

"Until the time came when the decisions would lie between you and your heart, Bianca. Would you have me believe that the lovely Countess del Toro fears—herself?"

"And have I nothing else to fear?"

Ricardo smiled wickedly. "No," he said. "Nothing."

"Still, it is necessary to avoid even the appearance of evil," Bianca persisted. "I would not set matronly tongues wagging because of some harmless escapade. You know how easily evil can be read into even the most blameless action."

"To be talk, there must be some knowledge of what happens," Ricardo said. "If they don't know, what can they say?"

"And you, of course," Bianca said scornfully, "can arrange it so they know nothing?"

Ricardo studied her pale, lovely face. Time now to change tactics, he thought. This line of procedure was getting him nowhere.

"I can arrange it," he said soberly. "But there is yet another side to this matter, Bianca. In a little while, you will go away—out of my life. And when you go something of my life will be gone. The better part, the fairest, richest part. I ask so little—a smile, a word, the joy of your nearness, nothing else."

Seeing the small smile trembling about the corners of her mouth, Ricardo knew before she spoke that he had won—the first engagement, at least. As for the future, if he were prudent, might not he gain all he hoped for, one small step at a time?

"I will go," she said at last, "but see that you are careful. I want no scandal attached to my name."

"Have no fear of that," Ricardo told her gravely.

"And see, too," she added, "that you do not forget yourself. It would pain me to have to end our friendship altogether, Ricardo, but end it I will if I must."

"With you," Ricardo said, "I am honor's soul and body."

That night, with the aid of Quita, Bianca slipped into the darkened street. She was heavily veiled, and wrapped in her thickest cloak, for the nights of Lima are bitterly cold. Outside in the icy darkness Ricardo sat impatiently on his horse, holding the bridle of another mount. Seeing Bianca, he smothered a glad cry and helped her up into the saddle.

Savage joy sang along the network of his veins. His mind went racing ahead filled with pictures that had him reeling in the saddle. If her face is so white, he thought, what of her body? He almost fell from the saddle, thinking of it.

Bianca put out a warning hand. "Are you ill, Ricardo?" she whispered.

"No. I am only overjoyed at your coming."

"Where are we going?" she asked.

"To a little place where the wine is good and the food excellent. A gypsy of Cádiz is there who makes music that tears apart one's heart." He felt very sure of himself.

If at that moment Ricardo could have listened to Don Luis as he addressed another sailor in Callao, he would have been somewhat less sure of himself. He would have discovered, as most of Don Luis's enemies had at one time or another, that it was a fatal error to underestimate him.

"I was told," Don Luis was saying to the sailor, who had been pointed out to him by the man who had brought him the message in Lima, "that you encountered a pirate vessel in these waters two days ago."

"Yes, my lord," the man said confidently.

"This vessel bore the name *Seaflower?*"

"That she did, and a bitter fight she gave us. We were off Chimbote when she bore down on us and . . ."

"The *Seaflower,*" Don Luis mused. "I think I know that vessel. A great ship of the line, is she not, mounting, say, sixty guns?"

"Right you are, my lord, and sixty-four-pounders they be. Why, I tell you . . ."

But Don Luis's great hand shot forward and caught the seaman by the throat.

"You miserable, lying dog!" he spat. "Who paid you to tell this monstrous lie?"

"My lord," the man gasped, "I speak truth—this great ship . . ."

"Whoreson!" Don Luis snorted, shaking the man until his eyes bulged from their sockets. "Don't you know that the *Seaflower* is a small brigantine, mounting no gun above thirty-two pounds, and that you and your master are the first of fools to think that you could trick me? Who paid you? Tell me, or you'll die!"

"I—I don't know him, my lord," the sailor gasped. "It was a young hidalgo of Lima. I don't know his name."

Still holding the man, Don Luis looked around for the man who had brought him here, but the second conspirator had vanished into the shadows of the water front.

"A young hidalgo," Don Luis said. "Hmmmm. . . . If that forked tongue of yours can manage a syllable of truth, tell me the color of his eyes."

"Blue, my lord," the wretch said hastily. "I noticed them, because they were most uncommon."

"And his hair?"

"As fair almost as that of a Dutchman or an Englishman."

Don Luis drew the wretch back and sent him sprawling with a tremendous shove. Then as the man attempted to rise he kicked him savagely in the face.

As he swung aboard his weary horse, he thought grimly: You are a fool, Ricardo—so young and already tired of life? . . .

Then he thundered away in the darkness, back toward Lima.

Bianca stood with Ricardo in the darkened entrance of a den of almost unbelievable foulness. They had eaten supper at a quiet inn, but Ricardo had insisted on showing her the seamier side of Lima. This place was dark and filled with the reek of stale pipe smoke, the stench of unwashed bodies, the mingled smells of wine and chicha—maize beer—and the nose-stinging scent of the vile perfume the women wore. Above the variously offensive odors, the noises blended into a nerve-shattering din. Some of these sounds, Bianca perceived, were intended to be music. Native performers blew into Panpipes of reeds of various lengths tied together with fiber; the quena flute lifted its weird wailing above the other anguished cries, while whistling pots shrilled, gourds filled with seeds or pebbles rattled, and trumpets of cattle horn blared. In a corner an Inca lad played an imported instrument, the *charango* of Bolivia—a kind of mandolin made of the shell of an armadillo—with a rapt and haunted expression on his dark face. Bianca had half-turned to flee from this place of terror when the music caught her. She hung there, one foot still raised to take the first step of flight, listening.

The music throbbed, wailed, rose and fell in the thick, smoky gloom. She could feel it possessing her, crawling insidiously along the network of her nerves. It had no harmony as such; it was direct, repetitive, hypnotic. Centuries of civilization, ages of restraint, slipped away from her like cast-off garments. She felt a wild impulse to leap into the center of the room, where the greasy flambeaux flared, and pound the earthen floor in a mad and savage dance. Ricardo bent down to her.

"Do you want to leave, Bianca?" he whispered.

"No!" she exulted. "No—this is magic, Ricardo!"

A lean figure out of an Inca carving approached them, pride of race showing in every line of his emaciated figure.

"A table, Titicaca," Ricardo said. "Wine—your best, man."

"Food?" the Indian grunted. Ricardo looked at Bianca.

"Yes, yes!" she said gleefully. "I'm starved again."

"Quinoa soup with peppers," the Inca suggested. "Cakes of *chunu*—maize?"

"Indian dishes?" Bianca guessed.

"Yes. They're delicious."

"All," Bianca said. "Bring them all."

Seated there in the throbbing darkness while the savage music entered her and beat along her blood, Bianca looked about. As her eyes grew accustomed to the darkness, she saw that there were other women present. Most of them were prostitutes, mestizas and mulattoes; but at a near-by table sat a woman as white as Bianca, and obviously of high station. The woman's eyes were feverish, darting through the smoke-laden gloom. Now and again she dipped her aristocratic fingers into a bowl and ate what seemed to Bianca to be a mess of red clay. Bianca turned her startled, questioning eyes upon Ricardo.

"Coca," he explained. "It produces a kind of sweet madness when its leaves are mixed with clay and chewed. The Indians use it as a specific against mountain sickness. Unfortunately, it is habit-forming, for it is the source of cocaine. That grand señora is doomed—she will die in shrieking horror before long."

"How horrible!" Bianca whispered.

The rattle of the gourds quickened, the *charango* achieved a wilder strain. There was a deep blare from the cattle-horn trumpets and a girl leaped into the circle of the flambeaux. She was entirely naked, and her supple young body had been anointed all over with oil. She planted her young feet firmly on the red earthen floor, and every muscle of her trunk undulated, beating savagely in tune with the music.

Bianca found, to her vast astonishment, that she was neither shocked nor offended. The Inca maid was indescribably beautiful, her pagan dance a votive offering to powerful mountain gods. It went on and on, the flutes and reed pipes silent, the *charango* still, only the pebble-filled gourds sounding now, and the llama-skin drums filling the dark air with savage frenzy. Bianca could hear the rasping of Ricardo's breath above the low thumping of the drums; she knew, without turning, that he was leaning forward, rapt, lost.

But at that moment a shrill shriek tore the close air in the little den and Bianca saw that the grand señora was swaying on her feet, tearing with clawing fingers at her garments. She wore very few, for a moment later she had joined the Inca maiden in the flickering light of the flambeaux, naked. This was indeed shocking. The Inca dancer was a bronze statue, oiled and glistening, so that her sex was submerged in the primitive surroundings, becoming unreal, so much a part of the mood and the music that seeing her one forgot that she was human and she became a work of perfect, savage art—a statue moving, a wild poem fleshed in life. But the whiteness of the other's skin was like a cry, her slender body demandingly, oppressively voluptuous. Against the primitive purity of the Inca, she was the decadence of civilization, the epitome of naked lust. Bianca got to her feet, but it was then that the señora's younger escort hurled himself upon her and wrapped her shameful nudity in the enveloping folds of his great cloak. She fought him fiercely, so that it was only after two other men rose to help him that she was finally subdued.

Bianca picked up her own cloak and was taking a step or two in the direction of the door when Ricardo touched her arm. In some curious way she felt unclean, as though the other's shame had been her shame, as though she herself had engaged in that sickeningly disgraceful performance.

"Wait," Ricardo pleaded. "Caviedes is coming!"

"Caviedes?" Bianca echoed.

"Juan Valle y Caviedes," Ricardo said. "See, he is entering now."

Bianca looked at the small man who stood dramatically in the doorway. His face was hideously marked with syphilis, his figure thin and bent, so that only his eyes seemed alive. But they were wonderful eyes, Bianca saw, strangely godlike eyes that soared above the dying wreck of his body as though they had a life of their own. The music crashed at once into silence. Every eye turned toward the doorway.

"Caviedes!" The name went up in a shout, a roar of welcome, bursting from the lips of every man and woman in the place. The Inca dancer crossed the room in one great bound, like the *grand jeté* of the classic ballet, and hurled herself into his arms. Caviedes stared down at her with contempt, then he opened his arms and let her drop unceremoniously to the floor. Men left the sides of their paramours to reach for his bony hands. He received their homage as his due. So a pagan god would receive mortals, Bianca thought, upon a rare descent from Olympus.

"Who is he?" she began, but Ricardo lifted a warning finger.

"Lima's greatest poet," he whispered, "though those fools who surround Monclovia don't know it. He can toss a gongoraism[1] with the best, though for the most part he scorns such folly."

"A verse!" a woman cried. "Come, Juan, give us a verse!"

Caviedes fixed her with an icy stare. "*Before* wine?" he drawled.

Instantly a dozen young hidalgos leaped forward, bottles and glasses in their hands. Caviedes tossed back the heavy cloak he wore to protect his thin body, seated himself at a table, and began to drink. He emptied glass after glass, tossing them down as though his very life depended on it.

"He is slowly dying," Ricardo murmured.

"Oh!" Bianca whispered.

"I think he wants to die. He holds himself guilty for his wife's death. You see how eaten up he is with French sickness? Well, he was contaminated by a woman of the town and passed the disease on to his wife. She died of it! He has never forgotten that. Monclovia's circle will not receive him because of the licentiousness of his life, but I think he lives this way to still the pain within his heart. And what a mocker the man is! He has set up a wooden beggar's stall in front of the Viceroy's palace. The soldiers tear it

[1] At that time Spain's best loved poet, Góngora, was widely imitated. He was noted for the intricate, involved, and tortuous nature of his verse.

down, but he sets it up again. He is so loved among the people that Monclovia dare not touch him."

"Bless you, my children," Caviedes mocked. "Now—a verse." He launched into a devastating attack on the medical profession, his favorite target. Before he was done, Bianca found herself laughing so hard that the tears tugged and stung at her eyelids. Then, almost without pausing for breath, Caviedes began another, describing the monumental stupidity and the trusting nature of a cuckolded husband. The laughter rose in waves and beat against the ceiling. Juan Caviedes looked about him, a sly grin on his ugly face.

"I now give you a piece in appreciation of those true benefactors of mankind," he announced, "the whores of Lima!" The poem held Bianca rigid in her seat. Caviedes left nothing to the imagination; his language was fluid, pungent, and exact. He described lovingly portions of the feminine anatomy that Bianca had not known had names—at least not such names as Caviedes gave them. This time the applause shook the room.

Bianca raised her white hands to cover her scarlet cheeks. Something in the gesture caught Caviedes' attention. When Bianca looked up, he was standing before her, peering down at her with rapt attention. A great fear entered her heart. She wanted to run wildly from the place, out of this fetid hole, out into the icy night, but for the life of her she could not move. Then Caviedes began to speak.

She realized at once that he was improvising. Others recognized this too, and one of his more ardent admirers seized a burnt-out torch and began to scribble the words hastily on a tablecloth.

This time, Juan Caviedes' voice was different: it was low, chaste, reverent. He began describing Bianca, comparing her face to dawn sunlight on the snows of the Andes, her hair to a starless night. Her eyes, he said, were limpid pools of pure darkness in which all man's ardent hopes sank down and drowned, never more to rise. . . . There was nothing in the poem of disrespect; here was another man speaking. Here, perhaps, was the Caviedes that might have been. The finished poem was an exquisite thing, a masterpiece of pure, exact statement, so that Bianca sat there with the unashamed tears streaking her pale face, feeling more humble and more honored than she had ever felt before.

She was conscious of the great and echoing silence. Everyone in the room sat as though stunned, caught up in the blinding recognition of genius. Her lips moved, and the corners of her mouth, smiling, diverted the track of her tears.

"Thank you, Señor Caviedes," she whispered. "I thank you with all my heart!"

This time the applause was a frightening thing. After the long, intense silence it echoed and reverberated, filling the room so that its pounding could almost be felt. As Caviedes made Bianca a low and reverent bow, no one in that room had eyes to notice the tall grandee who had entered; his footfalls were swallowed up in the stupendous outburst of sound.

Bianca became aware suddenly that something was wrong with Ricardo. He was on his feet, his blue eyes goggling. She reached up and took his arm to draw him down beside her, but he threw off her grasp so roughly that at long last, in deep puzzlement, she turned to look into the coldly murderous eyes of her husband.

Again the silence in the place crashed down, layers deep. Men stood up one by one and began to edge away. Alone of all those present Don Luis del Toro looked as though he were enjoying himself.

Ricardo's hand flew to the hilt of his sword.

"How now, godson?" Don Luis said, almost genially. "I have no wish to fight with you. There is no honor to be gained by spitting a sniveling whelp. Besides, I see no marks of rope burn on my lady's arms, or any other sign that she was abducted."

"Sir," Ricardo began, his voice high and breathless.

"A man fights, Ricardo," Don Luis continued gravely, "for the honor of his lady. Since it is all too apparent that mine has none, I see no cause to exert myself. I have never bothered to defend the honor of a whore, no matter how unprofessional her status."

Glancing down at the sheet-white horror in Bianca's face, Ricardo did the only thing possible under the circumstances. Drawing back his hand, he smote Don Luis a stinging blow full in the face. The Count smiled.

"I'm sorry that you did that, Ricardo," he whispered, "for now I must kill you. Come, my Bianca—or should I say *our* Bianca, lad? Yours and mine, and God knows how many others'—a pleasant thought, is it not?"

He took Bianca's arm in a grasp that for all its seeming gentleness had a grip like steel.

"Come, Bianca," he said almost gently. "It is time you were in bed. I hope it will not grieve you to sleep alone for just this once."

Bianca's gasp was a blade of fire entering Ricardo's heart.

"Now, see here, Luis!" he got out. "You wrong Bianca! Why, she is as pure . . ."

"As Caviedes," Don Luis finished for him. "Don't be impatient, Ricardo. I will meet you within the hour."

The time of waiting within the barred and shuttered confines of her room Bianca found agonizingly long. Actually, it was scarcely half an hour before Don Luis returned from his encounter with Ricardo. He strode into his wife's room with one arm hanging limp at his side, drops of blood dripping from his fingers. For an instant hope leaped in Bianca's heart, but Don Luis stilled it.

"The whelp fought well," he growled. "Too well—I had hoped to spare him."

"Then he is . . ." Bianca whispered.

"Yes, he is dead," Don Luis said slowly. "I shall order masses said for the repose of his soul. I loved him well."

"And yet," Bianca whispered, her voice freighted with horror, "you killed him!"

"Let us say," Don Luis growled, "that *we* killed him. Where is Quita? Order her to pack. We must leave Lima tomorrow."

"This—this murder of yours does not please the Viceroy?" Bianca asked. "Good! You should be hanged for it!"

Don Luis eyed his wife sternly, the pain from his wound visible in his face. "Let us not speak of hanging," he said quietly. "I might be tempted to use the whip you so richly deserve on your own fair back. If it is of interest to you, the Count of Monclovia has already absolved me of this. It is only that I do not want to flaunt your shame in the face of decent women that we are leaving so hastily."

Bianca looked at him, a smile showing on her ghost-pale mouth. "But flaunt it you must, Luis," she mocked, "for I fear that I cannot travel."

Don Luis straightened up, grasping his wounded shoulder. It pained him frightfully, but his impassive face gave no sign.

"Why?" he demanded.

"Because," Bianca began, then the words came out in a rush, "because I am with child!"

Seeing the joy leaping and flaming in his great dark eyes, Bianca felt that at some other time, under other circumstances, she could have forgiven him; but now the corners of her mouth lifted into a tighter curl, and her black eyes were as cold and cruel as death.

"I am disappointed in you, my lord," she said.

"And how have I disappointed you now?" Don Luis asked wearily.

"You have not yet asked who sired it," Bianca said ever so gently, "this child who kicks beneath my heart."

Don Luis lay back against the bedpost, naked anguish in his eyes. "And if I were to ask?" he whispered. "What answer would you give?" Bianca looked at him, her eyes cool and grave, the scarlet returning to her mouth, two bright spots of color burning in her cheeks. "Answer me!" Don Luis thundered. "Who fathered this bastard?"

"You, of course, my lord," Bianca said demurely, "who are so wonderously good at it. Though I doubt that this one will be as fair as your eldest, since I have not that worthless Frenchwoman's gold upon my head." Then she turned very quietly and went out of the room.

And Don Luis, hanging there against the bedpost, wondered as his blood-wet fingers loosed their hold and the roaring tide of blackness rose to engulf him which wound it was that bore him down—the one made by cold steel through his shoulder or this invisible dagger left twisted in his heart.

15

THE FRIGATE *Santa Elena,* Don Francisco Alvarez commanding, beat her way southward along the coast of Panamá. She had left Port Royal in Jamaica some days before, and after touching briefly at Porto Bello, was on her way southward to Nombre de Dios. Today, however, both the wind and the current were adverse, so that the frigate made very poor speed.

Nightfall caught Don Francisco and his crew some leagues from Nombre de Dios. Under ordinary circumstances, any of the Spanish commanders familiar with this coast would have proceeded without hesitation into the harbor and dropped anchor there, where they could await the coming of morning in perfect safety. However, the circumstances on this night early in July 1694 were far from ordinary. Don Francisco had been ordered from Spanish waters upon an official mission; neither he nor any member of his crew had ever sailed in the waters of the Caribbean before.

Being a man of sound practical sense, Don Francisco proceeded to do the worst thing he could have done under the circumstances: he pointed his prow toward the shore line, clearly visible off his starboard beam, and inched the *Santa Elena* in, taking careful soundings with a weighted line every few yards. When the depth seemed to him to be right, he ordered his crew to drop anchor and, lighting his pipe, settled down to take his ease.

The night was deep and soft. From the mainland a breeze brought the scent of dense, steaming vegetation, and the cry of the gulls circling like the ghosts of drowned seamen in the moonlight sounded mournfully through the still air. The stars were very big and close, like a Midas profusion of diamonds pinned in an endless black-velvet curtain, and the frigate creaked peacefully on her anchor line as she rose and fell in the easy swells.

Don Francisco's head fell forward on his broad chest and he slept. So did his entire crew, including the single lookout he had posted.

When he awoke it was to the scream of a man in the death agony. He stumbled clumsily to his feet and, seizing his sword, climbed out on deck, where his dazed eyes beheld his half-armed and totally unprepared crew being cut down by a legion of bearded fiends. With an oath, he sprang forward into the fray, only to be confronted by an apparition that quite unmanned him.

He had raised his slim Spanish sword only to have it met in the darkness by a blade of Toledo steel as fine as his own. Sparks flew from the impact, and Don Francisco realized at once that he was engaging a swordsman of no mean caliber. He found himself being beaten back, step by step, to where the light flooded out from the opened hatch of his cabin. He stepped back once more, furiously parrying that dancing blade which seemed everywhere at once. And at that moment someone came up behind him and laid a belaying pin over his head.

But just before the light went out inside his skull, Don Francisco had seen his apparition. The slim and graceful swordsman who had fought him with such deft and mocking skill was no swordsman at all, but a woman—a woman in boy's pantaloons and a tattered shirt, neither of which were sufficient to conceal the lissom quality of her beauty.

On the deck of the frigate the battle was over. Even in daylight, this crew, inexperienced in the ways of fighting buccaneers, would have been doomed; at night, bemused by sleepiness, they were like so many sheep. Rouge stood on the foredeck, her long red hair streaming over her shoulders, and addressed her buccaneers.

"Step lively now," she said. "Have you any further cause for grumbling? I got you off the *Seawitch,* though she flamed to her topgallant yards, and endured your goatish bleating across the rest of the sea. Now, look alive and pull hearty, lest what remains of my patience desert me. To your stations!"

The men swarmed upward amid the rigging, loosing a cheer that floated deep and lusty across the soft night air. Leaning over the bow, Rouge once more read the name of the frigate.

"The *Santa Elena,"* she mused. "I doubt there is any sainthood here. I christen her the *Gull,* for her broad wings will sweep the seas free of anyone who opposes me." She called the ship's carpenter to her side, ordering him to reletter the name in the morning.

She remembered the sufferings of those four days in the longboats after she had seen that every man had left the *Seawitch* before she herself left a deck that quite literally burned beneath her feet. Then the hunger and the snakes and the mosquitoes of the Panamá coast, where they had hidden themselves in the very heart of Spanish territory. Later she could think some more. Now there were things to be done.

"Bring the don aft," she said crisply to a seaman, and returned to her cabin.

The man saluted and went forward. After a few minutes he returned with Don Francisco. When the Spaniard was shoved unceremoniously into Rouge's cabin by the two villainous rogues who guarded him, he found her seated, her long legs propped gracefully on the carved oak table. That Don Francisco found this disconcerting was apparent. His hot little black eyes traveled over the long, sweet-curving length of thigh down to where her slim ankles disappeared into the gaping tops of her low jackboots. Rouge smiled at him, her green eyes brimming with mockery.

"Be seated, señor. I would like to ask you some questions."

The hidalgo made her a stiff bow and remained standing. Rouge nodded wearily to the guards, and the Spaniard found himself slammed vigorously into a chair.

"Will you have a tankard?" Rouge inquired. Don Francisco shook his head angrily. At once one of the guards was ready with a heavy pewter tankard. Rouge watched with quiet amusement as they forced the Spaniard to drink it down, sloshing it freely into his eyes, his mouth, and his beard.

"Now that we are done with the civilities," Rouge said, "we can attend to business. Where did you come from, señor?"

Don Francisco clamped his jaws grimly shut. Rouge lifted a weary eye toward the guards. Slowly they brought out their sheath knives. After a moment one of them leaned forward and plucked a hair from the Spaniard's heavy beard. A quick motion of the knife and the hair fell to the floor in two clean-cut halves. The Spaniard stared at it, a trace of sweat bedewing his forehead.

"I asked you a question, señor," Rouge said softly.

The Spaniard stared at the blue gleam of the knife blade and discretion won out over valor. "From Port Royal," he growled. "Your countrymen are more civil than you, señorita."

Rouge frowned. This traffic between Englishmen and Spaniards was not to her liking. Most Englishmen shared her feeling in this, she knew. Since the beginning of the long war of the Palatinate in 1688, all English sea dogs had had to swallow the bitter pill of finding themselves allies of the nation they hated above all others. Indeed, during every one of the joint forays against the French the English commanders had found it difficult to restrain their seamen from polishing off the Spanish long before their joint objectives were reached. Among the leaders, a frozen politeness was carefully practiced, but no power on earth could restrain the descendants of the sea hawks of Drake, Raleigh, Frobisher, and Hawkins from shouting "Papist dogs!" every time they sighted a Spaniard, or could prevent the crews of His Bewitched Majesty's galleons from replying "Filthy heretics!" with equal fervor.

"Then I am a truer Englishman than they," Rouge answered, "for I would have greeted you with roundshot the moment you hove to in the harbor."

"For which act," Don Francisco replied testily, "the authorities would have hanged you as they hanged that blond fiend your Captain Neilson captured."

Rouge's booted feet dropped smartly to the deck. She stood up and faced the Spaniard, the emerald blaze leaping in her eyes.

" 'Blond fiend,' did you say?" she demanded. "More of this, Captain! A tall lad with a sunburst of hair about his shoulders, and a face like a sea god come down to earth?"

"The señorita exaggerates," the hildalgo observed, "but otherwise the description fits."

"Did you hear his name? Was it Christopher? Or Cristóbal or Kit?"

The Spaniard looked at her, seeing the stark emotion written in her eyes. Then, with evident pleasure, he nodded.

"Yes," he said, "such indeed was his name."

Rouge felt the stiffness leaving her knees. They were quite boneless suddenly, watery and weak. She sat down abruptly.

"You—you saw him hanged?" she whispered.

"No," the Spaniard said regretfully. "He was being brought to trial the day we sailed. It was said that an Englishwoman was to give evidence against him, of mistreatment and dishonor suffered at his hands. The outcome was scarcely in doubt."

Rouge was on her feet again, her face crimson with rage.

"Rosalind!" she spat. "The lying, fork-legged wench! Rosalind Parish!"

"Again you are right," Don Francisco said. "Señora Parish was indeed the name mentioned. You are well acquainted with the gentry of Port Royal, señorita."

Rouge signaled the guards with a wave of her hand.

"Take him away!" she commanded.

After the Spaniard had been escorted from the cabin, Rouge sat before the great table staring blankly into space. She could feel the great scalding tears gathering just back of her eyelids, and blink as she would, she could not hold them back. She shook her head angrily, dashing the tears away from her eyes in a bright shower.

When last we met, she mused, I opened fire on him with intent to kill.

Why is it that now I weep for him? . . . She must think, she must. This whole matter must be made clear. But the stubborn thoughts refused to come. Instead, before her eyes rose the image of Kit mounting the gibbet, his blond head held high, pride in every line of his lean frame, no fear upon his face. She could see the hangman stepping up to him, see the loop of hemp in the man's hands, and . . .

But beyond that she could not go. She ground the knuckles of her hands into her eyes, trying to shut out the hideous picture that presented itself: Kit—tall, handsome Kit—swinging like a grotesque pendulum at the rope's end, his princely head bent sidewise at that terrible angle which has no counterpart in life. Her head went down on the oaken table and racking sobs tore unbidden up from her bosom. Then another thought, more horrible than any of the others, came to her mind.

"I crippled the *Seaflower!*" she whispered. "That was it! That stiff-necked fool, Neilson, could never have beaten Kit in a fair fight! But I— Oh, God, I! . . ." Her green eyes stared toward the bulkheads of the cabin like icy emeralds, hard and free of tears. And there, before her sight, she saw it all again, imprinted mercilessly upon her memory: her own corvette *Seawitch* flaming to its topgallant yards, and the thunderous backward recoiling bellow of her last broadside as her gunners poured their withering fire into the *Seaflower*. A gallant thing, this last gesture of defiance, heroic, magnificent—only it had sealed the doom of Kit Gerado as surely as though her hands had looped the hangman's noose about his neck. If the *Seaflower* had not been crippled by the last blast of her guns, Kit might have outfought Neilson's squadron; certainly he could have outrun them. She had done this. She, Jane Golphin, had murdered the man she loved.

Murdered him! And for what? For a house that he burned, not knowing that it was hers, for fields that he had destroyed in obedience to the orders of his superior officer in open warfare. What was a house that Kit should die for it? What was a cane field, ten thousand cane fields, the whole green earth to be compared to the lightest kiss from his firm mouth?

"For these paltry things," she whispered, "for these unbelievably petty things, I pursued him half across the sea and pulled him down to a death unworthy of a dog! Oh, Kit, my Kit. . . ." Her voice trailed off down a bright glissando of sobs, and her clenched fist beat a fierce tattoo upon the table.

She wept a long time until she had no tears left. When she at last attempted to stand up, she found to her surprise that she had not the strength to move her limbs, she who had prided herself on her lack of feminine weakness. Then a new realization came over her: she was whole again. She was a woman once more, wholly and entirely feminine, and she could admit clearly and simply something that in darkness and secret she had always known—that she loved Kit Gerado with all her heart.

She sat quite still in the darkness and stared at the dim bulkheads of her cabin, her mind moving along curious paths.

"I will return to Port Royal," she said aloud, "I will find Rosalind Parish and kill her with my own hands."

She stood up at last and went up on deck. "Put about," she said to the helmsman.

The man stared at her, his jaw dropping open. "Put about?" he demanded.

"Yes," she said quietly, "put about—back to Port Royal."

The man stared at her a moment longer, then shrugged. Lifting a hairy hand to his mouth, he bellowed: "Ready about!"

The crew scurried to their stations. The helmsman pushed the tiller down toward the leeward side and lifted his head again.

"Hard alee!" the helmsman roared, and brought the frigate around smartly. They were now sailing a broad reach with the wind abaft the beam. The wind held. Three days later they dropped anchor in a secret cove not far from Port Royal. Rouge told them to wait until she returned, or in the event she did not return, to remain there for four days and then sail without her.

Late that same afternoon, the Lady Jane Golphin, clad in a trim green riding habit that pointed up marvelously the color of her eyes, rode into Port Royal. She was greeted on every side by astonished people curious to know the reason for her recent disappearance and her activities during the past fortnight.

Rouge passed off their questions lightly. Of one, Gilbert Williamson, whom she knew better than the rest, she asked lightly: "Do you know the whereabouts of Rosalind Parrish?"

Williamson smiled at her. "I know there is little love lost between you," he said. "Still, if you want to see her, she lives at the house of Captain Neilson, having lately—and in some haste—married that gentleman."

Rouge laughed. "She wastes no time," she said.

She saluted him with her crop and drew in on the reins. Gilbert Williamson lifted a protesting hand.

"Stay awhile," he pleaded, but Rouge was gone, thundering off down the narrow street.

At the house of Captain Neilson, Rosalind herself opened the door, her single serving-woman being busy at other tasks. Rouge's hand vanished into her bag and her slim fingers closed about the butt of the slim silver-mounted pistol that she had hidden.

"May I come in?" she asked quietly. Rosalind stood aside and allowed her to enter. She pushed forward a chair. Rouge sank down into it.

"You know why I came?" she said.

Rosalind shook her head. "No," she whispered.

"Then will I inform you," Rouge said, speaking slowly, carefully, spacing her words so they came soft and clear and deadly calm. "Upon the commons a fortnight ago, a man was hanged." She paused, watching Rosalind's face. There was in it nothing but wonder and questioning. "I—I loved that man. He was a tall man, with a sea hawk's face and God's own sunlight on his head."

"Kit!" Rosalind breathed.

"Yes, Kit," Rouge said, and her hand came out of the bag holding the tiny pistol. "Before you die, explain to me why you sent him to his doom with your lies."

Rosalind was fighting for breath. "You're wrong!" she got out at last. "He wasn't hanged! He escaped. I aided him in his flight!"

The black owl's eye of the pistol wavered for a moment, then came steady again.

"You lie," Rouge said flatly.

"No, no!" Rosalind wept. "God help me if I lie! It's true I betrayed him, but only because he scorned me. Afterward I was overcome by shame and remorse. I slipped by night into the gaol and provided the means for his liberation—his and all his crew's. Believe me, Jane, he is not dead!"

Again the pistol wavered. "If that whorish tongue of yours is not speaking the truth . . ."

Rosalind strode abruptly to the door. She flung it open and called out to the old street vender who was crying his wares outside.

"Come here a moment. I have a question for you."

The old man shuffled forward, scratching his mangy head.

"There!" Rosalind said. "Ask him!"

Rouge looked at the old man and put the question to him.

"No, ma'am," the old man quavered. "That un got away clean. Stole his ship back and sailed her out past the harbor guards slick as a whistle! They couldn'ta come near to him—not that un!"

Rosalind went to a drawer and came back with a gold sovereign. She pressed it silently into the old man's hand. When she turned Rouge was standing beside her, her green eyes glistening with tears.

"I have never liked you," she said to Rosalind. "Yet from this hour we are friends. God bless you, Rosalind, for you have saved both his life and your own."

Rosalind put out her arms and swept Rouge into them. "Go to him," she whispered fiercely. "Give him all the love he should have, all the tenderness, and—and bear him many tall sons!" Then she fled sobbing into the other room.

Rouge stood staring after her for a moment. Then with swift, decisive steps she crossed the room and went out into the street to her waiting horse. The cobblestones echoed to the swift dancing clatter of the horse as she mounted. In a moment she was gone, thundering down the street in the direction of the hidden cove where the *Gull* lay. She would scour the Caribbean in search of Kit, and when she found him she would never again leave his side. "Pray God," she muttered, "that I find him soon."

She leaned forward over her mount's neck, urging him on with crop and spur and prayerful words.

16

AFTER HE HAD COLLAPSED in her bedroom, struck down as much by Bianca's words as by the wound that Ricardo Goldames had given him, Don Luis had lain near death for many hours. Bianca had pulled the bell cord and summoned his manservants. These, with the aid of the women, had put the heavy bulk of the grandee into bed and undressed him.

While they attended to him, Bianca knelt at an altar set into a small niche in her bedroom. It was not for Don Luis that she prayed, but for herself. Kneeling there before the image of the Virgin, with the flickering candlelight bejeweling the tears upon her face, Bianca fought her battle in silence and in tears. It was a grim struggle for all its saintly stillness, for Bianca was being assaulted by temptations as great as those hurled against Saint Anthony.

It would all be so easy, she thought as she prayed for guidance. She needed only to withdraw herself and Don Luis would die. Not one of the Indian servants was capable of nursing the Count, and the doctors of Lima were all Caviedes had said they were—and worse. Yes, she had only to let matters take their course and her husband would die. Then she could take ship to Jamaica and stay there awhile, waiting her chance to slip across the short stretch of sea in a coasting hoy into one of the blue harbors of Saint-Domingue. And once there . . . Her mind reeled, thinking of it.

However, Bianca was cursed—or blessed—with an extraordinarily lucid mind. A woman who withheld herself when she could save her husband's life was bloodguilty. To will his death, deliberately to let him die—how fine a line divided such an act from murder? To have Kit's strong arms around her, to feel his mouth upon her own—would she accept eternal damnation and hellfire for that? For a moment the hot rebellion in her blood shouted Yes! But then the training of the good Sisters of the convent and years of dutiful attendance at mass were too strong.

As she rose from her knees and approached the inert figure of her husband lying on the bed, a softer emotion awoke in her than even the mighty voice of her faith could inspire. She was moved by real pity for the big man who lay before her, his life visibly draining from his great body. As she knelt beside him, her deft fingers busy with the bandages and hot water and poultices that the servants brought her, she remembered that here indeed was her husband and her lord, the father of her unborn child. She remembered, too, that the outward harshness of his nature had never been directed at her, that Don Luis was, in fact, no better and no worse than any other grandee of his day. And, at the last, it came to her that her husband had spared Kit's life when he held him helpless. Could she, in honor, do anything else than help him now?

For three days and nights she did not leave his side. She got food into him, water, broth, and wine. When on the fourth morning she dozed off from sheer exhaustion, she dreamed that Kit stood beside her with grave approval in his eyes, but when she woke it was to find Don Luis's dark eyes upon her, clear and free of delirium and soft with tenderness.

"I have wronged you," he whispered. "Had you been what I thought, you would have let me die. Bless you, my little dove—and know that your small folly is forgotten."

Bianca put out her hand and took his. "I am glad, Luis," she said softly. "I would not have our son come into a house filled with strife. From this day on there must be no dissension between us. You must trust me, I will never betray you."

Don Luis's recovery was rapid, but because of Bianca's pregnancy they could not leave Lima for Cartagena. Soon, in fact, their positions were reversed. As Bianca grew heavy with child, the Count began to minister to her. By December of 1694, Bianca, in her seventh month, was rendered nearly helpless by her condition.

She awoke one morning during the Christmas week with the feeling that her head had been smothered all night in a blanket. Lima, cold Lima, where the temperature rarely rises above sixty degrees, was held suddenly in the midst of a dense and steaming tropical heat more reminiscent of

Panamá than of Peru. Outside her window she could hear the thud of running feet and the shouting of many voices.

At her puzzled nod, Quita opened the shutters and the voices came clear.

"El niño!" they shouted. *"El niño!"*

"El niño?" Bianca puzzled aloud. The words meant simply "the little boy" or, more likely at this season of the year, "the Christ Child." Yet why should they shout the name of the Christ Child with so much fear in their tones? She looked at Quita, but she was as mystified as her mistress. Bianca threw back her covers and put out her legs. Quita knelt and placed her soft slippers on her feet, and at that moment Don Luis strode into the room.

"What is it, Luis?" Bianca demanded. "Why do they shout?"

"They fear disaster," Don Luis growled, "and rightly, I am afraid. Don't you feel the heat?"

"Yes," Bianca said, "very much. What does it mean?"

Don Luis dropped heavily into a chair, his dark face troubled.

"Every year at this time," he said, "the winds blow from the north, from the hot regions about the equator. And with them they bring a back eddy of warm water that spreads over the cold offshore current. Once in every thirty years or so that north wind is much stronger than normal and the hot-water current increases a thousandfold. Men call the current *el niño,* because it comes most often at Christmas time."

"But why do they fear it?" Bianca demanded.

"Because it upsets all that is usual in Callao and Lima. Wait and you will see. You know it never rains here? Well—listen."

Bianca bent forward listening. Far off and faint there came the distant rumble of thunder, and on the roof sounded the first widely spaced spatter of the rain. The raindrops increased, became a downpour slanting straight down past the window in hard, exact lines. In five minutes the downpour had become a thunderous torrent so heavy that it was impossible to see even across the narrow street. The rain went on and on, hour after hour, with no apparent intention of slackening.

Bianca sat huddled in a chair while Don Luis, wrapped in his greatcoat, walked through the streets with other officials inspecting the damage caused by this unaccustomed torrent. On the coastal region of Peru, only fifty-two streams descend from the western slopes of the Andes to the ocean, and most of these dry up in summer. By November they have grown to thin brooklets, and by December they are usually in flood. But in December of 1694 they were raging cascades of boiling white water, inundating the surrounding territory for miles.

From where she sat, Bianca could hear the low crashes as the adobe buildings collapsed into muddy ruins. Lima was not built for heavy rains;

even some of its stone structures gave way before the torrents. In the Indian section not one of the plastered mud huts survived. The crazed Incas ran howling through the streets, and women and children drowned by the hundreds in the flash floods. From the window of her great stone house Bianca saw the bodies of pigs and chickens drift by in the flooded street, and now and again the small brown corpse of an Indian child. By nightfall her nerves had been reduced to a quivering mass of terror, and she wept aloud in Quita's arms.

All night the rains continued, but in the morning they ended as abruptly as they had began. Still the heat did not abate. In the coastal waters off Callao, the cold, greenish Peruvian current disappeared, to be replaced by a brownish, slow-moving southward current that was hot to the touch. The uncounted millions of microscopic sea life upon which the birds fed died and sank to the bottom, and the fish swam toward the open sea in search of cooler water. On the islands and promontories the myriad colonies of birds were abruptly deprived of food. Because of the tremendous demands of their great wing muscles, the sea birds spend every waking hour feeding, so in a matter of hours they began to die of starvation. Hundreds of thousands of them died, their feathered bodies making small mountains on their island nesting places. When the wind shifted and blew up the Rimac River toward Lima, the stench was past all belief or bearing.

"El niño!" the people wailed, *"el niño!"*

In the cathedral the Archbishop called on the people to pray and said this catastrophe was a punishment from God for Lima's many sins. The rains fell in torrents and disappeared as abruptly, leaving the streets filled with stinking yellow water and sticky black mud. Afterward, most maddening of all, came the insects. Because of its dry, cool air, Lima is usually free of flying pests, but now they descended on the city in clouds.

None of the fumigants that Quita burned in Bianca's bedroom seemed to do any good; the people of Don Luis's household were being devoured alive. The mosquitoes buzzed from dusk till dawn, and afterward the flies, the *colorojes,* took over, bringing sickness in their wake. Before a week was out the city was in the grip of an epidemic of smallpox. The Indians died like flies, and more slowly the Spaniards began to die too. It was this fact, more than Bianca's bitter pleas, that caused Don Luis to consider seriously leaving Lima at any cost. When at last the plague appeared in their very street and the death carts, piled up with cordwood stacks of bodies, began to groan through the mud before their very eyes, Don Luis could hesitate no longer.

In Bianca's delicate condition, it was a serious risk to move her at all, he knew. But if they remained in Lima, Don Luis ran the much greater risk of losing her altogether. So it was that early one morning he wrapped her tenderly in her velvet coat and lifted her into his waiting coach. They crawled over the eight long miles to Callao, but no matter how slowly they drove, Bianca was ghost-white and weak from repeated vomiting when she was lifted aboard ship.

Once clear of the harbor, it was better. Farther out to sea they found the cool currents again, and Bianca was more comfortable than she had been in months. But as they approached the equator the heat became an agony to her. It had been Don Luis's intention to remain in the new city of Panamá until the birth of the child, but Bianca would not hear of it. She stormed and pleaded until at last Don Luis gave in, and ordered the construction of a litter to bear her across the Isthmus to Porto Bello, where they could take ship for the cooler climate of Cartagena.

Bianca lay staring alternately at the leaf-fringed sky and the great vines that looked like serpents. Now and again she glanced downward at her swollen body and the rebellious tears came to her eyes. If, she reflected, it were Kit's child who kicked beneath my heart, I would be out of my mind with joy. As it is, I cannot even find comfort in the fact that the same blood will flow through its veins. . . .

The journey went on. On the morning of the fourteenth day Bianca was in the grip of a raging fever. Bending over her, Don Luis could see her parched lips drawn tightly away from her teeth and her fine head like that of a skull covered with white parchment. Opening his stone flagon, he forced the remainder of the carefully saved water between her teeth. Much of it ran out of the corners of her mouth, but she did not even stir. Don Luis turned on his drivers, roaring.

"Bestir yourselves!" he cried. "We must reach Porto Bello before dawn tomorrow!"

The men lashed the weary animals onward. By the time they stumbled, drunken with weariness, into Porto Bello, they had lost half the remaining mules. Even then Don Luis did not pause. He went on, carrying Bianca in his great arms when the second of the two mules that bore her litter died on its feet in the plaza of the city. Grimy, sweat-covered, he made his way to the house of Porto Bello's best physician, a Jew of Portugal, a man far in advance of his times.

"She has an even chance, I think," the doctor said after examining Bianca, "because of her youth."

"But what of the child?" Don Luis demanded impatiently.

The Jew shrugged eloquently. "That," he declared, "is in the lap of the gods."

Throughout the months of January and February 1695 Bianca lay in a comalike state in the house of the physician. The doctor himself was openly astonished that she did not die. Early in March her dark eyelids fluttered open for the first time, and Don Luis knelt beside her bed, the unashamed tears clouding his eyes. Gratefully, she put out a pale hand and stroked his head. After that her recovery was rapid.

Still, it was the first of April before she was strong enough to travel. They resumed the journey by easy stages, sojourning for many days at Nombre de Dios before proceeding southward to Cartagena. Never had Bianca dreamed that she would be glad to see the grim-walled city of Cartagena, but as the *Garza* slipped through the narrow opening at the Boca Chica and began to inch its way up the twisting channel, a feeling of peace descended upon her. Kit was gone, perhaps lost to her forever, but if that thought troubled her it also stilled the doubts and confusions that had so long racked her brain. She looked at her husband gently, almost tenderly. In all things have I failed him, she mused—and, so thinking, put out her hand.

"Home, Luis," she whispered. "It's good to be home."

Don Luis took the much-too-thin hand that she offered him and stood gazing at the pale, ethereal beauty of his wife. Like an angel come back from the grave, he thought, holding the slim hand hard in his grip, and wondering, with a quiet kind of terror, why she did not ask what had become of the child—the long-hoped-for son of his bosom, a babe as pale and lovely as the mother who bore him, who had come into this world on the second day of February 1695, and quitted it the same instant—without ever drawing the first faint breath of life. . . .

"Yes," he said at last, "it is good, my Bianca—wonderfully good. Come, the carriage awaits us."

17

EARLIER ON THE same morning that Bianca and Don Luis del Toro returned to Cartagena, Bernardo Díaz stood on the deck of the *Seaflower*. It was still dark, and he was checking the ship's position at sea. Now he lowered the cross-staff he had been sighting at a star and glanced wonderingly at the astrolabe. He looked at the needle, touched curiously with loadstone imbedded in a float of cork that floated in its bath of oil and water. Then, picking up a parchment chart, he traced the distance to the nearest shore with a pair of dividers. Again he lifted the astrolabe, hanging it on his thumb. Even with this most inaccurate instrument, affected as it was by the roll of the ship so that its usual error was as much as fifteen degrees, the results checked. He hurried forward to Kit's cabin.

"Do you know our position?" he growled. Kit nodded, a slow smile on his lean face. "When I said yesterday that there was scurvy among the crew, you said that you would make land and replenish our supplies, but why of all spots on this broad and miserable earth must you land at Cartagena?"

"I think you know," Kit said slowly. "When we embarked on this voyage my purpose was to gain the gold with which to establish myself forever on the lands the Sieur Ducasse granted me. I have obtained the gold and I am going back to Saint-Domingue, but first I intend to stop off at Cartagena."

"And your intention there is to deprive Don Luis del Toro of his wife?"

Kit studied Bernardo, small fires leaping in his eyes. "Let us say to deprive him of all his sorrows and all his joys forever," he growled. "Bianca is of but secondary importance."

"You will not leave her behind, will you?" Bernardo persisted.

"No, Bernardo," Kit said evenly, "but Don Luis comes first in my plans. After that, his wife."

"I think," Bernardo said with a grin, "that she will come willingly."

"I do not agree. This blood and slaying is likely to awaken within her so great a horror that she will refuse to touch my hand."

"Then why kill him?" Bernardo asked. "Think how much keener your vengeance will be if he lives knowing that each night she lies warm and panting in your arms! To a man of his tremendous pride wouldn't such a fate be worse than death? Take her away and leave him to spend his life in sorrow and shame!"

Slowly Kit shook his head. "Even if I wanted it so, she would not come. Night and morning at Cul-de-Sac I saw her kneel and pray. God is very close and very real to her. She never would break the vows she has taken." He stopped, a grimace of pain on his face. "Yet not even for her would I forbear. In Cádiz I swore that I never would rest until I had taken vengeance."

"So now?" Bernardo demanded.

"So now," Kit finished for him, "we will run the *Seaflower* in near the Santo Domingo section just past the Tenaza and lie at anchor there until nightfall. Then you will drop the longboat over and put me ashore. If I do not return by dawn, there will be little need of waiting. You will then deliver the *Seaflower* and her crew safely back in Saint-Domingue, and ask Father Dumaine to have masses said for my soul."

"*Smithers* will then deliver the *Seaflower* to her berth at Petit Goave," Bernardo corrected softly, "and Father Dumaine can include me in his prayers."

Kit was touched by Bernardo's unfailing generosity. He put out his arm and let his hand rest upon his friend's great shoulder.

"Your loyalty will one day be your doom," he said, "but it is true—I have need of you."

Bernardo stared eastward, toward the pearl-gray flush on the edge of the sky. "There is," he said, "one other thing that troubles me. You know, Kit, how many ships put in and out of Cartagena in the course of a day. What if the *Seaflower* is sighted?"

Kit frowned. "After we are put ashore," he said slowly, "the *Seaflower* must stand out to sea for some little distance—not far, but far enough to keep her out of sight of the walls. Most of the vessels lay a course broadside of the walls; otherwise it would be difficult to find the Boca Chica channel. By this means, she should escape all harm."

"Yes," Bernardo growled, "if these famished seahounds of ours can resist the temptation to drop a roundshot across some plate ship's bows while we are not there to restrain them."

"It's a risk we'll have to take," Kit said quietly. "Call Smithers aft."

The *Seaflower* held her course, angling sharply in toward the rugged shore. Off her port beam the sun broke water suddenly, a red-hot ball with blood across its face.

Later, above the mastheads the sky was blue and clear, utterly cloudless, with a fresh quartering breeze that sent them along at a merry clip. Now the mighty hill of the Popa grew out of the sea, blue, dim, and misty, discernible long before the closer-lying land at its feet could be seen. A low white edge, half imaginary, half real, broke the water before it and grew into a gray pile of rock—the mighty walls that had stopped Drake and Morgan and that had caused every other freebooter in the Caribbean to take a second thought before attempting the richest prize of them all. Here was the small outcropping fortress called the Tenaza, aimed like a pistol straight at their hearts. Below it they could see clearly the great dome of the Templo de Santo Domingo rising above the walls. Once it was in sight, Kit ordered the *Seaflower* to heave to.

By this time it was late afternoon and they could do nothing more than wait. Smithers put the *Seaflower* on a new tack so that they swept along the coast almost as far as the Boca Chica entrance. As they passed the Boca Grande, filled now with a mound of earth and rock, they could see the white sails of the native schooners flying like gulls over the surface of the Bay of Cartagena, though their slim hulls were hidden by the intervening land.

Then the helmsman put the whipstaff about so that they swung around and sailed back in the direction from which they had come. By the time the *Seaflower* had won her way back to the Santo Domingo section of Cartagena, it was dusk.

Kit looked at Bernardo, seeing his powerful hands clasping and unclasping. Across his broad chest he wore the crisscrossed leather belts from which his twelve great pistols were suspended. Kit had armed himself with two long pistols, stuck into his sash. In addition, both he and Bernardo carried daggers and cutlasses.

The tropic night crashed down and the palms that peeped above the gray walls were crowned with silver mist, the walls themselves becoming silver-gray, magically transformed by the moon's touch into things of beauty. Looking at the fair night, Kit sighed. It would have been far more to his advantage had it been clouded, the stars hidden and no moon showing. Once before such a night had almost cost him his life, but now there was no time for such reflections.

The longboat splashed into the indigo sea, and like grim shadows the oarsmen sat at their benches, their gnarled hands gripping the broad sweeps. The blades of the oars had been muffled with rags. Still, this was a perilous attempt, for one cry from a sentry would bring down upon them such a hail of shot that not even a ship of the line could survive. They moved out now from the lee of the brigantine, the men bending and straightening slowly, their motions stiff and hampered by their desire to avoid all sound. Quietly the longboat crept forward, making scarcely a ripple on the night-blue sea. Kit lifted his eyes toward the stars. They burned bright in the dark-blue vault of heaven. Who knew when, if ever, he would again see the stars? He lowered his head again toward where the moon track burned bright across the face of the waters. It was necessary for them to cross this, and there lay their chief danger. Here in the blue shadows of the night, the longboat was all but invisible, but there in the liquid silver of the moonlight they would stand out gigantic and black, a target for every eye that chanced to glance in that direction. Kit leaned forward.

"Double beat!" he growled. "In this moonlight, only speed can save us."

The men bent forward, grunting deep in their lungs, their belly muscles knotting with the pull of the oars. Then they hauled back and the longboat shot ahead, pushing its prow into the moon track like the point of a hard-driven knife. They raced full into the glow, running over the surface of the moon-silvered water like a gigantic water beetle. Then at last, utterly spent, they gained the protective shadow of the great walls.

"Skirt the edges on your return voyage and meet me here at dawn," Kit whispered to the boatmen. He and Bernardo went over the side, wading through the surf, their jackboots slung over their shoulders, their bags of powder and shot tied about their necks. Behind them now they could hear the low splashing as the longboat moved out, and though they would not have admitted it, a feeling of awful loneliness came over them.

The rough stones of the wall rose forbiddingly before their eyes. Exploring them with his fingers, Kit discovered that their very roughness was a help. Here were toeholds in God's plenty; an agile man could scale these walls with ease. Kit started upward first, with Bernardo close behind him.

Twenty minutes later they lay on their bellies on the broad top of the wall, gulping the air into their famished lungs. Lying there, the first thing to strike their ears was the ring of heavy boots against the cobblestones. Bernardo loosened his dagger in its sheath. Kit put out a restraining hand.

"No," he whispered. "Let him alone. His death would only set off the alarm. Follow me."

Kit crawled swiftly to the edge of the wall and let himself down, hanging by the tips of his fingers. Bernardo did the same, and the two of them hung there, listening as the sentry's footfalls went by with agonizing slowness, hammering through the red haze in their ears, beating against the white torture in the sockets of their shoulders. The sentry paused just above their heads to gaze seaward. Then, with a gusty yawn, he moved onward until his footsteps died out in the direction of the Tenaza.

Slowly they drew themselves up and, scuttling across the bright expanse of the top of the wall—broad enough to let two coaches pass abreast—they let themselves down into the welcome shadow of the other side. Now they had reached the streets and, passing in front of the great church of Santo Domingo, they headed toward the square. Here, the first thing that Bernardo saw was the building bearing the arms of the Inquisition. He shuddered as the two of them moved onward past the church of San Pedro Claver, named for that most saintly of men who had given his life to aid the black slaves. In the square crowned by Cartagena's great cathedral not a soul moved, for it was past the hour of the curfew.

Kit paused, frowning. How on earth was he to find the house of Don Luis? Without someone to give them directions they were hopelessly lost. As he pondered, the echoing footfalls of a guardia civil sounded in the street. Here indeed was a dilemma. If they asked directions of the guard, how could they prevent his arresting them for breaking the curfew? If they attacked him, he would almost surely cause an outcry.

Then, to Kit's vast amazement, Bernardo began to sing. As Kit's jaw dropped open, Bernardo winked broadly at him and shoved him back into the shadows. Then he meandered toward the approaching guard, the perfect picture of a man much the worse for drink. The guard stopped short, angry amazement on his dark face.

"Cap'n," Bernardo wheezed, "Good Cap'n—a favor, *por Dios!*"

"What is it?" the guard growled. "And what keeps you on the streets at such an hour?"

"Drink," Bernardo babbled sorrowfully. "I wasch at Rosita's house. You know Rosita, Cap'n?"

The guard's face relaxed a bit. Evidently he did know Rosita. This, Kit reflected with amusement, was a tribute to Bernardo's sagacity. Among all the whores in the great city of Cartagena there must be at least one Rosita.

"She did it, Cap'n," Bernardo went on. "Befuddled me wif drink, that she did—until I fell 'sleep, so help me. Then she tossed me out, wifout a taste of what I'd really paid for! Ever heard o' worse luck, Cap'n?"

The guard was grinning now. That this drunken fool had been cheated of Rosita's favors seemed to him infinitely amusing.

"You old he goat! Do you think that Rosita needs such as you? Now get on before I remember my duty and lock you up for being abroad at such an hour!"

"Cap'n," Bernardo quavered, "I'm stranger here—came from Santa Marta yesterday—but have a friend, coachman of Don Luis—Don Luis del Toro. He'll put me up—let me sleep in the stable. Will you direct me, please?"

"All right," the guard said. "It's not far, only three streets beyond the square. Now, here is how you can reach the house."

Bernardo listened attentively. Even Kit could overhear most of the words. He waited until after Bernardo had finished his profuse thanks and the guard had gone his way. Then he joined Bernardo and the two of them raced through the darkened streets toward the house. Upon reaching it they circled it three times, unable to decide which window opened into Bianca's room. Finally, in desperation, Kit loosed a handful of small pebbles against an upper window.

There was the quick flicker of candlelight, the window opened, and a woman stood peering down at them. Her dress, Kit saw with dismay, was the saya of an Indian serving-woman. He held his breath, expecting every moment to hear her voice lifted in a screech of alarm. But the woman stood there very calmly and studied them without haste. Kit realized that they were standing in a moon-washed street that revealed them as clearly almost as daylight.

"What do you want?" the woman demanded.

"A word with your mistress," Kit whispered.

Still the woman did not move. She stood like a statue of bronze and looked down on them with complete impassivity. The seconds ticked off on the clock of doom while she looked at them. Their breaths tightened in their throats, became a long-deep burning. Suddenly the Indian woman made a gesture, a little motion not unlike a start of surprise—or, more curiously, of recognition. She leaned forward, pressing her bronzed face against the bars.

"If the tall cacique will remove his hat . . ." she whispered.

Wonderingly, Kit put up his hand. The ostrich plumes blazed silver as he swept off his broad-brimmed hat. Then the moonlight was spilling down over the heavy, lionlike mane that fell in great curls about his broad shoulders, so that it was white-gold suddenly, shimmering in the sweep of light.

"You," the woman said clearly, exultation in her tones, "are the great cacique Kit, are you not? I've often heard my mistress speak of you!"

"Yes," Kit said, "I am he. And if you will conduct me to your mistress, I will reward you."

"My mistress's joy at the sight of you will be reward enough," the Indian woman said. "Go toward the stables and I will meet you there." There was the scurried rustle of her slippered feet and the candle glow disappeared from the window.

"You're in luck, Kit," Bernardo said with a grin. "This cuckolding of Don Luis seems to go easily."

"Don't speak of cuckolding," Kit growled. "I didn't come for that purpose. I came to kill him!"

Beyond the house, the night drifted black in the narrow alley, the smells of hay and animal dung stinging their nostrils. They scrambled over a low wall into the courtyard, and there by the gate the Indian maid awaited them.

"Come," she whispered.

Bernardo bent forward, seeing her youth, her proud and pagan beauty, and a low whistle escaped his lips. "You," he said, "what are you called?"

"Quita," the girl said. "Now if my lords will come."

"Wait," Bernardo said. "What of Don Luis?"

"He went this noon to the hacienda," the girl said, smiling. "He will return tomorrow."

"Then," Kit said, cold determination in his tones, "I will wait for him!"

"Kit," Bernardo implored, "don't be a fool! Take the girl and be off! That's revenge enough."

"I will be the judge of that," Kit said evenly. Then to Quita, "Lead on."

Quita led them to the enclosed patio and there she turned.

"Wait here," she whispered. When she had gone Bernardo turned to Kit.

"I'm going now," he said. "You need privacy and a guard, both of which I can provide, but please, Kit, don't wait for Don Luis!"

"Enough!" Kit muttered. Bernardo shrugged and walked out of the patio, looking for all the world like a benevolent gargoyle.

Kit strode about the patio listening to the hammering of his heart. All time seemed to have stopped, the flux of the universe frozen, and every breath had to be forced out of his lungs with great labor. The patio was a wilderness of tropical blossoms, but Kit did not see them. He moved back and forth like a caged animal, listening with his heart for footsteps long before his ears could catch their sound. Then he halted abruptly, for now unmistakably there came the sibilant whisper of slippered feet. Kit stopped his feet cautiously on the tiles and stood there, waiting. A moment later Quita appeared, leading her mistress.

Bianca stopped some distance from him. Quita smiled happily on them both and hurried away into the darkness. Still neither of them moved. Bianca's face paled, grew ghost-white, the color draining even from her lips. Her hand came up slowly in a curiously abrupt motion and rested at the base of her throat.

Kit could see her mouth moving, shaping the single word *"You,"* but it was a shape without substance, for no sound came from her lips, no sound at all. He stepped toward her, for the moment forgetting Don Luis and his revenge, forgetting even Rouge. Three feet from her he stopped, seeing her face paler, thinner than he had remembered it, her body wasted beneath her robe to a slimness that escaped emaciation by only a narrow margin, her small, exquisite head almost burdened by the foaming blue-night cloud of her hair.

She faced him wordlessly, without moving, until at last she put up her hand and touched his cheek, letting her fingers stray lightly over his face in sheer wonder at the evidence of her eyes. Then a sob escaped her throat, a high, hysterical sound like the wail of a violin, and she fell forward into his arms.

Kit held her close, stroking her soft hair while she stained his shirt front with her tears, her body quivering against his like that of a small doe on the hills who hears the horns and the hounds of the hunter. When her weeping had passed Kit lifted her face with his hand, and bent down to kiss her mouth.

"No!" she whispered. "You must not! I could not stand that. Dear Kit, have mercy on my weakness."

Frowning, Kit drew back a little. She rose on tiptoe without willing it, and her lips found his face, covering it with kisses—light as moth wings, brushing his eyes, his mouth, his throat.

"Oh, Kit, Kit," she moaned, "why did you come? I was winning, I was gaining peace—but now, now . . ."

Then ever so slowly she drew her face away, her eyelids coming open by almost imperceptible stages until her eyes looked up at him, tear-wet and glowing. She put her small hands against his chest and pressed so gently that it was a hint merely, a suggestion rather than an actual gesture of protest. Kit released her at once and stood back, her hands cradled in his great golden ones.

"You must not kiss me, Kit," she said quietly. "When I knew you at Cul-de-Sac I was a girl, with a girl's folly, but now I am a woman and a wife."

Kit smiled. "I see only that you are lovely—and dear to me."

"Please, Kit, be generous to me! I need your mercy. Do you know what your kiss does to me? It stops my heart and makes all my blood run molten in my veins. Would you make me turn away from God and damn my soul for love of you?"

"I know little of God," Kit said slowly.

"That may well be," Bianca whispered, "but only He in His infinite mercy can release me. I love you and I cannot help that. But now I want you also—and that is a great sin. I took my vows in good faith, always meaning to keep them. Don't, Kit—dear Kit, don't make me sin now!"

"I came," Kit said, his voice harsh and pained, "to take you with me out of this prison. I beg you to come with me. Don't deny me all chance of happiness."

Bianca gazed at him, her eyes soft with adoration. "It lies beyond my power to grant you that, Kit," she whispered, "even though to refuse you is a kind of death. I made my pledge in the cathedral in the sight of God, and while Don Luis lives I cannot do otherwise."

Kit's hand closed around the hilt of his dagger and gripped it until his knuckles whitened from the strain. "Then he dies!" he spat. "Nothing shall stand between us!"

Bianca's arms flew upward about his neck. "No, Cristóbal. Promise me you will not kill him. Swear by what you hold most dear that you will not lift a hand against him!"

Kit's thin nostrils flared. "You—you love him!" he said slowly. "*Madre de Dios!*"

"No, Kit," Bianca said softly. "It's you and you only that I love. Because I love you, I would not have you harm him—especially not him, for that is a sin greater than you know."

"Why so, Bianca?"

Bianca shook her head so that her hair shifted about her shoulders.

"You must not ask me. One day you will know the reason. But know only this—it does not concern me and lies only between him and you. Don't be troubled. Stay here with me while you can."

Slowly Kit sank down upon the stone steps of the patio and Bianca lay beside him, her head pillowed in his lap.

"Tell me about yourself," she said. "Tell me all that has happened to you since last I saw you. It would be a consolation for me, Kit—it would give me something to dream of and remember when you are gone."

Looking down into the angelic sweetness of her face, Kit made the attempt, but the words came out labored and slow, with scarcely any meaning or connection between them. A little frown knotted Bianca's brows.

"What of your Rouge?" she said. "You have said nothing of her."

"She is dead," Kit said flatly, his voice drained of expression.

Bianca's mouth formed a soft, rounded "Oh! . . . How did she die?" she asked. "You said she was very young."

"I killed her," Kit whispered. "Mother of God, must we talk of this?"

Bianca looked at him, her dark eyes widening. "Yes," she said quietly, "we must. Why did you kill her, Kit? Had she wronged you?"

Kit whirled upon her and for the moment his temper leaped out of his eyes.

"Never!" he said. "She was sweet and pure and . . . Forgive me, Bianca. Forgive me. It's a wound that will take a long time to heal. I fired upon a vessel not knowing it was hers. When I last saw her, her whole ship was in flames and my own craft was so crippled that I was powerless to help her."

"I see," Bianca said very quietly.

"You do not see!" Kit burst out. "How could you?"

"Perhaps I cannot see in the precise sense that you mean, but I do see why you stayed away from me so long and sent no word to me. I see clearly now that you have come at last to your second choice, having lost the one you loved most."

"I thought of you," Kit said contritely, "much and often."

"Do not lie!" Bianca whispered. "I hated her! I thought I would be glad if she were dead . . ."

"And you are not?"

"No. If ever I had been free to come to you, I might have won you from her fairly, but now what chance have I? What chance against the ghost that haunts you? What chance against a bright memory?"

Kit looked at her, and his eyes were very clear. "No chance at all," he said softly, "nor should it concern you. You cannot replace her—I do not want you to. I want you not as a substitute for Rouge, but for yourself. You are most unlike her, and though night can never take the place of day, a man needs both. I want you in my life to make a new life of it, a life entirely different from the one I would have had with her. And you should never try to seduce me from my memories. I shall be a better man because of them—kinder, gentler, I think, and more loving."

Bianca hid her face suddenly and her whole form was shaken with weeping. "Still," she said, "still you are free, and I am bound—and one day I shall lose you. Oh, Kit, Kit, promise me . . ."

"Gently, Bianca," Kit whispered. "Do not cry. What promise do you want?"

"What I have no right to ask," Bianca said through her sobs, "that you take no other wife, lest you redouble the barriers between us. I know I have no right to ask this, Kit. How can I doom you to loneliness? If you find another, go to her, find joy and—and happiness."

Kit drew her to him, smothering her sobs against his chest.

"Don't cry," he said gently, "for now upon my mother's grave I swear never to wed another while you live."

Bianca lay back contentedly, her head on his knees, cushioned in the soft cloud of her hair. She lay there a long time, studying him, and as he watched he could see her face change. Her lips softened, became more deeply scarlet, parting just a little until he could see a thin thread of pearl between them, and her breath came out slowly, deep-sighing, with a rustle in it. Her eyelids drooped over her eyes, and the pulse at the base of her throat was a visible thing, beating wildly.

"Go!" she whispered, her voice low and intense. "Go!"

Gently Kit lifted her to her feet. Then he touched her mouth, his kiss as light as a spring wind. He released her and took a stride away from her, one stride only, for then he heard her cry.

"Kit!" she cried, agony in her voice. "Kit—oh, Kit!"

He turned back to her then, and her arms were about his neck, brands of cool white fire, tightening more and more. Her mouth flamed upon his, soft lips parted, and her body through the flimsy stuff of her robe was one long caress, moving into his, working slowly. She drew away her mouth, but tightened her arms about him, and the small sweet-curving hollow of her waist undulated in a motion as slow and fierce as the pulse of life itself, so that through the velvet of his heavy, broidered clothing his body felt scalded.

He could feel the sweet fire running molten through his veins, and his hands tightened about her until her white flesh purpled under the grip of his fingers. But as she tilted back her head to receive his kiss he halted suddenly.

From the sea wall a sound rode in upon them—the slow-rolling, belly-deep boom of cannon fire. He hung there like one frozen, unwilling to let her go, but the sound came again, a mighty roar as the cannon on the walls smote the sea and the sky with their bass thunder. Her hands fell away from him, and the look on her face was one of stark terror.

"What—what is it, Kit?" she whispered.

"I can only guess," he growled. "But I think they have caught the *Seaflower* in their sights. I must go at once."

He released her suddenly, not even pausing to snatch one last kiss, and raced away through the dark corridors. Bianca stood very still after he had gone, knowing with a curious sense of certainty that her congealed breath would loosen after a time, that feeling would come flooding back, that these daggers of pain, being pushed slowly upward along her veins would, in another moment, drive through her fast-beating heart.

18

By the time that Kit and Bernardo reached the walls opposite the Tenaza, half the city of Cartagena was gathered there. They moved through the crowds with casual confidence, for no one had eyes for anything except the sea. In one quick glance Kit and Bernardo saw what had happened. There in the graying light of morning a great plate ship lay, listing far over to starboard, mortally wounded by the *Seaflower*'s guns.

His crew had been unable to resist temptation after all. Months at sea under Kit's stern driving, weeks of passing one rich prize after another with linstocks unlit and bronze cannon muzzles cold, had at last proved too much for them. Even the trusted Smithers must have succumbed.

Kit realized that they had signed their own death warrants, because in pursuing the treasure ship they had run recklessly inshore and the wind was from seaward. A little farther out, the great ship *Garza* lay. With any kind of wind the *Seaflower* could have shown so clumsy a vessel a clean white wake, but lying as she did to leeward, she had to claw off the lee shore, sailing close-hauled, working her zigzag tacks to within four points of the wind's eye. The difference in speed of a vessel working to windward and one sailing free before the wind is immense. Even the *Garza*'s great size and poorly designed hull did not slow her to the crawl to which the *Seaflower* was reduced.

Smithers undoubtedly was handling the trim brigantine with skill, but it was too late. The *Seaflower* was doomed. She lay between the great guns of the fortress and the mighty cannon of the *Garza*. Even as Kit watched, the great sixty-four-pounders in the fortress opened up, and the wall of smoke blotted out the ocean. As it cleared, Kit saw the geyser plumes of spray rising all around the *Seaflower* while her helmsman moved the whipstaff back and forth, trying desperately to escape. But there, beyond, the *Garza* waited. The guns in the Tenaza opened up again, their round balls rising black against the sky, seeming to hang there for one awful moment before they whistled downward to crash upon the brigantine. When the smoke cleared the *Seaflower* lay hull down on the water, totally demasted, wallowing helplessly in the choppy sea.

Now the *Garza* was bearing down for the kill. Kit watched her move in, only half hearing Bernardo's whispered, monstrously obscene Castilian curses; but when the great ship was close, to their astonished joy the whole side of the *Seaflower* exploded into smoke and flame. Smithers, gallant to the last, had let loose a broadside. They saw the *Garza* reel under the impact of the *Seaflower*'s fire, but she continued to come on, only slightly hurt by the *Seaflower*'s thirty-two-pounders.

When she was too close to miss, she squared off, sailing parallel to the *Seaflower*. Then her entire hull disappeared behind a wall of smoke and flame that reached as high as the yardarms of her topsails. The hoarse bass thunder of her guns, slow-rolling over the face of the waters, echoed hollowly in the sickened emptiness of Kit's heart. He saw the roundshot strike home, saw the masses of splinters leap from the brigantine's deck. At last, knowing it was inevitable, he saw the red and yellow tongues of fire leap up from her powder magazine—and the *Seaflower* was gone, only a white splotch on the sea's bosom marking her passing.

Kit leaned forward. Something in the *Garza*'s behavior had caught his attention. She was reefing sail, as though preparing to heave to. Kit turned a wondering face toward Bernardo only to be met by a look of complete incredulity on that worthy's own face. Still, there was no mistaking the *Garza*'s intent, for already they could see her longboat descending seaward on the lines of its davits. In spite of that tremendous explosion, some of the *Seaflower*'s crew must have survived.

"They would not let them drown," Kit muttered. "That would be far too kind a death. No, Bernardo, it is the gibbet for my brave lads, and all because of me."

"Nonsense," Bernardo declared. "They agreed to the risks when they signed on. The loss of the *Seaflower* is due entirely to disobedience of your orders. Lying to, out of sight of the walls, they would have been safe enough."

"That's true, but how much safer would they have been if I had not ventured into these waters! No, Bernardo, the fault is mine."

"Milk!" Bernardo spat. "Buccaneers don't die in bed. If it's not the blue sea's mouth, then it's the rope's end. Why concern yourself? If you had returned them safely to Petit Goave, they would have put to sea again until someday the gibbet got them. Besides, speculation is useless. We have ourselves to think of unless we want to end by being hanged too. Let's hurry to get out of this city."

Kit looked out to where the *Garza*'s longboat was moving back and forth. He counted silently each time she paused to drag an object from the sea. Five, he counted, five—but which five? Slowly he shook his aching head.

"Leave if you want to," he growled. "I'm staying."

"Fifty times we've had this out," Bernardo said flatly. "The answer is still the same. If you stay, I stay with you. My stars and yours have been linked too long for us to be separated. Come, Kit, let's hide until tomorrow. Then we will see what we can do."

They moved quietly through the milling crowds away from the sea wall, but they had gone only four squares when Bernardo, who was ahead, flattened himself against the wall of a building and signaled for Kit to do the same. As they stood there, hardly daring to breathe, a party of horsemen thundered through the street in the direction of the wall. At their head, towering in the saddle, rode Don Luis del Toro, Count of the Realm.

Kit looked at that burly, black-bearded man who time upon time had brought anguish and despair into his life, and his hand tightened on the butt of his pistol. But Bernardo's fingers were tempered steel on his wrists, holding him hard in a grip of incalculable strength.

"Not now," he whispered.

Slowly Kit's fingers relaxed their grip on the hilt of the pistol and the tight-knit muscles of his arm loosened.

"You are right," he muttered, "but one day it will be different."

"Perhaps," Bernardo said mildly. "But come, we must find the bridge that leads to the San Lázaro section. We can hide in the Cienaga, the marshes west of the city."

They hurried off, strain and anxiety apparent in their faces. By the time they reached the bridge it was night. They crossed boldly, knowing only too well that any furtive gesture would have instantly betrayed them. On the other side, they angled off from the road, wading through the sticky mud and marsh water until they came to one of the thousands of low islands of sawgrass that stood in the swamp. They lay down there, completely hidden by the man-tall grass; and despite the clouds of mosquitoes, so great was their weariness that they slept like men turned to stone.

During that same night Don Luis was busy. He strode slowly up and down before the five dripping buccaneers who had been dragged from the sea. As president of the Audencia, it was within his powers to question them, but thus far he had not uttered a word. His dark eyes glowed in his swarthy face as he continued his leonine pacing. Suddenly he halted before the tall figure of Smithers. His big hand shot out and yanked Smithers' shirt front open. Smithers' chest was bare of ornament.

"No crucifix," Don Luis said quietly. "No Saint Christopher, Saint Anthony, Saint Cecilia! Nothing! Observe this carefully, caballeros, for we have here, I believe, a case for the good Fathers of the Inquisition." He looked into Smithers' face, a mocking light in his eyes. Then, quite suddenly, he lapsed into English. "Whoreson," he said softly, almost expressionlessly, his words moving out through the fixed, almost peaceful smile on his lips, "what do you now think of your Captain Gerado who has betrayed you?"

"You lie!" Smithers roared. The instant the words left his lips he realized his mistake, for Don Luis turned to the *oidores* with easy grace and spread his hands.

"An Englishman, hidalgos," he said, smiling, "and hence a heretic. The good Fathers will no doubt be pleased." He made a gesture to the captain of the guard, and Smithers was dragged off in the direction of the courts of the Inquisition.

The same test applied to the other four produced a different result, because each of them had a golden crucifix hanging about his neck. However, one of them was a Negro, and to Don Luis this meant that he must be a runaway slave.

"This one," the Count drawled, "is obviously an escaped black. We will make an example of him as an example to our own slaves. To the rack with him!" He glanced at the others, his eyes filled with icy contempt. "We might as well hang these forthwith, unless you gentlemen insist upon a trial—which I think is plainly a waste of time."

The *oidores,* the lawyers who made up the Viceroy's privy council, the Audencia, shrugged their shoulders. The people plainly wanted a spectacle. Far be it from them either to interfere or to delay.

As the men were being dragged away toward the dungeon, another thought crossed Don Luis's mind. What of Cristóbal? What of that fine young lion cub, that fair and princely bastard he had himself made? Had he gone down with his ship? The Count felt something like pain at the thought. He wondered why he had not legitimated him long ago. What an heir he would have made! . . . But in the middle of these regretful thoughts a sudden suspicion stirred in his brain. His own captain of the *Garza* had declared that the black-bearded Englishman, Smithers, had been in command. The Spanish sea captain knew, for he had watched the *Seaflower*'s movements with contemptuous leisure through his glass. What, then, of Kit? Was he dead, killed in some previous encounter? Or was he very much alive—here in Cartagena?

The *Seaflower* had been cruising slowly off the coast. Why? Was she perhaps waiting for someone? Someone who, bone of his bone, blood of his blood, had the same lusts as himself? The cub—for so Don Luis always thought of his bastard son—had snatched the red-haired English girl from the sea. And certainly since that time at Cul-de-Sac, Bianca had never been the same. Had she not looked with favor upon Ricardo, who in his northern fairness resembled this Cristóbal Gerado who should have been a Del Toro? Could it be that now, even at this moment . . .

Don Luis turned a thundercloud face toward the struggling prisoners. Son or not, if Kit had touched his most precious treasure, he must die! He pointed a strong finger at the smallest of the pirates, a former Parisian sewer rat, who doubtless could be persuaded to talk quite easily.

"Take this one to the Tenaza," he growled, "I would like to talk to him."

Three hours later, Don Luis emerged from the dungeons beneath the fortress. The little Parisian had proved stubborn. It was not until they had applied the boot, that cunning device which left a man's foot a purpled, bloody, boneless mass, that he had spoken. Afterward, Don Luis himself had supervised the removal of the man's tongue. It would not do to have him babble before he faced the hangman.

As he thundered homeward, his dark face lined and troubled, Don Luis wondered how he would put the question to Bianca. She would, of course, deny it if it was true. How would he get the truth out of her? Threats meant little to his wife, he knew. Too often she had seemed quite willing to die. . . . When he strode into her bedroom he found her kneeling before the altar, her young face white and shattered with overwhelming grief.

"Was he here?" he roared, not even thinking to call the name.

Bianca turned her face with painful slowness. Her dark eyes rested gravely on her husband's face.

"Yes," she said very simply, no evasion or fear in her tone. "He was here."

Don Luis stood over her, towering into the shadows, his powerful hands clenching and unclenching, his dark face filled with a torment greater than the agony on the Parisian's when they had applied the boot. What now? If he opened the floodgates and let the green and sickening bile of jealousy flood out, what answer would she give? Knowing Bianca, he realized that she might lift her head and say quite simply:

"Yes, my lord, I have betrayed you. Now do with me what you will!"

And if she said that, what then? Punish her? How? What punishment could he devise that she would not welcome—yes, even death? Looking into his face, Bianca read his thought.

"No, my lord," she said quietly. "I have not dishonored you, but only because your son is more of a man than you, and did not take advantage of my weakness. If he had wanted me to bed with him, I would have betrayed you, but he was honorable. He, not I."

Don Luis stood gazing down at the slim figure of his wife and wondered if he could trust himself to speak.

"He was a fool, then," he said heavily, "for he has lost his chance. He, at least, will never have you."

"Is he—is he taken?" she whispered hoarsely.

"No," he admitted, "but he will be. And when he is he will hang."

Bianca looked at her husband, her eyes night-black, fierce.

"And when he is taken," she whispered, "I will see that you do not harm him. You will do as I say."

Don Luis stood staring at her for a moment longer before he whirled and started for the door. "For this alone," he threw back at her, "for these words of yours, his doom is sealed!" Then he strode away out into the coming dawn.

In the morning, after the age-long night of waiting, Kit and Bernardo stole out into the street, hearing the distant throbbing of the great drums that called the people of Cartagena to the city square. Now it would begin. Now these men who had followed him so long, charged with him through gun smoke, would die—ignominiously, ingloriously, terribly. And all because of him, because of the green lovesickness of his youth.

Kit and Bernardo reached the square, already closely packed, and saw at once that all preparations had been completed. The executioner took his time. At the foot of the gibbet, the kettledrums never ceased their rolling beat. Now they quickened as the first of the men was led to the scaffold. Step by step the man mounted upward, accompanied by a black-robed priest and two stout guards, and at every step the drums cried out in gloating triumph.

Kit tried to turn away his eyes, but he could not. There was the blare of horns, the roar of gunfire, and a mighty roll on the drums. Then silence. And black between them and the sun, the awful pendulum swung, amid a stillness so great that its very creaking could be heard.

The crowd was roaring now, hoarse-voiced, bestial. The second buccaneer followed the first, walking proudly to the scaffold. Kit was sure he heard the bone snap, even above the shouts of the crowd. In the echoing quiet after the beast bellows of the mob was stilled, two figures creaked gently at the rope's ends, their necks bent far over in that terrible angle which has no counterpart in life.

The little Parisian died badly. He had to be carried to his death, making hideous noises from the bloody, tongueless socket of his mouth. Now, at last, Kit found the strength to turn away. When he looked again, it was not yet done. The little Parisian's weight was insufficient to break his neck on the drop, and he hung there kicking, his thin face purpling slowly, until two soldiers, moved by some strange compassion, caught both his legs and swung downward with all their force.

Then they brought out the black. The Negro had been stripped naked, and his body was a magnificent thing, rippling with superb muscle, bull-throated, deep-chested, great of limb and thew, like a statue carved from ebony. Four helmeted Spanish soldiers hurled him flat on his back on a rack, and the cords were tightened about his wrists and ankles. Kit saw the executioners place their poles into the sockets of the winch and turn it slowly until the sweat stood out on the black body as the Negro was slowly stretched until every major bone had been dislocated. Then the chief executioner stepped forward. In his hand he held a long, limber rod of iron, no thicker than a man's thumb. Now, slowly, lightly, with apparent grace, he began to strike the Negro, and with every blow a bone was broken.

Kit could hear the black man's low, deep-throated grunting become louder, change into a heavy moaning, until at last the man's heavy lips tore apart and he loosed his last, piteous dying screech. When they cut the cords, he was a spongelike thing, lacking entirely in rigidity, so that when the soldiers picked him up he folded over in their grip like a dummy stuffed with cloth.

The hot tears stung and tore at Kit's eyelids, his face was ghost-white beneath his tan. So that was how his mother died. Suddenly, weakly, he bent down his head and retched on the earth. Bernardo put a great arm across his shoulder.

"Courage, Kit," he whispered.

The drums picked up their rolling again. This time it was different—a slow and solemn beat. Lifting his head, Kit saw a procession of friars of the Inquisition, and among them, stumbling blindly, so beaten, burned, lashed, and tortured that his bruised and branded face was almost unrecognizable—Smithers. He was not led to the gibbet; instead the friars drew him on to another structure, which up to now Kit had not noticed. It was a pole of iron girded with chains, and at its foot was a heaping pile of fagots. Kit had to grip Bernardo's shoulder hard to keep from falling. This, then, was the ultimate cruelty.

The executioner made short work of the business of binding Smithers to the upright rod. The torch was applied. The pitch-smeared fagots caught at once. The tongues of flame leaped up, caressing Smithers' bare feet. He seemed too numbed to care, but at last he stirred when the flames leaped upward to his knees. His mouth came open, and clear above the angry cackle of the fire Kit could hear the inrush of his breath as he gulped air into his lungs. His head went back, pressing against the iron pole, and the red maw of his mouth showed plainly, his lips drawn back from his yellowed teeth. But the scream never came out, for clearly, cleanly, across the square the crash of Kit's pistol sounded. The shot awakened echoes endlessly reverberating, and Smithers hung limply against the pole, a dark, spreading stain blossoming on his ragged shirt front exactly above his heart.

"Well done, Kit," Bernardo said.

There was no time for more. The outraged mob, thus cheated of its spectacle, was howling down upon them. With sword and cutlass Kit and Bernardo fought back, but there were too many. Except for the intervention of Don Luis at the head of a company of harquebusiers, they would undoubtedly have been torn limb from limb. Instead, bloody and bruised, they faced each other in the dank dungeons beneath the Tenaza, gazing up at the tiny square of light that filtered through the bars of the high window. That it was the last light they would ever see they had not the remotest doubt.

19

When Don Luis returned to his house that afternoon, there was no triumph in his stride. He walked slowly, almost dejectedly, his bearded chin sunk against his mailed chest. The executions had left him exhausted, the constant furor of the crowds had played more havoc with his nerves than he cared to admit even to himself. Luis del Toro was no longer a young man, and tomorrow's business was exceedingly distasteful to him.

Beyond the fact that the peace and serenity of his household would probably be wrecked forever after Kit's hanging, Don Luis found that he was loath to pass sentence on the young man for quite another reason. That reason seemed a curiously shameful one to him. It was simply that, try as he would, the Count could not help feeling a warm surge of love for his unlawful son.

He had fought Kit, true enough, but as one fences with a master, for the joy of the combat, watching with detachment even in the heat of battle the courage and the skill that nearly equaled his own. He had never hated as Kit had; rather his son's seamanship and courage in battle had filled him with pride. Kit's blond fairness, except for the golden tan the sun had given him, was so like that of Jeanne Giradeaux that Don Luis, looking at him, felt again a nostalgic sadness, remembering his youth. He had wronged the mother; must he now kill the son?

No, it would not be easy to hang Kit, yet what else could he do? The boy was indisputably a pirate, with many sinkings and pillagings charged against him. Perhaps he should be glad that Kit's simple dignity would assure his dying well.

As he entered his wife's room, he was a little surprised to find that she was fully dressed and calmly awaiting him. He had expected to find her prostrate, far gone in hysteria. She came forward to meet him, her face still and composed, with something regal in her stride.

"Is it true that he is taken?" she asked quietly.

"Yes," Don Luis growled, "and truer still that tomorrow he hangs."

Bianca studied his face, an expression in her eyes like that of one who gazes through bars at a caged and loathsome beast.

"Then he has already stood trial?" she said.

"No. Not until tonight, but the result is inevitable—he will be sentenced to be hanged."

Again that curiously cold stare.

"And you, as president of the Audencia, will of course preside?"

"Yes," Don Luis said. "Why?"

"Because you will take steps to see that he is not hanged," Bianca said calmly.

"And if I do not?"

"You want a son, my lord. If Kit dies, you will never again so much as touch me!"

Don Luis stared at her, his dark face heavy with frowning. "I believe," he said evenly, "that I have some control over that."

"You are mistaken, Luis. If you think you can force me, be warned. The instant Kit strangles on the gibbet, I will take my own life!"

"You wouldn't dare!" Don Luis thundered.

"Would I not?" Bianca whispered. "Since you are so determined to take his life, I will even precede him—now!"

Don Luis sprang forward in one great feline bound, his fingers closing on her wrist. He twisted cruelly so that the small vial that she had raised to her lips was turned upside down and the pale-green liquid spilled out, a drop or two falling on one of the roses that stood in a vase on the table. Before the Count's astonished eyes the flower began to wither, to droop—in half a minute more it was brown and sere.

"That is how I will die," Bianca whispered. "And you can't prevent me. I have twenty of these vials hidden about the house, and you'll never find them. So, my lord, if I am anything to you, you will spare him. If you say the fatal words you are condemning two—not one."

Don Luis studied the pale face of his wife, his own expressionless, but thoughts moved swiftly through his mind. He knew already that he was defeated; it remained for him only to retreat as gracefully as possible, and to extract what concessions he could from the situation.

"What if I do spare him?" he suggested dryly.

Bianca's dark eyes leaped. "You will find me from now on a good and dutiful wife," she whispered, "in all things."

Don Luis's mouth curved into a slow smile brimming with self-mockery. "My humblest thanks," he said, bowing his head in a burlesque of servility, "for your graciousness, my lady Countess. Now, if you will excuse me, I must return to the Casa Real."

With fear-constricted heart, Bianca watched him stride away. Kit's fate was in the hands of this man of tremendous pride, and only God and the Virgin knew what the outcome might be. Slowly Bianca turned back to her private altar and sank down on her knees.

Don Luis wasted little time on self-pity as he rode through the streets of Cartagena. He had reached an age and a degree of wisdom when such thoughts become superfluities. The business at hand occupied his whole mind. How, indeed, was his son to be saved? It was only because Kit had admitted that he was captain of the *Seaflower* that the *oidores* bothered to go through the formality of a trial. As he toyed with the question, Don Luis came upon the only answer. The gaolkeeper and the torturer of the Tenaza must be brought in to testify. It had been more than a year since the *Seaflower* had engaged in piracy. Don Luis was almost certain that there was no one in Cartagena except himself who had suffered looting at Kit's hands. The *Seaflower* had never, so far as he knew, ventured into these waters before. Therefore the whole defense must turn upon the fact that Kit was not aboard the *Seaflower* when she had attacked the plate ship, that the attack had been contrary to his orders. The little Parisian pirate had testified under duress that Kit's sole purpose in Cartagena was to visit a former sweetheart.

Don Luis made a wry face at the thought. Fortunately, the Parisian had either not known or had failed to reveal the name of the woman involved. That secret might yet be kept. Even the stiff-necked *oidores,* being Spaniards, were inclined to be charitable toward young love. Yes, such indeed would be the defense of his bastard son.

What troubled him was the fact that the same defense was also applicable to the Jew. Don Luis would have been delighted to torture Bernardo to death, but try as he would his logical mind kept reminding him that to condemn Bernardo Díaz was to tear holes in the argument that he was preparing for Kit's defense. Besides, here in the New World, the question of Judaism was rarely raised, the Jews being so few in number that no one could convincingly make a menace of them. There were even grandees so long away from Spain and young hidalgos born in the New World who had no anti-Jewish bias at all. Don Luis knew that while in Madrid or Seville it would have been possible to put Bernardo to death on the ground that his conversion was false, these Peruvian *oidores* would accept it at its face value.[1] No, regrettable as it seemed to him, Bernardo too must be permitted to live.

When Bernardo and Kit were led into the Casa Real, manacled at wrist and ankle and flanked fore and aft by helmeted and cuirassed soldiers, they presented a sorry spectacle. Ragged, begrimed, their faces marred with the dried smears of their own blood and the greenish purple of their many bruises, they contrasted strangely with the dignified *oidores* and their president.

Lifting his head, Kit stared coolly, almost insolently, into the face of Don Luis, holding his eyes so long that the Count flushed under the heavy weight of his judicial wig. Don Luis was seated on a dais, high above the rest of the court. From it he had upon one occasion defied the Viceroy himself and had won. Now, looking down into the icy-blue eyes of his natural son, even his lofty position was of no aid to him. He felt that he

[1] In the seventeenth century the Viceroyalty of Peru included all of Spanish South America. The Viceroyalty of New Spain (Mexico) included all of Mexico and Central America. Later, about 1718, the region we now call Colombia became a viceroyalty under the name of New Granada, but in Don Luis's time the citizens of Cartagena and Bogotá were considered Peruvians.

himself was on trial, that this tall, blond lion cub and the ragged Jew were weighing his fate rather than he theirs.

With a nod, he signaled to the clerk of the court to begin. Slowly the man began to read out the charges. To Don Luis's relief, they were few. Cristóbal Gerado and his mate, Bernardo Díaz, were accused of having unlawfully and willfully entered the waters of Cartagena in search of loot; of having committed the high crime of piracy; of having taken Spanish gold; and of having killed an Englishman who was being burned at the stake.

No reference, Don Luis noted, was made to Kit's former career. Indeed, he was little known in this part of the New World. In common with most pirates, he had allowed his prey to sail almost to his own doorstep before attacking them. Whatever was known of Kit's exploits was merely hearsay and rumor in Cartagena. Don Luis stared down at Kit, and in spite of himself a warm feeling of pride came over him. The erect boldness of Kit's carriage, the look of defiance on his face, his princely grace—all these had their effect. Perhaps he was growing senile, Don Luis told himself, but the emotion persisted.

Kit was, Don Luis mused, after all of good blood. The best of France and Spain flowed in his veins. This was not a peon or a slave, his very arrogance was lordly. . . . Suddenly Don Luis shook himself. He realized that the court was waiting for him to speak. He sighed.

"You have heard the charges," he said to Kit and Bernardo. "What is your plea?"

"Not guilty!" Kit snapped at him, and Bernardo repeated the words.

"You will tell the court," Don Luis instructed him, "why you entered Spanish waters."

Kit looked up into Don Luis's dark face. His lips curled in a mocking smile under the begrimed blond mustache. It would give me joy to tell you, he thought, but it's no concern to these others. No, I will not mention her name if it costs me my life. . . .

"My reasons," he said at last, speaking coolly, "are my own affair."

The viceregal prosecutor was on his feet now, his face dark with fury. "How dare you lie to this court?" he roared. "You came here to pillage and murder."

"Such was not my intent," Kit said quietly.

"You lie!" the prosecutor thundered. "As evidence there is your ship, sunk outside this harbor."

Don Luis looked at the young *oidor* appointed to defend Kit. As was usual in such cases, the man was distinguished only by his ineptitude. He sighed again and rapped with his mace.

"If the learned doctors and you, Prosecutor Godoy, will forgive me this irregularity," he said mildly, "I should like to point out that Captain Gerado speaks the truth."

The silence that followed this announcement was as profound as death. Bernardo turned to Kit, his dark eyes goggling.

Don Luis was continuing. "His Royal Majesty has often declared that these courts would temper their justice with mercy. In this matter there is little need even for that, for though I have hanged many a rogue, it is beyond my province to condemn a man for the folly of falling in love."

"If His Excellency pleases . . ." Prosecutor Godoy blustered.

Don Luis lifted a calm hand.

"Hear me out, caballeros," he said. "As many of you know, I have my own private sources of information. In this case they corroborate the captain's statement."

"If His Excellency would be so good as to elaborate," the prosecutor sneered.

"Gladly," Don Luis said. "Guards, summon the turnkey and the torturer of the Tenaza."

The court settled back to wait. The delay was short, for Don Luis had summoned the men before the trial, and they awaited their call in an anteroom. Under his skillful prodding, they told their story briefly, but well. At its conclusion the prosecutor was in a fury.

"Would you have us believe," he demanded, "that these villains were not aboard the ship, that they were on a peaceful errand, and that the crew mutinied in their absence?"

Don Luis bowed his head. "Such is indeed the case," he said simply.

Godoy controlled himself with an effort. "Might I be permitted to inquire," he rasped, his voice filled with biting sarcasm, "what interest my lord has in the case?"

"To see justice done," Don Luis said serenely.

"Justice!" Godoy shrieked. "He brings his lying hirelings and calls it justice! Why are you shielding this man, my lord Count?"

Don Luis stood up, towering on the dais. "I think," he said, his voice cold and deadly, his words glinting like steel being slowly withdrawn from a scabbard, "that the learned prosecutor exceeds his intent. Surely he does not intend to question *my* integrity?"

Godoy's knees turned to water suddenly. He was staring at that moment into the naked face of death.

"No, no," he protested, "it is only that the strangeness of it all . . ."

Don Luis waved his words aside. "In order to see justice done," he said slowly, "I shall forget your impertinence. I see here in this court the captain of the *Garza*. He is, I believe, an appointee of yours, my good Señor Godoy, sent by you to me not two weeks ago, when my own captain was sick with the fever. You believe him to be a truthful man?"

"Yes," Godoy said stoutly. "He is a man of honor!"

"Many of the *oidores* present heard his report to me," Don Luis said calmly, "but for the sake of the record I will have him repeat it. Captain Hernando, take the oath."

After the ceremony was over, the stout hidalgo stood at his ease before the court.

"Who was in command of that brigantine," Don Luis asked him, "when you fired on her?"

"The black-bearded Englishman," Hernando answered calmly. "I watched the whole thing through my glass. Of these two I saw no sign."

"Might they not have been below?" Godoy demanded.

"During a battle?" Hernando growled. "Any captain that did that would have his gullet slit by his crew within an hour. In my opinion they were not aboard."

"I don't care for your opinion," Godoy snapped. "Facts are what I want."

As if in answer to this testy remark, there was a sudden confusion at the door. Two of the guards raced outside. A moment later one of them returned. Bowing low to Don Luis, he craved the court's pardon.

"My lord, there is a woman outside who claims knowledge bearing on this case," he added nervously. Don Luis's dark face grayed. He was sure, beyond reasonable chance of doubt, who the woman was—Bianca. Bianca, the anguished murmur ran through his heart. What manner of man was this bastard of his that he could make her fling down her shame like a gauge before all the world? His concern at the moment was not for himself but entirely for his wife, who was prepared to brand herself an adulteress publicly if she could save Kit's life.

"I do not see," he began weakly, but Godoy had seen the naked pain in his eyes.

"Bring her in!" the prosecutor squealed triumphantly.

The guards disappeared through the door. When they returned Don Luis, who had been standing, sank weakly into his high-backed chair. The woman who was being led in by the guards was an ancient crone of a fishwife whom he had never seen before in his life.

"If you will be so kind as to take the oath, my good woman," he said with relief.

"That I will, my lord!" the woman squeaked. "Truth will out! I just want to say . . ."

"The oath!" Godoy barked.

The old crone raised her right hand and swore with calm conviction.

"Now," Don Luis asked gently, "what is it?"

"This pretty *niño* is innocent! Wasn't even on that boat. Stood alongside me while the fighting was going on, and when the little ship was sunk he cried."

"You are sure, grandmother?" Godoy demanded.

"Find me another such! Find me another *muchacho* with God's own gold on his head! Wasn't sure it was real. I didn't know hair could be that color. Why, yesterday when I saw him again, just afore he shot the Englishman, I was trying to feel it."

Don Luis bowed his head. How like a woman to mingle evil with good! True, she had saved Kit's life, but she had also reminded the court of the one remaining charge on which they could hold him. He felt very tired suddenly, and totally unprepared for the ordeal that awaited him.

As for Kit, he scarcely heard the remainder of his trial. His mind was a seething tumult of confusion as he tried to fathom the reason for Don Luis's having come so valiantly to his defense. Twice now this had happened, twice now this proud and violent grandee had spared his life. Why? In the name of God and the Virgin, why?

The trial lasted for hours. Godoy argued that Kit had killed a man in cold blood, for which the penalty was death. Don Luis replied that the man was a member of Kit's crew and that his death might be regarded as a fitting punishment for mutiny. Besides, rightfully, it was a matter that concerned only the English courts, as Kit had harmed no subject of the Viceroyalty of Peru.

He had balked the Inquisition in the rightful performance of its duty, the prosecutor insisted. This was indeed blasphemy.

All right, Don Luis said mockingly, to the lesser charge of blasphemy he would agree, but not to murder, for if the slaying of heretics was murder, he himself would have been hanged a hundred times.

This shot was a telling one. The *oidores* roared with laughter. The nonplused prosecutor had to swallow his pride and sit idly by while Don Luis sentenced Kit to six years at hard labor on the walls of the still uncompleted fortress of San Lázaro. Bernardo drew four years for aiding and abetting Kit.

As the court was dismissed and the prisoners were being led away, the sound of hoofbeats rang through the dark street. As the horse thundered around the corner, kicking up a small shower of mud, Don Luis recognized the rider. The premonition that had tortured him just before the guards had admitted the old lady had indeed proved to be true. Bianca sat on the racing animal.

At the risk of his limbs, Don Luis charged to the middle of the street and caught hold of the bridle. The beast reared, almost unseating Bianca, but Don Luis's tremendous arms fought him down again until he stood glistening with sweat and trembling all over in the light of the torches.

"Wait!" Bianca cried. "He must not be hanged! He is innocent! I can testify . . ."

Don Luis caught her cruelly by the arm and jerked her from the side-saddle, catching her as she fell. One great hand closed like a vise over her small mouth. Out of the corner of his eye he could see the exultant gleam leaping in Godoy's eyes. The man's thoughts could almost be read aloud: So, you cuckold! Of course you were sure of his innocence! You had your wife's confession to prove it. . . .

Don Luis sighed heavily. A hired assassin would cost him dearly, but he could not fan the flame of gossip by openly challenging the prosecutor. Of them all, he was sure, only Godoy had got the point. The rest stood there staring with open mouths, unable to conjecture the reasons for his actions.

"You are late, my Bianca," he whispered. "The lad is already saved. There is no need for your testimony." Then, very gently, he released her.

Bianca stood there, the red ridges of the grip of his fingers showing clearly on her white face.

"My wife has been very ill, gentlemen," Don Luis said quietly. "I hope that none of you will misinterpret this outburst. It is, I assure you, due entirely to overwrought nerves. Come, Bianca. . . . Come, *mi carissima.*"

He had spoken softly, but the underlying menace of his tone was unmistakable. He saw Godoy's face pale beneath the torch he held in his hand. A slow smile stole over Don Luis's dark countenance. Good! he mused, it would perhaps not be necessary to go to the trouble of hiring an assassin after all.

He helped Bianca to mount and swung himself into the saddle of his own horse. As they rode away, he could not resist watching her face. He knew that she would turn and look back at Kit, but he had thought that he himself would maintain his pride. But the look on Bianca's face unmanned him; slowly he swung in the saddle and followed her tender, anguished gaze.

Afterward he was sorry. Kit had stood there in his chains like a young god. For all the dried blood on his face, the tattered rags of his clothing, the mud and dirt matted into his blond hair and beard, he was still as slim and graceful as Mercury, as broad of shoulder and great of thew as a young Hercules. This one, Don Luis knew, would never bow. This one could never be defeated.

Perhaps, he thought bitterly, I should have had him hanged, after all. Then, touching his spurs to the horse's side, he thundered away in the darkness. After a moment, Bianca followed him.

20

Lady Jane Golphin sat in her garden under the shade of a wine palm. A ray of afternoon sunlight stole through the overhanging palm fronds and fell on her hair so that it blazed as bright as a brush fire. She sat very still with her slim white hands folded in her lap, though now and again she unclasped her fingers and toyed with the rich stuff of her dress, cunningly chosen to point up the matchless sea-green of her oddly slanted eyes.

At the moment, her face was pensive and sad, for her eyes rested on the rank weeds and sawgrass that had grown up in the burnt-out area where the manor of her plantation had stood. A new manor stood behind the garden in which she sat now, one larger and lovelier than the old. But the gaunt blackened rafters standing among the skyward-reaching bamboo shoots still remained to taunt her. She could have had them torn down; even now she did not understand the curiously elegiac mood that had caused her to leave them standing.

So has my life been, she mused. These charred timbers shall be its monument. . . .

After a moment, she turned and gazed at the white-painted exterior of her new home. It contained every comfort and luxury that money could buy, and yet, oddly, she hated it. There had been some question in Port Royal about the source of the money that had enabled her to rebuild so quickly and lavishly after the disastrous French attack from which most of the planters had not even now fully recovered. But there was always some question about Lady Jane Golphin. That a lady of her great beauty, culture, and many accomplishments had not yet married was a perennial topic of discussion at tea parties. Not even the most feline gossip of them all could deny the fact that she had suitors aplenty. That she had not yet wed was plainly through her own choice. Earlier, the most furious of speculations revolved about the matter of her frequent disappearances. On this score, the rumors had been as conflicting as they had been wild. One of the most popular had it simply and comprehensively that the lady was a witch, and disappeared to consort with her master, the Devil.

The more sophisticated gentry rejected this, of course. Yet even they were not able to come up with a more enlightening theory. But during the last year this peculiar habit of vanishing had apparently palled upon her, for since the early spring of 1695 Lady Jane had remained very quietly at home, supervising the reconstruction of her plantation.

Now, July fifth of that same year, all the work was done. The tall cane grew up in her rich fields, nodding all together with every passing wind. Her slaves were fat and glossy black and very well treated. Unlike the sullen demeanor so often noted among the workers on neighboring plantations, the servitors of Lady Jane Golphin often sang as they worked. Whatever the source of her mysterious wealth, it was apparent that she was growing richer by the season. This fact spurred on her suitors to redoubled activity, though it was not to be denied that many among them who were as wealthy as she sought her for herself alone.

She turned her head from the house and stared down the drive that led for two arrow-straight miles up to the manor. She leaned forward in her chair. Would God, she thought, that as little distance separated me from him I love. . . .

She straightened, frowning. On the sea in unclear weather, a distance less than that would be enough to make her miss Kit forever. Finding a needle in a haystack was child's play to finding a vessel whose course she did not know—course, or whereabouts, or base of supply.

Base of supply! She sprang up suddenly, her fingers gripping the flesh of her fair throat. Fool and daughter of fools! Why had she not thought of that before? Kit had sailed with Ducasse from Saint-Domingue! And among other things disclosed at the trial from which he had barely escaped with his life was the fact that he bore allegiance to the King of France! Where else then would he base if not at Saint-Domingue? Martinique? Guadeloupe? Saint-Christophe? These were possibilities, but Kit had been with Ducasse, and Ducasse was Governor of Saint-Domingue.

Already she was running hard toward the house. Now, finally, she would have her answer. Saint-Domingue lay across the channel, scarce a hundred leagues away. No more would she sit and brood in an empty garden, no more would she beat the trackless sea. Now, if God were willing, and French gallantry toward women—even women of their enemies—were unchanged, she could wait very quietly in the very port of call to which Kit Gerado must sometime return! The very thought made her almost sick with joy.

Inside her bedroom, she pulled off her garments in such savage haste that they tore in several places. Then, entirely naked and shivering from anticipation, she raced to a locked chest. Her fingers were clumsy with the key, and it was several seconds before she got it open. With true feminine lack of logic she took from it first a pair of barbaric earrings, great heavy circles of gold. Then, removing the dainty rosettes of pearl that so demurely adorned her ear lobes, she fastened the heavy hoops in her ears, standing slim and flower-petal white before her mirror, lithe-limbed, slender, soft-curving, like a sea nymph rising from the foam.

About the bright blaze of her red hair she wound a blood-red kerchief, and then only did she slip into the tattered shirt that clung about her bosom like a second skin, and the abbreviated trousers that, thin as she was, required an effort to draw on.

She was still barefooted when the trusted slave whom she had had summoned by her maidservant knocked on her door. He was admitted. Three minutes later, he scampered down the stairs, raced to the stables, and saddled two of the finest, swiftest horses. As Lady Jane drew on her jack-boots and hung her cutlass about her handspan of a waist, the slave was already thundering away in the direction of Port Royal. There he would move among the lowest dives of the water front. He would bend and whisper into a hairy ear and a strolling wench would be unseated suddenly as a bearded seaman rose to his feet and dumped her unceremoniously from his lap. He would murmur a few low words and a card game would end instantly with no question of stakes or winnings. He would raise a beckoning finger and half the tables of a grog-seller's inn would be suddenly deserted. Then he would steal out into the night, and a motley crew of the most villainous ruffians who ever cut a purse, or a throat, would materialize like shadows from Hades and creep silently after him. Knowing these things, Jane Golphin smiled.

"Ah, Kit, my Kit," she breathed. "You were with this Ducasse once. Pray God you are with him now."

She raced down the stairs to where the saddled horse waited, and pounded away toward that hidden cove where the *Gull* lay, tugging impatiently at her hawsers.

It took His Excellency Jean-Baptiste, the Sieur Ducasse, some little time to fathom the cause of the uproar that burst so suddenly on his peaceful realm some five days later.

"A woman, you say?" he growled. "What's that? An *English*-woman! Then she's a spy. Take her out and hang her directly!"

The captain of the guard smiled quietly. "I fear," he said suavely, "that if I were to hang so beautiful a woman, His Excellency himself might later call me to task for my impetuosity."

Ducasse looked up, a merry twinkle creeping into his little blue eyes. "Beautiful, eh?" he mused. "The English are not fools. Do you think they'd send an old crow to peck at us? No, *mon capitaine,* a swan would serve their purpose much better, knowing our well-deserved reputation in such matters."

The captain bowed. "A swan, your Excellency?" he said. "I assure you they have sent a bird of paradise!"

Ducasse allowed a bass chuckle to escape his lips. "That being the case, *mon capitaine,*" he said, "perhaps it would not be beneath my dignity to examine the culprit myself."

"Your Excellency knows your duty," the captain said, smiling. "But if I may be so bold, I might suggest that not even your Excellency has many such opportunities to wed duty with pleasure."

"You turn a nice phrase," Ducasse grunted. "Where is she?"

"Outside in the anteroom, awaiting your Excellency's pleasure."

"Then show her in, man! Show her in at once!"

The Sieur Ducasse had time for one quick pat at a stray curl of his enormous wig before Rouge entered his office. She was clad in a dress of green velvet, and a hat of the same material ornamented with peacock feathers. At once she swept down in a curtsy that would have been noteworthy even at the court of St. James. Courtier that he was, man of the world, Ducasse was for the moment completely nonplused. Then he recovered.

"We are honored, madame," he said in English. "That your masters had such respect for our taste as to send one of your beauty is indeed flattering."

Rouge smiled. "No one sent me, my lord," she said quietly. "I came of my own free will upon a most private errand."

Ducasse shook his head with heavy gravity. "I am, madame," he said, "as bemused by your loveliness as you could well expect—but not so bemused as to believe so transparent a fabrication."

Rouge stiffened. Her small head lifted on the snowy column of her neck, and her green eyes gazed fearlessly into the face of the Governor.

"If you will hear me out . . ." she said clearly.

Ducasse inclined his massive head with all the civility in the world. "To listen to your voice is a pleasure," he said. "It is as lovely as your fair person. Please continue."

"You have, do you not, among your subjects a young captain called Christopher Gerado?"

"Christophe!" Ducasse exclaimed. "But certainly! How do you know of him? Tell me." He stopped suddenly, awed by the great joy leaping and blazing in Rouge's eyes.

"Where is he?" she whispered. "Tell me, my lord! Lead me to him and you will give me back my life!"

"He is not here," Ducasse said, "but Petit Goave is his home port, and to it he often returns."

"Then I will wait," Rouge exulted. "Even if it is a hundred years, I will wait his return!"

Ducasse studied the small, lovely face with great care. "And what," he demanded, "makes you think that I shall permit you, an enemy subject, to remain in my territory?"

Rouge swept out an imploring hand. "Please, my lord," she said, with tears in her eyes, "do not send me away. If you think I have come to do you harm, imprison me—gladly will I submit to it. But do not send me away. . . . I love him so. Without him I shall die or go mad. . . . Have you never been in love?"

Slowly, softly, Ducasse smiled. "No, child," he said, "I shall not send you back, for already you have seen too much, and your masters would profit by the knowledge. Nor will I imprison you. I shall assign you a house in the town, and there you may stay until Christophe returns. He is a good lad, and much do I love him. I think, if you speak the truth, you may bring him happiness."

"You—you think I lie about this?"

Ducasse shook his head. "Either," he said crossly, "you are the world's finest actress, or you speak the truth. I cannot decide. Nor can I take chances. Our countries, unfortunately, are still at war. Therefore I must quarter guards with you, and keep this crew of yours under close watch."

Rouge bowed her head submissively.

"These guards," added Ducasse, chuckling, "will be men above seventy, for none younger would I trust to keep their hands off you. I must ask you to respect their old bones and not elude them. Have I your promise?"

"You have more, my lord," said Rouge, laughing, "you have my heartfelt thanks!" Then suddenly she went up on tiptoe and kissed him lightly on the mouth.

His Excellency's naturally florid complexion turned beet-red. "Captain!" he roared. The captain of the guard appeared and saluted. "Take this woman," Ducasse spluttered, "to the house that lies vacant in the Fifth Square—and be quick about it, for I fear I am bewitched!"

He stood there a long time after Rouge had gone, and gradually his face resumed its natural hue. Then the corners of his mouth crept upward into a low smile.

"Jean-Baptiste," he told himself, "you're a sentimental old fool—praised be all the saints!"

21

THE FORTRESS OF San Lázaro was designed to be the most imposing military structure in the entire Viceroyalty of Peru.[1] However, in July of 1695, when Kit and Bernardo were thrown into its prison camp, it was less than half completed. In one week, whatever feeling of gratitude they may have felt toward Don Luis for sparing their lives had vanished. The Count, they now believed, had merely considered hanging too kind a fate.

From so early in the morning that the stars still hung in the sky until so late in the evening that the moon had reappeared Kit and Bernardo worked on the walls of the fortress. During the day the sun shone above their heads and smote them, its glare so bright that all the sea and the land swam in a white-gold haze that took the edges off everything, so that sky and cove and slow-moving white sails on the bay had a curious indistinctness of outline, as though they were not quite real.

To view them with heat-stricken, bloodshot eyes did not help their clarity. Often, they danced crazily before the sight as the oxhide whips of the Spanish guards came down on their bare backs, the long, loaded lashes curling around their trunks so that even their bellies were striped. Their backs and shoulders were a mass of crisscrossed sores above which the *colorojes* buzzed endlessly. Even Kit soon learned to groan when he was struck, for if the soldiers did not hear a cry, they considered the blow too light and repeated it. It was hard to tell which part of the day was the worst. In the morning, in the soft-slumbering tropic dark, they worked in the quarry, bending and lifting the jagged stones until their hands were bloody masses that somehow healed and somehow managed to keep on moving. During the day the blinding heat was added to their other burdens.

They put the quarried stones in the oxcarts, groaning as their biceps and belly muscles knotted and protested, bending, lifting, the whole world a shifting haze of sweat-blurred agony, their bodies one long ache from sole to crown. They lifted stones that no one man should have been able to lift, the sinews of their loins threatening to tear loose, backs bowed, shoul-

[1] Now called the fortress of San Felipe de Barájas, it still stands in perfect preservation between the hill of the Popa and the old city. Completed in 1752, after nearly a hundred years of work, it cost 11,000,000 pesos and uncounted human lives.

ders ridged, thigh and calf thrusting upward against the inert mass, the thick hot stench of sweat and filth and fresh blood unnoticed in their nostrils, their momentarily superhuman strength begotten by the whistling, white-hot agony of the oxhide whips and foaled by the fury of their own impotent rage.

Then they would make their way to the fortress, totter on bare feet over the cobblestones and up into the hills, pushing against the clumsy wheels of the carts when they were stuck in the black mud—an event which happened with monotonous regularity—while the whips of the Spaniards sang through the air and curled about their bare backs, bringing blood. By now the cool darkness was gone, to be replaced by the merciless furnace heat of the sun.

They spread mortar and lifted the roughhewn stones into place. With hammer and chisel they chipped them into some semblance of squareness. For the most part, they worked without any gear or tackle. The helmeted soldiers, sweating under their heavy breastplates, were not disposed to be kind. The human cattle they drove were far cheaper than mules and oxen, and far easier to replace. The Chibchas, brought down from the cool blue reaches of their native mountains, felt it worst. They would have died even without the added burden of their labors. Week by week, it was necessary to replace the entire group of Indian slaves, who perished to a man under the blows of the sun and the whistling crack of the Spanish lashes.

Finally, the captain general in charge of the engineers gave it up. After all, his primary purpose was to build a fortress to protect the landward approaches, not to slaughter Indians. It was efficiency, not mercy, that moved him. He requested the governor of the province to give him a working force of Negroes. His request was promptly granted, for the fear of attack was a phobia in Cartagena. After that the work went better.

To the blacks, the mere eighty degrees of heat was as nothing. So well did they work that the captain general was inspired to grant them the same consideration that he extended toward his blooded Andalusian stallion—they, after all, were valuable animals, far more useful than the political prisoners and the Chibcha scum. He ordered his guards to use the whips sparingly, and doubled the Negroes' rations. It was this fact that saved Kit's and Bernardo's lives in the early days of their imprisonment.

Bernardo, being a man of immense goodwill, did not draw apart from the Negroes as did the other political prisoners. He moved among the blacks, talked with them in pidgin Spanish, laughed with them, attended to their illnesses, and gradually broke down their suspicions. In an unbelievably short time, he had won their trust—even more, their love. The affection they felt toward the little padre—for so they had come to call him—manifested itself in sharing their rations with him. Bernardo in turn shared with Kit. As a result, they lived. The other political prisoners died. By April of 1696, Kit and Bernardo were the only white prisoners left in the fortress. Even the guards had come to regard them as fixtures, and beat them almost as seldom as they did the Negroes.

The blacks trusted Kit too, but they never learned to love him. Kit was taciturn, not given to wordiness and display of emotion. At night he sat with Bernardo among the blacks in the prison camp inside the uncompleted walls of the fortress, but he said little, for his thoughts were far away. Neither he nor Bernardo was healthy; even with the gifts of the Negroes they lingered on the verge of starvation. Though in many places Kit's bones were outlined through his flesh, his muscular development approached that of Bernardo's, and where Bernardo's great strength was confined to his upper trunk, Kit had become a young Hercules, although a sadly starved one.

The problem of escape occupied his every waking thought. The tales of the buccaneers ran through his mind, a thousand stories of escape stirred in his memory. Kit tried. With a stolen chisel, he and Bernardo worked for four months to loosen the stones through a six-foot section of wall. They were discovered within two feet of freedom, and beaten almost to death. It was three weeks before they could even stand. Upon another occasion they made a break from the quarry, but a harquebusier put a ball through Bernardo's thigh.

Bernardo, Kit realized, would now be lame for life. To escape, Kit would have to leave his old friend, and that was unthinkable. As a result, he settled deeper into gloom and hopelessness. To make it worse, the dungeons beneath the fortress were now completed. As dangerous prisoners, Kit and Bernardo were locked in one of the new cells, and manacled to the walls with long chains. True, the Negroes now and again managed to slip food to them, but they were rapidly losing their last reserves of strength. Bearded, filthy, infested with vermin, they resembled nothing human, and the light in Kit's eyes was close to madness.

So it was that when the captain of the guard approached their cell one night in 1696 and announced a visitor, Kit refused to credit the man's words. Five minutes later he hung against the iron bars, looking like a blond ape, his face half-hidden in the golden sweaty tangle of his great beard, his matted, filthy mane covering his bare shoulders. Outside in the corridor Bianca stood, wrapped in her cloak, unable to speak because of the gasping flood of her sobs.

She had brought with her a basket of food. She passed the fine bread and wine and cheese and fruit through the bars, unable to force her shocked tongue to utter a syllable. As she stood there watching Kit wolfing down the food like a great beast, the stench from the cell beat sickeningly about her head. To this had her lover come—more animal than man, his grace and courtliness gone, his tongue so thickened by thirst and silence that when he spoke his formerly liquid Castilian was a guttural growl that sounded scarcely human.

"Bianca," he muttered.

"Kit," she wept, "Kit! Oh my God, what have they done to you?"

A slow smile moved amid the matted tangle of mustache and beard. "They have not broken me," Kit said slowly. "I am happy to see you. Nothing else matters."

Bianca's white hands reached between the bars and grasped his. She clung to him, going up on tiptoe so that her small mouth could reach through the bars, and kissed his bearded face. Bernardo, seated in order to favor his newly lamed leg, got up painfully and turned his back as he ate. At last Kit pushed her away.

"Don't add to my torment, Bianca," he said softly.

Bianca stood shuddering against the bars and the tips of her slim fingers traced the lines of half-healed stripes with a tenderness that was almost pain.

"You must escape," she whispered. "You must be freed!"

Kit shrugged hopelessly. "We've already made a dozen attempts," he said. "They have come to nothing. This place is too new and far too well guarded. If we were at the Boca Chica, we might have fled to the jungle that lies so near, and the sea is even closer. Old Don Sancho Jimeno and his garrison of ancient harquebusiers could not stop us." He sighed heavily. "But we are here. And here, I fear, we will one day die."

Bianca's pale face was radiant suddenly. "You will be transferred there!" she said. "So small a thing I can accomplish easily."

Kit's face darkened. Bianca saw the stricken look of jealousy flare suddenly in his eyes.

"No, Kit," she said gently. "Don't trouble yourself with such thoughts. I will have to make no new sacrifices."

Kit gazed at her, his face bleak and frowning. "Bernardo goes with me," he warned, "or I don't go."

"Very well," said Bianca with a smile. "You can have your precious friend—of whom I am sometimes jealous."

Bernardo turned around to grin wickedly at her. "I fear," he croaked, "that I am a little less pretty than you."

Bianca blew him a kiss. "God bless you, Señor Bernardo," she said gently, "for the many times you have saved Kit's life."

"And you, my lady," Bernardo replied, "for your graciousness."

Bianca stretched out her arms to Kit again. "I must go now, Kit," she whispered, "but before the end of this month you will have a chance at freedom. God and the Virgin grant that you win! I could not endure life if you were dead."

"Bianca!" Kit croaked, his voice failing him.

Bianca smiled up at him, blinking back her tears.

"You must escape," she whispered. "Now kiss me, Kit. I have to go."

Kit and Bernardo listened to her footsteps dying out on the stones of the corridor. Bernardo threw an arm across Kit's shoulder.

"You're a lucky man, Kit," he said, "to have a woman like that one."

That the task she had undertaken was no light one Bianca understood as soon as she looked into the frowning face of her husband.

"You want him transferred to the Boca Chica," he mused, "and the Jew likewise. Why, Bianca?"

"Because he is dying!" she stormed. "You promised to spare him. What does it matter that he escaped the gallows if they beat him to death at San Lázaro?"

"Would he be better off at the Boca Chica, or would he merely better his chances to escape?"

"He would get better treatment. The fortress there is completed. They would not drive him like a starved and naked animal."

"So? But why the Jew?"

"Because Kit will not leave him. Consider, Luis, Kit is your son."

Don Luis smiled at her, a dark and mocking smile. "My son—and your lover. An interesting situation, eh, Bianca?"

"I love him, I don't deny that, but that anything will ever come of my love is quite another matter."

"Then nothing has yet come of it?" Don Luis mocked.

"If you mistrust me in this, it reflects only the evil of your own heart," Bianca said tartly.

Don Luis frowned. "And if he were to escape?"

"It would be the best of all solutions. He would leave this land, and you would have no further need to trouble yourself."

This, Don Luis reflected, was true—if his fair wife did not fly away with Kit. His dark face relaxed suddenly.

"Very well," he said, "it shall be arranged—on one condition."

Bianca looked at him. When she spoke, her voice was high and breathless.

"And that condition is . . . ?"

"It is this," he said, smiling. "The day that Kit reaches the Boca Chica you will go with me to Santa Marta and there consult Mendoza, who, Jew dog that he is, is still the greatest physician in all Peru. If any man can cure you of your barrenness, he can. I ordered him to come here, but he makes excuses. And the captain general, a liberal-minded fool, sustains him in this effrontery. But no matter. What do you say to that, my Bianca?"

Bianca stood there facing him, unable to hide the pain in her eyes. At last she bowed her head. "Agreed," she whispered. Then she turned very slowly and walked away.

Don Luis took his time about writing out the order for the transfer of Kit and Bernardo. It would, he knew, cause much whispered criticism and, what was worse, speculation. Don Luis cared little about criticism, but speculation was another matter. He wanted no one to question his motives. So far Godoy, the viceregal prosecutor, had held his tongue; but in the general babble of public gossip he might feel safe to let slip a few veiled innuendoes, and once loosed, the scandal would spread like wildfire. Luis del Toro was prepared to appear a scoundrel, a petty tyrant, an oppressor of the innocent, but a cuckold—never!

His dark face creased with frowns as he laboriously wrote out the message in his own bold hand. Ordinarily, he would have employed a secretary, but this was too confidential a matter to trust to outside eyes. He finished the parchment, sanded it, dripped a blob of candle wax on it, and affixed his seal. Still the matter troubled him.

As he went into the street to deliver the order—for this, too, he would not trust to anyone else—his eyes fell on the rotund figure of Don Felipe Gálvez. Don Felipe was a great trencherman, with an extravagant fondness for wine and talk. In his youth, the story ran, the list had also included women, but as his girth and senility had increased Don Felipe had had to curtail his activities in that particular. In self-defense, he attempted to make up for his failings with his waspish tongue.

As Don Luis greeted him, the ghost of an idea began to dawn. Here was one of the greatest gossips and scandalmongers in Cartagena. Why not cap the prosecutor's tale before it had even been issued? It would drown the present scandal in a much greater one, one which, oddly enough, would reflect only credit on Don Luis's own virility. He took the fat arm of Don Felipe and steered him toward the nearest inn. Don Felipe came gladly, for something about Don Luis's expression intrigued him. The Count was plainly troubled with some momentous matter and needed a sympathetic listener.

Later, over the mounds of steaming viands, the talk was slow and hesitant. Don Luis allowed himself to be drawn out, inch by inch. Yes, it was true that he was greatly troubled. There was a matter in which duty conflicted with the dictates of his heart. Here he paused to sip his wine with maddening deliberation, a far-off look in his eyes.

A woman? No. At least no woman now living. This was an old tale, and a sorry one, which he hesitated to inflict upon his friend's kindly ears. (That those ears were agog and titillating he could plainly see, but he preferred to carry the pretense ever farther.) Ah well then, he would speak out, for Don Felipe was a man of discretion and the tale would go no farther. Don Felipe assured him with a fine excess of oaths that such was indeed the case.

The matter, Don Luis sighed, concerned a prisoner now held at San Lázaro, a blond lad who had been captured as a result of the *Seaflower* incident. Don Felipe was leaning forward now, his fat lips slack, his little pig's eyes filled with curiosity.

That lad, Don Luis said, his voice dropping into a conspiratorial whisper, was related to him by blood. He was in fact a—a nephew, although an unhallowed one. The pause before the word "nephew" was deliberately prolonged. Don Felipe, the Count knew, was nobody's fool. He would make the proper substitution for that transparent "nephew." How correct he was in his judgment of Don Felipe was proved a moment later. The fat grandee fell back in his chair, slapping his thigh and roaring with laughter.

"Oh come now, Luis," and he guffawed. "Your nephew! Now, really, who do you think will believe that?"

Don Luis's face assumed an injured expression. "I know," Don Luis said slowly, "that it's hard to credit that one so fair could spring from the swart house of Del Toro. But then, you have not seen his mother." He sighed heavily.

"But you have?" Don Felipe was grinning. "Nephew—pah!"

"Your skepticism is unworthy of you," Don Luis said with a slow smile that in itself was almost an admission of Don Felipe's surmise. "The point is that I cannot permit the boy to die at San Lázaro, nor can I order him released. So I thought of your friend and mine, Don Sancho Jimeno out at the Boca Chica. Out there Cristóbal might survive, as the tasks are less arduous. Later, who knows?"

"When the matter blows over, you might procure his release, eh, Luis? And even acknowledge him—as your nephew, of course," Don Felipe added hastily.

"Yes. What do you think of it, Felipe?"

"It does you credit. I'm sure that if it came to anyone's attention—not through me, Luis, of course—it would be well understood." He stood up, a pleased smile on his oily-fat face. "Yes, I'm certain it would be understood."

So it was that Luis del Toro went on his errand with a complacent look on his face. Let the prosecutor talk. His words would not be believed after Don Felipe had begun to gossip.

Two days later Kit and Bernardo were kicked awake by their guard much earlier than usual.

"Come," the guard growled. He made no attempt at explanation, nor did they ask for any.

As they reached the prison yard, a stir of excitement began to move sluggishly through their veins, for there they were flanked by a platoon, and a kettledrum sounded. They moved through the gate and down the hill into the dense jungle, stumbling wearily. Now and then a soldier prodded them with the butt end of his pike. At last they came to the shore of the bay. A narrow bridge connected it with the city of Cartagena, but they did not go up the ramp. Instead, they were ordered into a great pirogue waiting quietly on the water.

Late in the afternoon they came to the fortress on the tip of the peninsula, the celebrated Castillo de Boca Chica, against whose stout walls Drake and Morgan had hurled their furious assaults in vain.

The prow of the pirogue bumped softly against the quay, and a helmeted soldier made it fast. Then the guards scrambled ashore, dragging Kit and Bernardo after them. On the stones beneath their feet a vast replica of the royal arms was carved. They heard the slow, rattling clank of the great chains and the creaking of oak timbers as the drawbridge was let down. It came level and they crossed over, passing under the archway into the vast stone-paved courtyard of the fortress. There Don Sancho himself was waiting for them.

Kit was surprised that Don Sancho had come to meet them, but he did not know that the grandee had spent the last week vacationing in Cartagena, where Don Luis's carefully planted story was making the rounds. The Count could have done no better if he had employed the town crier, for Don Felipe Gálvez was constitutionally incapable of keeping a secret.

Don Sancho, of course, had heard the story. Despite his seventy-odd years, he retained a lively curiosity as to human affairs. Therefore he waited under the blinding glare of the sun to greet his new prisoners. The soldiers marched Kit and Bernardo up to him. The old man, still as fierce and strong as a sea eagle, studied Kit with intensity.

"Del Toro's bastard, eh?" he growled. "It could be. You have the build and the set of the Del Toro line. Well, Cristóbal, Del Toro or not, you can expect no favors from me!"

Kit took a staggering step backward, and the walls of the fortress, broader across the top than any street in Cartagena, reeled suddenly before his eyes. Del Toro's bastard! At last the mystery of his birth was explained. This man who had taken his mother's life, who had forced himself on Rouge, who had killed his entire crew, was also his father! It could not be—the whole idea was too fantastically cruel. Yet, completely, utterly, damnably, it fitted. Why else had his mother run down those stairs to check the grandee's horse that day in Cádiz? Why else had Don Luis on two occasions spared his life? Why else had Bianca whispered, "I would not have you harm him—especially not him"? He turned a stricken face toward Bernardo, but Don Sancho was speaking again, some of the sternness gone from his tone.

"Are you ill, lad? Yes, I can see you are." Then, turning to the soldiers: "Take him to his cell and see that he is well fed. It's not my responsibility to relieve Del Toro's conscience."

Afterward, in the cool darkness of their subterranean cell, Kit faced Bernardo.

"It's true, isn't it, Bernardo?" he asked. "Why didn't you tell me before?"

"I had no proof," Bernardo said, "although I suspected it. What now, Cristóbal?"

Kit studied the dim light filtering in between the heavy iron bars. "When we're free, I'll pay him a visit. It will be the last he ever receives," Kit said evenly. "Even though he is my father, I'll not spare him!"

Bernardo picked up the earthen vessels filled with coarse wholesome food.

"Eat," he said. "You will need your strength."

22

To HIS OWN SURPRISE, Kit found that he had no immediate desire to escape from the fortress of Boca Chica. Almost a year of semistarvation, brutality, exposure, and exhaustion had had a more serious effect upon him than he realized. Not only had his body been depleted, but also his mind, his spirit and his will.

Bernardo, on the other hand, had actually toughened under the ordeal. He had seen men die before. He knew that the bravest man on earth can be reduced to a gibbering idiot by long-protracted torture skillfully applied.

He realized that there is a limit beyond which no man can be expected to go, and upon entering prison late in his forties, still bearing the scars of earlier tortures and imprisonments, he had wondered whether he would be able to endure. That he had endured, that he was yet alive and in possession of his faculties, was a source of pride to him. Moreover, he was glad that Kit did not urge an immediate attempt at escape. Every day that they waited increased their chances for success.

Don Sancho saw that they were well fed; and at the Boca Chica, manned as it was by a skeleton garrison, there was little or no work to be done. Kit and Bernardo drew water from the well, tended fires, and cleaned the barracks. Those tasks done, they had many hours of leisure in which to recover their strength and explore the situation.

Because of the location of the fortress, they were confined to their cell only during the night. In the daytime they could wander about the vast, rambling fortification as they pleased. This situation was due in part to Don Sancho's knowledge of Kit's origin. Kit found this galling, but Bernardo accepted it calmly as a valuable asset. In their spare moments they made their plans. Bernardo drew a map of the Bay of Cartagena on a scrap of parchment, indicating their own position. Looking at the map, they realized that the land about Cartagena formed a hollow circle around the bay. Behind the fortress of Boca Chica extended the arm of the Terra Bomba peninsula, a dense jungle that led only northward to the city itself.

The plan Kit devised had nothing to recommend it but its audacity. Again and again Bernardo pointed out that its chances of success were so slight as to be almost negligible. But Kit was not to be deterred.

"In a mad world," he growled, "only greater madness succeeds!"

In the end, Bernardo was forced to give in. Kit proposed to scale the walls somehow and beat northward through the Terra Bomba to the city. Once there, a knife would flash in the darkness and Don Luis would render up his account before the throne of God. Then, with gold stolen from the grandee's coffers, the girl Quita would be dispatched to buy new garments and Indian dyes, which would darken the dangerous blondness of Kit's hair and beard.

He anticipated no difficulties from Bianca. She would journey with them to the great port of Santa Marta. There the three of them could buy passage to Santo Domingo. And as that city lay on the other side of the great island of Hispaniola, whose western half was occupied by the French colony of Saint-Domingue, it would be comparatively easy to bribe a coasting hoy to set them down in French territory. A splendid plan—except that there was not one chance in a million of reaching Don Luis's house in Cartagena without being cut down by the guardia civil.

To make it worse, how were they to escape from the Boca Chica in the first place? They might dive from the walls into the sea, but in the daytime either the shots of the harquebusiers would cut them down or the swift pirogues manned by the Negroes would catch them. Their only hope lay in avoiding being returned to their cell at night. In the darkness they might be able to climb silently down the walls, slip into the black waters, and gain the shores of Terra Bomba.

Their opportunity, when it occurred, came about through the purest chance. One afternoon while Kit and Bernardo were carrying their skins of drinking water to the sentries in the little rounded towers that marked the junction points of the corners of the inward-sloping walls, one of the soldiers drew Kit aside.

He had, he told Kit, spent his two-day leave in Cartagena. While there, a beautiful Indian girl had approached him. Apparently she had questioned him most deftly, for he had casually told her all about himself. Upon learning that he was attached to the garrison of the Boca Chica, she had begged him to deliver a note to Cristóbal Gerado. What she had given him in return, Kit could guess.

Kit listened with impatience to this wordy narrative. When the soldier finally passed him the note, he tore it open and read:

My Own:

When this reaches you, I shall be far away on a journey to the city of Santa Marta with my husband, there to consult the great physician Mendoza. I do not know when I shall return—if ever.

My anguished heart cries out to you—farewell, my Cristóbal. The vows I swore when I became Luis's bride are too weighty to be set aside even for a cause as great as my love for you.

Yet if God is just, He will grant you deliverance. As for the rest, I can only wait and hope.

Ever your

Bianca

Bernardo could see Kit's expression changing as he read the note, the pallor spreading under his tan, the fire of madness leaping in his blue eyes. But even Bernardo was not prepared for what happened. In two swift strides Kit reached the wall and split the blue waters in a dive as clean as any knife. Bernardo had no choice but to follow him.

That they did not die in the first two minutes of their swim was due entirely to Don Sancho's stern orders that Kit was not to be harmed. Before they were halfway across the channel, the first of the pirogues overtook them. After staring into the gaping muzzle of a musket, Bernardo allowed himself to be pulled aboard without a struggle, but it was not until the butt end of a pike had rendered him unconscious that they dragged Kit into the boat.

When they had been returned to the fortress, they faced the captain of the guard, for Don Sancho was enjoying himself with a new Chibcha concubine in Cartagena.

"So," the captain growled. "You love water, eh, Cristóbal? Well, you shall have your fill of it! Give them the Indian treatment, my lads!"

The soldiers of the guard roared with laughter. Kit and Bernardo were marched through the stone-paved courtyard and across the drawbridge spanning the moat that surrounded the inner walls of the fort. In the middle of the bridge they were suddenly halted. They waited there in the dense heat while the captain surveyed the scene. Apparently satisfied, he ordered the march resumed. They crossed over the moat and came to the gates of the outer walls on the landward side. Through these they also passed, coming out on the sandy beach of the channel.

They marched through the wet sand until they reached a spot where the palm trees came down to the edge of the sea. The guards pushed them through the low thickets of bamboo and reed without slackening their pace. Kit saw Bernardo bend down quickly and break off some lengths of reed, receiving a blow across the buttocks for even so short a delay. They emerged from the jungle at last and Kit saw that they had made a great semicircle, for the fortress of Boca Chica lay again before them.

As they approached it, another matter came to his attention. On this side of the outer wall was no wall at all, but a natural precipice, the inner face of which had been smoothed and lined with stones so that it formed the far side of the moat. One of the guards was paying out a great coil of rope so that it went down into the moat itself. The black-bearded captain bowed to them mockingly.

"If Señor Cristóbal will be so kind as to go down . . ." he said, a pleased smile on his dark face.

Kit had no choice. Very quietly he let himself down over the edge of the artificial cliff and went down the rope hand over hand. When his feet were almost touching the green-slimed, fetid surface of the water, he realized that it was not the Spaniards' intention to drown him immediately, because there in the side of the artificial precipice a low, stone-lined tunnel opened before his gaze. He swung himself into it and released the rope. Inside it was cool and dark. There were six inches of black mud on the floor.

The significance of the mud escaped Kit at the moment. He was too busy leaning from the tunnel's mouth, craning his neck to watch Bernardo's progress down the rope. He saw at once that he had little need for worry. The curious disproportion of Bernardo's build, with its immense arms and slight lower body, made the descent even easier for him than it had been for Kit. As he came down, blocking off the light from the opening, Kit saw that he still held the slim reeds. When Bernardo had swung himself safely inside, he tossed them aside.

"Thought they were going to drown us in the moat," he growled. "A man can stay under water a long time if he has a reed to breathe through. But I think these dons have other ideas."

Before Kit had the opportunity to reply, the rope came down again. At its end a wooden bucket had been tied.

"Take it!" the captain roared down at them. "You'll need it!"

Bernardo put out his long arms and took the vessel. He studied it in some puzzlement, then his eyes fell on the oozy slime of black mud in which they sat.

"Their mothers!" he spat. "The water of the moat rises with the tide!"

He stood up as far as the low roof of the tunnel would allow and examined the sides. From the watermark, he could see that the tide rose to within eight inches of the top of the tunnel. They would have to stand in a hunched-over position all night to keep their nostrils above the level of the surface. If they bailed with the bucket, they might be able to keep the water level a little lower. This, then, was the Indian treatment.

Without a word, Kit began to crawl toward the interior of the tunnel. About ten yards farther on it sloped downward a little, and here even at low tide there was a pool about eight feet deep. It was far too dark at this point to locate the watermarks, but Kit guessed that the tide came up here to within three or four inches of the roof. He swam across the pool and climbed out on the other side, but after twenty yards his journey ended abruptly, for the tunnel was closed off by a wall of stones.

Kit sat down weakly in the mud, feeling tears of frustration rising behind his eyelids. After a moment the fierce resolve that had possessed him since he had received Bianca's note came back. He turned and began the swim across the pool.

"It has no opening," he said calmly, "so we must think of another method."

Slowly, painfully, they returned to the mouth of the tunnel. Kit sat very still, his mind busy. At last his blue eyes cleared.

"If," he said to Bernardo, "the waters of the moat rise with the tide, there must be some connection between them and the sea!"

Bernardo looked at him. Then he nodded slowly. "There must be," he said, "but we must wait for night to look for it."

As night approached, the water began to rise in the tunnel until they sat in it up to their waists. Patiently, they waited until the edges of the tunnel's mouth were no longer discernible, till all was blackness without and within.

Silently, Kit waded through breast-high water and let himself down into the green-slimed moat. He began his slow, silent swim.

Bernardo followed, going in the opposite direction. Every few minutes they sank down and groped with their fingers along the outer walls. With half-hour intervals of rest, forced upon them by pure exhaustion, they kept this up all night. At the first flush of dawn, they were forced to admit defeat. If a passageway through the walls existed, they had not been able to find it.

They made their way back to the tunnel and entered it. The tide was receding now, so that once again they were able to sit. They had been there no longer than an hour when they heard the soldiers calling down to them:

"Had enough bathing, caballeros?"

Bernardo started forward, but Kit caught his arm. "Don't answer!"

"Say something, you stubborn swine!" the captain roared. "Don't force us to come down for you."

Bernardo watched in some mystification as Kit groped about in the water with his hand. A moment later, Kit gave a low grunt of triumph, for his fingers had come up holding the reeds.

"Come," he whispered and began to move away from the mouth of the tunnel. They reached the edge of the subterranean pool and waited there, holding their breaths in the stillness. When they heard the Spaniards splashing the waters, they slipped silently into the pool and sank to the bottom. Lying on the floor, they pushed the reeds upward until they protruded an inch or two above the surface.

It was not a pleasant feeling to lie as still as death with eight feet of slimy water above their heads and wait while the Spaniards moved nearer and nearer. Suddenly there was a great commotion almost directly over their heads, and the water was churned into foam by a man's wild thrashing: one of the soldiers had fallen into the pool. Fortunately, he wore no armor, or he would have been doomed. He bounded to the surface like a cork, and was drawn ashore by the shafts of his comrades' lances.

On the bottom of the pool, Kit and Bernardo could not hear his words, but if they had, they would have been comforted, for as he was drawn into shallow water, he cried: "If they're in that pool, they're drowned. By the Virgin, it has no bottom!"

Kit and Bernardo lay on the floor of the pool for another hour, drawing in their breaths through the tubes of the reeds. Then slowly, quietly, Kit swam upward. He put up his head, ducked under again, and waited. No sound came. He swam over to Bernardo's reed and gave it a triumphant shake. A moment later Bernardo's dark head broke the surface.

"So," he spluttered, "we've gained another night, but we're still inside these walls!"

"In that cell," Kit answered slowly, "no chance at all existed. Here, there's at least a possibility."

They settled down to wait for the coming of night. As the day wore on, they were conscious of their hunger and thirst. Their tongues thickened in their parched mouths until they could scarcely speak, and the growling of their empty bellies increased. The night, when it came, came with a difference. Whereas the previous night had been clouded, tonight the sky was clear and star-studded. The danger of swimming the moat was tripled, but it was also easier to discover their bearings.

Telling Bernardo to wait, Kit slipped into the black water. He swam below the surface until his chest felt as though it would burst, then eased his head up so cautiously that he made scarcely a ripple. When he had reached the far end of the moat, he was astonished by what he saw there. Here the wall slanted down. It was so low at one point opposite the second drawbridge that a man could easily scale it. He swam back to the tunnel and told Bernardo of his discovery.

After Kit had rested they moved out, swimming close to the inner wall so that they were in shadow, their hands pushing back the water so gently that they made hardly a ripple. At last they came to the place opposite the drawbridge. There they halted, prayerfully treading water, for black on the face of the moon-silvered moat they could see the shadow of the sentry on the inner wall. Going down, they sought bottom, and stayed there until the need to breathe became overwhelming. They popped up again, close to the slimy rocks. The sentry had not moved.

Nine times they went down and up before the shadow vanished. Kit struck out at once, underwater. When his groping hand touched the stones of the opposite side, he stole upward, scarcely daring to breathe. The inner wall lay blank and bare in the moonlight. The sentry had moved on about his rounds.

Kit waved frantically to Bernardo, who was clinging to the stones on the inner wall. Three powerful strokes brought Bernardo across the moat, and the two of them climbed out on the narrow ledge of rock beside the wall. Kit knelt down, signaling Bernardo to mount his shoulders. When he forced himself upright again, Bernardo's powerful hands easily reached the top of the wall. He drew himself up and, without pausing for breath, stretched a hand down to Kit. He pulled Kit up and then the two of them dropped down onto the silent sand of the beach.

Keeping just under the wall, they ran for the protective screen of the palm trees. Only when they had buried themselves in the overwhelming gloom did they stop to recover their spent breath.

"Now what?" Bernardo panted.

"We start for Santa Marta," Kit growled.

"No, Kit," Bernardo said. "Let us consider the matter with some care. We need weapons, clothing, food—maybe even gold—before we can start for Santa Marta."

Kit grinned suddenly, a light of mischief leaping in his eyes. "Thoughtful of Don Luis, wasn't it," he said, "to transport Bianca for us to the place of our departure. And one thing more, good Bernardo. In yet another way he can serve us."

Bernardo's dark face was filled with questioning. "How, Kit? In what way can Don Luis help us?"

"Simple. We return to our original plan. Cartagena is the last place on earth where the guards would expect to find us. And with Don Luis absent from his house, what's to prevent us from helping ourselves to all the things we need?"

A slow, crafty grin spread over Bernardo's dark face. "Excellent!" he exclaimed. "What a happy thought—to make Don Luis supply us with the sinews for our journey!"

"Let's start," Kit said, and got to his feet.

They moved through the tangled forest of the Terra Bomba at a rapid pace. It was soon apparent that it would be full daylight before they reached the walls of the city, so they decided to lie in the tangled bamboo thickets and wait for night. Their hunger was unabated, but they managed to find fresh water. After drinking all they wanted, they let themselves down into the little stream and washed away their filth. Refreshed, they lay on their backs and stared at the sky through the rents in the canopy of leaves. When it was dusk they resumed their journey, coming to the walls of the city just after nightfall. The gates were about to be closed; groups of stragglers were rushing to get inside so they would not be locked out for the night.

Boldly, Bernardo joined the throng, and a second later Kit followed him. So it was that they re-entered the city, and they went directly toward Don Luis's house. Since the incident of the sinking of the *Seaflower,* there had been no further hostilities near Cartagena. The citizens had sunk back willingly into comfortable apathy. Even the enforcement of the curfew had become lax. As a result, Kit and Bernardo were able to reach Don Luis's house without being stopped by a single guardia civil.

While Kit waited, hiding his blond hair and beard in the deepest shadows, Bernardo went to the stables. Here at last he was stopped, by a sleepy old caretaker. But Bernardo was ready for him. In a flash, the Jew's powerful hands shot out, and a moment later the caretaker was incapable of uttering a sound. Bernardo let him slip limply to the cobblestones, and relieved him of his ring of great keys.

He rejoined Kit, and the two of them studied the watchman. Finally, deciding not to take any further chances, they left him in the stable, trussed up with rope and gagged. Inside the house, they found cold meats and wines that were no doubt intended for the caretaker, for their quality was not of the best. Kit and Bernardo sat down and gorged themselves. Then, taking candles, they proceeded to ransack the house for valuables.

When they departed they were both decently dressed, with stout jackboots on their feet. They even took the additional precaution of trimming their hair and beards. Weapons they had found aplenty: two pistols apiece, daggers, cutlasses, and a long-barreled musket. In their duffle bags were flagons of wine, black bread, cheese, and dried fruits. That this supply was far too little they knew well, but they depended on the musket to supply them with game.

In the full light of morning they proceeded out of the city, walking leisurely through the crowds. Kit had his golden mane tied back in a great kerchief, and his beard and mustache were stained black with soot. They went down to the quay and hired a Negro boatman, who with the help of another black rowed them down the bay. Toward evening, they passed through the Boca Chica channel and were pleased to observe that there was no visible stir within the fortress from which they had so lately escaped. The belief that they were dead, then, had taken root.

When they reached the sea, the blacks continued rowing, bearing southward toward the Dique canal, which connected the Cartagena area with the Magdalena River, the arterial highroad to the interior of New Granada.

As soon as they came to the Dique, they ran into trouble. The Negroes refused to go farther and demanded their pay. Kit glanced at Bernardo, a slow smile lighting his eyes. A moment later the blacks found themselves staring into the muzzles of two great pistols. At Kit's command, the pirogue was edged into shallow waters; then, without more ado, Kit forced the Negroes over the side, and Bernardo took up the oars.

Looking back at the shivering Negroes, Kit was moved with pity. Reaching into the purse he had stolen from Don Luis's house, he brought out a gold piece and tossed it to them. The old Negro who owned the pirogue looked at it and his face lighted up; he had received twenty times his fare and the price of his homemade boat put together.

23

As Bianca stood before the cathedral in the plaza of Santa Marta, she shivered a little. In no way was her trembling caused by any chill in the air, for Santa Marta lies in a smiling horseshoe-shaped valley at the base of the towering Sierra Nevada de Santa Marta and is blessed with eternal spring. It was, she well knew, the doubt and confusion in her mind that made her limbs quiver so.

With slow, hesitant steps, she and Quita crossed the plaza, moving toward the fine old cathedral with its twin belfries. Slowly they mounted the steps. In the doorway Bianca paused before entering. The light was dim, and the air seemed cooler than outside in the square. Dipping her hand into the holy-water font, Bianca crossed herself and genuflected in the direction of the altar. Then, very quietly, she knelt before a lesser niche and tried to pray.

Her confused mind refused to shape either the words or the mental images of prayer. She was overcome by loneliness and fear. She had no way of knowing whether Kit had succeeded in escaping from the grim gray pile of the fortress of Boca Chica. Even now he might be lying dead of wounds suffered in the attempt. Or, God willing, he might be free and on his way to her. It was this last thought that sowed the blowing seeds of confusion in her mind. If Kit were free, if he were to come to her—what then?

Don Luis would never release her from her vow. Of this she was certain. She knew, moveover, that having sworn to remain faithful to her husband, to bear him a child if she could, she would not go back on her oath. Don Luis had kept his share of the bargain and she would keep hers. Though she loved Kit enough to give her life for him, though she shivered with ecstatic pain even at the thought of his arms around her, she was trapped by her vow. While Don Luis lived, she must remain his. Only Providence —or Kit—could find a solution.

There was, curiously, another side to the matter. Long ago she had discovered how much there was to admire about Luis del Toro. In truth he was a great man, considered against the background of his times. That his benevolence did not extend beyond the narrow limits of his own particular race, religion, and social position was in his own eyes only natural and right. If it had been suggested to him that the kindness with which he habitually treated Bianca, his friends, and even his blooded stallion, should be shown to heretics, Jews, and slaves, he would have dismissed the idea as insane. He might, for the moment, seriously consider better treatment for his mules, for they were valuable animals; but to feel humanitarian sentiments toward heretics and such seemed to him insulting to his Iberian pride, for, by inference, it would include this scum within the orbit of the human race. If such a belief were ever established, the status of all humanity would be lowered.

Bianca understood these feelings of his even better than he did himself, and she knew how futile it was to try to change his mind, so she left him in peace. But she knew also that to her he was kindness itself, gentle and tender. Whenever he lashed out at her with bitter words it was only because he was tormented by jealousy. Moreover, she was almost sure that Don Luis loved his natural son, and might, but for certain scruples and a very touchy pride, have owned him. Certainly he had once spared Kit's life of his own free will; and that second time when his eloquence had stirred the halls of the Casa Real in Kit's behalf—was it really only her pleas that had inspired him?

Groaning, she shook her small, lovely head. There was more to all this, much more. If Luis were to die, either by accident or by Kit's enraged hand, could she then go to her lover with unmixed feelings? After having been married to the father, after having more than a little *loved* the father, could she then turn to the son without having a secret feeling of guilt in the whole matter—as though the new relationship were a little beyond the pale? And it would be even worse if Kit killed Luis, for in that she, being the cause, would be bloodguilty also—and with the blood of parricide.

Her poor head ached so. As the stained-glass windows shifted with the light, their outlines growing blurred and confused, the outlines of her thoughts blurred, her mind blurred, so that the angels from the niches seemed to come down and waver vaguely at her right hand, their illumined smiles alive and inviting. She was tired, deathly tired. If Kit came, had she the strength to turn to his impetuous arms? How much easier to forswear love and lovers, forswear all men, and go to the beckoning angels, where she might forever rest.

Rest! That was it, rest! More than even love she needed rest—more than joy, more than the panting, pounding fury of passion, she needed peace. No longer could she stand as a death challenge between two strong men. She would go with the angels, and as a bride of Christ escape from doubt, confusion, and terror forever. . . .

She stood up suddenly, and so great was the joy on her face that her small countenance seemed to glow with unearthly light. Seeing it, Quita was frightened.

"Señora!" she gasped.

Bianca raised her hand.

"Hush!" she whispered. "They are calling me, Quita—the angels are calling. . . . Don't you hear them?"

"I hear nothing," Quita quavered. "Oh, Doña Bianca, come!" Then, taking her mistress by the arm, she drew her from the dim recesses of the cathedral.

That same afternoon, Don Luis finally obtained an audience with Dr. Mendoza. By the time he faced the great physician he was in a cold and towering rage, for he had been forced to wait in an anteroom while the doctor attended to the sufferings of beggars, stolid Chibchas, and Negroes afflicted with running sores. As much as he needed the great Jewish physician's help, he could not resist pointing out his monstrous discourtesy.

"They are all God's children, are they not, my lord?" Mendoza said gently. "I have great sympathy for the poor. My father, you see, was a swineherd."

Don Luis ground his teeth to stifle the furious burst of words that threatened to escape his lips. The advantage was all with the physician. Don Luis needed Francisco Mendoza, while Francisco Mendoza needed no man. There was perhaps a pride beyond pride in this flinging of his humble origin into the Count's face, as though he were saying: I came from nothing, yet you, with generations of wealth and power behind you, must come to me. . . .

Mendoza stood very quietly, eying the Count with something curiously akin to compassion. He understood how great a struggle Luis del Toro was having with his pride; but pride to him was nothing, so he waited very quietly for the nobleman to speak.

"I would like you to come to Don Avila's, whose guest I am," Don Luis growled, "to determine what causes my lady's barrenness."

Mendoza bent his head with courtesy.

"I am at your service," he said. Then he hesitated, a slow and secret smile lighting his eyes.

"What now?" Don Luis barked.

"If you will not take it amiss, I might suggest that unfruitfulness in a union is not always the fault of the woman. Sometimes the excesses of youth prove damaging to the fulfillment of later and more serious desires."

Don Luis snorted. "You need have no fear," he said. "My wife has already conceived, but the child was stillborn. Since that time, there has been nothing."

"I see," Mendoza said gravely. "I will see her tonight. And if you will permit, I should like to bring with me a young colleague, Dr. José Pérez, who is very wise in these matters."

"Bring the whole of Santa Marta, if it will do any good," Don Luis answered, and left the house.

To a woman of Bianca's modesty the very thought of being examined by a physician was an ordeal, but under Mendoza's grave and gentle manner she relaxed greatly. Pérez, however, she distrusted on sight. The man had a look of slyness and deceit about him; his gaze darted from object to object without ever coming to rest upon any of them. Bianca suspected that he was a charlatan, but in this she was wrong. José Pérez was as good a physician as existed in Santa Marta—which is to say that he was monstrously, criminally ignorant of many of the most rudimentary facts of human life and health. However, this ignorance was shared more or less completely by every other doctor in New Spain, even by the great Mendoza himself. What distinguished Mendoza from the rest was an instinctive sympathy and understanding that probed deep into human nature. Coupled with this, he had a healthy skepticism that made him realize his own ignorance and walk carefully in the face of it.

Mendoza examined Bianca under a huge sheet, without looking at her body at all. Pérez clearly found this disappointing, for Bianca's beauty had instantly inflamed him. But he was too wise to protest, the more so when he noticed that Mendoza's tactics had won Don Luis's unqualified approval.

The examination took a long time and was most thorough. Afterward, the men went out of the room leaving Bianca feeling sick with humiliation from the mauling and probing to which her body had been subjected. She was filled with curiosity to overhear the talk that was going on in the great hall, but she would have had to rise and dress herself, with Quita's help. Suddenly an idea struck her. With a quick gesture she pointed to the door, bidding Quita listen.

Quita smiled and hastened to obey. In common with most servants, there was nothing that she enjoyed more than eavesdropping, and to be told to do so made her pleasure complete. In the salon, Don Luis was listening attentively, his face heavy with concern.

"So far as I can find," Mendoza said slowly, "there is nothing the matter with the señora. She is young and capable of conceiving, although she is a trifle delicate."

"Then why have I no son?" Don Luis thundered.

"Frankly," Mendoza said calmly, "I do not know. There is an explanation

I strongly suspect to be valid in this case, but I hesitate to give it, because it could only prove offensive to you, my lord."

"Give it," Don Luis said dryly. "This is no time to consider delicacy."

"Your wife does not want a child. At least, not your child. Forgive me, my lord, but you asked me to tell you."

Don Luis, who had half-risen, sank down again.

"There are many different degrees of fertility in women. Your wife, I suspect, in all her life would bear no more than two children in any event. Now her fear of childbirth—or could it be some other confusion of her emotions?—acts as a powerful barrier to conception. If you will accept my advice, you will woo her once more as a tender lover. If this does not succeed, you should adopt an heir, for Doña Bianca will never conceive unless . . ."

"Damnation!" Don Luis spat. "This is old wives' babble!"

"Perhaps," Mendoza said calmly, gathering up his instruments, "but that is my diagnosis."

Don Luis looked at José Pérez. "And what," he demanded, "is your opinion?"

"It is different from that of my colleague," Pérez said without hesitation. "I should prefer to voice it only to my lord himself."

Mendoza looked at the younger doctor in some surprise. It had not occurred to him that the young man was an opportunist, seeking his own gain above all else. That this was so came to him now as a cruel shock. Being far too wise to expect human beings to be anything else but human, he bowed ironically and prepared to leave. Without moving from his chair, Don Luis tossed him a fat purse of gold, exactly as one tosses a bone to a hungry dog. Mendoza caught it deftly, and stood there looking at it a moment.

Then, very quietly and with immense dignity, he said: "Since I have accomplished nothing, I can take no fee. If you wish, you can give this to charity." He crossed the room and laid the purse noiselessly on a low table. Then he was gone, leaving Don Luis feeling fatuous, enraged, and ashamed, all at the same time.

Quita swung her lithe form deftly behind the door as Mendoza came out, then she returned to her post.

"And now that we are alone," Don Luis said, looking at Dr. Pérez, "speak your piece."

"It is not my intention to flatter my lord with untruths or half-truths," Pérez said. "Doña Bianca is indeed barren. Totally, completely barren. I wish to offer my lord two most useful suggestions."

"Go on," Don Luis said, his voice deceptively soft.

"My lord should petition the Archbishop for a decree of annulment. In cases of this sort, where there is no issue, the good Father is most amenable to suggestion."

"I don't like that," Don Luis said, with the same appearance of mildness. "You have another suggestion?"

Emboldened, Pérez plunged in. "In my work among the Chibchas," he said, "I have encountered rare and curious substances—poisons, if my lord does not dislike the ugly word—that bring death quickly and painlessly, with every appearance of natural causes. So freed, my lord might, after a short period of mourning, turn to a young and lusty lady who would assure him of many sons."

"Interesting," Don Luis said as he rose. "Very, very interesting."

Pérez, seeing the cold ferocity in his eyes, could only gurgle wordlessly as he backed away from the Count's powerful grasp. But Quita, on the other side of the door, could see none of this. Nor did she wait to hear more. Overcome with fear for the life of her mistress, she ran from her hiding place and told Bianca what she had heard.

"If," Bianca said sadly, "my husband wants to kill me, what can I do?"

"No!" Quita was weeping. "No, my lady! Only I will cook your food and serve your wine. You must touch nothing but what I bring. I will stop him! Oh, why didn't you go with the young cacique with the golden hair?"

"Hush," Bianca said gently. "Hush, Quita. The Blessed Virgin will protect me, for I am innocent of sin."

If Quita had lingered a moment longer, she would have heard the crash of overturning furniture as José Pérez scurried to escape. Don Luis caught him about the throat with one tremendous hand and lifted him clear of the floor, shaking him all the while as a terrier shakes a rat. When finally he released Pérez, the young physician collapsed into a gasping, sobbing heap at his feet. Don Luis kicked him contemptuously.

"Get up!" he snarled. "And thank all the saints that you still have your miserable life!"

Pérez scrambled to his feet and fled with such haste that he left both his instruments and his books behind.

The three weeks that followed were a period of slow starvation for Bianca. Quita was able to obtain but little food for her, and the succulent meals that were set before her went untasted. She made many excuses to avoid eating with her husband. Don Luis watched with gathering astonishment as his wife grew paler and weaker, failing before his eyes.

Finally he announced that they would go back to Cartagena, for the hot climate of Santa Marta was obviously making her ill. Bianca, who at last had been unable to find an excuse to stay away from the table, looked at him with horror. How could he be so callous? Then she rose from the table and, overcome with sudden weakness, fainted at his feet.

Don Luis knelt anxiously beside her. Grasping a goblet of wine, he started to force a little between her colorless lips. Instantly Quita was upon him. She struck the goblet from his hand so that it crashed into a thousand fragments, the wine making a bloodlike stain on the floor.

"Murderer!" Quita shrieked. "I will not have her killed!"

Don Luis stared at the lovely Chibcha girl, blank amazement in his eyes.

"What is this madness, Quita?" he growled. "Who said anything about slaying Doña Bianca?"

"You!" Quita whispered, her voice filled with horror. "I heard you—the day you plotted with that wicked doctor! He said he would bring poisons, and you could . . ."

Don Luis threw back his head and his laughter boomed against the ceiling.

"Bless you, Quita," he roared. "I should have you lashed for your impudence, but I forgive you. You make things clear." He looked down at Bianca, whose eyelids had fluttered open and who was staring at him curiously. "And you, my dove, also thought that I meant to poison you?"

Bianca struggled faintly in his great arms.

"Quiet, my love," he whispered. Then to Quita he said sternly, "Fill another goblet from the same flagon!"

Quita hesitated.

"Do as I say!" he thundered.

With trembling fingers the Indian girl obeyed. Then, taking the goblet, Don Luis raised it to his lips and drank half of it.

"Now you," he whispered to Bianca, placing the rim of the glass against her pale lips.

Slowly Bianca drank. It was cool and sweet, with no trace of bitterness in it at all.

"My heart is filled with grief," Don Luis whispered, his voice sinking to a bass rumble, "that you could think this of me. Did you know that Pérez barely escaped with his life? All these viands which all these days you have not tasted were both untainted and rich."

He stood up and lifted her tenderly in his arms. He looked back over his shoulder at Quita.

"And you, you untamed savage, go and prepare food for your mistress." Then he carried Bianca into her bedroom and put her down on the great bed. Bianca looked up at him, her dark eyes bright with tears.

"Forgive me, Luis," she whispered. "It is only that I knew how much you want a son."

"Trouble yourself no longer, Bianca," Don Luis said. "When we return to Cartagena, I will petition the good Fathers for a fair lad from the orphanage, and we will lavish our care upon him. Now eat and rest, so that you may be strong enough for the journey."

Lightly he kissed her, and getting up, beckoned to Quita, who was bringing steaming viands on a tray. The Indian maid knelt beside her mistress and Don Luis took his leave. But long before the hot broth was half gone from the bowl, Quita hesitated, the spoon of hammered silver poised in midair, for Bianca had turned aside her face. Quita leaned forward, listening to the quiet rustle of her breath. Then, very quietly, the maidservant got up and closed the curtains and tiptoed from the room, and on the great bed Bianca at last slept the sleep of deep peace.

24

On reaching the Magdalena, Kit and Bernardo started downstream with scarcely a pause for rest. Bernardo groaned at the killing pace Kit set at the paddles, but Kit dug in grimly and said nothing. And as they were rowing with the current, they made good speed.

They had assumed from the beginning that it would be necessary to travel overland from the shores of the river to Santa Marta, once they had reached the Caribbean coast, and to that end they had brought a large supply of gold, filched from Don Luis's strongbox. This gold was intended for the purchase of mules and other supplies. For this purpose it was more than sufficient, but to their pleased surprise they discovered that in a boat that drew as little water as their pirogue, it was possible to sail through the green Cienaga up to the very doors of Santa Marta itself.

So it was that on the second day of February 1697, after two long years of imprisonment, they set foot on the streets of their gateway to freedom. Here all things might be brought to a fitting conclusion—escape, vengeance, love.

Love? Kit mused. No, for my love is buried at sea in the *Seawitch*'s smoke and flame. Companionship and affection—many a man has accepted baser and less reasonable counterfeits for love, and these will serve me. These and the fulfillment of the solemn vow I made to Bianca when we last met that I would marry none other while she lives. And if I miss the sweet spring madness of my love for Rouge, this that remains, being less fierce, may prove more durable. . . .

They had come by this time to the house of Francisco Mendoza, for in Santa Marta they needed only to ask and a dozen leaped to direct them to his house, so greatly was Mendoza loved by the poor and humble he had so often befriended. His manservant, after studying Kit and Bernardo with some care, admitted them without question. Years in Mendoza's service had given him a keen insight into what sort of men the great doctor was willing to receive. These two, with the look of far horizons in their eyes, were the kind he most enjoyed, for he loved to hear the tales of seafaring men.

When they were ushered into his presence, he rose with courtly grace to receive them. His gaze flickered briefly over Bernardo's face and read there the signs of kindred suffering and brotherhood. But when he looked at Kit, a keen professional interest lighted his eyes. This one, he saw at a glance, was deeply troubled.

"Bring wine," he said, turning to his manservant, but Kit refused with a gesture.

"I'm afraid there is scarcely time for civilities. I beg your pardon, honored sir, but the information I seek of you is of great importance. Do you know the whereabouts of the Count del Toro and his lady?"

A little frown creased Mendoza's forehead. Then suddenly it vanished. "Has anyone ever told you," he countered, "that you resemble the Count to an astonishing degree?"

"I asked you a question, sir!" Kit spat.

The physician shrugged. "They are beyond your reach," he said dryly. Then softly, in the tone of a man talking wholly to himself, he added, "Doña Bianca is perhaps beyond any man's reach."

Kit took a step forward, deep concern in his eyes. "What do you mean by that?" he demanded. "She is not dead?"

"No, not dead, nor even dying. But I have no right to tell you these things. To a true physician, a patient's secrets are sacred. Why do you ask? Are you in love with her?"

"Why do you ask me questions," Kit growled, "when you have answered none of mine?"

Mendoza smiled. "Gently, my boy," he said. "You're distraught. I parried your queries only because if harm came to Del Toro or any other grandee through information given by me, my life would not be worth a piaster. I care little for my life, but many lives depend upon it. Sit and have wine, and I will tell you what I can."

Bernardo looked at Kit and nodded emphatically. Kit sighed.

"It seems," he said dryly, "that I have no choice."

Mendoza sipped the red wine the servant had brought and studied the two of them across the table. "Your coming," he said to Kit, "has been most opportune. It enables me to complete a diagnosis. I'm sorry. I can understand your impatience."

"Then for the love of heaven tell me where they are!"

"They have returned to Cartagena. I fear I proved a disappointment to the Count del Toro, for I could do nothing for his lady."

"Is she so ill?" Bernardo asked.

"She is not ill at all," Mendoza said. "Not in any ordinary sense. That's why I tell you this, for it violates no confidence. It isn't a physician she needs—a priest, perhaps. I don't know."

Kit, who at the mention of Cartagena had already got to his feet, stood still, listening.

"There is a confusion in her," Mendoza continued. "In her mind, I could say, but it's not wholly there. It's more of the spirit. What she wants to do she cannot, not because of her husband but because it runs counter to all the teachings of her lifetime. Now she no longer knows what she wants to do—most of all now, I think, she wants to escape, to be troubled no more. While I examined her she spoke once of angels. I fear that the tendency exists in her to take refuge in illusion."

Kit leaned forward, putting both hands on the table. "Are you," he asked, "suggesting that Bianca's mad?"

Mendoza shook his head. "No. Only that she could go mad, if her problem is not solved. There's nothing more hellish than warfare within the soul. But that, I think, is up to you. For as certainly as I sit here, you, young sir, are the root and branch of her trouble! Am I right?"

Slowly Kit nodded. "You are right," he admitted. "And even more right in the thought that I will be the solution of it. My thanks, good physician."

Mendoza took his offered hand. "One thing more," he said gravely. "In your solution, be not hasty or rash, or you'll force her into the very state we wish to avoid."

Kit and Bernardo bowed and took their leave. But Mendoza's final warning weighed heavy on Kit's mind. So troubled was he that he allowed Bernardo to persuade him to delay their departure until the next day. What Bernardo had in mind he did not voice. He hoped that given a whole night in which to ply the oil of persuasion, he might show Kit the wisdom of abandoning the whole thing and returning to Saint-Domingue. That Kit was determined to go back to Cartagena he knew without even having to ask.

Kit sat at a table in the inn, his viands and wine untasted before him.

Bernardo looked at him, trying to find an opening to begin his campaign. But Kit did not even look up. Finally, in desperation, Bernardo put out his hand to pluck at Kit's sleeve. It was then that the uproar burst on their ears.

Turning, Kit saw a thin, small individual who might have been the twin of the late Parisian sewer rat hanged at Cartagena by Del Toro, struggling in the grip of the burly innkeeper.

"But of course I have no money!" the little man screeched. "Tomorrow I shall have it—thousands! Name of a name! When I tell the captain general that the French are coming, he will reward me. Just you wait!"

Bernardo leaned forward, excitement moving in his dark eyes. "That accent!" he whispered. "Did you hear it?"

Kit nodded and stood up. Only a Frenchman would speak Spanish with that nasal tone. This would bear investigation.

"The French!" the innkeeper spat. "Pah! Beribboned jackanapes! Let 'em come! That doesn't pay for the good wine you've swilled . . ."

He stopped short, for Kit had touched his arm.

"If you'll permit me," Kit said, "this gentleman is a friend of mine. What's the extent of his bill?"

"Twenty reales," the innkeeper growled.

Smilingly, Kit passed over the money, adding a piece of eight for good measure. The innkeeper's bow after he released the seedy individual was magnificent. Kit took the small man's arm.

"Come," he said gently, "my friend and I would like to talk to you."

Flanked by Kit and Bernardo, the little man stumbled out into the night.

"You said," Kit suggested mildly, "something of the French. That interests us greatly. Please go on."

A look of greedy cunning stole into the man's little black eyes. "What's it worth to you?" he whispered.

"Another twenty reales," Kit declared.

The little Frenchman hiccoughed loudly, and the wine-perfumed cloud of his breath made Kit turn aside. "Make it twenty-five, señor," he whined "I've gone to great trouble."

"All right," Kit growled, "but not one centavo more. Speak your speech!"

Still the little man hesitated. Then with sly, drunken cunning, he extended his hand. Kit dug into his pockets and came out with the gold.

"Well, señor," the man began, "it's like this. I worked for Governor Ducasse—gardener, I was. And last month I got wind of something. Great ship came in from France, and what her captain told the Governor fair set him wild. They're planning an expedition"—his voice dropped into a conspiratorial stage whisper—"against Cartagena, no less! The minute I got wind of it I thought to myself, I did, here's your chance, Pierre! They hadn't treated me fair in Saint-Domingue, señor, that they hadn't."

"Get to the point, man!" Kit snapped. "What proof have you of this?"

"Name of the frigate from France is the *Marin*. Her captain is the Sieur de Saint-Vandrille. And here, señor, is the copy of the orders that Ducasse sent throughout the colony, calling every able-bodied man to arms."

Kit took the printed poster and read it. He passed it to Bernardo without a word.

"That," Pierre whined, "you must give back to me. The captain general will pay me thousands for that, señor, thousands!"

Bernardo, his dark face creased with frowns, passed the notice back to Kit. Kit's hands moved swiftly, contemptuously, and the paper was ripped from top to bottom.

"Señor!" Pierre shrieked.

Kit paid him no heed. Slowly, carefully, he tore the notice into tiny bits and scattered them in the gutter.

"You witless, treacherous, foul little dog!" he said quietly. So softly did he speak that long moments passed before Pierre realized that he had shifted into pure, accentless French, the tongue he had learned at his mother's knee. When the recognition at last struck Pierre, he collapsed into a shivering hulk of abject terror.

"French!" he whispered. "You're French! Oh, holy, blessed Mother of God!"

"A pity," Bernardo growled, shaking his head sternly, "but we'll have to kill him, Kit. He can't run around loose with that knowledge."

Kit nodded grimly and slipped his dagger out of its sheath. The blade glinted blue in the dim light of the lanterns, and the breath caught in Pierre's throat in a wordless gurgle. Then, as though touched by a bolt of lightning, the informer sprang backward and began to run swiftly through the dark streets. Without a word, Kit and Bernardo pounded after him. But fear lent wings to their quarry's feet. Kit and Bernardo were both much larger and heavier men than he, and he was drawing ahead of them with every jump. But as he rounded a corner, he burst almost into the arms of two soldiers of the guardia civil. He sidetracked beautifully and scampered away.

"Stop him!" Kit roared. "Stop that thief!"

At once the soldiers joined the pursuit. In three minutes they realized that they would never catch the swiftly running little man. They halted there in the street and leveled their muskets. The shots echoed through the narrow way, the echoes reverberating back and forth between the close walls of the houses. And little Pierre went over on his face and rolled, kicking up a small cloud of dust. He was dead when the four of them reached him. The men of the guardia civil looked at Kit inquiringly.

"If you will search his pockets," Kit said smoothly, "you will find twenty reales that he picked from my pouch in a tavern."

The soldier knelt and went over the body. After a moment he straightened. In his hand he held the money and some papers. He looked at the papers, holding them high to catch the glow of the lantern, and his face frowned with puzzlement.

"It's not Spanish," he growled.

Instantly Kit crossed to his side. Looking over the soldier's shoulder, he read swiftly.

"It's French," he said slowly. "A permit to leave the colony of Saint-Domingue. You've done well, Captain—apparently our small friend was also a spy."

A glow of triumph showed in the guard's eyes. Such things could mean a promotion. Seeing the look, Kit at once took further advantage of the situation.

"As to the twenty reales," he said, "I think it no more than fair that you and your brave companion keep ten of them as a reward for your trouble."

Wide, white-toothed smiles flashed in the guards' dark faces. They passed the money over to Kit, who counted out ten reales and gave the money to them.

"Adiós, caballeros!" He smiled and saluted them gravely.

"What now, Kit?" Bernardo asked as they walked away.

Kit grinned. "On to Cartagena!" he said.

"To Cartagena!" Bernardo gasped.

"Yes," Kit said, laughing, "with a slight detour by way of Saint-Domingue!"

They returned to their inn, which was much frequented by seamen, and listened carefully for talk of ships and sailing. But they had to linger in Santa Marta for over a week before they learned anything that would be of use to them. Then they heard that a large plate ship had left Cartagena, and would pause briefly at Santa Marta before proceeding to Santo Domingo and from there to Spain.

Santo Domingo, Kit reflected sadly, was on the opposite side of the island from Saint-Domingue, which meant more weary leagues of traveling. Still, so be it; in this he had no choice.

By dint of dropping a coin here and there in the right quarters, they obtained permission to see the captain of the *Santa Isabella,* as the great vessel was called. The captain told them bluntly that he had no right to take aboard paying passengers, but as they seemed likely lads, he would sign them on as seamen, but for the entire voyage—not merely to Santo Domingo.

"Look alive," he growled. "No French leave when we reach the island. I'm damned short of hands. If you must reach Santo Domingo, I'll bring you back from Spain on my next voyage—a little delay, that's all."

A delay, Kit reckoned, that might stretch into a full year or more. But what choice had they? Time was the vital issue. If he and Bernardo could not outwit this thick-skulled don, on their own heads be it. He picked up the pen.

"Agreed," he said with a sigh. "You drive a hard bargain, señor."

But by the time the *Santa Isabella* reached Santo Domingo the captain was occupied with other matters. Kit and Bernardo went about their tasks with seamanlike skill as the great vessel hove to in the harbor, waiting only for the dense tropical night to fall. Unlike the other seamen, they had not even asked for shore leave, which the captain had brusquely denied the others, fearful as he was of having to cross the broad Atlantic with too small a crew to handle the clumsy giant he commanded.

But late in the night watch, Kit and Bernardo went over the side, their pistols, powder, and shot in canvas bags they had tied on top of their heads, and the rest of the gold they had brought from Cartagena in leather sacks fastened to their belts. They swam through the warm water to the shore. Then they hid in the woods during the whole day that the captain searched the city for them.

Don Luis's gold solved everything. It brought them new garments, hats, and boots, and hired them the services of a coasting hoy that took them around the island almost to the borders of the French colony. There they hired a sloop, and beat their way into the harbor of Petit Goave through the greatest assembly of ships of the line their astonished eyes had ever seen in Saint-Domingue.

"Ah, Cartagena!" Kit whispered. "I slipped like a rat into your streets once. Now shall I loose thunder upon your head, and bury Luis del Toro under a mountain of smoking rubble!"

But Bernardo, who remembered the walls of Cartagena, said nothing. He had seen too many battles. He knew well that the outcome of this venture, like all others, lay in the lap of chance.

25

His Excellency Jean-Baptiste Ducasse, Governor of the colony of Saint-Domingue, was in a thoroughly vile humor. Usually a most temperate man little given to displays of emotion, on this seventeenth day of March 1697 he was having great difficulty controlling himself.

"Name of a dog!" he muttered as he strode up and down. "How much longer do I have to deal with this madman?"

The madman to whom he referred was His Lordship Jean Bernard Louis Desjeans, Baron de Pointis, whose formidable flotilla Ducasse could see from the window of his drawing room. He had first met him thirteen days ago on the Baron's arrival in Saint-Domingue, and every day had only added to his detestation of the man.

In the first place, De Pointis was cursedly secretive. Second, he was amenable neither to suggestion nor to reason. Third, he regarded his authority as being greater than and superseding that of Ducasse himself. Fourth, he was a martinet whose fantastic ideas of discipline had the whole water front in an uproar. The buccaneers loved Ducasse like a father. He jollied them, bullied them, and forgave them most of their minor transgressions, with the result that they had on several occasions, notably at Jamaica in 1694, waded through rivers of blood at his command.

But what had this noble of France, this Baron of the Realm, this stiff, ice-water-blooded aristocrat, done on his arrival? Almost on the first day, his officers, all as aristocratic as he, had arrested one of the bravest of Ducasse's buccaneers on the charges of being drunk and molesting a woman. Name of a name! When were the buccaneers not drunk? And as for the ladies of the water front, what honor did any of them have that needed protecting? Still, the thing had had grave repercussions, for a throng of bearded sea rovers had at once stormed the fort, intent upon releasing their fellow, and those stiff French fools had fired into that mob of roaring-drunk freebooters, killing three. For a time it had looked as though De Pointis would need the guns of his fleet to save his own hide. But for the diplomacy of Ducasse, the expedition would have ended then and there.

The expedition! Ducasse held his aching head between his hands. Damn his eyes to deep-blue hell, but this was a monumental piece of folly! If it were gold they wanted, with such a fleet as lay in the sunlight beneath his window they could sweep the Caribbean clean of the plate ships of Spain. But stubbornly, coldly, insanely, to insist upon attacking Cartagena itself! Mother of God, but they were mad!

If they were wise, they would forget this madman's dream of taking mountains of treasure all at one time. The obvious thing to do was to drive the Spaniards from Santo Domingo and raise the fleur-de-lis over all Hispaniola. Wealth, true wealth, consisted of trade and produce, not this delirium of gold fever in the blood.

A dry cough interrupted the Governor's unhappy reverie. His secretary stood there, waiting respectfully for his attention.

"Well," Ducasse snapped, "well, Paul, what folly is it now?"

A smile of real pleasure stole across Paul's emaciated face. "Madame Golphin awaits your pleasure, your Excellency," he said.

Slowly the Governor relaxed. "As lovely as ever, eh, Paul?"

"More lovely, your Excellency," Paul whispered, "if such a thing is possible."

The frown returned to Ducasse's brow, but this time it was tinged with a quizzical sort of amusement.

"I verily believe," he remarked, "that every man in the colony is in love with her. Yet she has behaved with the utmost circumspection. Though I've had to prevent four duels over her, it's well known that she herself has put a stop to ten. . . . Ah well, show her in, Paul."

A moment later, he was bowing grandly over Rouge's small hand. "You do me too much honor, madame," he murmured.

"Nonsense!" Rouge laughed. "If you were not so everlastingly busy, I'd visit you every day. Everyone knows that you are the most charming man in the colony."

Ducasse groaned. "For such overwhelming flattery," he said dryly, "I shall have to pay a high price. What do you want now, madame?"

Rouge's silvery laughter pealed against the ceiling. "Only to do you a favor," she said gaily. "Let me lead my sea hawks against Cartagena!"

Ducasse took a backward step. "Surely you are jesting," he said at last.

"No. I mean it. You would never believe that it was I who commanded the *Gull*. I want the chance to show you. Besides"—her voice dropped into an icy gravity that made the Governor shiver suddenly—"there is one particular grandee in Cartagena with whom I have an ancient score to settle —aside from the fact that I have no love for Spaniards at any place or at any time."

Ducasse looked down into the small, finely chiseled face with its oddly prominent bone structure over which the snowy skin was stretched tight in most intriguing planes and angles, so that it lacked the usual soft curves of femininity, but made up for this lack with a singular beauty all its own.

"I could use the *Gull*," he mused. "Still, consider what you're saying. If I permit this, you become guilty of treason against your own country. It is in alliance with Spain."

"If," Rouge said softly, "Kit ever returns, I shall become a citizen of Saint-Domingue by marriage, your Excellency. What does it matter if I do so prematurely—by my own hand?"

"What if he returns to the colony during your absence?"

"I'll risk it. Besides, I can easily leave word for him to wait for me here. Come, your Excellency, what do you say?"

Slowly Ducasse shook his massive head. "The answer is still no," he growled. "You're a brave girl, Jane. But I am a man, and though you plainly think me old, I can still value your beauty. I've seen small shot smash a man to bloody pulp. The thought of your being torn by grape or canister, or those lovely limbs of yours being mutilated by chain shot, is an utter horror to me. No, no, I cannot. Do not ask this of me!"

Rouge made him a short, mocking curtsy. "Yet I shall ask it again, your Excellency," she said. "I shall plague you until you give in. Farewell for now. But," she added with a smile, "you may expect me again tomorrow!"

Ducasse took her arm and escorted her through the outer offices to her horse. He stood there a long time watching her ride away before he turned back to his tasks.

"Damn my eyes," he muttered, "haven't I troubles enough?"

He had scarcely taken his seat before his desk and picked up the first of the mountain of letters that awaited his attention when Paul appeared again.

"Blessed blue-eyed pig!" Ducasse groaned. "What is it now?"

"Two gentlemen of the colony beg an audience with your Excellency. At least, they claim that they formerly lived here. But as to that I have my doubts."

Ducasse's mind was far away. Only the last phrase stuck in his thoughts like a burr. "Doubts?" he barked. "Why so, Paul?"

Paul leaned forward, speaking in an intense conspiratorial whisper. "One of them speaks French with a marked Spanish accent!" he said. "I think that these m'sieurs are spies!"

"Then send them in, by all means!" the Governor barked. "Spies, eh?" In his present mood the thought of being able to hang someone filled him with the keenest kind of pleasure. Paul returned, leading the two men.

"Monsieur Giradeaux!" Ducasse boomed. "And Monsieur Díaz! Name of an ancient camel, where have you two been?"

Kit smiled, a slow, quiet smile.

"In the bastion of your enemies, your Excellency," he said, "Cartagena of the Indies."

Ducasse lifted a thick red hand. "You too would mock me, Christophe?" he growled. "Enough and to spare have I had that accursed stone pile dinned into my ears! But I myself have sailed close by its walls. It could not be taken by the combined navies of the world. And you have entered it? Pah!"

"With your permission," Kit murmured, taking off his brocaded coat of somber blue, "I'll give you proof."

Ducasse sat there frowning as Kit's slim fingers loosed the buttons of his waistcoat, his silk-and-lace shirt, and his lace cravat. These garments had remained untouched at the inn of the Huguenot woman, jealously guarded by her throughout his absence. A moment later he stood before the Governor, stripped to the waist. His lean, sun-bronzed upper body rippled all over with long, graceful muscle, but when he turned his back, Ducasse drew in his breath sharply.

"Compliments," Kit said dryly, "of the captain general of the fortress San Lázaro of Cartagena, with an afterthought or two from the guards at the Castillo de Boca Chica itself."

"Mon Dieu," Ducasse whispered, "how you must have suffered!"

"Enough," Bernardo said dryly, "to make us hasten to offer our services to your Excellency the moment we learned of the proposed expedition."

A crafty little gleam stole into Ducasse's small blue eyes. He turned on Paul suddenly. "Please close all doors," he ordered, "and see that we are not disturbed!"

He led them over to a small table by the window and rang for his manservant. When the servant had come, he directed him to bring food and wine. Then he sat down, breathing heavily.

"This affair of the stripes is true, isn't it?" he demanded. "You did get them in Cartagena?"

"Your Excellency knows Cartagena?" Bernardo countered.

"Unfortunately, no," Ducasse growled. "I have passed its walls from the seaward side, that's all. And in this you two can serve me, if you speak the truth. Describe the inside of the bay to me."

"That," Kit said, "is easy. The fortress of Tenaza and the hill of the Popa you can see from the sea itself, and these you probably already know." Ducasse nodded. "But once inside the Boca Chica channel, past the fortress of Boca Chica—or more properly, San Luis de Boca Chica—one comes up the bay past the Terra Bomba, on the port side. A little farther north, to starboard one can see the Isla de Manzanillo, and directly opposite it on the left, the fortress of Santa Cruz. A little south of Santa Cruz lies the artificially blocked entrance to the Boca Grande."

"Enough!" Ducasse exulted. "You've been there! Can you make me a chart of these waters?"

"You have no chart?" Kit said incredulously.

Ducasse frowned heavily.

"There have been many changes since your departure," he said. "Today I have little authority. The Baron de Pointis has a chart—whose accuracy I question—but I am permitted not even one peek at it. I, Jean-Baptiste Ducasse, who know the Caribbean like the palm of my hand, am offered a captaincy in the French Navy! A captaincy merely! While he, the ancient fool, delegates to himself the title of General of the Armies of France by Sea and by Land! Insufferable!"

"You accepted this insult?" Kit growled.

"No. Since then the old fop has learned that nobody can control my buccaneers but me. Now, belatedly, he makes me cocommander in charge of the colonial forces."

"Ah," Bernardo breathed, "that's much better."

Ducasse looked at him. "Can you make me that chart?"

"Yes," Bernardo said. "And I'll warrant that it will be better than any other now existing."

"Good. You'll both stay here tonight, and I'll provide the instruments, inks, and parchments. Deliver the chart to me personally, and to none other."

He picked up a glass of the sack that the servant had brought during the conversation and drank it quickly. Then he looked at Kit, a merry twinkle in his small blue eyes.

"It lies in my power," he said, "to reward you at this moment—and such a reward as you could not dream of. But I talk too much. If I were to tell you of this, seven devils out of hell could not keep you here tonight. So—deliver my chart to me tomorrow and claim your reward."

Kit frowned. "I want no reward now," he said. "Just give me a commission. If my chart is of real value and my services are great enough during the expedition against Cartagena, I'll claim a reward. I mean to settle here, your Excellency. I'll need land on which to build."

"*Diablo!*" Ducasse snorted. "You shall have your commission, and if all goes well, your position here on Saint-Domingue is made. I have a brigantine that needs a captain of your ability, the *Providence*. It's a fast vessel, and you're familiar with brigantines."

"Agreed," Kit said, "if I can make Bernardo first mate."

"Of course," Ducasse said. "Where would you find a better?"

They both stood up and made a leg respectfully in the direction of the Governor, but he stopped them with a wave of his hand.

"In confidence now, lads, tell me," he whispered, "do you think that Cartagena can be taken?"

"Yes," Kit said. "If you don't try to batter your way through the walls. San Luis de Boca Chica is staffed only by a skeleton garrison, and old Don Sancho Jimeno, who commands that fortress, can easily be surprised. Once inside the bay, there are manifold avenues by which the city may be taken."

"Good," Ducasse grunted. "To your tasks, then!"

Early the next morning, Kit and Bernardo again waited on the Governor, and presented him with the completed chart. One glance at it told him that it was excellent. He launched into a profuse speech of thanks, but Kit interrupted him.

"I should like," he said, "to see my new craft. Where does she lie?"

Ducasse stopped short and clapped a broad hand to his forehead. "*Miséricorde!*" he gasped. "To think I had forgotten! Look you, Christophe, there is another matter more pressing than the brigantine that wants your attention. I suggest that you ride up to the old De Ville plantation this very morning. There is something there you must see!"

"Can't it wait?" Kit asked. "I'd prefer to see the *Providence*."

"Damn your eyes!" Ducasse roared. "You ride to De Ville's, Capitaine Giradeaux! And that is an order!"

Kit bowed stiffly.

"As your Excellency commands," he said quietly. Then to Bernardo, "You'll ride with me?"

"Yes," Bernardo said. "This mystery intrigues me."

The De Ville plantation, Kit remembered, had long been deserted. Therefore as he came to the gate, he drew up his horse with some astonishment. For the tangle of wild brush had disappeared, the road had been cleared and surfaced, and the twin lines of palms ran neatly up to the door of the manor, from which all the creeping vines had been cut away. Even from here they could see that the manor gleamed with a new coat of white paint and that the rotting timbers had been replaced. New panes shown in the window frames, and the lawns rolled fresh and green all about it. Not even in its heyday could the De Ville place have been more inviting.

Wonderingly, they passed through the gate and moved at a walk toward the house. The sound of the horses' hoofs must have carried, for just before they reached the door it opened, and a woman came out on the gallery.

Bernardo heard the agonized explosion of Kit's breath leaving his lungs and turning toward his young face, saw that all the color had drained from beneath the tan. Then he too looked toward the veranda. The woman who stood there was dressed all in white. She was swaying like a white orchid on a slim stalk, her hand pressed tight against her throat, and it was only when she began to run wildly toward them that Bernardo realized that her hair was like poinsettia petals, like hibiscus, like flame. Kit half leaped, half fell from the saddle, and took long strides forward.

"Kit!" Rouge called, her voice high, breathless; and the next instant she had hurled herself into his arms. Kit hung there, holding her, staring above the flame-red crown of her small head, feeling on his tongue and his lips like wormwood and gall the words he had uttered to Bianca: "Upon my mother's grave I swear never to wed another while you live."

Quietly he released Rouge and stood back, seeing that her beauty had in no way diminished, that indeed it had matured into a mind-stunning loveliness, and a sound caught in his throat that was halfway between a curse and a sob.

"I was a fool," Rouge whispered. "It was you—always and forever it was you I loved, though in my heart I denied it. But now I have found you and I will never leave you again—never as long as I live!"

Kit stared down at her, feeling his tongue curling and thickening in his mouth as it shaped the words he must say, the words he hated to say more than any others he had spoken in all his life.

"I—I found you too late, Rouge," he whispered. "I thought you were dead and I have promised another."

All the color drained out of Rouge's face suddenly, leaving it ghost-white. Then the glow of crimson flowed back suddenly, in small tidal waves of rage.

"Where is she?" she demanded, her voice high and breathless.

"In Cartagena," Kit said sadly, "and I have given my most solemn oath to come back to her."

"I see," Rouge whispered. Her eyes were star emeralds suddenly, jewel-bright with tears. "But there is nothing in this vow of yours, is there, Kit, which forbids you to kiss me—now?"

Kit bent down and found her mouth. It was warm and salt with the taste of tears. She drew back softly and stood there looking at him. So, Bernardo thought with bitter clarity, does a dying man look at the food and drink that could save his life. But Rouge was speaking again.

"Come up to the house," she said, "and tell me of this thing. I'm trying to understand, but I cannot. Yet I must! I must!"

Her slim white arm stole out and encircled his waist, and the three of them mounted the steps to the house. Kit told his tale, omitting nothing.

He began with the kidnapping of Bianca at Cul-de-Sac, and admitted freely that she had made him waver in his devotion to Rouge. As the sorry story unfolded, Bernardo thought he could discern a gathering paleness on Rouge's face. At the end she rose and stood looking at Kit.

"You will stay," she said, "both of you, for dinner. I must go and change now. Afterward perhaps we can straighten out this hellish confusion."

When she had gone, neither Kit nor Bernardo said a word. Bernardo drew out two long clay pipes, and after filling them passed one to Kit. They sat very still in the darkness, sending up fragrant smoke.

Afterward, neither of them knew who first heard that sound in the darkness, because they both looked up at the same instant. Rouge stood there in a gown that was like dawn mist and moonlight. It fell in clouds of misty whiteness, curling out in a great bell shape below her tiny waist, and her bare shoulders above the tight-laced bodice glowed pink-white and soft.

Kit sat like one frozen, holding the pipe in his hand; then he stood up, and the same instant her mouth was upon his, burning away his senses like all the fevers of the world. He did not know at what point Bernardo left them, but when at last, breathless, he drew away his mouth, they were alone. Rouge looked up at him, her emerald eyes dancing in her white face beneath the high-piled, smoothly coiled coiffure of her bright-red hair.

"You would leave me for another woman?" she whispered. "Can you, even if you would?"

Kit looked at her, and his eyes were naked with pain. "No," he admitted harshly. "I cannot, even though I break my most sacred oath, and become a man without honor, entirely damned!"

The sea-green blaze softened and darkened, and a look of tenderness spread over her small, strangely Oriental face.

"Which you gave unwittingly, not knowing that I lived," she said. "Let me go to her, Kit. Let me explain how it is with us. If she is a woman of honor, she will release you."

Kit searched her face with grave eyes. "And if she doesn't?"

"Then I'll set you free of her," Rouge said fiercely. "And she'll trouble you no more—you or any other man! The *Gull* is anchored in this harbor and I have men to sail her."

"Rouge!"

"I'll follow you to Cartagena, if I must. I'm still a ship captain, though I am a woman more." Suddenly, tenderly, Rouge stretched out her arms to him. "Forgive me, Kit," she whispered. "I am still more sea hawk than woman. Take me in your arms, and teach me to be gentle."

But Kit's fingers, inside the pocket of his greatcoat, fastened themselves around the single shred of gold cloth that was all that remained of the

Heron Banner. Bianca, poor lost Bianca, haunted perhaps with dreams and visions of illusion, must be attended to; and also, finally, the matter of Luis del Toro. Only then would he be free.

"No," he growled, "there will be years of time for such lessons, and now there are matters that cannot wait."

Rouge moved toward him. The moonlight touched her bare shoulders. The air was heavy with the perfume of tropical flowers, barbaric scents, rich with an opium-drugged compulsion. She took another step and her lips, soft-sighing, parting, blurring out of focus from too much nearness, drew out the last particle of clarity from his senses even before they touched his own. When she spoke her voice was husky, the words moving quietly through the scented rustle of her breathing.

"Will not tomorrow do?" she whispered. "Will not the matter wait?"

26

During the morning of March 20, 1697, while the great French fleet slipped out of the harbor of Petit Goave and headed westward toward Cartagena, Rouge was striding up and down the confines of her bedroom. Here of late more and more she found herself giving way to the hateful feminine weakness of tears. Never before in all her life had she been more troubled. She who had always taken matters in her own hands must wait here in this silent house, like Penelope spinning dreams of a lover who might never come back to her.

This would never do! If anything were true under the face of heaven it was that happiness belonged to those who grasped it with both hands. She could not wait here and hope that Kit would not be killed. She could not pace this floor and wish that Bianca would free him of his vow. Would she, if the situation reversed itself, release him? Would any woman who could have Kit Gerado give him up?

To Rouge there was only one answer. Already she was slipping the filmy nightdress over her head and racing for her sea chest. Before she reached it, she passed a full-length mirror illuminated by two candles. She stood still and gazed at herself, passing her hands down over her body, so slim and soft-curving that in the flickering glow of the candles it seemed the suggestion rather than the statement of womanhood. The terrifying thought struck her that perhaps Bianca was prettier than she, heavier, more voluptuously curved. And this, perhaps, Kit had already discovered for himself.

Whirling from the mirror, she tore open the sea chest and drew on her pantaloons and shirt. Whatever the comparison between her and her unknown rival, the matter must be put to the test immediately. She raced down the stairs, calling to her buccaneers as she ran. Here in Saint-Domingue she had kept them near her as house servants and bodyguards. And as they could freely consort with the women of the town, they had been docile.

Two hours later, the *Gull* stood out to sea on the freshening tide.

Kit stood on the poop of the *Providence* as the flotilla moved westward across the Caribbean. Bernardo was at his place on the quarter-deck. Knowing Bernardo's skill and seamanship, Kit trusted him to take command most of the time. From where he stood, Kit could see the great, beautiful ships of the line curving seaward before a freshening breeze: the *Sceptre*, the *Saint-Louis*, the *Vermandois*, the *Apollyon*, the *Furieux*, the *Saint-Michel*, great winged men-of-war these, none of them bearing less than sixty guns, or having a complement of fewer than three hundred and fifty men.

Behind them, with reef points taken to avoid outrunning the slower capital ships, moved the frigates *Mutine*, *Avenant*, *Marin*, and *Christ*. The *Christ* had been taken as a prize from the Spaniards, who had named this great forty-four-gun frigate, bearing two hundred and twenty sailors and men-at-arms, for the gentle Nazarene with no thought of either incongruity or irreverence. Among the other frigates, only the *Mutine* exceeded her in size, number of cannon, and complement.

After these straggled a motley flotilla of smaller craft, led by the bomb ketch *Eclatant*, which looked for all the world like a ship that had accidentally lost her foremast in a storm, for her towering square-rigged mainmast and her low lateen-rigged mizzen were set so far back that more than half the vessel did not lie beneath any sail at all. There was a reason for this, Kit knew. The tremendous mortar that was her sole armament was bedded in the great timbers of her foredeck. And as its great bombshell was hurled almost straight upward to crash down upon the walls and towers of a besieged city, a foremast would have been in the way. Still, the bomb ketch was a very ugly vessel, and awkward to handle. Kit had to keep the trim little brigantine *Providence*, which had less than half the displacement of his beloved *Seaflower*, under all reefs to stay in place behind the *Eclatant*.

The rest of the rear-guard flotilla was made up of two smaller flyboats, four traversiers (the small boats used in communication between the larger vessels of a fleet), and the fat-hulled *Drépoise,* the bearer of munitions and supplies.

The fact that he was taking part in one of the greatest naval expeditions of all time troubled Kit not at all. His mind was occupied by other and, to him, not less momentous matters. He was going back to Cartagena. Back to carry the city by fire and sword, level its fortresses, sack its houses. Earlier his thoughts would have been troubled by the visions of bloodshed, wholesale looting, murder, and ravishment that he was helping to let loose upon a peaceful people.

But any tendency toward mercy was checked by his memories of Cartagena itself: the people bellowing with joy in the streets as the dark silhouettes of his crew swung black against the sun from the towering gallows; the gleeful cries that had greeted every blow that landed on the helpless black gunner; and most of all the fiendish near-ecstasy of the populace at the sight of Smithers standing at the stake amid the devouring flames.

Beside him, Bernardo still limped. For this, thank Cartagena. Upon his own broad back not one inch of flesh was unscarred by the biting oxhide lashes. Yes, Cartagena! In Cartagena were lost years of his life. In Cartagena was the tender father who had begotten Kit in drunken lust and had then cast off the sweet, high-minded girl who had surrendered to him because she loved him too much to deny him anything. This was the father who had spurned the child of her love like a homeless cur, striped her across the face with a riding whip, and surrendered her to the torturers! In Cartagena was the man who had taken a gentle woman whom Kit had once loved—the man who with a brave show of kindness had spared him from the noose only to turn him over to the stone quarries, the walls of San Lázaro, and the never-resting whips of the Spanish guards. In Cartagena. Yes, in Cartagena! Bernardo, who could read Kit's expression, held out his hand.

"Easy, Kit," he said. "Too much thinking beforehand addles the pate. When the time has come, all things will be made right. Who knows? In the battle itself Don Luis may be killed, and so . . ."

He halted suddenly, staring at Kit. The great golden mane was thrown far back, and the hard young face was lifted skyward. Kit bent both arms at the elbow and clenched both fists with almost voluptuous slowness. His head rolled on the column of his neck, and his voice came out low and flat and calm, so that its very lack of emphasis made Bernardo feel cold all over, as though he had been plunged into a bath of brine and ice.

"With these two hands, Bernardo!" Kit said. "With these two hands!"

"No, Kit," Bernardo said sorrowfully. "Don't hold murder in your heart.

It will destroy you. I would not have your hands stained with the blood of parricide. I love you too well to have your soul damned in hell."

"He has injured you greatly, too," Kit snarled. "Do you forgive him?"

Bernardo looked away, his dark eyes calm and grave as they swept the surface of the sea. "I have forgiven him," he said. "Now in my old age I have forsworn greed, envy, and revenge." He smiled wryly. "All my former luxuries, for which I once lived."

The fleet swept majestically onward across the blue Caribbean. No enemy vessel opposed them. If any ship of Holland, England, or Spain sighted them, she at once cracked on all canvas and bore away at her best speed. On April 13 they sighted the mainland some four leagues eastward of Cartagena, between that city and Point Hicacos. Then the squadron reassembled at Sambee.

Kit knew it was foolish to try to batter down the thick walls opposite the Tenaza or the Santo Domingo section, but he suspected that such a man as De Pointis might attempt even this madness. What actually happened surprised even him, for the mighty eighty-four guns of the *Sceptre* roared out a challenge, and almost before the echoes of the broadside had died away, her longboats were over the side, racing for the walls.

Beneath the walls, the surf boiled white, and the first of the boats capsized at once. The others were lingering long enough to draw the half-drowned soldiers from the shallow surf when a signal gun from the *Sceptre* recalled them. Even so, it was a miracle that all six of the longboats reached the side of the great ship without being overturned. The *Sceptre* drew them aboard and stood southward toward the Boca Chica channel.

She veered seaward, firing as she passed, but her shots fell short, raising white geysers in the shallow water. Now the frigates *Saint-Louis* and *Fort* tacked in, and opened with all their port guns. Kit could see the clouds of dust rising from the walls where the thirty-eight-pounders smashed, but after they had passed there was no apparent damage. Momentarily, the *Fort* was aground, but by setting even her stuns'les she drew off. The *Saint-Louis* herself scraped bottom.

But the shallow-draft *Providence* could navigate in a heavy dew, so Kit rode her in and hurled his heavy mortar shells over the walls and into the city itself. It was only this last attack that forced the guns in the Tenaza fortress to bellow out their brazen answer; then the peremptory signal flags on the *Sceptre*'s masthead ordered Kit out again.

They had lain overnight at Sambee, and the whole day of the fourteenth of April was spent in desultory bombardment of the walls; but at high noon of the fifteenth all the ships dropped anchor in a vast semicircle ranging two miles out to sea and lying across the entrance of the Boca Chica channel. The frigate *Marin* pushed her prow into the channel itself, and lay there at anchor at its narrowest point, so that any Spanish vessel which attempted to escape would have had the instant attention of all her guns, which in turn would have brought down upon the Spaniards the whole French armada.

Toward nightfall, Kit saw through the glass a row of chaloupes, landing boats, putting out from the *Furieux*. Of these, only one was occupied by officers of the fleet, the rest being manned by Negro sappers. Kit saw Ducasse's imposing figure among the officers, and behind him Pally, who commanded the Negroes. Among the other officers was Beaumont, who commanded the Saint-Domingue brigade. Kit put down his glass with an oath. De Pointis, then, was only too willing to sacrifice the most gallant men of Saint-Domingue to make the first breach, keeping his perfumed fops from the court of Versailles entirely safe.

But when he lifted the glass again he saw among the officers the young Chevalier de Pointis, the nephew of the commander. This young aristocrat, Kit had suspected from the one or two occasions he had seen him before the fleet left Petit Goave, was a real man. Kit laid down the spyglass and called Bernardo to his side.

"You're in command now," he said. "I'm joining the attack."

"Kit," Bernardo began, but Kit lifted a warning hand.

"That is a command, Bernardo," he said quietly, "not a matter for discussion."

Bernardo saluted the young captain gravely, bleak misery in his eyes. Watching Kit go ashore without him was a chilling experience. How many years had he fought and suffered at the side of this great golden sea hawk? He shook his head sadly. Such thoughts had best not be dwelt upon.

As he slipped over the side into the longboat, Kit thought suddenly and with painful clarity of Rouge. The attack was going to be dangerous, almost suicidally so. For all the hideous confusion of his life, Kit did not want to die. Not with Rouge to come back to. . . . Bianca would release him. She must release him. And with his mother's death finally avenged and Ducasse's promised reward, all might be joy and peace.

During the night before the landing, eighty Negroes had hacked their way entirely across the narrow neck of the peninsula, so that Ducasse was able to station sentries at intervals a few yards apart from the shores of the ocean to the shores of the bay, thus effectively cutting off San Luis de Boca Chica from any aid that might reach it. Kit accompanied young De Pointis across the freshly hacked trail until the two of them reached the camp the

Negroes were making on the other side, around a bend just above the fort.

Walking up to a soldier, Kit requested the loan of a musket. Somewhat nonplused, the soldier passed it over. Kit was richly dressed, and the soldiers were accustomed to the whims of these gentlemen of France. Then very quietly Kit moved out of the camp. In all his finery, he went down on his belly in the mud and crept to within firing distance of the walls. He heard a slight rustle behind him and whirled, his dagger already out. The Chevalier de Pointis lay there behind him, his rich dress as mud-befouled as Kit's own, a grin on his handsome young face. However much of a stiff-necked old fool his uncle, the commander, may be, Kit decided, young De Pointis is indeed a man. . . .

Kit smiled back at him and the two of them looked up at the towering walls, coming clear in the breaking dawn. They could see the soldiers scurrying about, but Kit waited until the heavy, pompous figure of the captain of the guard, the same man who had given him the Indian treatment, appeared. Then the musket leaped to his shoulder and fired all at the same instant, without his even seeming to have taken aim. The captain of the guard reeled, and collapsed into the arms of one of the soldiers.

The whole wall exploded into fire, all of it aimed badly, showing plainly that the guards had not the slightest idea of the direction from which the shot had come. Then, almost as in answer, from the sea the hoarse booming of great guns rolled in. The *Saint-Louis* had opened up on the fortress, followed by the *Fort.* Half a minute later, the whole world reeled with bass thunder. The *Sceptre,* they both knew, had loosed a broadside.

They lay there in the mud and laughed aloud, their voices hidden by the thunder of the guns. They pounded each other on the back with muddy paws and roared.

Now it had begun. Now it had really begun.

27

By April 28, everyone in Cartagena realized that the city was doomed. San Luis de Boca Chica, the channel fortress that they had depended upon to keep the French out of the landlocked bay, had fallen with ludicrous ease. It had withstood only one day of pounding from the great ships of the line, then a wild attack from the landward side had overwhelmed it. It was scant comfort to them to learn that old Sancho Jimeno had fought like ten demons, so much so that De Pointis had given him back his sword and released him with honor and ceremony.

Even the early hope that had sustained them, of differences between the French regulars and the buccaneers, had proved of little account. True, De Pointis had driven the pirates back into the attack on the fortress with the flat of his sword when they had fled the battle. True, he had tied one filibuster to the stake and brought up the firing squad before the freebooters could be whipped into line. But somehow, somewhere, they had regained their courage, and crossing the bay, had swarmed over the lightly held hill Popa like a legion of fiends.

San Lázaro had fallen to a joint attack of buccaneers and regulars, and in this battle a wounded Spaniard had told of seeing in the forefront of the attack the blond young devil who had been held a prisoner at San Lázaro while he himself was a guard there. Everyone knew that this man, who was in some strange way linked to the Count del Toro, president of the Audencia, had perished during a later imprisonment out at the Boca Chica.

But had he? As the battle wore on, reports of his having been seen, always in the forefront of the fight, grew in frequency until at last they could no longer be denied. And now, with the great guns of La Motte Michel, commander of the Royal Battery, in plain sight across the narrow channel from the Getsémani suburb, thousands of the citizens could make out the tawny gold of his hair among the darker heads of his comrades. Of course several other of the Frenchmen were blond, but once a glass was leveled, there was no mistaking that face. He had been seen by too many of the crowd as he was being led away from that spectacular trial.

Now Coetlogon too had set up his lighter battery of twelve- and eighteen-pounders, for so close to the city had the Frenchmen come that even these light pieces were in range. Between the two batteries, the nine great mortars of De la Motte d'Hérans were rumbling, and Gombaud played his smaller high-trajectory pieces with exquisite precision. In the bay the bomb ketch spoke now and again with its brazen throat, and all the ships of the line stood behind it and hammered the walled city to pieces.

Much of the city was afire, making an evilly beautiful sight in the darkness, the gigantic flames blotting out the stars. From the walls the defending cannon split the night with their thunder. All the air was loud with the shrieks of the dying. That the city did not burn entirely to ashes was due to the circumstance that blew a blinding rainstorm up from the sea on the night of the twenty-ninth. During this, in the howling winds many of the citizens managed to escape the city in the darkness. While the French sentries huddled miserably under improvised shelters, their campfires drowned out by the rain, hundreds of Spaniards stole by them in the inky, rain-whipped night. Past the lines, they wound upward into the hills, and here most of the refugees drowned in the flash floods that turned mountain freshets into roaring cataracts.

On the morning of the thirtieth of April, several things happened. First of all, the brigantine *Providence* had ranged too close to the walls at Getsémani, and had been sunk by the guns of the city. As was not uncommon among sailors of that day, indeed of almost any day, most of her crew could not swim and perished with their vessel. Bernardo made a brave effort to keep the captain of the marines above water, but a sharpshooter put a ball through the old captain's head as they struggled in the water. Bernardo prudently dived, and swimming a long distance underwater, managed to gain the shore near the San Lázaro hospital.

Even as he drew himself ashore, wet and shivering, he saw Kit run out, fully exposed to the fire from the city, to hurl a hand bomb into a pirogue laden with explosives that the Spaniards were attempting to push under the bridge that connected the San Lázaro section with Getsémani. It blew up with a sound like the end of the world, and Bernardo was hurled several yards through the air to land almost at Kit's feet. Kit caught him by his long silver-threaded black hair, dragged him unceremoniously up the beach with musket balls kicking up the sand all around them, and tumbled with him into a sheltering trench.

Kit grinned at him, and took his place among a group of wild young chevaliers who were grouping to lead the attack. In these aristocratic young Frenchmen Kit had found a reckless courage that passed well over the border line of foolhardiness. And they, in turn, had adopted him as one of themselves. After the battle, they promised him gleefully, he should have a château near Versailles, all the money in the world, a title, and the prettiest woman in France for a wife, if their word with the King meant anything. Kit, who had his doubts, merely grinned at them, and took his place in line.

And now with Lévy, the bravest of all their commanders, at their head, they raced over the bridge toward the gates the heavy guns had pounded to pieces. But at the gates the Spaniards waited and loosed upon them the most withering musket fire they had yet encountered. Kit saw Marolles and Du Roullon go down, shot almost to pieces. Fouilleuse lay with splinters of bone protruding through his broken leg, and Montosier and Vanjoux had so many gunshot wounds that it was a wonder they lived.

Kit knew that without help in another moment they would all lie dead at the mouth of these broken gates, but in that instant Lévy had rallied the remainder of his forces and surged back to the fray. The Spanish fought back fiercely. Lévy got a musket ball through his neck, Frankin, his aide-de-camp, had his right arm broken, but they both continued to charge until they were carried off fainting from their wounds.

It was at this juncture that Kit saw Bernardo storming to his aid in a company of buccaneers, led by no less than Ducasse himself. Ducasse had been wounded in the attack on the Boca Chica, but he limped along firing his pistols and swinging his saber with fierce energy.

Still the Spaniards held, giving ground inch by bloody inch. Kit and young De Pointis fought side by side, for during the battle they had become as brothers. But above the noise of battle there rose a war cry that sounded like the shrieking of tortured souls in hell, and looking up, Kit and De Pointis saw Pally charging across the bridge at the head of his Negroes.

The blacks charged full into the musket fire, went down in rows, yet continued to charge over the bodies of their dead, so that the Spaniards had no chance to reload. At last the weary, heroic men broke, and the shrieking blacks pursued them through the narrow streets. Now the buccaneers of Ducasse joined the chase and Kit and young De Pointis were swept along with them, until they all piled up in wild confusion before the place where the Governor of the New Granada section had closed the doors between Cartagena and Getsémani in the face of his soldiers.

There was nothing for the Spaniards to do but to charge and die or to stand and be butchered. The Spaniards, being men of pride, charged. For eight terrible minutes they hurled back an attacking force of twenty times their numbers. Then they were overwhelmed and massacred.

Looking up at the white flags that at long last fluttered from the walls of the city, Kit could scarcely discern them through the scalding rain of his tears. For in his arms lay the body of the fair young Chevalier de Pointis, who had been shot through the heart at the last instant before the surrender.

28

THE GREAT GATES remained closed, however. When Kit saw two emissaries marching out under flags of truce to negotiate with the Baron de Pointis, who lay wounded on his litter, he decided not to wait any longer. The old general had not been advised of the death of his beloved nephew, and Kit felt moved with sympathy for him. Despot he might be, martinet and extreme disciplinarian, but after the first day of the attack there was no longer any question of his courage.

So, stumbling with weariness, sooted all over with gun smoke, through which his tears had left white streaks, Kit started toward Cartagena. It was here that Bernardo joined him. It was rapidly growing dark, and inside the city the renewed fires bloodied the skies with their glow. Slowly the two men circled the near-by walls looking for an opening. They had little difficulty in finding one, for there were places in the walls now where the great mortars had tumbled the stones down in avalanches of rubble, and over one of these Kit and Bernardo found it possible to climb with the easy motion of men mounting a low hill. Inside, the weary, blood-streaked, begrimed guards stared at them in astonishment, but made no move to impede their progress. Some of the soldiers, realizing the extent of their city's defeat, even saluted them.

It was easier still to find the house of Del Toro in the darkness, for almost the entire street on which it stood was aflame. Kit noted quickly that neither of the two houses that flanked it was yet burning, but if the wind held, it was only a matter of time before that entire section would lie in ashes.

They crept close to the house, their footfalls drowned in the crackling roar of the fires and the crash of falling timbers. Where the barred window had been was now only a great jagged hole, and inside much of the splendid furniture had been smashed to kindling by the shot that had torn through.

But when they rose from their crouching positions, their quarry lay before them, for there on the one unbroken chair in the room they looked into sat Luis del Toro, his proud head sunk on his great chest, his whole aspect so eloquent of defeat and despair that even Kit felt a momentary surge of pity move within his heart. Though I have sworn to kill him, he thought, if there is any way—any honorable way—to spare his life, I will spare him. . . . He leaned forward, peering intently at the suddenly aged man who sat amid ruins of his former grandeur at his banquet table—alone.

Don Luis sprang up at once, pistol in hand, and started toward the window; but he halted suddenly, for Kit had swung himself through it, his own hands resting on his undrawn-pistol butts.

"So we meet again, my esteemed father," he said quietly, "and for the last time."

Don Luis stood there, his own pistol lowered, a look of sad weariness on his dark face.

"So you know," he said at last.

"Yes," Kit whispered, "I know. Do you expect me to make a show of devotion? Raise your pistol, my father!"

Don Luis's shoulders stiffened, a slow, mocking smile curling the corners of his mouth.

"Is not this earth big enough for you and me, my son?" he said. "Go your way, for I do not want to kill you."

"Raise your gun, O begetter of bastards! Though I don't like to kill you in cold blood, I will if I have to."

"You are chivalrous," Don Luis said coldly. "And since it is forced upon me, I will take back the life I gave. But not with gunfire—that's no weapon for gentlemen. Besides, I have no skill with a pistol. You would have our encounter fair, would you not?"

Bernardo, who had crawled through the window, stood beside Kit, rubbing his numbed arm.

"Have done with the frippery," he growled.

"A moment," Kit said lightly. He took the two great pistols from his belt and laid them upon the table. Slowly, while Bernardo watched him narrowly, Don Luis did likewise.

"Take your choice, then," Kit smiled. "What say you, my lord? Sabers? Cutlasses? Rapiers?"

"Rapiers," Don Luis said softly, a slow, exultant smile on his face.

"No!" Bernardo roared. "By my masculinity, no! You are a good swordsman, Kit—but he is a past master."

Don Luis bowed with mocking civility.

"I will entertain any suggestion," he said quietly.

Kit's brow creased with frowning. Then suddenly light leaped and flamed in his blue eyes.

"My lord has lived in Seville and Cádiz, has he not?"

"Yes," said Don Luis. "What has that to do with this quarrel?"

"Then my lord has seen the gypsies fight. So will I fight with you, Luis del Toro—gitano-fashion!"

Bernardo could see Don Luis paling beneath his tan. With a lightning-like motion, Bernardo's hand swept down and came out with his dagger. He flipped it end over end so that it stood and quivered in the polished wood of the table. Kit did likewise with his own. The two were mates: Bernardo had purchased them at the same time, sheaths and all, in a bazaar of Algiers.

"Take your choice, my lord," Kit said softly.

Without even looking at the weapons, Don Luis stretched out his hand and picked up one of them. Its fourteen inches of glittering steel glinted evilly in the light of the candle. Kit walked calmly to the table and took the other.

"There remains yet a formality," he said. "Or have you forgotten?"

"No," Don Luis growled, "I have not forgotten."

Kit leaped up on the table, snatching two tapestries from the walls. One of these he wound about his left forearm, so that it made a protective bulge. The other he passed to his father. Slowly Don Luis followed his son's example.

Kit's eyes darted about the room until they fell on the great rope that pulled the bell which summoned the servants. One slash with the dagger and it fell. Kit knotted one end of it tightly about his left wrist. He played out a scant yard of the rope, and cut it off there. Then he held out the other end to Del Toro.

"This is madness!" Don Luis growled.

"Are you afraid, my father?" Kit said.

Angrily Don Luis picked up the rope and bound his own left wrist. Thus linked, they stood and faced each other.

"Now," Kit said, softly, almost peacefully, "now we can begin!"

The daggers flashed through the air and cut great rents in the heavy tapestries as the two men used them to screen their straining bodies. But at a yard's distance, it was impossible not to draw blood. There among the gutting tapers they moved silently except for hoarse grunts, locked in that strange dance of death, their leaps and capers gigantically magnified in grotesquely moving shadows on the walls.

This duel of the long knives was a thing of beauty, all grace and agility, thrust and parry, the furious stab caught harmlessly in the folds of the tapestry, the body hurled back to the limits of the rope's length to avoid the counterthrust, while blood and sweat mingled in glistening rivers on their faces.

A chair crashed over and was kicked aside. Don Luis's knife found the flesh of Kit's shoulder and sank in. Kit wrenched free, his silk shirt dyed crimson with his blood. Don Luis's cheek was gashed open from ear to jaw, and from the point of his Vandyke scarlet drops fell.

But no word escaped them, no cry, no groan. They halted briefly, breathing heavily like wounded beasts at bay, and started in again, each of them cut or gashed or stabbed in a dozen places. How it might have ended Bernardo could not tell, for Kit's lithe agility was made up for by Don Luis's gigantic strength. This one thing Bernardo swore in his heart—in one more minute his own pistol would deside the issue.

He took it out and cocked it, the loud click drowned out by the noise of the ferocious struggle. But it was in that instant that the cry came hanging high and shrill upon the air.

"Stop!" it rang. "Stop it, both of you, for the love of God!"

The two men halted, their fingers gripped on the hilts of the daggers, the great boles of their chests rising and falling with their labored breathing. Slowly their bloody, terrible heads came around, and there on the stairway they saw Bianca swaying, her lovely young face as white as death.

"I will not have it!" she stormed. "Do you think I find honor in being fought over like a scrap of flesh between two savage dogs? Know you, Luis, and you, Kit, that from this hour neither of you has in me an excuse for murder! For, as God lives, and upon the honor of His blessed Mother, I will go this night to the Sisterhood of Nuestra Señora de Cartagena—and over me, at least, there shall be no further bloodshed!"

She drew herself up until even her small figure seemed regal, and her voice came out high, clear, and marvelously controlled.

"Put down those knives!"

Slowly the tight-clasped knuckles loosened and both bloody weapons clattered to the floor. Bianca came down the stairs, step by slow step. But before she reached them she halted suddenly, her dark eyes enormous in her white face, staring past them, past even Bernardo, toward the window. Slowly Bernardo turned to follow her gaze, then his mouth dropped open, for there on the sill Rouge sat, her long, naked legs swinging shamelessly back and forth, her green eyes filled with savage joy, and two great pistols leveled in her hands.

"Your weapon, good Bernardo," she said evenly. "Drop it to the floor."

For all its calmness, there was no mistaking that tone. Bernardo let his pistol slide from his nerveless fingers. Rouge stared at Bianca, seeing her slim, lovely body, little hid by the filmy stuff of her gown, seeing her face, small, soft, heartbreakingly lovely, its whiteness startling in juxtaposition to the matchless, marvelous, vulture-feathered blackness of her long, deep-curling hair.

"I thank you for your vow," Rouge said. "It has saved your life. You're lovely, more lovely than I imagined. . . . But enough of this, for already the entire upper story of this house is afire, and we have little time."

As though to emphasize her words, the crackling roar of the fire sounded clearly above their heads and a tongue of flame leaped down the stairway so that it touched one of the heavy tapestries, which blazed up instantly like a pine torch. The three men surged forward at once, but Rouge's clear voice halted them.

"Not so fast!" she called. "There is still one small matter. I see, Don Luis, that you too recall my face. Good! Then I do not have to waste time in pretty speeches." She leveled the pistols at Don Luis's heart.

It was at that moment that Bernardo sprang at her, catching her wrists so that her arms were thrown upward, the two pistol balls plowing into the ceiling, making two heavy, downward-crashing showers of plaster. Afterward, he was at a loss to account for his action, except to say that there was something in Bianca's face that moved him—something not of this world, a reflection of an inward illumination passing all human understanding. It left no hatred in Bernardo's heart, not for Del Toro or for any other man or anything upon this earth save only of hatred itself.

The room was filled with acrid smoke now, through which they moved like dream figures, their struggles strangely diminished both in intensity and in importance. But Rouge twisted like a tigress in Bernardo's grip, her face contorted with rage. Forgetting the cord that held him bound to his father, Kit sprang forward to help subdue her. The bell cord brought him up short, and he turned. Don Luis was kneeling on the floor, his hand holding the dagger he had again picked up. He came up slowly, his intent masked by the murky smoke that half-hid his dark face. Then his arm moved and the bell cord parted. He stood facing Kit.

"All our lives," he said gently, "we have been so bound together, my son. My error lay in not drawing in upon the cord that bound you to me. Can you not forgive a man grown old and destroyed by his own pride?"

Kit stood there wavering, a fierce battle raging in his heart. He remembered his mother's face, cut open to the bone by this man's lash; he remembered Smithers amid the flames, and the small Parisian's agony as the noose strangled him to death; he remembered the walls of San Lázaro and the oxhide whips of the guards—yet in the end he was half putting out his hand when Bianca interrupted them.

"Farewell, my lords," she said quietly. "I must go now, for they are calling me." Then she turned and walked toward the flaming stairs.

"They?" Don Luis gasped. "Who on earth are they?"

"No one—on earth, my lord," Bianca said serenely, and turning, dashed up the fire-swept stairway. Don Luis was half a step behind her, and Kit upon his heels, but so great was the smoke and flame in the upper hall that it was impossible to see into which of the rooms she had gone.

"You take the right," Kit choked. "I'll take the left!"

The two men separated and disappeared into the smoke-filled, flame-swept rooms. Below them, Rouge had stopped struggling.

"Let me go, Bernardo," she said, weeping. "Let me go, for the love of God!"

"That you may go after him?" Bernardo growled, his own face ashen. "Never!"

"If he dies," Rouge whispered, "if for her sake he perishes, Bernardo, not one hour will I survive him!"

And if in answer to her words, they saw Kit, sooted all over, coming down the stairs with the still figure of Bianca in his arms.

"Dead?" Bernardo said.

"No," Kit croaked. "Take her, Rouge, and attend to her hurts." He looked about the room. "Don Luis has not come down?"

At Bernardo's quick, negative shake of the head, Kit whirled and started back up the stairs.

"Kit," Rouge shrieked, "do not go! Don't risk your life for *him!*"

Kit half-turned, and his eyes were blue glacier ice.

"You have my love," he said quietly. "Do not make me regret it!" Then he raced into the sea of flame. Bernardo surged up after him, and Rouge followed Bernardo. This time there was no difficulty in finding Don Luis, for his low, hoarse-voiced cries of agony guided them to the spot. Muffling his face with his arm, Kit plunged into the room, but when he was close Don Luis called out to him:

"Go back, my son. Go back, my tall son, for I am finished."

He lay on his back. Across his chest, pressing him down, was a fallen beam of quebracho wood, weighing hundreds of pounds and smoldering sullenly. Every bone in his upper trunk was crushed, and yet he lived. Kit took his arm and tugged fiercely, knowing as he did so that it was useless.

"My son," Don Luis whispered, "my son, go with God!"

Still Kit pulled at him fiercely, oblivious of the creaking as the great beams above his own head, weakened by the fire, bent slowly downward. It was at that moment that Bernardo and Rouge hurled themselves upon him, and drew him, struggling furiously, from the room. Outside in the hall he turned wrathfully toward them, but the words he was about to say remained forever unuttered, drowned unspoken in the avalanche of sound as the room they had left was buried under tons of masonry and charred timber.

They raced down the stairs, and Kit and Bernardo paused long enough to gather up Bianca. Then they all fled from the flaming house. Outside in the street they beat out the fire in their own garments and stood looking at the flames standing straight up in the still-breathing air and throwing great showers of sparks higher still. Then, with majestic deliberation, the outer walls began to buckle, crumbling slowly so that even their fall seemed prolonged, and the slow-rolling thunder of the impact as the house of Del Toro crashed into flaming rubble was almost an afterthought—an echo.

It was then that Rouge opened her lips and let out a cry, wild, high, hysterical wailing. Kit drew her to him, and she lay sobbing against his chest, unmindful of the blood and sweat to which she added her tears.

Bernardo stood looking at Don Luis's smoldering pyre, then, skeptic that he was, freethinker, the eternal alien scourged across the world, he lifted his head and whispered: "Forgive him—and forgive us, too, for the evil and hatred in our own hearts. We are as bloodguilty as he."

Then he and Kit bent and lifted Bianca, and started off through the flame-lighted streets. Rouge walked beside them, wiping the unconscious Bianca's face with a cloth torn from her gown. Softly, slowly, Bianca stirred. Her dark eyes came open and she stared up at them.

"Luis is dead?" she whispered. It was scarcely a question.

Slowly Kit nodded.

"I'm sorry," she murmured. "In his heart he was a good man." Then, seeking Kit's face, she said, "Take me to the good sisters, for there I was always meant to be."

Kit and Bernardo lifted her again and turned in the direction of the nunnery of Nuestra Señora de Cartagena. When they had reached it, Bianca stretched out her hand to Rouge.

"Be good to him," she whispered, "for this too was always meant to be."

Suddenly, impulsively, Rouge bent forward and kissed her. Then she waited while Kit and Bernardo carried Bianca inside the nunnery, standing there in a quiet kind of terror in the empty street, feeling utterly desolate and lost and horribly alone.

When she saw them coming out again, she took a running step forward, then she stopped short, seeing the pain moving in Kit's eyes. They walked through the darkened streets, but it was not until the broken walls were again in sight that any of them spoke. Shyly, softly, Rouge turned to Kit, and lifted her eyes, in which the tears hung glistening.

"Can you," she whispered, "still love me—remembering this?"

Kit turned to her, and in his clear blue eyes was the beginning of a great peace. Slowly, wordlessly, he drew her into his arms.

A
WOMAN
CALLED
FANCY

For My Mother

1

The Williamsons' farm lay on a hillside so that when it rained the water ran down and away from it. In fifty years it had worn out and starved out the three families who had tried to work it. The Williamsons were the fourth.

From where she lay, half hidden in the rank Johnson grass, Fancy could see the gaunt figure of her brother, Randy, bent tiredly over the handles of the plow. He moved along behind Mike, their lone mule, an animal so old that Pap, in his better moods, was fond of swearing he'd bought the critter offen a man called Noah, who'd brung him to Carolina on the Ark; and after him came Maw Williamson, her gnarled hands busy with the cotton seed. She looked, Fancy thought bitterly, a mite older than the mule, and not half as human.

It was hot. That was bad, Fancy knew. It had just turned planting time and already it was hot. Above her the sky was yellow-white, every bit of the blue washed out by the sunglare, and nowhere was there any cloud. Fancy narrowed her deep blue eyes to a squint, and peered upward into the limitless depths of the sky. Up there, tiny black dots moved in slow, lazy circles, so high up that only when she squinted could she see them.

"Damned old buzzards," Fancy muttered. "Circling up there a-waiting. Well, you won't get me. Rest of my folks can hang around here and rot; but not me. I'm going somewheres. Down to Augusta, maybe. Find myself a rich gentleman acquaintance and marry him—just you wait!"

She looked away from the all but invisible turkey buzzards, and picked up the ragged seventh-grade reader that lay upon her flat stomach. She had read it through so many times that she knew it by heart. And that, considered in its rightful place in the scale of things, was an accomplishment to be compared with the moving of a very small mountain. In seven generations of Williamsons, Fancy was the first ever to learn to read and write. She had done it herself, alone and unaided. If her pronunciation was often widely at variance with the actual sound of the words, the fact remained that Fancy could read a newspaper, on those rare occasions when anybody had a newspaper, and was always called upon to interpret the mysterious scrawls upon paper which occasionally came from the more adventurous sons and daughters of the hill people who had managed to escape.

But she put the book down after a moment and again stared up into the yellow-white sky. This time she did not squint, but looked upward with the opaque gaze of the dreamer. There were vague pictures moving in the light-flooded depths of space, and she was in each of them, striding lightly, gaily among handsome and beautifully dressed people, stopping now and again to exchange a word with some of the finest. Most of the people in these magic lantern pictures that Fancy's imagination cast upon the sky were young, handsome men. And they had one thing in common: they all adored Fancy.

This was the gulf that she had unwittingly opened between herself and her own: the wordless have not the materials for dreams.

The wind shifted, and jerked her back to reality. It came up the hillside from the hog pen below, and the smell of the razorback hogs and the slops upon which they were fed tugged at her nostrils. Fancy brought a grimy palm up and covered them. Then the wind died down, and the only smells left were the scent of the rank grass, and the sweat in her ragged dress.

Do nice folks sweat? she wondered. Reckon they must. But most likely they bathe twice a week and change all their clothes and use powder and perfume and even paint. Maw says that it's wicked to paint, but if I had my druthers—I'd druther be wicked than ugly.

Fancy lay there a long time, until some of the yellow-white began to spill out of the sky, and the blue crept back in and deepened. Turning her head a little, she could see that Maw and Randy and the mule were beginning to lose color, to blacken against the rim of the sky, the edges of them sharpening. After a while they were like those figures that that crazy artist who had traveled through the hills with the medicine show had cut from black cardboard with his little scissors. Only they moved still, jerkily, and above them was the pale glimmer of a star.

Fancy sighed and sat up. Time to be getting along home. Time to wake up Pap—if she could wake him up by now, after a day of sitting on the porch pulling on his brown jug. That was all Pap ever did. Life had put a curse on him, so that nothing he ever did came out quite right, and he had many sorrows that required daily drowning. In the meantime Maw and Randy ran the farm, with a little help from Fancy when they could catch her long enough to make her do it—which wasn't often, for among the things that Fancy understood was that a person who didn't know when to give up was a fool.

She started downward toward the house, the Johnson grass rippling against her skirt, walking slowly with short, mincing little steps, which she told herself was the way a lady walked. She was, if anyone had been there to see her, a sight to see. But there was no one there—no one to see the slight, small girl, just turned nineteen, whose hair was blacker than the wing feathers of a rain crow, and whose eyes, oddly, were the exact color of the evening sky come harvest time. Not that there hadn't been plenty of hill men who hadn't remarked these features, together with the mouth that was a mite too big for her face, and was the dark red of wild cherries, and looked a little sullen in repose.

Fancy had had her share of suitors—and more than her share it seemed to some of the other lonesome hill girls' way of thinking. They had come in droves: big, rangy boys with the knots of muscles jerking above their lean jaws, their eyes hot and honing; substantial farmers, already turned fifty and more, lean as the hills, with money in their pockets to buy Fancy aprons of crisp calico—even a preaching man or two. But Fancy would have none of them, much to Pap's outraged disgust. At nineteen, Fancy was already an old maid by hill standards. Maw, for instance, had borne her first stillborn infant before her sixteenth birthday, and continued to produce blue, strangled, pitiful little bundles of flesh, until finally, late in her thirties, Randy and later Fancy had miraculously survived. It was this long run of bad luck with children—valuable in the hills as hands—that had made a drinking man of Pap.

Now, in his old age, Pap had pinned all his hopes on Fancy. He had given her encouragement and help in shooing away the boys, but when she just as stubbornly refused to form a connection with some upright widower of sixty with money enough for Pap to borrow for seed and debts and whiskey, he had felt the sharpness of the serpent's tooth. Yet persuasion, threats, and even his big razor strop, availed him not. Fancy ran and hid, or stood and fought. At nineteen she was single still, and nary a prospect in sight.

The shadows lengthened out before her, blue on the path that led down to the house. Finally from a little rise she could see the house itself. She stood there looking at it. It had been built by the second of the three families who had preceded them, and it was old. To anybody else besides Fancy, that wouldn't have mattered much: most of the farmhouses were old. But Fancy dimly guessed that a house didn't have to be dilapidated or shabby; there must be houses with their shutters firmly attached, and whose roofs didn't leak. Ten years ago, when she was nine, the last porch step had rotted through, and Pap had been gittin' around to fixing it ever since. There were boards missing from the porch itself and the roof of it slanted down at a crazy angle, where two of the posts had been broken in a windstorm some four years before. Pap had just looked at that and picked up his jug. He hadn't even threatened to fix them.

Maw was too tired now to replace the oiled paper over the windows, so in the wintertime they froze and in the summer the bugs feasted off their unprotected hides. The house had never been painted in all its long life, and wind and rain had scoured it to a weathered gray that fitted into the age-old, tired hills, and which in spring, the flowering wisteria vine softened almost into beauty.

It was spring now, and the wisteria blew pale violet up to the mossy shingles of the roof; but Fancy couldn't see that beauty. Her reaction to the house in which she had been born was very simple: she hated it with all her heart.

She stood there looking at it for long minutes, then she came on down the path. When she was close, she saw that Pap wasn't asleep after all. He was sitting on a cracker box behind the screen of the wisteria talking to old man Wilkins.

Fancy's breath stopped still. Of all her suitors, old man Wilkins was the most persistent. She could see him now, sitting on the porch rail, stooped over like a red, bald turkey buzzard, moving his store-bought teeth loosely around in his mouth as he talked. Because of those teeth, nothing he said ever came out clearly. He talked, Fancy thought, as though he had a mouthful of hot mush. His faded blue shirt was as clean and pressed as ever, and his jeans were shiny at the knees and in the seat. His remaining wisps of gray hair were slicked down as usual with grease, and he fanned himself with his straw hat.

Oh no! Fancy thought bitterly. Oh God, oh Jesus, not again!

But it wasn't one of those things that running away from would help. Better to make an end to it right now. Better to tell that old buzzard that no matter what kind of a bargain he and Pap had struck between them it wouldn't do any good because she would never marry him.

Don't want an old man like him, she thought. Want myself a young man with blood in his veins, and not one of those hillbillies neither. A man who's polite and talks fair, and who'll take off his hat to me and bow and say, "Howdy, Miss Fancy—deelighted to make your acquaintance."

Old man Wilkins was grinning at her now, his store-bought teeth clicking up and down with the effort.

"Howdy, child," he snickered. "My but you're a sight for sore eyes!"

Fancy didn't answer him. His voice, she decided, sounded exactly like the whinnying of a horse. She stared at him, the corners of her mouth drooping a little into a grimace of acute distaste.

"Fan!" Pap wheezed; "ain't I done learned you to speak when you're spoken to?"

"See nothing, say nothing," Fancy said tartly. "And I sure Lord don't see anything right now—leaseways not nothing much."

"Now look ahere—" Pap began; but old man Wilkins laid a restraining hand on his arm.

"Young gals is like fillies," he whispered; "lots of spirit. Pays to gentle 'em. Take your time and they can be broke. . . ."

"Not by you!" Fancy spat. "Not never by the likes of you!"

"Now look ahere, Fan," Pap said in his whiskery quaver. "Mister Wilkins just paid you a mighty high honor. He come way over here to ask me for your hand. That ain't to be treated lightly—Mister Wilkins is a fine, upstanding man—a pillar of the church, and mighty respected in the community. . . ."

"Mister Wilkins," Fancy said coldly, "is an old goat who don't remember that he's sixty-five years old and that I could be his granddaughter. He may be a pillar of the church, all right, 'cause he spends most of his time leaning up against one, pinching young girls as they come out of meeting. And if he didn't have a heap more nerve than he's got common sense, he'd know I wouldn't have him on a Christmas tree."

Pap stood up majestically, swaying like an oak in a high wind.

"It'll pay you to curb that tongue of yourn, young lady," he growled; "'cause I already done give my consent."

Fancy stared at her father, her blue eyes widening.

"Pap—you didn't!"

"Yes I did," Pap said. "Time you stopped being so dadblamed ungrateful towards the folks what bore and raised you. Mister Wilkins already promised to take care of most of my heaviest burdens. . . ."

There was white fire in the blue eyes now, and seeing it, Pap quailed.

"Now Fan—" he quavered.

"Now nothing! So you aim to sell me like a horse to straighten out the mess your drinking got you into! And I'm s'posed to be grateful. For what, Pap? Tell me that. I never owned a dress or a pair of shoes what you paid for. I ain't never had nothing that you give me, except a mighty heap o' lickings! I'm s'posed to be grateful for that? I'm s'posed to be proud of the fact that all over the hills I'm known as that no-'count Rand Williamson's daughter? Don't you reckon I get tired of folks pitying me 'cause I come from dirt and ain't never going nowheres—leaseways so they think. But I am going somewheres, and not with this horny old buzzard, neither! I'll see the both of you laid out with your big toes pinned together before I'll let this old fool lay a finger on me!"

She whirled then and fled into the house, leaving a trail of half strangled sobs behind her.

"I'm mightily sorry," Pap said. "But don't you worry none. Her maw'll be home in a little while, and she'll talk some sense into her."

"She better," old man Wilkins growled. "You already bled three hundred hard-earned dollars out of me with your promises, and I ain't waiting a day longer—not nary another day!"

"Now don't fret yourself," Pap said soothingly, "Fan'll marry you all right. Just you wait till her maw comes home. . . ."

Hearing these words from where she stood just inside the hall, Fancy knew for the first time in her life the real meaning of despair. Maw wouldn't side with her either—not with so much money involved. Maw was an honest woman who hated debt. She'd be sorry to see Fancy wed to this sickening old man, but not sorry enough to discount the advantages of the match. And Randy would be worse than hopeless. After years of struggling with the worn-out washed away soil of their farm, he'd be willing to sell his sister for much less than that.

It would be dark in a little while—long before Maw and Randy came, Fancy reckoned. For a long time now, she had been telling herself that she was going to get away—that she was going down out of these red Carolina hills, down to where the Savannah River flowed slow and peaceful in the sun. Across the river on the Georgia side was Augusta—the biggest city that Fancy had ever heard tell of. There the rich, handsome young men she had dreamed of would be waiting. It had been a vague dream, more wished for than ever consciously planned. But old man Wilkins with his yellow false teeth clicking in his big, ugly mouth had put an end to that. The dream was a dream no longer. It was a plan.

It took her only a moment to gather her belongings into a bundle—her other dress, and the nice underthings that were not, like all her others, made of floursacking. Then she stole into the kitchen, and felt for the loose brick in the chimney. It gave under her fingers, and she drew out her treasure—the five dollars and sixty-two cents she had managed to save over a period of more than three years. She wrapped it in a bit of cloth and tucked it in her bosom. Then she went back into the hall and waited.

It wouldn't be fair to run away before Maw and Randy had had their say. Maybe she had misjudged them. Maybe they'd stick up for her after all. But if they didn't . . .

She saw them coming slowly, tiredly down the path just as she reached the doorway. Randy shuffled along, leading the ancient mule, and Maw walked with her head and shoulders bent, the perfect picture of the kind of weariness that has stopped hoping for rest or for anything better. Maw had stopped wishing, stopped dreaming so many years ago that the life had just about gone out of her. She didn't even talk much any more—as though even words cost her more effort than she could rightly afford.

Looking at her now, Fancy felt a wild surge of pity for this gaunt rack of bones and meager flesh that had given her life. Poor Maw, she mused, if I leave her, reckon she'll pretty nigh give up the ghost—sure Lord ain't nothing much left of her now.

I can't leave her, I can't! Fancy thought. But if she agrees with Paw she'll be sending me away anyhow—and the only thing I'll change will be the place where I'll be going. Old man Wilkins' place is nigh onto twenty miles from here anyhow, and Augusta ain't much further. Oh, Maw—it's up to you, now. You can lose me or keep me just by saying the word. . . .

"Sary—" Pap began.

"Yes?" Maw said tiredly, "yes, Rand?"

"Mister Wilkins is here on a mighty important errand," Paw said. "He's come to ask us for our little Fan. . . ."

Hypocrite! Fancy thought wildly. Mealy-mouthed hypocrite—why . . .

Maw turned her watery gray eyes upon the face of Fancy's ancient suitor.

"Well, now," she drawled, "I don't rightly know what to say. . . ."

"I'd be mighty good to your little girl," Wilkins put in quickly.

"Don't doubt that," Maw said; "only it 'pears to me that there's a mighty big difference 'twixt your ages."

"There was a big difference 'twixt ourn," Paw said.

"Twelve years," Maw said softly; "but Mister Wilkins got a much longer lead on Fan than that. 'Pears to me . . ."

" 'Pears to me he ought to be interested in a woman, not no girl," Randy put in hotly.

"Now wait a minute, you two," Paw growled. "There's a mite more to this than meets the eye. Mister Wilkins has agreed to take over our biggest debts, and it looks like to me that that ought to be thought about. . . ."

Fancy stared at her mother in the gathering darkness.

Oh, Maw, no! she prayed. Oh, Jesus, Maw—say no!

"Well now—" Maw began.

"There's another matter what ain't even been mentioned," old man Wilkins put in, "and what sure Lord ought to be. Right from the first Rand here entertained my suit right kindly—so much so that I let him have money from time to time. And that money up to today amounts to a mite more'n three hundred dollars—which ain't to be sneezed at, Miz Williamson."

Sarah Williamson turned and stared at her husband.

"Oh, Paw—no!" she breathed.

Pap squirmed upon his cracker box.

"It's a fact, Sary," he whispered.

"Of all the low down, ornery—" Randy began.

"Hush, child," Maw said gently. She turned back to old man Wilkins. " 'Pears to me," she said, "that you done took unfair advantage of Paw's weakness. But be that as it may, a debt's a debt—and we ain't got a Chinaman's chance of paying it off. Mister Wilkins, I give you my consent—mighty unwillingly. When you want the hitching to take place?"

"Right now—tonight!" old man Wilkins said; "I already waited nigh onto three years and . . ."

Fancy didn't wait to hear any more. She went down the hall and out the back door. She made a wide circle out and away from the house until she came to the place where the pines made night shadows across the little hollow where the hog pen was, and went down into that running. From there on, it was downhill all the way. Going down made it get dark faster. She was going downward and away from the setting sun. By the time the slope had lessened into near-flatness, all the blue had gone out of the sky and the stars hung low over her head and blazed.

She kept going. Like all the hill people, she was accustomed to walking miles on the simplest errand. But this one, she knew, was far from simple. Without even thinking about it, Fancy realized that she had taken her life in her two hands.

Have to get myself a job, she thought. Don't rightly know what kind—ain't never been learned to do nothing useful. I can sew a little and clean and cook—but down there they've got colored help to do those things. Maybe I can get myself a job in one of the mills—they don't hire nothing but white folks for that. . . . But that won't be no good either. Never meet anybody big or important like that. If I did they wouldn't pay me no attention sitting in front of a machine. I'd be a lint head, mill trash. Nope, got to think of something else. . . .

But thinking about it didn't help. The world past the rim of her hills was beyond Fancy. The very people who inhabited it were a strange breed, who refused to take exact shape even in her dreams. Besides, this part of the trail was strange to her. She needed all her attention to stay on it. Here the signs were less definite—much of it was overgrown, forming one of the barriers that the hill people kept between themselves and the outside. Over trails like these change passed but slowly, so that much of the speech and most of the customs of Queen Elizabeth's time were still a part of Fancy's life. The journey she was making at night stretched over more than miles—it covered centuries, too.

By the time that the black had begun to gray out of the sky, and the stars were dimming a little, Fancy gave it up. She was beyond pursuit now. And the ache in her legs crawled upward until she hurt all over and the tiredness settled down like a weight upon her eyelids, so that several times she lost the trail. Finally she moved off it and lay down under an oak. The grass grew tall and sweet-smelling there, and before she got through the first line of her prayers, she was asleep.

When she woke up, the whole world was washed in sunlight. Looking out from under the shadow that the oak branches made was like staring into a haze of gold. Over the field of high, waving grass, insects danced, suspended like motes in the light, and the air droned with their humming. On the branches above her, a bluejay scolded noisily, and a cardinal flashed from leaf shade to tree shadow tracing a trajectory like flame across the sunny places.

Fancy got up quickly and started to run out into all that excess of light. It seemed to be waiting for her, that wide, bright world, splashed with sun and dappled with shade. Even after she had no more breath left for running, she continued to walk very fast, until before she knew it, she was out of the hills altogether and there was the river before her, slow-flowing and muddy-golden in the midday sun.

Fancy stood quite still and gazed at the Savannah. It was the largest body of water she had ever seen in her life. From where she stood she could see the willows trailing their branches into the water on the Georgia side, and higher up, as the banks rose steeply along the Sandhill, the dogwood trees making spring snow, among the darker pines. She turned finally, and started downstream toward the bridges in the distance. She walked slowly, prolonging her moment, half out of fear, and half out of the unconscious desire to preserve it.

Then the bridge lay before her, arching up over the sluggish river, over the little fishing skiffs that drifted slowly downstream, toward where the spires of the churches and the tops of the taller buildings of Augusta showed above the dark green of the trees.

Fancy started up over the footwalk of the bridge. In the middle she stopped and gazed down curiously at one of the fishermen sleeping in a rowboat below. The man was black—inky-, sooty-black. Fancy stared at him with breath-gone fascination. In some of the lower hill towns there were signs: "Nigger, don't let the sun set on you in this town." Or: "Nigger—read and run; and if you can't read—run anyhow." But in the section of Carolina where Fancy lived, there was no need for such signs. Life was hard enough for white people; there was nothing for a black man to do.

So it was that the black fisherman sleeping in his rowboat was the first Negro that Fancy had seen in all her life.

She came down into McKinney Street, and walked down it until the bustle of Broad Street attracted her attention. It was packed from one side to the other with the wagons of the countryfolk come to town, for it was Saturday, the day for marketing. Fancy moved among the throngs of calico-clad women, and men in shiny blue jeans, their straw hats pushed back from their foreheads, engaging in long, slow talk on the sidewalks. The talk, what she could catch of it, was the same as at home—the weather, crops—a run of bad luck with the stock.

It came to Fancy suddenly that she was hungry, so she stepped quickly into a little restaurant run by an enormous Irishwoman, and parted with a single nickel for a cup of coffee and a roll. Then she went on east toward the spire of the Confederate Monument, reaching it just as the Dinner Car of the horse-drawn railroad pulled out for its run up to the Sandhill. The car bore a red flag, and was drawn by horses laden with sleighbells so that they jangled musically at every step. But it was the people on the car that caused Fancy to stop and stare in openmouthed wonder. The ladies were dressed all in white for the most part, and bore the sauciest little frilled umbrellas in their hands. Their bonnets were lace-edged too, or, if they were straw, had stuffed birds or bunches of artificial fruit upon them. All the ladies wore bustles, and their waists were scarcely a hand's span in width. Most of the men wore tall silk hats, and Prince Albert frock coats; a few were wearing the newer sack coat; but to Fancy, the strangest thing about them was their mustaches. The men of her native hills were either clean-shaven or fully bearded; therefore, to Fancy, this array of handlebars, mutton chops, burnsides, and even an imperial or two was a sight to see.

The car passed on up the street, and Fancy walked over to the monument, crossing one half of the street that Augustians proudly boasted was the widest street in the world. She stood there a long time gazing at the figure of the Confederate private, resting upon his musket and gazing with sad dignity back over the lost years. Circling the monument she read the names of General Lee and Stonewall Jackson under the figures that pictured them, and stared uncomprehendingly at the statues of Generals Cobb and Walker. She had heard about G'n'l Lee, and Stonewall Jackson, for Pap had fit somewhat ingloriously in that war; but the other two men meant nothing to her. She reckoned that they must have been great men, too, and turned away from the monument.

She had no aim in mind—no conscious plan. All she wanted to do now, today, was to see the city. Tomorrow was time enough for making plans. So she strolled slowly down Jackson Street until she came to Greene, and wandered eastward until she had passed all the lovely old houses, and had reached a place where the houses were shabbier and the speech of the people sounded foreign to her ear. She stared curiously at all the old Irishwomen, wearing quilted silk hoods of black, with "goffered" muslin ruffles around their faces, their stooped shoulders bent under their shawls despite the heat, and their work-worn fingers busy with rosaries, as they hurried to midday mass.

Fancy couldn't make them out, but she accepted them without too much wonder. This was her new world, and if such people lived in it they must be part of it.

Half an hour later, she had left "Canaan" and "Dublin," as the Irish sections were known, behind her, and was resting in the shadow of a house in the "Terry," watching the hordes of Negroes stream past, laughing, skylarking or simply walking. Fancy marveled at the black washerwomen who balanced huge bundles of snowy linen atop their heads, going by at a steady pace and sucking peacefully on their corncob pipes at the same time.

Then she straightened up, staring at the slant-eyed oriental, complete with a straw hat in the shape of a low cone, and a queue hanging down his back, moving with delicate little steps that scarcely stirred his bright-colored, baggy trousers. Behind him a mulatto girl walked at a respectful distance, and in her arms was a child whose hair curled more softly than her own tight kinks, but whose eyes had a definite slant.

Augusta sure is some place, Fancy thought. But before she could think any more, the roar of an angry bass voice sounded inside one of the houses, punctuated by high-pitched liquid tones. Then the door burst open, and a slim Chinese flew out of it, propelled by a massive boot, to sprawl in the street almost in front of the spot where she stood. The Chinese picked himself up and set off down the street at great speed. A moment later the door opened wide, and a man strode out on the veranda.

He was quite the biggest man Fancy had ever seen—and the handsomest, she decided a second later. He was dressed in a linen sack coat, and had a broad-brimmed Panama on his head. His hair was long, and dark, and his mustache was simply terrifying. Fancy guessed that he stood well over six feet tall, and the anger in his eyes made them magnificent.

"Where'd that Chink bastard go?" he roared; then his gaze fell upon Fancy. She could see the anger leaving his eyes. They widened and light leaped into them. He looked her up and down slowly, and nodded his massive head.

"Where'd you come from, little gal?" he said.

Fancy pointed indecisively.

"Over there," she whispered.

"Where's over there?" the big man demanded.

"Ca'lina," Fancy said.

"You got any folks in Augusta?"

"Nosir. I'm all alone here," Fancy said.

The big man put his head back and laughed aloud. It was a tremendous sound. To Fancy it sounded like thunder. It made her shiver a little as if she was cold; but she couldn't be cold, not in the pleasant sunshine.

"Duke," the big one chuckled, "this sure Lord is your lucky day!"

"Duke?" Fancy said. "Who's Duke?"

"I'm Duke," the big man said. "Reckon I'd better introduce myself proper like. Duke Ellis, at your service, Ma'am. Now what might be your name?"

"I'm Fancy," Fancy murmured.

"Damned right you are, but what's your name?"

"That's it—Fancy. Fancy Williamson."

Duke stared at her.

"Honeychild," he breathed; "I ain't never heard tell of a name what was more fitting and proper. Come along now—take my arm."

Fancy hesitated then slipped her arm easily through his, and they started up Campbell Street away from the Terry.

"Ain't nobody ever told you," Duke teased, "that blue eyes don't go with black hair? Appears to me that your folks kind of mixed you up. But baby-doll do I like the mixture!"

"Why'd you do it?" Fancy asked.

"Why'd I do what, Fancygal?"

"Kick that poor Chinaman."

"That blamed Chink ruined four of my best shirts. Got 'em all the way from Atlanta—ruffled fronts, too. So naturally he had it coming. Let's don't worry about him—we've got to attend to you—"

"To me?" Fancy echoed blankly.

"Yes, baby—to you. You're a mighty pretty little gal; but old Duke can't be seen round town with nobody dressed like you."

"What's wrong with my dress?" Fancy pouted.

"Everything," Duke said flatly. "Honeychild, you're as pretty as a speckled setter pup, but you just ain't got no style. And my lady friends got to have style."

"It's the only dress I got, except one," Fancy said sadly.

"That's all right, Fan," Duke said; "from now on you're going to have lots of dresses. We're going to stop by my house for a minute to pick up my buggy, then we're going straight up to J. B. White's Department Store. When we come out of there, ain't going to be a lady in Augusta finer than you—just you wait."

Fancy stared at him speculatively.

"You must be rich," she said.

"Now ain't you a smart one," Duke chuckled.

"Well–aren't you?"

"You're looking at the second richest man in Augusta, Georgia–right next to old man Phinizy himself. Four years ago wasn't nothing in my pockets except holes. Then a damyankee come down here and showed me how to get turpentine out of them trees on that no-good place of my paw's. Now they call me the Turpentine King. Folks what wouldn't spit on me before, bowing and scraping now, and siding up to offer me their hands. Damn them!" Duke added savagely. "Think I forget mighty damn easy!"

Fancy stared at him admiringly. In the back part of her mind there was just the ghost of a suspicion that it wasn't quite the proper thing for her to do to let this big man buy her dresses. But if she was going to be his wife, it wouldn't make much difference; besides whatever Maw and Pap considered proper didn't count any more. It Lord hadn't been proper for them to sell her like a hog or a sheep to that filthy old man Wilkins.

His wife. Mrs. Duke Ellis. Mighty fine ring to that. Come to think of it, he hadn't said anything about getting hitched. But he must have it in mind, she decided, or else why was he buying her clothes?

Two hours later, she came out of White's Department Store in a happy daze. She wore a dress that equaled and surpassed the ones that she had seen on those fine ladies this morning. Fortunately, fitting her had been an easy matter. Of course, she could hardly breathe with that corset pinching her waist so; but anyone with half an eye could see that her waist was slimmer than any other girl's on Broad Street. In a store window, she caught a glimpse of her bustle. Lord but she looked fine! And that little yellow straw hat, with the brim bent down back and front and that bunch of artificial flowers waving on the top. She'd never even seen a hat like this one, let alone worn one.

Duke's big hands were filled with bundles. Inside those bundles were six other dresses, innumerable petticoats, and the very finest underwear, trimmed with the nicest lace. Course, she had blushed a little when he'd bought those things, but a man had a right to pick out the best things for his bride.

Duke strode along beside her, grinning, his big cigar clenched between his even, white teeth. When they came to the buggy, he put the bundles in the back and helped her up.

"We'll drive over to Doc Beale's drugstore and have a soda," he announced grandly, "then I'll take you around town to see the sights. Dinner at the

Globe. That's the finest hotel in town. Can't nobody say that Duke Ellis don't treat his lady friends right."

Coming out of the drugstore, whose black marble soda fountain was still in that spring of 1880 one of the marvels of the city, always pointed out proudly to visitors, Fancy clung to Duke Ellis' arm and smiled up at him shyly.

"Reckon I'm fair about to bust," she said; "didn't reckon anything on earth could taste so good as that charcolate soda."

"Old Doc sure knows how to make 'em, and no mistake," Duke chuckled. "What you want to do now, little Fancygal?"

"Go riding," Fancy said without hesitation. "I'm plumb tuckered out from walking, and I'd sure admire to see more of Augusta."

"At your service, dollbaby," Duke said, and helped her up into the buggy.

He headed east, down Broad Street, pointing out the monument that she had already seen, and the celebrated haunted pillar, with its black imprint of a human hand near the base.

"They say a nigger who was being sold down the river away from his folks left that print there in his own blood. Ever since then everybody who's tried to move it has died—leaseways that's what folks say. I don't hold with such talk myself; but it does seem kind of funny that when the hurricane blew down the old market that pillar was the only thing left. . . ."

"Poor fellow," Fancy said softly.

"He was only a nigger," Duke said complacently. "Can't work up much sympathy for them burr-headed bastards myself. But folks hereabouts is mightily superstitious. Take Wylly Barron, for instance. He runs that gambling house in the Atkinson Hotel down on Carmichael's Range. Well, old Wylly's got his mausoleum all waiting for him down in Magnolia Cemetery. Had it built fifteen years ago, when a poor devil what lost his last cent playing faro swore that Wylly wouldn't have a grave to lie in, then went home and blew out his brains. Shook Wylly up, that did. So he built that there fancy marble tomb of his, and made a will saying that after he's laid in it, the key is got to be thrown in the river. Looks like that tomb's going to have a long wait—Wylly's as healthy as a horse."

"You don't believe in luck and signs?" Fancy said.

"No, baby—just what's betwixt my ears, and underneath my right fist. That's all the luck a man needs."

"Reckon you're right," Fancy said.

Duke turned northward and pointed out the bales of cotton blocking the sidewalks on both sides of Reynolds Street.

"Half the damned cotton in the world ends up right here, I reckon," he said. "Heck, it's getting late—and it's a long drive up to my cottage on the Hill."

Fancy stared at him. Then she shrugged. Well, if he wanted to show her his cottage, she'd be glad to look at it. Maybe he wanted her to stay there until arrangements could be made for the wedding. Sure would be a fine thing to be married to such a man as Duke—yes sir, it sure would. . . .

Duke swung the buggy in a wide semicircle that brought them through Telfair Street. As they passed the First Presbyterian Church, Fancy caught his arm.

"A wedding!" she said; "oh, Duke, honey, do let's wait and see it!"

Duke pulled the horse up, and stared at the people coming out of the church. Then he frowned.

"Them God-damned Brantleys!" he growled. "Be a good thing if this town was to get shut of 'em once and for all."

Fancy didn't answer him. She was too busy staring at the Brantleys.

The bridegroom was a tall, thin man, who, despite the fact that he was still young—thirtyish, Fancy guessed—was almost as bald as old man Wilkins. And the bride, half hidden in clouds of white veiling, was a girl not much older than Fancy. She looked like an angel, all pink and white like Dresden china, with masses of hair like pure sunlight peeping out from under her veil. But, somehow, Fancy had the feeling that she didn't look happy—not the way a bride ought to.

Then, a moment later, she saw the reason. Behind the newlyweds walked a young man—much younger than the groom, with a face so sad that just looking at it made Fancy want to burst out crying. For the life of her, Fancy couldn't tear her gaze away from that face. It resembled the groom's face so strongly that Fancy had no trouble in deciding that they were brothers. And it wasn't a particularly handsome face, either—the cheekbones were too prominent, and the mouth too wide, and tight-lipped, and droopy at the corners. It was a rawboned kind of a face, sort of like the pictures of Abraham Lincoln, except that the coloring was different—fair, instead of dark, with light, chestnut-colored hair and blue eyes. But it was the sadness in it that caught Fancy.

Bet my bottom dollar, she thought, that he's in love with her too!

"So Ty got her!" Duke chuckled suddenly. "Damned if I ain't glad. Ty ain't a bad sort. But that there Court . . ."

"Court's the light-haired one, with the sad face?" Fancy asked.

"Yep. And he's all Brantley—a no-good son of a biscuit eater if there ever was one. That old man's their paw—Jeff Brantley, and them two sad-looking female critters is the Brantley gals, Agnes and Saphira, what no man around here would have on a bet. That good-looking blond boy in the back is

Philemon, and that human iceberg walking 'longside of him is his wife, Martha."

"Who's the bride?" Fancy asked.

"Oh, that's Fern–Fern Vance. Used to spark her myself, once in a while. Poor thing, she had a hard row to hoe, being Matt Vance's daughter–and then getting herself hitched to a Brantley . . ."

"You don't think much of the Brantleys, do you?" Fancy said.

"Don't nobody hereabouts think much of 'em. One of the oldest families in the State–and used to be one of the richest. Only they're poor as Job's turkey hen now–which still don't stop 'em from trying to lord it over everybody else. Court and Ty've been feuding over Fern for years–Court was ahead, I think, till he got highfalutin notions and went away to Harvard College. Ty made good use of his time. . . ."

"You seem like you like Ty," Fancy observed.

"I do. Only Brantley worth his salt. Holds his cards close to his nose and his liquor like a gentleman. But that little snot-nose, Court–hell's bells, baby, I used to lick the pants off of him twice a week when we was kids, him and that Tommy Wilson, whose paw was pastor of that church. Him and Court was great pals–always mooning around reading poetry and stuff. Only Woodrow–that's his real name–not Tommy–has run off to Atlanta to be a lawyer. Heard tell he's gone into politics–"

"Why don't you like the Brantleys?" Fancy said. "They look like real nice folks."

"Well they ain't. There's a saying hereabouts: 'The Brantley women die by drowning, the men by bullets, fire and the sword; but no good ever come out of the breed–not yet nor ever will.' "

"Who said that?" Fancy demanded.

"Old Jeff, himself. Said it so often that everybody in town's got it down word for word just like I told you. And it's true, too. The Brantley women always do drown themselves. . . ."

"Why?" Fancy said.

"On account of their men. Them Brantleys sure got roving eyes and taking ways. You take Phil, for instance. He's got himself a highbrown down in shadetown and three off-color yard children. Only that Martha won't drown herself–she ain't got blood enough in her veins to care."

"I still don't see what you got against Court."

"Always held himself up as being so fine. Every time me or my brothers, Buck and Tom, would pass by Hiberion, he'd start his niggers to singing the 'druther song.' "

"The 'druther song'?" Fancy echoed blankly.

" 'Druther be a nigger, and work like heck,' " Duke quoted bitterly,

" 'than a poor Georgia cracker with a long red neck.' So naturally, I had to lick him. Now I'm top dog around here, and them Brantleys is plumb played out, only they don't seem to realize it. Still hold themselves up mighty fine!"

"Sure that Vance girl ain't the reason why you hate 'em so?" Fancy teased.

"Heck no! Pretty as Fern is, she couldn't of married anybody else—not being Matt's daughter. Matt was one of the biggest carpetbaggers in the State, and him and that nigger-loving Rufus Bullock—our reconstruction governor, was thick as thieves at a lawyer's funeral. . . ."

This, Fancy decided, was getting kind of mixed up, so she didn't ask Duke any more questions. Instead, she sat very quietly in the buggy and watched the houses drop away behind her until they were passing by the Negro shanties on the lower end of Gwinnett Street. Then, as the street ran through a vacant field, Fancy saw the flare of torches on the back of a wagon, and the short, powerful figure of a man haranguing the Negroes from it.

"A medicine show!" she cried. "Oh, Duke, let's stop and watch!"

"Some other time, baby," Duke said; "we got things to do."

Fancy looked back over her shoulder at the man on the medicine wagon. "What a funny little old man," she said.

"Heck, Wyche ain't old," Duke said. "He's thirty—the same age as me. He just looks that way. Funny thing about him—his folks are just about the richest people in Carolina—but Wyche ain't got a dime. His paw disowned him over some scrape he got into with a mill gal. Old man Weathers owns just about half of them Spartanburg mills. . . ."

"You know everybody, don't you?" Fancy said admiringly.

"Just about. Only there's just one person I'm interested in getting to know real good. And that party, little Fancygal—is you."

"Oh," Fancy said.

They drove up Walton Way past the miles of crepe myrtle that would bloom later in the summer, hiding the greens in the center of the street with their small, cerise blossoms, past the newer and more imposing houses built by the merchants and businessmen who had supplanted the old planter aristocracy, each with its white or pink dogwood blossoming in the front yard, and the rows of yellow jasmine, and flowering quince. As they approached the Sandhill section, with its distinctive cottages, all the earth flamed with color: giant magnolias towered heavenward, their branches bent under the weight of blossoms the size of small cabbages, creamy-white and heavy scented; spreading mimosa blew down the wind, with its fragrant powderpuff blooms and fern-like foliage; here were the smaller Japanese magnolias now, and weeping dwarf cherries, and redbud trees that were like deep pink flame. Along walls and fences the Cherokee roses twined, and golden masses of daffodil, crocus, forsythia, and marigold threw back the light.

"Lord," Fancy said, "what a pretty place!"

"There ain't nowhere like Georgia in the spring, babydoll," Duke said smugly. He sounded exactly as if he owned it all.

As one end of Lake Olmstead came in sight, Duke turned the buggy into a side road that wound out of sight into a pine wood. It was very cool under the trees, and the wind blew through them picking up the rich pine scent and the smell of honeysuckle. Fancy felt a little dizzy, and it came to her then that she hadn't eaten anything except that charcolate soda all day long. Duke had said something about taking her to dinner, but he must have forgotten it.

The sun had begun to set as they climbed up the crescent-shaped Sandhill, and now it was dark. There was the twitter of night birds among the trees, and far off and faint a whippoorwill cried out just once; then a mockingbird answered him, imitating the sound, a little sour and flat and not exactly on key.

Fancy felt cold, suddenly, and a little afraid. She turned and looked at Duke's face, illuminated briefly as he drew in on his cigar. She thought it had changed somehow. Duke was just as handsome as ever, but his face looked harder somehow, and his lower lip curled about the end of the cigar in a way that Fancy found vaguely disturbing.

Bet he can be mean as old Nick, she thought suddenly.

"How come you got two houses?" she asked.

"That one on Campbell Street belongs to all of us," Duke said, "though by rights it's mine–since I paid for it. But the one up here is where I hang out. I can put up with just so much of the folks then I get a bellyful. Look –you can see the house now. . . ."

By squinting a little, Fancy could make out the outlines of a Sandhill cottage, a type developed from a typical farmhouse but having lines so distinctively its own that it had earned its right to a name.

"We call this here village Summerville," Duke explained. "Reckon that was because folks used to live up here in the summer mostly to get away from the heat. Now lots of folks live up here all year round. Come on, lil' Fancygal, let's go inside."

He helped her down from the buggy, and she stood there waiting while he took her bundle out of the back. Then she walked a little ahead of him until she came to the porch and waited there while he unlocked the door. Inside, he scratched a match on the sole of his shoe, and lit one of the lamps. Then he lit several others and turned to Fancy with a broad grin.

"Well," he said, "what do you think of it?"

"Oh, Duke," Fancy breathed, "it's just too fine for words!"

The cottage actually was hideous; but Fancy had no way of knowing that. The heavy, ornate furniture, decorated with bows about the legs, and the painted fire screen and the tremendous gilt picture frames, and the wilderness of potted plants were all a legacy from her predecessor—one Myrtie Torrence, the last of Duke's many all too fleeting lights of love. Of course, Duke had bought the furniture, but Myrtie had selected it, so that the heavy hand of her ferociously bad taste lay over the decor like a blight. But Fancy had slept on corn shucks and sat on cracker boxes all her life. To her, they were beautiful.

Duke looked at her suddenly, keenly.

"Damned if you don't look right peaked," he growled.

"You didn't take me to dinner like you promised," Fancy said; "I'm right smart hungry, Duke."

"Oh damn!" Duke said. "I'm downright sorry, Fan. Maybe we can rustle up some grub out of the icebox."

Fancy followed him out into the kitchen and stood staring in awed admiration at the tremendous icebox, built to hold a hundred pounds of ice at one time. Up on the farm they had a spring house that really didn't keep things very cold so that food was always spoiling. But in this marvel of modern science, Duke had food enough to feed an army.

"Make a fire in the stove, honey," Fancy said. "I'll cook."

"Now ain't you a smart one," Duke beamed. "Just give me a minute."

Hungry as she was, Fancy didn't rush things. She wanted to show him what she could do. She fried the chicken in an egg batter, turning it a rich golden brown. She made hot biscuits, and steaming coffee, and green beans swimming in fat.

Duke tasted everything, then stared at her.

"Babydoll," he said, "you'n'me are going to get along."

"I hope so," Fancy said.

After supper, she washed the dishes, while Duke sat in his big easy chair and pulled at a bottle of bourbon. She took a long time about it, polishing each dish lovingly. When she came back into the parlor, Duke poured three fingers of bourbon into a glass, topped it with ice and water, and handed it to her.

"Here, baby," he grinned; "have a little pickup. You're going to need it."

"I—I don't drink," Fancy whispered.

"Time you was learning how," Duke said. "Go on, take it."

Timidly Fancy took the glass and tasted the drink. It burned like fire, going down. All the stories Maw had told her came back with a rush—of girls who took just one tiny, little one and then. . . . She looked at Duke and her blue eyes widened with real fear.

S'pose he didn't mean to marry her after all? S'pose he meant to get her drunk and—she groped for Maw's euphemistic phrase for that mysterious happening that caused girls to drop out of sight, ashamed to be seen again—and 'took advantage of her.' For a moment a lively curiosity over what were the precise details of being taken advantage of, almost drowned her fear. It must be plumb interesting, she decided, since it happened to so many girls.

But she didn't like the look on Duke's face. She had the funny idea that her clothes were not there any more. The way he looked at her made her feel naked. She didn't like the feeling.

"Sure is a pretty place you got here," she said breathlessly, and started walking around the room, still holding the drink in her hand. The minute Duke turned his head away from her just a little, she dumped the contents of her glass into one of the potted plants.

"Yessir," she said; "it sure Lord is . . ."

"Come here, lil' Fancygal," Duke said thickly.

Fancy noticed that his eyes were getting bloodshot. She shot a quick glance at the bottle. To her dismay, it was already three-quarters empty.

Duke got to his feet, swaying a little.

"I ain't drunk," he grinned; "I can down three of them and never feel it. Now, babydoll, how about a lil' kiss?"

Better humor him, Fancy thought fearfully. I'll let him kiss me just once and then I'll start talking about something real fast, and—but Duke put out his powerful arms and crushed her to him in a grip so hard that she was sure every bone in her body was broken.

She struggled with him soundlessly, but he caught her face between his fingers and forced her head back. Then he kissed her, hurting her mouth, tightening his grip about her waist until she could feel the breath leaving her body. Her head was enveloped in a fog of whiskey scent and her lips felt bruised. She was getting a little dizzy and she knew that she had to do something right away or—

Then, very quickly, she lifted both her feet off the floor. Duke had bent her so far over backwards, that even her slight weight was enough to make him lose his balance. He felt himself falling, and turned her loose, so that she had the chance for a half heartbeat to throw herself out to one side and away from him, before he crashed to the floor like a felled oak. He lay there for a moment, dazed, then he pushed up on his hands and knees, and rested there, hanging his big head and shaking it from side to side.

Fancy put out her hand and picked up the heavy brass poker that stood in the rack before the fireplace.

"Duke, honey," she whispered, "I'm awful sorry to have to do this; but I can't fight you no more—I can't. . . ."

Then she lifted the poker and brought it down across his head with all her strength.

There was a little blood, but not much; and he lay there breathing noisily out of his open mouth. Fancy bent over him, and her breath was a hot tangle at the base of her throat and her eyes were scalded. Then she turned and ran out of the door and down the winding road under the pines.

She fell more than once in the darkness, so that the new dress was ruined; but she kept going until she came out on the main road, and continued on down that, breath-gone and sobbing.

What am I? she thought miserably. What kind of a creature when my own folks put me for sale for a few dirty dollars, and the first man I meet thinks I'm only worth the price of some ruffled dresses? I'm me—a person, can't they understand that—not nobody's shoddy goods. I ain't to be pawed over and hurt and shamed—I ain't! I ain't! Oh God, oh Jesus, I'd druther be dead than held cheap. . . .

She had no idea how far she had gone when she saw the lights coming toward her. Then the terror was back again, and she turned to leap from the road, when her foot caught in a projecting root, and she sprawled on the ground, with a pain in her left ankle that was like fire.

The big grays that drew the wagon must have sensed her presence because they whinnied shrilly, and the driver pulled on the reins and got down. He came over to where she lay and stood there looking at her and she tried frantically to crawl into the brush, and screamed up at him:

"Don't you touch me! Don't you dare!"

"What's the matter, little girl?" the man said gently. His voice was as deep as Duke's, but ever so much more musical. Just listening to the sound of it made Fancy feel better.

"I hurt my ankle," she wailed; "and I'm plumb scairt and . . ."

"Here," the man said, "let me see."

He knelt down and his fingers caressed the injured ankle gently.

"Hmmn," he said; "bad sprain all right. Reckon I'll have to pick you up and put you in the wagon."

"No!" Fancy gasped.

"Don't be silly, child. I got mixed up with a young gal once and it cost me my birthright. Right now when I see a good-looking woman—I run."

Fancy felt the fear ebbing out of her.

"You must be Mister Weathers," she said.

He stared at her curiously.

"How'd you know?"

"Duke—" Fancy began and stopped in great confusion.

"So," Wyche Weathers said, "that's what you were running from in such an all-fired hurry. That overgrown polecat ought to be shot with slops and arrested for stinking."

He bent down and picked her up. Fancy was conscious of thinking, My God, he's strong! just before he laid her gently down in the wagon.

He stood beside it, looking at her, and the flickering lanterns showed on his face.

Such a strong face, Fancy thought, and a good one too. Bet he wouldn't mash a crippled fly—but he'd kill a man quick as a wink what got in his way. . . .

She studied him, seeing the enormously broad shoulders and the great arms thicker and bigger than Duke's, looking out of place on Wyche Weathers because he was scarcely a head taller than she was. She could see the white hair at his temples, and the small, neatly trimmed black mustache that outlined a mouth that was firm, but kind.

Wyche looked at her torn dress and all the kindness went out of his face, leaving it hard as granite.

"Did Duke Ellis—molest you?" he growled.

Fancy realized suddenly that she held a man's life in the hollow of her hand. It gave her a heady sense of power. But which man? Duke was so big and strong, and this short man, strong as he was, might not be able to—

"No," she said quickly; "I just got scairt and ran."

Wyche looked at her doubtfully.

"Your dress?" he said.

"I tore it coming through the brush," Fancy said.

"All right," Wyche Weathers said. "Come, let me help you up beside me and I'll take you back to your folks. . . ."

"I—I ain't got no folks," Fancy lied.

Wyche stopped still, staring at her.

"What on earth am I going to do with you?" he muttered.

"Take me away," Fancy begged. "Just take me a long way from here where he can't find me!"

Wyche Weathers studied that one for a long moment, then he sighed.

"All right, little girl," he said and taking her arm, half lifted her into the high seat beside him.

2

Fancy stood in the little tent about ten yards back of the wagon, and took off her clothes. Then she slipped on the tight-fitting little red pants, and over them the baggy oriental trousers that were made of some stuff like mosquito netting so anybody could see right through them. She took up the blouse, which, though thin, was not transparent, and drew it over her head. It was so short that it left her middle bare.

She worked furiously, putting on the ropes of bright glass beads, and the earrings that dangled more than six inches below each ear. After she had brushed her hair back out of the way, she put on her jeweled turban. These jewels were glass, too. Just before she adjusted the long, thick veil that hid all of her face but her eyes, she looked at herself in the mirror and blushed hotly. The only thing about her that was really covered up was her face. She didn't like the way the men looked at her. Something got into their eyes when they saw her rigged up like this—something hot and ugly. Looking at them, Fancy could see all the goodness in them drowning right behind their eyes, and the badness leaping up like fire. It was as if they stopped being men, and became animals; as if everything that had been done in the world to tame the ugliness down hadn't been much good after all.

And it was more than the way they looked at her. After each show, Wyche had to use his big fist on some one or two of them, liquored up and determined. She put out her hand and took up the little tin box. Then she drew the little key which hung around her neck on a chain out of her blouse and unlocked the box. Sitting there before the mirror, she counted the money. It came to more than five hundred dollars, and she had earned every penny of it herself.

That was the only thing that made it bearable. Never having had any money, Fancy had a good, sound appreciation for it. And except for letting her share a few of the expenses, Wyche wouldn't touch a penny of it.

"You made it yourself, baby," he said; "it's yours to keep. . . ."

Wyche was such a funny kind of a man. The way he treated her now—as if she was a queen or something. Of course, there might be something in his idea that it was she who drew the crowds; but he didn't have to be so gentle with her; that made her feel a little ashamed.

What made her more ashamed was the tight, grim-faced way the women looked at her. She could see their mouths moving, shaping the word, "Hussy!" every time she went into her dance. "Traveling round like that with two men," she heard one of them say once, "and one of 'em a nigger!"

Fat lot of good it would do her to explain that for the first two months they had been together, Wyche had slept on the ground next to Mose, leaving her the whole wagon to herself. It was only after she had bought herself this little tent with its folding cot, that he had had a comfortable place to sleep. After four months, the only time yet that Wyche touched her hand was to help her up and down from the wagon.

Fancy didn't want it any different from that; but she wanted folks to know what a real gentleman Wyche Weathers was. Being honest, she more than half realized that if Wyche had tried to change things, she would have agreed–out of gratitude; because never before in her life had anybody been so good to her. But Wyche didn't try to change things; he seemed to like them well enough just the way they were now. Fancy might have felt a little pique at his indifference, only Wyche wasn't indifferent. The look in his eyes had a glow to it whenever he gazed at her; half the time he seemed to be on the point of saying something–of asking her–but then his strong jaw shut tight like a trap.

Outside on the wagon now, old Mose was striking up a chord on his banjo. Fancy shivered a little. She was quivering on the inside like a marsh reed in a high wind, and she knew why. It was because they were back in Augusta again after four months of wandering. Augusta meant just one thing to Fancy–Duke Ellis. And she was mortally afraid of seeing his face in that crowd out there. Of course, with this veil over her face he might not recognize her, but then again, he might. There was no telling.

Quickly she put the money back in the box and locked it with the little key. All that money, and all because years ago old Liz Elberton had taught her to tell fortunes with a pack of cards. Fancy didn't hold with such foolishness herself, but a mighty heap of other folks seemed to. She had told Wyche's fortune about three months ago, and that had given him the idea for this outlandish getup.

"Heck, baby," he said, "you're a natural! With that hair and those eyes, you'll knock 'em dead! Make yourself a fortune, and help me make one too!"

In the end, Fancy had consented, reluctantly, more because she wanted to do something to earn her keep than for any other reason. She hated it with all her heart. In a few minutes now, Wyche would call out from behind the flickering lamps, made of wicks stuck in old bottles, "And now friends, I present to you Madame Scheherazade—mysterious daughter of the East! Knows all! Tells all! Past, present and future!"

That would be her cue to step out on the wagon and go into her dance, which wasn't anything but a sinuous wiggle in slow time to Mose's flute. Fancy was a good dancer, but this wasn't dancing. This was something else, aimed at getting that ugly look into men's eyes, and common sense out of their heads. It lasted only a couple of minutes; then the rush would begin as men came forward and plunked down their dollars to have Fancy read their future in the cards. Few of them left without making the suggestion that their future would be considerably brighter if she would consider taking a prominent if brief part in it; but Wyche had coached her well:

"I am dedicated to the gods," she would whisper, using the words that Wyche had made her memorize; "I am wedded to the mysteries. There must be no living man in my life."

Peeping through the curtain, Fancy could see Wyche arranging the jars filled with the ugly ribbons of tapeworms, pickled in alcohol. Where he had gotten them, Fancy did not know; but to the crowds he grandly proclaimed himself an expert who could cure them of such things. Next to them, he hung up the grisly human skeleton which had been worth its weight in gold to Wyche when he had specialized in rooking the Negroes; but since Fancy had joined his troupe, he played chiefly to white crowds. A Southerner born and bred, it would have been unthinkable to Wyche to have Fancy exhibit herself before the blacks.

But now Fancy had displaced the skeleton as his chief attraction; and Wyche made more money than ever. She saw his eyes narrow as he arranged the exhibit, and that look of cold contempt for everybody who drew breath came into them. It was the only thing about Wyche Weathers that Fancy didn't like. She suspected that it was put on, that down deep Wyche sort of felt the need of getting even with a world that had treated him so badly. At bottom, he was a good sort; she knew that well.

"Take 'em, honey," he used to say, "or they'll take you. Never give 'em an even break. . . ."

"I don't believe that," Fancy said. "Folks is mostly good when you get right down to it."

"Humph!" Wyche snorted. "Like Duke Ellis, maybe? Or like your paw who was going to sell you like a horse to a man old enough to be your grandfather?"

Fancy had to admit he was right about that. She was sorry she had finally broken down and told him the truth about running away from home.

"People aren't mostly good," Wyche said gruffly, "nor even mostly bad.

Trouble is they're a weak bunch of polecats who don't like their own scent. And the crazy thing about it, baby, is that they think nobody can smell it but them. So they got to hide things—got to play-act, puff themselves up big in the sight of their brothers. Folks don't hunger and thirst after righteousness, honey—they pant after applause, they thirst after self-importance. They'll lie, steal, cheat, sell themselves for vanity's sake. Ever notice how they tie themselves in knots reaching after a dollar? Preachers are always condemning the love of money, but money isn't important, not in itself; it's what it will buy that counts. . . ."

"Money won't buy everything," Fancy said.

"Damned little it won't. It'll buy what most folks want—it'll buy their brother's envy, and a sickening kind of fawning servility that most folks twist into respect. Hide your money in the ground, and nobody respects you for it; but buy yourself two dozen ruffled shirts, and a coach and four, purchase yourself the prettiest gal in town for your missus, and one a little prettier'n that for your light o' love, and they'll kill themselves in the rush to embrace your backside. Hell, baby, the more I see of folks the better I like old Mose and my mules."

"And me?" Fancy whispered.

"And you, baby. You, thank God, are different. . . ."

But I'm not, Fancy thought bitterly as she peered through the flap in the tent, or else I wouldn't get up there half naked on that there platform and let 'em look at me like I was a prize filly and they was snorting stallions. . . .

"Friends!" Wyche was beginning now, in his deep, rich voice, "I don't need to tell you what tapeworm can do to the human body! You have seen it with your own eyes—people wasted away to pitiful scarecrows, thin almost as Mister Bones here—" He tapped the skeleton playfully with his cane, and the spectators' eyes bugged out.

Fancy searched that sea of faces, but Duke was not among them; nowhere was there a mustache like that, or eyes with that hard, confident look. She sighed deeply from pure relief, and waited.

"But now, at last, I have made an end to these hellish tortures which for so long have devastated the human race. After years spent in the Far East, I have finally found a sovereign remedy! It was given to me by an old seer, a prophet of the occult whose life I once saved from the wild tribesmen of the desert! He lived scarcely a month after the rescue—just long enough to divulge to me his priceless secret, and to leave in my care, his beautiful daughter, Madame Scheherazade, whose knowledge of the occult equals if not exceeds that of her late, lamented father. . . . You will make her acquaintance in a moment; but first, let us look upon the lighter side of life. Music, Mose!"

The old black stood up, strumming his banjo; then with an agility astonishing in one of his years, he began a buck and wing that soon had the crowd calling for more.

"Mose is a wise man, too, in his quaint unlettered way," Wyche said genially. "For instance, Mose, why do old maids go to church so early on Sunday?"

"I reckon, boss, sah," Mose grinned, " 'cause they want to be there when the hymns is given out!"

"And why do old maids wear silk gloves?"

"That's easy, boss. It's 'cause they don't like kids!"

Many a time Fancy had heard Wyche groaning in real anguish as he copied his fearfully unfunny jokes from Thomas W. Jackson's *On a Slow Train Through Arkansas*. But the crowd loved them. It seemed to Fancy that it was the way that Wyche sprang them that made them go over so big. Now they were roaring with laughter.

"And now, friends, I give you that mysterious daughter of the East; that high priestess of the mysteries, to whom the future is an open book—Madame Scheherazade!"

Trembling all over, Fancy ran the few short steps to the wagon, and Wyche reached down and helped her up the ladder. Mose picked up his flute and began a wild wailing. Fancy closed her eyes and allowed her supple young body to quiver like an aspen in a high wind, and again the crowd roared. But it was a different sound now, a hoarse, ugly, beast bellow. Fancy could feel the men's eyes, hot upon her; but she didn't look at them—she didn't dare.

When at last Mose stopped playing, and Wyche started his chanted description of her powers, Fancy opened her eyes. She let her gaze pass over the faces in that crowd; then she stopped suddenly, held by one face, as though the pale blue eyes had turned her to stone.

It was a young face, haunted and thin, with big cheekbones, and hollowed cheeks, and a wide, tormented mouth. Under the tall hat, Fancy could see the chestnut hair, and the quick jerking of the knot muscle over the jaw, clear in the torchlight. It was a face she couldn't forget, a face she had seen before somewhere, had seen and marked, and that had troubled her in many a senseless dream.

And now, gazing into it, Fancy remembered just where she had seen that face. Even after all these months, that mouth hadn't lost the terrible sadness that she remembered. She had seen this man coming out of a church, at a wedding, watching his brother bear away the girl he himself loved. She searched for the name. Bran—Brantwell—Brantley! That was it—Courtland Brantley, whom Duke had hated so.

But how could anyone hate a man with a face like this—so pitiful, and so tender? It was the sort of face that made her fingertips itch to reach up and stroke his cheeks, that made her voice drop deep in her throat murmuring ancient, wordless, wonderful things. Looking at him now, Fancy found herself hoping that he would come to her little tent to have his fortune read. I could comfort him! she thought, I could drive out the misery. . . .

But she had almost given up when he finally did come. She had gone through her patter effortlessly, telling them all the things they wanted to hear: "You will obtain riches. Yes, yes, your sweetheart will come back to you. You will make a fortunate marriage—I see a tall, dark man in your life. . . ."

Lies, and rot and foolishness and she was sick of it! But when the last of them had gone, and he had not come, Fancy bent her head down upon the little folding table, and gave way to tears. She did not know how long she cried, but a hand rested gently upon her bare shoulder, and her head jerked upright, and joy leaped into her eyes and blazed.

"Why were you crying?" Court Brantley said.

"Because I'm plumb—" Fancy began and caught herself. She had started to say, "Because I'm plumb, downright lonesome," but people from the mysterious East didn't talk like that. "Because I'm lonely," she said in a husky whisper. "No one understands me. I—I need a friend. . . ."

A crooked grin twisted the wide mouth, suddenly.

"That shouldn't be hard, Scheherazade," he said. "Any man in his right mind would settle for even one of those thousand and one nights. . . ."

"You wish your fortune read?" Fancy said quickly.

"Not particularly," Court said; "actually I wanted a closer look at you."

"And now that you have seen me?" Fancy whispered.

"The catch is, I haven't. If only you'd take off that damned veil!"

"It is forbidden," Fancy said quietly, and began to spread the cards.

Court watched her, his pale eyes never leaving her face.

"There has been much trouble in your life," Fancy murmured. "You have returned recently from a journey . . ."

"Bosh!" Court laughed drily; "who hasn't?"

"From a far-off place—a place of snows. I see buildings, many buildings, a great city, and a—a school. Tell me, Mister Brantley, have you not returned from the University?"

Court's eyes widened.

"Well I'll be damned," he said; "how'd you know that?"

"But you have come home to sadness. I see a—a girl. She is fair, with hair like sunlight, and she is dressed all in white. A bride, Mister Brantley? But not your bride. The bride of another—one who looks much like you—

who bears the same blood in his veins . . . A cousin? No, closer than that —a brother!"

"Good God!" Court breathed. "I've never believed this stuff, still . . ."

"The voices speak to me, the cards do not lie. You love her, this fair girl whose name is that of a flower—Rose? Lily? No, no—not of a flower, but of a green plant that does not flower. . . ."

"Fern," Court groaned; "Fern Vance."

"So what is it," Fancy whispered, "that you wish to know?"

Court looked at her bleakly.

"How I can stop loving her," he said. "Whether there's any hope for me— No! Not that—she's my brother's wife, and I've got to stop thinking about her like that. But I can't. She's inside me, like fire—like poison, and I'm dying of wanting her so. Don't know when I've slept a night all the way through. I can't eat. I've got no mind for anything but her. That's it, Madame. Reckon I sound like a mighty big fool to you. . . ."

"No," Fancy said carefully, "only like a man in love. I will consult the cards. . . ."

She dared not talk too much. After three months of nightly coaching by Wyche, her command of 'proper talk' was still too unsure to risk it. But as she spread out the cards before her, her mind was racing.

It's her who's the big fool, not you, she thought. Any woman who could have married you and then let you go is a fool! If I'd been in her shoes, I'd have grabbed you so quick that . . .

"What do they say?" Court Brantley asked.

Fancy looked down at the cards, her young face frowning and troubled. They had a pattern. Usually the cards hadn't any pattern and she made up wild, improbable stories to tell her clients. But the cards that lay before her frightened her. It's all plumb downright foolishness, she thought. King of Hearts—that's Court. Jack of Clubs, that's his brother, followed by the Ace of Spades. Death. Then the Queen of Diamonds—that's her, damn her to hell, and back again. And the King of Hearts again followed by the Queen of Spades. Queen of Spades—a dark lady. Now who the devil—

Me? It could be. I'm dark—leaseways my hair is. Now she turns up again! Then Court, then—me, then her! Then her, and Court. Not me any more. And not the Jack of Clubs, his brother—not any more, not never any more because the Ace of Spades came and—Jesus God! Her'n' Court, and the Ace of Spades. Here it is again, her'n' Court and the Ace of Spades—and here I am again, but I'm all alone. . . .

She kept shuffling the cards, but the pattern held. Court, then Tyler— followed by death. Then Court followed by Fern Vance, followed by Fancy herself. Court and Fancy linked, paired. Then Fern Vance getting into the linkage, splitting it apart; then Court and Fern, and Fern and Court—then death, always death and Fancy left alone crying. . . .

"Well?" Court said evenly.

"I—I cannot read your fortune," Fancy whispered; "the cards are—mixed up, sort of. . . . Here, take your money back. Some other time, maybe."

Court stood up and pocketed the dollar.

"You," he said, "are a faker. But a damned clever faker. Good night, Scheherazade."

After him there were only a few more, and Fancy was able to go back to her tent and shut her ears to Wyche's lecture on the virtues of Doctor Weathers' Eastern Snake Oil. Before Wyche finished roping in the suckers, she had dressed in her own clothes again, and walked away from the noise and the shouting. She wanted time to think. There was something between her and Court Brantley. Something mightily powerful that got into the cards and made them fall like that. But cards were a joke, a trick, and had nothing to do with people's lives. Then why was she trembling so? If that were the pattern of the future, she could break it. All she had to do was to take one card, the Queen of Spades, herself, out of the combination and it was broken.

But she couldn't. There was that linkage between her and Court. Even if it didn't last long, it was there. And if that happened, it was the rest of the pattern she'd have to change—that Queen of Diamonds business, because that wasn't any good nohow, not with the Ace of Spades always there. Why this Fern Vance was a danger to Court! She could bring him death. Him and herself. But Fancy reckoned that wouldn't matter much to her, because she wouldn't believe it was really going to work out like that.

Her poor head ached so with all the thinking. She walked very fast away from the wagon until she came under the trees, and it was there that she saw him.

"Why, Mister Brantley!" she said.

"I was waiting for you," he said gravely. "Figured you'd have to come out of that stifling hole after a while. Come walk with me, won't you?"

"All right," Fancy said.

Court didn't say anything. He walked alongside her, towering up tall against the night, until they came out from under the trees into the fields, and the moon came up, too, red-yellow and huge, bigger than a pumpkin.

Court turned toward her, studying her face.

"I thought so," he said. "You're lovely. And young. That voice was a fake—it made you sound old. Who are you?"

"I'm Fancy Williamson," Fancy said. Then it all came out in a rush: "I'm from Ca'lina, and I can't really tell folks' fortunes. I knew about you before. . . ."

"I see," Court said, his face still and unsmiling. "But you wouldn't cheat me—why?"

"It—it wouldn't have been cheating," Fancy whispered; "I could have told yours. I don't know how come, but I could have. And I didn't want to."

"Why not?"

"Because—because I kept seeing myself in your fortune, and it didn't seem right proper to tell you that."

"You're telling me now."

"Now's different," Fancy said.

"You're Wyche Weathers' wife?" Court said.

"Oh, no!"

Court looked at her and his face was grim.

"You travel all over the state with Wyche and you're not married to him?" he asked sternly.

"What's wrong with that?" Fancy said.

"Plenty. You're young, but not that young. You must know what folks will think. . . ."

"I do know, and it riles me plenty. Not on my account, but on Wyche's. A truer gentleman never drew breath. Wyche ain't never so much as kissed me—I have that little tent all to myself, and he's never even seen the inside of it. 'Pears to me, Mister Court Brantley, that some folks got awful dirty minds!"

"People," Court said tiredly, "have realistic minds, mostly. All right it hasn't happened yet, but it will."

"It will not!"

"All right, all right—it's none of my business anyhow."

Fancy looked at him.

"What is your business, Court Brantley?" she asked. "What do you do, I mean?"

"I haven't any—really. I was planning to build a textile mill down here; but since Fern ran off with that precious scoundrel of a brother of mine, I've neither the heart nor the inclination. . . ."

Fancy caught his arm suddenly and clung to it.

"Then you got to get the heart!" she said almost fiercely. "You can't waste your life mooning over a girl you're better off without. You've got things to do, Tallman, and I aim to see that you do 'em!"

"Tallman? Why'd you call me that?"

"That's my special name for you. First time I saw you, I kept thinking, Gosh, how tall he is!"

"I see," Court said. "I'm flattered." But his voice sounded cold. "Come on," he said, "let's walk."

They crossed the field, and went through a grove of pines. When they came out of the woods this time the river was before them. The moon lay just beyond it, caught in the ragged pines of the Carolina hills. It left a yellow-silver track in the muddy water, and in the other places where the light didn't touch, the river was burnt copper, blue-shadowed by the low-hanging trees.

"Gosh!" Fancy sighed. "Ain't it pretty, Court? It's so—so romantic-like. . . ."

One corner of Court's big mouth twisted upward in a smile. Fancy didn't like that smile. It was hurt-ugly, pain-twisted.

"Reckon it is," he said.

The silence stretched out between them. Fancy felt like screaming. If only something would make a noise! In the stillness she could hear the rustle of her own breathing. It seemed to be coming disgracefully quick. And the muffled beating of her heart, racing like something half wild—could he hear that too?

"That's our house up there," Court said quietly.

Fancy looked up and saw the weathered old house sitting on a little hill about five hundred yards from the river. She saw that it had been beautiful once, and also that in a curious way it was still beautiful. It had a spirit of its own, like a grand old lady who had fallen on evil days. Its paint wasn't white any longer, but a soft, bluish-gray—and even from where she stood Fancy could see that the paint was chipped and cracked, and the house itself far gone in pitiful decay. She stood quite still and watched the rising moonlight crawling toward it. Then the light touched the house, and it blazed white once more, and the blossoms of the magnolias standing around it picked up the light, too, and threw it back in a glow like that of sea foam, pearls, snow. . . .

"Oh, Court," Fancy whispered, "it's lovely! What do you call it?"

"Hiberion," Court murmured, and his voice caressed the word, like a lover breathing the name of his beloved. "Reckon this is the end of it," he said sadly; "nobody's got the money to fix it up any more. It isn't even safe to live in now, but—"

"Then that's another reason you got to fight!" Fancy said. "What are you anyhow—a man or a mule? You got brains—use 'em! Go out and get the money. Start your mill, then fix up your house. Forget that girl—there'll be plenty more who'd be mighty proud to be your wife. . . ."

"They," Court said grimly, "would be mighty big fools, considering my chances."

"Oh, you!" Fancy said in exasperation. "Come on, let's be getting back now."

"No," Court said, "let's sit down by the water, and look at the moon."

"All right," Fancy said.

They sat on the root of an oak and gazed out over the water. Fancy could see the grief coming back into Court's face, there in the moonlight. She put out her hand and laid it gently upon his arm.

"Tell me about her," she said.

"There's not much to tell—not that a man can put into words, anyhow. Why do you want to know?"

"So—I can find out," Fancy murmured, "what it is about her that can 'most kill a man down inside his heart. Reckon if I knew that I could bring him back alive again. 'Tain't much fun keeping company with a ghost."

"You want to bring me back?" Court said. "Why, little Fancy?"

"Can't answer that—not right off the reel. Don't rightly know myself. Reckon it's 'cause I got a mighty heap of pity for suffering. Suffered a right pert myself. . . ."

"Well," Court said, "she's a little bit of a thing—no bigger than you are, all white and pink and golden. . . ."

The sound of his voice made Fancy shiver. Oh God, oh Jesus, she thought, if I could only make him sound like that when he's talking 'bout me!

"She never had much of a chance—not with being the daughter of the rottenest carpetbagger that ever abused the sovereign State of Georgia. Folks don't forget those days easily. I know—I grew up during them. Maybe that's why she was content with becoming the wife of a Brantley. . . ."

"And take her chance ending up in the river?" Fancy said.

Court stared at her.

"So," he said, "you know that too!"

"Reckon there ain't much about you I don't know."

"Why, Fancy?"

"Right now, I'm listening—you're talking."

"All right. Fern grew up to daily slights and insults. She was left out of everything—she never had any friends, except Ty and me. It made her a little queer—too silent, and a mite too intense. It was settled all along that she and I were to get married. Then I went away to Harvard, and something I said in a letter gave Ty the idea that I was getting hitched to a Yankee heiress. That did it. He told Fern. I think she married him out of pique. . . ."

"And were you?"

"Was I what?"

"Getting hitched to a damyankee?"

"Blazes no! I used to see Hester, my employer's daughter, once in a while; but there was never anything much between us."

"I doubt that," Fancy said drily.

"Why?"

"Because 'twixt you and most any girl there'll always be something much going on."

Court looked at her.

"Including you, Fan?"

"That's plumb, downright unfair! All right Mister Tallman Court Brantley, since you've got to be so blamed nosy–including me. Now take me back to the tent; I don't like being made 'shamed of myself."

"No," Court laughed; "I think I'll shame you a little more. It might be –fun."

Then, very quickly, he took her in his arms and kissed her.

Fancy wrenched herself backward and away from him. The next instant colored lights exploded inside his head, as her small, hard right fist landed high upon his jaw. Court put his hand against the place where she had hit him, seeing her standing there both fists doubled and ready, and lightning in her blue eyes.

"Well, I'll be damned!" he whispered helplessly.

"You," Fancy said flatly, "shouldn't ought to have done that."

"Why not?" Court said.

Fancy looked at him.

"There's a lot of bad things in this world," she said; "but I don't reckon there's anything worse than being kissed because a man thinks you want him to–except one thing, Court. . . ."

"And what's that?"

"Being kissed by a man what closes his eyes and thinks about somebody else whilst he's kissing you! I'm me, Tallman! I ain't Fern Vance. I got more blood and breath and blazes in me right now than she'll ever have if she lives to be a hundred! Now take me back, Court–and I hope I never see hair nor hide of you again!"

"All right," Court said quietly.

It wasn't until they were in sight of the medicine wagon that he spoke again.

"Did you mean that?" he said.

"Did I mean what?" Fancy asked.

"About never wanting to see me again?"

Fancy looked at him and the dark red corners of her mouth trembled a little.

"No," she said, "reckon I was trying to fool myself. Never was much good at it. But I don't want to see you right soon. I want to see you when you're over her—when you're capable of loving again—not before. . . ."

"And then?" Court whispered.

"Reckon I'll learn you what a kiss ought to be like. What it feels like when a body means it."

Court grinned at her then, a crooked, engaging kind of a grin.

"Couldn't you," he said, "give me a small sample—right now?"

"No!" Fancy began; then a little flame showed in her blue eyes. "Why not?" she said, and putting up her arms, she drew his face down to hers. When she turned him loose finally, letting his lean face slip gently upward between the palms and fingers of her two hands, he leaned back against a tree and stared at her.

"My God!" he whispered.

"Told you, Court," she said. "More breath and blood and blazes than anybody in this whole blamed world!" Then she turned and ran away from him through the ghost-shadowed trees.

When she came out into the clearing Wyche was waiting for her. At the sight of her the sick worry in his eyes vanished and thunder and lightning took its place.

"Where the devil have you been!" he roared.

"Out walking," Fancy said tartly. " 'Pears to me you're spreading yourself mighty wide, Wyche. Ain't nobody appointed you my keeper."

"Sorry," Wyche said shortly. "I've just been worried sick, that's all. Thought maybe you'd run into Duke and—"

"Duke!" Fancy said. "Why Wyche, honey, I'd forgotten all about him. Jehosiphat! I could of bumped into him at that. I'm mighty sorry, Wyche—didn't mean to give you a turn. . . ."

"It's all right," Wyche said. "Your supper's ready, baby. Sit down and eat. Afterwards I want to talk to you."

"All right, Wyche," Fancy said.

All the time while she was eating, she could see him watching her. There was a funny look on his face—half fearful, half tender. She finished her supper, and sat there, waiting.

"All right, Wyche," she said.

Wyche leaned across the table and took her hand.

"Fan, baby, I've been a fool," he said. "Thought I could go on living in the same world with you, seeing you every day and not have it get me. Reckon I've been in love with you for a long time. . . ."

Fancy's blue eyes widened, and her breath caught somewhere deep in her throat.

"Knew I'd have to tell you some time," he went on; "but I figured I didn't have the right. I'm too old for you—that's one thing. And being dragged all over the face of this filthy earth, living from hand to mouth, without even a pillow to put your pretty head on, or a roof to keep out the rain—that's a mite too much, to my way of thinking. . . ."

Fancy looked at him, but she didn't say anything. She didn't know what to say.

"When you walked off like that tonight, it came to me how it would be without you. The whole damned world went hollow, Fan. There wasn't any light anywhere—just emptiness, and that darkness that Moses talks about in the Bible—the kind you can feel. So—right then I knew you had to be mine if anything was to make sense any more. I know you don't love me, but I'm hoping maybe you can learn to—not the man I am right now, not old Doctor Snake Oil Weathers; but the man I was—the man I'm going to be again. . . ."

"You couldn't be any finer," Fancy said, "than you are right now. To me you're just about the best man in the world—and one of the nicest. . . ."

"No," Wyche said somberly; "I've been a hypocrite and a coward too long, baby. Thought I could run away from myself, but I couldn't. I was always there, pointing the finger of shame at myself. Nobody ever made himself bigger than the next man by cheating him; a framework of lies is a mighty flimsy foundation to build a life on. Reckon I always knew that—but I didn't care. Now I do care, and that's your fault, baby. . . ."

"What do you aim to do?" Fancy asked him.

"Go back to Spartanburg. Go to my father, ask him for a job. Hell, I'll doff bobbins to get started. I'll win him over again. Heck, it won't be hard—I happen to know he wants me back again, now that Sue has run off with that drummer. . . ."

"Sue was the girl who . . . ?"

"Yep. Paw's a right smart businessman, but he doesn't know a thing about women. . . ."

Fancy looked at him.

"Why wouldn't you marry her, Wyche?" she said.

"Sue was right smart free with her favors. I doubt seriously that I was actually the guilty party; but I was rich, and old Ted Weathers' son—which made me the most likely prospect. . . ."

"You mean to take me with you?"

"No. Paw wouldn't cotton to the idea. I've got seven hundred dollars saved—first money I've kept since I've been on the road. That was your doing, too. When I saw how you hung onto a dollar, it shamed me into doing the same thing. Now here's my idea: there's a woman in Atlanta named Tess Fullbright. She's a good, motherly soul who runs a respectable boarding house. I want you to take this money and stay there until I come for you. It won't be long, baby—I promise you."

"Couldn't I," Fancy whispered, "stay here? I like Augusta."

"And run the risk of having Duke Ellis get his filthy hands on you? Fat chance, Fan—it's got to be Atlanta."

"All right, Wyche," Fan said; "but I won't take your money."

"Why not, baby?"

"Like you said, I don't love you. I might learn to; but then I might not. I don't want to be held to a promise. If I'm still there when you come, you'll know I'm yours—all yours, fair'n' square. If I've gone don't look for me, Wyche—it wouldn't do no good. . . ."

Wyche's face was terrible suddenly.

"There's somebody else?" he said. "Another man?"

"Yes. And it ain't Duke Ellis, which is what you're thinking. I don't want to call no names, Wyche, 'cause I ain't sure. I know I love him; but I don't know if he loves me. I got to find that out. If he don't, I've got to learn him to—or try to, anyhow. Maybe it won't work out. Maybe I'll change my mind. If I do, I'll be waiting. . . ."

Wyche's eyes were bleak with misery.

"That all the hope you can give me, baby?" he said sadly.

"Remember what you said about being a hypocrite? Can't lie to you, Wyche—I think too much of you for that. I'm just trying to be honest. I'm plumb, downright sorry, but that's the way it is. . . ."

Wyche got up slowly.

"I see," he said. "But just one more thing, Fan, baby. Don't settle for nothing less than the real thing. Whoever this man is, make him put a ring on your finger, and stand up before the preacher. Promise me that—the real thing or nothing. It just isn't smart otherwise. And tell him one thing for me—if he tries to play fast and loose with you, I'll find him. I'll find him if he tries to hide in hell itself. . . ."

"And when you find him?" Fan whispered.

"I'll kill him," Wyche said. "'Night, Fan."

"'Night, Wyche," Fancy answered; but her voice was so low he didn't hear her.

3

When Fancy got up the next morning, she saw that Wyche hadn't done anything about getting ready to leave Augusta. She looked around for him, and saw him sitting under a tree, peacefully smoking a cigar.

"'Morning, baby," he said as she came up to him, and started to rise.

"Don't get up," Fancy said. "Wyche–"

"Yes, Fan?"

"How come you ain't getting ready to pull out?"

"We're not leaving–not until tomorrow, anyhow. And–"

"But, Wyche," Fancy wailed, "you said you was sick of cheating people! You said it last night. And I'm sick of it, too. Sicker'n you, maybe. You don't have to get up and wiggle around before a passel of menfolks with almost nothing on. . . ."

Wyche studied her, his brown eyes tender and grave.

"You hate that, don't you?" he said.

"Yes. Most anybody would."

"That's another thing I like about you," Wyche said. "You're modest–really modest. It isn't anything you've been taught. It's just in you, that's all. You're a funny kid, Fan. You aren't dry behind the ears; yet in some ways you're as old as the hills. You always try to do what you think is right, don't you?"

"Yes. But, Wyche, about tonight . . ."

"We're giving our farewell performance, baby–free. I'm going to give the suckers all that fine, bottled branch water for nothing. I'm donating Mister Bones to the Medical College here. I'm selling the mules, and taking Mose with me for my personal valet. Then you and I, Fan, are going to get aboard a train."

"Do I," Fancy said in a low voice, "have to dance?"

"Yep. Put your heart into it tonight, baby. You'll be doing them a favor. Give 'em something to remember. Most of those poor, lecherous devils are starved for beauty–fresh young beauty like yours. Up there, behind those lanterns, you're every man's dream girl. You're beauty, and passion–tenderness and flame. That's what they want, but they don't know how to say it. They don't even realize what being tied to their timid, duty-bound wives has done to 'em. If any one of 'em ever in his whole life got a caress he didn't have to buy, he'd die happy. . . ."

"To buy?" Fancy said. "But you said—"

"That some of 'em's married? Right. Only there're various kinds of coin that a man has to pay his way with, Fan. For most of 'em the coins are patience and resignation—to the woebegone, sullen, dutiful, holier-than-thou expressions on their spouses' faces when they slip into their arms. They've got an inkling that love oughtn't to be like that—that it should be joy given and taken—shared. So all their lives they feel cheated by the counterfeits they have to accept—at some dim-lighted brothel off a side street, or their little sacrificial lambs' frozen faces as they prepare to do their repugnant duty. . . ."

"You're a funny man, Wyche," Fan said.

"Am I? Funny—amusing; or funny—odd?"

"Both. And funny wise, too. Wyche—"

"Yes, baby?"

"You said I always tried to do right. But what is right, Wyche? I used to think I knew; but now I ain't sure. . . ."

Wyche stared at her, his strong, square face working.

"You *are* in love with this man, aren't you?" he said gruffly.

"Yes, Wyche," Fancy whispered.

Wyche looked away from her toward where the sun was coming up over the pines.

"Being in love makes you unsure," he said quietly. "He stretches out his arms and you want to jump right into 'em. That's perfectly natural, Fan, baby; but society is agin it; and this time, society's right."

"Why, Wyche?"

"Several good reasons, too long to go into, and which wouldn't interest you. I'll tell you the one that I think will: when a man's in love, he wants to keep the one he loves—and cherish her. He wants to build a picket fence 'twixt them and the world. He doesn't want it temporary, secret, hidden. He wants the world to know. The one he loves is somebody to him, not a thing to be taken, used and tossed aside. Hell, I'm not saying he shouldn't be interested in your pretty ankles and what a nice sway your bustle's got. That's part of it, too; but only a part. The rest of it is the long years ahead, the laughing together, and the crying, bringing up your kids, nodding together under the lamplight when your heads have turned white, and finally lying together forever in the long dark. . . ."

"But Wyche," Fancy said, "s'pose I can't have those things? S'pose all I could look forward to is a little while with him? Shouldn't I take a little happiness in place of none at all? Is that wrong, Wyche? What is wrong and right, that's what I want to know?"

"The question of Pilate," Wyche groaned. "Only he wanted to know what truth was, which is only another way of saying the same thing, I reckon. Fan, I can't answer that. You have to answer it for yourself. All I can give you is a rough rule of thumb to go by. The whole history of man, baby, has been made up of his efforts to raise himself up from the ape he was into something approaching the angels. Somewhere along the line he acquired himself a brain that could think. Of all the animals he was the only one who knew he had to die, and he hated it. He's built the world we know by refusing to accept the blind accidentality of fate; by never admitting that he was a pallid worm crawling over the surface of a half burned out cinder in space. He couldn't be little, couldn't sink into dust. Something in that awful, blind cosmos had to care about him, so he invented God. Maybe there is a God—I don't know; but the very conception is noble. Man stopped gibbering around in trees, he came down to earth and mastered it; he stopped crawling on all fours, he stood up and looked at the stars. . . .

"The point is, baby, the ugly, clownish ape-thing we were had a hunger after dignity. He'd licked the saber-tooth tiger and the woolly mammoth with nothing but his brain against their awful strength. He had a right to his pride. And every time he's let go of that pride, every time he's lost that dignity, the world has sunk in blood and chaos, the light has gone out, and men have groped in darkness for hundreds of years. . . ."

He looked at her tenderly, keenly.

"So here's my rule of thumb, baby: anything that exalts that dignity of yours, be it chants and ceremonies, a ring on your finger, the white of a veil, is good: anything that debases it—is bad. And you have tremendous dignity, Fan, baby; I've never seen anything like it in anybody so young. . . ."

"Thanks, Wyche," Fancy said gratefully; but her voice was sad.

"I know I haven't made you happy," Wyche said; "I only hope I've made you strong."

Fancy put out her hand and let it rest on his arm.

"I reckon maybe you have," she said. "You've given me something to hang onto, Wyche. Now, whatever happens, I'll be thinking: I can't shame Wyche, I can't!"

"You can't shame yourself, baby," Wyche growled; "it ain't in you to. Come on, now—let's go get something to eat."

They had supper at the Globe. Fancy was dressed well enough for that now, and her manners were at least as good as those of the wives of many back-county planters. They didn't talk much. In fact they were sitting there over their coffee, when Fancy looked up and saw that man coming toward them. That man. It was a funny thing that those were the exact words that her mind formed in connection with him, for she couldn't remember ever having seen him before in her life. Yet she had the feeling that she would have known that freckled face anywhere, it and the eyes that smiled even when the rest of that thin, exceedingly handsome face was still, and the carrot-colored, thick-curling hair.

"Howdy, Wyche," the man said. His voice was like the rest of him, high-colored, warm, with a half suppressed chuckle in it.

"You buzzard," Wyche said.

"Now, Wyche," the tall man said, "you ain't got no call to low-rate me like that—'specially in front of a lady. Haven't taken notice of you letting any suckers off scot-free yourself. . . ." He looked at Fancy, and that infectious grin that demanded an answer was there on his face.

"Howdy, Ma'am," he said, "I'm Jed Hawkins. Hope you'll forgive my introducing myself this way, but since Wyche here clearly has no intention of doing it for me, I reckoned I'd better."

"I'm Fancy Williamson," Fancy said, and put out her hand. "Pleased to meet you, Mister Hawkins."

Jed Hawkins took her hand and held it a long time.

Wyche groaned.

"Now I've got to ask you to sit down," he said. "Reckon that's the only way short of mayhem I can get you to turn Fan loose."

"Mayhem," Jed grinned, "wouldn't do. It would have to be murder."

"Don't tempt me," Wyche said.

Jed drew a chair from one of the nearby tables, and sat down. He didn't say anything. He just sat there, looking at Fancy.

"I—I've seen you somewhere," Fancy said. "Leaseways, I kind of think I have. . . ."

"Right," Jed said. "Savannah, Macon, Waycross, Columbus. I'm a traveling politician, Miss Fancy. And every time I heard your show was going to be some place, I kind of made it my business to be there, too. . . ."

"That's downright flattering," Fancy said. "Wish I could believe you was telling the truth. . . ."

"The truth and Jed Hawkins," Wyche said, "ain't even on speaking terms."

"What was that saying about 'honor among thieves'?" Jed groaned. "Wyche, as one crook to another, you ought to treat me a little whiter'n that."

"And have you make off with my girl? Not on your life, Jed. I'm having enough trouble in that direction right now. . . ."

"Do tell!" Jed grinned. "Handsome young feller like you?"

"Wouldn't be so bad," Wyche said soberly, "if men like you meant her any good. But Fan's no more'n a kid, Jed—and real inexperienced. But there's one thing I want to get straight right now. I know you don't know a lady when you see one; but Fan's a lady. A true-born, honest to God, lady. So I don't want any free and easy tomcats like you hanging around. Understand me, Jed?"

Jed stared at him.

"All right, Wyche," he said quietly. "You've had your say. So now I reckon I'll have mine. You're dead, damned wrong on several counts. Number one, because I ain't had any particular hankering to chase after any real ladies before, don't amount to a hill of beans in this case. Knew the first time I laid eyes on her that this little girl was a lady. Heck, man, anybody who's got one good eye can see that; and ain't a blamed thing wrong with my sight. Number two, I don't mean Miss Fancy a bit o' harm. Fact is, I mean her all the good in the world. . . ."

Fancy looked at him. It wasn't, she realized, a hard thing to do. Jed Hawkins was one handsome man. A mighty heap handsomer, for instance, than Court Brantley. Not that it made any difference. Nothing made any difference as far as that was concerned.

"I think," she said, "you'd better explain yourself, Mister Hawkins."

"I aim to. Straight. Wyche, you know that being single doesn't help my political chances. I ain't very old, and folks have the curious idea that a young bachelor is a mite too unsteady for public office. . . ."

"I get your drift," Wyche said grimly. "Go on."

"On the other hand, a highfalutin aristocrat wouldn't do me any good with the folks who're my chief support. So I've kind of been on the lookout for a—a bride. I won't lie to you, Ma'am. First time I saw you, I looked you over with the cold eye of calculation. Can't say I fell for you at first sight. I didn't. But it took just one of them cute little dances of yours to warm that cold and calculating eye up a mighty heap—yessir, a mighty heap. . . ."

"So?" Wyche said brusquely.

"I just moseyed over here, and butted in to ask the little lady one thing: whether I couldn't see her once in a while. Whether we couldn't get better acquainted. After that, who knows? She might not like my looks or my style. . . ."

"And you," Fancy smiled, "might not like mine, knowing me better. . . ."

"Fat chance of that," Jed Hawkins said. "Now you tell me, Miss Fancy—what kind of a chance have I got?"

Fancy looked at him with grave eyes.

"None," she said.

Jed stood up slowly.

"Congrats, Wyche," he said.

"Not me," Wyche groaned, "some other polecat."

"In that case," Jed grinned, "I'm going to keep on hoping. Wyche, here, is a mighty good man, for all that he's a mite unfriendly. If it was him, I'd give up. Somebody else—no. I can give somebody else a run for his money."

"Not this—somebody else," Fancy said. "You coming to the show tonight?"

"No'm. I'm due back in Savannah tonight. That's my home town. Next time you're down that way, I'd sure admire to squire you around. . . ."

"There won't be any next time," Fancy said.

"I'll keep hoping," Jed said. "My luck's always been good. . . ."

"Don't depend on it," Fancy said.

"I got to," Jed murmured. "I'm sunk now. Seeing you this close, talking to you—I'm sunk. Scheming's all gone now, Miss Fancy. It's just you. 'Bye, now—both of you. You'll be seeing me. . . ."

As Fancy watched him walk out of the dining room, her face was puzzled.

"Does he," she said, "always go around proposing to girls he just met?"

"No," Wyche said. "Jed's got a reputation of being cagey—hard to get. Many a little filly's set her cap for him before now. Only he wasn't having any. Damned if I don't believe he means it!"

"He's nice," Fancy said. "Most any girl would take a shine to him. So good-looking and all. Still . . ."

"Still there's this other bounder," Wyche said. "That's it, isn't it, Fan?"

"Yes, Wyche," Fancy said, "that's it."

Wyche looked at her a long time and very intently. But he didn't say anything. He stood up at last and took her hand. They went out of the Globe together and started walking back toward the place they'd left the wagon.

On the way, they passed Court Brantley. He stopped still and looked at Fancy, seeing her in daylight for the first time, her clear young beauty unmottled by the flambeaus. And he frowned, thinking:

If she's no good, it sure hasn't marked her. That's a child's face—a sweet child at that. God, but she's pretty! Blue eyes with black hair is unusual—sets her off. And her skin's like a blonde's. White as—as—and it came unbidden to his mind—as Fern's. But he didn't want to make that comparison.

It was, to him, a kind of blasphemy to compare any mortal woman with Fern.

As for Fan, one sight of him and there was a sunburst in her cheeks. She looked away from him quickly, hoping that Wyche wouldn't see.

Wyche didn't. He was too troubled in mind to notice the people they passed.

Peering through the flap of the tent that night, Fancy was frightened by the size of the crowd. It looked like everybody in the world was there. Even from where she stood, shivering behind the tent flap, she could see Court Brantley, and after that she didn't look for anyone else. She could hear Wyche making his farewell speech. It was, she realized, a curiously honest speech, for Wyche hinted that most of the benefits to be gotten from any medicine lay in the minds of those taking it. "Have faith," he said, "and it will help you the exact extent of the amount of faith you have." He made none of his usual extravagant claims for the medicine. The crowd sensed his mood and was restless.

He didn't even call upon Mose to dance or to crack any of their miserable jokes. At the end he said very simply: "And now, the young lady known as Madame Scheherazade will entertain you with her dance of the mysterious East. She will not tell fortunes, tonight—nor any other night in the future. For this, my friends, is her last appearance before you—and mine, as well."

Fan could hear the disgruntled mutter rumble through the crowd. She could feel her heart beating like a wild thing, and despite the heat there were beads of icy perspiration on her forehead.

Mose picked up the flute and began, and Fancy raced over to the wagon and Wyche helped her up. This time she didn't close her eyes: she looked straight at Court Brantley. She couldn't make out his face, because he stood too far away from the lanterns, but she had the feeling he was frowning. Then, very slowly, she began to dance to the music of Mose's flute.

Tonight, for the first time, she actually listened to it, and her dance was beautiful. She had no idea what she looked like, but Wyche did. He thought she looked like a bride in some strange, primitive rite, entertaining her future lord. He tried to follow her gaze to see whom she was doing it for; but it was too dark, and the faces of all but the men in the first two or three rows were hidden. Wyche found the dance strangely touching. Even Fancy's young, inexperienced awkwardness was moving. It was like an oriental child bride trying to please, but betraying her innocence of the sensuality she had been trained to imitate with every gesture.

Then he heard a high, nasal tenor voice saying: "That her, Duke?" And looking out he saw the three men pushing their way through the crowd.

Duke was the only one of the Ellises that he knew; but he guessed at once that the other two men must be his brothers, Tom and Buck.

He loosened the buttons of his frock coat, getting ready to take it off. Then Duke Ellis elbowed his way into the front row and stood there looking at Fancy.

"Hell, yes! It's her all right," Duke bellowed. "Now where'n hellfire is that polecat, Weathers!"

Wyche stepped forward easily from the shadows alongside the wagon. "Right here, Duke," he said quietly, "though how you can smell another polecat through your own scent is more than I can see."

"Well, well," Duke grinned; "if it ain't the little Doc, himself! Nervy little fellow ain't you, stealing my gal!"

On the platform, Fancy stood still, too frightened to move. The men in the front row broke away from Duke and Wyche like a wave. Only Court Brantley stood where he was; then after a second, he started forward.

"Hiyah, Fan," Duke laughed. "Time you came on back home, babydoll. Been looking all over for you ever since you run away from our cozy little cottage."

Court had moved up now so close that the light of the lanterns showed on his face. Fancy saw him stiffen when he heard what Duke said, and something inside her died, terribly.

Oh, no, Court! No! she cried inside her heart. He's lying, it wasn't like that at all—it wasn't!

"Appears to me," Wyche said, "that Miss Fancy's got a perfect right to say what she wants to do."

"Nobody asked you, little Doc," Duke said evenly. "Now move out of my way. I don't aim to hurt anybody so small."

"You mean you don't aim to get hurt, don't you, Duke?" Wyche said almost gently.

Duke stopped short and glared at him. If he had ever before bothered to notice Wyche, he would have seen that the short man was as big around the chest as he was, and was better muscled, with even bigger arms. Fancy had thought to herself more than once that the top of Wyche Weathers looked like it had gotten joined to the wrong bottom, for only Wyche's legs were short. And they were thickset and powerful.

"You're asking for it, Doc," he said. "Well, I'll make this short. Got better things to do. . . ."

Then he swung his big right fist like a sledge-hammer, all of his weight behind it. But Wyche wasn't there any more. He weaved downward to the left, letting Duke's blow whistle over his shoulder, and came up almost from the ground with his left so that it buried itself in Duke's middle. Duke doubled, and Wyche crossed with his right, the sound of the blow carrying clearly. Duke's big head turned halfway round on his neck, and he went down like a pole-axed bull.

The men crowded back, staring. Not Duke Ellis! Not the man who had spread terror from Pinch Gut to the Sandhill. Not the man who had wrecked half the taverns on Carmichael's Range single-handed. But a second later, a look of pleasure came into their eyes. More than one man there remembered how Duke's big fist felt. And to see him sprawled out in the dirt was a real pleasure.

Duke sat up shaking his head. He stared at Wyche with astonished eyes. He had never been hit so hard in all his life.

"You want some more?" Wyche said.

"Why you stinking, ornery, woman-stealing little polecat!" Duke roared and came up off the ground in a rush. But a heartbeat later he was back on it again, for Wyche waited until he was close enough, and jabbed through Duke's clumsy defenses, with maddening ease, flattening Duke's nose against his face; then hooking a right to his jaw turning it sideways just far enough so that the left hook could turn it back again, then right, and again the left, smooth-working, swinging, Wyche's fists, the size of small hams, landing right, left, right again so fast that it was for all the world as though he were punching a bag in a gymnasium. Duke Ellis didn't land a blow. He hung there, his eyes glazing over, taking it; until Wyche stepped back and dropped his hands to his sides, watching with cool amusement while the big man bent forward slowly, as though bowing to Fancy, and continued on down, gathering speed as he went, until he toppled to the ground.

"Reckon that settles that," Wyche said, "unless you other two polecats want a taste of the same."

Tom and Buck didn't answer.

Wyche turned toward the wagon, and put one foot on the lowest step, before Fancy screamed:

"Look out, Wyche!"

He half turned, but he was too late. Buck Ellis lunged forward, the blade of the spring-operated pocket knife clicking open as he touched the catch on the handle. Wyche's big fist grazed his jaw; but the blade, all eight inches of it, disappeared into Wyche's flesh, low on the left side.

Wyche backed away from Buck, holding his side, and Court Brantley came up from behind and slashed the knife out of Buck's hand with one blow of the short gutta percha cane he carried. Tom Ellis started for him. Then he stopped short, and Fancy saw the reason: Court was holding a short, ugly little pistol with four barrels mounted in two pairs one above the other pointed straight at his chest.

"Don't come any closer, Tom," he half whispered. "Shooting an Ellis would give me a hell of a lot of pleasure." He looked toward where Wyche leaned up against the wagon, the color draining out of his tanned face. "'Tend to him, Fan," he said; "he's hurt bad."

Fancy leaped down from the wagon, and clawed at Wyche's clothes with frantic fingers. They were wet, sickeningly wet.

"Got to sit down, baby," Wyche whispered; "can't stand any more."

He slumped down to the ground, and Fan tore off her veil, holding it against the wound.

"Reckon I'm done," Wyche muttered. "Fan, baby—" Then he went down.

Court stood there listening to Fancy's helpless crying.

"Oh Wyche, honey, don't die—not over me don't die! I ain't worth it—I ain't! Oh God, oh Jesus, Wyche!"

Court turned away from her.

"Some of you men go get Sheriff Bowen," he said. "And one of you get Doc Blumfeldt."

By the time the sheriff and the doctor got there, Duke was up again. Court held all three Ellises before him at pistol-point while the sheriff clicked the handcuffs about their wrists.

"You Ellises have gone a mite too far this time," the sheriff said; "if Weathers dies, by God, I'll see that you swing for it!"

"He won't die," Harry Blumfeldt said; "he can thank his wonderful constitution for that. All right you men, help me load him on the wagon. One of you drive to the hospital. I have to stay back with him."

"All right, you three," Sheriff Bowen growled; "get moving. Thanks, Court—you acted like a public-spirited citizen."

"Just a minute, Sheriff," Duke said. "Let me tend to one little personal matter, before you drag me off. The little lady's a friend of mine. Surely a Southern gentleman like you won't stand by and see her left without a cent and nowhere to stay. . . ."

"All right," Bowen said; "but make it fast."

"Be a good scout, Sheriff, and take my wallet out of my breast pocket. That's it. Now my keys, out of the side. Give 'em to her. Fan, honey, these are to the cottage. You stay there till I get out . . ."

Mutely Fancy took the wallet and the keys, and went back to wiping Wyche's face with his own handkerchief. Then she saw Court staring at her, and realized at last what she held in her hand.

"No, Duke, no!" she cried; but Court turned away from her, his thin face filled with disgust. In the driver's seat, the man who had taken the reins flapped them over the backs of the mules. The wagon moved off through the dark, with old Mose trotting behind it.

Fancy wanted to jump out of it and run to Court, but she couldn't leave Wyche. There goes my future, she thought, and turned back to the unconscious man. But from time to time she turned her head toward where Court Brantley's tall figure stood in the darkness, now that the lanterns were gone. She kept watching him until she couldn't see him any more. And it came to her then that the place where he stood was awfully dark—the darkest place, maybe, in the whole wide world.

Then the wagon went around a bend in the road, and she couldn't even see the place where he stood.

4

"It was mighty white of you to write me about my boy's misfortune, Mister Brantley," Ted Weathers said to Court. "Yes, sir—mighty white!"

Court looked across the aisle of the train at the pullman berth in which Wyche lay. Wyche had his eyes closed, and his massive frame seemed drained of strength.

"Isn't it a little dangerous," Court said, "to move him so soon?"

"Well, the docs did want me to wait; but I've got to get him home where he can be properly attended to. Besides, I've wanted him back for years. 'Pears to me I treated him mighty harshly. I mean to make it up to him now—if it's the last thing I do."

"Is he conscious?" Court asked.

"Not fully. The doc gave him a little something so that he wouldn't feel the jolting of the train. He'll be back in Spartanburg before he comes to himself. Anyhow, I'm mighty glad to have him—it's been five years, Mister Brantley. . . ."

"I know," Court said gravely. "There's one thing I think you'd like to know, Mister Weathers: Wyche was planning to come home of his own accord. The night he was attacked—he'd already announced he was giving up the medicine show."

"Was he now?" Ted Weathers' powerful old face brightened; then a worried look came back into his eyes. "But this—this girl," he muttered; "heard tell the fight was over some girl."

"In a way it was," Court said smoothly. "It seemed that—this girl had previously formed a connection with a local man. They quarreled, and she ran away from him. Then she joined Wyche's troupe—in a purely professional capacity. She was much younger than Wyche, and he seems to have treated her in a fatherly sort of way. That's what she says—and I believe her. In fact," and Court forced a convincing chuckle, "she seemed a mite disappointed."

He could see the old man's face clearing with relief. Strange how the desire to believe a thing increased a man's credulity. . . .

Outside the window, the conductor bellowed: " 'Board!" and Court stood up.

"It's been nice meeting you, Mister Weathers," he said; "and give Wyche my kindest regards when he comes around."

"Thank you, my boy," Ted Weathers said. "If there's anything I can ever do for you—if you should ever need a job or anything . . ."

"Thank you," Court murmured. "Take good care of Wyche. He was a friend of mine."

When the train had gone snorting and puffing out of the station, Court Brantley stood there a long moment looking after it.

"So long, Wyche," he murmured. "You're out of this now—back in the lap of luxury. While I—oh hell, thinking about it does no good. . . ."

He started walking slowly through the town, back toward Hiberion. What went on inside of his mind was a kind of ugliness, but he couldn't stop it. They're all alike, he thought, women are all alike. Fern lying with the sanction of church and state in my brother's lecherous arms, and Fan up there in that little cottage of Duke's on the Sandhill—waiting. Why am I concerned about that? Fern now, was something to me; but this little fluff of hill trash was nothing and less than nothing. Yet it hurts, damn it! I was beginning to believe her—she swore there was nothing between her and Wyche. Maybe there wasn't. Wyche was a strange man. But she didn't swear anything about Duke Ellis and she took that money and those keys without a murmur. . . . Watch it, Court, boy. When are you going to grow up? You should know by now that virtue's always a lack of opportunity, or the product of fear—never a real inclination. . . .

But Fern. My little Fern—with that blonde hair like new moonlight, and skin like snow with a dawn flush on it. How could she? How in the name of all that's decent and holy could she turn to Ty? She knew Ty—she wasn't fooled. She knew that he was all Brantley—blood and bone of this centaur breed of ours. But am I any different? I've tried to be. Hell of a heritage to live down, though—seven generations of men who died in those atavistic, ceremonial brawls we call duels, and always because of their poaching upon the preserves of men who were their neighbors and friends. Not counting the ones who broke their necks leaping from second-story bedroom windows, or were shot in the back while running away from their discovered dishonor. . . .

Some family, we Brantleys. The men a breed of satyrs, and the women haunted by a suicidal mania. The Brantley women die by drowning, Father says. And by poison, leaping from high places and any other method that's convenient. He laughed aloud. Fine lot I've got to offer any woman—and I've been eating my heart out because two of 'em beat me at my own treacherous game. . . .

He came to the gate of the house, and stood there looking at it. He had the feeling that he was seeing it, really seeing it, for the first time since he had come back from Boston. That was crazy. He'd been back better than six months now; but it came to him that he had never really looked at Hiberion in all that time—never seen it with eyes stripped of illusion, divested of emotion.

Well, he was seeing it now, and the sight made him sick. Hiberion had been a name that had meant something in Georgia once. Had been. But not now. The slim Doric columns that had soared up for two stories to hold up the roof above two lovely porches were chipped and cracked, and there was green mold in the cracks. The white paint was a dirty gray now, peeling in tattered flakes, and the upper porch hung down at a crazy angle, all that was left of it, that is. Its floor had rotted through, and somebody—the Negroes, or perhaps even the family itself—had been using the timbers for firewood. The delicate filigree tracery of the ironwork balustrade that had surrounded it was still intact, but it was red with rust.

There was Spanish moss dripping from the eaves, and through the roof of the porches, Court could see the sky. The bronze knocker was gone from the front door, and the holes from the bolts that had held it had been greatly enlarged by rot.

The grass on the lawn stood up waist-high, and the bird bath was choked with weeds. None of the riot of flowers that had surrounded the porch showed, gone, too, a prey to neglect and despair. Around the house, he remembered, the fields had stretched out time out of mind down to the banks of the Savannah. But the fields were gone now, filled up with ugly little breezeway and dogtrot houses, with shotgun cabins, even; and instead of the scent of jasmine, the rank stench of collard greens cooking assailed his nostrils.

He was aware of a movement in the tall grass and weeds that choked what had been the finest yard and driveway in the State of Georgia, and a sow marched triumphantly before him, her litter grunting and snorting behind him. Pigs, by God! In Hiberion's front yard. " 'If ye have tears,' " Court quoted, suddenly, bitterly, " 'prepare to shed them now!' "

It had been bad enough when he left, eight years ago. But he had been so little prepared for this that in all the months he had been home he had shut his mind to it, had refused to see it as it was.

He started walking once more toward the porch and stood looking up at the giant magnolia tree that stood beside it. The tree was as beautiful as ever with its glossy oval leaves, and its huge, heavy blossoms whose petals were like woman's flesh, creamy-white and soft; and the scent that came down from them was a thing that overpowered the reason.

He went up the steps, feeling them giving under his weight, their strength and solidity gone. When he reached the lower porch, he realized that it too, had rotted through, and that all the Brantleys had been able to do about it was to bridge the gap with rough-hewn planks. He pushed the door and it opened with a creak that was an agony to hear; then Court stood once more inside the foyer of the house in which he had been born.

He kept quite still, holding hard against the pain and sickness inside his chest, seeing the great patches of plaster that had fallen from the walls and the ceilings. The fine old wallpaper, brought from England at great expense, hung down in tattered ribbons; the wide, curving staircase, that soared unsupported in sweeping spirals to the upper floors, had a ten-foot section of its balustrade missing. That staircase had been the glory of the house, like the magnificent chandelier of cut Belgian glass that now was a tattered ruin, with numerous strings of crystal missing.

Court went very quietly up the stairs toward his father's room, but before he had reached it, he heard the old man weeping.

"How are the mighty fallen!" Jeff Brantley cried. "I should have been killed at Atlanta! I should have died in my blood on a muddy field with a Yankee bayonet through my guts! That it should come to this! Oh the shame of it all!"

Court stepped into the room. It was a little better than the rest of the house, but even so it was sad to see. Saddest of all, perhaps, was the face of his father, lined and sunken, a ruin, too, like Hiberion, a breed that had died at Appomattox Court House, that lived on only in this quaking ghost. Court glanced at the thin, shapeless figures of his sisters, at their pale faces, which even to call plain was a kindness.

It was Saphira who saw him at last.

"So you're home at last," she said tiredly. "Father, here's Court."

"Court?" the old man quavered, and Court knew that this time again his father wasn't going to remember him. He had been through it all before, but it wasn't pleasant.

"Court?" Jeff Brantley mused. "Oh yes, Court—another of my sons. The one that ran away to Boston. The one that had to become a Yankee and go to Harvard College. . . . Oh, how sharper than a serpent's tooth is an ungrateful . . ."

"Hush, Father," Agnes said.

"I will not hush! Let me howl like old King Lear. Let me bare my shame to all the world. Come here, Court. Let me look at you. Let me see what they've done to you, up there in that heathen land."

Court started toward the trembling old wreck who had been a Brantley, who had sat on his horse with the best of that centaur breed, who had been proud, and brave and fiery and handsomer far than any of his sons. Halfway across the room, he could smell the liquor fumes. Jefferson Brantley was drunk.

"Yes, Court," he whispered, turning his watery blue eyes upon the tall figure of his son. "You came back. That's good—that's better than the others did. Tyler running off to Martin in Savannah, and Philemon—Philemon—"

"Father!" Agnes and Saphira chorused.

"I'll not be silenced! Philemon wallowing with his nigger wench and begetting children with her! There are black Brantleys now—you know that, Court? The finest blood in Georgia is flowing now in nigger veins!"

Of course Court had known about it. He had been told the whole story with delicate malice by Fern the very day he got home. But it wasn't a thing that talking about helped. Nothing helped things like that really.

"Father—" he began.

"Tyler now," Jeff Brantley said, "I'd have expected this of him. He's a raffish nighthawk like all the Brantleys . . . but not Phil. Phil was always good. Should have known better, though—it's in the blood. The Brantley women die by drowning; the men by fire, bullets, or the sword—those that escape hanging, that is. But no good ever come out of the breed, not yet, nor ever will. . . ."

Agnes came up to Court quickly and whispered in his ear:

"We've been keeping it from him for years. But Mary Jane, our washerwoman, told him about it this morning. Oh, Court, why do niggers love so to be the bearers of evil tidings?"

"Revenge, perhaps," Court said, "for the way we treat them. Who knows?" Then to his father, he said: "Now, Father—it's not as bad as all that—"

"Not bad? Do you mate a thoroughbred with a jenny? Or the sons of men with female apes? Not bad, Court? I should have strangled in my mother's womb before I lived to see this day!"

"Well," Court said, "it's done now, and sitting here crying over it won't do any good. There's a lot more to be done around here than moaning over Phil's misdeeds—"

"You should talk!" Jeff Brantley roared. "You were the first of my sons to run away and leave us in poverty and despair."

Court could not repress a smile despite his misery. His father still talked, as always, like a back-county orator.

"And the first to come back, Father," he said gently.

"That's true, that's true," the old man sighed. "Only what are you going to do, Court? What can anyone do now?"

"Well," Court said, "for one thing, I'm going to try to raise some money to build a mill—"

"A mill!" Jeff exploded. "Oh no—not another one! Not another of my sons stooping to engage in trade!"

"Engaging in trade," Saphira put in drily; "Father's quaint way of describing that store Phil was smart enough to set up. Have you been up there yet, Court?"

"Once or twice," Court said. "I didn't linger. Stores depress me—especially Phil's kind of a store."

"You're as bad as Father. Phil's done right well, Court. It's his money that has kept us eating and put clothes on our backs. In fact Father couldn't afford the disgusting state he's in right now if it weren't for Phil."

"I gather," Court said, "that you don't entirely disapprove of Phil, Saph."

"No, I don't. Any man who married Martha Tilton would have done the same thing. Of course, it's unfortunate that Phil had to turn to this colored girl. But he's been married to Martha six years, and still not a child in sight. Besides his mulatto yard children are quite pretty; I've seen them."

"Saphira!" Agnes said.

"Why not?" Saphira said. "Why shouldn't I see them, Agnes? After all, they are our own flesh and blood."

"I think," Agnes wept, "that you're being perfectly horrid."

"All right, I'll be horrid then. We've lived in illusion too long, my dear sister. Notice the crowd of men outside beating a path to our door? We're too good, we Brantleys. Good for what? You know why we're still here in this drafty, hideous old house, listening to the wails of this drunken old weakling who sired us? Because nobody would have us, my darlin' sister. Sneer at Phil's high-brown wench if you want to; but she's better than us. She could at least get a man. Can you? Can I?"

"That, Saph," Court said quietly, "is quite enough."

"It is enough, isn't it, Court? It's a heap too much to my way of thinking. I'm through with this life. I'm going out and get myself a man—any way I can get him. In wedlock or out of it. And I won't be choicy. Any man I can get will do—even an Ellis. . . ."

"How are the mighty fallen," Jeff Brantley moaned.

I could have stayed in Boston, Court thought. With a little encouragement my friendship with Hester Snow could have ripened into something. I could be sitting down right now to a good dinner looking at her across a Hepplewhite table under candlelight. But I had to come back to a girl who wouldn't wait for me, to this plantation overgrown with weeds and white trash, to this lovely old house through which the wind blows without hindrance. I had to come back to this sodden old wreck of a father, to these two disappointed harpies I call sisters, to those tart-tumbling gallants, Tyler and Phil. It's something to be proud of, this family; there's nothing finer than this Brantley breed. . . .

"Please," he said tiredly, "we've quarreled enough, don't you think? I'm very tired. . . ."

"I'm sorry, Court," Saphira said at once. "That was rotten of me. You must be hungry, too. Anything to eat in the house, Ag?"

"Well," Agnes said, "there's some greens and sidemeat and corn pone. I'll make Court some coffee . . ."

"Nigger food!" Jeff Brantley snorted.

"No thank you, girls," Court said politely. "I'm not hungry now. I'm a little too tired to eat anyhow. I think I'll go out and wander around a bit."

"But Court," Agnes protested, "you just said you were tired."

"I am, but it's not the kind of tiredness you can lie down on. I'm all kinked up. I need to move about."

"Go see Phil," Jeff Brantley said suddenly. "Talk to him, Court. You always had great influence over him. Maybe you can get him to give up his wench. Maybe you can get him to see the light of reason."

"I'll try," Court said; "I'll stop by Ty's, too; I want to talk to him about the business I'm planning."

"Didn't you hear Father say he's down at Melody, Uncle Martin's place?" Saphira said. "Uncle Martin's sick, and our precious brother is trying to persuade him to leave Melody to him—instead of to all of us."

"I don't believe that," Court said. "With all Ty's faults, he wouldn't. Fern go with him?"

"Aha!" Saphira laughed. "So the wind blows still to that quarter! No, Court, darlin', she didn't. She's at home now, all by her pretty little self. Now you can establish a new record even for the Brantleys. Your brother's wife—that would be interesting, wouldn't it?"

"Saph, you're a devil," Court said; "I have no intention—"

"Haven't you, my saintly brother? Then you're the first Brantley in history who hasn't. Besides, I don't believe you. Considering the fact that you so nobly came to the defense of Wyche Weathers' fancy woman last week —or was she Wyche's? I heard she was originally Duke Ellis'. Anyhow, she's most likely yours by now—since Wyche is in the hospital, and Duke's in jail. What about it, Court?"

Court's face reddened; then, suddenly, he smiled.

"You won't believe me, Saph," he said, "but she isn't. Anyhow, thanks for the suggestion. Come to think of it, it's a mighty good idea."

"Court," Agnes wailed, "don't you go and get yourself in trouble! Somebody in this family has to stay out of trouble."

"Why?" Saphira said. "Appears to me it's a heap more fun to get into it—deep. Come on, Court, I'll walk you to the door."

They came out on the porch, and Court looked at Saphira, thinking: you've got grit in your craw; no wonder you're my favorite relative. But Saphira's hand was gripping his arm, hard.

"Court!" she whispered; "is that her?"

Court looked up, and saw Fancy standing at the gate looking at the house.

"Yes," he said brusquely, "that's her all right."

"My, she's pretty!" Saphira said. "Go ask her in, Court. I'd like to meet her."

"No!" Court said. "You don't want to meet that kind of a woman, Saph. Leave it to me—I'll attend to her."

"She doesn't look bad," Saphira said. "She looks like a child—sort of scared. Why, Court, she has a sweet face! I don't believe the things people are saying about her—I really don't!"

"Now, Saph—" Court began; but Saphira wasn't there any more. She was running down the path toward the gate.

Court started out behind her, then he slowed to a walk. He'd be damned before he made a scene. Let Saph meet Fancy if she wanted to. Not much harm could come of it.

"Hello," Saphira said breathlessly; "I'm Court's sister, Saphira. You're Fancy, aren't you?"

"Yes'm," Fancy murmured. "Mighty proud to make your acquaintance, Miss Saphira. . . ." Then, very shyly she put out her hand.

Saphira took it in a grip that caused Fancy to wince.

"How pretty you are!" she said. "Black hair and blue eyes—that's an odd combination, but it's lovely. I wish I were pretty. Oh well, there's nothing can be done about that. I do hope we're going to be friends."

"Me too," Fancy said.

That's Saph, Court thought. A tongue like a fiend out of hell, and the best, kindest heart in the world when you get right down to it. I'm glad she's being sweet to Fan. The poor kid needs it.

"I wish I could ask you in," Saphira rushed on, heedlessly, "but–"

"I know," Fancy said. "Court won't let you. He–he thinks I'm–bad."

"Well, aren't you?" Saphira demanded. "I should think it would be very interesting to be bad. I've often thought I'd like to be–very much."

Fancy stared at her, then at Court.

"Does she mean that, Court?" she asked.

"Reckon she does," Court grinned.

Fancy put out her hand and let it rest on Saphira's arm.

"Can you tell when a body's lying, Miss Saphira?" she asked seriously.

"Of course I can. I'm a woman, aren't I?"

"Then listen to me: I have never let a man so much as touch me in all my life. . . ."

"Ha!" Court snorted.

Fancy whirled and faced him.

"Listen to me, Tallman!" she said. "You're the first man I ever even kissed! Course Duke Ellis kissed me once, but that was 'cause he was twisting my arm fit to break it; and afterwards I hit him on the head with a poker to stop him from doing anything more! I let you kiss me, and that was the first time! And I kissed you, and that was the first time for that, too!"

"You expect me to believe that?" Court said.

Fancy looked at him, and her mouth tightened.

"No, I don't," she said flatly. "That would be too much to expect, 'specially from a high and mighty Brantley. Reckon I'm a mighty big fool to care. But then I am a big fool as far as you're concerned, Court–so right now, I know exactly how Lem Waters felt. . . ."

"Lem Waters?" Saphira said.

"Yep–neighbor of ours in Ca'lina. They found him a-lying 'longside of Hannah Murray, and her dead–shot to death. Lem was drunk, and there was one bullet gone from his gun. Well–they hung him. Come protracted meeting time, Hannah's husband, Tim, got religion, and confessed that he'd shot Hannah, seeing her walking with Lem in the moonlight. That bullet Lem shot lit in a tree. But right now, I know how he felt sitting there in his cell a-waiting. You see, Court, nobody believed him either."

"Court," Saphira said, "she's not lying! Can't you see that, you big dumb ox? She's not!"

Court looked at Fancy, but he didn't say anything. He just stood there looking at her, and after a while he spoke to her very gently, but all he said was:

"All right, Fan, I'll take you home now."

They started off together walking slowly, and Saphira hung over the gate watching them. I believe her, she thought; don't know why I should, but I do.

Court didn't look at Fancy, or even speak to her; but from time to time he glanced at her out of the corner of his eye. His face was puzzled. Looking at her made it a hard job to do any kind of thinking at all. He kept seeing that her skin was just as white as was Fern's, except that the coloring of the cheeks and the mouth was warmer and richer, and that her hair was so black it looked blue. Every time he glanced at her he had the funny feeling that her eyes didn't belong to her; they were startling behind her sooty lashes, being the exact color of an October sky when she looked at him, and like flashes of light when she moved them.

Her mouth's too big, he thought, and sort of sullen. I've never seen that exact shade of red before. But that wasn't what he wanted to think of—he had to decide really whether or not she was telling the truth. She couldn't be. No man on earth would travel around for months with a girl like this one and not—Then, too, hadn't Duke given her his wallet and his keys and hadn't she taken them?

There was beyond this something else, something frightening to think about. Suppose she was telling the truth? What then? He thought about his choices in the matter if she were. They were very simple, and both of them very unpleasant: He could be all Brantley and heap upon her the misery that came to every woman who loved a Brantley without thought of herself, or he could play the fool and marry her and be forever the laughingstock of the whole town.

"Oh damn!" he groaned, and seeing her looking at him, he realized he had spoken aloud.

"Court," she said very simply, "why won't you believe me?"

"You took his wallet," he said, "and his keys."

"I know. I was beside myself what with poor Wyche hurt so. There was two hundred and fifty dollars in that wallet, Court. Here it is—count 'em and you'll see I haven't touched a red cent of that money."

As he took the wallet, it came to Court that he had absolutely no way of knowing how much money had really been in that wallet. But looking at Fancy, he knew suddenly she was telling the truth. About this, at least, she was telling the truth.

He handed the wallet back to her without even opening it.

"Why?" he said.

"I don't want to be beholden to Duke," she said simply. "Took this money back to him three times at the jail, but he won't take it."

"But you stay at his house," Court said.

"Yes. Tried to pay him rent, but he laughed at me. One sure thing, Court, I'm going to be gone from there long before he gets out of jail."

"Why do you stay there now?" Court said morosely.

"Where else could I stay? Can't come stay with you, Tallman. Can't stay in the streets. Leaseways, up there, I'm safe. Folks hereabouts so scairt of Duke, that they leave me be. That's the only good thing," she added bitterly, "I ever got out of knowing him . . ."

Court looked at her. He was frightened. He couldn't exactly put into words what he was afraid of, but he knew that if he started believing Fancy he was going to be in trouble—bad trouble.

"Why'd he say you were his girl?" he demanded.

"Reckon I was, kind of. I thought old Duke was just about the finest gentleman I'd ever seen. Way he talked, I thought he aimed to marry me. Then he got me up to that little old cottage of hisn, and tried to make me drunk and grabbed me. I hit him with the poker and ran. That's how I met Wyche."

"And he, of course, was not your beau either?"

"Wyche wants to marry me, Court," Fancy said gravely; "and he's willing to wait. He ain't one for putting in a crop before he's built a fence—not that I'd let him if he was. . . ."

Court stared at her, and nodded slowly.

"You know, Fan," he whispered, "I believe you. Damn my hide for a stupid fool, but I do!"

"Oh, Court, honey, I'm so glad!" Fan said; "I'm so blamed glad I'm scairt I'm going to cry. Heck, I am going to cry, darn it!"

They were passing the railroad station, and the train from Atlanta was in. But Court didn't pay any attention to any of the dozens of people he knew who were getting off of it. He stepped up close to her and took her in his arms. When they came apart finally, he heard the sharp intake of breath behind him and a woman's voice gasped:

"Why, Court! Court Brantley!"

Court turned his head slowly and looked over his shoulder. Fern stood there, her small, slippered foot beating a tattoo on the cobblestones. Behind Fern were still others, the women's faces twisted with rage, the men trying to keep the look of envy out of their eyes. Court turned then and made Fern a deep bow.

"I suppose," Fern said, "that you make a habit of kissing women in public places!"

"No," Court said; "no, my dear sister-in-law—not all women. Just the pretty ones who don't belong to me. The ones who do, I kiss in private. Of course, I'll admit the classification can be stretched a mite."

Fern took a backward step.

"Oh!" she said. "Her! That woman! Why, Courtland Brantley!"

Court grinned at her wickedly.

"Now look, Mrs. Brantley," he said, "Mrs. Tyler Brantley—you've no call to take on about Fan like that. Appears to me you've thrown away your right to be concerned about anything I do. And Fan's all right. At least she's honest, in her curious way."

"Honest!" Fern said. "Her!"

"Yes, her. It was because she'd just convinced me of that that I kissed her. I know the truth when I hear it, having had some recent experience with liars."

"I suppose," Fern said, "that you'll end up married to this—this circus snake dancer!"

Court looked at her.

"I could have done worse," he said quietly. "Reckon the way little Fancy made her living is kind of irrelevant. The point is, Fern, honey, I kind of think that she tells the truth—that she'd keep a bargain. I know some people who can't keep bargains, who forget important promises, whose sacred word doesn't mean anything. Maybe I'm no judge of such things, but I don't think Fan comes off so badly by comparison."

He turned to the others, smiling peacefully.

"And now that you've all had your fun," he said, "don't you think youall had better run along home? Night air's bad for the health, I'm told."

The crowd began to move off slowly. Ceremoniously Court turned to Fancy and offered her his arm.

"Oh, Court!" she said. "The way you took up for me—it was just grand!"

Court looked back over his shoulder and saw that Fern was still standing there. As he looked at her, the last ray of sunlight came through the open ends of the depot and lighted her face. She was crying.

Seeing her cry made Court feel good all over. It was, he knew, a bad, ugly sort of feeling—a cheap kind of triumph. But he couldn't help it. After what he had come home to, it felt good to make Fern cry.

A little while later, walking through the gathering darkness with Fancy, after they had got down from the horsecar that had taken them up the Sandhill, Court didn't feel so good about it any more. You're a bad loser, Court Brantley, he told himself, and that was a mighty ugly thing. What good is it now to hurt Fern? What good is anything now, anything in this whole damned dreary world, now that she's gone?

Fancy tightened her grip upon his arm, and rubbed her soft black hair against his shoulder. He was so tall, this Court Brantley. Tall and brave and gay—a real gentleman. The Brantleys were the finest people in the state. Real quality, no mistake about that. But that girl—that Fern Vance who'd married his brother Tyler. She was so pretty. A body hadn't ought to be that pretty—it wasn't right. It wasn't fair to the rest of the women in the world—it wasn't fair to Fancy to have that white and golden beauty 'twixt her and the man she loved. . . .

Court had spoken to her right short like, though. But why? He had sounded a mighty heap like a hurt and disappointed man. I'll fix that! Fancy decided; I'll make him forget her if it's the last thing I do. . . .

But when they had come to Duke's cottage, the moon was already up and she could see his face. It frightened her. Fancy hadn't known any Brantleys before or else she would have recognized that look. Fern could have told her about it—Fern, and any of a legion of other women, living and dead, who'd seen that look on a Brantley's face. The Brantleys weren't the smartest folk in the world or the bravest or the best, as Fancy believed; what they were actually, was unbeatable—they were just a little too much for most other people; without knowing or caring how and why, they made better men than they, back water—give ground.

Fancy fumbled in her little handbag until she had found her keys. She unlocked the door and turned back to Court.

"'Night, Court," she said quietly.

"'Night?" Court laughed. "Heck, Fan—the night's not even a baby, yet. But you and I, honey, are going to age it—fast."

Then he stepped up to her and took her in his arms.

Fancy didn't fight him. She didn't because she didn't want to. And, after a minute or two she knew that what he wanted was what she wanted too, as much as he did, maybe, or even more. But Wyche Weathers had given her something; he had strengthened something that she herself had. And what he had given her was a very good thing, for even in the midst of this —this new thing that spun the night about her head, that made her want the dying, the melting, the awaited hurt, it came to her and cried out fiercely: no, not like this! In a veil, in the church—for always, not a play-toy, not your easy woman, Court Brantley, no more than Duke's—your woman, yes, because I love you; but only when you love me back, when you're willing to build that fence and stand up 'longside of me proud for the world to see. . . .

She tore free of him and stood there shivering and crying a little until her breath came back and then she said:

"No, Court—not like that. Not even you—like that." Then she turned and went through the door and slammed it shut and locked it behind her.

She stood just inside the door and listened to his breathing. It was an ugly sound. He didn't move or say a word. She stopped her own breath, holding it hard in her throat until she hurt from holding it so. There was a hot tingling feeling crawling over her flesh, and at the same time it was cold, too, so that she felt like she was scalding and freezing; but outside the door Court Brantley didn't move. Then, very quietly, she heard him turn, and his footsteps went slowly, lumpily across the porch and down the steps. She heard the gravel on the walk crunch once or twice, and the harsh, rusty squeak of the gate hinges. Then it was still.

She let her breath out, little by little. There was no sound in the room, no sound at all except the noise she made breathing, and the hammering underneath her ribs. She took a step toward the door, then another, and her fingers closed over the knob. Then, quite suddenly, her knees gave way, and she went down in a little heap before the door, one hand still stretched out and up, holding the doorknob, the knuckles of the other rammed into her mouth, trying to keep from crying aloud; but it was no good.

She let it out then, ugly and choked and noisy like a whipped child.

"Court!" she cried. "Oh, Court, Court, Court. . . ."

Then she lurched to her feet and went to the side window where she could see the road, curving down and away from the cottage in the moonlight. Court was walking down it, his head bent, shuffling his feet in the dust like an old man, and everything Wyche had told her, everything that she herself believed was nothing and less than nothing, and she hurled herself against the door, twisting the key with stiffened fingers, and ran out of the house.

But, when she got to the gate, she saw it. A smart little road wagon came up the road toward Court. It was drawn by two dappled grays, and as it stopped, the moonlight came down between two of the pines, and fell upon the head of the girl who drove it. Where the light touched her hair, it looked like silver. Fancy stood there, watching her talking to Court. Then Court climbed up into the seat beside her, and she pulled the horses around in a wide circle, heading back down the road.

The moon still shone on the road after they had gone. But somehow a grayness had got into the light, dimming it. Fancy couldn't understand that. All she knew, as she turned away from the gate and started back toward the cottage was that the edges of everything were unclear, that there was no purity to the moonlight, or even to the light of the stars. . . .

5

Fancy looked at Court, seeing him sitting there upon the big Morgan that was the last of the fine horses for which the Brantleys had been famous. His face was frowning and sad. How long had it been? Six weeks now—maybe a little more. Lately he seemed to have given up trying—he just sat on the porch and talked to her, telling her his dreams. He's got big dreams, too—mighty big ones. A great cotton spinning mill to give jobs to the poor folks hereabouts—course it would make him rich, too; but he really didn't seem to care so much about that.

He's good, Fancy thought, down deep he's good. Here lately he's been treating me so sweet like. If only I didn't know about him going to her house, too—and her married to his brother! But he wouldn't—Court wouldn't, not my Court, not the one I know—better than he knows himself. Holding him off was the right way to handle him, only it was so blamed hard. How do you hold off a man you love? How do you make him keep his distance when what you wanted was him up close, so close, holding him hard and never letting go?

Only that would be the surest way of spoiling it. What she had right now wasn't much, but it was something. It was a chance, and it was getting better all the time. He's beginning to believe in me, now, she mused; he's kind of thinking that even if I ain't his kind I could learn to be. I could get to be a lady, too. I read all those books he brings me, and I try so hard to speak fair. He'll see some day that I wouldn't shame him—that I could move among all his fine friends and be at ease, that nobody'll ever know that I was just a hill girl from Ca'lina, that they'll think I'm a lady born. . . .

"This the place, Court?" she asked.

"Yes. This is Dry Gully. Notice how it runs, Fan—clear up to the river almost. If it weren't for that little hill there, the river would run down into it. That's what makes it perfect."

"How come, Court? I don't rightly understand."

"Textile mills," Court explained patiently, "are run by water power. That canal down in Augusta was dug more than forty years ago for the same reason. It furnishes six hundred horsepower; but just look at the way this gully falls down and away from the river. Why it would be a millrace,

Fan. It cost them a fortune to dig that nine-mile channel down in the city, and this one, short as it is would furnish more power—much more. A thousand horses at the least, or I miss my guess. I could build a series of dams, and spill the water over the wheels, and . . ."

"But there's no water in it," Fancy said.

"I know that. Look at the bluff, Fan. A few hundred sticks of dynamite and the whole thing would go up in the air, and let the river through. Don't you see?"

"I see all right," Fancy laughed. "I see you're one smart man, Court. Tell me one thing, though—who owns this land?"

"I do. I bought it as soon as I got back—took a lot too much of the money I'd saved. That's why I've got to borrow more."

"I've got four hundred dollars," Fancy said seriously. "Would that do?"

"Bless your sweet little heart," Court laughed. "No, Fan, it wouldn't —to build the kind of textile plant I have in mind would cost in the neighborhood of one hundred thousand. Fat chance I've got of getting that much."

"Why not, Court? The mill would pay it back in no time at all."

"Right. But you think the bankers believe that? I've maps to show this gully. I've led them over the whole thing point by point: see here, this natural canal doesn't even have to be dug—it's there waiting. One hour's blasting and you have more water power than all of Augusta—enough to power all the openers, breakers, finishers, cards, drawers, rovers, spindles, looms that a first-class mill requires with that. . . . Heck, Fan, do you know what I'm talking about?"

"No," Fancy said seriously, "I don't, Court."

"Neither did they. I'd start to describe all that beautiful machinery to them—tell them exactly what each one does, and they brushed me aside with, 'So sorry, but we can't see our way clear at this time'—or: 'Sorry, Mister Brantley, but since you don't have any security. . . .' "

He turned to her, his face flushed and angry.

" 'Security.' What the hell do they want—a pound of flesh? What's a man's knowledge and integrity if not security? But they can't see that. What they want is mortgages and Hiberion is already mortgaged to the hilt. I've nothing left to pledge. That fine family of mine has already mortgaged away my life and my future—almost before I was born. They sold me and my future down the river to pay gambling debts, to buy off outraged but surprisingly reasonable husbands, to try to hold onto a kind of life that was dead and rotten fifty years ago. . . ."

He pulled out his handkerchief and mopped the beads of sweat from his brow.

He's so wonderful when he's mad, Fancy thought. If there was only some way I could help him; but a hundred thousand dollars! Heck, there ain't that much money in the whole wide world. . . .

She rode the little mare she had rented from the livery stable up close to him and put one gloved hand on his arm.

"Don't give up, Court," she said. "You can do it. I know you can. If anybody in the whole state of Georgia can do it, you're the one. Wish I could be some help to you, instead of just getting in your way—don't look like I'm much good to you in no way atall."

Court looked at her.

"You're the only person in this whole filthy world who is any good to me, Fan," he said quietly. "You believe in me—and I need that, 'cause I don't really believe in myself. You stick by me although I've tormented you enough to make you hate me a thousand times over. I actually think you're really fond of me, though for the life of me I can't see why."

"No, Court," Fancy said, "I ain't fond of you. Not just fond of you. I love you. There's a mighty big difference 'twixt the two words to my way of thinking."

Court grinned at her, mockingly.

"You sure don't act like it, sometimes," he said.

"That's where you're wrong," Fancy said. "Love is for keeps, Court. This—this other thing isn't love. It can be mixed up with love, and it ought to be. Between people who love each other, reckon it can be downright beautiful. But people what love each other ought to be proud of that love—proud enough to make it a going concern, not something cheap. The way I feel about you, Court, is a mighty handsome thing; the way you feel about me—ain't. . . ."

Court stared at her.

"You know, Fan," he said, "sometimes I think you're a thousand years old."

"I'm nineteen—and that's old enough. The way I love you, Court, honey, ain't simple. I want too many things. I want a house and kids and you walking 'longside of me to church, feeling proud that I'm yourn. . . ."

"Yours," Court corrected her.

"All right, yours. Like I said, the way I feel about you is beautiful, and I don't want it dirtied. Only you make it so hard for me. . . ."

"How, Fan?"

"In a way that shames me to think about, let alone say. Folks have been saying for years that men and women are different. Course they are, but not as much different as folks like to think. Men are supposed to be wild, and spirited and a little bad—but not women. Only that ain't—isn't—so. I know that now. You taught me. I've got a mighty heap of wildness in me, Court, and a lot more badness than I'd like to have to answer for. You kind of reach that, Court. From all I hear tell about youall, it's you Brantleys' greatest talent. Youall can make any woman feel like a hussy and be glad of it. . . ."

"Fan," Court said, "Fan, honey . . ."

"Wait, Court. I haven't finished having my say, yet. The times I've kept you outside that little cottage haven't been 'cause I didn't want to let you in. It would be a relief to let you in and get it over with—it would be nice not to have to feel so choked up and miserable all the time. But it ain't that simple. I don't want you like that. I don't like the idea of slipping around and being scared, and hoping that I don't have a shamed yard child, that you don't think enough of to own. . . ."

Court looked at her, but he didn't say anything.

"And I don't like playing second fiddle. I hate knowing that the only reason you come around at all is that the girl you love is married to your brother. I know you go to see her. I don't think nothing much happens betwixt you. Leaseways I hope not. I'm just living in hope, Court, that all that can be changed. . . ."

"You're a funny kid," Court said; "but damned if you aren't kind of fine at that."

"Yep, I'm funny. Likewise I'm a fool. I keep on hoping with everything against me. I didn't come from nowhere. My folks are hill trash. I don't have book learning. I can't even talk fair. The main reason why you never even thought serious like about taking me home with you is 'cause you think I'd shame you in front of your fine friends. . . ."

"You are nobody's fool," Court said grimly.

"Ever thought about one thing, Court? I learned myself to read and write without ever being inside a school. Just listening to you, I'm getting so I talk better. Don't you see I'd have sense enough to keep my mouth shut until I learned the ways of your kind of folks? It ain't where a person comes from, but where she's going that counts—and dangblast it all, I'm going up! With you, I hope; without you, if I have to. Come on now, let's go back—I've dangled my heart on my sleeve enough for one day."

Court rode along beside her silently, his forehead creased with thinking.

"You know, Fan," he said, "there's a lot in what you said. Where a person ends up is the important thing after all. Folks around here would die in their tracks before they'd admit it; but three-quarters of the aristocracy of Georgia were jailbirds and debtors who were shipped over here from England because they didn't have what it took to get along over there. I've heard my mother say when she was good and riled that the first Brantley was a common cutpurse, let out of Newgate Prison on his promise to leave England—and the girl he married was a slattern whose morals weren't anything to shout about. I kind of believe her. The Brantleys got to be rich and powerful, but lesser folk would have been hanged out of hand for half the things they did. . . . Yep, we're haunted by our origins, our souls are twisted because a tavern wench got tired of being paid for casual loves; there's a devil in us because a London cutpurse went unhung. . . ."

The way that they rode looped down Walton Way into Gwinnett Street, and cut through the edge of the Terry. Fancy looked at the Negroes curiously. Then, suddenly, she drew the rented mare up, and laid a hand on Court's arm.

"Those kids," she whispered. "My, but they're pretty!"

Court looked at the two little mulatto girls playing in a hard-packed dirt yard.

"They ought to be," he said bitterly; "they're Brantleys, too."

Fancy turned and stared at him.

"My brother Phil's yard children," Court said. "We're a tribe all right."

Before he could say anything or put out his hand to stop her, Fancy was down from the mare and running hard toward the wooden gate. A moment later she was kneeling in the dirt beside the two little girls, holding them both in her arms. They stared at her, their eyes round with wonder. Then one of them smiled.

"Lady," she said, "pretty lady . . ."

Court got down from the Morgan and strode over to where Fancy knelt. He stood there frowning at her; but when she looked up he saw her eyes were bright with sudden tears.

"Oh, Court," she whispered, "they're beautiful! They're just too beautiful for words!"

Court looked at the children. It was the first time he had seen them up close. They were the color of dark honey with the sun shining through it, and their hair was only a shade darker than that. He put his hands on their heads, feeling that hair as fine and soft as cornsilk, without even a trace of a kink to it, and it came to him that Fancy was right. The children were beautiful. And all they could look forward to, he realized bitterly, was to fall into the lecherous hands of some diseased black or twanging poor white and bring forth more victims to the eternal degradation to which we've consigned them. . . .

"I wish they were mine!" Fancy said fiercely. "Niggers or not, I wish they were mine!"

"Thank you, Ma'am," a soft voice said behind her. "You sound like you mean it. And that's a powerful nice thing for a white lady to say."

Fancy turned her head and stared at the young mulatto woman who had spoken. She had a baby in her arms, a child fairer than the others, with bright blue eyes, contrasting strongly with his pale coppery skin. Fancy got up at once.

"Let me take him!" she breathed. "Oh please let me hold him, won't you?"

Silently the young woman passed the infant over, and Fancy hugged him hard, crooning to him softly.

"Howdy, Mas' Court," the woman said. "This lady your Missus?"

"No, Belle," Court said gravely.

"Sure Lord ought to be," Belle sighed. "The way she do love chillun! I do declare, it's the beatingest thing I ever did see."

"What do you call them?" Fancy said. "They're such darlings!"

"I called the boy Dred, Ma'am. But I got real fancy with the girls. I call 'em Angel and Delight."

"Such pretty names," Fancy sighed, "and downright fitting, too."

Belle laughed pleasantly, completely at ease now.

"They sure Lord have taken to you, Ma'am," she said. Then peering more closely at Fancy's pale face: "You hongry, Ma'am? You looks right peakish to me."

"I'm starved!" Fancy said.

"Then you come right on in. I got dinner pretty nigh ready. You, too, Mas' Court . . . that is, if'n you don't mind."

Court frowned. He had doubtless eaten food prepared by Belle's hands many times when she had been a servant at Hiberion. What real difference did it make to eat it in her house? Southern custom was against it, but Southern custom had been against his going away to Harvard; it was against his going into the textile industry, and any of a thousand things he wanted to do. He smiled a little sheepishly.

"I don't mind, Belle," he said gently. "But don't go to any trouble."

"No trouble a-tall, Mas' Court. Youall just sit right there and play with them kids. I'll whip you up something nice in two shakes of a jackrabbit's tail."

She was as good as her word. Minutes later she laid the food before them—a half spring chicken apiece, golden-brown, rolls so light that they seemed weightless as they lifted them to put the butter in, and so hot that they reddened the tips of Fancy's fingers. There were peach preserves beside the plates and string beans with a piece of salt pork in them and coffee that was black and scalding and perfect.

"Belle, honey," Fancy sighed, "it's 'most too pretty to eat!"

"Tastes better'n it looks, Ma'am," Belle laughed. "You dig right in."

Afterwards, Fancy had a hard time getting up out of her chair.

"I'm fair about to bust!" she said; but a minute later she was romping with the girls over the well-scrubbed floor.

"We'd better be going now, Fan," Court said. "Thanks for the dinner, Belle—it was mighty good."

"You're welcome, sir," Belle said. "'Bye Ma'am."

"Can I come and see them sometimes?" Fancy asked breathlessly. "They're so sweet, and I do love them so!"

"Yes'm," Belle whispered, blinking back the tears. "God bless you, Ma'am! God bless your good, kind heart. . . ."

"I don't understand it," Court said as they rode away. "Belle's not pretty. I've seen any number of high-brown wenches who are prettier'n her. What the devil possessed Phil to . . ."

"She's kind of restful like," Fancy said. "Didn't you notice that, Court? And from what you've told me about Phil's wife, she's awful hightoned and fidgety. Maybe your brother needed somebody restful around him."

Court looked at her.

"You," he said with mock severity, "you are exactly one thousand years old!"

"Court," Fancy said.

"Yes, Fan?"

"What are you going to do about those kids? If you stand back and let folks kick 'em around the way they do most niggers you ain't the man I thought you were!"

"I mean to do something for them," Court said, "or see that Phil does. Send them to a good colored school, Hampton or Tuskegee, maybe. I've been planning to ride up to that store of his for some time. Want to come along?"

"Yes," Fancy said. "Where is it?"

"In Pinch Gut," Court said.

"Pinch Gut?" Fancy said, "what a funny name!"

"It is, isn't it? It seems that during one of our eternal floods, a Jew named Asher loaded all the foodstuffs his boat could hold and went from house to house giving it to the starving people. Gave away his entire stock of merchandise. They say he kept saying: 'Oi, oi! the poor pinched guts!' That's how the section got its name."

"Poor folks live there, don't they?" Fancy said.

"Yes," Court said; "but most of Phil's clients are farmers—'croppers and small acreage men. They come in on Saturday and let him cheat them—and he's got them so buffaloed that they think he's doing them a favor."

"You don't think much of your brother, do you?" Fancy said.

"Nor of myself. The world would be better off if somebody blew the whole shooting match of us plumb to hell."

"I think you're wrong about that," Fancy said, "and I aim to prove it."

When they came to Phil's store, Fancy was disappointed. Instead of the fine establishment she had expected, it was a ramshackle building filled to bursting with all sorts of goods. Here were plowshares and harnesses and hoes. Under glass, put there, Fancy guessed, to keep the flies out, which it didn't, were loaves of bread, and hogsheads of flour and sugar and tubs of lard stood opened in the aisles. There were smoked hams and sides of bacon hanging from the ceiling, most of them green with mold, and bolts of cloth filled the shelves. But above all the many smells, one stench rose up overpoweringly so that all the air was thick with it.

Fancy saw Philemon Brantley standing behind the counter. He was as tall as Court, and far handsomer. He was lean and broad shouldered, and his rich blond ringlets crowned a face that Fancy decided was a sight too good-looking for a man.

"Howdy, Court," he said. "Time you were paying me a visit. Jehosiphat! Who is this? No, don't tell me—it must be that girl everybody's connecting you with . . ."

"Miss Williamson," Court said stiffly, "my brother, Philemon. Phil, meet Fancy."

Phil put out a powerful hand and gripped hers hard.

"Howdy, Miss Fancy," he grinned. "Sure Lord wish I'd seen you first! You're about the prettiest little thing these old eyes have feasted upon in many a year!"

"Well you didn't see her first," Court said. "Besides you're tied up enough. Saw those yard children of yours on the way up here, Phil."

"Did you now?" Philemon said. "Cute little beggars, aren't they? More'n half the time I forget they're niggers."

There was, Fancy was sure, not even the tiniest bit of shame in his voice.

"What's Martha got to say about them?" Court asked.

"Nothing. What could she say? But it appears to me this ain't the kind of thing we ought to discuss before Miss Fancy, here."

"She was with me," Court said; "she saw them first. . . ."

"They're too sweet," Fancy said. "I just love them!"

"Me too," Phil said. "I feel kind of sorry for those kids, though. Hell of a thing to be born black."

"They're not black!" Fancy said.

"I know, I know. It's just a way of speaking. Much good it'll do them that they aren't."

"Phil," Court said slowly, "you have got to do something for those kids."

"Sure, sure, but what?"

"Give them an education. At least do that."

"All right, but where? You know of any school for niggers hereabouts? Besides, I'm not sure it would be good for them anyhow. Put ideas in their heads—make them uppity. And the South's a mighty bad place for uppity niggers to have to live."

"They don't have to live in the South, Phil."

"Jehosiphat! You're mighty concerned about those kids, aren't you?"

"I am. And I'm going to see that they get a chance, even if you won't, Phil. Race is one thing; but blood's thicker than water, boy."

"All right," Phil said cheerfully; "you do it, then. I don't mind."

Fancy wrinkled up her nose.

"What's that smell?" she asked.

"Guano," Phil explained. "Nowadays it's well nigh impossible to get a decent crop without it. The soil's bled white. Stinks like blazes, doesn't it?"

"Sure does!" Court said. "Let's get out of here!"

But before they could get away from the stench of the fertilizer, a man came into the store—a poor white that reminded Fancy so much of her Pap that her heart ached at the sight of him. The man was tall, but so bent over from his labors that his actual height seemed shortened by half a foot. His neck was red and seamed by wind and sun, and his adam's apple jerked fearfully as he came toward them. He held a hat in his hand, and he kept twisting it.

"Mister Phil," he began.

"I know, I know!" Phil snapped. "You want an extension. Why, damn it to hell, Adams, what do you think I am—a charitable institution?"

"No—sir," Adams said doubtfully. "But I got to have another loan, Mister Phil. Crops didn't do so well last year, and if I don't git some guano down, the seeds I put in ain't going to grow. You can't let me down now, sir. How you ever expect me to pay you off if I don't raise a crop?"

"I've been carrying you on the books for four seasons, now, Adams. If you'd attend to your farming instead of hossin' around with the old woman and raising a passel of bare-assed younguns you can't feed, you'd do better."

"I reckon I can't help that," Adams said tiredly. "Them there's the ways of nature. Mister Phil, for God's sake . . ."

"All right, all right! Good thing for you I got a kind heart. I hold mortgages on your last three crops. Reckon you'll have to give me a note on your land and your mules. Don't reckon I'll take one on your old woman, seeing how you've plumb wore her out with younguns."

Adams smiled feebly at this last joke.

"Sure," Phil said affably, "take all you need. I'll have Lawyer Cummings draw up the papers. You come in here tomorrow and sign them."

"All right, Mister Phil. Thank you, sir—thank you kindly. What your time prices going to be this time?"

"Forty percent, you lucky devil. Most of the merchants are charging fifty-three; but as I said, I've got a kind heart. How's Sal and the younguns?"

"Right pert, thank you. One of the gals ain't so good though. She's got a misery in the chest—yesterday she was a-spittin' blood. . . ."

"You send her right down to Doc Blumfeldt," Phil snapped. "Damn it, man, why didn't you tell me about this before? Tell Doc to send me the bill. I'll take the money out of your worthless hide, later."

Adams' thin face broke into a wide, grateful smile. For a moment Fancy was sure she saw tears in his eyes.

"Can't thank you enough, Mister Phil," he husked. "Mighty white of you, sir—yessir, mighty white!"

"Forget it," Phil said grandly. "You seen anything of that good-for-nothing Tom Watts?"

Adams hesitated.

"Yessir," he said, "sure have. He's kind of hiding out from you, sir—seeing as how he can't pay. He's afeared he'll lose his land."

"Damned right he'll lose it," Phil said. "But what can I do? I can't carry him any longer. Tell him to come on in—I already talked to Burke Cameron, and he's got an empty shareholding out on his east section. Nice house on it, too; heap better than the one Tom's living in now. Hell, 'cropping ain't so bad. Tom will be better off as a tenant for Mister Cameron than he ever was on his own. . . ."

"I'll tell him," Adams said. "You sure are good to us folks, Mister Phil."

He left the store then to get one of his grown sons to help him carry out the hundred-pound sacks of guano. Court looked at his brother, his whole face pale with rage and shame.

"Forty percent!" he said. "And a mortgage on his land for a few bags of that filth. God in glory, Phil—what's come over you?"

"Got to live," Phil said complacently. "And I'm good to those ragged-assed crackers. They're the worst people in the world to collect from—worse than the niggers, even. What in hellfire's wrong with you now?"

"Sick," Court said. "I'm puking sick. Our folks have had their faults, but mostly they were the kind of faults a man could understand—like getting mean drunk and wrecking a saloon, and chasing after anything in skirts. But they were brave men in their way. They might kill a man over his wife and take his last cent in a game of cards. But they never figured they had to live at the cost of blood spitting from a young girl's lungs, or children getting soft bones and potbellies from eating swill. Not even the Brantleys were that rotten low!"

Phil's face reddened.

"You're a fine one to talk, Court," he said. "However I do it, I'm the only one who's been keeping the family alive, while all you do is to chase from vinegar bend to bitter creek after this little bit of hill trash, here!"

Fancy saw Court's mouth tightening, and his hands doubling into fists, so she stepped in quickly and caught his arm.

"No, Court," she said quietly. "Don't fight him—not over me. If that's what he thinks, let him. Come on now—let's get out of here."

But it wasn't until Fancy stumbled as they stepped out on the sidewalk that he saw her eyes were tear-blinded. He turned to go back into the store, but Fancy looped both her hands through the crook of his arm and swung down hard.

"No, Court!" she said. "I told you—no!"

"Damn him to hell and back again!" Court roared. "What right had he . . ."

"All the right in the world, I reckon," Fancy said wearily. "We were poking our noses into his business—so we kind of had it coming. Anyhow, Court—I had to find out some time. It's better that I found out now. . . ."

"That you found out what?" Court demanded.

"How your family feels about me. Take me home, Court—I got packing to do."

"What the devil do you mean, Fan?"

"I'm getting out—Court. Out of your life. All I could ever do for you would be to spoil your chances and make you 'shamed. I—I love you too much for that. . . ."

"God damn it, no! I'll show them. We'll go down right now and find Reverend Mister Barrish. They'll have to accept you, Fan; damn them all to hell, I'll make them!"

Fancy looked at him wonderingly, and her blue eyes were very wide. Then, slowly, she shook her head.

"No, Court," she said.

"I thought you said you loved me?"

"I do. More'n anything in this whole blamed world. More than life itself. Too much to cheat you. Too much to let you marry me because you're mean-mad and hurt. If the day ever comes when you want to marry me—for good reasons, like loving me, and thinking that nothing's any good without me, I'll marry you. But until then, no, Court."

Court studied her small face.

"You're something kind of special, aren't you?" he said gravely. "Promise me one thing, Fan. . . ."

"What's that, Court?"

"That you won't run out on me. Give me time to fix things up—straighten out my crazy, snake-bit hound dog's mind . . ."

Fancy waited a long time before she answered him.

"All right, Court," she breathed. "I won't run out on you 'cause I can't. I'm your prisoner, just like you had me locked up in jail. Got to be near you, got to see you, got to touch your hand—I can do without food and water better'n that. I think sometimes if I had to go 'way where I couldn't see you no more, I'd plumb curl up and die. . . . Now take me home. I got to be by myself for a while."

On the porch of the little cottage, Court kissed her solemnly, and turned to go.

"What you going to do now, Court?" she asked fearfully.

"I'm not going to whip Philemon, if that's what you're thinking. I mean to have a talk with my brother Tyler. He came back to town yesterday. If we can get this business about my Uncle Martin's place straightened out, maybe I'll have enough security to make a start. Anyhow, it's worth a try."

Seeing him riding away down the road, Fancy thought suddenly, wildly, I'm a fool! A mighty big damned fool! I could have had him—he'd have learned to love me afterwards. . . . Oh God, oh Jesus, why didn't I?

Court didn't have to go to his brother's house to see Tyler. He met him walking down Broad Street, a valise in his hand.

"Don't tell me you're going back already, Ty?" he said.

"Yep," Tyler grinned, pushing his hat back on his bald head. "Uncle Martin's a mighty sick man. Might kick off any minute. I got to be there to show him how us Brantleys love him!"

"You bastard," Court said. "How you love Melody, you mean."

"Now don't be so finicky, Court," Tyler laughed. "You wouldn't want to see him leave that lovely plantation to an orphan home, would you?"

"No, I wouldn't," Court said honestly, "still . . ."

"I'm being plumb, downright practical. And I am good for the old man. You'd think I was his maw, the way I gentle him. Come on, boy, let's go into Riley's and have a snort of bourbon and branch water."

"Won't you miss your train?"

"Hell, no—I got an hour yet. Come up here to try to get Fern to go with me, but she won't budge. Thought for a while you had something to do with that—unprincipled scoundrel and lady-killer that you be; but Saph told me about your little bit of fluff from the Ca'lina hills. Black hair and blue eyes—boy! When do I get to meet her?"

"Never, if I can help it. How long you plan to be away this time?"

"Long as necessary. Can't tell, boy—the old man's weakening fast. Still, he might last another month or so. . . ."

"I see," Court said drily. But inside his heart he was crying: don't go, Ty! Don't leave Fern here alone any more. She's been dangled in front of my eyes too much now. You're my brother. Of course you're a polecat and worse, but what Brantley isn't? It won't be good for you to go away again. You're my brother. We're the same flesh and blood. But I'm a Brantley, too, remember. How in hellfire do I know I can keep my hands off her even if I want to? And I do want to. She loves me—me, not you, you bald buzzard! She's admitted it to me, hanging in my arms a-crying! But she's good and sweet and loyal, and she'll hate me. I don't want that. Don't want any bad blood between us. Because what will happen will be killing business, and our whole history's muddy with ill-spilt blood. . . .

"Come on," Tyler said. "A little bourbon will cheer you up."

"All right," Court said. "But this time, I'm buying."

They walked up Broad Street toward Campbell, and turned down it once they had reached the saloon. Then they went in the swinging doors, and stood together at the bar, resting a foot upon the brass rail.

But the liquor did Court no good. All his Brantley blood rose up in him hot and angry. He looked at his lean, pale face in the mirror that hung behind the bar. His wide mouth was twisted in a scowl, and his brows crowded his eyes.

Still he lifted his glass with a steady hand and proposed a toast.

"To you and Fern," he said.

"And Melody," Tyler answered. "Unc hasn't said so outright, but he's hinted that he's leaving the place to you'n'me, Court. We're going to be rich, boy."

"Fat lot of good that'll do me," Court said.

"Why not? Then you'll be able to build your mill."

Court looked at him, hard.

"So you know about that?" he said.

"Yep, Phil told me. Appears to be a right smart idea. Do us Brantleys a mighty heap of good and no mistake. You can count on my help, Court."

"Thanks," Court said ironically, lifting the clear amber liquor to his mouth. He gulped it down, feeling it choking off his breath like fingers of fire; then that passed, and it lay in his belly like lava, from which fumes rose black and evil into his head.

I can count on your help. Your help. Know how you can help me, Ty? Give me my Fern back. Give her back, damn you! My mill. My big, sprawling mill with the machines clattering and the white fluff growing smaller and smaller until it's no more than a single thread winding itself onto the bobbins. Like life, Ty—you card it free of illusions, you comb it clean of dreams, you twist it tight, rove it down, spin it down until it's narrow and fine and has direction, then you warp it with the threads of other people's lives, pulling them down off the creel, winding them on the beam, then you weave them into the pattern of your destiny, all the bright and dark threads and when you're through, you've got something fine. . . . Hell yes, I'm drunk. Going to get drunker yet. Only in this case, you ugly, bald-headed buzzard of a brother of mine, the only thread I need is missing; you, Ty, have stolen the golden skein.

There's a code, I know; I'm supposed to be gallant and wish you luck, and keep my chin up and breathe the air. Only I'm a Brantley, too, and we Brantleys talk about gallantry, never act it and I don't wish you luck a damned bit and what the hell good is the mill anyhow without Fern for whom I was going to build it? The mill was going to give me back Hiberion, white under the trees, with the music and lights and dancing in the big hall. But I don't care about Hiberion, Ty—it's dead; it's lost its soul. I'll get it back, I reckon. I'll build that mill. But every time I look up, I'll be listening for Fern's footstep on the stair. I'll be watching for her to come and sit down across the table from me so I can see that hair soft golden under the candlelight, and hear that lovely voice of hers saying what she says to you, now, my brother—or at least what she's supposed to. . . .

"I reckon," Tyler drawled, "you've had enough."

Court threw back his head and laughed aloud.

"More than enough, Ty," he said. "Of the bourbon, of the Brantleys, of all the things that have happened to me."

"Go home, Court, boy," Tyler said. "Don't slip your block. Go home and stick your head under the pump. Drink yourself a quart of scalding black coffee. You'll feel better in the morning."

Or worse, Court thought. But aloud he said mildly, "Reckon you're right, Ty. Now you go catch your train."

Court rode very quietly under the pines, with the river rolling on toward the sea on his right hand. It was rising now, but this year it wouldn't be very bad; the signs were against it. Still it boomed bass-voiced and angry, and the drifting logs ground their ends ragged against the Sand Bar Ferry landing. There was a mule, dead and floating, being borne southward on the flood, and behind it a coop of chickens came, the rooster standing on the wire top and crowing lustily.

Like me, Court thought, crow while you're drowning, boy! Crow your lungs out and who'll hear you? Not the river, not the pine trees, maybe not even God. . . .

But where the road wound downward from Augusta, it was quieter under the trees. The scent of honeysuckle drifted sweet, and yellow jack in the pulpits brightened the swampy places, and along the roadside were wild verbena, red clover and reddish grass. Court felt himself growing quieter, too, there in the cool shade, where the winds came down brimming with pine scent and all the air was clean and good.

When he came up the drive to Hiberion, he suddenly touched his crop to the Morgan's flank, and came thundering up to the gate in a cloud of dust. When he was close enough, he hauled back on the reins and the great stallion lifted, flying over the broken gate, thudding to earth beyond it, and pounding around the house to the stable. Court sawed at the bit cruelly, and the horse reared, pawing the air and neighing shrilly.

That was a mighty fool thing, he thought; but I had to let it out somehow. . . . He fought the horse down, and dismounting, led him into the stable. Then he took the saddle off, threw a frayed blanket over the Morgan's steaming sides and walked up to the back porch.

Inside the kitchen, Saphira saw him coming.

"You're late," she snapped. "Here I've been slaving over this range like a nigger, and nobody shows up to eat. Father, dear Father—is not hungry. He prefers a liquid diet. And our sweet, delicate Agnes has a headache. Wonderful things, headaches. They allow you to lie on your back and pity yourself, and at the same time avoid doing any hard work. You hungry, Court?"

Court glanced at the greasy, lumpy corn pone growing cold on the stove, the turnip greens with the white fat congealing on the top, and the thick piece of sidemeat, white and salt and disgusting. Nigger food, his father had said; but even Negroes ate better than this.

"No," he said quietly, "I'm not."

To his chagrin, Saphira started to cry.

"I'm no cook," she wailed. "I'm the only decent white woman in this town who has to do her own cooking. We can't afford a colored woman. We can't even afford our laundress, except that Phil pays her. I can't even go to church any more, because I've made over those rags of mine so many times that even the children snicker when they see them. I'd like to get married, Court; but who'd marry a woman with hands like these? And nobody wants a woman my age, especially when she's so broken down with scrubbing floors and making beds and cooking and nursing a drunken old imbecile that . . ."

"Saph, please," Court said.

"It's the truth," Saphira said. "Now where are you going?"

"Up to see Father," Court said wearily.

"He's in no fit condition to see anybody. He's quiet now, but this morning there were lizards in his room. Lizards! Now, Court, I ask you. . . ."

Court didn't answer her. He was already halfway down the hall toward the stairs. As he passed Agnes' room, he could hear her crying. It went on and on, never rising, never falling, in a dull, endless monotone. He stopped quite still and listened to his sister's weeping; then he shook his head and went on up the stairs. No wonder Father's drunk, he thought, and pushed open the door.

Jefferson Brantley sat in the big chair with his head sunk forward on his chest. He was asleep and as he slept, he snored. His mouth hung open, toothless and weak, and a thin line of saliva crawled down the corners of his mouth into the dirty whiteness of his beard.

Court stood there looking at his father, his chest tightening so it was hard for him to breathe. He took a step forward, two. The old man did not even stir. Then Court put out his hand and took the second bottle from the table, the one that had scarcely been touched; and, putting it in his pocket, went back down the stairs.

He started walking then, toward the center of town, stopping every few feet to take a long pull at the bottle. Drink it down, Court, boy, he railed at himself, get yourself some Brantley bravery. Drown your mind in this gut-corroding poison—it stops thinking, boy, it stops it dead in its tracks, and after a while, you're free. After a while you forget about Fern lying soft and acquiescent in your brother's hairy arms. After a while Hiberion's beautiful again as it was when you were a child, and being a Brantley means something. . . . So drink deep, Court Brantley, and when you're drunk enough go find yourself a girl on the town. That to a Brantley fixes everything. That always was our sure cure for hunger and hopelessness, lost love, and present despair. . . .

But he wouldn't. He knew that. It wasn't as easy as all that with him. He was a Brantley, all Brantley, but he was something else too. Something different. Reckon I've got a weak stomach, he thought; but it wasn't that, either. What it was wasn't simple. It was complicated in the same way that he himself was complicated. Inside his head was a brain that worked like no other Brantley brain had worked before it. Inside his body were nerves stretched tighter than nerves ought to be stretched and still hold together. Depending on how things (and people) struck them, they twanged like music, or jangled in discord. And not just anybody could strike that note. No hot tangle of alien woman's flesh, rented for an hour. Not for him. The woman had to mean something, be somebody. And it came to him that had Fern been as ugly as homemade sin, he would have loved her still.

Ty was gone. Back to Savannah. Back to keep his ghoulish watch beside his uncle's bed. Fern was alone in a house on Telfair Street, and he, Court Brantley, was drunk—mean drunk and full of hell. This, Saphira had said, would mark a new low, even for the Brantleys. It wasn't a thing to be thought about; he must push it out of his mind—go back to Riley's, blind himself into speechlessness and stupor. But his footsteps traveled, steady and slow, down McIntosh Street, past Broad, past Greene, until he stood on the corner of Telfair looking at the light that shadowed in her window. . . .

Being alone was one of the bad things. Fancy knew that. It wasn't late yet—only a little after nine o'clock. Maybe he would come back again. It would be a good thing to sit on the porch and hold his hand and not even talk. Just knowing he was there was a kind of a comfort. Where was he now? With her? Oh God, oh Jesus, Fancy prayed, please don't let him be—anywhere but with her. It wouldn't be a good thing, on a night like this most anything could happen and afterwards there would be killing.

For a half-second the image of Court Brantley lying dead in his blood rose up in her mind so clearly that she was sick. She got up from her chair and went to the edge of the porch and clung to one of the pillars until the dizziness went away. And, as she straightened up, she heard the sound of the horses.

She went down the porch steps so fast that she almost fell; but she caught her balance and reached the gate running and threw it open. Then she stopped. Horses. Two of them from the sound. The irregular clip-clop of a team, and the sound of wheels whispering through the sand. But Court always came horseback, riding his big Morgan like a prince. She didn't know anybody who drove a team, and this was the last house on the road, so—whoever it was had to be coming here. Fancy stood very still waiting until the little road wagon came round the bend and she could see the woman who sat in the driver's seat. And even through all the questions that rose in her mind, one thing sang aloud: he's not with her! He's not, 'cause she's here!

Fern drew the wagon up before the gate.

"I hardly expected," she drawled, "to be greeted with so much enthusiasm. However . . ."

"You're here, and it can't be helped," Fancy said. "Come in, won't you? Or would you rather sit up there on that wagon and feel high and mighty?"

"You have spirit, haven't you?" Fern laughed. "As a matter of fact, I will come in. I have a certain amount of curiosity—and it isn't often that one gets the opportunity to see the inside of a—love nest."

"Then come and take a good look," Fancy said. "Reckon you'll find it kind of dull though—can't be much of a love nest where a woman lives alone, can it?"

"That," Fern said coolly, "depends."

Fancy put up a hand and helped her down.

"Started to let that one pass, but I reckon I won't. Just what does it depend upon, Mrs. Brantley?"

"Why upon her visitors, of course—and on just how long they stay."

Fancy looked at her. This one, she decided, has a tongue like a snake. For all her looking like an angel out of Glory, she's bad—she's mean bad, and capable of wrecking most anything to get what she wants.

"But I don't have visitors," she said simply. "Just one visitor. He's all I'm interested in. Reckon you're interested in him, too—for all that you've got no right to be. So let's bring it right out in the open, Mrs. Brantley—let's talk about your brother-in-law. That's what you came way up here to do, ain—isn't it?"

"You are quite right," Fern said.

Fancy pulled up one of the big rockers on the porch.

"Sit down," she said.

Fern slipped gracefully into the big chair.

"I," she said, "don't know quite how to begin. . . ."

"Then I'll do it for you. You came up here to get me to give Court up. You were going to tell me that since I'm not quality, and because Augusta people with tongues joined in the middle and loose on both ends have done a mighty heap of mean talking about me, I might kind of hurt his reputation, and keep him from doing what he aims to. . . ."

"You are a mind reader!" Fern breathed.

"Your kind of mind. Small, greedy, and kind of dirty. The main trouble with all of those things is that none of 'em is so. Want me to tell you what is so?"

"Why yes, I think it would be very interesting."

"You're in love with Court yourself. You married Ty because you was mean-mad and hurt, thinking Court had ditched you. Now you're sorry. You want Court back, and you aim to get him. Your husband ain't no hindrance. To your kind of woman a husband never is. Too easy to fool. You're the kind what passes along every twisted lying thing what folks say about a girl like me—a girl what has no man to shoot or horsewhip folks who use her name in public; and goes right home to wait for your lover to slip into your house the minute your husband is out of it. . . ."

"Go on," Fern said.

"All right, Court comes to see me. But he sits right there in that chair you're sitting in, and never sets foot on the inside of the house. Maybe he kisses me good night—which ain't wrong, seeing that I'm a single girl with a right to a gentleman friend. What riles me up plenty is that when he leaves here, where he can't come inside, 'cause I don't aim to make of myself nobody's easy woman in spite of all the talk—he goes right smack dab down to your house where he can come in, and does! So now, Mrs. Brantley, while we're on the subject of giving Court up, why don't you give him up? Appears to me that I have more right to him than you. Tell me, why don't you?"

Fern looked her straight in the face, and her eyes were utterly naked. "Because I can't," she whispered.

"I see," Fancy said. "So it's like that, eh?"

"It's like that. I was going to say all the things that you mentioned. And, in all fairness, most of them are true—you wouldn't be good for him and you know it. You're not his kind. But you're not stupid. What's the good of lying to you. I do love Court. I always have. I expect to go on loving him till the day I die. If it's any comfort to you—there's nothing actually between Court and myself—which is why I believe your fantastic story of his never entering your house. I know from experience that he's an honorable man. But tell me one thing, Miss Williamson—do you mean to marry Court?"

"Yes," Fancy said, "if he'll have me—yes."

Fern stood up. There was something curiously unreal in the grace of the motion. She lifted one hand and patted a stray lock of her silvery blonde hair back into place.

"I don't think you will," she said quietly. "I don't even think that there's much danger of it. But if the danger ever arises, I'll prevent it. You see, Miss Williamson, Court loves me, too. That there's been nothing between us is my doing—not his. So if I ever think that he's getting too lonely, too desperate—I'll—remedy the situation. Good night, Miss Williamson. You've been very kind."

"There ought to be a name," Fancy said bitterly, "for women like you—but offhand I can't think of it."

"So little imagination," Fern Brantley said. "What a pity!"

I feel sick, Fancy thought, death-sick. How can you fight a woman like this one? Used to dream about people like these—so fine and sweet 'cause they didn't have to root hog or die like us. But where we get mean-mad and liquored up and raise holy ned, the meanness inside of people like her stays there and kind of festers so that everything they touch or even breathe on—dies. . . .

"I'm glad we understand each other," Fern said. "In your quaint, unlettered way, you're not unintelligent. I think you know now that you can't win. So, good night again, Miss Williamson—and I hope that you won't think too badly of me. . . ."

Fancy watched her climb into the smart little wagon.

"I don't think about you," she said, "in any way a-tall. Maybe, like you said, I won't win; but it won't be because I stopped trying."

She turned then and walked back into the house, hearing the sound of the wagon turning on the road behind her. By the time she reached the porch, the sound of it had dimmed, so she turned once more, thinking:

There's no way to get down there now. The horsecars aren't running. And me like a big fool, turned that horse back to the livery stable. If I went what could I do, anyhow?

But all the same she knew she was going. There was no question about that. She went into the house and changed her shoes, selecting a pair that were low and comfortable, suitable for walking. Then she tied her big hat under her chin and started out. The walking itself was a good thing; it required enough attention to keep her from thinking too much. But she knew somehow, in a way that left absolutely no room for doubt that something was going to happen that night—she could feel it in the very marrow of her bones.

It had been a long time now since she had done so much walking. By the time she came down into Augusta, it was very late and she was tired. She leaned against the foot of the fire alarm tower, called Big Steve by everybody in Augusta.

Then it came to her that standing on this brightly lighted corner of Greene and Jackson Streets wasn't the smartest thing in the world for her to do—so she moved on slowly, wearily in the direction of Hiberion.

When she got there, it was dark. She stood at the gate a long time, looking at the house, thinking: I've been a fool. You can't just go to a man's house in the middle of the night and ask for him. His folk'll think you're crazy or worse. And Court would get mighty mad. . . .

Nothing for me to do but turn around and go back, she mused. But that was all of seven miles, and she was so tired. . . . She started walking, just the same, away from the house back toward the river, but she hadn't gone fifty yards, before she heard the rich, dark voice chuckling:

"Looking for Mister Court, lil' Miss Fancygal?"

Fancy whirled and stared into the face of the old Negro woman. She knew this old scarecrow, old as the hills, and black as original sin. Everybody in Augusta knew old Maud. They all said that the old woman was crazy; but Wyche who was very friendly with old Maud laughed at the idea.

"Crazy like a fox," he said. "Maud just won't take low for nobody—and since she's near eighty, and a woman, nobody's got the heart to put her in her place. So to hide the fact that they don't know how to handle one old colored woman who thinks that whitefolks are both fools and hypocrites and says so, they take refuge in pretending she's insane."

"No," Fancy snapped at her. "Anyhow, what's it to you, old nigger-woman?"

"Ain't a thing, honeychile. I just happens to be on your side. And I hate to see you a-worrying thataway when you ain't got a thing to worry about —not a thing."

"What you mean I ain't got nothing to worry about?" Fancy demanded. " 'Pears to me I got plenty!"

"Just 'pears that way—that's all. Lil' gal, you got everything. You got a face like an angel out of Glory, and a figger what would make the 'Piscopal minister lay his Bible down. You got a way o' walking what would make a young man itch all over and plumb nigh drive an old man wild. So how come you worrying?"

For the life of her, Fancy couldn't keep from smiling.

"Can't help it, old woman," she said. "I kind of think I'm going to lose my best gentleman friend."

"And I kind of think you's crazy, 'specially if you's talking about Mister Courtland Brantley."

Fancy looked at her.

"How'd you know it was him?" she said.

"Got ways of knowing. Listen to me, chile. Done knowed them there Brantleys since 'fore they knowed themselves. Ain't never been one of them, from their great grandpappy right on down, what a pretty woman couldn't wind round her little finger. You listening, honey?"

"Yes'm," Fancy whispered, "I'm listening."

"Good thing you is. 'Cause I'm agonna set you straight. Ain't never been no woman what had any luck with a Brantley—you know why?"

"No," Fancy said. "Why?"

" 'Cause the wrong kind of gals married 'em—poor lil' critters what couldn't manage 'em nohows! Listen to me. Just like old Mas' Jeff says, the first one of 'em mated with the devil's daughter and the strain is in the blood. But I kind of think you's a match for Mister Court. First place, he ain't as wild as the rest; secon', you got spirit. Wild devil horse need a wilder mare. Be good for Mister Court if you was to git him hooked—heap better than gitting shot over his brother's wife. . . . But listen to me, chile—don't let him get too close beforehand—not even 'cause you loves him, and he wants to—or maybe 'cause you wants to, which though folks won't admit it, sometimes crosses a woman's mind. Marry him, lil' Miss Fancygal! Make him stand up in front of the preacher man. Git him hooked legal—then give him hell!"

"How can I?" Fancy said. "He don't love me none. . . ."

"Then he's a mighty big fool—'cause he sure Lord ought to. You's a mighty sweet lil' old gal. But just the same it's your bounden duty to hook him—'cause he needs you, Miss Fancy—you be good for him. That lil' yaller-haired gal his brother married is going to ruin him sure. She ought to know that one Brantley is more'n any woman can handle, let alone two!"

"Is he," Fancy breathed, "with her—now?"

"Don't know. Saw him a-heading in that direction, 'bout an hour ago—maybe two. If'n he is—you go right in that house and pull him out—yank out some of that yaller hair whilst you's at it. Snatch her bald-headed—teach her some respect—go on, lil' Miss Fancygal, go fight for your man!"

Fancy stood there a long moment after Maud had gone, disappearing quickly into the night. Then she, too, turned, and started walking toward Telfair Street. But this time she went very fast.

The minute she got to the house, she saw him. He came through the gate so fast that he was almost running, and something caught hold of Fancy's heart and tore until she could feel the sinews giving and the inside of her lungs filled up with brine and fire and there was a taste in her mouth like blood.

The cards were wrong, she thought. They said afterwards. Only there wouldn't be any afterwards. There won't be anything else after tonight, not even me. . . .

Then she turned up McIntosh Street toward Broad and Reynolds. She went down Reynolds past East Boundary into the countryside where Hiberion was, and on past it until she came to the place where the willows were and the Savannah flowed quietly, blue-golden in the night.

Court slowed his pace after a time. Above his head the great stars hung low and close, so close that he could almost touch them with his outstretched hand. The earth rolled away under his feet, and the sky swung about his head in ponderous rhythms. But it was no good, none of it was any good, or even real. Nothing was real except the sickness down inside of him.

That was a near thing, he thought bitterly. Another minute and it would have happened and damn my stupid hide I don't know whether I'm more ashamed of the fact that I nearly pulled another rotten Brantley trick, or of getting cold feet and running out of there like a man pursued. She was willing—great God—she was willing! And now I'll die remembering her mouth like that, and the way her eyes looked melting under her lashes.

. . . I should go back. Who'd know? Ty would never find out and . . .

Ty, my brother. There are many kinds of dishonor, but this one, I reckon, beats them all. . . . I've got to get out of town, leave Augusta—go back to Boston . . . marry some Yankee girl, bank the fires that consume me with her; but Fern—yes, Fern—oh God, oh Jesus, I—

"Looking for your lil' Miss Fancygal?" old Maud drawled.

Court looked at her.

"Yes," he said tiredly. "Where is she? You've seen her?"

"Yep, sure Lord has. She gone to the river—like all the Brantley wimmen. Look for her there, Mister Court Brantley—look for her there!"

Court caught hold of the old woman's arm, holding it hard.

"Where?" he roared; "where'd you see her?"

"Turn me loose, Mister Court," Maud said drily. "You's hurting my arm. Then I'll tell you, but not until then."

Court turned her loose.

"Down in back of your house," old Maud said. "I seed her standing out in front looking at it a few minutes ago. Then she started running—straight for the river. I 'spects you better be getting down there, Mister Court."

Court didn't answer her. Already he was off, running down the road in the direction of Hiberion. He passed it and went on down the gentle slope until he came to the clump of willows.

Almost at once he saw Fancy. She was sitting under a tree, her back resting against the trunk, staring out over the water. Court stopped short. Then he started walking toward her.

Fancy heard him and looked up, her face white and still, the corners of her mouth down-drooping, her lips trembling.

Court knelt down beside her and caught her shoulders hard with his hands. But she turned her face away from him.

"No," she said.

Court sat down beside her.

"What's got into you, Fan?" he said gruffly. "What made you run off like this?"

"None of your business," Fancy said.

"Well, I'll be damned," Court said. Then he put out his arms to seize her, but her hands came up, raking at his eyes.

Court stared at her.

"You *are* riled up!" he said.

She turned toward him, her young face bleak and fierce.

"No," she said, "just hurt, that's all. Still don't know me, do you? Still think you can come to me with her kisses all sticky on your mouth!"

"So that's it," Court said.

"That's it, all right. I ain't going to preach at you. You know what you're doing, I reckon. Just going to tell you a few things—like how it feels to love a man what doesn't love you back. It's no fun, Court. I found myself walking by your house at night—just to look at it. It's a mighty nice old house. And I kind of started to wish that I lived there—with you. That I was really yours—that's not it exactly. I reckon what I really mean is that I wish you were mine, like I'm yours. I belong to you, Court; but you don't belong to me. You don't belong to nobody, I reckon, excepting maybe—her."

"No," Court said, "not even to her."

Fancy leaned forward suddenly, and pillowed her dark head on his knees. She hid her face and whispered: "Found myself a-wondering the other night how it would be to have your baby. I'd like that, Court; I'd like it very much. . . ."

"Good God!" Court said.

"I know, I know," she went on. "You think I ain't fitten. But I'm more fitten than her—than a woman what marries one brother and plays fast and loose with the other!"

"That isn't so, Fan."

"Think I'm a fool? Saw you coming out of her house two o'clock this morning. But no matter. What you do isn't my concern any longer."

"Why not, Fan?"

"It's her you love, not me. Not this damnfool hill gal mooning around dreaming how it'd be to hold your son in my lap—and him so little and sweet with light-brown hair like yours and a mouth like yours and eyes. . . ."

"Fan, for the love of God!"

"I'm sorry, Court, if I shocked you. Shocked myself, too, when I thought of it. But that's how I feel—all gentle like and tender, a-looking at you. All wanting you and not wanting you at the same time. Know what? It's even nice just like this—a-sitting here looking at you. You don't have to say anything, do anything—to make me happy. All you have to do is to be here, alive and breathing the same air I breathe. . . ."

Court didn't say anything. He looked at the delicate white oval of her face, framed in her black hair.

Fancy took his big hands and turned them over, palms upward. Then she ran a soft finger over them.

"Rough," she said. "You worked hard once, Court. These ain't gentleman's hands. Yet you are a gentleman—a real gentleman through and through. Even I can tell that. Sometimes I want to cry, looking at you. You look so sad and mad with yourself for getting mixed up with poor white trash like me. And I look at you and think, How beautiful he is! Like an angel sent down out of Glory. Only your eyes got a little bit of devil in 'em, Court. And your mouth—why it's the wildest, cruelest, sweetest, wickedest mouth in the whole wide world!"

She bent down suddenly and kissed his upturned palms. Court felt something stirring in him—something like pain. He put his hands under her armpits and stood up, raising her with him until she was facing him. He stood very still, looking down at her. Fancy did not move or speak, but lay back against the circle of his grasp, and the big tears hung in her black curling lashes, and made streaks down her face.

"Now what the devil are you crying for?" Court blustered.

"Because I love you so much," she wept. "I love you so hard I want to die!"

Court kissed her.

"No," she whispered, "not any more. Don't kiss me again, Court. It hurts too bad. Thought I could give you up—thought I could let her have you and stand by and see Tyler kill you and laugh. But I can't. I got to stop that two-timing hussy. I got to keep you safe. All right you don't love me, but I'll learn you to—you've got to see the light of reason, Court. There's only one way to fix things so she can't get her thieving hands on you—so that you won't even want her no more. . . ."

"And what's that?" Court asked mockingly.

"You can marry me," Fancy said.

Court turned away from her very slowly, and his face was terrible.

"Court," Fancy said. "Don't look at me like that. I'm shamed to my soul, that I had to say it, but it's true. I'd make you the best and sweetest and most faithful wife in the world. We're alike, you and me—we suit each other. . . ."

Court started to move off then, under the dark trees, where the first morning light was beginning to show.

"Court!" Fancy said. "Court—where're you going?"

"Home," Court growled. "After this, I'm going to get drunk."

Fancy stood up, facing him. She had a little lace handkerchief in her hand. Her fingers moved, tearing it to shreds. When she spoke finally, her voice was little more than a whisper.

"Good-bye, Court," she said.

"You'll be seeing me," Court mocked her.

"No, I won't," Fancy said. "Know why, Court? 'Cause deep down inside, I'm yours. That makes me one of the Brantley women, doesn't it? And you know what happens to them!"

She whirled then, almost before the words were out of her mouth, and hurled herself down the steep slope, running very fast, stumbling over roots and stones until she came to the river and went into it still running, splashing it up about her in great silver sheets, until it was above her knees, her waist, her shoulders.

Court came after her. As he splashed through the muddy water, he could see her small head, black against the water, her long hair floating out behind her in a cloud, then she threw herself forward and the yellow water rose up like wings, and came down closing, and the eddies moved out in circles, spreading, spreading, out to the shores of forever.

Court went in then in a clean dive, and swam powerfully under water, his fingers groping, groping until he could stand it no longer and had to come up for air. As he gulped his lungs full, he saw Fancy break water, yards downstream, her white arms thrashing helplessly about. He started after her, eating up the distance with mighty strokes, and caught her just as she went under again, fastening his fingers cruelly in her hair. Then he started for shore, dragging her behind him. He got her out at last, and struggled up the slope. Then he lay her face downward across a log and pumped at her back until she turned her head on the side and vomited black water and started to cry.

He picked her up, and marched up to the house with her. Saphira heard him kick the door open and started down the stairs.

She saw Fancy lying drenched in his arms, and stopped still.

"Oh, no, Court!" she whispered. "Not another one!"

"She's all right," Court said. "Take care of her, won't you, Saph?"

"Why certainly. The poor little thing! What made her do it, Court? Tell me, what?"

"That," Court said, "is none of your damned business, Saph." Then he put Fancy down upon his sister's bed.

She lay there upon the bed shivering, her lips blue with cold, until he covered her with a blanket, and went out of the room and came back with some whiskey.

"Here," he said, "drink this."

Fancy drank the whiskey, never taking her gaze from his face. Her blue eyes were very big behind her sooty lashes, and the look in them was a thing that Court wasn't going to want to remember.

"Don't try that again," he said. "Promise me, Fan—don't try that again!"

"You love me, Court?" she said. "Say you love me—even if you lie!"

"I love you," Court said. It was almost the truth. He bent down then and kissed her lightly. Then he started for the door.

"Where are you going?" Saphira said.

"To get some dry clothes," Court said. "Then—out."

"You coming back?" Fancy asked faintly.

"No," Court said.

Fancy raised herself up on her elbows.

"Come here, Court," she said.

Court walked back.

"Now kiss me," Fancy said.

Court bent down and kissed her lips. He straightened up, staring at her. He hadn't known there was that much tenderness anywhere in the world.

"That's how I love you, deep down inside," Fancy whispered. "All soft-like and sweet. Oh, Court, if you only love me, too . . ."

"If he doesn't," Saphira said angrily, "he's a fool!"

"I do," Court said; then very quietly, wonderingly, half to himself: "God help me, I really do!"

He got up then and walked out of the room. Saphira sat on the bed and put her arms around Fancy. And Fancy rocked back and forth on the bed, hugging her knees with joy.

He didn't come home all that day. When it was night, Fancy went out to find him. She had gone to her cottage first, and changed her clothes, putting on a dress of scarlet lace that did wonders for her complexion. Her hair was smoothly knotted in a little bun on the base of her neck. Then she climbed upon the nag she had rented and rode back down the hill toward Augusta.

She found Court where she expected to find him, standing in front of the bar in Riley's Saloon on Campbell Street. Riley looked up in astonishment as she entered, holding the rag he was wiping glasses with in mid-air.

"Now what th' divil is all this?" he roared. "No females is allowed inside me bar!"

"I—I want to talk to him," Fancy said, pointing.

"You talks to nobody in me place," Riley said. "Now git out of here before I summons the law, and have you pulled in as a common—"

"Softly, Riley," Court said. "You're talking to the girl I'm going to marry."

"Th' divil you say!" Riley bellowed. "You're in no fitten condition to know what you be a-doing! And be damned and be jasus if I'll be a party to . . ."

Court grinned, swaying a little as he spoke, "You aren't a party to anything, Riley."

"You mean to stand there and tell me that you're going to git yourself hitched up to that—"

"Now, now, Riley," Court said, "no hard names. Appears to me that Fan's a heap better than the fine ladies of this town who think that a nicely printed piece of paper gives them the privilege to sneer at her. A piece of paper whose provisions they abuse constantly in their husband's absence.

Well, little Fan's going to have her little piece of paper. And I don't think she'll abuse it—being a curiously honest girl. Will you, Fan?"

"Never," Fancy breathed. "Oh, darling, I'll never leave your side. . . ."

"Come on, Riley," Court said, "shut up your grog shop for the evening. You're going to be best man—and a witness. No argument, now."

Riley didn't argue. In fact, he was moved to do what he hadn't done in twenty years. That is, he took a drink of his own poison. Then he shut up shop and followed Court and Fancy to Hiberion.

Court tiptoed up the stairs, taking care to wake neither his father nor Agnes, and came down with Saphira. She came running into the kitchen and threw her arms about Fancy.

"I'm mighty glad!" she said. "You're going to be good for Court—I just know you will!"

"Just a minute, everybody," Fancy said quietly. "Saph, honey, is a fire laid in that stove?"

Saph looked at her wonderingly.

"Yes," she said; "why, Fancy?"

"Light it," Fancy said. "Where's your coffee pot?"

"Over there," Saphira said. "But, Fan, I don't understand . . ."

"Appears to me that Mister Riley here said the only thing that made sense all evening. He said Court's in no fitten condition to marry anybody. I don't want him to wake up tomorrow and be sorry. So I'm going to make him some coffee—strong as the dickens and black as old Maud. After I get him sober, if he still wants to marry me—all right. If not, I won't be around to bother none of you. Mister Riley, I'm sorry to keep you waiting; but I kind of think you agree with me—don't you?"

"I do, Ma'am," Riley said, "and I want to say I'm sorry, Ma'am—I kind of had you wrong."

"I'm used to that," Fancy told him.

Half an hour later, Court Brantley gulped the last of four cups of steaming black coffee, and sat there shaking his head.

"Court," Fancy said tremulously, "do you remember what you said—in Riley's?"

"Heck, yes," Court grinned; "I was drunk and I wanted to marry you. I always get my best ideas when I'm drunk. Come on—let's go. . . ."

"Where?" Fancy said.

"To Judge Harris, of course. He's the nearest Justice of Peace, isn't he?"

"You mean that, Court?" Fancy said.

"If I don't, I'm crazy—and I don't think I'm crazy. Come here, Fan."

Several minutes later, he looked down into her eyes, that were hazed over with tears.

"Do I mean it?" He looked at her tenderly.

"Yes," Fancy said. "Yes, oh yes!"

When Riley left the parlor of Judge Harris, he ran all the way home. Mrs. Riley listened for a breathless five minutes. She didn't even wait until morning. Neither the whispering wires of the telegraph nor the even newer telephone that Augustians were only beginning to get used to after four years of watching a few advanced citizens grind a crank and shout into a long-necked mouthpiece, could have spread the news faster. By mid-afternoon of the next day, the only people in Augusta who did not know it were the dead in the local cemetery.

It had, of course, certain consequences. Among other things, Fern Vance Brantley took to her bed and stayed for three days. And for all of that time, not for a minute did she stop crying. . . .

6

So I WAS DRUNK, Court thought bitterly, but I wasn't that drunk. Can't even tell myself I didn't know what I was doing. I knew all right—Fan saw to that. Mighty decent of her—or mighty smart—which? Now I can't say she tricked me, 'cause she didn't. Outsmarted myself, I reckon. Any way I play it, it comes out wrong. If she's honest, she's still a millstone around my neck, because she's going to keep me from reaching the very people I need to go to for help. If she isn't, I've been the world's biggest fool. . . .

Wonder what in hellfire got into me? Reckon I was lonely and there was that business about Fern, but even so was that reason enough for this? I'm a failure, but the Brantleys have mostly always been failures when it came to anything practical. Yet not one of them, not a single one that I ever heard tell of ever made this kind of a mistake. The Brantley women have always been something—something very real and sweet and fine, and our mistake has always been on the side of not treating them as well as they deserved, of making the lives of good women into pure hell while we followed our natural bent on the side. We're a proud, wild, wrong-headed breed all right; but none of us has ever been this stupid before—not a single one. . . .

He looked at Fancy as she bent over the black iron range. Her face was flushed from the heat, and her black hair hung down stringily into her eyes as she worked. Court noted with acute distaste that there were yellow sweat rings at the armpits of her dress. She looked, he thought, like what she was—white trash.

But, he had to admit, it was not her fault. That stove was enough to drive a mule mad. It was very old and it never drew properly, and either burned or undercooked the food. Fancy could cook, he knew that. And she had thrown herself wholeheartedly into the role of wife and homemaker. Truthfully Court had no complaints. That made it worse. If Fancy had turned out badly as he had confidently expected her to in her new position as his wife, he would have felt better about the whole thing. But she had tried so hard to live up to what was expected of her, and on the whole her failures had been few.

Court suspected that the dismal little shotgun house he had rented on the edge of town gave her as much of the horrors as it gave him; but so far she had not complained. Duke's cottage had been so much more comfortable. That was another thing that bothered Court. Did she ever in her mind make comparisons?

"Oh, Court, honey," Fancy wailed suddenly, "I can't do a thing with this stove!"

Court got up and worked gingerly with the damper. Finally the fire caught up and blazed.

"There," Court said, "nothing to it, Fan."

"I'm so dumb!" Fancy quavered. "I try so hard to do everything right—for you, Court—and it looks like everything I try turns out a mess. Reckon you're plumb, downright sorry you married me. I make you such an awful wife. . . ."

"No," Court lied, "far from it, Fan. You're just tired, that's all. Besides it won't be like this all the time. One of these days real soon you're going to have a colored woman to cook for you, and a decent house to live in, and a maidservant to clean. . . ."

"Oh, darlin', will I?" Fancy breathed. "That would be just too wonderful. You're smart. Soon as you find somebody who's got sense enough to back you with that mill, we'll be just about the richest folks in town. I'll have the finest, nicest clothes—all silks and satins, and all the best people in town will come to call. . . ."

That, Court thought grimly, will never happen—no matter how rich we get. Didn't know you had ideas like that, Fan. Guess all women are alike in some ways. They never learn anything in this town, but they never forget anything either. When I do make my pile, we'll have to go away, little Fan—far away where people never saw you dancing half naked on the back of that wagon. . . .

He stood up and reached for his hat.

"I'm going out for a while," he said. "Couple of things I've got to attend to. . . . See you later, hon. . . ."

"Court," Fancy whispered, "know what? This is the second time this week you've started out of the house without even offering to kiss me good-bye."

Oh, damn, Court thought; but aloud he said mildly: "Sorry, hon—got a lot on my mind, I reckon. Come here and kiss me then, because I have things to do."

Fancy slipped into his arms, and her mouth clung to his with easy, accustomed passion. That way she never fails me, Court thought wryly; God, no—not that way. . . .

"See you later, Fan," he said, and went out the door.

Court had nothing to attend to and nowhere to go. He had to get out of the house, that was all. Away from the smells of cooking and poor ventilation. Away from Fancy's woebegone little face, trying so hard to be cheerful. Away from anything that reminded him of his folly.

He started walking through the shaded streets of the town, feeling the thick heat of the Georgia summer beating down upon his head. He had the curious sensation that the streets through which he passed emptied themselves as he entered them; and a little while later he saw that he was right. He turned quickly into the upper end of Broad Street. The scattered crowd of passers-by suddenly and with a single mind discovered they had business elsewhere. Court found himself striding through a street emptied of all but the aged and the infirm. And they had all become concerned with the ancient, fly-specked signs in the show windows. . . .

Rage mounted up out of his collar and beat about his ears. So they'll snub me, he thought bitterly. Who do they think they are? I had more than half decided to leave this town, but I'll be damned if I will now. Going to build that mill if I have to steal the money to do it. I'm going to get this damned place so sewed up that they'll have to come a-running when I crook my little finger. I'll fix it so that these pious old she-dogs will have to dance attendance upon Fan—damn their hypocritical souls. . . .

But a little while later the rage drained out of him, and he was oppressed with an awful sense of loneliness. Here, a few blocks away on Greene and Telfair Streets were the houses of his friends—men and women whom he had played with in childhood, schoolmates, good people all of them, and he realized suddenly that there was no longer any house in Augusta with the possible exception of Hiberion itself that he could enter and be welcomed. And for this, he had only himself to blame. Of all the Brantleys, only he had crowded the town too far. Of course the sins of the family had been many and black, but they had stayed within the larger, looser boundaries of convention; theirs had been the sins expected of a vigorous headstrong breed. But this was too much; Augustians might whisper behind their gloves and fans about his openly consorting with a woman like Fancy; but asking them to accept that woman upon their own level was something else again. . . .

He got tired of his aimless wandering finally, and started back to the little house where his wife waited. He looked at his watch and swore bitterly under his breath. He had been gone far longer than he intended. Fancy must have had his supper ready for him hours ago, and to Fancy the little suppers she fixed for him were very important. They were an expression of her love for him; burnt offerings, he thought wryly, upon the altar of domesticity.

When he came into the house, he found her crying.

"It's all cold," she wept; "and I tried so hard to keep it warm. The one time it turned out well, too. Oh, Court, why couldn't you come back on time?"

"I got all tied up," Court said. "It's all right, hon—I'll eat it cold."

"No, you won't!" Fancy said. "My husband is not a-going to eat cold food!"

I could have done worse, Court thought, as she busied herself, thrusting the pots and pans into the oven, and poking up the dying fire. Oh yes, I could have done much worse. . . .

Later, Fancy sat across the table from him and watched him with her great blue eyes as he ate. She ate very little, but it pleased her greatly when Court had, or feigned, a good appetite. Tonight, Court forced himself to eat two helpings of everything, though he really did not feel like eating at all.

When he had finished and sat down in the big rocker, she brought him his cigar case and stood behind him with her arms around his shoulders.

"Court," she said plaintively.

"Yes, hon?" Court said.

"Myrtie Torrence was by here today and she said . . ."

"The devil you say!" Court roared. "How many times do I have to tell you I don't want you associating with Myrtie Torrence?"

"But Court," Fancy said, "I really don't have any girl friends, and I couldn't rightly put Myrtie out. It would of been a mighty mean thing. She ain't really bad, and—"

"All right, all right," Court said. "What did she say?"

"A lot of things. But only one of 'em made any sense to me. Court, why don't we live up at the big house? It is part yours, ain't it?"

"Myrtie put that bee in your bonnet?"

"Yes. Why can't we, Court?"

"For one thing, my father lives there. For another—so does my sister Agnes. Saph, of course, is all right—she liked you. But you don't know Agnes or my father."

"But it's such a big house. It's got lots and lots of rooms."

"Damn it all, Fan, you're no fool! You know what would happen if I brought you there?"

"What, Court?"

"My father would have heart failure. And Agnes would walk out into the street. You're a good kid, Fan; but people are the way they are. They don't forget things easily."

"I see," Fancy said sadly. "Court, ain't there no way we can win them over?"

"None," Court said grimly.

"Not even if you was to get rich and . . ."

"I said none," Court growled.

Fancy didn't say anything more.

Looking at her, Court had the thought that even when it was still her face was lovely. Given a little better chance in life, given the good fortune to have been born into a different estate, Fancy might have queened it over Georgia society.

"You're going up there tomorrow?" she asked.

"Yes," Court said. "It's about time I paid the folks a call."

"Oh," Fancy said. "You won't be long, will you? I do get so lonesome, Court."

"No, Fan," Court said gently, "I won't be long."

"Want to hear me read now, Court? I've been studying real hard."

"Yes," Court said. "You can read to me, Fan."

Fan went and got the book and sat down on his lap. That was one of the first things that Court had done, once he'd gotten used to the idea of being married to her. If he were going anywhere, his wife couldn't shame him. So he had begun teaching Fancy. He was surprised at how much she knew already and how quickly she learned. Listening to her now as she raced over the page, making only a very few mistakes in pronunciation, Court nodded his head in slow approval.

She'll make it, he decided. Oh, yes—Fan'll make it all right. . . .

That night it took him a long time to go to sleep. And when he did sleep he dreamed. He wasn't afraid of his family, but this first visit to

Hiberion after his marriage was something to think about. He had no guarantee that his father or Agnes wouldn't show him the door. Yet he had to go. Common courtesy demanded that much.

He dressed very carefully in the morning. Fancy sat upon a low footstool and watched him. He kissed her lightly and went out walking under the great oak trees whose leaves hung down listlessly from the heat. Not a breath of air was stirring, only the zigzag lines of heat rising from the cobblestones as he crossed the street, only the sun beating down mercilessly where there were no trees, and he remembered wryly his father's story that in the beginning the devil had been given both Georgia and Hell, and after spending one summer in Georgia he had promptly rented it out and lived in Hell. At the moment, Court didn't doubt it.

He took a longer time to reach Hiberion than he could remember ever before having taken. Even then he stood in front of the gate a long time before he pushed it open.

Hell, he thought, it's done now. And nothing they can say or do can make any difference. So thinking, he mounted the steps to the front porch and opened the door.

Agnes and Saphira were both sitting in the high-ceilinged living room, crocheting. Agnes saw him first and stood up, letting her work fall to the floor.

"Court!" she exclaimed. Then: "Oh, Court—how could you!" Then she turned and ran up the stairs. Saphira got to her feet more slowly, and came toward him with a slow smile that was half tenderness—and half spite.

"The prodigal returns," she said. "Well, Court—welcome home. Sit and chat with me a spell. . . . You must have *so* much to tell me!"

"I don't have a blamed thing to tell you, Saph," Court said. "How's Father?"

"Prostrated. How'd you expect? He declares that his sons will put him in his grave yet. I think he slightly underestimates his daughters—or at least one of his daughters. How was she, Court—fun? Now you can tell me the things I ought to have learned from my husband. Only I don't have a husband. So you tell me."

"You are mad."

"Then I'll ask Fancy. She'll tell me. I'll get her to teach me the secret of her black arts."

"You don't need any teaching. All it takes is the temperament and the inclination, and you, Saph, darling, have both. Father's upstairs?"

"I told you he was prostrated. But don't go yet, Court. Seriously, I'm curious. You're happy?"

"Very," Court said. "Fan's really been wonderful. Don't think I could have found myself a better wife if I had searched the pages of the Almanach de Gotha."

"Trying to convince yourself, Courtie-pie? You don't sound that happy. Fan's a sweet child—but she's a child. And I'll bet you're too strait-laced to teach her all the tricks you've learned from your lights o' love. Well, you've succeeded in out-Brantleying the Brantleys, with, of course, my hearty approval. That's quite an accomplishment."

"I am going up to see Father now," Court said, "with your kind permission, Saph. . . ."

"Or without it, brother dear. I shall be waiting for you when you come down."

Jefferson Brantley, Court observed the moment he entered the room, was neither more nor less prostrated than he had ever been. And what was wrong with him was the pint and a half of bourbon he had consumed as usual, rather than any sorrow.

"Court," he said. "Glad to see you, boy. Heard you'd gotten yourself married and to a rather disreputable woman at that. Well, I'm not going to quarrel with your choice. A good man can do wonders for a woman who loves him—set her feet on the right path, raise her up again to respectability. Shows you're honest at least—that you don't regard your fellow human creatures as mere playtoys for your pleasure. That's good. Have a drink, son—have a drink!"

Court picked up the bottle of bourbon and poured himself a stiff one. He hadn't expected this. Not this.

"Perhaps this will change the Brantleys' fortunes," Jeff Brantley went on. "We've been rather cruel in our dealings with women, Court, boy—yessir, rather cruel. Our wives have suffered—and the lesser women who have given way to our impetuosity have suffered even more. Yessir, son, the Brantley women die by drowning—we drive them to the river, or to the madhouse. We're a satanic breed; we've got centaur blood in our veins. Well, here's to you, Court, boy—to you and your new bride!"

Court lifted his glass to his lips. But he didn't drink. He heard the noise start below.

"Don't you go up there!" he could hear Agnes' voice shrieking, "don't you dare!"

"Now, Ag," Saphira laughed; "she's a perfect right to—"

"Now what in the name of the lustful daughter of Satan who gave birth to the first Brantley is that?" Jeff Brantley roared.

Court took a stride toward the door, but he was too late. Fancy stood in the doorway, clad in an enormous black hat with quite outrageous yard-long ostrich plumes, and holding a feathered muff of the same black plumes in her hands. Her dress was of black silk, plentifully garnished with even blacker sequins, and it was cut in extreme décolletage, being intended for dancing instead of street wear. Court knew that dress and that hat. Fancy had bought them out of her own savings, and he hadn't had the heart to tell her how bad they were. To her simple country heart, they were elegance itself. She probably saw Myrtie Torrence in that professional tart's costume, Court groaned, and thought it looked so fine. . . .

He started toward her grimly, but his father's anguished quaver stopped him dead in his tracks.

"This the girl you married?" the old man whispered. Then, suddenly, astonishingly recovering the full power of his lungs, he roared: "You're welcome to visit me any time you like, Court boy, but get that—that—creature out of here!"

Court could see Fancy quite visibly crumpling under the impact of the old man's savage scorn, so he came up to her and took her gently by the arm. She did not say a word as he led her down the stairs and out into the street, but came along quietly in all her bedraggled finery, her tears streaking her pale face.

When they reached the little house, Court looked at her.

"Go wash your face," he said coldly. "And take off those rags and burn them."

"But Court . . ."

"Do as I say! They make you look like—like the kind of woman Myrtie Torrence is."

"Oh, Court—no!" Fancy said. Then she ran into the bedroom and shut the door. He could hear the water splashing in the basin on the washstand. He sat down miserably in the big rocker and thought about the expressions on the faces of all the people they had passed in the street. He knew then that he was doomed in Augusta. If he ever wanted to get his mill started, if he ever were to rise in life, he'd have to go somewhere else. He knew that now.

Fancy came out of the bedroom then, wrapped in a soft, pink robe. She looked absurdly young and penitent and fearful all at the same time.

"Court," she said timidly, "I'm so sorry. . . ."

"It's all right," Court said gruffly. "You had to find out some day."

"But I shamed you, Court. I shamed you in your own house in front of your father. I reckon I got too lonely—and started thinking about what Myrtie said and . . ."

"And you came to my father's house," Court finished for her. "He and my sister behaved precisely the way I told you they would. You got your feelings hurt, damned badly, which was what I was trying to avoid. Oh well, it's done now. Let's forget it, shall we. . . ."

"I can't forget it!" Fancy cried. "I'm so shamed I could curl up and die and . . ."

Court stood up then, and took her in his arms.

"Forget it, Fan," he said.

But the next day, he noticed the change in her. She was silent. Moodily and sullenly silent. The breakfast she gave him was awful. Court thought she hadn't tried to make it any better. He stood her pouting until mid-afternoon, then he spoke to her sharply.

"What the devil's the matter with you, Fan?"

"A whole lot of things," Fancy said tartly. "Been thinking what a fool I am. What call had your pap to speak to me like that? After all him and all the Brantleys except your brother Phil is poor'n Job's turkey hen. How come they hold themselves so fine?"

"Look, Fan—" Court began patiently.

"You, too!" Fancy raged at him. "You stood there and let him call me bad names and never said a word—nary a living word! I reckon you're shamed of me, Court Brantley. Reckon the best thing for me is to get myself out of this house right now!"

"Fan, for God's sake!"

"Thought I was doing myself proud when I married you! Well, I didn't. You ain't got a ghost of a chance of doing anything big in this here town. You know why, Court Brantley? In the first place, you ain't got it in you, and in the second, nobody's going to give you a helping hand—because of me."

"There are," Court said, "other places. . . ."

"You've been to 'em, and what good did it do? I don't aim to be poor all my life—and that's all I'll ever be with you. I'll be slaving over that miserable, rotten little stove till the day I die. And you ain't even got the gumption to get out and get yourself a job of work. What we going to do when your savings are gone, Court? Tell me, what?"

She is more than a little right, Court thought bitterly, on all counts. So, now the honeymoon is over.

"You can leave," he said coldly, "any time you want to, Fan."

The rage went out of her at once, like air from a pricked balloon. She started to cry, terribly. Court went over and took her in his arms.

"I'm mean," she wept. "I'm meaner'n a sidewinder! And you, Court, honey, are just about the sweetest and the nicest and the best . . ."

"No, Fan," Court said gently. "Reckon most of what you said was just about right. But I haven't given up trying. And you mustn't give up either.

If we can't make it here in Augusta, we'll go to Macon or Savannah or some other place far enough away so that nobody ever heard of us. We can start clean, that way. Make a new life for ourselves. Come on, now—dry your eyes."

Fancy obeyed. But that night, for the first time since they had been married, she pushed away his encircling arms.

"Just don't feel like it, Court," she whispered. "I'm plumb wore out, and I don't feel so good. . . ."

Yes, Court decided, the honeymoon was definitely over.

He couldn't sleep. He kept thinking about what Fancy had said. He thought about it a long time and very carefully. And the next morning he got up and caught a train for Atlanta.

But a week later, sitting in his room on the sixth floor of the Kimball House, Court was ready to give it up. He had his shoes and socks off and was bathing his swollen feet in a basin. He had no idea how many miles he had walked, or how many men of wealth and prominence he had talked to. Now, from the railroad depot diagonally across Pryor Street, he could hear the whistle of the trains.

Go back North, Court Brantley, he told himself angrily. Go back where you've got a chance!

It didn't help to be a Brantley. Not here in Atlanta. They had the fever here already. There were all kinds of factories and plants in and around the city. And that prophet of Southern industrial progress, Henry W. Grady, had bought a one-fourth interest in the *Constitution*. From the editorial chair, he was shouting industrialization to the rooftops. Court, earlier in the week, had visited the offices of that newspaper, and Grady, himself, had offered support.

But even that hadn't helped because of two things: the capitalists of Atlanta were quite willing to back another mill—in Atlanta. They had no intention of seeing the profits and wages going to benefit another section of the state. That was the first thing. The second was that too many of them knew the Brantleys of old.

"Court Brantley—Brantley did you say? Not old Jeff Brantley's boy? I knew your father well, son. Finest horseman and best shot in the state. And women—Lord! So you want to go into business—W-e-l-l, now—that's right strange. First Brantley I ever heard tell of that had any interest in making money—mighty good hands at spending it, though. . . . Now, son, don't take on. I've got nothing against your family. I'm sorry, son, but since you put it that way, I'll have to admit that I would rather invest money with people who have a better reputation for steadiness. Fine people, the Brantleys; but you got to admit that all of 'em I ever heard of was a mite wild."

The dead hands of the past, strangling the future. The sins of the fathers. . . . Oh, hell, Court thought, I'm going home.

It was hard, telling Fancy of his failure. What made matters even worse was the fact that that very next morning, Tyler came back from Savannah. He stood on Court's front porch at half past eight in the morning, tall, lean, hook-nosed and laughing, the sunlight gleaming on his bald head. Seeing him there, like that, Court groaned. In all of Tyler's thirty-seven years of life, nobody had ever been able to pull him out of bed before noon.

"This the lil' gal you married?" he grinned. "Mighty nice. Yessirreebob-tail, mighty nice! Sweetest lil' bit o' fluff I ever did see. But tell me, boy, all things being considered, did you have to make it legal?"

Thereupon, Court hit him.

Tyler wiped the blood that was streaming from his nose, and the wide grin never left his face.

"Why you snotty little pup," he laughed, "I used to tan your hide come weekdays or Sundays, and I can do it again."

"Think so?" Court said, and started out of the house.

But Fancy caught hold of his arm.

"No," she said. "You ought to be used to what folks think about me by now, Court. Don't take on about it. Shouldn't rile you up none, nohow—'cause you more'n halfway believe the same thing yourself. . . ."

"Fan, please," Court said.

"It's all right, Court," Fan said quietly. "One of these days you're going to find out that I didn't lie to you—that I'm not and never was the kind of woman you think, then you're going to be mightily ashamed of yourself." She stopped talking and put out her hand.

"Howdy, Mister Tyler," she said. "Mighty proud to make your acquaintance."

"Likewise," Tyler grinned. "Sorry I opened my yap like that, Ma'am; but bedeviling Court is one of life's dearest pleasures."

"How's Fern?" Court asked.

"Just fine. In fact, she's sitting out there under the oak waiting on me."

"I'll go invite her in," Court said. "Excuse me a minute, hon."

He started down the walk toward the gate, and Tyler came with him. Fancy watched them go, her face troubled. Didn't ask me to come along, she thought. Thought marrying him would be enough; but it isn't. Got to work at it yet—got to get her out of his mind. . . .

"Look, Court," Tyler said as they came up to the buggy, "I got news for you, boy—big news!"

Court ignored him.

" 'Lo, Fern," he said.

"Court—" Fern whispered.

Tyler looked from one of them to the other, and he didn't like what he saw.

"I said I had news for you, Court," he said drily. "Would you like to hear it? Or would you rather just stand there and make sheep's eyes at my wife?"

"Mighty pleasant occupation," Court said. "All right, Ty—what's your news?"

Tyler grinned shamelessly.

"Uncle Mart," he said, "kicked off a week ago and left Melody to the two of us."

"Why, Tyler!" Fern said sharply, "is that any way to talk about your uncle's passing?"

"Reckon it isn't, honeychild," Tyler said; "but the old man wasn't doing any good here below. He'd been sick a long time, and I reckon going was a relief to him. Sure was to me," he added, looking at Fern. "If I had had to stay down there one minute longer without seeing your pretty face, I'd just about busted a seam."

"Tyler Brantley!" Fern said.

"Come into the house and have a seat," Court said. "It doesn't seem right somehow to stand up out here talking about Uncle Martin like this. You, too, Fern; you'd be mighty welcome."

Fern shook her head.

"No, thank you, Court," she said stiffly; "I'll wait right here. You boys run along and have your talk."

Court looked at her.

"Why won't you come in, Fern?" he said. "Because of—Fan?"

"Because of Fan," Fern said flatly. "Marrying her was your business, Court. But associating with her—would be mine. Go ahead, youall. I'll wait."

Court stood there a long moment, then he turned back toward the house. Tyler looked back at his wife and whistled softly.

"Boy," he said to Court, "you sure got yourself in a spot. Reckon you better take lil' Fan to some other place where she ain't so well known."

Court's face was bleak and fierce.

"Be damned if I will," he said. "Money talks, Ty. And before I'm through I'm going to own this town—lock, stock and barrel. Then watch them. They'll put up with Fan all right; they'll come a-crawling on their bellies to kiss her fingertips."

Tyler shrugged.

"Can't blame you for being pig-headed," he drawled. "I'm right pert stubborn myself. Runs in the family. But it 'pears to me that you're barking up the wrong tree this time, Court, boy. This here is bigger than you. There are rules, you know—main one is not to get caught. But you got yourself caught, and that's bad. On top of that, you forget one thing: never has been a man born what needed a home or a family. Most men get them accidentally, because some smart little filly holds out long enough and teases bad enough to convince him that her particular equipment must be a heap better'n any other gal's—which it ain't, as he soon finds out. Marriage, Court, is woman's vested interest. She's the only one what gains a damned thing by it. And she gains a hell of a lot—security—financial that is—and freedom to give way to her natural impulses, 'cause she's got a man to hang the results of her sins on, even if no two of 'em remotely resembles the other. What I'm driving at, boy, is that nothing on earth is meaner and fights dirtier than a good woman—and little woods fillies like Fan are her natural enemies. She can smell 'em five miles to the windward. They're always there, a-threatening to break up her closed corporation, and she doesn't like it one damned bit. The men, now, that's different—they'll cotton up to a cute little bit of fluff like Fan in a minute, but if you think any woman in this town is going to accept Fan, even if you roll her in diamond dust and gild the seat of her pants, you're crazy!"

There was, Court realized grimly, a lot of truth in this.

"Come on up to the house," he said. "Fan'll be wondering what we're standing here jawing about."

"With pleasure," Tyler said. "I'm right smart partial to your little Fancy myself."

"Come in, Mister Ty," Fancy said shyly. "I'm mighty glad you're here. We ain't had no visitors in the longest time."

"I aim to," Tyler grinned. "'Sides I'm hungrier than a hound dog on a nigger 'cropper's section, and believe me, that's some hungry!"

Fancy's face brightened at once.

"I'd be mighty proud to fix some breakfast for you, Ty," she said. "Your brother don't rightly 'preciate my cooking."

She went into the house, and Court and Tyler sat down on the steps.

"Reckon Melody is saddled with mortgages, too," Court said, "like all the big plantations nowadays. . . ."

"Not so many as you'd think," Tyler said. "I got some ideas about that, boy. Given my head, I'll clear them off in less than a year."

"Tell me about Melody," Court said.

"Tell him about Melody!" Tyler echoed, rolling his eyes skyward. "Ask me to tell you about heaven—that's easier. Court, boy, that there Melody is just about the prettiest spread of land these famished old eyes ever feasted on—lying there in the Savannah river bottom, a-stretching itself out in the sun from vinegar bend to bitter creek, plumb from hell to breakfast! Black bottom land, Court; hell, you can smell the good stuff in it. Every inch of topsoil what's washed from these starved-out holdings up here around Augusta is piled up down there eighteen inches deep—cotton grows so damned fast that you throw in the seed and jump back to keep the stalks from cracking you on the jaw."

"Yet," Court drawled, "there are debts. . . ."

"Your Uncle Martin," Tyler said, "knew about as much about planting as the left side of my hindquarters. His methods—" Tyler stopped, groping for the words—"Heck, the only way I can describe them is to say that they existed in a state of urinal poverty. Doggone! That's what I call turning a phrase. I sure put that plumb politely!"

"But you could do better?" Court said.

"Court, boy, if I don't clear that place of debt in one growing season—hell's bells, if I don't show us a good-sized profit, I'll lay my worthless carcass down in a coffin and let you nail the lid shut."

"You've got your chance," Court said. "I'm no planter, God knows. But Ty, if you can't straighten that place up, I'll have to sell my half to raise the money for the mill."

Tyler stared at him in genuine alarm.

"Don't do that!" he said. "Don't you even think that way! Why, Court, boy, that there plantation is a-going to make us so damned rich. . . ."

"All right, all right," Court said tiredly. "Take the damned place. Run it for a year and show me the profits. You've got the land in your blood, Ty—like all Southerners. I'm sick of the old life. While I was up North, I saw a few things, including why they were able to whip the pants off of us. We've got to have more industries down here—we've got to give these rednecks half a chance at a decent job and wages in their pockets. The South's got to have enough to eat in its belly for once in its history—all the South, Ty, not just a few fortunate aristocrats."

"Damned if they didn't make a Yankee out of you, up there," Tyler grinned. "You sound like one of those abolitionists."

"I am," Court said, "but it's human misery I'm trying to abolish, Ty—the misery of white humans, just like you and me. Maybe I'll even get around to the blacks, before I'm done."

"Do tell!" Tyler chuckled. "I'll be right there when you do—to wave you good-bye as you start off on your journey—a-riding on the topside of a fence rail, all dressed up in that suit of tar, and all them pretty feathers!"

"That won't happen," Court said. "Ty, how'd you happen to marry Fern?"

"How'd I happen to beat your time, you mean? You helped—writing home about your pretty Yankee heiress."

"That was a lie!" Court growled.

"Well, maybe I did exaggerate a mite—but all's fair in love and war, boy. Appears to me you ain't got no right to complain."

"I'm not complaining. I'm just remembering what you said. Stuff like marriage being a woman's vested interest."

"Don't miss a thing, do you? It's the truth, boy. But the point is, what in hellfire makes you think any Brantley's got a mite of sense in his head as far as women are concerned—even me?"

"You were talking mighty wise a minute ago," Court said. "Thought you were above such things."

"Well, I ain't. That little yaller-haired filly gave me the itch so damned bad I nearly went plumb out of my mind. I was plumb burning to find out if her hidden talents were as delectable as they looked from the outside. Course I hinted more than once that between such high-minded, modern enlightened people as her and me, the book and the preacher weren't really necessary; but Fern wasn't having any—not that girl!"

"So, like the rest of us damned fools, you had to build your fence around her to find out that her talents were just as mediocre as any other woman's?" Court mocked him.

"Partly," Tyler drawled; "but only partly. As a matter of fact, Fern ain't mediocre. But there's more to it than that. I just like to have that little gal around anyhow. She's stimulating. She'll help me git up and git somewheres. Besides, boy—ever thought about the fact that after us there ain't no more Brantleys? Phil and that girl he stole plumb out of the chilling room of the Augusta ice plant ain't got a chit or a child—and you and Fancy ain't likely to do no better. Seems like it's up to me to keep the breed going."

"Phil," Court said, "has done that already."

"You mean his nigger yard children? Hell, boy, they don't count. What this town needs is a passel of true-born Brantleys to turn it up on its ear. So it's up to me—if you'll give me half a chance."

"Me?" Court said brusquely; "what the devil do I have to do with it?"

"You know damned well what you have to do with it," Tyler said calmly. "Fern ain't over you, yet. And there ain't a doggoned thing you can do about it." Tyler grinned half teasingly, half fondly at his younger brother. "I'm getting old—and you always was a heap prettier'n me. So lay off, won't you? Give me a chance to set Fern right."

Fancy put her head out of the door.

"Your breakfast is ready, Ty," she said. "Come on in, won't you?"

"Sure Lord will," Tyler groaned. "My belly was just asking my backbone whether my throat was cut."

Court stood up along with him.

"That—business we were talking about," he said; "don't worry about that, Ty—I have no intentions at all in that direction."

"Good!" Tyler said, and they went into the house.

Half an hour later, he sat back, the last hole in his belt completely bypassed.

"Honeychild," he said, "sure you don't want to leave this nitwit and run off with me? Girl what can cook like that—whew!"

"Ty, you're the beatingest old thing!" Fancy giggled. "It's sure nice to cook for a man what enjoys it."

"I always enjoy your cooking," Court pointed out.

"You!" Fancy snorted. "You eat like a bird, Court."

"I will try to do better in the future," Court said.

Tyler pushed back his chair and got up. Court walked through the hall with him, and a moment later Fancy came, too, putting the dishes she had started to gather up, back on the table.

On the porch, Tyler stood a moment, looking at the two of them.

"You swing a wicked fist, boy," he said, feeling his swollen nose gingerly. "Good-bye now." He crossed the porch, and started down the steps, but on the second one he turned.

"Oh, by the way," he said, "heard they turned Duke Ellis loose this morning. Didn't have a thing to hold him for—'cepting disturbing the peace. He was unconscious when Wyche got knifed, so they couldn't hold him for that. Good-bye, honeychild—you, too, Court—be seeing y'all."

Then he turned very quietly and went down the path out of the yard.

7

There was no wind. The flame in the kerosene lamp stood straight up. Above it, Court Brantley's face glistened with sweat. He sat across the table from Fancy and in his hands he held a revolver. He worked over it very carefully, oiling it, then slipping the cartridges one by one into the chambers, and giving the magazine a slow, deliberate whirl with his thumb. He picked up an oily cloth and began polishing it, although it already glinted bluely in the light of the lamp.

"Court—" Fancy got out, "oh, Court . . ."

"Yes, Fan?" Court said somberly.

"Maybe he won't come . . ."

Court stood up slowly and walked to the windows. There was no moon and the chinaberry tree hooped its umbrella shape, black and tremendous across half the sky. Under it the shadows were inky, sooty, crawling with secret, unheard sounds. A man creeping up through that blackness with a gun in his hand would have all the advantage, Court knew. Even if I blew the lamp out now, he'd still be able to see better. Wearily he turned back to Fancy.

"He'll come all right," he said.

"Maybe he won't," Fan moaned.

But he would. Court knew that. Duke Ellis was no coward. Buck and Tom, yes. Without Duke they were nothing, and less than nothing. But not Duke. Duke was something—absolutely something. Looking out of his window into the crawling dark, Court Brantley thought that the something Duke Ellis was, was a thing the human race should have gotten rid of twenty-five centuries ago. Well, it hadn't; and what lay between him and Duke now was killing business.

He, Court, had married Fancy. But he knew exactly how much difference that would make to Duke. Tonight, within hours, minutes, maybe—one of them was going to die. Tonight, in this year of Our Lord, 1880, in modern times, in a civilized country, he and Duke were going to pump bullets into each other's guts until one of them went down and stayed.

And to the victor would belong the spoils.

Looking at Fan, seeing her face white in the lamplight, her black hair running off unedged into the blackness behind it, her full, sullen mouth trembling in little uncontrolled jerks at the corners, Court wondered. If Duke gets me, he thought, will she step across me and fly into his arms? Will she? Why not? He was something to her once, how much I don't know, will never know, don't even want to know. I'm a Brantley and any pretty woman can lie to us and make us believe it. It's bad enough to die any time in any way even when you're dying for something, but I never thought I'd die like all the rest of the Brantleys in dubious battle over second-hand goods . . .

He looked at her.

I shall save one shot, little Fan, he thought. And if I live long enough, I'm going to pump it right between those lovely breasts of yours. You'll lie beside me, Fan, in the long dark, and I'll share those lips of yours, but only with the worms, the dampness, and the crumbling mold. . . .

Fancy backed away from him.

"Court," she whispered, "don't look at me like that! Oh, Court, honey, you make me plumb scairt!"

"Don't be frightened, Fan," Court said gently. "There's nothing to be afraid of. Not now, not any more."

"But I am scairt!" Fancy wailed. "Right then, I thought you was going to kill me."

Court shook his head.

"No, Fan," he said. "Not now. Not until you deserve it."

Fancy stood there looking at him, her fine nostrils flaring with her breathing. Then she came up to him, her face very white, her blue eyes behind their sooty lashes, enormous in her small face. She was so close to him that he could feel her breath rustling against his throat.

"Duke can't win," she said quietly. "Maybe we'll all lose, but he can't win. I'm not a thing, Court. Not nothing a man can have for fighting over—like two dogs a-snarling after the same bone. I'm me, darling—and maybe I ain't much, but I'm all yours."

"Suppose," Court said cruelly, "he kills me?"

"Then he'll have to kill me, too. Kill me—or watch me night and day. 'Cause I'm a Brantley now, Court, love—and the Brantley women always know just what to do."

"You'd die because of me?" Court demanded.

"That's one way of putting it. I don't think about it like that. What I think is I couldn't live without you. Not one minute, Court."

Court looked at her. Then he put down the gun.

"Come here, Fan," he said.

She came away from his kiss, crying. He held her by the shoulders, hard.

"Go to bed, Fan," he said. "It's going to be all right—believe me."

"All right, Court," she whispered. But she didn't believe him. She didn't believe him at all. . . .

Court sat in the big chair, waiting. His eyelids stung. They felt as if they had sand under them. His head nodded once or twice. He stiffened his neck until his head jerked against the taut-held muscles. Then, ridiculously, it was morning, graying in through the windows, and the gun lay on the floor under his loosened fingers, cold and unfired, and Duke Ellis had not come.

But he did come in the afternoon, in full sunlight, as Court, who knew the man, should have known he'd come. He came up the path, slowly, dressed in a suit of the finest white linen, a cigar stuck between his teeth at an angle, having somehow an air as jaunty as a plume.

He stopped on the porch long enough to fan himself with his soft, rich

Panama hat, then he lifted his big hand to knock on the door. But he never brought it down, for Court stepped out on the porch and faced him.

Duke looked him up and down slowly.

"Where's Fan?" he drawled.

"That," Court said, "is none of your damned business, Duke."

"Now do tell!" Duke said. "That's a mighty poor way of greeting an old friend. What I want to know is how come it ain't, Court?"

"Fancy happens to be my wife," Court said. "I don't think I'd have to tell anybody else this, Duke; but I know you. I don't want you hanging around my place. I don't want you trying to see Fan. If you do . . ."

"What?" Duke drawled. "Tell me what, Court, boy? Sounds right pert interesting."

"I'll kill you," Court said. "I'd do it now and save myself future trouble, but I see you don't have a gun."

"A gun?" Duke chuckled. "Since when did I need a gun for one puking puppy of a Brantley? You Brantleys are played out. Not that you ever was much, Court. Anyhow, so's you'll know, I'm taking Fancy back, any time I get the notion to."

"Why don't you get that notion now?" Court said quietly.

"Some other time," Duke said. "Ain't had my vittles yet. Course I could break your stiff Brantley neck on an empty stomach, but it'll be more pleasurable after I've et."

Court looked at him.

"I am not that particular," he said. "I'll send you and any other Ellis whatsoever to hell any time at all. Before breakfast or after it. I'm warning you, Duke."

"Well, I'll vow," Duke said happily, "that you do talk big for such a little fellow. All right, boy, I'm warned. I'll tend to you later. You—and Fan." Then very calmly he turned and walked down the steps and out of the yard.

Court watched him go, his own fingers tightening on the trigger of the pistol he had in his pocket. Couldn't miss him from here. He's half as big as a barn anyhow and I could drop him now so easy that . . .

Only I can't. All the men that we Brantleys have killed—not one of them ever died with a bullet in his back. Or unarmed. No—we've always faced them down on the Sand Bar Ferry and took their shot first and then shot back, sometimes even with a bullet already in our guts. The Brantleys don't run to cowardice or murder. Which is the reason, maybe, that so many of us have died violently in very bad ways.

He turned then and went back into the house.

There began then what Court always thought of afterwards as the bad time. For Duke Ellis stayed in town and did nothing—absolutely nothing at all.

The heat lay along the land like a blanket, and the chinaberry tree in the yard sent down its thick, sickening scent. The river grew shallow and stank and there were mud flats in the middle of it. And the rains did not come. Night after night the moon came up big and yellow, dimming the stars. The songs that the Negroes sang down in the Terry seemed to get sadder each time Court heard them. And Court Brantley sat by his window each night, holding the gun in fingers that dripped with sweat, but Duke did not come.

Every day, all day long in the thick heat he did not leave the house. Outside the sun flamed down, smashing the red Georgia earth with hammer blows. Nothing moved. Even the crows were still in this heat-killed, sun-stricken land. Court ate nothing, wasting away into gauntness, and Fancy's sullen mouth drew down more and more at the corners. And always they quarreled. One minute they were still, and the next the air was alive with sharp and bitter words that ended with Fancy sulking in a corner or dissolved in acid tears that settled nothing and left her eyes reddened and ugly.

But at night they did not quarrel. No, never in the night.

The days crawled into weeks until it was fall, but the heat did not lessen. When the rains finally came, they came in great thunderstorms like those of midsummer that turned Fancy's face ghost-white with fear. Having to stay there like that in that ugly little house was a bad thing. Court hated the sight of her, now. He wondered if he couldn't go to Savannah, Macon, Charleston—any place where there might be men with money who would listen to him.

He came into the house one day with the rain dripping off his broad-brimmed hat, and looked at the dinner that she had fixed for him. He didn't even sit down.

"Fan," he said, "I'm going down to Savannah. There's a man down there—a friend of Tyler's . . ."

"Oh, Court," she whispered, "no!"

"I've got to go some time," Court said. "Looks like old Duke has just about given up. You stay in the house, and you'll be safe."

"Please, Court," Fancy said, "please, darlin'—don't go! I'm scairt! He might come. . . ."

"He won't come," Court said, and went into the bedroom to pack his bag.

When he came out, Fancy was curled up in the big chair. Her mouth was sullen.

"Go on," she said, "leave me. But I want to tell you one thing, Court Brantley. Won't be my fault what happens."

"I know," Court said; "nothing ever is from a woman's point of view. I'll be back in two or three days. You stay in the house, Fan."

"I won't promise you," Fan said tartly.

In Savannah, it was the same thing again—failure. Court rode out toward Melody, telling himself that he wanted to talk to Tyler; but it was Fern he wanted to see.

Melody was a beautiful plantation. Riding through the mile-long drive bordered with water oaks that led up to the house, Court had the feeling that it was even more beautiful than it had been before. The oaks dripped gray moss that shredded the morning sunlight, and on both sides of the road, the fields stretched away out of sight, with the cotton plants, bursting with bolls, standing in the cleanest rows he'd ever seen, and the earth between was blacker than the heart of darkness. It was good land, rich bottom land, river silt piled up with the compost of all the earth that the Savannah drained. The yield, he could see, would be great.

But there was something else about Melody—the miles of fences freshly whitewashed, the clipped, pruned, orderly look about it—all the thousand small evidences that here was the hand of a master planter. In his uncle's time, it hadn't been so.

Ty's good, Court admitted. Now if he can only give me a lead on something . . .

But there was something missing. For the life of him Court couldn't tell what it was. Then the house came in sight as he turned a bend in the road and he knew quite suddenly what it was.

Nobody sang. You expected singing on the land. The field hands timed their work to the rhythms of the lead hand's song. Negroes sang all the time: when they were happy, when they were sad; when they were sick, or drunk, or dying. Something had to be mighty amiss for a black man not to sing. But he didn't see anything wrong—not at first, not until he was only fifty yards from the house.

A line of Negroes crossed the road with hoes in their hands, and picking sacks slung from their shoulders. They looked up at him, sitting on his rented horse, and Court saw that their eyes were dead. The brownish whites of their eyes were red-streaked and dull, their gaze listless. There was not a fat man among them. Some Negroes ran to fat. One of Martin's best workers had been a black who weighed three hundred pounds. But these hands weren't fat. They were black skeletons walking. They were a line of unkempt scarecrows. They were filthy. His uncle's hands had been decently dressed in blue jeans or overalls, but these had rags and gunny sacks for clothes. Looking at them Court felt sick.

Then the last of them crossed over into the field and a white man came behind them. He was tall and dressed in faded khaki, and a double-barreled shotgun lay in the crook of his arm. He had a muleskinner's whip about fifteen feet long coiled about his shoulder. And he had three dogs with him: two bloodhounds and a bull mastiff.

Court looked at the dogs and the sickness left him. What took its place was a different thing. Like murder.

Bloodhounds were bad enough. Court knew that bloodhounds wouldn't attack a man. They'd only track him to hell and begone, corner him, and wait for the man and the mastiff to come up. The mastiff. Big as a yearling calf. Ugly. Able to pull a full-grown man down and worry him to death.

His feelings must have showed in his face, for the man stopped and looked at him.

"Now who in hellfire," he drawled, "might you be?"

Court looked him up and down, slowly.

"That," he said very quietly, "is none of your God-damned business."

He could see the overseer's hand tightening on the triggers of the shotgun. And he didn't have a pistol. He had left it behind with Fan.

"Reckon I'll have to make it my business, Mister," the overseer said. " 'Pears to me you're trespassing."

"And it appears to me that you're exceeding your authority. Whoever told you to stop and question people on the drive?"

"The owner," the overseer said. "Mister Brantley."

"The half owner," Court corrected him. "You're looking at the other half right now. And if you aren't off this place by sundown, I'll take the greatest pleasure in throwing you off, personally."

"I reckon Mister Ty'll have something to say about that," the overseer said.

"Reckon he will," Court said. "But if he doesn't sing a tune I like, I'll throw him off along with you. Now get out of my way; you're blocking the road."

The overseer fingered the gun. Court touched his heel to the nag's flanks and bore down upon him. Then the man stepped aside. Court rode on toward the house thinking what a wonderful target his back made at that distance. But he didn't turn his head. The man stood there looking at him; then, swearing softly, he plunged on into the field after the blacks.

The house had been painted. It had the same trim, well-kept look as the rest of the plantation. Court got down from the horse and climbed the porch steps. He pushed open the screened door and went in.

Tyler was sitting before the dining room table, his food untouched before him, staring off into space.

"You bastard," Court said.

Tyler grinned at him, wearily.

"Funny thing," he drawled; "I've just been calling you that same thing. But now I'm willing to apologize—'cause I see I had you wrong. Sit down, boy. I'll have Matilda rustle up some vittles."

"No," Court said. "We've got a crow to pick, Ty."

"Thought so; but what I want to know is—is it the same crow?"

"Those Negroes," Court growled; "convict labor, aren't they? Farmed out to you?"

"Yep," Tyler said. "Different crow . . ."

"All right, what's yours?"

"Fern."

"Fern?"

"Yep, Court. She left me. Got the Pinkertons out a-looking for her. They trailed her far as Boston, then they lost her. Boston—that's what made me think it was you."

"Well, I'll be damned," Court said.

"Don't reckon you were planning to join her later, were you?"

"First I heard of it," Court said.

Tyler looked at him.

"You're telling the truth," he said at last. "That makes it worse. Don't reckon I'll ever find her now. Though it's kind of nice not to have to shoot you, boy. Blood is thicker than water, ain't it?"

"Sorry, Ty," Court said quietly. "I'm mighty, damned sorry."

"You are, like hell. Oh, skip it. Now, what about the niggers?"

"Get rid of them. Get rid of that redneck. He was itching to take a shot at me."

Tyler put out his hand and took a cigar out of the box on the table. He stuck it into the side of his mouth and passed the box over to Court.

"Sit down," he said. "Have a smoke. No need your being so riled up over something you don't know about, and damned sure don't understand."

Court sat down. He took a cigar. Tyler bent forward and lit it.

"Well?" Court said.

Tyler took his wallet out of his breast pocket and counted out ten new one-hundred-dollar bills.

"Here," he said, "that should run you for a while."

Court looked at the money, then pushed it back toward his brother.

"Don't change the subject, Ty," he said.

"Hell, it's yours. Part of an advance the Savannah factors offered me against the crop. Go on, take it—I know you need money."

"I do," Court said, "but not this kind."

"What other kind is there? It's all dirty. Look, boy, to make a profit after paying off our debts, I had to cut expenses to the bone. That's how come I got those convict niggers. All right, it ain't right. I feel sorry for those poor devils, too. But you're young, Court. You got a mighty heap to learn. Show me anything on this God-damned earth what ain't got a little evil mixed in it. The line between what's good, and what ain't is mighty unclear. Look, right now—by November, in our first growing season, I'm going to pay off all the debts and show a profit, too. Next year, maybe, we'll clear enough to start your mill. Is that good or ain't it?"

"It's good, Ty—but not like this."

"I'll send those jailbirds back to the pen right after next harvest, Court. I don't want 'em around. By then, we can afford to hire hands—pay 'em good, too. I want you to build your mill. Even if the money did start off wrong, what difference does it make when it ends up right? Them nigger jailbirds catch hell—all right. But you think my getting rid of 'em is going to do 'em any good? They'll catch it somewhere else—more hell than here, because I keep a kind of tight rein on that redneck. Besides, here, they're making it possible for somebody to have a chance. . . ."

"How?"

"By getting us started to build that mill of yours. That mill will do the whole town a mighty heap of good like you've been preaching for years. What's more it'll keep on doing those starved-out crackers good; be the first time in history they ever got enough to eat. And the money they spend will do the merchants good, and through them, the whole town. Like I said, I won't renew my contract with the State after next harvest time—a year from now."

"And that overseer?"

"State man. He goes with the niggers. You'll buy that?"

Court looked at him. No unmixed blessings. In a few years, with luck, he could start to build his mill. He could remain in the land he loved. His sons would grow up Southern men. The Brantleys would again be a power in the State. And Hiberion would again be what it had been. No more pine-barren children, spitting death from their lungs. No more supply store with his brother living by choking the life out of the starving. It was good. From this there would come good. This blood money, earned in the hot sun under the chain-gang guard's lash. This filthy pile of paper that had cost the blood beaten out of black men's backs—and inside them no more singing.

But Tyler had said there would be no more of that. No more after a year. Slowly Court put out his hand and picked up the money.

"I'll buy it," he said. "Hope you find Fern."

"Me too," Tyler said.

8

THAT WAS a mighty foolish thing, Fancy thought. How come I had to go and say that? Telling Court what happened wouldn't be my fault. . . . Now s'posing something was to happen? S'posing Duke was to come and—oh Lord, oh God, oh Jesus, no!

Court would think I planned it. No matter what, he'd always believe that I cottoned up to Duke—that I opened up the door and let him in. Only it ain't a-going to be like that. Duke come here while Court's gone, I'll kill him. Can't do that—I'll kill me. Better be dead than shame Court. Be no good nohow a-sitting here seeing him looking at me—thinking. . . .

She got up and walked to the window, holding Court's revolver in her hand. It was too big. She could scarcely lift it. Going to get myself a gun of my own, she thought. Little lady's pistol what I can handle.

She turned back and looked in the bureau drawer under the pile of socks until she found the money. Then she went out of the house and started walking toward the upper end of Broad Street where the pawnshops were. They had pistols there, she knew that.

The shopkeeper looked at her through his thick spectacles.

"What can I do for you, Ma'am?" he said.

"I want a gun," Fancy blurted. "A little old gun—what I can handle."

The storekeeper stared at her. She saw him looking at her hand where the ring was.

"Planning to shoot somebody?" he said.

"No," Fancy said. "My husband travels—and I'm just plumb scairt in that house all alone. Feel better if I had a gun."

"That's right," the storekeeper agreed. "Mighty heap of prowlers and vagrants about these days. I can see your point, pretty little girl like you. . . . All right—which one?"

"That one," Fancy said and pointed.

The storekeeper got the small revolver with the ornamented stock, and the trigger that folded forward without any guard.

"Bullets?" the storekeeper said.

"Yessir."

He got down a box of the tiny cartridges, and laid them beside the gun. "You know how to load it?"

"No," Fancy said, "show me, please."

He did, and Fancy went out of the store with the little pistol in her handbag.

She didn't want to go back home. Not now. It was mid-afternoon, and she didn't believe that Duke would come in the daytime. Besides, she didn't like to stay in the house alone.

Now where could she go? She couldn't visit Myrtie Torrence, because Court wouldn't like that. Myrtie was bad, just like Court had said. Fancy shook her head thinking of it. How come a girl like Myrtie could do such a thing? Myrtie was pretty and soft-spoken, and always acted nice around Fancy. It was a hard thing to understand. What love was, what a body was made for, couldn't be bought and sold. It was a good thing, kind of holy, even, 'cause that was how life started—a new life, part of Court, and part of me, and the rest of it God and the angels. Anybody who'd ever seen a child, sleeping in his mother's arms could understand that. How could people put a price on such a thing?

But thinking about children gave her an idea. She hadn't seen Belle and those kids of hers in the longest time. Well, she'd go see them right now. She'd hold little Dred in her arms and rock him to sleep. And anybody what didn't like it because those kids had a drop or two of the wrong kind of blood could go hang!

She loved them. More than that, they meant something to her. What they meant was a thing she couldn't exactly put down in words, because she didn't even know the words for it. But what it was, was a simple thing. They stilled her hunger for children of her own.

Today, as Belle's little house came in sight, she realized that for the first time. Oh, Lord, she prayed silently, why can't we have one? A little boy what'll look just like Court. So little and sweet. One I can hold and sing to, and love. . . . He'd need me. Court doesn't need me or even really want me, I reckon. But a baby'd change all that. Man can't hate the mother of his son. . . .

"Howdy, Miz Fancy," Belle said. "Thought you'd plumb forgot all about us."

"That's something you don't need to worry about," Fancy said. "Can't forget those kids. Can't get 'em out of my mind. How are they?"

"The girls are fine; but Dred's been a mite poorly lately."

"Sick?" Fancy said. "Oh, Belle, why didn't you come to me before now?"

"Don't take on so, Miz Fancy. Reckon it's 'cause he's teething. Though he do feel awful hot. . . ."

Fancy went into the house at once without saying anything else. She bent over the crib and picked up the child. He was burning with fever, his tiny face flushed.

"Belle!" Fancy said, "this child's sick—death-sick! You run right out of here and get the doctor!"

"Miz Fancy," Belle said sadly, "I ain't got no money for no doctor. . . ."

Fancy stared at her.

"You mean to tell me that Phil . . ."

"Mister Phil would give me some all right. He's good that way. But he ain't been around here lately—and I can't go up to his house and ask for him."

"I've got some," Fancy said. "Now run!"

"Doctor ain't a-going to come in no hurry for colored folks," Belle said. "Do my best, though."

"Tell him," Fancy said, "that Mrs. Courtland Brantley wants to see him—right away. Tell him it's a—a emergency."

Belle went out of the house at once. Fancy turned back to the child thinking, That was a real proper word. Court would be proud of me, if he'd heard me say it. Then she began to strip the clothes off the feverish little body.

Twenty minutes later, Belle was back with Doctor Benton. Fancy could hear his voice, gruff and angry, saying:

"You told me Mrs. Brantley, gal. Who're you trying to fool? Mrs. Brantley doesn't live in a shotgun cabin in the nigger section!"

"She's in there, all right," Belle said. "You go see, Doctor."

Fancy got up and walked to the door.

The doctor took off his big hat.

"Howdy, Ma'am," he said. "What's the matter? You get sick all of a sudden while you were passing through?"

"I'm not sick," Fancy said. "It's a child—her child."

"Well, I'll be damned!" the doctor exploded. "You don't mean to tell me you made me drop everything to come attend to a pickaninny!"

Fancy stared at him.

"I sent for you to come attend a baby," she said. "A helpless baby who's death-sick. But right now I don't think you could do any good. Man with that kind of a heart couldn't do nobody any good. You can go. I'll get somebody else."

Doctor Benton studied her. Then he said:

"Where's the child?"

"In here," Fancy said and led him to where little Dred twisted in his crib.

"Light skin," Doctor Benton muttered, "blue eyes. Another Brantley yard child, by God!"

"Another baby, what's sick," Fancy told him. "Now you get busy, damn you!"

Doctor Benton examined the baby. Then he opened his bag and took out a bottle of pills.

"Give him this," he said. "Cut the pills in four pieces. Crush one of the pieces. Give it to him in water. *Boiled* water, dammit! Every half-hour till the fever breaks. Bathe him with cool water and alcohol. That'll help. You got sense enough to remember all that, gal?"

"She's got sense enough, all right," Fancy told him. "But *I'm* going to do it. Now how much do I owe you, Doctor?"

Doctor Benton got up and snapped his bag shut.

"Not a red cent," he growled. "Charge it up to my bad heart." Then he marched out of the house.

Fancy turned back to the baby.

"Get a pot of water on the stove," she snapped. "Quick, Belle! You got any rubbing alcohol?"

"No'm," Belle whispered.

"Then take this and get some. Go down to Oertel's Drugstore. But put the water on first."

"Yes'm," Belle said.

It was after midnight when little Dred began to sweat, and a half-hour later, he was sleeping peacefully, cool and quiet.

Fancy was tired—dog-tired; but she knew she had to get home. Even then she didn't think about Duke Ellis. She was thinking about Doctor Benton, wondering what made a man get like that. But he ain't all bad, she thought; he's got shame left. I reached that. Good thing—else that poor little fellow would be dead by now. . . .

She walked on. Wonder when Court's coming back? Lord, I do miss him so. Wonder what he's doing right now? If he even thinks about me?

Court was thinking about her all right. He had gotten back to Augusta a little after ten that night. Coming into the house and finding Fancy gone hadn't been a good thing. The waiting had been worse. He left the house at midnight and went down to Hiberion. But Fancy hadn't been there. Then, gripping the gun in his pocket, he went to the Ellises'. Duke wasn't at home, either. And there was the thing that Fancy had said: "Whatever happens, won't be my fault, Court."

Walking the dark streets of Augusta, Court Brantley was just a little crazy. All the things he'd thought, all the times he'd cursed himself for a fool for marrying Fan, were gone now. He was sick inside. He was filled up with death and bitter hell. And only one thing would do the way he felt any good.

Killing.

But he couldn't find Fan or Duke. Not anywhere at all.

Fancy trudged along, so lost in her own thoughts that she didn't hear the buggy until it drew up alongside her.

"Howdy, Fan," Duke said.

Fancy looked at him and kept on walking.

Duke flapped the reins over the horse's back, lightly. The buggy moved off slowly, keeping pace with her.

"Riding's better than walking," Duke said.

Fan didn't answer him.

"Don't you trust me?" Duke said. "I wouldn't do you no harm."

"No," Fancy said.

"I'll take you home," Duke said earnestly. "I swear by my mother I'll take you home."

Fancy looked at him. Then she remembered the little pistol in her bag. And it was a long way home.

"All right," she said tiredly. "But don't try nothing, Duke. You do, and you'll be sorry."

"I won't try nothing," Duke said.

Fancy climbed into the buggy.

Five minutes later, they passed Court Brantley, standing in the shadow of an unlighted street.

He came after them, running.

But Duke was driving fast.

At the house, Duke got down and helped Fancy from the buggy.

"Good night, Duke," she said. "And thanks. I'm surprised. Didn't know you could be decent."

Duke looked at her and laughed.

"Said I'd take you home, didn't I? But I didn't promise nothing after that. Nary a damned thing."

Then he stretched out his big arms and picked her up, as lightly as a leaf.

"Duke!" Fancy said. "Please, Duke!"

"Please what?" Duke rumbled. "Don't tell me to let you go, 'cause I ain't a-going to. Thought you could run out on me, eh? Got yourself married to a real aristocrat! Mighty fine, ain't you? Only, baby, you're my kind.

Soft little boy like Court Brantley don't know how to treat you. Big damn fool even to try. . . ."

"Duke," Fancy wept, "oh, Duke, please!"

"Which way is the bedroom, hon?" Duke chuckled. "Kind of ironical, ain't it? Thought he could balk Duke Ellis, huh? Well I laid off a long while, but it's time I learned him! Which way, Fan?"

Fancy's blue eyes narrowed. They looked shrewd, but Duke didn't notice that.

"In there," she said.

Duke marched into the bedroom.

"Now," Fancy whispered, "put me down, Duke. I ain't a-going to fight you. Know it ain't no use."

"Now you're talking sense," Duke said, and put her down.

Fancy's hand went into the bag and came out with the little gun.

"You get out of here, Duke," she said. "Get out or I'll kill you. I ain't fooling. Get out."

"Well, well, well," Duke grinned. "Good thing that the light is on, or I wouldn't even be able to see that little toy. Don't reckon it can shoot nohow."

"It can shoot all right," Fancy said. "Be mighty sorry to kill you, Duke. But I will. Believe me, I will."

"That lil' toy couldn't even dent my hide," Duke said, and started toward her.

Fancy backed away from him.

"Don't come no closer," she said.

Duke took another step, and stopped, his eyes widening.

"Now," he growled, "what the devil is that?"

Fancy half turned to see what he was staring at, and he was upon her, his big hands twisting her wrist until the little gun clattered to the floor.

"Now, babydoll," he said, "you're going to pay for that—with interest!"

"Turn her loose, Duke," Court Brantley said.

Fancy's lips moved, shaping his name.

"Court," she whimpered. "Oh, Court . . ."

"True to form, eh, Fan?" Court said. "The minute my back was turned . . ."

"No, Court!" Fancy said. "Oh, no, darlin', no!"

Duke looked at the gun in Court's hand. It was very steady, pointing at his heart. Beads of sweat broke out on his forehead.

"Reckon you got me dead to rights, Court," he said. "Only there's two things I'd like to ask you."

Court nodded.

"Let Fan out of here," Duke said. "Don't reckon even one of you Brantleys is up to shooting a woman. . . ."

"And the second?" Court clipped the words.

"Give me a chance at my gun. More sporting that way, it 'pears to me."

Court looked at Fancy, seeing her lips blue, her whole body shaking. "Get out of here, Fan," he said.

Duke pulled his own big Colt from the pocket of his pants. He looked at Fancy and grinned.

"Blow the lamp, honey," he said; "then git!"

Fancy looked at Court. Her eyes were imploring.

"Blow it out, Fan," he said.

Fancy bent over the lamp, but she couldn't blow it. She didn't have the breath.

"Blow it!" Court said.

All the breath came out of her at once. The flame bent back against the wick, scattered. And the darkness came down.

She ran out of the bedroom, through the other room, and out on the porch. She leaned against the pillar trying to get her breath back. From where she stood she could see the chinaberry tree humping its umbrella shape, black and tremendous across half the sky.

She didn't think about anything at all. She didn't feel. She just hung onto the pillar so hard that her nails broke against the wood.

It was quiet. From the hills above the town she could hear the whippoorwill crying. Then a mockingbird answered, closer at hand, imitating the sound. He didn't get it quite right. He was a half note off, and a little flat.

A dog howled.

Death, Fancy thought, that's the sign of death. Oh God, I—

Then there were the shots.

Fancy clung to the pillar, hearing them, feeling them. Her body jerked each time they came.

Then—silence.

But she couldn't move. She had to move, but she couldn't.

Then she tore herself away from the pillar and ran back into the house. Into the bedroom. She put her hand out and groped across the table until she found the box of matches. Her hand shook so that she dropped them, spilling them all over the floor. She bent down and found a couple. The first one broke. The second one flared briefly, while she lifted the shade and ran it along the wick. The wick spluttered. Caught. Fancy turned the knob. The glow spread through the room.

They lay on the floor—both of them. Fancy didn't move. Then Court

Brantley put one hand down and pushed himself up halfway. She ran to him and put her arms around under his chest and pulled.

"Get your hands off of me," he said.

Fancy stepped back. Her hand felt funny. When she looked at it, she saw it was wet. Wet and sticky and red. She looked over at Duke Ellis. He lay in the other corner with a grin on his face and four little blue-rimmed holes in his chest. He was dead.

Court got up stiffly and went out of the room. But when he got to the porch, he had to sit down. Fancy followed him.

"Court," she whispered, "Court . . ."

Court looked at her.

"You little tart," he said.

"No, Court," she said. "It isn't like that. You're wrong, Court. There wasn't nothing. . . ."

"I saw you in his buggy," Court said.

Fancy sat down beside him, and pillowed her head on her knees. The way she cried now was a bad thing. Court couldn't bear listening to it.

"Wait here," he said. "I'll be back with the sheriff."

Then he lurched down the steps. The pain in his shoulder had been very bad to begin with and now it was worse so that he had to lock his teeth together to keep from groaning. Every time he took a step, he jarred the wound so that he could feel the smashed splinters of the bone digging in. The blood pumped out faster. He could feel the sickness starting down in the pit of his stomach. There was a gone, hollow feeling spreading out in both directions from his middle so that when he moved his legs he didn't feel them. But the black shapes of the trees jerked toward him and passed and fell away behind him and the road curved out before him.

She looked so small, sitting there. So small and childlike. Crying. Innocent-looking. Sweet. What made her do it? God in Glory, what?

How far is it? Got to rest—got to. Don't sit down, boy. Never get up if you do. Lean back against this tree—that's it. Steady now. Can't be much further. Christ! Didn't know a man had so much blood. . . .

The inside of his sleeve was sticking to him along all its length, but he had a feeling now the flow was slowing. He moved off again, almost running, his head low, snatching the air into his lungs in great gulps while the far stars and the black-shadowed trees and the shapes of the houses did a slow and stately dance before his eyes, and the road curved out white before him and curved again and there was the sheriff's house.

He walked up on the porch. Hammered at the door.

The sheriff came down in his nightshirt with his thin, hairy legs sticking out from under it, and stood there yawning at him with a lamp in his hand.

"Who is it?" Sheriff Bowen said. "Court! Court Brantley—what's the trouble, son?"

"I killed a man," Court said. "Duke Ellis."

"You don't say! Well, I reckon I ain't surprised. Somebody was a-going to do it sooner or later. But how come it was you, son?"

"Good and sufficient reasons," Court said. "He's up at my house. You coming?"

"Just a minute till I get dressed. Come on inside, boy."

"I'll wait here, thank you."

"You ain't a-going to run away?" Sheriff Bowen said.

Court laughed bitterly.

"The time to run was before now," he said. "Why in hellfire would I come to tell you if I meant to bolt?"

"That's right. Set down there in the rocker. You look plumb tuckered out. I'll only be a minute."

Court sat down. He felt sick at his stomach. The bleeding had stopped, but the shoulder was bad, very bad. He heard the little whimpering sound start and after a moment it came to him that he was doing it. He set his teeth hard and straightened up in the chair, staring out into the night.

Sheriff Bowen came down, hitching a last gallus over his shoulder.

"Where's your gun, boy?" he said.

"Right here," Court said, and passed it over.

"Well, I reckon we'd best be getting down there. Son, I'm plumb sorry it's you what done this. Your paw and me was boys together; don't reckon I know a finer man."

"Thanks," Court said drily. He got up stiffly and came down the steps with the sheriff, but in the street, in spite of all his efforts, he swayed a little.

The sheriff looked at him.

"You drunk, son?" he said.

"No," Court said, "not drunk."

When they got to the house, Court dropped down on the steps.

"I don't want to go in," he said. "I don't want to see it—again."

Sheriff Bowen looked at him, then shrugged. Court heard his footsteps receding as he went through the front room. Three minutes later, he was back.

"Where's your wife?" he drawled.

"Gone, I reckon," Court said tiredly.

"This on account of her?"

"Yes. Duke was—molesting her."

"With, or without her consent?" Bowen snapped.

"Without, of course," Court said. "He thought I was out of town and kind of broke in. . . ."

"I see." Then he passed Court back his gun.

"Better load it, son," he said. "Tom Ellis is out of jail now—and old Rad ain't no slouch with a gun. Other than them, you ain't got a thing to worry about. Ain't a jury in the whole South what wouldn't bring in a verdict of justifiable homicide in a case like this." He lowered his lantern suddenly and stared at Court's left hand.

"And self-defense," he added. "You come along with me to Doc Brewster and git that fixed. Wasn't going to take you into custody, but I reckon I better. Keep you up at my house. You ain't in no fitten condition to defend yourself. I'll send a wagon up for Duke in the morning." He looked at Court. "And when it's over—go easy on that little gal, won't you?"

Court stared at him. He thinks I'm lying, Court thought. He thinks I caught them together. That's what they'll all think. Everybody—the whole town.

"Don't worry," he said, "I will."

9

"I CAME as soon as I read it in the papers," Wyche Weathers said. "Always thought Court Brantley was a good sort. But then I read the other part—about Mrs. Courtland Brantley—née Fancy Williamson. . . . So I caught a train."

"I'm glad," Fancy whispered. "Oh Wyche, I'm so glad."

Wyche looked at her. Then he put his hand in his pocket and came out with a packet of letters, tied with a string.

"Wrote you to that boarding house in Atlanta. They came back. So I wrote you here—General Delivery. Figured you'd ask at the Post Office. I figured wrong. Picked these up myself this morning. Don't know why the devil they didn't return them. . . ."

"Give them to me," Fancy said. "I want to read them."

"No," Wyche said. "Water under the bridge, Fan."

"I'm sorry, Wyche."

"Don't be. You told me the score before I left. And you did it right, married him. These go in the grate. Now, tell me about it. Knowing you, I know you weren't playing around with Duke Ellis. I'd bet my life and my hope of heaven on that."

"Thanks, Wyche," Fancy said.

"What's the trouble, baby?"

"Court doesn't believe me. He won't even see me when I go to see him."

"Then he's a fool. Why won't he?"

"He—he saw me in a buggy with Duke Ellis—that night."

"Damn!" Wyche said. "What the devil were you doing there?"

"I'd been down to that colored girl, Belle's house. Her baby was sick. I got a doctor for her. On the way back, Duke offered me a ride. Swore he'd be good."

"And you believed him?"

"I had a little gun in my handbag, Wyche. Figured I could take care of myself."

"I see. Can you prove that you were at Belle's house?"

"Yes. Belle will tell them. . ."

"No good. A colored woman's word ain't worth a dime in court."

"The doctor," Fan said. "Doctor Benton."

"Good! Come on."

"Where're we going?"

"Down to Bob McCullen's office. He's Court's attorney. I want him to know this."

"Why?"

"Got a hunch that District Attorney Carter's going to say some mighty mean things about you."

"Oh, Wyche, no! Why should he?"

"To pin a murder charge on Court instead of justifiable homicide. Next year's election time, Fan. He can see himself in the governor's chair. And this case is big. If he can make the jury believe that your marriage wasn't exactly—legal, the whole thing becomes a scrap between two men over a woman—of, I'm sorry, Fan—of doubtful virtue. You see?"

"I see," Fancy said. "But my marriage to Court was honest and I can prove that, too."

"How? They're saying about town that Court was drunk."

"Riley stood up with us. He saw me pour a whole pot of coffee into Court first to get him sobered up. I made Court ask me again, Wyche, after he was sober. Judge Harris can testify whether or not Court was drunk. And Saph."

"Saphira? Hell, baby, that's best of all. His sister. Good! Right now I feel damned good. Carter hasn't got a chance."

"Wyche, won't they say that—that you'n'me were . . ."

"You bet your boots they will. But I'm going to demand to be called. Another reason I want to see Bob."

Fancy looked at him. He was dressed up. Fine—real fine. The nicest clothes she reckoned she'd ever seen on a man.

"You look mighty nice," she said. "Heap of difference from the way you used to look."

"Thanks," Wyche said. "Things have changed, Fan. I run the Weathers Mills, now."

"You run them? But I thought . . ."

"That my old man was mad at me? Heck, he was. But he got over it when he found out the truth about Sue Wells. Then he saw the handwriting on the wall, baby. Six months before I got hurt, he suffered a light stroke. While I was laid up, he had another one. Nothing much, left him with a twitch in the right corner of his mouth, and the shakes in his hands. . . ."

"Wyche, he ain't a-going to die?"

"No. The doctors say he can live to be ninety, if he's careful. But being careful includes giving up running the mills. So soon as I got up, I took over. The old man's as pleased as punch at the way I handled things. So he signed over the mills to me. I'm his only child anyhow, and he was going to leave them to me when he died. Mills are making more profits now than any time in their history. The old man brags about me all over town. About once a month he comes down and interferes with what I've changed. We argue like hell, then he grins and admits that I'm right and goes out and brags some more about how smart his boy is."

"That's wonderful, Wyche. Sure wish that Court . . ."

"That Court what, Fan?"

"Could get started with his mill. He owns a piece of land up in Dry Gully that would make a perfect mill site. Only nobody'll back him. The Brantleys have got too bad a reputation."

Wyche looked at her.

"Want to show me this place, baby?" he said.

"But, Wyche—what about Lawyer McCullen?"

"Heck, Bob'll be in his office all day—we got time. I want to see this place."

"Why?"

"Because it'll tell me a few things about Mister Courtland Brantley. Things I need to know."

"What kind of things, Wyche?"

"How much he knows about textile mills. A good site means a whole lot. You can locate a mill most anywhere, Fan—but a man who knows the business will put his plant close to a source of cheap power. Come on, I got this buggy for the length of my stay."

"All right, Wyche," Fancy said.

Looking at him, as they drove northward out of town toward Dry Gully, Fancy was thinking: I was a fool. Knew what kind of man Wyche was. Knew he'd get there. But love and horse sense's got mighty little to do with each other. Man like Wyche—good, kind-hearted, sure. Got grit in his craw. Got get up and get in his make-up. Smart—steady. But I'm in love with a man that's crazy wild like all his family, and who'll never get anywhere, and who's 'shamed of me. Only he can look at me and I melt all over. What can you do against a thing like that? . . .

"This the place?" Wyche said.

"Yes—little further up. We'll have to leave the buggy though."

"All right," Wyche said, "come on."

A few minutes later, they stood above Dry Gully, looking down into the steep, twisting ravine. Wyche didn't say anything.

"Court says that water used to run through here once," Fancy said. "Water from the river. Then something—an earthquake maybe, raised up that bluff, and cut it off. Says that a few sticks of dynamite could blast through that bluff and the water would race through down here—real fast. Fast enough to turn the mill wheels and run all the machinery for a mill."

"He's right," Wyche said quietly. "Seen a lot of mill sites in my day, but I've never seen a better one than this. He'd have more power than he could possibly use. Heck, baby, this gully would run three full-sized mills, let alone one."

"That's what Court said."

"How much does he need?" Wyche said.

"A hundred thousand dollars," Fancy said sadly.

Wyche grunted.

"He's got it," he said.

"Oh, Wyche!" Fancy said. "Wyche, honey—you don't mean . . . ?"

"That I'll back him? Heck, no, baby. Far as I'm concerned, Court Brantley is an unknown quantity, beyond the fact that he evidently knows the textile business. What I'm backing, is you, Fan. Want to see your future assured. It'll be a straight business deal—Court'll have to pay me back say—seventy-five thousand, and keep me in on this as minority stockholder. But I want the thing set up so that no matter what happens to him, you'll be protected. And if he has an ounce of sense in his head, he'll see it my way."

"Wyche," Fancy said, "I don't know what to say."

"Don't say anything—especially not to Court. Let me talk to him. You put it to him, and he'll get his back up, sure. Come on, now. We got to see that lawyer."

Bob McCullen looked up as they entered. Fancy thought he looked worried.

"Howdy, Mrs. Brantley," he said. "And Mr. Weathers. Glad to see you both. Yessir, mighty glad. Hope you can help me out. The case comes up tomorrow, and I haven't a thing to go on—not a thing."

"Why not?" Wyche said.

"Court clams up every time I ask him questions. He's not doing a blessed thing to make it any easier. Ordinarily it would be an open and shut case. Unwritten law, you know. But Carter's got something up his sleeve beside his arm. He's going around grinning like a crazy bobcat."

"What could he have up his sleeve, Mister McCullen?" Fancy asked.

Bob McCullen looked at her and flushed.

"Ma'am," he began, "I don't exactly know how to put this. . . ."

"Speak your piece, man," Wyche growled.

"The fact is, Ma'am, that you're the big question mark in this case. Nobody in Augusta knows anything much about you, and what they think they know sure Lord doesn't help. . . ."

"I see," Fancy said. "I used to dance on the back of Wyche's Medicine Wagon—and tell fortunes. That makes me—bad. A man's got a right to protect his wife, if she's a good woman—if she's really his wife. But if a man in high society marries a nobody, that's different. If the whole town believes he only married her because he was drunk and crazy, that's different. And when the man who got killed was supposed to have been more'n a mite friendly with her before she got married, kind of throws your unwritten law out of kilter, doesn't it?"

"You have stated District Attorney Carter's case—beautifully," McCullen groaned.

"All right," Fancy said. "Only the trouble with all that is that none of it is so. I never had anything to do with Duke Ellis—never in my life. Not him nor any other man. When I met Wyche, here, I was running away from Duke after I had hit him on the head with a poker to keep him from—I don't have to say what, Mister McCullen. . . ."

"Which only brings up another point, Mrs. Brantley—the question of your relations with Mister Weathers here."

"Let her tell you the whole thing, Bob," Wyche said. "The whole dadblamed story. It's kind of sad—how a whole town can go out of its way to persecute an innocent kid on nothing more than hearsay. How her marriage has been hurt by gossip, completely unfounded gossip. Don't interrupt her; just listen. Then call me to the stand. Let me have my say. Call

Judge Harris who married 'em, and Riley the saloonkeeper, and Saphira Brantley, then see if that polecat Carter can make of this marriage a drunken farce. Call Doc Benton to prove where Fan was on that night, and the colored woman Belle—Doc's word will make hers stick. Then call Fan to the stand, and see if even those stupid oafs they'll make a jury of won't be able to see she's telling the truth."

"I could use more light," Bob McCullen said, "and less heat, Wyche."

"Tell him, Fan," Wyche said.

When she had finished, Bob McCullen leaned back, grinning. Then he got up and went to the telephone. He turned the crank and barked into the mouthpiece:

"Operator, get me Burt Benton's office. Number? Hell, honey, I can't be bothered looking up numbers. You get it—there ain't that many telephones in town."

That next morning was bright. The courtroom was packed. Sitting beside Wyche, Fancy could see people who looked important; people dressed in their finest clothes. The case was big. She remembered what McCullen had said to Wyche as they left the office:

"Heck, Wyche, put your money up. For a case like this, I ought to pay you. If I'm not sitting in the governor's chair next term or the one after directly as a result of this case, I'll resign from the bar."

Fancy looked at all those people. Some of them she recognized. Philemon and Martha. Jed Hawkins. It gave her a queer feeling seeing him here. Agnes and Saphira. Tyler. Old Jeff wasn't there. Home, drunk, Fancy guessed. Across the aisle on the front row sat Rad and Sary Ellis. Fancy couldn't keep from looking at them. She thought she'd never seen a man look madder than Rad Ellis in her life; but Sary Ellis' face was sad—terribly sad. Fancy couldn't look at her. With all his faults, Duke had still been her son. Tom, Duke's brother, sat beside them; but Buck was still in jail. It would be years before they let him out, Fancy reckoned. . . .

But some of these folks were mighty fine. She looked at them keenly, studying their clothes.

"The Brewsters," Wyche whispered; "the Wagoners, the Waltons, the Phinizys, the Cummings—the flower of Georgia, Fan. This case is really something. Saw folks outside from Macon, Waynesboro, and Brunswick—got here too late to get in. Why right now you can name your price for a seat in any of the windows. . . ."

Bob McCullen paused by their seats and whispered to Wyche.

"Notice the crowd?" he said. "And you asked me about my fee!"

"Couldn't we," Wyche asked wearily, "kind of keep Fan out of this as much as possible?"

"Are you crazy, Wyche?" Bob said. "That's going to be our main defense. The unwritten law. Leave it to me, Wyche. I'll do it right. Play for sympathy for her. The poor, downtrodden lower-class girl who never had a chance. Build Court up big, too—his decency, his nobility in marrying her, the respect he showed for her simple, innate goodness by making her his wife instead of just sneaking around like so many of our so-called respected citizens. Boy, I won't leave a dry eye in this courtroom!"

"Don't doubt it," Wyche said grimly. "Notice that Tom Ellis is leaving the courtroom?"

"Damn!" Bob McCullen said. "Not even waiting for the trial, is he?"

"Do you think what I think?" Wyche growled.

"Yes. Probably gone to round up some of his boys. Mob violence. Well those Ellises aren't popular—don't reckon they'll get very far."

"I have a mighty shiny piece of persuasion in my pocket," Wyche said. "You have the police ready, Bob."

"Right," McCullen said.

Judge Richardson was entering the Court now, and all the people stood up until he was seated. Then the bailiff began his cry:

"Hear ye! Hear ye! The case of the People of the State of Georgia versus Courtland Brantley, charged with the murder of Duke Hently Ellis, on the night of September 7th, this year of Our Lord, 1880! The Court is now in session!"

Fancy put out her hand and gripped Wyche's wrist, squeezing it hard.

At once Granville Carter, the prosecutor, was on his feet.

He turned to the Court and looked each juror in the face, slowly. Then he began.

There were, he told the jury, and the spectators, in the city of Augusta, two well-known families. The members of one of them had been citizens since the founding of the city; the others, late-comers, had had the sagacity to found the great turpentine industry upon which so many of the good people of Augusta depended for livelihood. One of these families, being aristocrats, had been venerated, though throughout their history, they had lived the lives of drunkards, profligates, and lechers. . . .

Fancy stared at him.

"The Ellises," Carter went on, "though vigorous, high-spirited men, given to the playful excesses of youth, have aided in keeping Augusta economically upon her feet, despite their humble birth. They are the type of men who have made our democracy great, while the Brantleys have produced nothing, and destroyed much! Who is it, I ask you, that have driven their wives to suicide or the madhouse? Which of these two clans has figured in scandals without number, in endless duels, in drunken orgies? Which, I ask you?"

Bob McCullen got slowly to his feet. He looks lazy, Fancy thought. But that other lawyer's awful. They listen to him and Court ain't got a chance. . . .

"Your Honor," McCullen said quietly, "I object. It seems to me that the learned counselor is laboring under a wee mite of a misapprehension. Didn't the bailiff read a charge against Court Brantley? Or was it against his ancestors? Maybe we ought to recess while my eloquent opponent goes down to Magnolia cemetery and digs 'em up so that they can be properly charged. . . ."

"Objection sustained," Judge Richardson said. The whole courtroom rocked with laughter.

McCullen made the prosecutor a sweeping bow and sat down. Granville Carter's face was beet-red.

"I see," he grated, "that we have to deal here with the tactics of a mountebank!"

Judge Richardson leaned forward.

"Mister Carter," he said, "you will please withdraw that remark, or I shall be forced to hold you in contempt of Court."

"Very well, then," Carter snapped; "I do withdraw it. Is my worthy opponent satisfied?"

"Quite," McCullen said.

"My opening statements," Carter went on, "were intended merely as introductions to more pertinent matters. From past experience, I know exactly what to expect in this case. Counselor McCullen intends to sway you with his matchless eloquence; he intends to portray the defendant in the role of the poor, deluded husband, defending the sanctity of his home; he intends to work upon your sympathies for his distinguished lineage, his good looks—to present Court Brantley, in fact, as a man of probity and honor!

"It must be, therefore, regrettably, my task to prove to you that such was not the case! I am going to prove to you that the poor, unfortunate young man who was brutally bereft of his life in the full bloom of his youth was merely trying to repossess what was rightly his! I tell you, Gentlemen of the Jury, that it is known by nearly everybody present here that a common-law relationship existed between the deceased and the woman called Fancy. I tell you further, that the defendant, Courtland Brantley, took advantage of Duke Ellis' absence to alienate the notoriously fickle affections of the woman, Fancy. . . ."

"Your Honor," Bob McCullen said, "I reckon I'd better object again. Mrs. Brantley ain't on trial here. Her husband is. Besides which, Prosecutor

Carter's remarks are downright ungentlemanly—even if they were true, which they aren't. Furthermore, they have very slight bearing on the case, if any."

"Will the prosecutor," Judge Richardson said, "please explain the pertinency of his procedure to the Court?"

"It's very pertinent, Your Honor!" Carter said. "I intend to prove that far from being a case of an outraged husband rightfully defending his home, that Court Brantley actually engaged in a marriage of doubtful legality for the purpose of safeguarding his hold upon his paramour, and that upon learning from the deceased that he intended to have back the woman on whom he had much more valid claims, Courtland Brantley did willfully murder Duke Ellis! Yes, I said murder! And I intend to win from this Court the highest penalty—that Courtland Brantley be hanged by his neck until he is dead!"

"Objection overruled," Judge Richardson said.

Carter turned, smiling.

"Call Courtland Brantley to the stand!" he said.

"Courtland Brantley to the stand," the bailiff echoed.

Court got up and walked to the chair. The bailiff lifted the Bible and said: "Do you solemnly swear to tell the truth, the whole truth, and nothing but the truth, so help you God?"

"I do," Court said.

"Mister Brantley!" Granville Carter began, "I want you to answer me carefully! Isn't it a fact that you met the woman, Fancy, during the absence of Duke Ellis? Answer me, isn't it?"

"No," Court said, "it isn't. Duke was right here in town when I met—my wife. He didn't leave until later. Reckon I had a hand in his leaving though. That was when he and his brothers got high-spirited—I believe that's what you call it, sir—and tried to murder Wyche Weathers. I sort of helped send them to jail."

"You answer my questions!" Carter roared. "The information I want, I'll ask for!"

"And what you don't want, you'll conceal," Court said drily.

"Mister Brantley," Judge Richardson said, "please confine your remarks to answering Attorney Carter's questions."

"Yes, Your Honor," Court said.

"Courtland Brantley," Carter began again; "did you not pursue this woman," and Carter pointed at Fancy, "until you succeeded in your sole aim—which, due to the fact that there are ladies present, I can only hint at—not state?"

Court turned to the Judge.

"Do I have to answer that one, Your Honor?" he asked.

Judge Richardson nodded.

"Well, Attorney Carter, I'd better warn you that I can't answer that with a yes or no. It's a little more complicated than that."

"Answer my question!" Carter roared.

"All right. I did pursue Miss Williamson night and day. And my motives don't do me any credit. I'll admit that. But that I succeeded in my aims—no, sir. Miss Williamson shamed me out of 'em. She pointed out to me that I had unmarried sisters; that I sure Lord wouldn't like it if any man tried with them, what I was trying. She reminded me that she was all alone in the world—and that people had been using her name mighty unkindly already. . . ."

"Ha!" Granville Carter snapped, "you expect these gentlemen to believe that?"

"Why not?" Court drawled, "since it's the truth?"

"Will you tell the Court, please, just where you were on that evening that this so-called marriage took place?"

"No," Court said grimly.

"Then I will!" Carter shrieked. "You were in Riley's saloon. Furthermore, Gentlemen of the Jury, the aristocratic Mister Courtland Brantley was so drunk at the time he could scarcely stand—thus conclusively proving that he had no intentions of marrying this woman in the first place. Isn't that the truth, Court Brantley!"

"No!" Court roared.

"This marriage which the defendant did murder to defend, or so we're asked to believe—started in Riley's saloon. The woman, Fancy, dragged him from that saloon, and married him before he could recover his senses. You can readily see, gentlemen, how a handsome young aristocrat must have seemed quite a prize to her. Furthermore, Riley himself, our good barkeep, upon whom, God knows, I wish to cast no aspersions stood as witness to this touching and sacred ceremony! Gentlemen, I ask you! Your witness, Counselor!"

Bob McCullen got up.

"I notice," he began, "that Attorney Carter has carefully refrained from determining exactly what happened the night of September 7th, which after all, is what concerns us here. But I'm going to follow the line of questioning he has indicated. I'm going to for two reasons: Attorney Carter has persistently and with malice aforethought, tried to blacken the name of a sweet, innocent girl whose only crime was that she was poor and from a humble background. And my second reason is that Counselor Carter's procedure is made to order for determining my client's innocence . . ."

McCullen was good, Fancy could see that. But he had gone through a long list of questions before she realized how good he was. He asked Court questions about his marriage. Then he dismissed him from the stand, and called Riley, Saphira and Judge Harris to back up what Court had said.

"That takes care of the drunken marriage," he said. "But I've got to take care of something else. Attorney Carter said first that Mister Brantley was safeguarding his hold on his paramour—and then contradicted himself by saying that the defendant married Miss Williamson because he was drunk. I'm going to finish the job, with the Court's permission—even if this line of questioning doesn't seem exactly germane. We believe in the sanctity of womanhood down here, Your Honor—and I mean to see that no slur is cast upon this woman whose only mistake has been to underestimate our feeble understanding—and who has committed no sins!" Then he turned to the bailiff. "Call Mrs. Courtland Brantley to the stand," he said.

Fancy got up. She could feel the trembling down inside her. The way the people looked at her! Like—like their eyes were hot. She understood why Bob McCullen had gone so far as to pick out her dress. It was black and plain and simple. He'd even made her brush her hair down tight, too, so that her face looked like a child's.

"Mrs. Brantley," McCullen said, "what exactly was the relationship between you and Duke Ellis?"

"There wasn't any," Fancy said. "I met him when I first came to town. He made a big fuss over me—bought me things, made out like he aimed to marry me. Then he tried to get me to drink liquor, and grabbed me—I—I—got away from him and ran. That was how I met Mister Weathers."

"I see," Bob McCullen said. "Why did you come to Augusta, Mrs. Brantley?"

Fancy told him, trying hard to use proper speech. She could see after a while that folks were believing her. Some of the women were crying, as she told how she ran away from a loveless marriage, only to land in even worse trouble.

"Reckon I was foolish," she said; "but I'm a hill girl, with no booklearning, and I thought folks mostly meant what they said. I trusted Duke Ellis, and I was wrong. Then I trusted Mister Weathers, but that time I was right."

She told them about her travels with Wyche. How he'd respected her, given her her own private quarters, protected her from bad men. He'd asked to marry her, but by that time she'd met Court Brantley. She told them how she hated to do that dance, but she didn't know any other way of making money—and there were worse ways.

"What I didn't figure," she said in a barely audible voice, "was because I did something that looked wicked, folks would think I had to be bad. . . ."

She straightened up and looked at the hushed spectators.

"There's one thing I'd like to say," she said quietly; "I hope Your Honor'll forgive me if it ain't in order. I'd like to ask you folks, all of you, to give me a chance. You've got fathers and brothers and husbands to take care of anybody who uses your name in public. I—I haven't anybody. The things I've done came of not knowing—not out of badness. Didn't know what they'd lead to—didn't realize that my husband's life could be put in danger because he tried to protect me; that a whole case could turn on whether or not I was worth protecting. That wasn't a fight 'twixt two men over a—a street woman. That was a man trying to defend his home."

She had them now, and Carter saw it. He was on his feet crying, "Object, object!" before she could finish her words.

"Overruled," Judge Richardson said.

"Mrs. Brantley," Bob McCullen said, "was the night of your marriage the first time Court Brantley had asked you to marry him?"

"No sir. It was the second."

"What happened the first time?"

"I—I turned him down. Not because I didn't love him. I did—I do—so much! But because he asked me for the wrong reasons. Had an argument about something with his brother Phil, and Phil made a remark about me. Court was set to show him—to show the whole town. But I couldn't marry him because he wanted to show people. It had to be because he loved me—no other reason."

"I see—but you were convinced he did love you, after you and his sister had sobered him up that night with black coffee, and he asked you again?"

"Yes. I tried to let him alone before. But every time I saw him, I loved him more and more. And then I saw some other girls paying attention to him, even some who had no business to, 'cause they were already married, and I got so jealous I thought I'd die. So I got real riled up and had some hard words with him, but he only laughed at me for being so foolish. But, Your Honor, I was so sad and mixed up 'cause I thought I'd lost him, that I told him I was going to be like the rest of the Brantley women, and I ran and jumped in the river. Court saved my life then. . . ."

"Your Honor," McCullen put in smoothly, "we are prepared to introduce two dozen corroborating witnesses, who saw the defendant walking through the streets dripping wet with Miss Williamson in his arms."

"That won't be necessary," Judge Richardson declared. "Proceed," he added.

"That was when he decided to marry me. Reckon that kind of forced him into it—'cause I really ain't his kind, and Court could have most any girl he wanted. But afterwards, he was so good to me! He knew I didn't know anything, so every night he would sit down and bring out the McGuffey Reader and teach me to read and spell and even to figger a little. . . ."

"And this, Your Honor," McCullen said, "was the marriage that my distinguished opponent would have you believe was no marriage at all! This tender, heart-warming romance, in which a man of honor tried to lift up a simple, lovely woman to his own high estate in life! This is what Prosecutor Carter tries to reduce to mere bestial lust! Your witness, Counselor! I'll get back to the night of September 7th, after a while."

Granville Carter stood up. Fancy thought his face looked ugly.

"Mrs. Brantley," he said, "I'm not going to take you back over the points that my opponent has introduced so skillfully—though I doubt most of them. I'm going to take up the night of September 7th, 1880—a few hours before the murder. Isn't it a fact," he thundered, "that you spent those hours away from home—in the company of the murdered man? Answer me, isn't it? And isn't it also a fact that your husband, along with half a dozen other citizens, whom I have here in this Court, and whom I will call upon to testify, saw you riding through the streets at a most unseemly hour in the buggy with Duke Hently Ellis? Did he not then follow you home from your rendezvous with the man who, despite all testimony to the contrary, had once been very dear to you? And did not the fatal shooting take place," Carter paused, spacing his words with terrible clarity, "in the bedroom of your home?"

Fancy looked at Bob McCullen. He was grinning. Carter had slipped his head into a noose of his own making.

She looked the prosecutor straight in the face.

"I was in Duke's buggy that night, late. That's true. And he was killed in my bedroom. That's true, too. But none of the rest of the things you've said. Not one of 'em is true. . . ."

"Ha!" Carter exploded; "you expect anyone to believe that?"

"Yessir," Fancy said evenly, "I do. I'm not quality. Never learned how to lie and cheat like quality folks do. Folks who know me, know that."

"Then maybe," Granville Carter sneered, "you'd better tell us exactly where you were."

"I was at the house of a colored woman named Belle Fisher. Her baby was sick. I got Doctor Benton to come and 'tend to it. Then I 'tended to it myself until after midnight. . . ."

"You can prove this, Mrs. Brantley?" Judge Richardson asked.

"Yes, Your Honor."

Bob McCullen stood up.

"If Your Honor will allow the irregularity, I'd like to make a motion that Belle Fisher and Doctor Benton be called to the stand."

"Permission granted," Judge Richardson said.

Fancy kept watching Court's face during their testimonies. It was stony, unchanging. He doesn't believe them, she cried inside her heart, he thinks they're put up to say that!

But Carter was not satisfied. He called Fancy back to the stand.

"I think," he said, "that the Court would still like to know what you were doing in Duke Ellis' buggy."

"I was walking home from Belle's. It was late, and I was tired. Duke came by and offered me a ride home. Spoke real nice, but I didn't trust him, not at first. Then he swore by his mother that he'd be good and take me home. After we got there, he told me that he hadn't sworn anything about after that. Then he picked me up and walked into the house with me. That was when Court came home. . . ."

Carter dismissed her. Then Bob McCullen called Court once more to the stand.

"I found my wife," Court said, "struggling in Duke Ellis' arms. I started to kill him then. But Duke asked for a chance. . . ." Then he told the story of the duel in the dark. He didn't say anything much about his wound; but McCullen dragged that in, too. The lawyer called Doctor Brewster to the stand.

"An inch lower, and it would have been fatal," the old doctor said. "As it was, Court had damned near bled to death when he got to me. Pretty brave boy, I'd say—walked all the way up to Sheriff Bowen's and back to the house with the sheriff without saying a word about a wound of a type that three times in my experience I've seen put men in their graves. Obviously Ellis fired first, because Court's bullets killed him instantly—he couldn't have fired that shot after he'd been hit."

Sheriff Bowen was next. He testified that Court had made no effort to run away, that he had reported the killing to him, and had given up his gun without protest. He described the scene at the house, and stuck to every detail under Carter's furious cross questioning.

Carter was beaten and he knew it. But he tried hard. He called back every witness. He tried to find holes in the testimony. He kept it up so long that Bob McCullen was moved to drop a bombshell. He asked the Court's permission to call Sary Ellis, Duke's mother, to the stand.

As the tiny, frail old woman took her seat, there was not a sound in the courtroom. Looking at her, Fancy thought, Oh no, this is mean, this is too mean, not that poor old lady, grieving for her boy. . . .

"Mrs. Ellis," McCullen said, "I'm sorry to have to call on you. I sympathize, and I'm sure everyone here sympathizes with your grief. You're a good woman, and a fine mother. I called on you because I know you're not vengeful—that you don't want to see a man punished unjustly, not even over your son.

"But the prosecution has tried to color the whole case with the idea that your boy was only trying to take back a woman who'd been his common-law wife. Mrs. Ellis, this is painful, I know; but you and your son were unusually close. How much did you know of Duke's private life?"

"Everything," Sary Ellis said tiredly; "Duke warn't close-mouthed."

"You knew about Myrtie Torrence?"

"Yessir. Him and me had words over that. Tried to get him to straighten up and do right."

"Then you—didn't agree with your son's behavior?"

"No, sir. Duke was mighty wild. Knew he'd get hisself kilt if he kept it up. Cried over that boy many a night—over all my boys. . . ."

"Your Honor!" Carter spluttered, "I—"

"Sit down, Attorney," Judge Richardson snapped. "The testimony is germane. You introduced this line of questioning yourself."

McCullen smiled.

"Mrs. Ellis, did your son at any time say anything that led you to believe that a—relationship existed between him and Miss Williamson?"

"No, sir. He was all steamed up over that. Said she'd balked him. Said she was the sweetest, best lil' gal he ever did know, and that he'd even get hitched with her before he'd let anybody else have her. 'Maw,' he used to say, 'you ought to meet her. She's driving me wild. . . . Done looked all over the State for her, and ever' time, I just misses her. But she's a-coming here,' he said—'then I'm going to get her. Going to bring her here for you to see. She ain't like my other gals,' he said. 'Maw, you'll just love her.' "

The old woman turned and looked at Fancy, seeing her sitting there, crying from joy. "I kind of reckon he was right," she said sadly. "That little girl would of been the making of him. . . ."

The jury was out less than five minutes.

They filed back in, and Fancy strained forward, a tiny white line around the corners of her mouth.

"We find the defendant," the foreman said, "not guilty!"

Fancy collapsed against Wyche's shoulder, shaking all over. Then all the people started shouting and laughing and crying at the same time, and men fought their way forward to shake Court Brantley's hand.

Court shook hands with them, thinking: you polecats. You'd have watched me hang with just as much glee. It was a good show, wasn't it? Either way it came out it was a good show, and none of you, not a clinking one gives two hoots up a hollow stump that it was my life that was in balance here. . . .

When he left the courtroom, a free man, he saw Wyche Weathers waiting for him with Fancy. Tyler and Philemon were there, and several other men —friends and schoolmates of his.

"Heard tell," Wyche said, after he'd almost broken Court's hand in his grip, "that Tom and Rad Ellis and a bunch of their cronies is out to get you. Me'n' the boys decided to walk you and Fan home, and stay there with you tonight, seeing that you're in no fit condition to defend yourself."

Court looked at Fancy and frowned.

"Thanks, Wyche," he said. "That's mighty decent of youall."

"I'd like to be excused, if you don't mind, Court," Tyler said. "Got a little crow to pick with that there shyster, Carter."

"No you don't!" Court said. "There's been killing enough, Ty. You come along with the rest. It's been a long time since I had a chance to talk to you fellows, anyhow. . . ."

" 'Pears to me," Nick Cohen drawled, "that we might not have to sit up tonight after all. Them Ellises ain't waiting for night. Here they come now."

Fancy saw them, then, heading toward the place where she stood with Court and the others. Tom Ellis was leading them, and behind him came old Rad.

The crowd that still packed the courthouse square fell apart. Fancy saw men pushing their womenfolks into buggies, and fat, rich-looking men running off like clumsy bulls.

Tom came on, drawing ahead of his followers.

"We want Court Brantley," he said. "And we aim to get him. You fellows give him up peaceable like, and won't nobody git hurt."

Wyche stepped out of the group.

"Now do tell!" he drawled. "Reckon I'd better tell you a thing or two, Tom. Court was tried fair and square for killing that hound dog of a brother of yours, and acquitted by due process of law. That's enough for me and every other law-abiding citizen in this here town. We ain't giving him up, Tom. And you and them rednecks you got with you better turn right around and git out of town while you can. . . ."

"Take care how you talk, Wyche," Tom said. "They's more of us—and we're armed."

Wyche loosened his frock coat so that the butt of his big revolver showed plainly in its holster under his armpit.

"Reckon you think we ain't?" he said quietly. "Another thing, Tom. You'n' your brothers have made this town a mighty unpleasant place for decent folks ever since you come out of them backwoods where you belong.

We'd be mighty happy to be rid of you Ellises once and for all. There's more'n twenty-five men here, and I'm going to tell 'em right now that if you start anything half of 'em is to aim for you, and the other half for old Rad. And out of all these fellows, somebody ain't a-going to miss. Reckon I've said my say. You want Court, here—come and get him!"

Fancy moved over to where Court stood and put her arm through his. He didn't move. Then he put his hand up and pushed her hand down and away from his side.

Tom stood there, staring at Wyche.

They're nothing, Fancy thought. Like Court said, without Duke, they're nothing.

"You win—this time," Tom said. "But you ain't heard the last of this, Court Brantley—you neither, Wyche!"

"I'll wait," Wyche said.

"I feel like a fool," Court said, "standing here letting you stick up for me like that, Wyche. Don't reckon you fellows will have to stand guard over me tonight. Those yellow polecats won't come back."

"Don't think they will," Wyche agreed; "but Ty and Phil and me'll walk you home just the same. And we'll kind of set on the porch. The rest of y'all hear any shooting tonight, come a-running—all right?"

"All right," the others said. "So long, Court. So long, Ma'am—good luck."

Luck, Fancy thought bitterly; I'll need luck. He ain't right yet. Wouldn't let me take his arm—even after what Maw Ellis said. . . .

"Don't mean to horn in on your talk with Fan, Court," Wyche said; "but I got to get back home. I got some business to talk over with you. Fan showed me that Dry Gully of yours, while you were in jail. That's the best damned mill site I ever did see. How much will you take for it?"

"It's not for sale, Wyche," Court said.

"Didn't think you would sell it, and I don't blame you. All right then, boy—here's another proposition. How about letting me advance you the money for that mill? I don't even want it all back. I aim to keep a minority share in the concern—that's how good I think the chances are."

"No, thank you, Wyche," Court said quietly, "I owe you enough already."

Wyche stared at him.

"You owe me?" he said. "For what?"

"Those witnesses you bought. Belle. Doc Benton. Maybe even old lady Ellis. They must have cost you plenty, Wyche. I'm grateful, of course. You did it for Fan—I know that. Even so it was mighty handsome of you, 'cause it was your chance to have me out of your way."

Wyche's big fist doubled. Then he loosened his fingers, slowly.

"You better thank God for that bad arm, boy," he said quietly. "I sure

Lord was tempted to separate your fool head from your worthless shoulders."

He looked over at Fan, seeing her face white, the look in her eyes like that in a trapped animal's, dying in terrible pain.

"I withdraw my offer," he said. "But I'm going to make another one—for Fan's sake. Since you've shown me that you ain't got sense enough to appreciate what you've got, I'll put it this way: I'll advance to Mrs. Courtland Brantley, any time she wants it, the entire amount of money needed to build a textile plant in Dry Gully—that mill to remain in her possession, and in the hands of her heirs—forever. She can hire you as general manager, if she wants to. She can even sell or assign you a minority share. But it's got to be down in black and white that Fan keeps the controlling interest. Because I don't trust you, Court Brantley. I don't think you're wicked. You're something worse—you're a fool."

Court looked at Fancy, mockery in his eyes.

"Well, Fan," he said bitingly; "want to be a rich mill owner?"

Fancy didn't answer him. She was looking straight at Wyche.

"No, Wyche," she said; "not like that. It's got to be Court's."

"Pearls," Wyche said bitterly, "at the feet of swine." Then he turned and marched away from them.

"Ty," Fancy whispered, "Phil—I don't think they'll come back. I want to be alone with Court for a while. He's got a gun. If you hear shooting, you can come with the others. . . . All right?"

"All right," Tyler growled; "but I don't like it. I don't like it at all." He looked at his younger brother. "For the record, boy," he said, "Wyche is right. You're a fool."

Then he and Philemon turned and went away together.

Inside the house, Fancy came up to Court and stood there looking at him.

"Court—" she said.

Court didn't answer her.

"I'm glad you got off," Fancy said breathlessly. "I reckon I would of died if they had sent you to jail or—oh, Court . . ."

Court moved past her deliberately and sat down in his big chair. Fancy moved over and stood in front of him. Court didn't even look at her. He groped in his pocket with his one good hand and came out with a cigar. At once Fancy ran into the kitchen and came back with a match. She lit it, and held it out.

Court drew his head back and looked at the match in her hand until it burned down to her fingertips. She dropped it, shaking her hand, and blowing on her burned fingers. Then he put his hand in his pocket and came out with his own matches and lit his cigar. He shook the match out and threw it out into the yard. Fancy came up to him in a rush and put her arms about his neck.

"Court," she whispered; "I'm so glad you're safe. Oh, Court, honey, I'm so glad!"

Court put up his right hand, and locked the fingers around the flesh of her arm. Then very slowly he pulled her arm away from him.

Fancy stood there looking at him. Then, very quietly, she turned and walked into the bedroom, and closed the door behind her. She lay there all night, awake, listening every time he moved in the big chair in the next room. Then, just before morning, she got up again.

She came into the room, and walked over to the chair. He was awake, but he didn't move. Fancy bent down and took the dead stump of the cigar out of his mouth. Then she kissed him, achingly, longingly.

Court's mouth was as cold as death.

Fancy stood there looking at him, trying to keep from crying.

He got up out of the chair, easing his heavily bandaged left arm up with the aid of his right hand. For a moment, pain showed in his eyes. Then he straightened up and went on out the door.

It was quiet in the room after he had gone. Fancy stood in the middle of the room for a long time. Then she couldn't stand up any more so she went and sat down in his big chair. She sat very still, with her hands on the two arms of the chair and stared out into the empty yard.

And the sun came up over the chinaberry tree like a blast of trumpets.

10

It wasn't until she saw Jed Hawkins coming up the path toward the house that Fancy remembered that he had been at the trial. That wasn't strange, after all that had happened. She watched him coming toward the porch, and she didn't move. Her mind was too sunk in dull misery for that. Court was gone—God knew where—hating her, believing her guilty of all the ugly things that Lawyer Carter had said about her. All she could think of, seeing Jed now, was that he had acted mighty funny afterwards.

He hadn't come forward like Wyche and the other men to help Court out. She hadn't even seen him after the trial. He had simply slipped into the crowd and disappeared. Wouldn't have done Jed any good to try to help, Fancy thought. Court would have just spoke mean to him like he did to Wyche and made one more enemy. And Court had enemies enough already—all the Brantleys did. Still it was mighty ungentlemanly of Jed not to help. But then she stopped thinking about it altogether because Jed was standing there on the porch looking at her.

He wasn't smiling, and that made him almost a stranger. He had the kind of a face that was meant to smile. When it was serious he looked different somehow. Older—harder, she couldn't decide. . . .

"Fan," he said.

"Yes, Jed?"

"Heard that husband of yours had left you. That so?"

"Yes, Jed."

"Good. Good riddance for bad rubbish. Listen, Fan. . . ."

"I'm listening," Fancy said.

"Damn! When you look at me like that you make it hard for me to talk. My tongue gets thick. And I'm supposed to be the original silver-tongued boy. . . ."

"Get to the point, Jed."

He leaned forward and took her hands.

"Come with me, Fan," he said tensely.

Fancy tried to pull her hands back, but she couldn't. He was holding them too tight.

"I'm a married woman, Jed," Fancy said. "You want to make of me all the things that mean old lawyer said?"

"Heaven forbid. Look, Fan, let's reason this thing out. You're married—legally, technically. Only you ain't—not by a long shot, when your husband gets in a huff and leaves you. I'm a lawyer, remember. Even under the law that changes things. I've got friends in high places. This here marriage of yours can be dissolved because of Court Brantley's action. I'm not asking you to do anything dishonorable. Appears to me all the dirty tricks have been done to you already."

Fancy didn't say anything. She just sat there looking at him.

"I don't want to make a mistress of you. If I wanted a mistress, you think I couldn't have half a dozen right now?"

"No," Fancy said, "I don't think that."

"All I want you to do is to come with me to Atlanta. I'll put you in a nice respectable boarding house with a bunch of other working girls. Woman there watches over them better'n their own mothers would. Then I'll petition the Supreme Court for an annulment or a divorce. And I'll get it for you, too. Then, after a decent interval, you'n'me can get hitched—

legal and proper. And damn it, honey, we'll stay hitched until Gabriel blows that horn of his. . . . Come on, Fan—what do you say?"

"No, Jed."

Jed stared at her, wonderingly.

"Why not, Fan?"

"He—might come back," Fancy said.

"Good God!" Jed exploded. "Hell, Fan, where's your pride?"

"Haven't any. People in love never do."

"Oh, damn!" Jed Hawkins said. He straightened up, and watched her face. "All right," he said, "but I'm not giving up, Fan. I'll wait. You just might change your mind. . . . I don't believe you dislike me."

"No," Fancy said, "I like you very much."

"Thanks," Jed said drily. "That gives me a hell of a lot of hope. Anyhow, just in case you do change your mind, I'll give you my address in Savannah."

"I don't want it," Fancy said. "I'm not going to change my mind."

"Suppose he doesn't come back?"

"No, Jed."

"Fan, honey—isn't there any way on earth . . ."

"Yes, Jed. Just one. If you ever hear that I'm a widow—wait two, three years, then ask me again. I like you a lot—better'n anybody else next to Court, except maybe Wyche . . ."

"Third fiddle!" Jed groaned; "that's a fine thing."

"No—second maybe. I don't like Wyche that way. He's a fine man—a mite too fine for me, maybe. He's like a big brother—or a father. Don't think I could ever think of him any other way. . . ."

"'For this relief, much thanks,'" Jed quoted bitterly. "So now I'm supposed to spend my life waiting around for somebody to shoot that Brantley polecat."

"You aren't supposed to spend your life doing anything as far as I'm concerned," Fancy said. "Your life's your own, Jed Hawkins. Smart thing for you to do is to forget all about me. Find yourself some nice, sweet little girl and . . ."

"You stop talking damned foolishness, Fan."

"What's foolish about that?"

"Everything. You've got me as mixed up as a snake-bit hound dog baying a summer moon. Got your face in my eyes like two silver pennies. I'm blind, honey. Every time I look at another woman, all I see is—you."

"I'm sorry, Jed."

"Don't be. Loving you is a kind of a glory. Living on like this, hoping against hope, is God-damned awful, but I wouldn't live any other way. Every morning is a new day, and the sun comes a-blazing with hope. I keep telling myself, today it'll happen—something will change, something will. . . ."

"But it won't, Jed," Fancy said; "you've got to see that."

"I'm blind, honey," Jed said. "I told you that before. 'Bye, now. I've bothered you enough for one day."

Fancy didn't think about him much after he had gone. All she could think was: Where is Court? Where is he now—right now, this minute? What's he doing, thinking, feeling . . . ?

Court Brantley at that moment stood in the cupola above the dome of the State House and looked out over Boston. He did this every time he came there. It was a kind of a ritual with him. He had been in the city three days now, but this was the first time he had gotten the chance to do it.

Maybe that's why I haven't had any luck, he thought. Hope this changes it. God knows it needs to change. . . .

He looked down on the Common, seeing most of the expanse of fifty acres that slopes down from the State House to Boylston and Tremont Streets. He could see the broad estuary of the Charles, with the Harvard crews rowing on it, and he had almost the feeling of being home.

He couldn't see Harvard from where he stood. It was too far away; but he had visited the campus already, walking the lanes alone, looking at the place where of all his life he had been happiest. Court loved Boston. It was the only city he could ever remember where he had been entirely at peace. There was something about the old city, with its rows of well-built brownstone and brick houses, each with its two squares of neatly trimmed grass between it and the street, and all the quiet, cultured people he had grown to like so well, once their almost impenetrable armor of reserve had been broken through. Life went smoothly here; he had been a fool ever to leave it. He could remember how the quiet and dignified servants had opened the doors for him in the homes of his friends; homes so solid and forbidding from the outside, yet radiating warmth and welcome on the inside. He remembered his friend, Stan Woodbury, standing under the plaster cast of the *Winged Victory* of Samothrace on the high, marble mantel, and lifting his glass of steaming punch to drink his health.

Those were good memories. Much better than his last ones. But he didn't like to think about that.

As he came down into the street, he had the feeling once more that he had behaved badly—that Wyche hadn't lied and Belle hadn't lied and Doc Benton hadn't lied and that nobody had paid them. Fan—least of all had she lied. He couldn't explain it even to himself: the wave of revulsion that had risen up in him afterwards, the natural, instinctive Brantley cruelty.

Well, it was done now. Fan was down in Augusta and he was in Boston—more than a thousand miles away. He'd come to get backers for his mill. Afterwards, I'll make it up to her, he thought. Poor kid, she's sure seen hell on account of me. . . .

He started walking rapidly toward State Street, where the business offices of Woodbury Textiles Incorporated, were. Stanton had slid easily into the position his father had reserved for him. And, Court had found out, he had done well. His fortune, now, was one of Boston's largest.

Court arrived with minutes to spare. But the bespectacled young man who served Stanton as clerk and receptionist did not keep him waiting. He had, he informed Court, orders to show Mister Brantley in at once.

Stanton Woodbury stood up the moment Court entered the oak-paneled office, his hand outthrust. He had put on flesh with the years, but his ruddy face was the picture of health.

"Court!" he said. "This is a pleasure!"

Court took the hand Stan put out to him and shook it hard.

"Sit down," Stanton said. "Have a cigar. They're good Havanas right off the very last boat."

Court took the cigar and sank down in one of the leather-covered chairs.

"It's good to see you, Stan," he said quietly.

"Same old Court," Stanton said cheerfully. "A little thinner, maybe. Big a devil as ever, I'll bet. They'll never forget you at Harvard, Courtland."

"I was kind of hoping they would," Court grinned.

"We'll have to get together and talk over the old days," Stanton said. "But Rileton, my clerk, says you wanted to see me on business. What's it all about?"

"I've been trying to raise the money to build a textile mill, near my home in Georgia. So far—no luck. I need a lot of money—nearly a hundred thousand. People don't listen to that big a proposition easily, Stanton. I've been trying for years. I've seen every man of wealth in the whole South. No luck. It's a perfectly safe deal, Stan. With cotton growing right in my back yard, the mill would show a fantastic profit. Labor's cheaper down home, too; but you know all that. The point is, as I said before, it's a perfectly safe investment; but I've been turned down all over town, and I don't know why. So I thought of you. Would you consider it, Stan?"

The smile left Stanton's face, and he looked at Court, soberly, seriously.

"The answer, old boy," he said quietly, "is no. But I'm going to be a little different from the others. I'm going to tell you why. And after that, I'm going to make you a counter-proposition. All right?"

"Shoot," Court said.

"Since you Southerners got interested in textile manufacture, we've lost a fistful of money here in New England. The conditions down there all favor you: climate, cheap labor, and accessibility of raw materials. If we could compete with you on anything like an even basis, I'd let you have the money in a minute. But, Court, I think that when you consider the matter, you'll see that it just isn't sound business to finance something that's going to cut your own throat."

"So," Court said, "that's it!"

"That's it, all right. I'm sorry to have to tell you that you haven't a Chinaman's chance of raising that money in Boston. Give it up, Court—it's a bad deal."

"I reckon I'll have to," Court said sadly, "if that's the way it is."

"That's the way it is. But don't look so downcast, old boy. To me, you're a gift from the gods!"

"What do you mean, Stan?"

"My manager in chief of all my mills has just retired. He was a crotchety old beggar anyhow; I'm glad to be rid of him. But I've been driving myself mad trying to find a man to replace him. Court, old boy, the job is yours if you want it. You know more about mills than I'll ever learn. I'll give you fifteen thousand dollars a year to start with. What do you say?"

Court frowned.

"Damned if I know what to say. I've been offered three jobs since I've been calling on folks trying to raise that money. I turned them all down because I thought that I would be able to raise it, finally. But now, I don't know. . . ."

"Believe me, Court, you won't be able to," Stanton said seriously. "It's a good position and I don't believe you can call the pay bad. Besides, it would be wonderful if we could make a proper Bostonian of you. This town needs a little of your spirit. What do you say?"

Court got up slowly.

"Give me a couple of days to think about it, won't you, Stan? If I take that job, it's going to change my whole life. A man oughtn't to do a thing like that too fast."

"Right you are, old boy," Stanton Woodbury said cheerfully. "You can drop in on me here when you've made up your mind. Or you can telephone me. The office has one of those infernal machines, now. Ah, progress! By the way, Court—where are you staying?"

"The Vendome," Court said. "See you, Stan."

He didn't go back to the hotel at once. Instead he went back to the Common and sat down on a bench. Near him a group of children were feeding the pigeons. It was a clear, autumn day, with just a hint of a bite to it. Court stared straight ahead of him without seeing anything at all. He sat there until he began to feel stiff, then he got up and started up Beacon Hill. That part of the Hill had already been overrun by the Irish. If the signs meant anything, the rest of it would go, too. No longer would it be the dwelling place of aristocrat, poet, philosopher, and sage. The old order changeth, he mused. But not to change was, in the long run, a kind of death. . . .

I've changed, he thought. I've gotten harder, and meaner'n Satan himself. . . .

But for the life of him, he couldn't come to any decision about the job. I could send for Fan, he thought; nobody knows her here, and it would be much better. . . . But he couldn't make up his mind. Maybe, he thought, because I don't really want to make it up. . . . So he turned and went back toward the Vendome.

As the hotel came in sight, a sudden oddity of memory struck him. Martha, his sister-in-law, had asked him where he would be staying in Boston. On the surface, there was nothing queer about that. Nothing—but the way she had asked it. A little too intensely. A mite too much interest. Then it was a little strange that she had asked him at all. Martha Brantley wasn't going to write him any letters. Phil, either. The Brantleys never wrote letters. Then why the dickens had she wanted to know?

He had asked her that same question, and her answer was queerer than her question: "I've got reasons," Martha had said.

He shook his head, thinking about it. Women loved to appear mysterious. Once inside the hotel, he dismissed the matter from his mind and went straight to his room. He pulled off his shoes, his coat, and his tie, and stretched out on the bed, staring at the ceiling.

It was a hard decision to make. He had dreamed about that mill so long. Even when he'd been an undergraduate at Harvard, he'd haunted textile mills, and learned all he could. Afterwards he'd worked for Jonathon Snow and really learned the business. Then there had been the trips to Atlanta, Savannah, Macon—even Charleston, all failures. He hadn't wanted to come North for capital. He had wanted to keep the Yankee mill owners out of it. But they were the only people he knew who might be interested. Or so he had thought.

Of course, he could get the money from Wyche Weathers. Or rather, Fan could. But he couldn't do that. It was unthinkable. You didn't take money from a man who is in love with your wife. Not even from a man like Wyche, who almost certainly would never try to do anything about the way he felt. And the terms Wyche had set were downright insulting.

I insulted him first, Court thought bitterly, reckon he had a right to hit back at me. . . .

The half healed wound in his shoulder ached dully. His head ached, too. Groaning, he got up from the bed, and picked up a glass from the dresser. He opened his valise, and took out the bottle of bourbon. But he never got it open, partly because it was a hard thing to do with no strength in his left hand, and partly because a bellboy knocked on his door while he was still trying to get it open.

"Lady to see you, sir," the bellboy said. "Downstairs in the lobby."

Court groped in his pocket and tipped him. Then he put his shoes and his tie and his coat back on. It took him a long time because his left hand was awkward and weak. And all that time he was thinking, Now who the blazes? Can't be Hester, because I heard yesterday that she'd married Horace Clayton. All the rest of the girls I knew here didn't know me well enough to look me up at my hotel. Come to think of it, that's a funny thing for any Boston girl to do. . . .

But he was halfway down the stairs before it hit him. No Boston girl. No girl reared in the rock-ribbed conservatism for which Boston was famous would even think of such a thing. But a girl who'd lived all her life outside the pale of society because of the fact that her father had been a New Englander and a carpetbagger, might think of anything. "They trailed her as far as Boston," Tyler had said. "Then they lost her. Boston. That's what made me think it was you."

She stood up as he came into the lobby, and extended one small, gloved hand.

" 'Lo, Court," she said.

Court didn't answer her. He just stood there looking at her. She was dressed all in brown and the color became her. It matched her eyes, for Fern was one of those rare blondes with brown eyes so dark they look almost black. Her brown velvet hat had red and yellow artificial flowers in it. The angle it was cocked at above her silvery blonde hair was damnable, Court thought. She had on a brown plush pelisse instead of a coat, with big sleeves that fitted the upper part of her arms, the rest of the sleeves forming the back and sides of the cape itself. It was trimmed with brown beaver fur. So was her skirt. Her collar was beaver, too. It fitted close around her neck. She'd tied it with a tie of light brown silk. As she came toward him, Court could hear the ruffles of her silk petticoat rustle as she walked.

"I said, hello, Court," she whispered.

"Come on," Court said, "let's get out of here."

He stepped to the edge of the sidewalk to call a cab, but she stopped him.

"I have a buggy," she said. "There it is—over there."

Court looked at it. It was a smart little rig—spanking new. The horse that drew it was something, too.

"I see," he said; "you're making your stay here—permanent."

"Yes, Court."

Court helped her up into the buggy, then he climbed up beside her.

"Suppose," he growled, "I were to write Ty. . . ."

Fern smiled at him.

"You won't do that," she said. Then she flapped the reins over the horse's back.

Court didn't say anything. He sat back watching her. It came to him that Fern knew Boston as well as he did. She paused at Old North Church, from whose tower Paul Revere's lanterns had been hung. Then she turned the horse slightly eastward to Old South Church and the State House from whose balcony the Declaration of Independence had been proclaimed. They stopped at the Granary Burial Ground, almost under the shadow of the tower of the Park Street Congregational Church that Sir Christopher Wren had designed.

"I want to stop here," Fern said.

Court stared at her. Then he got down and swung her down after him. She took his arm, keeping the other hand in the fur muff and they went through the graveyard together. Court looked at the headstones. They were weathered, chipped, brown. And on nearly every one in this section was the name, Vance. Most of the dates were from the time of the Revolution or even before. Three of the stones listed battles in which the men lying below had been killed.

"Funny," Court said, "I never realized. . . ."

"That Father was a Bostonian? It isn't strange. Nobody ever bothered to find out anything good about us. The Vances of Boston. Only I was born in Augusta, Georgia, of a Southern mother, who hated my father."

"My God," Court said. Then: "Are all your folks buried here?"

"No," Fern said. "Only the first ones—and not all of them. Some of them are over there. . . ."

She pointed to King's Chapel, not a stone's throw away. King's Chapel, Court knew, had been the church of the Tories.

"King's men, eh?" he said.

"Yes, Court. Your precious Civil War that you Southerners will never be done with fighting wasn't the only one in which brother took up arms against brother. Two of my great granduncles died in the same battle—on opposite sides. I only hope they didn't kill each other. Come on, let's go."

"You had a point," Court said, "in bringing me here."

"Yes. Boston is my home. It always has been, I reckon. Father used to bring me here often as a child. He left me a brownstone—on the Hill. And a trust fund that'll take care of me the rest of my life. Here, I have friends—like the Woodburys. I'm accepted. . . ."

Court stopped her.

"Did Stanton tell you that I—"

"No, Court. I had a wire before you even left Augusta."

Court stared at her.

"Martha!" he exclaimed.

"Yes, dear—Martha. She hates Ty almost as much as I do. She hates all the Brantleys, including that precious husband of hers—except you. She thinks that you and I were made for each other. I agree with her."

"But," Court said, "I have a wife. You have a husband."

"I know," Fern said. "Come on."

They rode toward the Charles. Neither of them said anything.

Court put out his hand and laid it on Fern's arm.

"All right, Fern," he said. "Speak your piece."

"All right," Fern sighed. "You have a wife. I have a husband. Let's take them up in that order. Your wife. A nobody from the Carolina hills. A medicine-wagon mountebank who danced nude before hundreds of men."

"Not nude," Court said.

"Almost. Required precious little imagination on their part. Duke Ellis' mistress. Wyche Weathers' mistress. Your mistress. Your marrying her, Court, was one of the most fantastic businesses I ever heard of. . . ."

"Go on," Court said grimly.

"A woman who made you do murder. Who nearly got you killed. The list is endless, but that's enough. Too much, to my way of thinking."

"And Ty?" Court said.

"A drunkard. A balding satyr. An ugly egotist who imagines himself to be God's gift to women. . . ."

"You married him, remember."

"I know. On the rebound, Court. I was a fool."

"Go on."

"A man whose manners would disgrace a pig. Sloppy, unkempt. Loud, boorish, vain. A man," Fern paused, looked at him, "who isn't even a man any more. Not even half a man. . . ."

"What the devil do you mean, Fern?"

"You stopped in New York for a week, didn't you?"

"Yes, why? I was laid up—my arm went back on me. What's that got to do with it?"

"Tyler stayed in Augusta. He made all his trips between Riley's and Hiberion on that big Morgan of yours. Somebody—who didn't know you were out of town, took a shot at him. You do look alike, you know. And everybody knows that horse. In the dark it must have been easy for him to get confused."

"You're lying," Court got out. "Dammit, Fern, you're lying."

"No, Court. Martha wired me this morning. Told me to tell you. The man who shot at him didn't hit him. Only that Morgan of yours reared and threw him—not all the way. His foot got caught in the stirrups. The animal dragged him half a mile. His back is broken—he'll be paralyzed from the waist down—the rest of his life. . . ."

Court stared at her.

"And your reaction to the news," he said flatly, "is to desert him."

"I'd done that already. I see no reason to go back, now. Pity is a kind of sentimentality I can't afford, darling. The point, Court, which you've been so stubbornly evading, is that there's no reason for your going back. I had dinner with the Woodburys last night. I dropped a hint or two that you'd do admirably for that manager's job Stan is trying to fill. Stan was delighted. And what makes it perfect, Court, is the fact—" She stopped, looking at him.

"I'll bite, Fern. What makes it so perfect?"

"The fact that nobody in Boston, so far as I know, has the slightest idea that you're married. Do they, Court?"

"No," Court said. "Not a living soul in this whole blamed town." Then very quietly he got down from the buggy.

"There's a word," he said, "for what you're suggesting, Fern."

"There is? What is it, darling?"

"Bigamy," Court said.

"A word," Fern said tensely, "made up of sounds, letters, syllables. Meaning as little as any other word. Meaning nothing considered against the actuality of—us."

Court lifted his broad-brimmed hat.

"Good-bye, Fern," he said.

"Where are you going?" Fern said.

"Back to the hotel. Then home. I'm going to see what can be done for Ty. I'm going to ask my wife to forgive me." He smiled, suddenly. "She should be grateful to you. You've made me appreciate her."

Fern shrugged.

"A risk I had to take," she said calmly. "But don't say good-bye, Court. Good-bye is the wrong word."

"Why is it, Fern?"

"Because you'll come back." She pulled at the reins, turning the horse gently around in the direction from which they had come. When she had him all the way around, she pulled up, briefly.

"Oh yes, Court," she said; "you'll come back." Then she drove off in the direction of Beacon Hill.

"Fan," Tyler said, "I'm dry as a bone. Get me a drink, won't you?"

Fancy went back into the kitchen and came back with a glass of water. She put one hand under Tyler's head and raised him up so that he could drink.

"Damn!" Tyler swore. "Call this a drink, babydoll? Ain't Court got no bourbon in this shack?"

"Yes," Fancy said; "but you can't have it. Doc Benton says it's bad for you."

"To heck and tarnation with Doc and what he says! Fan, a spot of bourbon and branch water wouldn't harm a baby, let alone . . ."

"No, Ty."

Tyler watched her, moving about the room, and his eyes were dark with adoration.

"Anybody ever tell you," he whispered huskily, "that you're an angel?"

"Don't be silly, Ty," Fan said.

"My brother," Tyler said, "is a fool. A hairy-eared jackass. A mule. A stubborn, good-for-nothing, Brantley mule. Than which there ain't no worse breed. . . ."

"That's enough, Ty," Fancy said.

"He'll be back, though," Tyler said. "Not even a Brantley could be that stupid. Any day now the doorbell'll ring and . . ."

Fancy sat down on the edge of the bed and wiped his face with a damp cloth.

"You—you don't hurt none, do you, Ty?" she said.

"No," Tyler said. "Wish to God I did, Fan."

"Why?"

"Pain would mean feeling. And there ain't any feeling. Did you see Doc Benton sticking pins in my feet and legs? Just like puncturing so much beef. Didn't feel a thing. Fan, remember what I asked you?"

"Yes. Only you don't have a gun any more, Ty. I took it last night and threw it in the river. Didn't see how you could get to it, but some fool might give it to you. Couldn't have that, Ty. You see, if you blew out your brains in my bedroom, I'd have to clean up the mess."

"I'll have to think of some other way," Tyler said cheerfully. "Can't mess this place up. Not after the way you've fixed it up."

Fancy looked around the room. It glowed with fresh paint. There were curtains, that she had made, on the windows, and hooked rugs on the floor. Belle had made the rugs. They were real pretty, Fancy thought. Outside in the yard, she had a flower garden. There weren't many flowers blooming in it, because late October was a little cool for them, even in Georgia; but next spring it was going to be something.

Next spring. If there ever were any spring again.

Looking at Tyler lying there, she felt like crying. But she couldn't. That would be bad for him, too. She'd brought him down from Hiberion when she saw how low his spirits were. Agnes' hysterics didn't help. Nor old Jeff's drunken wailing. Saph had been mighty fine, though. She still came in at night to sit with her brother. Other people came, too. Mister Wittly, the Episcopal Minister. And that, Fancy was beginning to see, was a good thing.

People were changing. Getting to be on her side. Old Mrs. Cummings had passed by last week and seen her up on that ladder, in overalls, whitewashing the house. She'd stopped and stared. Then she'd climbed out of her buggy and come into the yard.

"God bless you, child," she'd said; "you've got spunk."

Fan took her in to see Ty, and she'd prayed over him. Then afterwards, she'd gone out and told the members of the Ladies Auxiliary:

"We good Christian people of Augusta have done that girl wrong. Everybody has deserted poor Tyler but her. If you want to see goodness in action go up to Court Brantley's little house. Go there and be convinced, like I was, that she's innocent of the things we've said about her."

I've got friends now, Fancy thought. I've got a chance. I've got everything but what I need most, want most—everything, but—Court.

She saw that Tyler was sleeping at last, so she put her face down against the covers and cried very quietly. She didn't make any noise. Nobody could hear her. She was sure of that.

But she felt hard hands gripping both her arms, and she came up, winking her eyes, trying to get the tears out of them, trying to see. And when she did see, she started crying harder than ever.

"Court!" she sobbed. "Oh, Court, honey, sweetie, Court . . ."

Court held her against his chest, tight.

"Come on," he said, "let's get out of here. We don't want to wake him."

They went out on the porch, and Court held her and kissed her but she couldn't stop crying.

"You came back," she said. "Oh, honey, you came back!"

"Stop it!" Court said gruffly, "and listen to me! I've been a fool, Fan. Didn't know until the other day, just how big a fool. I'm going to ask you to forgive me. I want to make it up to you. 'Cause Wyche was wrong about one thing: I can recognize a pearl when I see one. Will you forgive me, Fan?"

"Forgive you?" Fancy whispered. "You're back and you talk about such foolishness? Oh, darling, there's nothing to forgive. . . ."

Inside the house, Tyler groaned.

"Fan!" he called. "Where are you, baby?"

"Coming, Ty!" Fancy said.

They went in together, and Court stood looking down at his brother.

"Is it bad, Ty?" he said.

"You bastard," Tyler said.

"Look, Ty," Court said, "it won't stay like this. I'm going to get the best damned doctors in the world, and . . ."

"With what?" Tyler said. "I made a crop before this happened. Paid off my debts. But no profit, Court. Not even money enough for seed for next spring. What are you going to pay 'em with, boy? Your looks?"

"No," Court said. "I'll get the money, Ty. Don't worry about that. It may take me two years, but I'll get it. I'll see you on your feet, walking, if it's the last thing I do."

"Big words, boy. How's Fern? You saw her in Boston, didn't you?"

"Yes," Court said, "I saw her. You want me to write her?"

"No," Tyler said. "I never want to see her again. Not as long as I live. Kind of expected that you'd stay up there, too. Would have been downright cozy for you two. Me crippled, and Fan tied down here taking care of me."

"I came as soon as she told me about you, Ty," Court said quietly. "It's better like this. Fern—in Boston—and us, here. Take it easy, boy. I've things to do."

Court and Fancy went back out on the porch, and stood there, looking at each other.

"Fan," Court said, "I've got to go away again. Right away—tonight."

"Where?" Fancy said.

"Spartanburg."

"No, Court! You're not going to Wyche and . . ."

"Yes, Fan. I'm going out and get you that mill. I'll manage it, if you'll hire me. Think I'll do, bosslady? I've had a lot of experience and . . ."

Fancy looked at him. Then she shook her head. Slowly.

"No, Court," she said.

Court didn't say anything for a long while. Then, he said, very quietly: "Why not, Fan?"

"I know you. You're all Brantley—a mighty heap too much, sometimes. The mill's all right. It's a mighty fine idea—but not this way. Not with you eating your heart out over the way you had to get it. Learning to hate Wyche, who's always been your friend. Maybe even hating me because the mill would be mine and the only way you could get it would be through me. It just isn't worth what it would cost . . ."

"I see," Court said. "You prefer for Ty to stay crippled to save my feelings. You'd rather us stay poor than to make this little sacrifice."

"It's not little. And the trouble is you can't make it—not for keeps. Right now—sure. But later on, you'd get to thinking. Besides, Court, if you'd use whatever that is you've got betwixt your ears you'd realize that there's another way."

"Such as?" Court said.

"Melody. Ty can't farm it. You're going to let it go to seed? All right you don't have any money, but you could even sell part of it to get the stuff to plant the rest. And any banker would let you have a loan if you gave him a mortgage."

"That's true," Court said, "still . . ."

"Still nothing! Listen to me, Court Brantley. I lived on a farm all my life. I know as much about planting as you do—more maybe. Ty's got it out of debt. First growing season we could make us a handsome profit—four or five seasons we'll have enough money to start building the mill, and Melody as security to borrow more."

"What about Ty's share?"

"Make him part owner of the mill. Pay him—do anything; just you get going!"

Court looked at her a long time.

"All right," he said. "I'll do just that."

11

But it wasn't that easy. Nothing ever is. You make your plans, then all the things you hadn't figured on kick them into a cocked hat. Things like the boll weevil. Like the supply merchant whose interest rates, apparent and hidden, were never less than forty percent, sometimes as high as eighty. Like the sharecroppers, white and black, beaten down by the heat and the kinds of things that they ate until it took three of them to equal the work of one Yankee farm hand. Things like the other most important fact of all, that Courtland Brantley was a gentleman born and bred and cotton planting in the 1880's called for a taskmaster meaner than a sidewinder and tighter than the Georgia Railroad Bank.

So that first season they failed. Miserably. Completely.

Sitting in the house, just before that second planting season they talked it over. It was raining and that didn't help. It had been raining too long. By now even the sound of it got on their nerves.

"You can do it, Court," Fancy said; "I just know you can."

Court looked at her.

"Yes," he said, "I can do it. But do you know how, Fan? Do you know how Tyler made this place pay?"

"No," Fancy said, "how did he, Court?"

"He used convict labor farmed out to him by some of the crookedest officials that ever disgraced the State of Georgia. Five out of six plantation owners hereabouts do that still. You pay those crooks a pittance, and they send you the dirty, starved-out niggers, complete with an overseer—with a whip."

"Oh, Court—no!"

"Damned right they do. Even your highfalutin friends, the Gilmores, use convict labor. And do you know who has his crooked fingers deep into that stinking mess? That would-be lover of yours—Jed Hawkins."

"I'm glad you said would-be," Fancy said tartly. "Besides, I don't believe Jed would do a dirty trick like that. Why it's no better than slavery."

"Why pretty it up? It *is* slavery. Hell, it's worse. In slavery times a good Negro was a valuable possession. You fed and clothed and petted him like a good horse. But who gives a damn what happens to these chain-gang niggers? Kill 'em off, work 'em, starve 'em, beat 'em to death. There're always more. And don't take up for Jed Hawkins. If I see his red freckled face around here one more time, I'm going to remove his spots—with buckshot."

"Don't be a fool, Court," Fancy said. "Jed means nothing to me."

"Oh no? Seems to me you do a sight more cottoning up to him than is necessary or seemly. I tell you, Fan—"

"Don't tell me. I'm sick of your telling me. I married you, Court Brantley, because I loved you. I do still, which is downright foolish, maybe. But you haven't anything to fear from Jed Hawkins. I like Jed, but it doesn't go any further than that. But every time you sit here snarling at me over your own mistakes and failures, I like him a little better. It isn't Jed you ought to be afraid of, Mister High and Mighty. It's your own stupid, stubborn, stiff-necked self!"

Court looked at her. Then he grinned, wryly.

"You sure have got guts," he said.

"Thanks," Fan said. "Court—please don't let's fight any more. That's all we've done all winter. We got to make some plans. There ought to be some way we could make a go of Melody."

"There are several," Court said slowly, looking away from her, "but they all stick in my craw like bile. All right, we've got one advantage down here in these bottom lands—we don't have to buy guano—not yet. But we have to buy damn near everything else at rates that would make any Ohio farmer reach for his teamster's whip. So we have to reduce expenses—which means taking it out of the hides of our people. And they're good people, Fan, black and white, they're all good."

"I know," Fancy said sadly.

"Their living standards are the ones they got used to in slavery. The Negroes, anyhow. The whites didn't even have it that good. You'd think a body couldn't live any lower than that. But they can. Every planter who doesn't use convict labor has proved that. All right, corn pone, molasses, collard greens and fatback gives the grown-ups pellagra and the kids soft bones—even when they have enough of it to fill their bellies. But now, cut out the collards—you need even that little garden patch to plant more cotton. Don't ever give 'em enough of the other swill—hell, Fan, even the hogs refuse it. In the wintertime give even less. Don't listen to 'em whining from hunger—it might soften your heart. And planters with soft hearts don't make profits. . . .

"Cabins don't cost much to build, do they? Hell, even that little is too much, now. You've got to make a profit, remember. The supply merchant is breathing down the back of your neck, and the damyankees with their railroad freight differentials, and their factories that make the things he sells, and their high tariffs are breathing down his. So you don't build your 'croppers' cabins even as good as nigger slave cabins were built before the war. You build 'em like hillbilly cabins, stand green pine planks on end, running 'em vertically, and make 'em a one-room box that after one season of rain and sun has warped and shrunk so that the winter rain blows through it without hindrance and the wind plays tunes up and down their backbones. . . ."

"Court, it doesn't have to be like that. I tell you . . ."

"Doesn't it? Ever seen the Tilton hands? God damn it, Fan, even a nigger should have a suit of overalls once in a while. Not now, not down here. Put gunny sacking on him. Let him make his shirt from flour bags. Shoes? Hell, I bought the black bastard a pair three years ago. If he was big enough jackass to wear 'em every day, let him do without.

"Oh, yes, Fan. I keep the books. And my 'croppers, black and white, can't read or figure. I can do it all right. I can get the money to build my mill. Only every time I see my face in the mirror afterwards, I'm going to get sick—puking sick."

"There's some other way," Fancy said stubbornly. "Some other decent, honorable way."

"Is there? At best it's no good. I'm no damned planter. The old place was gone before I was born. I hate it. Getting out of bed before sunup, pounding on the doors of the shanties, dragging old women and kids barely toddling out to the fields, standing over them all day cursing at them, driving them worse than animals. God damn it now, Will, get the lead out of your black ass! Get moving, Ras, what the hell do you think this is—a square dance? And you, Tildy, you're missing a sight more weevils than you get. Look at that damned grass—which one of you burr-headed black bastards plowed this row? You think I like that, Fan? Hell, the mill's not worth that—not even that."

"Then what are you going to do?" Fancy said.

"I'm not going to plant this season. I'm going out and raise that money for the mill even if I have to put a gun in their faces! Stealing is better than this. There's a sight more risk to it, and a hell of a lot more honor."

"Then I'll plant," Fancy said. "I can do it. I was raised on a farm and I know how."

Court looked at her narrowly.

"Damned if I don't believe you could," he said. "But we'd have to go further into debt to get supplies, and we'd be the laughingstock of the county—a woman running a plantation."

"Who cares about that? I can do it—without abusing the hands, or starving them. And it would leave you free to try to raise some money elsewhere. Court, give me a chance. All along I've been nothing but a drag on you. I want to help you. It would make me mighty proud if I could . . ."

"I'd be away all summer," Court said. "And if I came back and found out that Jed Hawkins had been hanging around here, I'd have to shoot him."

"And you," Fancy said bitterly, "would have to go to Boston. So I reckon I'd have to shoot Fern. Only shooting's too good for her. Reckon I'd just notch her nose and her ears, cut her tongue out, scratch out her eyes and snatch her bald-headed."

Court looked at her. Then he started to laugh. He stretched out his arms and drew her to him. She could feel his body against hers, shaking with laughter.

"I don't have to go to Boston, hon," he said. "Fact is, to Bostonians, the Southern mills are a threat. I wouldn't have a Chinaman's chance there. New York—Philadelphia, Baltimore. God knows where else. But not Boston. That I promise you."

"And if Jed comes here while you're gone, I'll chase him off even if I have to put the hounds on him. I promise you that, darling. Is it a deal?"

"It's a deal," Court Brantley said.

Afterwards, after he had gone, Fancy was sorry. She knew farming all right, but not big farming. It was ten times harder and more complex. And doing it herself, she learned how right Court had been about the bitter needs that had all but destroyed all over the South the ancient sense of *noblesse oblige*. To keep alive now, with high tariffs, time charges, taxes, high freight rates, and the boll weevil destroying a quarter of the crop, it was dog eat dog down to the naked bone.

But Fancy was a woman, and that made a difference. There was a way—so simple that the men never thought of it. Fancy deliberately ignored cotton's endless demands for land and more land until nobody even had flowers around their doors any more, planting the white enslaver up to their porches. She returned a full twenty-five acres to the growing of foodstuffs. All kinds of foodstuffs. She diverted some of the money she borrowed into a small dairy herd. And chickens. She put the old men and women and the children into the garden acreage. And she fed her people, after the quick-growing truck vegetables were up, better than any hands had eaten in the South in fifty years.

Twenty-five acres hardly scratched Melody's boundless sweep. But it made the miracle she was praying for. It and Fancy and God. It changed sullen, shuffling hands into workers who loved the ground she walked on.

Who never had to be cursed or driven. Who worked from before dawn until after dark—singing.

Then there was nothing else to do, after the crop was in but wait for cotton weather. Fancy knew the signs, and waited. She wanted that long, hot dry weather. She prayed for it. While it's damp, early planting time, springtime, raining, the crop gets a good start. But so do the weevils and the weeds, and the grass. But when the dry weather sets in you work like a dog, like a Negro, like an ox. It's nip and tuck, between the cotton and the weevils and the weeds. You don't let up a minute all day every day. Fancy knew that, and she waited.

She rode out every day with the black hands, making them turn over a row or two, so that she could feel the earth, seeing when it was dry enough. Then one night, she got on her horse and rode around to all the cabins, telling the tenants to be ready. This was it.

She knew that absolutely, perfectly without even knowing how and why she knew. Something about the air—so hot and dry you had to sit on the back porch and gulp at it to get enough. Something about how the sun went down flaming orange down the sky. The lightning bugs bobbing over the Johnson grass. The frogs begging for rain, deep-voiced and moanful. The way the corn curled up from the heat.

She was up before the sun, out in the fields with the Negroes and the white 'croppers—the two races in different fields, of course. She knew better than to work them together. She watched them pushing the plows between the rows turning the grass back into the soil, and behind the big, earth-breaking plows the women and children came, digging out the ugly boll weevils. Fancy didn't say a word to them, she just sat there on the horse, watching them. But she had a hog already killed and roasting over the barbecue pit, and watermellons, and fish a-frying. They worked like dogs, like demons, singing all the time, grinning up at her. After a while, she got tired of sitting there. So she got down and bent through the rows with the black women, breaking every law of etiquette ever heard of in the South, every custom, and tore the ugly weevils loose until her fingers ached. And the hands kept working faster.

They piled the weevils up and burned them with coal oil. They smelled awful, burning. The water boys came and went, bringing the buckets. Some of the Negroes didn't drink. They just poured it over their heads and let it soak their shirts for coolness and kept on working.

They had lunch in the middle of the fields, and afterwards Fancy went over and worked with the white 'croppers. They hadn't been working so fast, but after she joined them they started to work as fast as the blacks or maybe even a little faster. And that night, they all sat down to the barbecue, the whites on one side, the blacks on the other. And they all told jokes and sang.

But Fancy couldn't sleep. She went out to the barns and watched old Josh rubbing down the mules so they wouldn't get too stiff. Then she went out into the fields and under the light of a moon you could read a newspaper by, she started picking more weevils. One of the house servants missed her and came looking for her. When she saw what her mistress was doing she went back and roused out the others, roaring at them, black arms akimbo on her massive hips:

"Lil' Missy ain't a-going to lose this heah plantation! Not with that kind of spirit! Git up, you lazy rascals and let's go help her!"

They did. By morning they'd almost cleared the south acreage of the pest.

And the next day, red-eyed, sleepless, Fancy started all over again.

So it was that when weeks later, Jed Hawkins rode out to Melody, he stared at Fancy with real concern. She was down to skin and bones. Her white skin that wouldn't tan, because she had a blonde's lack of pigment despite her black hair, had reddened and blistered and peeled, so that her blue eyes looked twice as bright.

"My God!" Jed whispered. "You—you look like a damned cracker!"

"Which is exactly what I am," Fancy said. "Didn't you know?"

"Yep. But you never looked like one before. All you need now is a corncob pipe between your teeth, or a wad of snuff under your lower lip. Fan, for the love of God, do you have to do this?"

"Yes."

Jed stared at her, his face working. He looked hurt and mad, and sick all at the same time.

"The woman I love," he said, "down on her hands and knees in the rows with the niggers—for that long-tall polecat. And him gallivanting around begging for money to start a mill, and letting his wife do his work. . . ."

"That's enough, Jed Hawkins!" Fancy said.

"It's a damned sight too much to my way of thinking. Fan, how long are you going on being such a fool?"

"As long as he's alive," Fancy said, "and wants me."

"Jesus!" Jed said.

"What would you suggest? That I leave him and run off with you, and live in luxury off the money you get out of farming out your convict niggers?"

"So," Jed muttered, "you know about that. . . ."

"I know about that and a lot more of the dirty, rotten things you've done, Jed. I'm sorry I found out. I like you a mighty heap. It shames you for me to work in the fields like the poor white trash I am; but it sure Lord shames me to have a friend of mine turn out to be a sidewinder and a polecat and a dirty, rotten crook. Reckon that makes us even, doesn't it?"

"No," Jed said. "After today, I'm getting out of that shady deal. I'd rather be tarred and feathered and ridden out of town on a rail than have you hate me, Fan."

"I don't hate you," Fancy said; "I like you. I don't expect folks to be anything much. When they are, it always surprises me."

"Prepare to be surprised," Jed said. He came toward her, his eyes pleading. "Fan—Fan, honey," he said.

"No, Jed. There's just one thing you can do for me. Get off of Melody and don't come back until my husband's at home. I don't want talk. And I want to keep your friendship. Court's got a good gun eye and a mighty short temper. And there's been enough killing—over me."

"Right," Jed said sadly. "But one of these days . . ."

"Forget it, Jed," Fancy said, and put out her hand.

Jed took it, feeling it rough, toil-worn, calloused. He held it a long time, looking at her. Then he swung himself into the saddle and rode away without saying anything at all. Not even good-bye.

By the end of August, Fancy knew she had won. The crop, she could see, was going to be more than double the yield that Melody had ever produced before even from its entire acreage. And before it was all picked, Court came home.

She could see from his face he hadn't got the money. It was worn with bitterness. And when he looked over the fields, white with the bursting bolls, seeing the pickers working smoothly, rhythmically in time to the lead hand's song, he didn't congratulate Fancy or thank her or even say anything about the thing she had done.

That hurt. Fancy brooded over it while Court attended to the picking, baling and ginning, and rode with the long line of wagons into Savannah to the factors to sell it. When he came back Melody was out of debt. He had bought supplies for the next season, and paid off all the debts and they still had a small profit. But he didn't thank her. And then, finally, Fancy knew why.

He had failed. She had succeeded. He was a man, all man, and a Brantley—prouder even than other men, and it had taken his wife, this hill girl he had married to show him how to run a plantation. He was, deep down inside, grateful to her. But he would never forgive her. Never.

When he came back from the factors, his face was black with anger. He came up to Fancy and caught her by the wrist, hard.

"So," he said, "Hawkins was out here! First thing I heard in town was . . ."

"You are hurting my arm, Court. Turn me loose."

"He was out here, wasn't he?"

"Once. And I sent him packing. I'm sorry I did now. I was a fool."

Court turned her loose and stared at her.

"You mean that?" he said.

"Yes, Court."

"Might I ask why?"

"Yes. You're an honorable man and a gentleman, but you're not nice. You're meaner than old hell. Jed is a crook and a scoundrel, but he's nice. Very nice. He thinks nothing on earth is too good for me. Came out here and saw me working in the fields with the hands, and he almost cried. You don't give a damn about that. You don't even care that I saved Melody for you—that I gave you the chance you needed. Jed thinks nothing's too good for me—you, I reckon you think everything's too good for this poor white trash you made the mistake of marrying."

Court stepped back and stood there, bleak misery in his face.

"You're right, Fan," he said. "I haven't even said thank you, have I?"

"No, Court—you haven't."

"Then—why didn't you run away with him when you had the chance?"

Fancy looked at him and her blue eyes were very clear.

"Because I love you, Court—not him," she said simply. "Funny I have to tell you that."

The next second she was in his arms, held so hard she couldn't breathe.

"You won't be sorry, Fan," he muttered hoarsely—"not ever!"

After that, it all went very smoothly and very well. Court learned what Fancy had to teach. He humbled himself even to asking her advice on the crops and the weather, and the next season the profit they made was better than fair, and the one after that it was so good that Court could buy guano to fertilize the already rich land so that at their fourth picking time the other planters came out to look at their fields with wondering eyes.

They didn't make enough money to start the mill. Not yet. But at the end of their fourth year at Melody they had an excellent chance of getting it. If in the fifth season they had any kind of luck at all, if the weather held, and they beat the weevils, and the high spring grass, if . . .

"Just one more year, Fan," Court said. "Just one—that's all."

Fancy didn't answer him. She came up to him and tied the white tie that he had been struggling with for nearly five minutes. Then she stepped back and looked at him.

"Now," she said, "now you really do look nice. You'll be the handsomest man at the Gilmores' tonight."

Court grinned at her.

"No I won't," he said. "Know who's going to be there? Your light o' love—Jed Hawkins. Sometimes I think I ought to shoot him offhand and save myself the trouble of doing it later—when he's deserved it."

"That," Fancy said, "will be never. Besides, he can't deserve it without me being mixed up with him some way, and I don't aim to get mixed up with anybody. You're enough trouble, Mister Courtland Brantley." She stopped and stared at him. "You know," she said softly, "that's plumb, downright strange."

Court ran the comb through his hair.

"What's strange, Fan?"

"That we—haven't had any children," Fancy said. "It's been five years, Court."

"We're young yet," Court said; "I've known of cases where couples after fifteen years . . ."

"Court—"

"Yes, Fan?"

"You aren't sorry, are you?"

"Sorry about what?"

"That you married me. I'm just getting so that I can mingle with your kind of folks without making a fool of myself. And—you ought to have a son."

Court turned around and looked at her.

"It could be my fault, Fan," he said. "The Brantleys are an old, and worn-out line."

"You—worn-out?" Fancy said; "ha!"

Court picked up her evening wrap and held it out for her. Fancy slipped into it and sighed.

"Five years," she said.

"Five good years," Court said. "One more will make six. If I hadn't had to borrow to run that first year, we'd be away from here now."

"I'm glad we're not," Fancy said. "Didn't know I could love any place on earth like I love Melody."

"We'll keep it," Court said. "We can come down here in the summer, as soon as the mill gets to running smoothly enough."

"Court," Fancy said, "what do we need with a mill—now?"

That was the wrong thing to say. She saw that at once. Court had that mean Brantley look in his eyes, and that stubborn set to his jaw.

"We don't," he said flatly. "We're on the top of the heap right now.

Melody is a success. I could get any price I named for it. But it isn't that simple. What does a man need with any particular woman as a wife? Or with any of his dreams?"

"I don't know, Court," Fancy said. "I'm sorry I asked you that."

"It's all right. And the answer to that question is that he really doesn't need any of those things—except that something inside of him dies if he doesn't get them."

"You'll get your mill," Fancy said; "I just know it."

"Thanks," Court said. Then he looked at her with grave eyes.

Fancy was dressed all in white. The dress was made of white satin, cut just a little way off her shoulders, very tight in the waist, and decorated with lace that was just off white. The collar was of lace, and the short sleeves that came to a little below her shoulders were trimmed with it. Great masses of the same lace went around her hips and were tied in a bow at the back, and then trailed down alternating with the white satin to make her train. More of the lace was sewn in foot-wide ruffles all around the full skirt, and the hem of the ruffled satin skirt was edged with it. Fancy had a puff of ostrich feathers and aigrettes in her black hair. She looked, Court thought, damned lovely.

"Merry Christmas, darling," he said, and kissed her.

It was Christmas Eve of 1885, and they were going to the Gilmores' to a party. The Gilmores were a power in Savannah, but right from the start they had accepted her. That was one of the things Fancy liked about Savannah. Nobody down here knew her history. Except Jed. And he wouldn't tell it. None of them had ever seen her dressed in those baggy, transparent trousers, doing that awful dance on the back of Wyche Weathers' Medicine Wagon. She was Court Brantley's wife, and that was enough. All the women went out of their way to be nice to her, including the ones who were too nice because they were envious. They—the envious ones—were looking for an opening, a chance to get in their barbs; but Fancy never gave them any. She had learned the difficult trick of answering questions very politely without telling the person who had asked them what he wanted to know. So it was that all their efforts to find out who she was, what her family connections were, how she had met Court and any of the ten thousand other things they asked her that were none of their business, met with the same lack of success. They never gave it up, being Southern women and endlessly curious; but they never found out anything.

It was raining when they came out of the house, and the air had that bottom land chill to it. In other places the cold was dry and biting, but in that part of Georgia it crept in upon you through your very pores until after a while your bones ached with it. But Court had the closed carriage brought around and wrapped her in the buffalo skin robe; so it wasn't too bad.

She was nervous about going to the Gilmores'. They had the finest house and their plantation was the biggest of all and they were richer than anybody else. One of the Gilmore girls had been in love with Tyler and she never failed to ask after him with real sympathy. But all the while she was busily engaged, perhaps unconsciously, in transferring her affections to Court. Which, Fancy realized, wasn't at all hard to do, because Court was ever so much better looking than Tyler, and besides, he had all his hair.

Amos, the Gilmores' butler, announced them, and Fancy could see people all over the place turning to look at them. When they did, the same things always happened: the women's eyes narrowed a little, and their gaze traveled quickly up and down her, so that tomorrow her gown would be the subject of many a conversation. But the men's eyes widened, and when they looked at her, it wasn't the gown they saw. They were indulging themselves in the pleasant masculine speculation over how she must look out of this gown and indeed out of any gown whatsoever. When she had been younger, before she had married Court, Fancy had hated that look; but now she had gained a certain security of spirit, and knowing how men were, and how natural and right it was for them to be like that, even, in the case of this tall man she loved and had married, how exceedingly pleasant it was to be wanted until you began to want back, she gloried in it.

She was a grown woman now. She didn't place too much importance upon female envy or male desire, but she wouldn't have been a woman if she hadn't liked being the object of both attitudes. Then she saw Jed Hawkins looking at her, and a little spot of color came into her cheeks, and moved upward until it reached her eyes. She had, oddly, the feeling that it wasn't right for the young lawyer-politician to look at her like that. She didn't know why. The reason was very simple: Jed Hawkins existed for her as a person. The others didn't.

Jed disturbed her. He was tall—not so tall as Court, but still tall. And he was so good-looking that in spite of all the times she had seen him, his looks still surprised her. Looking at him now, she had again that feeling of annoyance that he always provoked in her. She had worked and fought and studied to gain her easy assurance, and Jed wrecked that in half a second. She couldn't understand it. She loved Court Brantley more than life itself, but every time she came into a gathering where Jed was, she found afterwards that she could remember precisely what he had worn, whom he had danced with, and every careless word he had said. Jed had red hair and freckles. Jed had a most engaging grin. He had two ways of talking. At the Gilmores', he talked like the cultured, educated man he was;

but when he made a speech, he twanged like a backcountryman, became deliberately ungrammatical, and talked about his 'Pap,' who he swore had been a sharecropper, spat tobacco juice through his teeth, hitched up his galluses, and told them he had been twelve years old before he had ever worn anything but a gunny sack, and eighteen before he crowded his big feet into shoes.

All of which was a pure lie. But it got the votes.

He's nothing but a crook, Fancy thought hotly. But that grin of his is kind of cute, the other part of her mind said. She had those thoughts about him and they horrified her. They rocked her hard-won assurance to its foundations because it made her think that she was wicked. She didn't realize, being a woman of her generation, that no man born of woman has ever been able to rid himself of his natural inclination toward polygamy. The best most people are able to do is to refrain from acting upon it. She didn't even suspect that the same nature that had given her certain natural responses to being looked at certain ways, to being kissed, to being caressed, was entirely too efficient to place the key to those responses in the hands of any one man. A species was too damned difficult to evolve to have it perish from lack of propagation while its members spent lifetimes hunting around for their one and only true love. . . .

Decency was never lack of temptation, but Fancy didn't know that. I'm bad, she thought, I'm awful bad; but all the time, she was looking at Jed Hawkins out of the corner of her eye.

She danced the first waltz with Court. Then Court went away to dance with Laura Gilmore, and Fancy saw Jed coming toward her. She wanted to run, to hide. Then she realized that she was being a mighty big fool, and took the hand he held out to her, and swirled into the giddy strains of the waltz.

"You're beautiful," he said.

"Please," Fancy said, "don't make fun of me."

"I'm not. I mean it. Also, at the risk of having you think me a blackguard, I'm going to tell you I love you."

"Take me back," Fancy said.

"No," Jed grinned. "You know I'm a scoundrel now. So I'll make the best of it. If I could steal you from your husband, I'd do it. If I could find out what nights he's away from Melody . . ."

"Jed Hawkins!"

"Don't act so shocked," he said. "I'm only telling the truth. And the truth is always respectable."

"Nothing about you is respectable," Fancy said.

"You're mean," Jed teased; "now I'm going to get even!"

He whirled her through the door into the dining room. Then he kissed her, a long time, and very thoroughly. And when he turned her loose, she didn't slap him. Jed had already raised his hand to point at the mistletoe as a means of defense, but then he saw he didn't need to. So he took her arm, and drew her through the dining room and out on the big gallery that went all around the house. He started down the steps toward the garden.

"No!" Fancy whispered. "Oh, no, Jed!"

"Oh come on," he said. And Fancy went.

He kissed her again. She kissed him back very honestly. He tightened his arms about her waist, and kissed the hollow of her throat, her bare shoulder, the nape of her neck, and finally raised his head to find her mouth, but the moonlight was very clear and he saw that she was crying.

"Now what the devil . . ." he said, and turned her loose.

Fancy went on crying.

"I'm sorry," Jed said.

Fancy didn't answer him. She couldn't. She was crying too hard.

"I said I was sorry," Jed said, desperately. He was lost. This was out of his depth. A belle of Savannah might slap your face when you kissed her, but she wouldn't cry. Not like this.

And it came to him that he was in a bad spot. Because of this nothing—this thing that hadn't happened, he was now in danger of being shot or horsewhipped by a man who came from a family known for its murderous tempers.

"Please stop crying," he whispered. "Fancy, please!"

He took out his handkerchief, and dabbed clumsily at her cheeks. His freckled face was so filled with concern that he looked funny. Fancy suddenly found that she wasn't crying any more. She was afraid that now she was going to laugh. But then she remembered that she had allowed him to bring her out here without resistance, that she had kissed this man who was still a stranger, that she had liked kissing him very much, and after that she didn't feel like laughing.

"Take me back now," she said.

He took her arm and they went back into the dining room. "Let's not go in together," Jed said, and Fancy looked at him.

Why, she thought, he's afraid! He's scared stiff. . . . Then she stepped very quickly ahead of him and went back into the ballroom. Court was dancing with one of the McQuinizys. He seemed to be enjoying himself.

I'll go to him, Fancy said. I'll tell him I have a headache.

But she didn't have a headache. All she had was this sick feeling. This feeling of being dirtied in some peculiar, unseen way. By herself. By her own act. Jed had only been a man, playing a man's game. But what had she been—and what was the name of the game she had been playing?

I'll stick it out, she thought. I won't spoil Court's fun.

She danced with several of the guests. Jed didn't come near her for a long time. When he did, she started to refuse to dance with him, but it came to her that he might think she was afraid. So she got up and danced with him. He didn't talk at first. He seemed to be thinking, sketching out in his mind what he was going to say.

"I'm sorry," he said at last; "but only that I made you cry. I'm not sorry I kissed you. I'd do it again. I'm going to do it again the first chance I get. . . ."

"You won't get another chance," Fancy said.

"Why not? You didn't seem particularly offended—not at first."

"I wasn't," Fancy said. "That's why you won't get another chance."

"Want to bet on that?" Jed Hawkins said.

Going back home in the carriage, Fancy lay back against the cushions, listening to Court's cheerful whistling. He was a little drunk, and he looked very happy. Fancy pretended to be asleep, but she kept watching him.

He's so fine, she thought. He's got some funny ways, but he's all man, mine. He's worth ten of that damned little. . . . Oh God, oh Jesus, why did I have to think of that? All it proves I reckon is that from white trash, comes more trash. And me thinking I could be a lady. . . . Made Court kill Duke Ellis, but that wasn't my fault. I felt terrible over that, but what I felt was pity, not shame. But this—what in heaven's name got into me? Oh, Lord, please don't let me ever do anything like that again!

Court opened the door for her, and they climbed the stairs together. Fancy took off her wrap and stood there watching Court while he yanked off his tie and his stiff-bosom shirt. Then he flopped down into the armchair and pulled off his shoes.

"Thank God," he said. "Now I can breathe!"

Fancy stood there looking at him a long time. Then she went over and sat on his lap. She put up both her hands and held his face between them. She came up very slowly from his lap, so slowly that Court didn't know the precise instant that her mouth closed over his. But afterwards he knew.

Afterwards, when the night was graying into morning. When he was very sweetly, softly, loosely, warmly, completely dead. When there wasn't a muscle left in his body. Or a nerve. Or a care.

"Court," Fancy whispered.

"Yes, Fan? Yes, darling, honey, sweetie . . ."

"Court, listen! Let's go back to Augusta. Right now—tomorrow. Let's start the mill. We've money enough—almost. And most anybody would lend you the rest now."

"I thought—" Court said.

"Don't think! Let's go!"

Court raised himself up on one elbow and looked at her. He could see her very clearly. There was light enough for that now.

"Thank God from Whom all blessings flow," he said fervently.

"Are you that glad I changed my mind?" Fancy said.

"I am glad. But that wasn't what I was thanking God for. . . ."

"What were you?" Fancy said.

"For giving me eyes," Court laughed and put out his arm to her. She came to him and lay with her head pillowed on his shoulder.

"Fan," Court said, "why do you want to go all of a sudden? Only last night you said . . ."

"I know. But now I want to. I can't stand this place any longer!"

Court raised himself up and stared at her, frowning.

He was no fool, and Fancy knew that. In about a minute he was going to start asking some very pointed and leading questions which it wouldn't be good or wise or safe for her to answer. She knew how to stop that. But it wasn't all calculation. With his face frowning and intent, Court Brantley to any woman—any real woman—was irresistible.

A minute later, he discovered he wasn't dead after all. Not completely.

12

FANCY sat in a big chair on the rise about one hundred yards above Dry Gully. She sat very still, with both her hands resting on the handles of Tyler's wheelchair. Everybody else was standing up.

Except us, she thought, except us two cripples. Then it came to her that that was a bad thing to think—that what was wrong with her was not like being crippled. It was, actually, a kind of glory.

But Fancy was young. On that July day of 1886, she was only a few months past her twenty-fifth birthday. And all her life she had been slim and good to look at. It was kind of hard to believe that very soon now, in a month or so, she'd be slim again. She'd be slim, and Court would have his son, and everything would be just about perfect.

She could see Court standing with Philemon and Martha and the mayor and several other important people. Below them, in the valley, was the mill. It was the biggest building that Fancy had ever seen. The hills on both sides were covered with people—mostly the men and women and children that Court had already hired to work in Dry Gully Mill. For more than two weeks now, Court had been teaching them to use the machinery. Fancy had wanted to watch that, but he wouldn't let her. Of course, most of the machines couldn't be worked anyhow, because they didn't have the water power yet; but Court had even got around that by having a little steam engine brought into the plant to turn them over enough for the people to learn to work them.

He'd used up a thousand dollars worth of cotton that way; but those folks sure had learned fast—Fancy had to give them that. Many of the women in that crowd, Fancy knew, were wearing dresses from the cloth they had made while learning. It wasn't good cloth, but they were proud of it. They and their sons and their husbands had made it down to the last thread.

Tyler half turned in the wheelchair and looked at her.

"Feeling all right, babydoll?" he said.

"Just fine, Ty," Fancy said. But she wasn't. She felt terrible. Her legs hurt, and her feet and ankles were swollen. She had a misery in her back, and she was so heavy that it was uncomfortable to move. But she was very happy. On the inside she was melting with happiness. Every time the child stirred, she could imagine what it was going to look like. It would be a boy, and right from the first it was going to look just like Court. It was going to be so sweet to hold it in her arms and sing to it and feed it and watch it kick and laugh and gurgle. It wouldn't cry much—not Court's son. No, it would laugh all the time and be happy and she was going to love it so. . . .

She looked at the mill wheels waiting in the gully for the first rush of the water. The dams stood there, bone-dry and dusty. But in a little while they were going to blow that bluff sky-high and the water would come tumbling in and the mill wheels would turn over. A little further up on the ravines and hills, she could see the half finished houses that Court was having built for the mill workers. They weren't much, but Fancy knew they were a heap better than anything these folks had had before. In the middle of the hollow square that Dry Gully Village would form, two bigger buildings were going up—one a church, and the other a school. That was mighty nice, Fancy thought. Court sure was taking good care of his people. But she looked over at a still larger building that stood a little further off, and frowned. The General Store, Philemon Brantley, Manager. That was Phil's own idea, and Fancy didn't like it. He'd told Court it wasn't a good idea to make the mill people go all the way down to Augusta to buy their stuff. He'd even promised to run it fair and square, but Fancy didn't believe him. She didn't trust Philemon. He just didn't have an honest face. . . .

Agnes and Saphira were coming up the hill now. They had on new dresses, and there were two escorts with them.

"Look at 'em," Tyler snorted, "proud as punch of themselves. Got themselves a couple of beaux. Hell, baby, ain't they got sense enough to realize that them boys are just cutting themselves in on a good deal?"

"I think they have got sense enough," Fancy said quietly. "But I think now they don't care much. They're both over thirty, remember. Besides Saph's friend is right nice."

"Breath and britches," Tyler said, "that's all, Fan."

"What else is there to a man?" Fancy mocked him.

"Nothing, I reckon," Tyler said sadly. "And in this case the britches don't even work."

"Ty, please! Don't take on. You know Court's doing all he can."

"Yep. Damned fine of him. Sending me all the way to the University of Edinburgh in Scotland, because Doc Fleischer said that O'Donnell of the Scottish Medical College was the one man on earth who could operate on me and get away with it. Doing it on borrowed money—money he can't rightly afford to use—and the mill still in the gambling stage. . . ."

"No it isn't," Fancy said. "This morning Court showed me more than two hundred orders that had come in. Most of them from Atlanta and Birmingham, and other places where they make ready-made clothes—and linen. We've been getting orders right along. A few of them from as far away as New York and Chicago."

"Two hundred orders is chicken feed, Fan, baby. What about the rest of the year?"

"Court says it's simple arithmetic that we'll make a profit of fifteen percent clear the first year, and double it the next. Phil agrees with him, and Phil is one smart businessman."

"One smart crook," Tyler said; "but he knows how to milk the suckers."

Fancy put her hand on Tyler's arm and squeezed it hard.

"Oh, Ty!" she said, "here they come!"

The two men climbed the rise with the heavy black box between them. A plunger stuck up out of the top of it, and the men were unrolling the wires as they came up the hill, paying them out behind them.

They came up to Court, grinning.

Even from where she sat, Fancy could hear them.

"Here you are, sir!" they said. "It's all yours."

Court put his hand on the plunger. Then he straightened up and said something to the men. They grinned at him and picked up the box again. Fancy could see that they were coming straight toward her. Court came behind them a little more slowly.

When he was close, he smiled at her. Fancy didn't like that smile. It wasn't altogether a good one. She thought that his face looked hurt, smiling—and a little bitter, too.

"It's your baby, Fan," he said. "Blow it!"

"No, Court," Fancy said. "I couldn't. I just couldn't. It's yours—all yours. You've done so much and waited so long. . . ."

"Put your hand on the plunger, Fan," Court said.

Fancy stretched out her hand and let it rest on the wooden handle, but she couldn't push it in. For the life of her, she couldn't.

Court bent down and covered her hand with his own.

"Now, baby," he whispered. "Now!"

Then he pushed her hand down, hard.

Fancy saw the earth leap up in the narrow place that was all the diggers had left between Dry Gully and the river. It went up high in a black, solid cloud, and afterwards she heard the boom of the explosion. It felt like someone had cupped two big hands, and pounded against both her ears at the same time. It crowded down inside of her body so that the child stirred, and she hurt, suddenly.

"The water!" Tyler roared. "God, boy—the water!"

Fan saw it then, tumbling through the gap in a yellow torrent, pushing the red clods of earth ahead of it, spreading out between the broken earth rubble the dynamite had left. It ran very fast in the sunlight until it came to the first dam and stopped there. Then it began to rise in the channel. Fancy watched it creeping up the dry, dusty wall of the dam until it got to the top and ran across that, and fell down the other side with a roar that she couldn't hear very well because the explosion had deafened her.

Her fingers worked on Court's arm as the water hit the first of the mill wheels. Even from where she sat, Fan could hear it creak. Then the bucket-shaped upper blades filled up and the wheel began to move ever so slowly as the weight of the water tripped the buckets over, spilling the water down and out and the next bucket-blade filling up and spilling and the next, and the wheel turning now, faster, faster. . . .

Fancy looked at Court and saw that his lips were moving, shaping words. But they never came out. She could hear Philemon's husky:

"Good God, Court, look at it! There goes the second wheel!"

The second wheel's blades dipped into the whirling millrace, so that they were pushed around by the force of the current; but beyond that was another dam with even more of a drop. The water went over it and now the biggest of all the wheels began to turn, ponderously, and even further down the last wheel was beginning to stir. The people on the hills saw it turn too, and now they took off their hats and cheered.

Then all at once, without anybody saying anything to them at all, they came together in bunches and formed into lines, and the lines moved forward raggedly down the hill, and crowded together in front of the mill's gates.

Court looked at Fancy and saw that she was crying, and a little way off Phil was trying to dry Martha's eyes and Agnes and Saphira were bawling in each other's arms.

"Stop it, you all!" Court roared at them. "We've got enough water!"

"Can't help it!" Martha sobbed. "After all we've been through to see this started—to know we're going up again. Court, you'n' Phil will be the biggest men in the State!"

"Oh yes, you will!" Fancy breathed. "The biggest man in the whole South, Court—not just in Georgia."

Court stared at her.

"I don't know," he said. "I don't even think I care. See those folks down there going through the gates? Well some of those families, working together, are going to have more money at the end of this week than they've ever seen in any one year. I wonder what it'll do to them. . . ."

"I'll tell you," Tyler drawled. "The women are going to blossom out in shoes too tight for their feet, and fancy dresses and all kinds of gewgaws. The men'll be buying bowler hats and striped pants, and nickel cigars. There is going to be a mighty heap of drinking done, and somebody's going to use a knife on somebody else, and there'll be a shooting scrape or two, maybe, and Myrtie Torrence and gals like her are going to get rich. . . ."

"Who is Myrtie Torrence?" Martha asked.

"Our local daughter of joy," Saphira told her without batting an eye.

"Saph," Court said, "one of these days I'm going to take a buggy whip to you."

"Why?" Saphira said. "Appears to me there's a heap less harm in saying what she is than patronizing her the way you men do."

Court took half a step toward her, but Fancy caught his arm.

"Leave her alone, Court," she said. "This is such a wonderful day; don't let's spoil it."

Court smiled at her.

"You're right, Fan," he said. "Come on, all of you, and I'll show you Dry Gully Mill going full blast!"

"It's not dry any more," Martha said. "That's just about the wettest gully in the State of Georgia."

Fancy got up slowly, looking down at the earth. Even the special dresses didn't do any good, she knew. I'm just plumb, downright ugly, now.

Philemon got behind the wheelchair and pushed Tyler down the hill. Then they went into the mill, together with the mayor, and Mister Phinizy, the banker, and the pastor of the Episcopal Church, and all the people who were anybody in Augusta. They went past all the whirring, clattering machinery. Fancy looked at it in a way that made Court think she understood it. Then they stopped before the slashing bath, and Agnes asked:

"What on earth is that for?"

"They're starching the yarn to make it strong," Fancy said, and Court stared at her. Of course there was much more to it than that. The hot, bubbling bath that the yarn went through had other things in it besides starch. There were lubricants in it, and a preservative and—but Fancy was right in the main. Slashing yarn, when all was said and done, was starching it.

"How the devil did you know that?" Court said.

"My Aunt Tilly used to work in Horse Creek Valley Mill," Fancy said. "I used to go over there and take her stuff Maw had baked. I even doffed bobbins myself a couple of times in rush seasons."

"I see," Court said.

Fancy thought he sounded mad.

They all stayed until one o'clock when the whistle blew for lunch. But when the workers poured out of the gates into the open air, they found that sawhorses had been set up, and long planks stretched across them, and a crew of Negroes in white aprons and caps were busy with the pigs spread out over the pits. They all started toward the pits, but long before she got near them, Fancy could smell them. They smelled wonderful. There was a black iron pot where the Negro cook had put in the heads and the livers of the hogs mixed up with beef and seasoned with a lot of different kinds of hot spices to make the hash. The pot was propped up on bricks over a low fire, but beyond that was a big fire of oak logs that the Negroes kept blazing by throwing in new logs as fast as it burned down even a little. They didn't cook anything over this fire. One of the cooks came and went, taking the clear, glowing embers from it with a shovel. He spread the embers out in the bottom of the pit. Over the pit the pigs turned on green hickory spits. That way the pork was cooked in clean, smokeless heat. Other Negroes stood by the pits and didn't do anything but turn the pigs over and over again. There was one man who stood next to the pit with a mop made of clean rags tied to a hickory stick. He kept dipping his mop into a pot filled up with vinegar, salt, pepper and spices, and smearing it all over the roasting pigs. The pigs were turning golden-brown and their skin puckered up in little blisters that would become very hard and dry and would crackle when you ate them, Fancy knew.

"You women will have to serve," Court said. "We've got to start these folks off feeling good."

"Oh, Court!" Agnes said, "not in my nice new dress!"

"Dress be damned," Court said. "These pine-barren crackers are a touchy lot. They're prouder'n all hell. You'll find the majority of the men who come up to get served will call me by my first name. In their way, they're the world's staunchest democrats, within certain limitations, of course."

"Limitations?" Fancy echoed.

"You've got to have the right color to your hide, and belong to the right church. Beyond that, a man can be poorer than the dickens, or richer than old Commodore Vanderbilt, and they'll treat him just about the same. Of course, they'll listen a little more carefully to the opinions of a man who's rich and powerful; but the next day, when they repeat those opinions, they'll give them as their own—and believe it. Here come the others, now."

Fancy looked and saw buggies and carriages and riders still coming into the mill grounds. All the people got out of their carriages or off their horses and came forward to shake Court's hand.

Court introduced her to Judge and Mrs. Richardson, though he didn't need to, because Judge Richardson remembered her from the trial. But he was too polite to say anything. She shook hands with Bob McCullen, Joe Cummings, all the Phinizys, the Waltons, and Tom O'Mallory. After that she lost track of the names. A big stage came up and an orchestra climbed out of it, and a brewery wagon brought keg after keg of beer.

Fancy was surprised to see how all the fine ladies in their new summer dresses joined in and heaped up the plates of the mill workers. Then the mayor got up and made a speech; he said that Court was a public benefactor. After a while, Fancy stopped listening, because the speech was dull.

Fancy saw Court standing up now, but when he started talking, it was to the mill workers, not the important people, that he spoke.

"I don't have to tell you," he said quietly, "what the price of guano is today—or what kind of a crop you can grow on these starved-out lands without it. I don't need to remind you what your chances were of keeping your lands another two years, or even another one when the supply storekeeper tallied up his accounts. You know these things as well as I do. You've seen the red earth bleed away along the gullies, and the crops come in smaller every year. You've seen the blights come, and the cotton fail. You've heard your children crying in the night from hunger, and put your hands over your ears because there was no food. Your old woman got a misery in the chest. Your oldest daughter died—spitting blood. . . .

"Then you lost the land and became a 'cropper on another man's place. That was bad even when he was a good man, because the mills up North set the prices on his bales. When he was a bad man, the exact difference between you and the niggers he used to drive before the war was the color of your skins, that was all. . . ."

Fancy could see them nodding, as Court touched their deepest fear.

"That's what this mill is for, folks. No more depending on the weather, praying there won't be a drought, that it won't rain too much, that the Savannah'll behave itself and not sweep you clean away. No more hoping that you'll make enough bales to pay off the debts and have a little something left over besides. Every week now, you're going to have cash money in your jeans—money to buy food, and clothes—to call the doctor if your folks get sick, money to lay aside for your old age. More money than any of you have ever seen.

"This mill doesn't belong to me. Not alone. It belongs to you—all of you. Now let's see what you'll make of it!"

He sat down then, and Fancy caught his hand and squeezed it hard, and all the mill workers stood up and cheered him so loud that Fancy couldn't even hear herself think.

All the barbecue was gone by now, and one of the storekeepers set up a row of caged turkeys, and Court pointed out a wagonload of borrowed guns. The mill workers, hill men all, could shoot. None of the turkeys got past three contestants though only the head was in sight.

Then the orchestra started up, playing the toe-tickling hill tunes. One of the oldest mill workers started calling the sets and Fancy was astonished to see that all the fine ladies danced with the sweaty, linty mill hands. She wished that she could dance because she did love dancing, but it was too late for that now. So she sat beside Tyler and watched Court dancing with the mill girls. She didn't like the way they looked at him—as if they could eat him with a silver spoon, but Court looked bored, so she felt better.

She heard Tyler swearing softly under his breath.

"And I used to be the best God-damned dancer in the State of Georgia," he said.

She laid a hand on his shoulder.

"You'll dance again, Ty," she whispered.

"No," Ty said. "No, babydoll—I'll never dance again. All I want to know is why in hellfire that Ellis bastard had to be such a rotten shot!"

"That's a wicked thing to say, Ty," she said gently. "Wicked and foolish.

Dead you wouldn't have a chance. But now there's still that doctor in Scotland, and you've still got hope. . . ."

"No, Fan," Tyler said. "I haven't any hope–nary a drop. I'll be sitting here in this dangblasted wheelchair till they roll me through the pearly gates–or into bottom pits, which is a sight more likely. Don't reckon it'll be too long, neither. A man don't hang around when he ain't got nothing to cling to."

"Ty, please," Fancy began; but the whistle blew, and the music stopped. Court stood up and raised his hand.

"Go on playing!" he called. "We'll make cloth tomorrow!"

The dancing lasted until after dark. When it was over, Court got up and told his workers that they would be paid for the whole day, and they all clapped and cheered.

Even after that, when Fancy rode back with Court to Hiberion, the carriages of the important people followed them, and the party went on in the big hall until morning. The hall had been cleaned, and a few repairs had been started on it.

"It's beginning to look like its old self again," Thomas Cummings, Joe's father, said. "Tell you what, Court–suppose I send a crew of men down from my lumber yard tomorrow. Good carpenters, all of them. Fix the old place up . . ."

"I'd like to," Court said; "but every cent I have is tied up in the mill and–"

"Hell, boy," Tom Cummings boomed, "your credit's good. Pay me when you get it. Take two years–heck, take three. You're the biggest man in Augusta now; you can't go on living in this old barn."

"Thanks, Tom," Court said, "that's mighty kind of you."

Agnes and Saphira were surrounded. Agnes was flirting with all the young men, but Saph's gaze rested only on Peter Lewis' face. Fancy soon found out that neither the fact that she was Court's wife, nor her delicate condition stopped the young men from paying her compliments.

"Ma'am," young Joe Cummings was saying; "I'm plumb, downright sorry that Court saw you first. Now if it had been me . . ."

"You'd have tripped over your own big feet," Fred Walton chuckled. "One good thing, though–old Court's going to be mighty busy with that mill. So if you ever get lonesome, Mrs. Brantley, just let me know; I'd be mighty proud to squire you around town."

"You sure don't aim to live long, Fred," Nick Cohen said.

"Oh well, a short life, but a merry one, I always said," Fred laughed.

Life is going to be good now, Fancy thought. Oh yes, it's going to be good.

In the morning, she was sure of it. Because that next morning, the noise of hammering woke her up. When she looked for Court, she found that he was already gone. She put on her robe and went downstairs. The whole house was filled with carpenters. They had torn both of the rotten porches down, and were putting up new ones.

Inside the hall, other men were ripping down the last of the wallpaper, and knocking down the broken plaster. The furniture had been covered, but the floor was white with plaster dust. Two men excused themselves and went past her up the stairs and started squinting along the broken section of the balustrade, and one of them made marks upon a piece of paper.

Two others came in with a tall ladder, and began rigging a block and tackle over some scaffolding to let the damaged chandelier down to the floor. Another man was taking the broken windowpanes out one by one. It seemed to Fancy that they were tearing the house all the way down instead of building it up. But all the broken things had to be cleared away before they could start to fix things.

She went up to her room and got dressed. When she came down again Agnes was watching the work. Saphira wasn't there, because Saph didn't live at Hiberion any more. She lived with Tyler in the cottage where Court and Fancy had spent their honeymoon. She took good care of Tyler, Fancy had to give her that. A few minutes later, Jefferson Brantley came tottering down the stairs, leaning on a cane.

"Court's a good boy, Missy," he said. "What in tarnation did you say your name was?"

"Fancy," she told him.

"Fancy. Yessir, Court's a good boy. Best of the Brantleys. Reckon he took after his maw. Never thought I'd live to see this day—never thought it. Now Hiberion's going to look like it did before the damyankees came down here and ruined everything."

"Father," Agnes said crossly, "you talk too much!"

"Why? She ain't a Yankee. She's as Southern as you are, Missy. Course she come from a poor family, but that doesn't matter." He turned to Fancy, smiling. "We'll make a Brantley out of you yet. We can do it, too. You've got the makings. Got the build and the carriage and the grace. Don't reckon Court went far wrong, marrying you. But then, us Brantleys always did pick out the best. Got a talent for horseflesh and women."

"Thank you, sir," Fancy said, laughing.

"Course I'm mighty sorry Court has to get his money by engaging in trade. No occupation for a gentleman. We Brantleys have been planters for well nigh onto two hundred years, most of it right here on this spot.

Ty was the only one of my sons who was carrying on in the old tradition. Poor Ty—didn't seem to have no luck, nohow. But Court's a better man than Ty. Course he's made his mistakes. . . ."

"Father," Agnes snapped, "will you please hush!"

"Reckon I will," the old man said. "Didn't mean to hurt your feelings—Fancy. There! I got it!"

"You didn't hurt my feelings," Fancy said. Then seeing he was turning, trying to go back up the stairs, she took his arm.

"Here," she said, "let me help you."

"Thank you, daughter," the old man said, and his old eyes misted over, suddenly. "Nobody's tried to be nice to me in so long," he quavered. "Nosirreebobtail, Court didn't make no mistake in marrying you—no mistake at all. . . ." He leaned forward suddenly, until she could smell the whiskey on his breath.

"If it's a boy," he whispered loudly, "name him after me, won't you?"

"I will," Fancy promised. "And after Court, too. Courtland Jefferson Brantley—how's that?"

"Just fine," Jeff Brantley said. "Yessir—that's a mighty fine name."

For the rest of the week, when Court came home, late at night, he was too tired even to talk much. But from the few things he said, Fancy gathered that things weren't going as well as he had expected. Finally she got it out of him.

"It's the damned climate," he said. "I thought it would be an advantage, Fan; but it isn't. There's so blamed much static electricity in the air that the yarn breaks if you look at it hard. I'll have to go down and see old man Phinizy tomorrow."

"Why, Court?"

"We'll have to put in humidifiers to moisten the air. You'd think that in a river valley it would be wet enough, but it isn't. And that won't be good for the workers."

"You mean the dampness will make them sick?" Fancy said.

"Damned right it will; but what choice have I?"

"But Court—they're humans, just like us. Some of 'em are little children!"

"I know, I know! But Fan, they were starving before the mill came. It's a choice of evils. I'll have to hire a company doctor to take care of them. Not all of them will get sick, and even so, it's better than starving the way they used to."

"Reckon you're right," Fancy sighed; "but it's a pity—isn't it?"

"Yep. But the point that's worrying me right now is the fact that I'll have to borrow more money. That's why I'll have to see Mr. Phinizy."

"He'll lend it to you, won't he, Court?"

"Sure. There's no doubt of that. He's a mighty fine man. But what's worrying me is having to pay it back."

"You'll do it, Court," Fancy said; "I just know you will."

Court's lips brushed her cheek, and he was gone. Fancy stood there staring after him. He didn't used to kiss me like that, she thought.

She didn't go upstairs again, but stood in the hall looking at the repairs the workmen had already made. There was so much more to be done, but already she could see how it was going to be. It made her feel good all over just to look at it. She was going to live in a house now, the kind of a house that she had dreamed of.

She turned at last to go up the stairs, but before she reached them she heard the sound of high heels. So she came back toward the door, thinking that it was Saphira, and she was glad. She liked Saph. But in the doorway she stopped. It wasn't Saphira.

It was Fern.

"Mind if I come in?" Fern said. "No, don't answer that. You've an uncomfortable habit of telling the truth. And I shall come in for a moment. Is Court here?"

"No," Fancy said.

"Too bad. I did so want to see him. I hear he's done it—built his mill and all. I wanted to congratulate him."

"That wasn't all you wanted," Fancy said.

"How true," Fern sighed. "And I always do get what I want, did you know that? But don't worry, I'm very patient. I can wait—for years."

"You'll have a long wait," Fancy said. "Too long, to my way of thinking."

"Who cares about your way of thinking—Mrs. Brantley. I suppose I have to call you that. It has a singularly ill-fitting sound—applied to you."

"Don't you think you're wasting your time?" Fancy said quietly. "My mother always told me—see nothing, say nothing. And dirt is still dirt even when it's all dressed up and speaking proper. Appears to me you'd look a mighty heap better in folks' eyes if you'd go and take care of your own husband—who needs you."

"Thanks for the sermon," Fern said, and stepped past her into the hall. She looked around her, seeing the scaffolding, and the partially completed repairs. Her brown eyes lighted.

"Hiberion restored," she exclaimed. "You know, Fan, I've dreamed of this. Only it was I who lived here in those dreams, not you."

She turned and looked at Fancy, seeing her in the light of the gaslights clearly for the first time.

"My God!" she whispered.

"Yes," Fancy said, "I'm going to have a child—his child. Now how long do you think you're going to have to wait, Fern Brantley?"

"Too long," Fern said. "I'm afraid you've won. The Brantleys have great pride of family. They might betray their wives with a casual light o' love—but not one of them has ever left the mother of his sons. I congratulate you. I didn't believe it was possible. Now if you'll be so good as to tell me where Ty is . . ."

"I'll do better than that," Fancy said; "I'll drive you over there."

"But you're in no condition to—"

"Don't worry about my condition, Fern. I'm white trash from the Carolina hills, remember. We have our babies and go on plowing. Come on."

"Even so," Fern said as they walked toward the stables, "I don't see why you're putting yourself out this way—for me."

"I'm not putting myself out. This is going to be plumb, downright interesting. Reckon I've got a hankering to hear what Ty says when he sees you."

"I can imagine," Fern laughed, "that he won't be overly polite. But why should that amuse you, when it isn't going to bother me in the least?"

"We'll see," Fancy said.

When they reached the cottage, Tyler was shaving. He looked at Fern and closed the razor, taking a long time about it. Then he laid it very carefully on the washstand, although one half of his face was still covered with lather. Saphira stood up and stared at them, but she didn't say anything either.

"'Lo, Ty," Fern said.

"Get out of here," Tyler said. He didn't raise his voice.

"No, Ty," Fern said; "I've come—home."

"I said—get out."

"But, Ty," Fern said, "you need me now. You can't expect Saph to—"

"When I was a man," Tyler said, "I needed you. Now I don't. I don't need anybody but the sexton to toll the bell, and the Reverend Mister Wittly to say a prayer. I don't want you now. I hate the sight of you. Looking at you makes me sick—puking sick. Now will you go?"

"No," Fern said.

"I reckon you won't," Tyler said. "It gives you a delicious tingle way down in your little pink guts to see me here crippled—less than half a man, doesn't it? And you won't go back to Boston. That would take you too far away from my precious brother. You little witch. Don't you see you haven't a chance now? Court's a fool, all right. Before you might have been able to steal him away from the sweetest, best little gal who ever drew breath

—the Brantleys have always been weak in that direction. But do you think you can steal him from his son? I ask you, Fern—do you think that?"

"No," Fern replied almost inaudibly. "No, Ty—I don't think that."

"Good. Stay in Augusta if you want to. But not here. Being hanged would be a blessing to me—a whole lot better than sitting here rotting. And if you stayed here, you couldn't sleep. You wouldn't—dare."

"All right, Ty," Fern said, "if that's the way you want it."

"That's the way I want it," Tyler said.

That month of August was one long nightmare to Court Brantley. Nothing seemed to go right. There was too much time and labor lost because the raw cotton did not flow smoothly enough from bale to finished cloth. There were still too many trucking operations, and the loss in unsalvageable lint was high. So Court shut down parts of the mill for a few days at a time, and changed things. He moved the openers, breakers, intermediate and finisher pickers into the carding room and connected them to the big carding machines by a chute; then he had a hole knocked in the wall between the carding machine and the drawing equipment, and fed the cleaned fiber slivers into the drawers mechanically; but the combs stopped him—as they were used only for the very finest fabrics. He worried over that problem for a week, but finally had to content himself with a v-shaped conveyor line into the roving, spinning, spooling, twisting, warping and slashing processes. He set up an endless smooth-flowing chain movement on the last three processes, warp drawing, mercerization and weaving, and last of all he reorganized the cloth room where the finished bolts were prepared for shipment.

By the time he was through, the whole month was spent; but the work served its purpose: the mill produced a quarter more fabric than it was designed for, and the supposedly undiminishable material losses were cut a full five percent. And Court had done another thing, too: he had kept himself from thinking throughout the more than twenty days that Fern, his brother's wife, waited for him every night outside the gate. Those hour-long rides with her were something he didn't like to think about. He was all Brantley, and Fern was lovely; but there was Fancy at home waiting to bear his son. That stopped him. Nothing else could have.

Still it wasn't a good thing to ride with her night after night down by the river where the willows were and the water went by murmuring. When the moon pulled itself loose from the river, and the silver spilled down, and the wind talked in dark voices, what could he say to her? What were the words?

I want you I need you I love you. But not spoken. I always have I always will and what has happened is an ugliness but it's a strong thing and I cannot break it. It is flesh of me now blood of my blood bone of my bone my big dreams and all the far, sweet hungers. It's a woman waiting. A good woman, true to me, in whom I can find no blame. A woman who loves me needs my love, who deserves a better man than I. The mother of my son to be, Fern, and that's a strong thing. A woman whom I ought to love but cannot (but only because of you because of you) and all the oft-mouthed words—honor, faith, decency—meaning nothing, Fern, meaning everything. I can't say them, don't know what they mean, they have departed from the house of my fathers and all that is left is I cannot because there will be a son of my loins and that is stronger than this—than even this. . . .

But all he said was, gruffly:

"Come on, we've been out long enough."

And all Fern said was:

"All right, darling—whatever you say."

Meekly.

He came home that night of August 31st and lay beside Fan in the dark a long time before he went to sleep. And even when he did sleep, hands caught hold of him and shook him. They were very big hands and they didn't have any arms or face or body. They held on to him very tight and shook him so that every bone in his body rattled. Then he heard Fancy scream.

"Court!" she cried. "Court! Wake up! Oh—Court—the house—the house!"

He sat up in bed and the hands let go of him.

"What's the matter with the house?" he said.

"I—I think—it—it's falling down!" Fancy said.

"You're dreaming," Court said; but there was the enormous shaking again and the pictures fell down from the walls and the bricks came down from the chimney and hit the roof and it was still again so that he could hear his own breathing, then one more brick fell.

"Come on," he said. "We'd better get out of here!"

They went down the stairs very fast but when they were halfway down it started again and the windows crashed in and there was the smashed tinkle of broken glass and the big door slammed open without anybody's touching it. Court pulled Fancy away from the house, seeing the shapes of the trees bending far over as though there were a hurricane but there wasn't any wind. Then one of the biggest broke in half and came down making a noise like thunder. Behind the house in the quarters, they could hear the Negroes screaming, then the horses started screaming too, and there is no sound anywhere worse than that. It stopped, then started again. Court pulled Fancy further away from the house but he had to stop because the ground at their feet opened up in a wide chasm, so deep it had no bottom; then it closed up again and they couldn't even see where it was.

"Court!" Fancy cried. "Your father!"

Court started running back toward the house, his dressing gown flapping about his long legs. Fancy stood there looking after him, hearing the Negroes screaming, and watching Hiberion sway from side to side and inside glass breaking and the booming noise from underneath the ground.

She was standing there like that when she felt the first pang. She sat down at once, waiting. She remembered that Maw had said that after the first one it took hours, sometimes all night, so she didn't worry about that part of it. She was too busy worrying about Court.

Then she saw him coming out of the house with Jeff Brantley in his arms, and when they were close she could hear the old man shouting:

"What's the matter with you, boy? Here I was sleeping the sleep of the just and you come a-busting in and snatch me out of my bed like a wild man! You drunk, Court? You must be! Look not upon the wine when it is red. . . ."

Then it stopped, and Fancy started to laugh. She didn't know why she laughed. She felt more like crying.

But she knew that Maw was wrong, because the pangs hadn't stopped, they were coming quicker now, and she tried to time them, and then she was scared. Because they weren't fifteen minutes apart like Maw had said, nor even ten, nor five. They were coming one after the other.

"Court," she said, "you better get Doc Brewster. I—I think it's coming."

Court stared at her.

"What's coming?" he said.

"The baby. Oh, Court, hurry! It's coming soon!"

Court started off, and the minute he left the house, the ground started to shake again. He ran through the streets toward the doctor's house, dodging the bricks from falling chimneys, and jumping over the rubble where whole walls had fallen down. When he got to Broad Street, he saw that people had left their houses and were putting up tents in the middle of the street. He heard voices:

"Worst quake in the history of the State!"

"The hospital's overflowing—don't know how many's dead. . . ."

"Tell me the colored folks have started a prayer meeting in the middle of the Terry. They aim to keep it up all night!"

"Damned if I blame 'em!"

"I'd say a prayer myself—if I knew a prayer. . . ."

Court Brantley was saying a prayer as he ran. He didn't need to know one. It just came.

But he couldn't find Doc Brewster. Doc was far too busy. He was treating the injured, riding through the broken streets, giving help where it was needed.

Just before morning, it started to rain. The sky opened up and the rain came down in sheets. Court trudged through the mud back to Hiberion, afraid to look, afraid even to ask; but when he got there, Fancy was lying under one of the trees with the child in her arms. She was wrapped in three blankets.

"Aunt Matilda helped me," she whispered. Then she started to cry.

"Oh, Court," she sobbed; "it–it's a–girl!"

Court bent down and pushed back the blanket and gazed at the tiny wrinkled ugly thing Fancy held. It had a button for a nose, and its eyes were shut tight so he couldn't see them. But its mouth was like a rosebud, and its head was covered all over with long, soft curling black hair. Like Fancy's. Even then he knew his daughter was going to be beautiful. He felt something come loose inside of him, and he was filled with something like singing. He leaned forward and kissed Fancy's mouth. She opened her blue eyes and stared at him.

"I'm glad," he said. "She's just like you. God, baby, I'm glad!"

Fancy stared at him unbelievingly. Then very slowly she smiled.

"The next one will be a boy, honey," she whispered; "I promise you."

"And the one after that?" Court teased.

"Whatever you want, darling," Fancy said.

13

It was a good thing, Fancy saw, that the men hadn't got any further with the repairs to Hiberion. Because now, they were going to have to do them all over again and more besides. She was lying on a couch in the hall, because Court didn't want her taken upstairs until he was sure that the house hadn't been weakened by the earthquake. The Negroes were cleaning up, and Lynne lay beside her, sleeping peacefully. Every minute or two Fancy would pull back the blankets and look at her.

So little and so sweet. There are a lot of ugly things in life, Fancy thought, but a lot of beautiful things too. This was one of the beautiful things. Of course Court teased about the baby's being red and wrinkled and ugly, but Fancy couldn't see that. She was sure that she had never seen anything quite so lovely.

She heard Court's booted feet on the half finished porch. He came through the door, his arms filled with flowers.

"How nice!" Fancy said, "are they for me?"

"Course not," Court laughed. "They're for my little sweetheart there. You play second fiddle in this house from now on, Mrs. B." Then he bent down and kissed her.

Aunt Matilda took the flowers and went to look for a vase. It took her a long time to find one that wasn't broken. Court sat on a chair beside the couch and poked at the baby's tiny hands with his finger, trying to make her grab it, until Lynne woke up and howled.

"She's a Brantley all right," Court grinned. "Noisy little beggar, isn't she?"

"Court," Fancy said, "what about the mill?"

"It was untouched," Court said. "Apparently the quake didn't extend that far."

"Thank goodness," Fancy said.

Court sat there looking at the baby and grinning. Fancy thought he looked right foolish, but she reckoned that all new fathers looked that way.

Court stood up finally.

"I have to be getting back," he said. "The mill's going full blast, Fan. We won't even miss a day's production."

He was bending down to kiss her good-bye when they heard the sound of high-heeled slippers clattering up the porch steps and Saphira came into the house.

"Thank God you're here!" she said. "Oh, Court—you've got to come at once!"

"Where?" Court said. "What's this all about, Saph?"

"Ty," Saph whispered. "Half of the house fell in last night. He wasn't hurt, but I couldn't move him. Everybody was so scared I couldn't even get help. . . . And this morning early it rained so. . . ."

"Is he sick?" Court said.

"Terribly. He's got to be moved up here. That house is dangerous and he's burning up with fever and. . . ."

Court turned to one of the Negroes.

"Tell Ernest to hitch up the carriage," he said.

It wasn't until then that Saphira saw Fancy lying on the couch. She came up to her at once, and when she was close, Fancy lifted the baby up so that Saph could see her.

"Oh no, Fan!" Saphira said. "Don't tell me! When?"

"Last night," Court grinned. "Didn't you hear the celebration? We kind of shook up this town, I'm told."

"Oh let me take him! He's beautiful! Oh, Fan, you darling, I'm so happy I'm going to cry. . . ."

"It is not a him," Fan said sadly. "It's a girl, Saph. I called her Lynne."

Saphira stopped and stared at her, then she smiled broadly.

"Good!" she said. "There's been too blamed many Brantley males now. Come to Auntie, Lynne, and let's start showing the world what a female Brantley can do."

"Saph," Fancy whispered, "what about Ty?"

"He's very sick," Saphira said, "and the awful thing about it is—he—he's glad of it, Fan. . . ."

"Does she know?" Fancy said.

"No. He won't let me send for her. Fan, I'm scared. I don't like the way Ty looks. It's a dreadful thing to want to die."

"We'll snap him out of that," Court said. "Here's Ernest now. Come on, Saph, we'd better go get him now. We'll pick up Doc Brewster on the way."

Two hours later when they came back with Tyler, two of the Negroes had to carry him into the house and upstairs to bed. When they passed the couch where Fancy lay, she could see his face. Then she was sure.

"Why," she said aloud so that the sound of her own voice startled her a little, "he's going to die."

Hearing her say that, Court stared at her, and Fancy could see that he knew it too. There was no doubt of it; Tyler Brantley was dying.

Doc Brewster came down the stairs looking a little sick himself.

"Doc," Fancy whispered, "is there any hope?"

"None," Doc Brewster snapped. "Ty's a strong man, and even in his present condition he ought to make it. But he won't. He won't because he doesn't want to. I've seen cases like this before. And every time I meet up with a new one, I say the same thing. I swear I'm going to quit practicing medicine and take up planting!"

"But you never do," Fancy said.

"No," Doc Brewster said; "I never do. Now I reckon I'd better check up on you and the little lady."

There were times during the next five days when they began to hope. But when Tyler started to go, he sank very quickly. Fancy saw Court tearing through the hall on his way to get the doctor. He didn't say anything to her, but she knew. So, although she wasn't supposed to, she got up and went up the stairs.

Tyler looked at her out of eyes that burned like lights in the sockets of his skull.

"Fan," he said, "babydoll."

Then he made a grimace that she knew was meant for a smile.

"Ty," Fancy said, "please try. We all love you so. For us, please try. If you don't, we'll never feel right again. . . ."

"Fern," Tyler said. "Get Fern."

"All right, Ty," Fancy said.

She sent one of the Negroes over to the boarding house where Fern was staying. Fern came at once. She got there only a little after the doctor, himself.

Doc Brewster took one look.

"Pneumonia," he said. "He hasn't got a chance."

In the doorway Agnes and Saphira started to cry, and Court's face was hurt-ugly. But Fern Brantley didn't cry. She just stood there, looking at her husband.

My God, Fancy thought, how can she . . . ? But then she saw that Tyler was trying to force himself up on his elbows. Doc Brewster tried to push him back, but he couldn't. Even dying, Tyler was too strong.

"Fern," he said, "Fern."

"I'm here, Ty," Fern said.

"Loved you," Tyler said. "So much. You left me. All right. Just want to tell you one thing. . . ." His mouth opened, gulping at the air. It wasn't a pleasant thing to watch. Then his voice came back. When it did, it was clear and strong.

"You're going to see hell, Fern," he said.

Then he died. Like that. Like someone turning off a light. It was so quick that none of them knew it except Fancy. She was watching his eyes. She saw them stop burning, dim. She walked with quick, jerky steps over to the bed. Then she sank down and pillowed her face against the covers.

Behind her, Agnes started to scream, but the sound of it was cut off suddenly, as Saphira brought her hand hard across her sister's mouth. Fancy turned her face so that she could see Fern.

Fern hadn't moved. But all the color had gone out of her face. Even her lips were white. Then without saying anything at all, she turned and went out of the room. Fancy could hear her footsteps going down the stairs. The front door slammed, then there was the whirr of wheels on the drive.

Court knelt down beside Fancy and put an arm across her shoulders. "Poor Ty," he whispered.

"He was a good man," Fancy said.

They buried Tyler Brantley among his ancestors in Magnolia Cemetery. All the Brantleys were there, and they wept for him. All the Brantleys except one—the one to whom he had given his name. For Fern had taken the train for Boston the same night that he died.

Going back from the cemetery to Hiberion, Court tried not to think of her. He tried very hard and very sincerely. But all the way back to Hiberion, one thing echoed through his mind like a refrain:

She's free now. Fern is free. . . .

14

THE EARTHQUAKE, actually, hadn't done too much damage. It was centered near Charleston and the shocks that had struck Augusta had been relatively weak. A few citizens had been hit by falling bricks, or cut by flying glass. Nobody had been killed. But many buildings had to be torn down as a result of it, and the topography of the whole region changed. The Sandhill rose many feet, and the downtown district of Augusta dropped, so that afterwards, buildings in the lower section of the city that had never been visible before could be seen from the hill. Of course, it did cause a few deaths, indirectly, Tyler Brantley's, for instance.

All that winter the work went on at Hiberion. By spring it was finished and the gardeners started landscaping. Fancy took an active interest in this, because she had her own ideas how she wanted the place to look.

Court was too busy at the mill to pay much attention to the house. All the advantages he had thought would come from having the mill located close to the cotton fields proved in practice to be no advantages at all. The differential in freight rates that Northern railroad owners saddled on the South, canceled out the advantage of being close to the cotton. The high static electricity in the air forced him to install expensive humidifiers, and the climate, which he had boasted of to Stan Woodbury, was so depressing to human spirits that his workers turned out to be less than half as productive as the Yankee mill workers he had known. Yet, he made a profit. The wages he paid his hands—wages no better and no worse than those paid by the rest of the Southern mill owners—made that certain. Court didn't feel bad about it. He was a man of his times. Grover Cleveland sat in the White House, ready to use the bayonet upon men who struck for better wages, and the people of Court's native Georgia were getting ready to elect John Gordon, of the famous triumvirate, to the governor's chair, knowing that he had gotten rich from his share of farming out convict labor. And bad as the wages were that Court paid his people, they were better than they had ever had before. No, Court didn't feel bad; he felt like a philanthropist.

It was April of 1887 when they finished the restoration of Hiberion. By early June, the gardens were done too. From her window, Fancy could see nearly all of it. She glanced quickly at Lynne, sleeping like a cherub in the wicker crib beside the big bed. Lynne was so beautiful. She had Fancy's black hair and blue eyes, but the expression in them reminded Fancy of Court. Looking at her, Fancy fairly ached to pick her up; but she did not. It was much better for the child to sleep.

She turned once more to the window, looking toward the river where the willows were. They reminded her of women washing their long hair in the water. Outside on the lawns the sunlight dappled with leaf shade lay along the moist green of the grass. Fancy let her gaze wander over the formal garden with its winding brick walks, broken into different levels, connected by low steps. There were fountains down there now, flashing in the sunlight. There was also a little garden house in the Japanese style, built of diagonal lattices with a pagoda roof. Fancy loved her garden house. It was very cool there, and she could sit and watch the little cherubs mounted on stone dolphins out of whose mouths the water arched into the goldfish pool. There were water lilies and hyacinths in that pool and the fish were so tame that they came up and nibbled at her fingers when she trailed them in the water.

She got up from the window and started out of the room. She wanted to go out into the garden now, and stand again to look at Hiberion under the trees. Then she decided that she'd better take a parasol, because it was already hot. She turned and hurried to her closet without even pausing to look at the blue wallpaper with the silver fleurs-de-lis in it. All the furniture in her room was Louis Fourteenth—delicate and fine, brushed very thinly with white so that the gilt underneath showed through. There was a crystal chandelier in the ceiling, a copy of the one in the big hall, but much smaller of course, and the pictures on the wall and her mirror had massive frames of the same rococo white and gilt.

She had picked out the decorations herself, which had surprised everybody because she wasn't supposed to know about such things. She didn't know really, but since the mill had become a going concern, a great many doors had been opened to her, and she had copied everything that she liked best in the houses of the wealthy people.

Her blue and white and gold room became her, but Court was a little out of place in it. He didn't complain, because he had his own retreat in the library on the second floor. It was paneled in dark oak, and had a rack for Court's assortment of fine guns, and another rack for the pipes he had taken to smoking. Fancy hated those pipes. Not only were they smelly, but she had heard Fern say once during those terrible five days while they were trying to keep Tyler alive, "I love to see a man smoke a pipe—especially a tall man. They're so becoming. . . ." And a couple of months later, Court had taken up pipe smoking.

The library was crowded from floor to ceiling with books. Although Lynne kept her busy, Fancy had read many of them. Some of them she didn't understand, but she was beginning to. She had found Shakespeare hard going, but Court had read some of it aloud to her, and she had caught the lovely music of the poetry—deep-voiced and strong, like the sea, and after that, whenever she didn't quite understand a passage, she tried reading it aloud. It nearly always helped. The Bible and Shakespeare were her favorites. She was slowly working her way into other books as well, and without her even knowing it, the books were changing her. By great effort, she had mended her speech to the extent that it was now usually more precise than Court's, although she didn't have half his vocabulary.

She went down the stairs. As she came down the staircase that spiraled down into the big hall without anything holding it up that a person could see, she could see Court in the dining salon, having breakfast with Governor Gordon. The governor had come last night with several members of his staff. They were, Fancy knew, only a few of the hundreds of guests that would fill up the great hall tonight. There was going to be a reception in honor of Agnes and Saphira and their new husbands. The girls were getting married this morning—both of them.

The breakfast was being served, Fancy saw, not on the big banquet table, but on the smaller one that had a revolving circular leaf in the middle, so that if anybody wanted anything, all he had to do was to give the leaf a whirl and the dish he wanted would fly around in front of him. And there was plenty of food on it—too much to Fancy's way of thinking. There was oatmeal and bacon and eggs, or ham and eggs, if a guest would rather have that. At the moment, the governor was almost hidden behind a stack of buckwheat cakes soaking in butter and syrup, while a pile of biscuits stood smoking on a platter beside him. The servants ran back and forth between the dining hall and the kitchen, keeping the plates filled. But those senators and lawyers were emptying them almost as fast as they were being filled up.

Court wasn't eating much—as usual. He never ate much, Fancy knew that. He sat there talking to his guests, with a big cup of scalding coffee in his hand; but the slice of smoked ham and the one thin pancake on his plate went untouched.

He'll never get fat, Fancy thought. That's good; I hate fat men.

While she was standing there on the stairs, watching them, a servant came in with a stack of letters. Court put them aside, barely looking at them and went on talking. But he glanced at the top one and something about it made him frown. He picked it up, and looked at the writing. Then he said something to the others—an excuse, Fancy thought, and opened it. He read it quickly, and even from where she stood, Fancy could see his face change.

But only for a moment. It was so quick that she thought she was imagining things, and tiptoed on down the stairs and out onto the veranda. It was cool and white and there was no way that anybody could tell that it hadn't been built along with the rest of the house. Fancy stood there, looking up at the graceful Doric columns, then she went out into the front yard where the rose bushes were, and stood by the bird bath looking back at Hiberion.

It was something now. Really something. Just like it had been—only better. For the gardens were finer than the original ones. Court had hired an Italian landscape artist, whom Stanton Woodbury had recommended, to do them.

"Yep," old Jeff Brantley said; "Hiberion wasn't this pretty before. Court's outdone us. It's kind of different, but I like it."

As she walked toward the gardens, she could see that even the outbuildings were finer than many a house that the quality of Augusta lived in. Then she went down the first of the low steps and took her seat in the pagoda-roofed garden house and looked out across the pool on the side view of Hiberion.

She loved Hiberion now. It was the kind of house that she had dreamed of. Only it was more than she had dreamed of because she hadn't been able to imagine anything like this. She thought about the girls, and made a face. She didn't care much for the men they were marrying. Both Thomas Wilson, Agnes' fiancé, and Joseph Plainfield, whom Saphira was marrying, seemed a little too sharp to her. They had both jumped at the high-paid jobs Court had offered them in the mill. Tom Wilson was the worse of the two. Joe wasn't so bad. Fancy thought that she might even learn to like him eventually.

She got up after a while and came back to Hiberion. There was so much to do. Most of it could be done without her help, but tonight had to be just perfect—for Court's sake. This reception for the girls was going to put him back where he belonged—right on top of the heap. Everybody was coming. They said that Court could deliver the vote of all of Richmond County through his mill workers. In a close election, that meant he could actually see to it that the man he wanted sat in the governor's chair. And Georgia elections were pretty nearly always close. People were saying that he was the richest man in the State, which wasn't so, because rebuilding Hiberion and improving the mill, and paying the interest and part of the principal on the debt had left them with precious little money. Enough to make the show that was expected of them—but not much more. Next year it would be better, and the year after that and all the coming years would be better and better until finally they would be as rich as people thought they were now. But Fancy knew it was a good thing for them to think so—Court could get the loans he needed, and the help of people who wouldn't lift a finger if they knew how things really were. . . .

Fancy made her way into the kitchen where the regular cook, Tildy Mae, and a crew of five more, hired especially for the occasion, were already hard at work. The baking was being done now, the pound and raisin cakes, as yellow as old gold with thick dark crusts were coming out of the oven. Tildy Mae was busily stirring the chocolate frosting for the chocolate layer cakes, and another girl was making a snowy covering of confectioner's sugar, egg whites and shredded coconut for others. Pies cooled on all the window sills and half grown black boys took turns at the cranks of the ice cream churns. Once the ice cream was hard, it would be packed in ice and rock salt and taken out to the spring house to stay frozen until tonight.

The other foods, the ones that had to be served hot, would have to wait until after the guests came, but the scalding, plucking, and cleaning of plump frying chickens filled the back porch with steamy, unpleasant odors. Boys ran back and forth to the smokehouse and came back laden with hams, many of which were rejected by Tildy Mae after one contemptuous glance. Potatoes were being peeled, and the yams were already being boiled into softness. Tonight they would be candied, and come out a golden-brown, silvered over with a rich crust of sugar, and dotted with spices. Bottles of wine were being brought up from the wine cellar and hurried down to the spring house to cool in the cold water. Later they would be thrust neck down into the buckets of ice that Jonas was busily cracking on the back porch, while the delivery wagon from the Augusta Ice Company unloaded still more cakes.

"Anything I can do?" she asked Tildy Mae, timidly.

Tildy Mae gave her a look that was only a little short of a glare. All black house servants were a little arrogant, and the cooks were the worst of the lot. And their snobbery was colossal and complete. Everybody else in Augusta might forget that Mrs. Courtland Brantley wasn't really 'quality';

but Tildy Mae wouldn't forget it. And she wouldn't let the rest of the Negroes forget it either. Only Matilda, Lynne's nurse, was immune to her influence. As for the rest, Fancy had to call twice to get an answer; to be sternly demanding to get any kind of service at all. If it hadn't been for Matilda and Belle and her children, Fancy might have developed the same feelings about Negroes that everybody else had. But they, and her own good heart prevented that.

"No'm," Tildy Mae said sullenly. "Just get yourself all hot'n' bothered in here, Ma'am. You go rest and 'tend to your dressing—I'll take care of things down here."

"All right, Tildy," Fancy said; "but see that it's done right."

As she left the kitchen, she pretended not to hear Tildy swearing under her breath.

She went back out into the garden and got Moses to cut the flowers for the tables and mantels. Then she went back upstairs and bathed, and started dressing. It was almost time for the wedding. When Court came into the bedroom, she was already dressed, and Candy, her maid, was putting the finishing touches to her hair. Candy had drawn it back from her ears and curled it into a bunch of soft, cascading curls down the back. These were held tightly close to their roots by a small, light blue ribbon, and Candy at the moment was fluffing the front of her hair into bangs, which lightly shadowed her forehead. She had a string of pearls around her neck, and two big pearls set in her earrings. Her dress was light-blue silk, cut low and square across the bodice, and edged there with shimmering white lace. The same kind of white lace was made into an outer skirt that covered but didn't hide the blue silk skirt beneath it and was tied in an enormous lace bow above the bustle. Her slippers were a darker blue, and her soft kid gloves that went up above her elbows a delicate off-white.

Court stood there, staring at her.

"You're lovely," he said. "Blue becomes you."

"Thanks, honey," Fancy said. Then to Candy: "You may go now."

Court sat down tiredly and felt the bristles of his beard.

"Damned lot of trouble," he said. "I'll have to shave again."

"We couldn't do any less for the girls," Fancy said. "Go on and shave and I'll help you get ready."

She went out to the upstairs hall closet and got his dress suit. When she came back, Court was burning something in the grate.

"What's that?" Fancy said.

"Nothing that concerns you," Court said flatly. "All this rigmarole because the gals are getting hitched. . . ."

While he was in the bathroom, Fancy laid out his dress suit. It was jet black with an even blacker silk braid running down the sides of his trousers. The trousers fitted very tightly, but thin though Court was, he had well-shaped legs. Fancy was glad of that. She didn't want him to make a poor appearance. The lapels of the jacket were of quilted black satin, and the stiff-bosom shirt was made of the finest kind of linen. Fancy laid the white piqué bow tie and the high, stiff winged collar and the stiffer cuffs on top of the shirt. Then she opened the little plush-lined box containing his diamond studs and cuff links.

He'll look so nice, she thought, as she put out his black silk socks and the patent-leather pumps with the black grosgrain bows on them.

"Oh, bother!" she said as she saw the jacket of his business suit lying in a heap where it had fallen from the back of the chair where Court had tossed it. She bent and picked it up and as she did so, her gaze fell on the grate. Whatever it was that Court had been burning had gone out, and it hadn't burned all the way up. She picked it up quickly and saw that it was part of an envelope. There was no letter in it. When she looked again, she saw that Court had burned the letter separately from the envelope, and that it was gone—only a heap of gray-white ash was left to tell where it had been.

She bent over the ash, seeing the words, "My own darling—" on the very top where the good rag paper had hung together in spite of the burning. Then she made the mistake of touching it, and it went to pieces so that she was left only with the piece of the envelope in her hand. The postmark hadn't burned. It said, "Boston, Massachusetts, June 10, 1887." And in the corner that was burned a part of a name was left: ". . . . tley," it said. She knew what it was then: Brantley. Fern Brantley.

She felt sick. So sick she had to sit down. Then she heard Court coming out of the bathroom, and got up quickly.

"What's the matter, Fan?" he said. "You look like something's bothering you."

"No," Fancy lied. "It's nothing, Court. I—I guess I'm just nervous, that's all. All these important people coming and . . ."

"Don't let it fret you, hon," Court said. "Come on, now—help me into my monkey suit."

A few minutes later, Fan gave a last pat to his bow tie and stepped back to look at him. He looks like a prince, she thought. My prince, mine. And nobody in the whole wide world is going to . . .

"Well, Fan," Court said gravely, "how do I look?"

"Beautiful," Fancy breathed.

"Beautiful?" Court said. "That's a funny word to use about a man."

"But you do," Fancy said; "you look beautiful, Court—just too beautiful for words. . . ."

Court looked at her. She was crying.

"Now what in hellfire ails you?" he said.

"I'm scared," she wept. "Oh, Court, honey, I'm scared stiff!"

"Don't be," Court said gently. "You've changed, Fan. Now you can hold your own with any of them. You can talk as nice, and you're a hell of a lot prettier and . . ."

"I'm not afraid of them," Fancy sobbed. "I'm scared of losing you!"

"Hell, baby, you couldn't give me away. Besides why are you scared of losing me all of a sudden?"

"You're so handsome. And all of those women are in love with you and you really don't love me, and besides you wanted a son instead of a daughter and . . ."

"Stop it!" Court roared. "You'll be a mess." He caught her by the shoulders, hard. "Fan," he said, "look at me."

She turned her face back toward him.

"There's time for a son. We're both young yet. So don't think about it now. And I'm not going to leave you—not ever."

Fancy looked at him. Her blue eyes were very clear.

"Not even—for Fern?" she said.

Court stood very still for a long, long time. Fancy could hear the clock on the mantel ticking. The sound of it filled the room.

"Not even for Fern," he said. Then he walked away from her to the door. "You come down as soon as you can," he said.

Fancy didn't remember a thing about the wedding afterwards. She seemed to be watching, but her eyes were shut off from her mind. After it was over, she told Court she had a headache, which was the truth, and went upstairs and lay down until it was nearly time for the reception.

Then she dressed again in another dress, all white, and came down the stairs. The big hall was crowded with people and snatches of talk came up to her.

"Yes sir! Cleveland's a good man! Honest as they come. I thought that scandal about the kid had finished him, but he came back fighting. Sure has made us one damned fine President—sure has. . . ."

"They say that Court's the power behind General Gordon. I wouldn't know, but . . ."

"And his wife, my dear—have you seen her? A nobody from Carolina! With all the nice, sweet girls we have here, you'd have thought he'd . . ."

"Laid the cornerstone two years ago under McDaniels; and believe it or not, Tom, the last time I was in Atlanta the building was damned near completed. It's the finest capitol building in the nation, sir—not even excluding Washington! I tell you the State of Georgia is progressing like nobody's business!"

"Well, now, John Gordon has been mixed up in a few shady deals—like that business of farming out convict labor. But on the other hand, who started the Georgia School of Technology, and the Georgia Normal and Industrial College? Got us a Federal grant for the Agricultural Experimental Station; those things aren't to be sneezed at, I say. . . ."

"Progress—that's what it is, boy—progress. Never will forget the day they turned on them newfangled electric lights atop of Big Steve on the corner of Greene and Jackson Streets. And the other day I talked to a man clear 'cross town—called him by telephone from Oertel's Drugstore. No sir, not even New York's going to outdo us down here in Augusta. . . ."

"Now it depends on how you look at it. Maybe education does make niggers uppity. But that there Paine Institute has been running all of four years now and a more quiet, orderly set of young niggers you'd never hope to see. . . ."

"And my dear, the minute Court got his hands on some money—these fellows rushed right in and married those two! If it hadn't been for Court, those two faded wrecks would be old maids today. . . ."

"There he is now! Oh, Sarah, isn't he the darlingest thing!"

Yes, Fancy thought, there he is. And he is the darlingest thing. But he's mine. Don't forget that. Don't any of you uppity females forget that.

Then she moved through the crowd and took Court's arm.

"So here you are," Court said. "I was getting worried about you, hon. Gentlemen, allow me to present my wife."

Fancy could hear the talk dying. All over the hall it died. And one by one they turned to look at her. Many of them had seen her before—at Court's trial. But many of them had not. And they, the ones who had never seen her before tonight, had the funniest expressions on their faces. Fancy thought that they looked stricken.

"Why," a whisper came over to her, "she *is* pretty! I'd heard she was, but I never would have believed it!"

And a man's snort, answering:

"Pretty, hell! That there girl is beautiful."

She could see the women looking at her dress, as if they were memorizing it. Tomorrow, she thought, they'll be telling each other what I had on, right down to my skin. But she made herself smile when Court introduced her to them and tried to remember their names. She couldn't, though. There were just too many of them.

Then Ernest, the butler, announced that dinner was served. Fancy and

Court led the guests into the big dining salon. There was too much food, and too much wine, and too many people, so that Fancy couldn't eat anything. Besides, the men kept proposing toasts to the happy couples, so that even only sipping each one to be polite, she found that her head was spinning. She wasn't having a good time. She kept remembering a pile of ashes in the bedroom grate, and a half burned-out envelope postmarked Boston. Then she looked up and caught Saphira's eye. Saph was sitting next to her Joe, but when she looked at Fancy she winked her eye. Somehow, after that, Fancy felt better. She smiled at Saph, and looked at old Jeff Brantley, sound asleep over his half filled plate, his old fingers wrapped around his empty champagne glass.

Now the Negroes were coming with the desserts, chocolate layer cake and raisin cake and sweet potato pie, and coconut cake and huge bowls of ice cream. Behind them came more waiters with a big cut-glass bowl filled with sillabub, heavy cream whipped very stiffly with sugar, and dashed with sherry.

Fancy ate a dish of ice cream and that took care of the wine. On her left, a fat woman confessed that she was 'fair about to burst.' Fancy thought she looked it.

Then the dinner was over, and the Negroes took all the tables out of the hall and the dancing started. It came to Fancy that she seldom got a chance to dance with Court. Nothing in their life together had been normal or ordinary or usual enough for that. But, now, swinging through the first waltz with him, she remembered all the times they had danced during the five years they had lived at Melody. Those had been the good years. The best. It was fun dancing with Court. He danced beautifully. So, for that matter, did she. She could see that people were stopping to watch them.

Then he bowed to her and was gone. He had to dance with the other ladies; she knew that. But every time his partner happened to be young and pretty, Fancy stiffened and missed a step. I'm being a fool, she told herself, but I can't help it.

Then Court did a funny thing. He stopped dead in the middle of a dance and stood there staring at the door. He whispered something to his partner, one of the pretty young McQuinizy girls from Savannah, and walked toward the door. Fancy looked after him. Then she, too, stopped dancing.

For Jed Hawkins stood in the doorway, looking over the gathering with a mocking grin on his face.

"You'll excuse me, won't you?" she said to her partner, and started off after Court.

When she was close, she saw that Jed wasn't dressed for the evening, and she realized suddenly that it was strange that he wasn't. That business suit he had on meant only one thing: Court hadn't invited him.

Invitations had been sent to everybody of any importance in the State. That should have included Jed. He had been a State Senator twice now. In spite of his youth, people were mentioning him as a likely prospect for the governor's chair. . . .

Thinking about it now, Fancy remembered positively that his name hadn't been on that list. She had checked it over with Court herself. She should have noticed the omission then. But when she had left Savannah, she had pushed Jed Hawkins out of her mind. And so many things had happened afterwards: Lynne's being born, Tyler dying like that, so terribly, the mill. She realized that the thought of Jed hadn't entered her head in nearly two years. That was a good thing. It meant that what had happened between them had had no real importance. She was glad of that.

Then she saw Court's face. He hadn't forgotten. He had left Jed's name off that list on purpose.

It made her feel good right down to the tips of her toes. Court cared enough about her to be a little afraid of Jed's boundless charm. Then she remembered that letter with the words, "My own darling—" still showing on the thick gray ash, and the envelope postmarked Boston, and what got into her then was a kind of meanness she hadn't known she had.

"Congratulations, Court," Jed said. "This is sure one fine turnout. Yessir, mighty fine. . . ."

Fancy could see Court struggling with himself. But for all their faults the Brantleys had always been gentlemen.

"Come in and join us, won't you, Jed?" he said quietly.

"Don't reckon I'm dressed right for—"

"Oh, bother!" Fancy said. "You look a sight better than three-quarters of the men here. Come in, or I'm going to be mighty mad at you, Jed."

"That does it," Jed grinned. "What's the occasion, Court?"

"My sisters," Court said, "got married today—both of 'em."

"Well now, reckon that does call for a celebration. Happened to be down in Waynesboro on business; but I came the rest of the way up here to see you two—youall and the new addition. Is she like you, Fan?"

"Very much," Court said.

"Then I reckon I'll wait," Jed said, "till she grows up. Missed out with her maw, but me'n' little Lynne are going to come to an agreement right now."

Fancy took his hand.

"Come on," she said, "I'll show her to you."

Court looked at her.

"No, Fan," he said; "Jed hasn't even had a drink, and you can't leave your guests. It would be downright impolite."

"Oh, bother my guests!" Fancy said, but Jed shook his head.

"Court's right, honey," he grinned. "Besides which, if you were to drag me upstairs, every woman in the house would start speculating on just what we were going to do up there. And the conclusions they'd arrive at would be mighty interesting; but they sure Lord wouldn't do you any good. Besides which," and that engaging grin of his widened, "when folks crowd Court here into shooting me, I aim to be guilty as hell. That would be worth dying for. So, honeychild, I'll just mosey up and see my little sweetie pie myself after a while. Her mammy's with her, isn't she? Good—then me'n' my future sweetheart can chat in private. . . ."

"Jed," Fancy said, "you're so blamed sensible that it hurts. And I think I mostly hate people anyhow. . . ."

"Why?" Jed said.

"They get things so mixed up. They interfere where they've got no business to. They—" she looked Court straight in the face, "write letters and say things they shouldn't, and try to steal what sure Lord doesn't belong to them. Yes, I hate 'em all right. Especially women."

Court's face was stony. He didn't say anything. Jed looked at him, then back at Fancy.

"I think I'll take that drink now, boy," he said.

Fancy waited until Jed had had his bourbon and branch water, and had chatted for a while with Court. Then she went up to where the two of them stood.

"Come on," she said, "you haven't danced with me yet."

Jed glanced uneasily at Court. The look on Court's face delighted Fancy to the bottom of her soul. What she was doing, what she was going to do, was foolishness and worse, but she didn't care. Court had hurt her too much and too often. Time she paid him back. With interest.

She danced with Jed. She tilted her head back and laughed. She was gay—too gay, so that the frown on Court's face got blacker by the minute. Then, seeing that he was dancing with one of the ladies present, at the other end of the hall, and couldn't see her, she tightened her grip on Jed's arm.

"Come on!" she whispered, "let's go out in the garden."

"No," Jed said; "'tain't safe. Court wouldn't like it. Wouldn't myself if I were in his shoes."

"Oh, bother Court and what he doesn't like!" Fancy said. It came to her then, that she meant it, and that was a funny thing. And right then she learned something—something that every honest woman knows but precious few will admit—that nobody on earth is capable of loving another person all the time, or even as much sometimes as she does at others. Any two people who live together have times when they're mighty close to hating each other, and that's a natural thing. Thinking about it, Fancy got a glimpse of something else: that the time could come, when after years of worshiping Court Brantley and getting only bits and scraps and cold left-overs of affection from him, she wouldn't care any more. One morning she would wake up and be free. Like that. It was an awful thing to think, so she pushed it from her mind.

She took Jed by the hand and led him out a side door into the garden where the fountains were. They were white in the moonlight, and the roses next to them were white, too, so that out there it was very pretty.

Jed stood by the pool and stared at her.

"You're lovely," he said. His voice sounded strange. Deep, kind of. Hoarse —a little strained. "God, but you're lovely!"

"Thanks, Jed," Fancy said.

"You didn't bring me out here," he said, "for a tête-à-tête. Now did you?"

She recognized that tone now. Jed was angry. With her.

"No," Fancy said.

"Court made you mad. Some young filly or another's been writing him letters. I gathered that much. So you thought you'd use me—to kind of even up the score. Not that you give one hoot up a hollow stump about me. . . ."

"Should I?" Fancy said.

"No. Not according to the rules. But I don't play according to rules. Neither do you. Found that out the last time we—went into a garden."

"I'm sorry, Jed," Fancy said.

"Don't be. Not now. Be sorry later. I'll do all the sorrowing necessary for tonight."

"Why?" Fancy whispered.

"Because the girl I love thinks I'm something to be used. Because she ain't above playing children's games. You kick my dog, I hit your cat. Hell, baby, what do you think I am?"

"A very nice man," Fancy said. "A man who ought to find himself some nice, sweet girl and . . ."

Jed snorted.

"While you're still alive and in the same world with me?" he growled. "Come on, Fan, let's go back in. . . ."

Fancy looked at him in wonder.

"Aren't you," she said, "even going to try to kiss me?"

"No. Reckon I do have rules after all. One of them is, I only kiss gals who want me to. Me, special. Meaning it—not for a lark. I don't play children's parlor games, Fan."

Fancy got up very slowly from the bench. It had all gone wrong. She felt like a fool. Feeling like that, mean-mad and ugly, she'd wanted only to hurt Court. And she had ended up by hurting Jed—and herself.

The worst of it was that when they came up the path, they saw Court coming toward them. He stopped and stood there, waiting.

"This," he said quietly, "sure doesn't look good, Jed."

"Damned right it doesn't," Jed said, "and the hell of it is it only looks that way. What kind of a fool do you think I am, Court Brantley?"

"Don't know," Court said. "What kind are you?"

"A mighty big one, I'll admit. But not the kind who plays a hand he ain't got a Chinaman's chance of winning. If I started something with this girl whose only fault is she's crazy enough to be in love with you, I'd take her so damn far away that you'd never find her. Not just out into your pretty garden, Court—halfway across the world."

"I see," Court said drily. "Then why did you come out here?"

"So she could cry on the shoulder of a friend she trusts over a man who ain't got any better sense than to try to keep up something he ought to have dropped years ago. Who don't know the difference between a blue diamond and polished glass. Hell, boy, I can't take Fan from you—though I wish to God I could. But you can throw her away. And you're doing it—damned fast."

"I think," Court said, "that you're wearing your welcome mighty thin, Jed."

"Consider it plumb wore out," Jed said. " 'Night, Fan. When you've had enough of this arrogant jackass, just sing out. I'll be waiting. . . ."

Then Court hit him. His left hand jabbed out very fast, the forearm stiff, traveling no more than eight inches, with all Court's weight behind it, pivoting off the ball of his left foot, without any warning, smooth-working, fast, and Jed Hawkins went down into the rose bushes.

He floundered there, breaking the stems so that the white blossoms showered petals. Like snow, Fancy thought, crazily, like snow. Then he was up again, swinging both arms like a windmill, clumsily, and Court Brantley laughing a little, boring in, hooking short rights and lefts to his middle until his hands came down, and then swinging very smoothly and very hard, so that Fancy thought sure the blow would tear his head off; but Jed Hawkins got up again, even after that.

She couldn't stand it. She loved Court, but this wasn't fair. Court was bigger and stronger, and ever so much better at this, and Jed's face was already bad to look at, bleeding from the nose and the corners of his mouth and his eyes closing.

"Stop it!" she screamed at Court. "Court Brantley, you stop it!"

Court didn't even look at her. He moved in on Jed, catlike, his face absolutely murderous. She could see that Jed was out on his feet. This time Court didn't try to knock him down. He just hooked Jed's head, back and forth, right, then left, each hook setting it up for the next so that it was getting to be a bloody mess and Fancy couldn't stand it.

She whirled between them, raking her long nails down Court's face, bringing blood. Court Brantley had been a gentleman all his life, but five minutes ago, he had stopped being one, had become something else, something very ugly that Fancy had no name for. He felt her nails dig in, and he brought his opened right hand up hard, the back of it smashing across her mouth, so that she went down into the thorny bushes, and lay there.

That stopped it.

"You bastard," Jed Hawkins whispered.

Court didn't say anything to him. He put out his hand to Fancy, but she refused it. As she got up, the rose bushes tore her dress, and there was mud on it and her face was a mess, with the red mark of his hand across it, the lips swollen and trembling.

"I'm sorry, Fan," Court said.

She didn't answer him. She got up and started back toward the house and then she saw it. Her guests, all her guests. At the windows. On the little veranda on the side of the house. And moonlight so bright you could read a newspaper by it.

Court looked at Jed Hawkins.

"You," he said, "get out of here."

"Don't worry," Jed Hawkins said, "I'm going."

Fancy stopped on the path, looking at all those people. Her face felt like fire, and the rose thorns had scratched her arms. But she wasn't thinking about that. She was feeling cheapened, dirtied. Down deep. On the inside, where nothing would ever do it any good.

Like a street woman being fought over by a couple of drunken brutes. Like—like—like hill trash, the image came unbidden into her mind. They see through me now. I'm not nobody, just a thing my husband has to fight other men over and slap around to keep straight. Oh God, oh Jesus, I—

Then she put her head up high and walked toward them. Very calmly. Straight. She looked at them all, one by one, straight in the face, coming toward them very slowly, so that they dropped their gaze and opened a way for her.

She went through the crowd without saying anything or looking at them until she came to the big stairway. That far, she carried it off. But she broke there. She covered her face with one arm, and ran up the stairs, blindly, trailing a glissando of broken sobs behind her.

Court came in, and turned to his guests.

"Mighty sorry, folks," he said. "Took on a spot too much, I reckon. Me'n' Jed had words, and Fan tried to separate us. . . . My apologies. . . ."

"It's all right, Court," Bob McCullen said. "Reckon we all get riled up, once in a while. . . ."

But it wasn't all right. And, looking up that stairway where Fancy had fled, Court had the feeling it never would be. . . .

15

IT WAS RAINING. It seemed to Fancy that all she had done that summer of 1888 was to quarrel with Court and listen to the rain. She hadn't quarreled with him about Fern or any other woman. Their arguments now were about the mill. They had started because Fancy wanted to learn something about a mill—how it was run and all. And now that Lynne was able to walk a little, Fancy didn't have too much to do. Matilda took care of the child, and that left Fancy with an awful lot of time for thinking.

One of the things that she thought was that although Court was young and strong, she'd be in an awful mess if anything ever happened to him. She knew a little about the mill, but not enough to run it if she had to. So she started in to learn. And that was one of the strange things about Fancy—whatever she set her mind on learning, she learned very thoroughly. She started going down to the mill, and getting the girls to teach her to run the light machinery. By the time that Court, who was busy in the office, found it out, she could run every piece of machinery in the plant that was operated by women.

She knew how the heavier machines worked too. She stood by and watched the men operate them and asked dozens of questions. And when Court came home at night she asked him from whom he bought the cotton, and how much he paid for it, and how to tell good cotton from bad. Court answered her questions and also told her how he sold it, and to whom, and how much he got for it.

"Of course," he said, "there's the matter of freight rates, and wages to the hands, and doctor bills for the sick, and the salaries of the teachers in the mill school, and the preacher's salary, too. And you've got to figure in a certain amount of loss in lint, and repairs to broken-down machines and—say, why the devil do you want to know all this, Fan?"

"I just want to know, that's all," Fancy said.

But the next day he walked through the plant and found her doffing bobbins along with the bobbin boys. He stood there watching her.

"Learning the business from the ground up, eh, Fan?" he said. "What's the matter—planning to take over?"

"No, hon," Fancy said. "Just thought it would come in mighty handy to know how to run this place if you got sick or something. . . ."

"I'm not going to get sick," Court said. "And ladies in your position don't doff bobbins. I won't have my wife lowering herself so."

"Lowering myself? How can I do that any more? Appears to me you've done enough slapping me before all those people at your sisters' wedding," Fancy said. "Suppose you had an accident? Suppose you even got killed? Don't you see, Court, that I'd be helpless? Anybody could come in here and cheat my eyeballs out, and I wouldn't know the difference. That is, I wouldn't have known the difference. I do now."

"You," Court said, "could always call in your beloved Jed."

Fancy looked him in the face. Calmly.

"Jed doesn't know one blamed thing about a mill," she said.

"Then you could call in Wyche Weathers. He does. And he's just as ready as Jed to take you off my hands. Or perhaps any of half a dozen other men that I don't know about."

Fancy didn't say anything for a long while. She needed the time to get the shake out of her voice. But she didn't get it out. Not entirely.

"White trash from the Carolina hills, eh Court?" she said. "Still think I'm no good, don't you? All right. Wyche writes me. And not one of his letters ever started off, 'My own darling—' like that two-timing Fern wrote you! But you know that; you've seen every letter he's ever written me. There wasn't a thing in them that I couldn't have read to Lynne. And Jed doesn't write me at all."

"You didn't have to show me your mail," Court said stiffly. "I didn't ask. Anyhow, after this, you stay home where you belong!"

"Who's going to make me?"

"I am," Court said.

"I don't think so," Fancy said quietly; "I don't think you're man enough."

They made it up after a while, without ever saying, "I was wrong; I'm sorry." They made it up by letting the matter drop. But it came up again and there were more quarrels. And all that summer and into the fall, it rained.

Because of the rain, Court took some of the stronger men out of the mill and raised the level of the bluff between Dry Gully and the river, thus making a very effective levee out of it. There was some grumbling about that down in Augusta. Augusta didn't have a levee, and throughout its history from the time of the Yazoo Freshet right down to 1888 the town had been flooded many times.

"It'll raise the water level down here sure as shooting," the older citizens complained. "That upper valley used to be a natural spillway and kind of kept us from having bad floods down here. But with this here levee of Court's piling it up, we're sure to get washed out, come any kind of high water. . . ."

"They're right," Court admitted to Fancy when she asked him about it, "but without the mill, where would the town be? The Ellises have moved on. They've cut over, bled white, and ruined the woodlands for miles around. Nobody ever thinks of blaming them for the fact that they've tripled Augusta's flood danger by denuding the earth of its natural barriers, the trees. Besides, I've got sluice gates and spillways that I could open if it got too bad. And dangblast it, Fan, why the devil don't they build a levee to protect the city? They've been talking about it for a hundred years!"

He was smart, Fancy had to admit that. And the best thing about him was the way he handled his workers. He acts, she thought, like he's their father, and him only thirty-six. Everybody right down to old Maud thinks nothing of walking into Hiberion and telling him his troubles and asking him to help him. And he always does. Court's a good man. I guess I wasn't rightly cut out to make him the kind of wife he needs. Everybody in town, except children and the colored people, calls him by his first name. The colored people too, only they put Mister in front of it. And every man in the mill can stop work and come into the office and make a suggestion or a complaint. And he'll listen to them, too. If he can't do what they want, he'll explain why just like they were the president of the bank or the chairman of the board of directors.

The mill hands loved the ground he walked on. Fancy knew that, and she knew why. It was mighty hard to hate a man who would shut up shop any time he felt like it and give a picnic or a barbecue for all his hands. Many a time Fancy had heard him walking down the line and calling out:

"Ned, Tad, Lester—you boys go home and get your shotguns and meet me in my office in an hour. Heard there's a mighty heap of quail out by the old Brewster place. . . ."

The men swore he was the best shot in Richmond County.

"Yessir, you ought to of seen him! Ten miles we tramped and him not even breathing hard. Reckon he got twicet as many birds as the rest of us put together. And when ole Tad here come out with a jug of corn likker, he took his swig right along with the next man, not even wiping the bottle with his hand. Ain't many big men like ole Court, I'll tell you. . . ."

"When my Sal come down with the misery in the chest, he come over to the house and brung his wife with him, and her this big with child. Fair thought he was going to bust out crying when he looked at poor Sal. Had Doc Brewster over quicker'n a wink, and all the medicines that could be fetched up from Augusta. Course it didn't do no good, Sal ups and dies; but it sure Lord warn't because Court warn't in there a-trying. . . ."

The minister at Dry Gully Church called him a gallant gentleman. Fancy had heard him say that many times. She often went to church in Dry Gully, because the simple, forceful preaching was more to her liking than the dignified services of the Episcopal Church in Augusta. The teachers at Dry Gully School could never praise him enough. Court wouldn't have liked such praise, so Fancy didn't tell him about it. And his people thought it wasn't any more than the truth, so they didn't tell him either.

It was a funny thing, Fancy said, that everybody loves him and can get along with him except me. I love him, too; but I sure Lord can't get along with him—not longer than a week at a time. . . .

So things went smoothly for Court Brantley. When a union organizer showed up and tried to unionize the mill, the workers beat him up and threw him out. He made the mistake of calling Court an "oppressor of labor." Court didn't think of himself as an oppressor of labor. The little houses that he had built for his people were miserable shacks—even he knew that; but they were tight against the wind and the rain, and they were painted, a thing the mill people had never even hoped to see. His workers, called pine-barren crackers, white trash, rednecks, by the great and proud, were treated like men and women by him. Besides, they were so used to freezing in the damp Georgia winters, and roasting in the summer sun, that any degree of comfort seemed real luxury to them. And the houses he gave them, perched upon the Godforsaken ravines and red hillsides, were better houses than most of the small farmers of Georgia lived in, and were not even to be spoken of in the same breath with the miserable shanties in which the 'croppers shivered in half the year and baked the other half.

Even the wages Court paid, twenty-five cents a day to bobbin boys, forty to sixty cents a day for spinners, and seventy cents to one whole dollar for weavers, seemed like a lot of money to the poor whites he hired. The three-dollar-a-day men, the trained mechanics who kept the machinery running, became the big men of Dry Gully. They ordered tailor-made suits from Augusta, and smoked nickel cigars.

So, if an entire family, from ten-year-old Willie, busy at doffing bobbins, to seventy-year-old Grandpaw, slowly sweeping up the lint while Maw twisted lint and Paw wove, had to work sixty-eight hours a week to meet even their simple wants, it must not be imagined that they thought of Court Brantley as a mighty mean man—since other mills not too far away paid less, and other workers had a seventy-two hour week.

Therefore, when Sal came down with a misery in her chest and lay there a-spittin' blood, Lester Watts didn't blame Court Brantley. When Ted Spink's kid was born a queer, still brat who would never be right in the head, Ted didn't even connect it with the mill. Not that, nor the pains in his back and the ringing in his ears. He never saw the sun any more from one week end to the next, but neither Ted nor Lester nor any of the others knew that sunlight had anything to do with health. Sow belly or fatback and greens and corn pone might and did riddle his family with pellagra, but what else had he eaten before he came to Dry Gully, and whenever before had he had so much?

These things, the preacher told him, were visitations from God for his sins. And if Ted sometimes wondered when he ever got the time or the energy to commit any sins, a little thinking could call to mind some mighty good substitutes: the time he got drunk down in Augusta and was thrown out of Riley's Saloon, that painted little daughter of joy he got mixed up with the Saturday night he managed to slip his block, because Lu wasn't feeling up to going into town, the crap game he got into in back of Riley's, that had his whole family eating stale cornbread for a week, washed down with water, which at least cost nothing. . . .

If Ted had asked Court, Court would have sworn at him and told him he was entitled to a couple of sins; but Ted was mightily afraid that Court might find out what he'd been up to. Like all the mill workers, Ted rated Court only a little way beneath God. How the devil did he know so much? Which member of the family was sick, and Sary Lou's marks in school, and old man Spink's rheumatism. Like the other day when he'd stopped by the creel, and said:

"Now look here, Ted, I know a man's a man; but if you keep on going down to Myrtie Torrence's place, like you did last Saturday night, you're going to catch something you don't want and bring it home to poor Lu. . . ."

Ted had stood there, staring at him in wonder.

It was very simple, really. It did something for a mill hand's pride to be on friendly terms with Court. They talked their heads off to him. If anybody in the mill, down to the smallest bobbin boy did something out of the ordinary, Court knew about it the first thing in the morning. And Court had a wonderful memory. Besides, he thought of them all as being his family, and was always asking after them, getting the details of their lives outside of the mill, which, being a Southerner, he never thought of as being none of his damned business. And he was always giving them advice.

"I know what I'm talking about," he said to a group of younger workers as they sat around the campfire after a 'possum hunt. "I made some damn bad mistakes myself not too long ago. I'm not setting myself up as a plaster saint. I couldn't; you fellows know my history much too well. But a man who can't profit by his own mistakes is a fool; and a man who's got sense enough to learn something from somebody else's is plumb, downright smart. That's all I'm trying to do—smarten you boys up a bit, that's all. . . ."

They nodded in sage agreement, chewing on their blades of grass.

And still it rained. Fancy thought if she heard the sound of it any more, dripping off the eaves of the house, she'd go fair out of her mind. It gave her much too much time for thinking and wondering and one of the things she wondered about was how Maw and Pap and Randy were making out, over there in Carolina. She remembered how bad those first years at Melody had been for her and Court, and Melody was a good plantation, rich, black bottom land. That hillside farm of Pap's was worse than bad—it was terrible.

So that morning, just before Court started out for Dry Gully, she spoke to him about it.

"I feel kind of ashamed," she told him, "that I haven't been back to see my folks. Wrote 'em once or twice, but they didn't answer. I really didn't expect them to—they're mighty poor hands at writing."

"Why don't you run over there?" Court said. "It's not too much of a drive. Take Thomas and the closed carriage. Spend a few days with them."

Fancy looked at him.

"Thanks, Court," she said. "Thought maybe you'd raise some objection, but I should have known better. You're glad enough to get me out from underfoot, aren't you?"

"I didn't say that," Court said.

"Know you didn't. Didn't need to—it's true enough, though. All right, it doesn't matter. I meant to go anyway. And, Court . . ."

"Yes, Fan?"

"I should take them something—something nice. . . ."

Court put his hand in his breast pocket and came out with his checkbook. Then he went into his study and scrawled his name at the bottom of a check. But he didn't write in any figures. He left that part blank.

"Here," he said. "From what you've told me about your folks, they're probably in damned bad shape financially. Straighten 'em out. Pay off their debts. Buy that brother of yours some decent stock, and some good farming equipment. A tract of better land, too—if you want to. Spend what you have to—it's yours anyhow. Never could have made it without you. . . ."

Fancy got up and kissed him, hard.

"Never will understand you," she said, winking back her tears. "Half the time I'd like to shoot you, then you go and do something like this. . . ."

"Don't mention it," Court grinned. "I always want to shoot you—in the daytime."

"Court Brantley!" Fancy laughed. "What a thing to say!"

She started out early that next morning. Thomas had a hard time getting through, because most of the Carolina lowlands were already flooded. A couple of times they had to be hauled out of the mud by the local farmers with their teams. But when they got up into the hills it was better. At least it was better at first but afterwards it got worse because the hill trails really weren't made for such a fine carriage.

But Thomas was a good driver and they made it, although it took them all day to go the twenty miles.

The first thing Fancy saw when she got home was that the house looked a little better. The porch and the steps had been repaired, and all the windows had oiled paper in them. A wisp of smoke curled up from the chimney and she could smell collard greens cooking. Thomas helped her down from the carriage, and she went up on the porch and knocked.

A young woman answered the door. She was skinny as a rail fence and had hair like wet straw. Her lower lip bulged over a wad of snuff. She had a baby in her arms.

This, Fancy thought, this is what I would have looked like—if I had stayed. . . .

The young woman stood there looking at her, her jaw dropping open, so that Fancy could see her bad, uneven teeth.

"Good evening," Fancy said. "Mister Williamson at home?"

"Yes'm," the girl said; then she turned back toward the room and called: "Ran—dee! Company!"

Randy got up and came to the door. Just looking at him, Fancy wanted to cry. He looked so—so beaten. Two other children came with him, clinging to his knees. Their clothes were made of sacking, and their feet were bare.

"Howdy, Ma'am," Randy said politely, but his eyes were puzzled. It was dusk, but there was light enough to see.

"Randy," Fancy whispered, "don't you know me?"

"No'm," Randy said. "Got a feeling I've seed you somewheres, Ma'am, but I can't rightly place you. . . ."

"May I come in, please?" Fancy said.

"Why, shore, Ma'am!" Randy said. "Our little shack ain't much, but we'd be mighty honored. . . ."

But the minute she was inside, where the lamp was, Randy stopped dead. His mouth worked several times before he got it out:

"Fan! Great, jumping Jehosiphats, Sal—this here's my sister, Fan!"

"Howdy, Ma'am," Sal said. "Mighty proud to make your acquaintance."

Fancy took the thin calloused hand. The children came up to her timidly.

"This here is Ted—and this is Lester," Randy said proudly. "The baby's a girl. We called her Lucy. Children, meet yore Aunt Fancy."

Fancy knelt on the well scrubbed floor and kissed them.

"I—I didn't bring them anything," she wailed; "I didn't even know about them." Then she got up, looking at Randy.

"Ran," she whispered, "what about Maw?"

Randy looked down at the floor.

"Gone," he said, "these six years, Fan. Didn't seem to have much heart for living—after you left. . . ."

"And, Pap?"

"The year after that. Took to drinking worse than ever after Maw died. Got liquored up one day whilst I was out in the fields and wandered off. Took me three days to find him. Never would of, I reckon, wasn't for the buzzards. . . ."

"Oh, Randy, no!"

"They hadn't got at him," Randy said quickly. "They was still up there —a-circling."

"Thank God for that," Fancy said.

"You shore do look fine," Randy said. "Married?"

"Yes. A fine man, Randy—didn't have much when I started with him, but now he's one of the richest men in the State. . . ."

"You always was lucky," Randy said.

"Ran—how's the farm?"

"We can eat," Randy said tiredly, "that's about all."

"Tell me something," Fancy said; "you know of any good land hereabouts—for sale?"

"You planning to farm, Fan? As I recollect, you never had much use for it."

"No, Ran," Fancy said, "I'm not going to farm—you are."

It took him a little while to get her meaning. When he did, lean, work-hardened man that he was, he cried a little. Sal cried a great deal.

"I'd sure admire to kiss you, Ma'am," she blubbered; "I surely would!"

Fancy kissed her.

They all sat up late that night, talking. Randy offered to fix a place for Thomas to sleep in the barn. But Thomas gave one look at the dirty straw and his broad nostrils flared.

"No, thank you, sah!" he said; "I'll bunk in the carriage." Thomas was a house Negro—and had been one all his life.

The next morning Fancy and Randy drove out to old man Wilkins' place. It was in a valley, and was the best farm in the entire county. But old man Wilkins had died five years ago, and left a young widow, younger than Fancy. Unable to farm the place herself, she had married again, but she had followed her heart instead of her head, and the man of her choice was a dreamy youth who liked to sit and watch the sun go down over the mountains. When, driven by his bride's tongue-lashing, he'd tried to work the place, he'd doubled up over the plow and started coughing—blood. So, the Wilkins place was for sale.

When Fancy got back into her carriage to drive home, Randy Williamson was the owner of the best farm in the county, the children had shoes and store-bought clothes for the first time in their lives, and Sal had three new dresses. And the stonecutter in the village was hard at work on a marble headstone to replace the simple wooden cross over Maw and Pap's grave. . . .

But it didn't stop raining, down in Augusta. By the tenth of September, the Savannah crept up over its banks and flooded the city. On the eleventh, it was thirty-eight feet high. Fancy lay awake all the first part of the night listening to the noise in the darkness. She could hear the water, and the people crying, and men shouting. People passed by on rafts and in boats.

Court was awake too, listening; but he didn't say anything to her. Along about eleven o'clock one of the Negroes came and knocked on the door and told them there was a man downstairs to see Court. Court slipped on his dressing gown and went downstairs. He stayed a long time, and when he came back, he started to get dressed without a word.

"What's the matter, Court?" Fancy said.

"Bunch of people up at the mill," Court said. "They want to open the sluice gates to relieve the pressure down here. I've got to go up there, quick!"

Fancy was already out of bed.

"I'm coming too," she said.

"Don't be a fool, Fan," Court said. "It's going to be a whole lot of trouble getting up there—and the mood those folks are in, it might be dangerous."

"I don't care," Fancy said; "I'm coming."

"All right," Court said; "on your head be it."

It was a lot of trouble getting up to Dry Gully. The water in the streets of Augusta was so deep by then that part of the time the horses had to swim. The canal banks were still holding. After they let go, not even a horse could have got through.

Fancy was wet and cold and miserable by the time they reached the mill. Court turned to Brayton, his assistant manager—the man who had brought the message.

"Where are they?" he said.

"Over there," Brayton said, and pointed.

Fancy could see the group of men standing in front of the mill. They had shotguns in their hands. She thought that something about some of them looked familiar, and when she got closer she saw what it was. Leading the group were Tom and Buck Ellis.

"All right, boys," Court said; "speak your piece."

A man named Ronald Raeburn stepped forward.

"It's this way, Mister Brantley," he said. "We're already under water down in Augusta. . . ."

"I know that," Court said.

"But now the city engineer says the canal banks are threatening to let go. If they do that, it'll be the worst disaster in the city's history—Lord knows how many people will get drowned. So we figgered—"

"You figured?" Court said; "or Tom and Buck Ellis figured—which?"

"Well now, Tom did say . . ."

"I don't give a damn what he said," Court said quietly. "I know what's on his mind. This looked like one damn fine chance of getting even with me by ruining my mill beyond repair. That business about relieving the pressure down below is just so much hogwash."

Then Joe Cummings stepped forward.

"No it isn't, Court," he said.

Court looked at him.

"You, too, Joe?" he said.

"No—not me, too. You'll notice I don't have a gun in my hands. I came with the others because I agree that there might be a chance to keep those banks from collapsing. Thought I could talk to you man to man—as a friend. I don't hold with using force. I don't even have a gun with me."

"All right," Court said. "Know what it'll cost me if I open those gates?"

"Yes. And I know what it'll cost the folks down in Augusta if you don't, Court. Their lives. Don't think Dry Gully Mill, important as it is, stacks up above that. What do you say, Court?"

"No," Court said.

"Then by God," Buck Ellis said, "we'll damned well see that you open them!"

"I'm outnumbered, Buck," Court said; "but somebody's going to get hurt if you try it. And given my choice, reckon you've got a pretty fair idea who that somebody'd be."

"Come on, boys," Buck Ellis said, "let's take him!"

Fancy put up her hand.

"Wait a minute, boys!" she said.

The men stopped, looking at her.

"Joe," she said, "is that the truth? Folks will get drowned if we don't open the gates?"

"Yes'm," Joe Cummings said.

"What guarantee," Court growled, "do I have that those banks won't let go even if I do open them?"

"None," Joe said honestly. "It's a chance you'd have to take. But it's a good chance, Court. It's the only decent choice."

"Standing there jawing," Tom Ellis said. "Let's get started!"

Court put his hand inside his coat and let it rest there.

"No, Court," Fancy said. "Don't pull a gun. Not for this. Not over a thing like this."

Court stared at her.

"You against me, too?" he said.

"No," Fancy whispered, "not ever against you, honey. I'm always for you. It's not being against you to tell you that you can't let people get drowned on account of buildings or machinery. Please, Court . . ."

Brayton looked at Court, helplessly.

The squareness went out of Court's shoulders. He slumped forward a little like a man who was very tired and very old.

"Open them, Brayton," he said.

"Yessir," Brayton said. "Right away, sir!"

Court looked at the group of men who stood before the gates of the mill. "Now, if you—gentlemen will excuse me, I'm going home. Stay and amuse yourselves. I expect you'll find the spectacle mighty interesting. . . ."

He turned and rode away from the gates. Fancy turned her horse's head and rode after him.

"Court, wait!" she called.

Court pulled up his horse and waited.

"Court, I—" Fancy began; but Court didn't say anything. He just looked at her. He sat there like that a long time, looking at her. Then he flapped the reins over the Morgan's neck, and the two of them started off together toward the city.

But when they came down off the Sandhill, they couldn't go any further. The streets had been filled up with water before but now they were mill-races, torrents. While they were sitting there, looking at the flood, a man came up to them.

"You folks better turn back," he said. "The canal banks gave way half an hour ago—God knows how many folks have drowned!"

Fancy turned toward Court, but he didn't even look at her. Then she started to cry.

But he still didn't say anything, no word of comfort—nothing at all. He just sat there listening to her cry and looking at the dark waters. Then, finally, he turned his horse away from the flood.

"Come on," he said, "we'll stay at the Lewises' tonight."

"Oh, Court," Fancy whispered; "I'm so sorry!"

"You're sorry," Court said. "That helps. That helps one hell of a lot. Come on. . . ."

Riding through the streets on the morning of September thirteenth, after the crest of the flood had passed and the waters had receded, Fancy knew that nothing would ever be the same or even right between them again. She kept looking at Court out of the corners of her eyes, seeing his face drawn, tired, grim. She reckoned he hadn't said five words to her in all of the two days that they had stayed at the house of their friends. Never, she thought bitterly, will he forgive me for this. . . . Still it was a chance, and as Joe Cummings had said, it was the only decent choice. Only it turned out to be a useless one, and we're right back where we started from with the mill ruined and us loaded down with debt. . . .

When she got back to Hiberion, she felt like crying all over again, seeing the furniture on the ground floor wrecked and six inches of stinking red mud all over everything. So more to help the way she felt than any other reason, she called the servants in and started to clean up. By mid-afternoon, Hiberion began to look a little better.

Court drank a cup of black coffee and headed back toward the mill. When he came home that night, his face was a little less grim and Fancy almost started to hope. Still he sat through dinner without saying anything until she couldn't stand it any longer.

"Court," she said, "is it—bad?"

"Not as bad as I expected," Court said. "Only four machines are ruined beyond repair. But they happen to be the biggest machines in the plant—and the most expensive. I'm going down to the bank to see about a loan tomorrow morning. If I get it, I'll have to go North—to New York, I reckon, and order some new ones. We've only been set back about five years by your generosity, Fan."

He stood up, looking at her.

"Incidentally," he said, "ten people drowned, in spite of our opened sluice gates. And the damage to the city is a little over a million dollars."

He stood up then and left the dining room without even saying good night.

A week later, he sat in the offices of Bryant and Sons, manufacturers of textile equipment in New York City.

"Sorry, Mr. Brantley," Fred Bryant said, "but that particular type of creel is made only by Satterlee of Boston. I think you'll find his roves and cards about the best, too. Wish I could help you, but we specialize in lighter machinery for smaller plants than yours. . . ."

Court got up.

"Reckon I'll have to go to Boston, then," he said.

"Yes," Fred Bryant said, "Boston's your best bet."

When he came out on the sidewalk, Court stood still, looking at the crowds.

Boston.

The one place on earth I shouldn't go to right now. Not now, not feeling like I do.

It's business. It's in Fan's interest. . . .

Boston.

I'll be there a day at the most. Then I'll catch a train and hightail it back to Augusta so fast that . . .

Boston.

He hailed a cab and went back to the hotel. He took a stiff drink of bourbon, and repacked his bag.

Why doesn't he come home? Fancy thought. It's been a month since I heard from him last. Said he couldn't find the machines in New York, and he'd have to look elsewhere. But where is elsewhere? She's up there. And Boston isn't far from New York. Surely it shouldn't take Court a whole month to buy four machines. . . .

I'd go looking for him, if I knew where to look. But New York's a big city, and Boston's a big city. . . .

Boston. Always Boston. God Almighty why doesn't he come?

He did come home two days later, looking so tired and sick that Fancy didn't have the heart to question him. The machines arrived almost the same time that he did, and thereafter Court was in the mill morning and night seeing that they were set up properly.

Once the mill was in working order again, he drove himself and his men almost to the breaking point. He did well, too, Fancy had to admit that. They were getting so many orders now that the mill had a hard time handling them all. And every time he got his hands on some money, Court paid it back to the bank.

When it was over, when things had eased a little, Fancy didn't ask Court whether he'd been to Boston or not. Many times she wanted to, but she didn't ask him. Court didn't tell her, either. And that was just as well.

16

"IT'S BEEN a long time," Wyche Weathers said.

"Seven or eight years," Court said. "Thought you'd scratched us off your list, Wyche."

Wyche grinned at him.

"Nothing like that, boy. Just had all I could do keeping my head above water last year. I'm going to remember '93. That was some panic—five hundred banks went down, eight thousand businesses—a heap of the big railroads. . . ."

Fancy came up and leaned against the back of Court's chair.

"But you didn't," she said, "neither of you."

Wyche looked toward where eight-year-old Lynne was sitting on the floor, reading a book.

"She's lovely," he said. "Going to be prettier'n you, Fan."

"Thank you, Wyche," Fancy said.

They were sitting in the dining room of Hiberion. It was a spring day early in 1894, and Wyche had come down that morning from Spartanburg to visit them. Fancy was very happy over the way Court had received him. Court was behaving very well. Then it came to her that Court had never been actually jealous of Wyche. He knew he didn't have to be. I wonder, Fancy thought, how he'd act if this were Jed?

Jed was in town, too. She knew that, although she hadn't seen him. She very much didn't want to see him. She hoped he wouldn't come to Hiberion. It had been very peaceful lately, and she didn't want any trouble with

Court. Right then, of course, to her disgust, Wyche had to go and mention it.

"Heard tell Jed Hawkins is in town," he said, "rallying himself around whooping up the niggers."

"Yes," Court said, "there's a move afoot to disenfranchise them. I'm for it. The poor bastards don't know what to do with a vote."

"I'm not," Wyche said. "Take it away and they'll never get it back. By the way, Court, how are your sisters?"

"Just fine," Court said. "They aren't here any more. Did you know that?"

"No," Wyche said, "I didn't."

"Those fellows, Wilson and Plainfield, didn't work out in the mill. For different reasons. Wilson was a mite too sharp. Wanted to cut too many corners. But Joe was a good sort. He quit because he got to thinking about things and decided that he oughtn't to be making his way on my bounty. So I helped them some more—in a way that was right smart business, Wyche. I set 'em up in a ready-to-wear clothing manufacturing business. They've a big store in Savannah, and a factory. Joe and Saph live out at Melody, now, and keep the old place in good repair. They don't do much planting, though. Joe's too busy for that."

"I see," Wyche said. "What about Agnes and Tom?"

"They live in town. A damned good arrangement, Wyche. Agnes wants to shine in society—and no two married women can live in the same house. Besides, an angel out of Glory couldn't get along with Agnes, anyhow."

"Court," Fancy said, "is that any way to talk about your sister?"

"It's the truth," Court said.

Wyche looked at Lynne.

"Funny you haven't had any more," he said.

"It is," Court said. "Damned if I can understand it. Fan and I both love kids. Given our choice, reckon we'd have half a dozen by now."

"I'd settle for one more," Fancy said; "just one—if it were a boy."

Wyche looked at her, thinking: How nice she talks. Poised, too—you'd think that she'd been born here in Hiberion instead of Court. Women are funny that way. Given a role to play and they play it to the hilt. Little Fan in the role of Grand Duchess—great lady. Only she's not acting any more. She's it. Last time I saw her, it was an act. Not now. It's the way she is, the way, maybe, she was born to be—given the chance. Funny how people like her can come from nowhere, out of the most unlikely surroundings, from a family that in ninety-nine generations produced nothing of note before. Then, on top of the dung heap—a rose. Among the quacking ducklings—a swan. . . .

"Give yourselves time," he said. "You're both young, yet."

"No, Wyche," Court said. "Leaseways I'm not. I'm forty-two."

"And I'm thirty-three," Fancy said. "It's getting to be too late, Wyche. It's got to be within the next three or four years or not at all. Doc Brewster says—that reminds me, I have to go see him. . . ."

"Why?" Court said.

"General checkup. Headaches, bad digestion—and I've been losing weight. He's been after me to come in for weeks, but I just haven't got around to it."

"What did he say," Wyche asked, "about women in general I mean? You were going to tell us, then you interrupted yourself."

"Oh, yes. Doc Brewster says that it's not good for a woman past thirty-five to have a child. Some do—in their forties even; but it's not good for them."

"It's worse for the child," Wyche said. "By the time he's in his teens, he has parents who are old enough to have been his grandparents. Too big a gap—it makes for bad relations. People that far apart just don't think alike. A woman that long out of her girlhood can't remember how she felt when a pimply boy took a shine to her."

He looked at Court, gravely.

"Too bad about your father," he said.

"No it wasn't," Court said. "Father died happy—roaring drunk and full of hell. Besides he lived to see Hiberion restored, and something like the old life come back again. And he was proud of me before he died. All in all, it was a good way to go, Wyche. We all did our best for him, and there are no regrets. . . ."

"Good," Wyche said. "What do you think of Atkinson, Court?"

"I don't know. They say he's a good man. But he's depending mighty heavily on the colored vote. Those all-night picnics are a scandal. He gets the niggers drunk, then buys their vote at a dollar a head. Hawkins is acting for him around here, which is enough to set me against him. I don't like Hawkins."

"Why?" Wyche said.

"He's a crook. And there are other reasons. Let's not talk about it. To hell with politics anyhow. . . ."

"Wyche," Fancy said, "did you go to the Columbian Exposition in Chicago?"

Lynne put down her book and jumped up.

"We did!" she said. "We went to the Egyptian village. Mama smoked a water pipe. It made her sick. But Daddy had the most fun of all. He stood around and watched the naked ladies wiggling their stomachs—like this."

Then she showed him.

Wyche threw back his head and roared.

"Lynne," Fancy said, "why don't you go and practice your piano lessons?"

"Because I don't want to," Lynne said. "I hate the piano. I hate lessons anyhow. I have to take too many of them. Music and singing and dancing and French—I hate French most of all."

"Who makes you do all that?" Wyche said.

"Mama. She's mean to me. She doesn't love me like Daddy does. He brings me candy and Mama takes it away. Says it isn't good for me."

"Well, now," Wyche said, "your mother knows best. Reckon she's just trying to make a lady out of you."

"Don't want to be a lady. I want to go West and be a cowgirl and shoot buffaloes—and Injuns."

"Lynne—" Fancy began.

"Oh, leave the child be, Fan," Court said.

Fancy didn't say anything. Wyche looked from one of them to the other, then he turned back to Lynne.

"What else did you see at the World's Fair?" he said.

"I rode on the ferris wheel," Lynne said. "So did Daddy and Mama. They went with me. They were scared stiff, but they wouldn't admit it!"

"Reckon I'd have been scared, too," Wyche said. "Tell you what, honey. Let's go down in the parlor and you play the piano for me. I'd sure like some pretty music."

"That's a trick to get me to practice," Lynne said. "But I'll do it for you, Uncle Wy. . . ."

She didn't play badly, but she'd never make a pianist. Wyche could see that. She'd be able to entertain a drawing room full of friends and relatives who were not too critical. But nothing more.

Court sat there smiling. To him it was all right. Everything that Lynne did was going to be all right with Court. But Fancy frowned every time Lynne stumbled or missed a note.

She wants too much for that kid, Wyche thought. Not having had it herself, she wants Lynne to have it. Everything—the whole world. And it can't be done. It'll turn out badly—with the child hating her. Kids are a hell of a lot more like weeds than like flowers. Can't prune 'em too close. Got to let 'em grow.

"How's that, Uncle Wy?" Lynne said.

"Beautiful, baby—just beautiful. Now if your paw'll let me use the telephone, I'll send for what I brought you."

"Send for it?" Lynne said. "Couldn't you have brought it in your pocket, Uncle Wy? Or is it too big?"

"It's too big," Wyche said. "Where's the phone, Court?"

"Out in the hall," Court said. "Help yourself."

Wyche came back in a few minutes, and sat down, looking at Fancy.

She's better now, he thought. The years become her. And she'll keep on getting better and better. By the time she's old, she'll be a queen. A real queen—with grace and dignity. . . . Then he saw Court looking at him.

"She's something, boy," he said. "You ought to be mighty proud."

"I am," Court said. But Wyche didn't like the way he said it.

"Show Uncle Wyche how well you can read, darling," Fancy said.

"No," Lynne said, "I won't!"

"Lynne!" Fancy said.

"It's all right, Fan," Wyche said. "Some other time."

Fancy didn't say anything else, and after that the doorbell rang. They still had the big knocker on the door, but now Court had had electric lights put in, and an electric doorbell that rang in two places at once—in the hall and in the pantry. Ernest came out of the pantry and went to the door. He came back into the parlor with his eyes opened wide.

"Marse Court!" he said. "Man out there with a pony! Say he was told to bring it here."

"A pony!" Lynne squealed. "Oh, Uncle Wy! You darling!" Then she threw both arms around his neck and kissed him.

"Come on," Wyche grinned, "let's go see him."

They all went out of the house together. There was a colored boy standing in front of the gate holding a Shetland pony. The pony was spotted and glossy. He was hitched to a little wicker cart.

"Oh, Wyche, you shouldn't have!" Fancy said.

"Why not?" Wyche said. "Nothing's too good for the little princess."

"Mighty handsome of you, Wyche," Court said. "Come on, let's have a look at that thing."

But just as he reached the gate the telegraph boy came riding up on a bicycle.

"Telegram for Mister Brantley," he said.

Court took the telegram, and tossed the boy a coin. Then he opened it.

Wyche saw him stiffen. The color went out of his face. Then he straightened up and looked at them.

"Court," Fancy said, "is something wrong?"

"Yes," Court said slowly. "There's some trouble in New York. I was kind of—depending upon getting the Mosher and Levine cotton goods contract. Means a hell of a lot to me. I'll have to go to New York tonight—and the bad part about that is that there isn't a train out of here before two-thirty in the morning. I'll have to put in another bid—see if I can't swing things my way."

He's lying, Wyche thought. He's on top of the heap now. He's doing better than I am, and I ain't doing bad. The state my mill's in, the loss of one contract or of ten wouldn't make any difference. We've both got more business than we can rightly handle. Besides, from all I've heard, he was cool as a cucumber last year right smackdab in the midst of the worst panic in fifty years. Made himself a profit when everybody was losing the shirts off their backs. He wouldn't get that excited over business. No sir, it's something else.

"Court," Fancy whispered, "will you be long?"

Seeing her face, Wyche had to turn away. It wasn't good to see her look at Court like that. With her heart in her eyes. Breaking there.

Whatever this tall bastard's up to, Wyche decided, she knows—or at least suspects. God damn him to bitter hell, I'll . . .

"No, hon," Court said. "A week—at the most."

"I'll get your things together," Fancy said.

"All right," Court said. "Tell you what: you do it now, and we can all go out and have some fun tonight till train time. Go to one of your friend Jed Hawkins' nigger picnics. They tell me they're a sight to see."

"All right, Court," Fancy said.

"I have to run back out to the mill and give Brayton some last-minute instructions," Court said. "Want to come with me, Wyche?"

"Heck no! I'm on vacation. Don't want to see the inside of another blasted mill till I get back to Spartanburg."

"Suit yourself," Court said. "Wyche, stick around while I'm gone, won't you? I don't like leaving Fan alone. There's one certain party around who has given her trouble before. . . . What I mean is . . ."

"Don't say any more than you want to, Court," Wyche said. "I'll 'tend to things."

"Thanks," Court said.

In half an hour, after he had gone, Fancy came back down the stairs.

"All packed," she said. "Wyche . . ."

"Yes, baby?"

"You know what Court was talking about?"

"No."

"Jed Hawkins. Court thinks Jed's in love with me."

"Is he?"

"Yes. But the bad part about it is that Court thinks that I—"

"Do you?"

"No, Wyche. Tell you what—let's take a little ride. I want to talk to you. Alone, I mean. The servants around here have mighty big ears, and they repeat everything they hear."

"All right, baby," Wyche said.

They started riding down Broad Street. When they got to McIntosh, Fancy turned the buggy into it.

"It's good to see you, Wyche."

"Thanks, Fan."

"You know, Wyche, sometimes I think I've been a fool."

"Why, Fan?"

"Letting you go for Court."

"You love him, Fan. Don't forget that. Don't ever forget that."

"I know. I love him. But is that enough? Love isn't everything. 'Specially not one-sided love."

"One-sided?" Wyche said.

"He doesn't love me. He pretends to, but he doesn't." Fancy thought suddenly, sharply about that time that Court had hit her, at Saph's and Agnes' wedding, before all those people. She started to tell Wyche about that. But she didn't. It wasn't a good thing to tell anybody. Especially not Wyche. . . . "For all I know," she whispered, "he might be carrying on with that Fern. He goes North every year and stays for the longest times. Wyche, how far is Boston from New York?"

"Far enough. Two—three hundred miles. Don't know exactly. Why?"

"His letters come from New York. He writes me once a week, sometimes twice. They're postmarked New York. They're written on the stationery of the hotel he says he stays at. . . ."

Wyche looked at her.

"Just what are you driving at, Fan?" he said.

"Trains go very fast, Wyche," Fancy said.

"Oh," Wyche said, "you think that he—"

"Goes up to Boston between times to see her. Or that she comes down to New York—and stays with him. There—I've said it! Oh, Wyche, how awful!"

"You mustn't think such things, Fan," Wyche said. "I don't believe anything like that's going on. You're just upsetting yourself like this for nothing. Forget it. Everything's going to be all right."

"All right, Wyche," Fancy said. "But there's another thing. . . ."

"What's that, baby?"

"He—he's turning Lynne against me."

"How?" Wyche said.

"He spoils her. Every time he comes into the house he brings a new toy —or some candy. Doc Brewster says candy is bad for her teeth—that she should have very little of it. So I have to take it away from her. Then she runs to Court and he takes her side. If she's bad, I have to punish her. Court won't. All the things she needs, I have to see that she gets—like her music and deportment and all the other things a young lady needs. Being a child, she doesn't want those things. She doesn't realize how important they are. So she throws tantrums. Then Court says, 'Come on, baby, let's go for a ride.' And he takes her down to Oertel's and fills her up on ice cream sodas. . . ."

"Fan, don't you think that maybe you're being a mite too strict?"

"You men!" Fancy said; then she smiled at him: "Reckon I am, Wyche," she said. "I missed so much when I was a child. There've been so many times when I didn't know what to do—or the right thing to say, and I was so afraid and ashamed I could have died. I've learned to get along with Court's kind of people. I know how to keep from embarrassing him now. But it came hard, Wyche. I had to get after I was grown, the training I should have had as a child. I had to learn proper grammar and which fork to use and how to greet people. Court and I have been married fourteen years and it's taken every one of them for me to learn the simple, ordinary things a girl in my position should have known already. . . ."

She smiled at him.

"Of course," she said, "in my case it wasn't anybody's fault. Mine, maybe, for aiming so high above me."

"Baby," Wyche said, "there ain't anything above you—except heaven, maybe, and God's own angels."

"Thanks, Wyche," Fancy said. "Reckon we'd better turn back now."

Back at the house, Court was waiting to take them to the political picnic Jed Hawkins was staging for the Negroes. They got into the buggy and drove down to the Terry. Court was right about that picnic.

In that election year of 1894, the white vote was so hopelessly divided that the blacks without knowing it, held the whip hand. But Jed Hawkins was taking care of that. He was running for state comptroller, and he didn't mean to let the colored brethren keep his fingers out of that rich pie.

He had a whole wagonload of beer, and even a few hogsheads of corn liquor. There were torchlights all around the picnic grounds, which were packed with a milling throng of black humanity.

They were, Fancy saw, feeling their oats. They were laughing, skylarking, pushing each other. They formed lines to the beer wagon, where a grinning cracker who, had it not been for the necessities of politics, would not have spat upon them, served them foaming glasses of beer.

There was a barbecue going on, too, and Jed, himself, was making a point of heaping the plates of his dark constituents.

Court frowned, looking at it.

"The bastard," he said. "I've been as good a friend to the colored folks as they've ever had in this State. But I don't believe in dropping the line like that. Any time a white man starts getting that damned friendly, it's time for those poor devils to look out. . . ."

"Damned right," Wyche said.

Fancy didn't say anything. She was too busy watching the show. A Negro with a banjo got up on the wagon and began to play. And right away, a crowd of youngsters started to shuffle, and do a buck and wing. They were very good at it, and Fancy enjoyed watching them. But then she saw young Dred standing on the edge of the crowd. His face was something to see. It was filled with disgust. If he could, Fancy realized, he would have killed every one of those dancing youngsters.

She felt afraid suddenly. She had talked to Belle many times, and she knew that Phil's illegitimate son was growing up a rebel, filled with hatred for the system that held him bound to a race for which he felt no kinship, and for the customs of a region that denied every outlet to the pride of manhood he instinctively felt.

"He's going to get hisself kilt!" Belle had wailed. "Oh, Miz Fancy, the whitefolks going to kill him sure!"

Fancy looked around the crowd. There were many whites present, come, like Court and Wyche and herself, to see the show. She recognized the Ellis brothers. That was bad.

But the banjo playing was over now, and Jed Hawkins climbed up on the wagon. He was in fine form. He told them how important the ballot was. He urged them not to waste it. He cracked bad jokes that had them all roaring.

"I know the problems of you people," he cried; "I've summered and wintered with you! I had a good mother, rest her soul, and she done her best for me. But ever' living thing I know 'bout gitting along with folks—"

He can talk better than that, Fancy thought bitterly. What does he want to talk like a colored man for? Then she knew. It was a trick. Jed Hawkins was full of tricks.

"Ever' living thing, I tell you—I learnt at the knee of my good ole Mammy! Yessir, Aunt Hannah taught me to respect myself, and other people! She was just a little ole black woman with no booklarnin'—but inside her heart, folks, she was just as white as I be! I tell you, my old Mammy—"

He staggered back suddenly, and clapped a hand to his head. When he drew it away, Fancy saw the little stream of blood in the light of the lanterns.

Jed bent down and picked up the stone.

"Who threw this?" he roared. "Which one of you God-damned burr-headed black bastids . . ." Then he caught himself. "Sorry folks," he said; "I thought I was amongst friends. . . ."

"You is!" they called to him. "Here's the one, Mister Hawkins! This damfool little ole yaller nigger, here!"

Fancy saw Dred struggling in the clutches of two powerful blacks.

Court looked at Wyche and nodded. Wyche put his hand inside his coat.

"Come on," he said.

They walked without haste to where the two Negroes held Dred. But when they got there, the Ellises were before them.

"All right boys," Buck Ellis said, "give him to us. We'll learn him."

The Negroes thrust Dred forward. Then Court stepped between Dred and the Ellises.

"I'll take him," he said quietly.

"Now do tell!" Tom Ellis said. "How you Brantleys do stick together! Take up for your own, don't you, Court? Even when what's yourn is half nigger and a bastid."

"I said I'll take him," Court said.

"You'n' who else?" Buck Ellis snarled.

"And me, Buck," Wyche Weathers said. "We don't want no trouble—don't like to see nobody hurt. But if anybody gets hurt, I'll give you just one guess who that body's going to be."

The Ellises fell back, half a step.

"Come along, Dred," Court said.

They moved easily through the crowd. The Negroes opened to let them through. They could hear the white men muttering. But there were ten blacks to every white, and nobody knew exactly what to expect. When Court and Wyche got back to the buggy, Fancy was already in it, waiting.

Court half lifted, half threw Dred into the back of the buggy.

"Now what?" Wyche said. "Them Ellises are going to get themselves a mob together so damned fast that . . ."

"I know," Court said. "Hiberion, first, Wyche. I'm going to give you a horse. You take this fool boy up to the mill. Hide him in the shipping room. Stay there with him until almost train time. Then bring him to the depot by some roundabout way. . . ."

"They'll come to Hiberion," Wyche warned.

"I know," Court said. "I can handle them."

"Oh, Court, no!" Fancy said. "They'll wreck the house! They might even shoot . . ."

"I'm not going to fight them, Fan. I'm going to invite them in—let them search the place. Give them a cock and bull story about sending the boy away with one of the servants . . ."

"That makes sense," Wyche said. "But how are you going to take a nigger-boy on the train with you? They'll make a fuss—send him to another car. . . ."

"The conductor won't know Dred," Court said. "Who's going to tell him the boy's colored?"

That was true, Fancy realized. Even with his dark olive complexion, Dred was much more white than black.

She looked at the boy. He was crying very softly.

"Dred," she whispered, "why did you do that?"

"Could of said my ole colored nurse, Miz Fancy!" Dred sobbed. "Didn't have to call her his ole black Mammy. They always calls us names—Uncle, and Auntie and boy even when we's a hundred years old! Ole black Mammy, ole black Mammy! Bragging 'bout her heart being white. If having a white heart makes a body act like whitefolks do, I hope to Jesus that mine is black as night!"

"You shut your trap, boy," Court growled. "You've done enough harm."

"Yessir," Dred whispered; "I'm mighty sorry, Mister Court."

Fancy watched Wyche riding away fast on Court's big Morgan, the boy clinging to him, looking so small and pitiful. She couldn't have felt any worse if Dred had been her own child.

She was there beside Court when the Ellises came with the mob. She watched the yard filling up with lean, hard-eyed white men, shotguns slung over the crook of their arms. Buck Ellis had a muleskinner's whip.

"Bring him out, Court Brantley!" they roared. "Bring out the little yaller bastid!"

Court stepped out on the veranda and faced them.

"He's not here," he said quietly. "I sent him away. Listen to me, men! He's only a child and—"

"He's lying!" Buck Ellis cried. "He ain't had time to!"

Court raised his hand.

"Gentlemen!" he said, "I invite you all to come in. Search the house if you like—and the outbuildings. I tell you the boy's not here."

They came into the house, looking a little sheepish.

"Get whiskey," Court said out of the side of his mouth to Fancy.

She went into the pantry and came back with her arms full of bottles.

"Don't drink it!" Tom Ellis said. "He's trying to give that little nigger time to git away!"

"Hell, Tom," one of the men said, "for a snort of that good bourbon, I'd let most any nigger git away. Some of you boys mosey 'round the place. We'll save your drinks till you come back."

Some of the men moved off. Fancy poured them tumblers full of bourbon.

"Thank you, Ma'am," they said politely. One of them whispered to her: "We warn't going to kill him—jest tan his hide a little to teach him some sense."

Fancy didn't answer. Then the others came back.

"He ain't here, boys," one of them said.

"'Pears to me," Tom Ellis said, "that we ought to hold Court Brantley accountable for gitting him away!"

Court put his hand inside his coat.

"I invited you in peaceably," he said evenly. "I didn't aim to kill a white man over any nigger, not even one I've got some interest in. But this is my house. My wife's here, and my daughter. That's a different story. There's only one of me to a hundred of you. But I'm not going out of this house with you on my own hook. You can take me out feet first, but as God sits in Glory, some of you are going with me—the same damned way."

The men looked at him, indecisively. Then there was a little noise in the doorway. Fancy saw Jed Hawkins standing there, a little white bandage around his forehead.

"Look, men," he said, "as the injured party, 'pears to me I ought to be heard in this matter. . . ."

"Why shore, Jed," one of the men answered, "speak yore piece!"

He sounds relieved, Fancy thought.

"I got a little bump on my head. That ain't proper grounds for a lynching. I'm a Southern white man, and I believe in keeping the niggers in their place. But I ain't taking to heart what one fool kid did—'specially not that kid, 'cause that was his white blood talking. Proud white blood. The best. Let him go. And I won't look kindly on any of you raising a hand against Mister Brantley here. I admire and respect him. And I honor his wife, who is the finest, sweetest lady who ever drew breath! So I'm asking you, as a favor to me, to go home peacefully. Mister Brantley'll send that boy away, and keep him away—won't you, Court?"

"Yes," Court said, "I'll do that, Mister Hawkins."

"Hell, he's talking sense," one of the men said. "Let the little nigger go! I say. Who's with me?"

"Me!" they all cried at once, "I am! Let him go!"

All except the Ellises.

"Have a drink, Jed," Court said; "and thanks. That was mighty white of you."

"Don't mention it," Jed Hawkins said.

The men stayed a half hour longer until every drop of the bourbon was gone. Then Jed Hawkins went away and took them with him.

Wyche brought Dred to the depot through the back streets, but he didn't need to. He could have ridden down the middle of Broad Street itself.

After the train had gone, Fancy stood there with Wyche. She was crying.

"Wyche," she said, "does it have to be like this?"

"Reckon it does, babydoll," Wyche said. "Transplant the same number of Negroes to New York or Boston in proportion to their numbers as we have here and I wouldn't give a fig for their chances. Hell, during the draft riots in New York, in the Civil War, they killed more niggers in one night than we lynch in the South in ten years. Burned a colored orphanage with all the children in it . . ."

"How awful!" Fancy was horrified. "But you sound like you're defending the way we treat them down here."

"I'm not," Wyche said. "I'm just talking about human nature. What in hellfire would happen to those pine-barren crackers if they didn't have the blacks to look down on? They'd go crazy—or revolt; because even European serfs don't live any worse than they do. Having the Negro to feel superior to kind of makes it up to them. I don't hate any man. There're an awful lot of Negroes I'm damned fond of, who're really friends of mine. I'm fond of 'em like I'm fond of my white friends—in exactly the same way, not like these planter aristocrats who have pet Negroes like they have pet hounds. What I mean is I have black friends—like old Maud, for instance, who manage to like me in spite of the fact that my skin's the wrong color from their point of view. But I have to admit that blacks and whites can't really live together. Not now, not ever. A Negro is just too damned physically, visibly different from a white man. Notice I said physically. I've known black boys who were in the first rank intellectually, which makes life damned miserable for them, the poor bastards. . . ."

"Wyche," Fancy said, "you say the strangest things . . ."

"I know. But the main trouble is that the Negro in the mass is actually inferior to the white man in the mass, theories be damned."

"I don't know, Wyche," Fancy said.

"Don't get me wrong, Fan. I know how fond you are of Phil's yard children. I didn't say he was born that way. I sorrowfully and shamefully admit we made him that way. You can break the spirit of a horse. What do you think it does to a bright boy to know it would cost him his life if he ever reared up on his haunches and acted like a man? Being bought and sold like mules did something to them. And even after that was over, the system we worked out to bolster up our uncertain vanities kept up the dirty work. It's like Dred was saying: you don't ever call a black man, 'Mister.' Up to forty-five, he's 'boy'; and after that he's 'Uncle.' The ones you know, you call by their first names—no matter how slightly you know 'em. The women are Mary Jane while they're young, and after that they're 'Mammy' or

'Auntie.' We carry the thing even to such extremes of pure damned pettiness. We put them in places like the Terry—and keep them there. We deny them anything like comfort. Heck, we've got it fixed so they don't even get enough to eat. Then, when they rear up and act like the beasts we've made of them, we lynch them with a barbaric savagery that would disgrace a Sioux. I don't like it, Fan. Never did, never will. A man pulling off his cap and shuffling his feet, and getting off the sidewalk to let me pass doesn't make me feel good inside. Hell, he makes me feel sick."

"Wyche," Fancy said, "we'd better drive by and let his mother know he's safe. Reckon she's nearly out of her mind by now."

"All right," Wyche said.

It was a long time before they could get Belle calm enough to understand them. When they did, she started crying all over again—this time from joy.

Wyche looked at Angel and Delight, and then back at their mother. He didn't say anything for a long time, and when he did, all he said was:

"These kids getting any schooling, Belle?"

"I was sending 'em to Miss Lucy Laney's School on Gwinnett Street," Belle said, "but Mister Phil didn't like the idea. Said too much schooling was bad for 'em."

"You send 'em back."

"Mister Phil won't pay for it, Mister Wyche. Course Miss Laney would take 'em for nothing, but I ain't got the heart. . . ."

"Send 'em back," Wyche said. "I'll pay for it. After they finish there—send 'em somewhere else. Hampton, Tuskegee, Howard. I'll pay for that, too. Then we'll see."

Fancy stood up, and put both her arms around his neck. Then she kissed him, hard. On the mouth.

"Wyche," she said, "you're just about the best man in the world!"

"Do that again," Wyche said, "and I'll turn out to be the worst. Come on, let's get out of here."

He helped her up into the buggy.

"I feel like I've been torn to pieces inside," Fancy said. "Oh, Wyche, I don't think I'll ever be whole again."

"That," Wyche said, "is the South, Fan. That's part of its ancient charm."

When they got back to Hiberion, the house was dark. But when they came up on the big veranda, they heard a noise. Just a little noise—like the creak of one of the rocking chairs. Wyche put his hand inside his coat where his gun was. Then a man came out of the shadows and stood in front of them. Dark as it was, Fancy could see the white of the little bandage around his forehead.

"Fan," Jed Hawkins said.

Wyche took his hand out from under his coat.

"This is one hell of a time," he said grimly, "to pay a call, Jed."

"I know. But I had to see Fan—Mrs. Brantley. It's important, Wyche. Fan, could you spare me ten minutes—just ten—" he looked at Wyche, "alone?"

Fancy stared at him, trying to make out the expression on his face. But she couldn't. It was too dark.

"All right," she said, "come in, won't you?"

The three of them went into the big hall together.

"You'll excuse us, won't you, Wyche?" Fancy said.

"Sure, baby," Wyche said. "You see, I've got two advantages over Court. I ain't married to you. And I know for a fact you can be trusted. However, I can't say as much for this—politician. If you need me, Fan, just sing out."

"I won't need you," Fancy said. "I trust Jed. You go to bed, Wyche."

"In a little while," Wyche said. "After I hear you come up those stairs."

Jed looked at him as he went up the stairs.

"Thank you for what you did, Jed," Fancy said. "That was mighty fine of you."

Jed didn't answer her. He kept looking up the stairway. He looked worried.

"Fan," he said, "what's Wyche Weathers to you?"

"An old friend," Fancy said simply, "nothing more."

"Good!" Jed said. "Lord, but I was worried. Right when I'd found out I had a chance—he had to show up. . . ."

"A chance?" Fancy said. "What do you mean, Jed? You think because Court's out of town—by the way, how did you know that? You must have known, or you wouldn't have come here."

"I was in the depot when the train pulled out," Jed grinned. "Kind of thought he'd put that bastard of Phil's on it. But I was downright surprised when he got on it himself—with a valise."

"And you think that because he isn't here you can—"

"Oh, no," Jed said, "nothing like that, honey. Know you better than that. You wouldn't play that kind of a game. You're too smart."

"Not too good, eh Jed? Just too smart."

"Both, maybe. Fan, look at me. You think that if I needed a casual light o' love—a one-night-stand, I'd come to you?"

Fancy looked at him wonderingly.

"No," she said, "I don't think that, Jed."

"Hell, Fan, women like that are a dime a dozen. But you ain't a dime a dozen. Folks don't know how to count high enough to set a valuation on you."

"Thanks, Jed."

"Don't thank me. Thank God—He made you what you are. The first time I saw you all I could think was: Why in hellfire did that long-tall, no-good, overbred, mangy hound dog of a Brantley have to see her first!"

"Jed, it's awful late. Get to the point, won't you?"

"Just wanted to ask you something, honey. Fan—if something were to happen between you and Court—where would I stand?"

Fancy stared at him.

"But nothing is going to happen between Court and me," she said.

"I wouldn't be too sure of that," Jed Hawkins said.

Fancy took a step toward him so that she could see his face better.

"You know something," she whispered. "Something that I don't. All right, Jed, what is it? Tell me."

Jed shook his head.

"No, Fan," he said.

"Why not?"

"Against the rules, honey. I don't play that way."

Fancy sighed.

"All right, then—don't tell me." She smiled at him. "Reckon you're something kind of special, Jed. This is the second time tonight you've proved that. First when you took up for that boy, and now when you've got something on Court—something that you think maybe would even break us up, and you won't use it. You're a bigger man than people think, Jed Hawkins."

Jed frowned.

"I ought to let it go at that," he said, "but you're the one person on earth I can't lie to. All right, I do know something. But the reason I ain't going to tell you is not because I'm too honorable. Hell, honeychild, I'd lie, steal, blaspheme, cheat, and abuse orphans to get you. But I'm not going to do this. I'm not because it just isn't smart."

"Why not?"

"I think you'll find out yourself. You're nobody's fool. And I know damn well that if I were the one who spilled it, you'd hate me. You'd think I took unfair advantage of the situation—and you'd be dead, damned right. Which is the only reason I don't take unfair advantage. Which is the reason I'm going to squat my hindquarters right down in a room at the Globe—near a telephone. . . ."

"You think I'd call you?"

"I hope you'll call me. I hope you'll remember that there's a redheaded, freckle-faced son of—of his mother, who loves you more than life, or fear of death or hope of heaven. Who'd never do to you what's being done to you now. Who asks only one thing—that he be given the privilege of spending the rest of his life worshiping you, the way you ought to be worshiped. . . ."

"Thanks, Jed," Fancy whispered; "you—you're mighty sweet. . . ."

"Then you'll call me?"

"I don't know, Jed."

"I'll be waiting," Jed said, and half turned toward the door. Then he turned back, his face working.

"I'd kill that long-tall son of a bitch," he said, "if I thought you'd forgive me for it. If I thought you'd understand. . . ."

"Understand what, Jed?"

"That I was doing it for your sake—not for mine."

"Jed," Fancy said, "I'd better tell you something."

"Speak your piece, honey," Jed said.

"It wouldn't make any difference why you did it—if you harmed Court. It doesn't even make any difference what he's doing. You see, Jed—I love him."

Jed looked at her a long time until it got so quiet that she could hear him breathing. Then he moved, breaking the silence.

"I'll still wait," he said. Then he turned very quickly and went through the doorway without saying anything else at all.

17

FANCY thought about what Jed Hawkins had said. But it wasn't the kind of thing that it did any good to think about. If she kept on brooding over it, she would have to do something: go to New York, maybe, and find out if Court really was at the hotel, and if he were, whether he was there alone. She didn't want to do that. She hadn't been very happy with Court, but she kept on hoping. Maybe things would change. Maybe he would forget Fern. Maybe . . .

But three weeks went by and she didn't hear from him. Not even a postcard. She almost made up her mind that she would go, that even finding out couldn't be any worse than this terrible wondering, but she kept changing her mind until the worry made her sick.

Nerves, she told herself, and dismissed the idea of calling Doc Brewster.

But the headaches went on and the sleeplessness until she knew finally that she would have to call him, or she was going to get really sick, the bad kind of sickness—the kind that was inside her mind and heart and would kill her finally, taking a very long time in very bad ways, so she went downstairs into the hall where the telephone was. She had even put her hand on the crank when the doorbell rang.

She answered it herself instead of waiting for Ernest to come from the back of the house. Saphira stood there with her husband, Joseph Plainfield. Joe looked so all-fired pleased with himself that Fancy felt like strangling him.

"What's the matter with you?" she said. "You're not becoming a papa at this late date, are you?"

"Nothing like that," Joe grinned. "It's business, Fan. Heck, honey, it's a gold mine, right here in Augusta all these years—right under our noses and we didn't see it!"

"What," Fancy said, "has been right here in Augusta under our noses that we didn't see?"

"The climate, honey! Remember that big old house Major Tully built for Mrs. Tully just before the War? Well, after the Major died, the old lady had to open the house to paying guests. Last time we were here, last February, remember? Me'n' Saph happened to stop by there to sort of pay our respects. Do you know where most of her guests come from?"

"No, where?"

"New York. Boston. Philadelphia. Rich folks trying to get away from those terrible winters they have up there. One of Court's best friends—man by the name of Woodbury—Stanton Woodbury, is up there right now. Had a talk with him this morning. Of course he's only been there since March, and he's going to have to go back to Boston any day now, but he swears he's going to spend the entire winter down here next year. Didn't Court tell you?"

"No," Fancy said, "he didn't."

"Funny. Mister Woodbury says Court was up to see him a couple of days before he left for New York. They were classmates at Harvard. Appears to me that Court ought to have had him and his Missus out to the house. . . ."

"Well, he didn't," Saphira said, "so he must have some reason not to."

"I don't see your point," Fancy said. "The climate—rich people from the North, and Mrs. Tully's house on the Hill. What's it all about, Joe?"

"Fan, honey—don't you see? It would be doggoned easy to convert that house into a first-class resort hotel. I'm going to dicker with Mrs. Tully. Even if she won't sell, I'm going to ask her to let us put money into expanding it. Build a tennis court, bridle paths, more rooms, a decent lobby. We'd make a million!"

"I would like," Fancy said, "to meet Court's friend."

"That's easy," Joe said. "We're going up there tonight. Mrs. Tully is giving a party for her guests. No reason why you shouldn't come along."

"Think it would be all right, Saph?" Fancy said.

"Of course, darling. We've already felt Mrs. T. out on this proposition—that's why she invited us. As a relative of ours, you'll be more than welcome. So get out your best bib and tucker and come along."

I really don't feel up to it, Fancy thought, but there's something behind Court's not inviting them here. He's not that ashamed of me. I wonder if what Jed . . .

She dressed carefully that night. She put on her dress of rose silk with its bertha of Irish crochet lace. Her hat was trimmed with the same lace and had pink velvet bows. Her belt was made of pink velvet, too, and the dress had heavy pouch-shaped sleeves that the fashion designers called bishop sleeves. They fitted very tight about her wrists above her white gloves. The dress was tight about her hips, drawn in with a yoke made of scallops corded with the pink velvet, but it didn't have any bustle, because after 1890 fashionable ladies didn't wear them any more. The skirt came down to the ground and had deep, inverted box pleats. She looked very nice and she knew it.

Stanton Woodbury knew it too, the minute he saw her.

"Gad!" he said, forcing his bulk up out of the chair, "what a pretty woman! Who the devil is she, Mrs. Tully?"

"Why that's Mrs. Brantley," Mrs. Tully said. "My dear—come here a moment, please—I want you to meet Mister Woodbury."

Fancy came across the floor from where she had been standing with Joe and Saphira, and put out one gloved hand.

"I'm very glad to meet you, sir," she said. "My husband—"

She didn't finish what she had started to say. Stanton Woodbury didn't let her.

"Brantley?" he boomed; "you must be related to Court. Finest chap I know. Friend of mine—has been for years. Often dine at his house on Beacon Hill. His wife's a charming girl."

"You must have the wrong Brantley," Mrs. Tully said. "This is—"

"No, I don't! Court Brantley. Classmate of mine at Harvard. Came from right here in Augusta. Has a textile mill down here—lives here part of the year. Right?"

"Right," Fancy whispered. "Now if you'll excuse me . . ."

"No you don't! I want you to meet my wife. Any relative of Court's is a friend of ours. Oh—Lizzie!"

"Yes, dear?" Elizabeth Woodbury said.

"Meet Miss Brantley—relative of Court's. Beauty, isn't she?"

"She is indeed," Elizabeth Woodbury said. "You're not his sister are you, dear?"

"No," Fancy said, "I'm not. Your husband is—a little mistaken. It's Mrs. Brantley—not Miss."

"Oh, then you must be his brother's wife?"

"No," Fancy said, "I'm not his brother's wife either. . . ."

Mrs. Woodbury looked uncertain. Fancy had answered her questions, but she didn't know anything.

"Just say," Fancy said quietly, "that I'm the wife—of—of a distant relative. But I'm terribly fond of Court. Would you mind giving me his address in Boston? I'm planning to go up there in a few days. . . ."

"Not at all," Stanton Woodbury said. "It's—here, I've got it right in this little book."

"May I copy it, please?" Fancy said.

"Sure thing—go right ahead."

Mrs. Tully didn't say anything. She couldn't. She was in a state close to apoplexy.

"What a strange girl," Mrs. Woodbury said, when Fancy had gone back to Saph and Joe. "Why I do believe she's leaving! And she just got here. . . . There was something odd in her manner, too. The way she answered me, why—"

Mrs. Tully recovered her voice.

"I reckon," she said, "I reckon you'd act odd too, Mrs. Woodbury, if you'd just been told that your husband had another wife in Boston!"

Stanton Woodbury's jaw dropped open.

"You don't mean—?" he said.

"That girl is Court Brantley's wife. His lawful wife—unless he married the other one first. But that's not likely, since he's been married to this one for fourteen years."

"The cad!" Stanton Woodbury boomed. "The bounder! And to think, Lizzie, we've entertained them in our home many's the time!"

But Elizabeth was looking toward the door.

"Poor little thing," she whispered. "Poor lost, hurt little thing. . . ."

"Fan, you're the limit!" Joe Plainfield said. "You knew how important this was to me, so what did you do? You got a headache, and have to leave."

"Hush, Joe," Saphira said.

"I lied about the headache," Fancy said. "Just take me to the trolley line, Joe. Then you two go on back."

Joe stared at her.

"If you don't have a headache," he said, "then what the devil ails you?"

"There isn't any word for it," Fancy said. "All I can tell you is how it feels."

"And how does it feel, Fan?" Saphira said.

"A little like dying. No. More than a little."

"Fan, you were talking to the Woodburys. What did they say to you? What did they tell you? Tell me, honey. Don't sit there looking like that. God, Fan, you frighten me."

"Don't be frightened, Saph," Fancy said. "Here's the trolley line now. Go on back to the party. Enjoy yourselves. I–I'll be all right. . . ."

"You're sure, Fan?" Joe said. Even he looked worried now.

"Quite sure," Fancy said.

But when they got back to the party, Saphira and Joe went straight to Mrs. Tully and she told them. Saph gripped Joe's arm, hard.

"We'd better get home, Joe," she said.

"Good God! You don't think that she'd–"

"I don't know. I don't know," Saph whispered. "All I know is that we'd better get moving–fast!"

When they got to Hiberion, they came up the stairs at once without saying anything to anybody. Fancy was in her room, packing.

"Fan, honey," Saphira said, "you're not–?"

"Going up there? Yes, Saph."

"But, darling, what good would it do?"

"No good, Saph. But I've just got to see for myself. I won't do anything wrong. I won't shoot her–though I feel like it."

"Court's the one who ought to be shot," Joe Plainfield said, "or at least horsewhipped."

"And tarred and feathered to boot," Saphira added bitterly. "Oh, Fan, baby, I'm so sorry!"

"Don't be. I'm all right. I'm going to be all right. It–it takes a little getting used to, that's all. . . ."

"But, honey–what are you going to do?"

"Nothing, everything. Leave him, I reckon. He doesn't want me. He never did. I'll get a divorce–so he can have her."

"A divorce!" Saphira said.

"Yes. Shocking, isn't it? They'll be calling me a gay divorcée in town, now, and whispering about me behind their fans. Shooing their men out of my way. And I won't have any friends."

"You," Joe said, "will always have friends, Fan."

"I don't care about that. That's the outside part. It's what's inside that's bad. The remembering. How glad I used to be to see him when he came home from—the North. How I used to fly into his arms. The same arms that had just—turned her loose. . . ."

"Fan, for the love of God . . ."

Fancy put out her hand and let it rest on Saphira's arm.

"You've been good to me, Saph. You always were—right from the first. Thank you for that; and try not to think too badly of me. . . ."

"Of you? It's that hound dog of a brother of mine I'm thinking about! And what I'm thinking would sure Lord curl his hair!"

"Want me to go up there with you, Fan?" Joe said. "In a case like this you need—"

"No, thank you, Joe. I won't need anybody. I'm not going to do anything. Just pay them a little social call. Very politely. We'll sit and chat, and maybe have tea. Then I'll come home—and afterwards I'll go away for a while."

"Away?" Joe said. "Why?"

"To get her divorce, silly," Saphira said. "She wouldn't want to get it here. Think of the scandal!"

"Well, that does it," Fancy said, and snapped the valise shut. "Mind driving me to the depot, Joe? There's a train at midnight."

"Not at all," Joe said.

"Fan," Saphira said, looking at her, "how can you be so calm!"

"Calm," Fancy whispered. "That's the wrong word, Saph. Killed is better."

"Oh, Fan!" Saphira wailed.

Later she looked at them, standing in the garish glow of the electric lights, under the big iron shed of the depot. There was the light, and there was the shadow, and there was nothing in between. Nothing between joy and disaster. Then the train started moving, and the lights jerked backward one by one. Fancy turned and waved at them.

She came up to the brownstone house on Beacon Street in the afternoon, and stood there looking at it. Then she went up to the door and rang the bell.

An Irish girl opened the door.

"Yes, Mum?" the girl said.

"Is Mr. Brantley at home?" Fancy said. Her own voice surprised her.

"No, Mum. Mrs. Brantley either. You want to leave your card, Mum?"

"No," Fancy said. "Have you any idea when they'll be back?"

"Not soon, Mum, you can depend on that. What with Mrs. Brantley being in the hospital, and Mr. Brantley attending the Textile Manufacturers Association meetings, and visiting her between times, there's no telling when he'll be home. . . ."

"In the hospital?" Fancy said. "Is she ill?"

"Oh, yes, Mum! Thought we were going to lose her, sure! And all account of that awful gas jet. She had the window open, and it blew out. Wouldn't have made much difference, only feeling cold, the poor thing, she got up and closed the window, not noticing about the jet. Of course, Bridget—she's our cook, does swear that it wasn't no accident; but, faith, Mum, when you're as old as Bridget, you get to taking queer notions, I do say. . . ."

"But she's better now?"

"Out of danger, the doctors say. 'Twere Terence, our coachman, who thought of sending the Master that telegram. That's Terence for you, Mum, great presence of mind, I always did say. . . ."

The telegram. That telegram. God, how smoothly Court had lied! But there was one more thing she had to find out. It wouldn't do any good, but she had to know.

"Why," she said, "does Bridget say the—gas was no accident?"

"Because of the quarreling, Mum. But then, married couples always do have their differences, don't they? I'm not the one to put much importance on such goings on. 'Tis a sad life, she's had, though—the poor thing, what with Mr. Brantley being away so much, down there in Georgia among all those heathen Southerners. . . ."

"Yes," Fancy whispered, "I guess her life has been sad, come to think of it."

"Who'll I tell 'em was here, Mum?" the Irish girl said.

"Just—a woman they used to know. A woman called—Fancy. Tell them that. They'll understand." Then she turned and went back down the steps.

"Fancy," the Irish girl said to herself. "Bless me, but that's a funny name!"

On his way to the hospital, Court again had that feeling of being trapped. Fool, he told himself, this was what you wanted—remember? You went through hell when you heard she'd married Ty. Only Ty was the lucky one. He's dead and out of this. . . .

Or maybe I'm being unfair to Fern. Maybe she wouldn't have been like this if things had taken their normal course. This jealous shrew with a viperish tongue. All right—why shouldn't she be? What have you given her, Court Brantley? A precarious hold on the fringes of your life. Months of absence—then a little stolen time granted each year with ever greater reluctance.

All that time alone—no wonder she broods. That explains the imaginary ills, I reckon. My God, her medicine chest should supply a dispensary! She faded so fast, too. Five years older than Fancy—and you'd swear the difference was fifteen—or twenty. Querulous—quarrelsome. And I can't leave her. Haven't the heart. What would she do now? She gave me her life on a silver platter. Pretty as she was, rich, she could have had almost any man even after Ty died. But now . . .

He shook his head, thinking of it, and went into the hospital. As he walked toward the desk, it came to him that the people who thought the world well lost for love never really reckoned the cost until afterwards. And afterwards was too late.

Fern was propped up on the pillows. She watched him out of the brown eyes that were always opaque now, that always hid something. She was so thin that it hurt to look at her, her skin drawn tight over cheekbones and jaw, the cheeks themselves hollow, and the little web of lines crawling away from the corners of her eyes. Court bent down to kiss her, thinking: Once she was beautiful—once, but she turned her face a little aside so that he only brushed the corner of her mouth.

"Did you bring my things?" Fern said. Her voice was high and harsh. It grated on his ear.

"Yes," he said tiredly.

"You don't seem to be a bit enthusiastic about taking me home," she said.

"I'm just tired, Fern," Court said. "I had a hard day."

"You're tired all right," she said, raising herself up a little, searching his face; "but it's me you're tired of, isn't it, Court? Answer me! Isn't it?"

Court stood there looking at her. But he didn't say anything. He just looked at her.

Then she started to cry.

But Court had seen her cry before. Too many times. That weapon was blunted from overuse.

"Oh, come off it," he said. "Here're your things—get into them. I'll wait outside." Then he turned and marched into the hall.

He could hear her in there, sniffling and sobbing a little, and he knew how her face was going to look afterwards, her eyes red, with puffy lids, and those lips he had wasted so many years dreaming of, would be sullen and moist and trembling. And he hated Fern suddenly with a hatred that was absolutely bottomless, that was equaled perhaps, only by the hatred and contempt he felt for himself.

I should go home to Fan now I should get down on my knees and kiss the hem of her skirt and rise and thank God for so blessing me I should never leave her again no never leave her always stay where she is where goodness is and sweetness and devotion and faith. . . . But I'm trapped. I'm saddled with these the wages of my sin these so heavy wages which are nothing so simple and final and acceptable as death. I loved her wanted her had to have her but it wasn't that easy. Didn't know I would become involved in this clinging endless suffocating battle of wills, this conflict that has no end and no victory. Well, I asked for it. Little Fern. A doll of Dresden china. Pink and white and golden. Lovely. Desirable. Where has she gone? By what alchemy, what metamorphosis did this weeping witch take her place?

Then Fern came out of the room and took his arm.

On the way home they didn't talk. But when they were almost there, Fern reached over and touched his arm.

"That drugstore," she said; "I've got a prescription—something for nerves that Doctor O'Brian gave me."

"Nothing—dangerous?" Court said.

"Oh, no. He took all those awful pills away from me. Besides, darling, I—I wouldn't do that again. . . ."

"You'd better not," Court said. Then he took the prescription and went into the drugstore.

When they got home, she was quiet. She lay back among the pillows, listening while Court read to her. She even achieved a certain wan beauty. Looking at her, he could even remember what she had been like—before. Her brown eyes had lost a little of that pleading, dog-like look that so infuriated him, and a little light showed in them. A little secret glow, as though she had mastered something finally—and was content.

"Court," she said, "ring for Mary, won't you? I'd like a cup of hot tea ever so much."

Court pulled the bell cord, and went back to the novel he was reading to her. It was sickening stuff, but she liked it. It described the last agonies of a woman dying for lost love. . . .

Then Mary came into the room.

"Yes, Mum?" she said.

"Bring me a cup of tea, Mary," Fern said, "like a good girl."

"Yes, Mum, right away, Mum," Mary said, and turned to go. But in the doorway she paused. "Oh, sir," she said, "there was a lady here asking after you and Madame. . . ."

"A lady?" Court said.

"Yes, sir. A very pretty lady. She didn't want to wait. So I asked her her name, and she said the funniest thing. . . ."

Fern looked at Court.

"What did she say, Mary?" Court said.

"She said to tell you she was the woman called Fancy. Said you'd understand. Oh, sir—do people really have names like that?"

"Reckon they do, Mary," Court said. "Now go get that tea, please."

He turned and looked at Fern. The big clock on the mantel ticked, filling the room with the sound. Then, very slowly, Court turned and started toward the door.

"You—you're going to her," Fern said. It wasn't a question.

"Yes," Court said, "I'm going to her. Now. I should have gone long ago."

"And you won't be back."

"No," Court said, "I won't be back."

Fern leaned forward and hugged her own knees. Then she laughed. It was a clear sound, surprisingly strong.

"You're wrong, Court," she laughed. "You're coming back. You're coming back and this time you'll never leave me."

Court shrugged.

" 'Bye, Fern," he said.

But she didn't answer him. She just sat there, laughing.

Fancy sat in the little parlor, watching the door. He's had time enough, now, she thought. Even if he didn't catch the train until the next day, he's had time enough. I could go now. I should go now. But I can't. Not till I've seen him. Not till he's told me why. . . .

Only he won't. The Brantleys never explain why they do the things they do. They don't even know why, maybe. And Court's too stiffnecked to try to explain. Wouldn't do any good anyhow. I wouldn't have him now. Not now—not knowing at last exactly where I stand with him. No. I'm going to walk out of his life as quietly as I came into it. I'm going to take with me precisely what I brought. My clothes, and myself. . . .

So many things I can't take. All the years. The way we felt—or at least the way I felt. Oh God, oh Jesus—where is he? Why doesn't he walk through that door and . . .

But he didn't come.

Fancy got up and went to the telephone. She turned the crank and gave the operator a number.

"Jed?" she whispered.

"Fan! Fan, baby—you called me! You did call—"

"Yes, Jed—I called you. You were right—on all counts. I found out—and I called you."

"Fan, honey, darling—"

"Wait, Jed—let me talk. Let me say this before I lose my nerve. Jed—I—I'll meet you in Aiken—tomorrow. . . ."

There was a long silence. The wires crackled. When Jed spoke again, his voice was hoarse, and deep.

"For keeps, Fan?" he said.

"Yes, Jed—for keeps."

Then she hung up the phone.

She started to pack, but she couldn't finish it. She felt too sick—too hurt-sick to do anything. She went into Lynne's bedroom and looked at the child sleeping, one clenched fist over her eyes.

I'll miss you, darling, she thought. But you're his—and it's him you love, not me. I can't take anything of his with me when I go—not even the child he gave me. . . . I helped him get all those things, but he doesn't know that or believe it, and was always ashamed of me. He's taught you that, without even meaning to. . . . So, good-bye, my darling—try not to hate me—too much. . . .

She started to cry. Not wanting to wake the child, she went back to her own bedroom and lay down upon the bed and cried all night.

In the morning she was too ill to move, but she dragged herself up and went down and had breakfast with Lynne.

They were eating when Court walked into the dining room.

"Daddy!" Lynne squealed. "You're back!"

Court bent down and kissed her. Then he straightened up.

"'Lo, Fan," he said.

"'Lo, Court," Fancy said.

"Lynne, run upstairs for a while," Court said. "Your mother and I have things to talk about."

"All right, Daddy," Lynne said.

They went into the little drawing room.

"Well, Fan?" Court said.

Fancy just looked at him.

"Don't you have anything to say?" Court said.

"What's the good of talking now, Court? It's done. We're finished. We've been finished for a long time. I guess I knew it. But I kept hoping. Foolish of me, wasn't it?"

"No," Court said, "it wasn't foolish, Fan. I kept hoping, too."

"Only it isn't any good any more, is it?"

"I reckon not."

This idiotic conversation, Fancy thought. This solemn talk where we say everything but what we can't say. And what we can't say is sure Lord what we ought to. . . .

"Now what, Fan?" Court said. "What do we do now?"

"You don't do anything, Court. I'm leaving. Now—today. Go and get your Fern—put her in this house. This house I helped you rebuild. And I hope it will haunt her!"

"Fan," Court whispered, "don't go. . . ."

Fancy stood up, looking at him.

"Don't go? Stay here, you mean? Stay and remember—that to you I was always the woman you married by mistake—always the poor white trash you were ashamed of? The one you could slap in the face before all your friends? No thank you, Court. I'm taking nothing with me—except a few clothes. I'm leaving you everything—even the child you've taught to hate me—"

"Lynne doesn't," Court began; but the door flew open and Lynne came into the room.

"Let her go, Daddy!" she cried. "I do hate her! I do! I do!"

"Lynne—" Fancy said.

"I hate you! I hate you! You're wicked! You danced naked on a circus wagon! Tildy Mae says you're nothing but a wh—"

Then Court slapped her, hard across the mouth.

She fell back, looking at him. She stopped crying. She was too surprised to cry.

"You hit me!" she said. "Daddy—you—you hit me. . . ."

"I know. And I'll do it again if I ever hear tell of your speaking to your mother like that. Listen to me, Lynne. Maybe your mother has been strict with you; but right now it appears to me you needed it. Your mother is a good woman, Lynne—the best. Now tell her you're sorry!"

"I—I'm sorry, Mother," Lynne got out, then she ran, wailing, from the room.

Court walked over to the bell cord and pulled it. Ernest came into the room.

"Tell Tildy Mae to come here," Court said.

Then he leaned back against the wall, waiting.

Tildy came shuffling up from the kitchen, her face sullen.

"Yessir?" she said.

"Lynne just repeated some remarks," Court said, "that you made in reference to Mrs. Brantley . . ."

"Lord, Mister Court, I never . . ."

"Shut up! You get your things and get out of here, Tildy. And mighty damned quick, too, or so help me God, I'll take a buggy whip to your black hide. You heard me, get!"

Tildy got.

"Court," Fancy said, "I've been planning to do that for years."

She started toward the stairs.

"Where're you going, Fan?"

"To get my things," Fancy said.

"Fan," Court whispered, "please . . ."

"No, Court."

"Then go, damn you! I'm not going to get on my knees if that's what you want. . . ."

"No, Court—that's not what I want," Fancy said.

Sitting in the hack, on her way to the depot, Fancy thought about it. It had started off cool and quiet, and that was the way she had wanted it. But then it had become ugly. Loud and ugly. Cheap. Funny—marriage was a thing that you went into feeling almost holy about, something you meant to last, that had dignity about it. But when it was broken it always ended like this in very bad and ugly ways that afterwards you didn't like to think about or want to remember.

But she would remember this, she knew that. She would remember it all the rest of her life. It would leave a sickness in her. A hurt that she would one day die of.

When she got to Aiken, two hours later, she went into the lobby of the hotel and asked for Jed. He came down in two minutes and took her by the arm. They came out on the sidewalk together.

It was there that Court Brantley met them.

Fancy couldn't bear to look at his face. But she couldn't turn away. It was bad to look at. A man dying on the inside. Terribly.

He put his hand inside his coat, then Fancy spoke to him:

"Take your hand off that gun, Court," she said. "You have no right to—now."

Court looked at her. At Jed. Jed's face was white. He was shaking.

"How long has this been going on?" Court gritted.

The way Fancy answered him was wrong. She knew that. But Fancy was a woman.

"Wouldn't you like to know," she said.

"I—I haven't a weapon," Jed said. "Give me a chance, Court. You wouldn't . . ."

"Go get one," Court said. "I'll wait."

"No you won't, boy," the deep voice said.

They all turned then and saw Sheriff Bowen standing right behind them.

"Aren't you a little out of your jurisdiction?" Court growled. "This is Carolina, Sheriff—not Georgia."

"Yep, I know that. Can't even arrest you, Court. Hell, son, I don't want to. I didn't come to meddle in your private affairs—though it's a good thing I got here when I did. Warn't even in no hurry until I saw you riding away from the house hell for leather like that. Good horse you got—eighteen miles in a little over an hour and a half. . . ."

Court's face was puzzled.

"Then what did you come for?" he said.

Sheriff Bowen looked at Fancy.

"Hope you'll forgive me, Ma'am, but I got to lock your husband up for something mighty bad. Only I don't want to be the one who has to break the news to you. Court Brantley, you acted right honorable the last time you got in trouble. I'm going to ask you to act that way again. First I'm going to ask you for your gun—not as the sheriff, but as your friend. I got no authority over here, and you don't have to give it to me. But if you don't, I'll have to try to take it. . . ."

Court stared at him.

"Ain't as young as I was, and I reckon you're quicker on the draw than I be. Still, if you don't give me your weapon, I'm duty and honor bound to try to take it."

Slowly Court drew the pistol out and passed it over, butt first.

"Thanks, son. Now I'm going to ask you to step over there, and tell your wife—apart from me and this gentleman, just what you was up to in Boston. She's going to find out, remember. Just rather that you told her."

"I know, Sheriff," Fancy said.

"Mighty sorry, Ma'am. I was hoping you didn't—that even Court here didn't know."

"I don't," Court said, "at least not what you're arresting me for."

"I ain't. Got no right to here. All I'm doing is asking you to step over to the sheriff's office here, with me, and turn yourself in. And you don't have to do that. Only that'll put me to the trouble of going to get him and a posse to hunt you down."

"That won't be necessary," Court said. "But don't you think you ought to tell me what I'm supposed to turn myself in for?"

"On second thought," Sheriff Bowen said, "you could come back to Augusta with me and let me arrest you there. . . . Nope. Better here. Away from all the wagging tongues. . . ."

"Sheriff," Fancy said, "for the love of God!"

"Get to the point, man," Jed Hawkins said. "What for?"

"Murder," Sheriff Bowen said.

"Who?" Fancy breathed.

"Old Matt Vance's daughter. Got a wire from Boston yesterday asking me to apprehend Court, here. Only he hadn't got back yet. Figured there was some mistake so I wired back asking for details. Got 'em this morning—night letter. Yep, pore little Fern's gone all right. Poison. That's how come I knew Court didn't do it. A gun, yep. His big fist maybe—if she got him real riled up. But poison—no. Ain't a man's weapon. A woman. A little effeminate sneak. But not Court Brantley. Still I got to lock him up till this is cleared up. . . ."

Fancy turned to Jed and put out her hand.

" 'Bye, Jed," she said.

Jed took her hand and held it.

" 'Bye, Fan," he said. "I could lick everything but this—everything but your God-damned decency . . ."

"Thanks, Jed," Fancy said. Then she put her arm through Court's. "Come on," she said, "let's go turn you in so I can get busy. I've got work to do."

Court looked at her.

"All right," he said.

18

Fancy stood outside the prison and looked at it. It was ugly. Prisons are always ugly, but the Boston jail was even uglier. It was dark, and massive and barred. It had the smell of a prison.

I won't cry, Fancy thought. I won't. But that took some doing. Up until this morning, she had had some hope. Surely, sooner or later, somebody—the judge, the jurors, the attorneys, would recognize the letter Fern had left for what it was: the product of a sick and vengeful brain.

"If anything happens to me, it will be foul play. Arrest my husband, Court Brantley. He has threatened my life several times, as he is in love with a woman in Georgia, and wants to get rid of me. . . ."

Such a flimsy thing. A few words scrawled on a piece of paper by a woman with death already in her. Surely nobody . . .

But they did.

Fancy had thought of everything. She had sent to Georgia for her wedding license, to prove that Fern had lied about that one thing at least. If they could be made to believe that she lied about that, then perhaps . . .

But Court wouldn't let her use it.

"It wouldn't change anything, Fan," he said tiredly. "A man is just as likely to kill his paramour as his wife. Why blacken her name? She's dead. . . ."

And this morning the district attorney had called the pharmacist to the stand. He had recognized Court as the man who bought the sleeping tablets. That did it.

Before now, there had been hope.

Standing there before the prison it hit Fancy, suddenly. She wasn't going to be able to free Court. They, presently, were going to take him out of this grim pile, and hang him by his neck until he was dead.

"Oh, no!" she wept. "No, God, no!"

She could hear the echoes her crying made.

She straightened up suddenly and walked into the prison, her face pale, still. She said the few necessary words to the desk sergeant, and then followed the turnkey down the corridor between the iron barred doors. The turnkey opened the cell door and let her in.

" 'Lo, Court," Fancy said.

" 'Lo, Fan."

He was thin. He hadn't shaved. There was gray in his hair now. A lot of it. Just looking at him was bad.

I won't cry. I won't!

"Fan—Fan, baby . . ."

She ran to him, put her arms around him, feeling his ribs standing out, even under the coarse stuff of the prison shirt.

"It's going to be all right," she said breathlessly. "We'll get some new evidence. We'll . . ."

"No, Fan."

"You mustn't give up, Court! Oh, darling, you mustn't. . . . You're all I've got. You're all Lynne's got. Court, isn't there anything you may have forgot? Anything at all that would make them see . . ."

"No, Fan."

She did cry then. Terribly.

Court stroked her hair.

"It's all right, baby," he said. "I had it coming. I'm not guilty of killing Fern. But I'm guilty of worse things: hurting you, being blind, being a fool and a coward. . . ."

"You're not a coward—you were always brave and fine and . . ."

"I could shoot a man. I could even face a mob. I've that kind of guts. So does a savage—or an ape."

"Court, please!"

"That kind of courage has always wrecked men and nations, hon. What I needed was the quiet kind of guts—the kind that sticks to what's right in spite of all kinds of temptations. And I didn't have that. I didn't even have sense enough to look at you and to look at Fern and see which of you was real and true fine and which was mighty shoddy goods. Took me two months to find out. But after that, being a Brantley, I was trapped. By pride, by pity, by refusing to admit I'd been taken. . . ."

"That's over with, Court," Fancy whispered, her cheek against his face in spite of his coarse beard. "I only missed being as big a fool by an accident. Don't let's talk about that. Let's talk about the future. Let's think; let's plan. . . ."

"The future," Court said. "There isn't any future, Fan."

"Court, for God's sake . . ."

"Don't let them make Lynne ashamed of me, Fan. Take her away if you have to. Bring her up to be like you—just like you—so damned wonderful that the world will have to kneel at her feet. . . ."

"You mustn't say such things, Court. . . ."

"Oh, yes. I must. I should have said them long ago. Years ago—when I knew already that no man on earth from the beginning of time was ever so blessed. I fretted myself over the mill, over piling up money, while all the time I had a treasure beyond price in the crook of my arm. Took me a long time to see that. I was too concerned with things like where you were born and who your folks were and the way you talked. Tormented you into changing, into imitating the dress and airs and talk of women not fit to kiss your shoe soles. Even that didn't hurt you. It couldn't. What's inside you can never be hurt or broken or dirtied. I don't know what it is. A reflection of Glory, maybe. Some of that kind of fire that burns where God is—the kind that can't burn out. . . ."

"Court—"

"Yes, Fan?"

"It can go out, though. It will—if you let them do this to you. . . ."

"There isn't much," Court said wearily, "that I can do about that, hon."

Fancy put up her arms and pushed away from him.

"I can," she said. "I don't know what it is yet I'll have to do, but I can—and I will!"

Then she kissed him, hard, and ran to the door. The turnkey opened it and let her out.

She got a hack almost immediately. When she was inside, she gave the driver the address of the house on Beacon Street. Whatever it was that would free Court would have to be there. Something Fern had overlooked. Something she had forgotten.

She wasn't that smart, Fancy thought. She was never that smart. She can't win now. You can't let her, God. If You let her drag him down to death after her, what good are You, God? Tell me that. What good?

Mary Jane answered the door.

"Oh, Mum," she said, "ain't it just too awful! Her dead and them aiming to hang the Master, and he never did it. I tell you, Mum—he never!"

Fancy felt something inside her loosen. Here was hope. Mary Jane was on her side.

"Could you let me in?" she whispered, "I want to search the house. Maybe I could find something—anything. . . ."

"I'll do better than that, Mum. I'll help you."

Four hours later, they had to give it up. There was nothing. Fern had been thorough.

Mary Jane made tea for Fancy in the servants' quarters. Fancy was sipping it, without tasting it, without noticing what was around her, too hurt-sick to care when Terence, the coachman, came into the room.

"Good evening, Mum," he said.

"This is Terence," Mary Jane told her. "Terry, we've been trying to find something—anything to prove that the Master was innocent. Do you know, could you tell us . . ."

Terence did a funny thing. He looked quickly over his shoulder. Then he went to the door and looked out, up and down the hall. He came back into the room and bent over close to Fancy's ear.

"Ask Bridget," he whispered. Then he turned and walked out of the room.

"Bridget!" Fancy said, "where is she, Mary?"

"In the kitchen. She would know something all right. She and Madame was this close. All the rest of us worshiped the Master. But Bridget hated him. 'Twas her idea that he was unkind to Madame. And Bridget fair doted on Madame. . . ."

But Fancy was already racing toward the kitchen.

"Bridget," she said, "please—I've got to talk to you. . . ."

"I've nothing to say to the likes of you, Mum," Bridget snapped.

Fancy stared at her.

"But," she whispered, "they—they're going to hang him, Bridget! If there's anything you know—anything at all that would help . . ."

"I don't know anything," Bridget said.

She was lying. Fancy could see that.

"You—you'd let an innocent man—die?"

"He let her die—the poor, sweet little thing. And do you know where she died? In these two arms, Mum—while he was off running to your arms—to the arms of his kept woman! Faith, and I hope that they do hang him. 'Tis a pity that they can't hang you, too!"

Fancy knotted her fists so hard that her nails broke against her palms. But she spoke softly. Gently.

"Did he give her those pills?"

"I ain't a-saying," Bridget said. "That's for the law to decide."

They would finish it tomorrow. Tomorrow the defense would sum up its weak plea. Tomorrow the district attorney would be a tower of scorn. The jury would file out. And Bridget stood there with Court Brantley's life in her big, red hands.

Then Fancy had it. The way. It had been there all the time.

"You don't approve of kept women, do you, Bridget?" she said.

"Approve! Faith and they should be horsewhipped—one and all!" Bridget said.

Fancy turned to Mary.

"Call Terence," she said.

Terence came.

"Can you drive me to the Vendome?" Fancy said. "I have something over there I want to show Bridget. Something I hope will change her mind. . . ."

"Certainly, Mum," Terence said.

They were back within the hour. Fancy walked straight up to Bridget and laid the scroll of parchment in her hands.

"Read it, Bridget," she said grimly. "Read it aloud."

"Know all men by these presents," Bridget read, "that this twelfth day of August A. D. Eighteen hundred and Eighty, I, Judge J. Lister Harris, hereby certify, that Courtland Brantley and Miss Fancy Williamson were joined in the Bonds of Holy Matrimony, to which fact, attested to by the hereunder signed witnesses, I hereby sign my name, and set my seal. . . ."

Bridget gave the certificate back. She was shaking.

" 'Tain't so," she whispered. "It's a fake, I don't believe . . ."

"Ever seen an official State Seal, Bridget?" Fancy said. "Were you ever married?"

"Yes, Mum. My poor Tim died years ago. . . ."

"Then you've seen a wedding certificate?"

"Yes'm." Bridget's voice was weaker now.

"All right. Court Brantley and I have been married these fourteen years. If necessary, I can bring to Boston these people who witnessed the ceremony. Fourteen years ago, Fern Vance was already married to—Court's brother. Have you ever seen *her* wedding certificate, Bridget? Have you?"

"No'm. . . ."

"You couldn't have, because she hadn't any. You don't approve of kept women, do you, Bridget? Well, who was the kept woman? Who tried to keep my husband away from me, after having tricked him into this ugly relationship that he didn't even want? Who was it that came to his hotel after him—knowing that he had a wife and a child? Who, Bridget? You were talking mighty big a little while ago—where's your brash tongue now?"

"I don't believe it!" Bridget cried. "Her so little and sweet, and doting on him so. . . ."

"Did he," Fancy said quietly, "kill her? Answer me, Bridget—did he?"

"Yes! Anyhow, 'twere the same thing!"

"Ah! The same thing. But it's never the same thing, Bridget. Did my husband give that cheap little cheat you were so fond of—those pills?"

"I ain't a-saying," Bridget said.

Fancy turned to Terence.

"Terence, go call me a policeman," she said.

"You can't!" Bridget said. "There ain't no law . . ."

"Oh, yes—there's a law all right. Material witness. As such you can be held until you decide to talk—to tell the truth. If you don't talk, you can be held for obstructing justice. If you lie—that's perjury—five to fifteen years. Well, Bridget?"

"He—he drove her to it!" Bridget sobbed. "Always a-threatening to leave her and niver come back! She—she asked me for some water—Mary wasn't here—and I saw her open the bottle. I never dreamed she was a-going to take them all. . . ."

"Terence," Fancy whispered, "get me some paper, and a pen. Now Bridget, tell me all about it—just like it happened. I'm going to write it down. Mary and Terence will have to sign it as witnesses. . . ."

"Will they," Bridget got out, "put me in jail?"

"Not if you tell the truth. You'll have to come to court tomorrow and testify there. That's all. . . . Thank you, Terence. Now Bridget, begin at the beginning. . . ."

"I didn't know about that note," Bridget wailed. "Faith and me sainted mother, if I knew that! I only read about it in the papers afterwards. . . ."

But you would have let him die, Fancy thought. She must have had something after all to win such loyalty.

"It's all right, Bridget," she said, "just start talking. . . ."

Afterwards, she was very tired. She was tired all over. The reaction had her. But she had no time to stop. She finally reached defense attorney

O'Conner by telephone. Then she walked all the way to the jail, because it was too late to get a cab.

They wouldn't let her see him, of course. It was long after visiting hours. But the desk sergeant took her note in to him.

When she got back to the Vendome, she couldn't sleep. In a few hours now it was going to be tomorrow. There was going to be a tomorrow, now. The sun would come up. Life would go on. Her life.

For that was what Court Brantley was to her, anyhow. Her life—all of it.